AWAKE AND SINGING

7 Classic Plays from the American Jewish Repertoire

Aaron Hoffman's *Welcome Stranger* (1920) uses vaudeville humor to depict American anti-Semitism. It portrays the confrontation between Isidor Solomon, a proud Jewish peddler, and small-town bigots, led by an anti-Semite, who turns out to be a Jew himself.

Counsellor-at-Law by Elmer Rice (1931) deals with some of the same issues in the very different milieu of New York City, where a prestigious and accomplished Jewish lawyer tries to secure a foothold in an alluring but hostile society.

Clifford Odets's *Awake and Sing* (1935) is a watershed American Jewish play. Its authentic portraits of three generations of a family in the Depression-ridden Bronx marks the debut of characters who were to become staples on the American stage.

Morning Star by Sylvia Regan (1940) dramatizes the lives of a plucky widow and her extended family. Their fortunes are shaped by momentous events, from the Triangle Shirtwaist Fire, to World War I, to the Great Depression.

Home of the Brave by Arthur Laurents (1945) brings to the stage the all-American platoon. A young soldier loses a cherished buddy, but gains a new understanding of what it means to be a Jew.

S. N. Behrman's *The Cold Wind and the Warm* (1958), a retrospective of the author's youth in Worcester, Massachusetts, previews the 1960s' celebratory explorations of ethnic roots. This moving, frequently humorous memory play is peopled by characters whom Saul Bellow found "immediately familiar."

Paddy Chayefsky's *The Tenth Man* (1959), like Anski's Yiddish classic *The Dybbuk,* centers around the exorcism of a troublesome wandering soul. But unlike the homogeneous community of *The Dybbuk*, Chayefsky's characters seek spiritual peace amid the fragmenting demands of contemporary urban America.

Ellen Schiff, Ph.D., is a former professor of French and literature. She is the author of *From Stereotype to Metaphor: The Jew in Contemporary Drama,* an associate editor of *Jewish American Women Writers,* and a contributor to many books, among them *Anti-Semitism in American History,* and *Handbook of American Jewish Literature.* Her essays and articles on theatre of Jewish interest have appeared in a wide range of periodicals, including *The New York Times, The Massachusetts Review,* and *Studies in American Jewish Literature.* A consultant on theatre to the National Foundation for Jewish Culture, she lives in the Berkshires.

AWAKE AND SINGING

7 Classic Plays from the American Jewish Repertoire

EDITED AND WITH AN
INTRODUCTION BY

Ellen Schiff

A MENTOR BOOK

MENTOR
Published by the Penguin Group
Penguin Books USA Inc., 375 Hudson Street,
New York, New York 10014, U.S.A.
Penguin Books Ltd, 27 Wrights Lane, London W8 5TZ, England
Penguin Books Australia Ltd, Ringwood, Victoria, Australia
Penguin Books Canada Ltd, 10 Alcorn Avenue,
Toronto, Ontario, Canada M4V 3B2
Penguin Books (N.Z.) Ltd, 182–190 Wairau Road,
Auckland 10, New Zealand

Penguin Books Ltd, Registered Offices:
Harmondsworth, Middlesex, England

First published by Mentor, an imprint of Dutton Signet,
a division of Penguin Books USA Inc.

First Printing, March, 1995
10 9 8 7 6 5 4 3 2 1

Cover illustration by Jim Parker

(The following page constitutes an extension of this copyright page.)

REGISTERED TRADEMARK—MARCA REGISTRADA

Library of Congress Cataloging Card Number: 94-77538

Printed in the United States of America

Once more, for Mort—
and once more, because of him.

Contents

Acknowledgments

A number of people helped me resolve to do something about the need to define and illustrate the phenomenon of American Jewish drama. There are the many who, over the years, indulged and encouraged my resistance to the ready assumption that a Jewish play means a Yiddish play. Then there were the thirty-five lifetime theatergoers in my 1992 Lenox Elderhostel, The Coming of Age of American Jewish Theatre. They brought to the classroom an impressive range of informed opinions and no hesitation about expressing them. With exemplary generosity, they invited spirited discussions (Is *Death of a Salesman* a Jewish play? How about *Two for the Seesaw*?) and never settled for fuzzy or arbitrary answers. So I begin by thanking all those people who share my love for the theatre, whose interest substantiated my commitment, and whose probing questions guided my investigation.

I am grateful to the National Foundation for the Humanities for a research grant in 1991–92 which made possible trips to libraries and archives. The staff of the Billy Rose Theatre Collection at the New York Public Library for the Performing Arts, Paula Shoots of the Williams College Theatre Library, and Louise Ouellette of the interlibrary loan department at North Adams State College lent unfailing cooperation. Brooks McNamara of New York University offered valuable advice on anthologizing.

My thanks to my editor, Arnold Dolin, for his sensitive attention to the manuscript and assistance with permissions. I am much beholden to Florence Eichen, Eleanore Speert, and Henry Wallengren, who guided me across the often exasperatingly tricky shoals of permissions. I gratefully acknowledge the permission of Walt Odets to quote material from the unpublished early drafts of Clifford Odets' *Awake and Sing!*, and of Sylvia Regan Ellstein to reprint the songs by Abraham Ellstein and Robert Sour used in *Morning Star*.

A number of friends and colleagues actively supported the project. Deep appreciation goes to Alan Berger, Michael Bloom, Alan Brody, Stanley Chyet, Lewis Fried, Martin Halpern, Carole Kessner, Lawrence Langer, Roberta Levitow, Sanford Marovitz, Nahma Sandrow, Edith Sobel, Janet Sonenberg, and Michael Taub. Len Berkman, whom I can never thank enough, found yet more ways of being indispensable.

Ann Shapiro graciously provided both hospitality and sound counsel on the manuscript. Sara Horowitz and Robert Skloot were unstinting in their advocacy of the book and their critical reading of its introduction, which also benefitted from the substantial editorial advice of David Delman. My daughter, Stacy Schiff, took time from her own book to comment on mine. In addition to offering gratitude to those who read my writing, I extend appreciation to Walter Bode, who guided my reading.

The warmth and humor of my family were a constant source of perspective and sustenance, and I thank them lovingly. As I do Mort, whose inspiration gives everything purpose and savor.

Introduction

Today's *New York Times* Arts and Leisure Guide lists sixteen plays written by Jews, but, as the joke goes, who's counting? It is an apt comic irony that over the course of the twentieth century, the contribution of Jewish playwrights to the American theatre has become so conspicuous that it generally passes as an unremarked fact of national theatrical life. However, the millennium—as a major new talent has reminded us—approaches, and it presents a fitting moment to acknowledge that contribution. Since the popularity of Jewish dramatists is so intertwined with the proliferation and success of explicitly Jewish plays (like half of today's sixteen), it is also time to recognize properly and at last what can now be seen as a tradition of American Jewish plays and playwriting.

The American Jewish repertoire is, in fact, a national treasure some eight decades old. It consists of a large and ever-growing body of plays—there are already several hundred—that explore some aspect of the American Jewish experience, and that are written in English, usually by Jewish dramatists, for the general theatregoing public. A major goal of this collection is to illustrate and pay tribute to the development of this canon. The present volume brings together seven important works that appeared between 1920 and 1960. A forthcoming companion volume will demonstrate continuity through a selection of American Jewish plays from the last four decades.

I

Acknowledging the tradition of the American Jewish repertoire begins, of course, by considering the context in which it developed. That means paying attention to both the "American" and the "Jewish." Jewish participation and presence have been so constant in the indigenous American theatre since its coming of age in the post-World War I years that it took the perspective of an outsider, British director Tyrone Guthrie, to observe that if Jews withdrew from the American theatre, it "would collapse about next Thursday."[1] While Guthrie was no doubt referring to a whole range of Jewish activities—from artistry, to administration, to audience support—the role of Jews in the making of American theatre is difficult to overestimate. From producers and impresarios—Erlanger, Zimmerman, Belasco, the Frohmans, the Shubert brothers—to the writers and performers who animated this country's vaudeville circuits, burlesque and musical halls, and experimental pioneer theatres, Jews have worked shoulder to shoulder with fellow Americans in the making of what we can finally call a national theatre.

Their efforts did not occur in a vacuum, or, for that matter, in a climate of tolerance. Nativism, well-entrenched as the twentieth century got under way, manifested itself in its first decades as what historian John Higham terms "inflamed racial nationalism."[2] Though the resurgent Ku Klux Klan and various ideological firebrands threatened all foreigners, Jews were the specific target of new quotas and restrictions on immigration that, in 1924, effectively ended their mass influx to these shores.[3] Higham records the nation's most severe eruption of anti-Semitism in the years surrounding World War I, the pestilence breaking out again "in the 1930s, stimulated by the Great Depression and the example of European fascism."[4]

While racism made inroads in the arts as well, it did not deter Jewish playwriting. In disregard or defiance, distinguished critic and author Gilbert Seldes used the pages of *The Menorah Journal* in 1922 to implore dramatists to translate to the stage "the poetry and the richness and the hard certain solidness of our fantastically mingled existence [as Americans and Jews]."[5] Nonetheless, intolerance probably accounts for the timidity or ambiguity with which some dramatists treated ethnicity, a practice that continued well into the 1960s. So, for example, transparently Jewish characters are named Jim Knight and

Charlie Tyler in Samuel Shipman's *Cheaper to Marry* (1924). Or they have Jewish names but no Jewish substance, as in Edna Ferber and George S. Kaufman's *Minick* (1924). Or they have Jewish identity so thin as to be meaningless, a signature practice of the prodigiously successful Kaufman.

The early years of the century also ushered in significant changes in the uses of leisure. Cultural historians note that Americans were increasingly drawn to passive diversions. While theatregoing was already well-established among the elite, after the turn of the century it became more and more a source of popular entertainment. Interestingly, Russell Lynes credits the invention of the phonograph and later, film and radio, with "creating a mass audience of listeners and watchers out of a people who . . . seem to have preferred to do rather than to be done by. . . ."[6]

The growth of audiences was crucial among the many factors fostering the development and popularity of all the arts. The role of Jews as arts patrons, especially German Jews, who had prospered since their arrival here earlier in the nineteenth century, has been well documented. Less spectacular, but equally consequential, were the cultural and recreational habits of the newcomers from Eastern Europe. Irrespective of the work they did in this country, many immigrant Jews brought with them middle class tastes. These included a frequently indulged partiality to theatre, to which the enormous popularity of the Yiddish stage well into the 1930s bears testimony. It is no surprise that this predominantly East European immigrant population has also contributed importantly to the ranks on both sides of the footlights of American theatre, including many of the playwrights who are our concern here.

Since the 1920s—the date by which "the American theater began to function as a world-class vehicle of dramatic literature"[7]—Jews have been writing often and with distinction for the American stage. That they have earned a warm welcome is confirmed readily by a few statistics. In 1969, critic and editor Otis L. Guernsey Jr. tallied up the playwrights whose work had been selected as Best Plays most often during the first half-century of the authoritative *Year Book of the Drama in America* and found that one-third were Jews. George S. Kaufman, cited eighteen times, was followed closely by Moss Hart, Lillian Hellman, and S. N. Behrman. Since the establishment of the Tony Awards in 1947, plays and books for musicals written by Jews have been nominated virtually every year; by 1990, some thirty had won. Elmer Rice, the first Jew awarded the Pulitzer Prize for drama—for *Street Scene* in 1929—heads a roster that currently includes seventeen Jewish laureates.

To arrive at the focus of this book, however, we need to cull from the multitude of works for the stage written by American Jews those plays which, by virtue of their explicit Jewish content, constitute the American Jewish repertoire. Making such distinctions can be controversial. For some, a Jewish play is anything written by a Jew, a judgment that does not consider whether Jewishness infuses the work in any meaningful way. For others, no play written in English can be a Jewish play, an issue to be addressed shortly. The matter is further complicated by the existence of countless works by Jews whose subjects or characters are not specifically Jewish, but whose themes and values undeniably are.

For example, Jews contributed heavily to the drama of social consciousness and political activism that reflected the turbulent climate of the 1920s and 1930s. Numerous plays dramatize the plight of America's downtrodden, typically portrayed as victims of capitalism. Elmer Rice's panorama of New York tenement life, *Street Scene*, portrays urban frustrations and violence. Industry's unconcern for the individual is appropriately represented through the depersonalized expressionist style of Paul Sifton's *The Belt* (1927) and Rice's *The Adding Machine* (1931). The despair and fury that fuel workers' revolts furnish the subject of John Howard Lawson's *Processional* (1925), set against a West Virginia mine strike; Albert Bein's *Let Freedom Ring* (1935), a reckoning of the shattering cost of job action for southern mill workers; and, perhaps most famously, Clifford Odets's agitprop play about a taxi drivers' walkout, *Waiting for Lefty* (1935). The socio-political bias of these works reveals a traditional Jewish emphasis on human worth, equity, and moral rightness. The cry for social justice is taken up by Claire and Paul Sifton in their scathing indictment of the human tragedy of unemployment, *1931* (1931); by John Wexley, responding to the Scottsboro case in which nine blacks were wrongly convicted of rape, in *They Shall Not Die* (1934); and by Albert Maltz, in his depiction of the bitter life of coal miners, *Black Pit* (1935).

Concern with ethical behavior finds eloquent and sustained expression in the works of Arthur Miller, whose early play *They Too Arise* (1936) deals with a small manufacturer whose Jewish values put him at odds with the strike-breaking tactics of his corporate colleagues in the garment industry.[8] While Miller did not again focus specifically on American Jewish life in subsequent works until the recent *Broken Glass* (1994), his entire canon is informed by his preoccupation with individual integrity and social responsibility, concerns which, he makes clear in his autobiography, derive from his Jewish heritage.[9]

The Jewish love for music added another dimension to socially conscious drama. Harold Rome's revue *Pins and Needles* (1937) presented the garment industry through the eyes of its workers. With a cast of amateur players drawn from the International Ladies Garment Workers Union, the show had a run of 1109 performances. Marc Blitzstein's *The Cradle Will Rock,* though developed under the sponsorship of the Works Projects Administration, a federal relief project, made a searing anticapitalist statement that provoked government watchdogs to attempt unsuccessfully to squelch its premiere in 1938. Better known and decidedly better natured in its satire of governmental irresponsibility was *Of Thee I Sing* (1931) by Morrie Ryskind, George S. Kaufman, and George and Ira Gershwin, the first musical to win the Pulitzer Prize for drama. But Jewish activity in American musical theatre—from Irving Berlin and Jerome Kern to Jerry Bock and Sheldon Harnick and Stephen Sondheim—provides the rich subject of other volumes. Until very recently, the musical stage did not depict American Jewish life in any substantial way.

The presence in the national repertoire of so many dramatizations of Jewish social and political concerns does not eclipse the body of plays of *explicit* Jewish content, the American Jewish repertoire, which is our subject here. Still, it is worth noting that the sheer volume of plays in English *by* Jews may be responsible for diverting attention from the important number of plays *about* Jews that is only now attracting well-deserved notice. But there are other factors as well.

The very use of English as the language of Jewish plays presents one issue. Ethnic writing in English is sometimes seen as a dilution of the national identity typically conferred by language. For example, critic Robert Alter finds that, "though Jews have lived in many different cultures and have been profoundly influenced by them, they have never created a distinctly imaginative literature except in indigenous Jewish languages."[10] But what *is* the "indigenous Jewish language" for American Jews, who often have none other than English?

To answer that question is to recognize an international phenomenon. The native languages of many countries have come to function admirably as vehicles for "distinctly imaginative literature" by and about Jews. Significant works in all the literary genres provide examples. To cite a few for the theatre: the English-language drama showcased in this collection has its parallels in Canada in the plays of Aviva Ravel and Larry Fineberg, and in England in those of Arnold Wesker and Bernard Kops. The Jewish stage speaks French in the plays of Liliane Atlan and Gilles Ségal; German in those of Nelly Sachs and Peter Weiss; and Spanish in the Argentinian theatre of Diana Raznovich and Jorge Goldenberg.

Casting doubt on the Jewish authenticity of works in non-exclusively Jewish languages or challenging the contribution of such works to the Jewish literary tradition can only skew the evidence and scant the art. Surely both cultural and aesthetic considerations are better served by accepting these works for what they are: reflections of every dimension of Jewish identity and Jewish life in pluralistic societies. What more appropriate medium than the vernacular of the countries where Jews are citizens could there be to express the dominant theme of modern Jewish creativity: the imperatives and difficulties of dual identity?

A second issue arises in distinguishing American Jewish drama as an entity. It may be pushing at an open door to argue that American Jews have already created out of their own lives a "distinctly imaginative literature" in English. The legitimacy of American Jewish fiction, poetry, and film rarely needs defending. These genres are validated by wide attention in critical discourse, by their conspicuous presence in university curricula, and in routine references in the popular press. Curiously, however, American Jewish plays are regularly overlooked as a component of American Jewish literary creativity.[11]

There are several explanations. Historically, theatre has been held in low regard, considered less literary, hence less consequential, than fiction and verse. Drama critic Walter Prichard Eaton once observed, "To take the theatre seriously always surprises many serious people."[12] A more contemporary attitude takes the opposite stance while paradoxically working to the same end: it considers theatre too elite to rival film as a major force in popular culture.

Then too, prefixing "American Jewish" before such words as "play," "drama," "theatre," or "repertoire" often provokes dissent. The "American" notwithstanding, the association of Jewish theatre with the Yiddish stage is inevitable and unyielding. Semantics is partly to blame. When, for instance, in 1980 the newly formed Jewish Theatre Association of the National Foundation for Jewish Culture convened the First Jewish Theatre Conference and Festival, it felt obliged to explain its use of the term. The JTA acknowledged the common tendency to substitute "Jewish" for "Yiddish,"—as in, "Do you speak Jewish?"—an interchange that proves mischievous in referring to the theatre. Declaring its concern "with all theatre expressions which relate to the Jewish experience, life, and culture," the JTA devoted its event to "exploring the dimensions of Jewish theatre." The Festival's four jam-packed days of performances, readings, demonstrations, workshops, and panel discussions served up overwhelming evidence of the breadth and depth of Jewish theatrical activity—all of it in English.

Although English has superseded Yiddish as the Jewish lingua franca (Israeli scholar Moshe Davis observes that English "is the mother tongue for the majority of world Jewry"[13]), the conflation of "Yiddish" and "Jewish" persists. It is nowhere more enduring than in reference to the theatre, despite the profusion of plays of Jewish content in English and the diminished availability of Yiddish productions. Potential ticket-buyers regularly call the box offices of the Council of Jewish Theatres, the network of producing companies across North America that has succeeded the JTA, seeking assurance that their productions are in English. At least some of the tenacity of the confusion lends itself to explanation.

First of all, the Yiddish theatre has not disappeared. It lives in the annual productions of New York City's Folksbiene, the oldest continuous theatre in the United States; in the programs of the Joseph Papp Yiddish Theatre; and in revues like those of Moishe Rosenfeld and Zalmen Mlotek. Yiddish classics, translated into English, endure in print (notably, Joseph C. Landis's collection[14]) and are smartly refitted for the stage. New York's Jewish Repertory Theatre scored a tremendous hit in 1983 with Nahma Sandrow, Raphael Crystal, and Richard Engquist's *Kuni Leml,* based on Goldfadn's famous farce. The JRT initiated its new space in 1992 by commissioning a fresh adaptation by Stephen Fife of Sholom Asch's powerful *God of Vengeance*. Joseph Papp's production of Leivick's *The Golem* at the Public Theatre in 1984 was hailed by the *New York Times* as "a play of imperishable ideas." Still, Irving Howe's observation about the extraordinary classic *The Dybbuk* can be extended without exaggeration to the Yiddish repertoire itself. Howe writes of Anski's work that "for all its brilliant darkness, it offered no path of development for the Yiddish theatre: it was a work sealed into the past, which could be imitated but not enlarged upon."[15] However heartening late-century Yiddish theatrical activity (it includes reports of a new play in Yiddish by the prominent Israeli dramatist, Joshua Sobol), it is neither substantial nor prevalent enough to support the claim that "Jewish theatre" means exclusively the Yiddish stage.

The persistent identification of Jewish theatre with Yiddish also may be attributable to a faculty much prized in the Jewish world—memory. New York's Second Avenue and its equivalent centers of Yiddish theatre across the country remain a treasured part of the recollections of many American Jews, frequently because their earliest, most indelible impressions of theatre were fashioned by the Yiddish stage. Nor is this an experience unique to senior citizens. Emily Mann, born in 1952 and one of the most versatile playwrights and directors working today, recalls that she knew where she wanted to spend her adult professional life when, as a teenager, she saw Anski's *The Dybbuk* and "fell under the spell of the girl in white." Mann's experience echoes that of innumerable Jewish artists who have brought to their careers in the American theatre the vitality, the cosmopolitanism, the artistic standards, and the social consciousness of the Yiddish stage at its finest. It is quite possible that simply because the remembered excellence of the Yiddish stage remains so vivid and so prized, it continues to cast its shadow across any other theatre that calls itself Jewish.

It is useful to bear in mind that though the Yiddish and the American Jewish stages have had much in common, particularly in the first decades of the twentieth century, they are poised on separate axes and serve different constituencies. The Yiddish theatre is particular; it faces inward. Like all theatre, the Yiddish stage works because it entertains, and to that end, the American Yiddish stage graciously makes provisions for theatregoers who are, as Moishe Mlotek puts it, "Yiddish-impaired." Still, its appeal is keenest for those who can appreciate the nuances of its language and rejoice in hearing it spoken or sung well. It is likely that these are members of the audience whose pleasure is sharpened by the realization, at some level, that the Yiddish stage fulfills what Francine Prose, in a very different context, calls a "moral and spiritual obligation."[16] Nourished by memory, animated by historical consciousness, the Yiddish stage comments, in straight plays as in musical revues, on traditional Jewish mores and values. It revivifies not only roots, but the places where roots once flourished. Observing the distance of the Yiddish stage from contemporary life, Yiddish theatre historian Nahma Sandrow writes, "I have never yet had a chance to see a serious Yiddish drama that was not set among Jews in Eastern Europe half a century ago or more."[17] With the destruction of these communities in the Holocaust, Yiddish plays can scarcely be viewed without evoking poignant awareness of a world obliterated.

The Yiddish stage comes as close as any in the modern world to replicating the original function of drama, to affirm the identity and beliefs of a people. It energizes its legends: biblical patriarchs who comport themselves with all-too-human impropriety, fathers who err because they are overambitious for their offspring, children who thwart their parents by hiding money in graves. How can one not relax and rejoice where it is acceptable (and often funny) to see Jews portrayed with all their warts and foibles? Yet how can one not admit that this special kind of gratification in the theatre is an ethnic secret, impenetrable by general audiences, as well as by many Jews, in a multicultural society?

Just there lies a problem. Linguistic barriers made the Yiddish theatre a safe place to laugh at Jewish foolishness and weep at Jewish misfortune. That haven is compromised (some would say threatened) when such frank portraiture of Jewish life is made accessible beyond the "in" group. The sensitiveness of Jews to their public depictions has exacted formidable demands on those who would write about them in the vernacular. When Aaron Hoffman's charming *Welcome Stranger,* the first play in this volume, played in New York in 1920, it raised Jewish hackles. The New York audience at a special Jewish New Year's performance laughed heartily, but somehow missed the play's strong defense of ethical and self-assured Jewish behavior. Instead the audience complained that Hoffman had turned his back on the opportunity to "do the Jew in America a fine service by explaining his attitude toward the age-old racial antagonisms his people are supposed to have created."[18] The same touchiness has created painful chapters in theatre history. Witness the fate of Rudolph Schildkraut's world-renowned production of Sholom Asch's *God of Vengeance,* the plot of which involves a Jewish brothel keeper and his lesbian daughter. When the play arrived in New York in 1922, discomfited uptown Jews turned its English language debut into an historic moment: the first instance in American jurisprudence of a play's being closed down and its principals brought to trial on obscenity charges.

Viewed from this point of view, American Jewish theatre can be seen as a challenge to Jewish exclusiveness. From its inception, the American Jewish stage faced in exactly the opposite direction from the Yiddish—outward. Where the Yiddish stage is particular, the American Jewish theatre is representative. Its vanguard was vaudeville, where the personal stories of Jewish comics so resonated with the analogous experiences of other new Americans that they made of the Jew what Alfred Kazin has aptly termed the "representative national entertainer."[19] By mid-century, Jews as entertainers had forged their way into the center of American life. Meanwhile, history ushered in what Leslie Fiedler called an "apocalyptic period of atomization and uprooting" in which "the image of the Jew tends to become the image of everyone."[20] Jews in the theatre were quick to employ the perspective of that identity. They have used the stage to reflect on the world as they saw it and as it saw them—as Americans and as Jews, identities not always compatible, and for that reason, eminently representative of all who, for any of myriad reasons, feel conflicted, alienated, and vulnerable.

However, the distinctions made here between the Yiddish and the American Jewish repertoires, and the argument for the legitimacy of the latter as unquestionably Jewish, are not meant to imply that the two are mutually exclusive. Contemporary Yiddish-English revues consciously borrow from the American stage. For instance, in their adaptation of Itsik Manger's biblical poetry for the Joseph Papp Yiddish Theatre's *Songs of Paradise,* Miriam Hoffman, Rena Berkowicz Borow, and Rosalie Gerut incorporated rock and roll, gospel, and "traditional Jewish beats."[21] The influence in the other direction is far more consequential. As we have already noted, many of the makers of American Jewish theatre came from Yiddish-speaking homes in which attendance at the Yiddish theatre was a cherished custom.[22] The repertoire itself, including some of the plays anthologized here, demonstrates that the Yiddish theatre's bequest to the American Jewish stage extends well beyond the older institution's stock of plots, characters, legends, and music. The legacy includes informed respect of the Old World repertoire, especially the inspiration of the modern European masters of dramaturgy and production.[23] And one thing more: a level of artistic achievement, notably on the part of its actors, that earned the respect of this country's reputation-making drama critics, a predominantly non-Jewish coterie (e.g., Alexander Woollcott, Stark Young, John Mason Brown, Robert Benchley).

While the dazzling achievements of the Yiddish theatre

may persist in blinding some theatregoers to any "other" Jewish theatre, that reputation is perceived by many, English-language theatre practitioners among them, as a heritage to build on. For what finally defines American Jewish drama and sets it apart from the Yiddish is precisely the dual citizenship explicit in its name. Nathan Glazer and Daniel Patrick Moynihan have usefully pointed out that changes wrought on immigrant cultures as they integrated into American society may have "transformed [them] into something other than what they had been in the old country [but they] did not make them any less distinctive or identifiable—or any less significant to those adhering to them."[24]

The American Jewish stage tells the story of Jews in America. It is customarily the product of Jewish playwrights collaborating with non-Jews in the production of scripts typically populated by both Jews and non-Jews, enacted by casts in which Jews do not always play Jewish roles, and performed for audiences and critics comprising the gamut of American theatregoers.

The dual identity often provides the substance of plays. As the works by Hoffman, Elmer Rice, and Arthur Laurents demonstrate, American Jewish drama often grows out of the playwright's experience of being Jewish in a pluralistic country whose liberties, like its prejudices, are exactly what provoke him or her to ponder what being Jewish means—and to work out the conflicts on stage. One of the most intriguing phenomena of American Jewish theatre history is the use artists have made of their freedom to decide how to write as a Jew, or even if they should. Their choices range from Montague Glass and Charles Klein's exploiting the good-natured vulgarity of their eponymous buffoons, Abe Potash and Mawruss Perlmutter, to ignoring Jewish subjects almost entirely, the option exercised by Gertrude Stein and Lillian Hellman. A much-trod middle ground is that taken by all the authors included here: their classic Jewish plays are part of canons that include works without any Jewish content.

Indeed, as the earlier-cited plays and musicals of social conscience from pre-World War II illustrate, it was more common for Jews to write *out* of their American Jewish experience than *about* it. The 1960s and 1970s produced vast changes in the manner in which Jews perceived themselves and were, in turn, perceived, and predictably, those decades became a turning point in the development of the American Jewish repertoire. It would require momentous political, social, and cultural upheavals before America's Jewish playwrights and their audiences began to expect—indeed, to take for granted—Jewishness as an integral part of plays by Jews. But that is the subject of my next volume.

II

The plays in this anthology were selected to represent the range of topics and themes, dramatic styles, and social attitudes that characterize the American Jewish repertoire between 1920 and 1960. In subject or in point of view, each play incorporates what sociologist Steven M. Cohen and political scientist Charles Liebman call the "competing impulses: the urge to *integrate* into modern America and the urge to *survive* as Jews."[25]

A number of criteria determined the choice of plays. Works presented as classics must have considerable artistic value and the enduring power to please. These seven are so endowed. It is gratifying to unpack them from the attic to which the theatre (especially in the United States) all too promptly consigns even the excellent as it caters to the public's insatiable appetite for the new. It is true that contemporary theatrical styles and vastly increased production costs heighten the challenge of producing works with casts as large as some called for here. Nevertheless, they still work. *Awake and Sing!* has had several recent major revivals, in New York (1984) and Chicago (1992); Lincoln Center Theater opened its 1989 season with a production of *The Tenth Man;* and *Counsellor-at-Law* was successfully mounted in the 1993 seasons of the Shaw Festival and the Williamstown Theatre Festival. Production considerations aside, these plays retain a dramatic vitality and the capacity to entertain that reading easily evokes.

In content as well as style, the collection aims to reflect the evolution of American Jewish life from the second decade of the century through the threshold of the turbulent 1960s. The goal was to suggest the breadth and diversity of the American Jewish experience that dramatists have presented to the general public. Plays, like other creative works, have estimable value as documents, though "documents" seems a stodgy term to apply to the lively artistry on view here. Still, these plays attest to the values, institutions, and both seminal and daily events that shaped American Jewish life in the first half of the twentieth century: immigration, family life and generational conflict, the Great Depression, "making it" in America, anti-Semitism, the Jewish community in cities as well as small towns, the Triangle Fire, and the two World Wars. (The century's paramount Jewish phenomena—the Holocaust and Israeli statehood—were rarely treated on stage prior to the 1970s.)

A major contribution of Jewish playwrights to the American theatre has been revising and increasing its census of Jewish characters, so as to depict Jews more credibly. The scripts in this volume were chosen to represent this broader, more widely varied population. It includes, among others, the Jew in business and the military, as lawyer, rabbi, scholar, and artist, as disillusioned greenhorn and disenchanted modern professional. There are several views of changing gender roles and images, and of the pious elderly hard put to cope with the indifference of a determinedly secular world. It is intriguing to find early appearances here of fresh characters who will have long stage lives, though sometimes in the reduced dimensions of stereotypes; Odets's and Regan's Jewish mothers and their daughters offer apt illustrations.

Given the historic stage career of the Jew as rascally clown and the widespread image in American culture of the Jew as comic, it seemed essential to choose plays that treat even their humorous characters with dignity. For that reason, the language of some of these scripts warrants comment. A number of the characters speak English that betrays minds still working through Yiddish syntax and vocabulary. This definitive version of *Awake and Sing!* is a fine example, and even it anglicizes dialogue that was in early drafts much more liberally punctuated with Yiddish. The distortions and solecisms that result have an authentic ring, and sometimes, as in the Behrman play, a comic one. However, the speakers' idiom is not intended as the source of mocking humor, in the style of Potash and Perlmutter's fractured language. Nor is it designed to be cutely endearing, like Molly Goldberg's malapropisms. Rather, these characters appear earnest about expressing themselves in the language of their new country. In doing so, they make a statement that goes beyond what is needed to make themselves understood on the other side of the footlights.

Because this volume is conceived as part of a larger project that represents the development of American Jewish plays and playwriting to the present day, it was naturally essential to identify the pioneers and shapers of the tradition. The headnotes to the plays detail the considerable and varied contributions these seven dramatists have made to the American Jewish repertoire, as well as to the American theatre generally. The confidence and flair with which they presented their subject opened the way for the stylistic innovations and ever more candid and diversified theatrical representations of American Jewish life in the last four decades of the twentieth century. While affirming the preeminence of these seven playwrights and of the works gathered here, this collection makes no claim of inclusiveness. Readers may well cite other influential dramatists and fine early plays about American Jewish life. Further substantiation of the sturdy base of the American Jewish repertoire can, of course, only be greeted with applause.

With its unmistakable vaudeville humor, Aaron Hoffman's mischievously titled *Welcome Stranger* (1920) presents an early view of an American Jewish experience which, for all it was typical, often escapes literary notice. Its protagonist, Isidor Solomon, typifies countless aspiring entrepreneurs whose response to opportunities was limited only by their imagination—and by how much merchandise they could carry as they peddled through hamlets and hinterlands. Solomon exudes the qualities that constitute business aptitude: vision, social skills, and the courage to take risks. Like many resilient newcomers, he is willing to pick up and move, but determined to put down roots where he sees they have half a chance of taking hold. The play's title is not its only comic paradox. Hoffman appropriates the freedom of America's stage to dramatize American intolerance. There is a second delicious irony in his setting this play about anti-Semitism in New England, the new Zion originally settled by seekers of religious tolerance. And a third in Solomon's flight from bigotry in Boston, a city historically famed for its insistence on fair play and freedom from oppression.

The sleek Manhattan offices of George Simon, Elmer Rice's eponymous *Counsellor-at-Law* (1931), seem more than a few hundred miles from Isidor Solomon's New England village. Still, the upwardly mobile Simon copes with the same problem as his rural co-religionist: securing a foothold in an alluring but hostile society. Though the lawyer has the advantages of education and cosmopolitanism, his two adversaries are as formidable as village anti-Semites. The first is the patrician WASP society where, despite his showy successes, fortune, and the armor of intermarriage, Simon will never achieve the acceptance he craves. The second is his personal value system, where decency battles ambition for primacy. Simon brings to the practice of law a thorough grounding in Jewish morality, but his relentless drive to the top occasionally leads him to betray those values, as well as himself. His capacity for kindness and his sophistication notwithstanding, Simon's relentless ambition anticipates the opportunistic Jewish scrapper at the center of John Howard Lawson's *Success Story* (1932). (Overzealous achievement was hardly uncommon among first-generation Americans.) There is biting irony as well as remarkable courage in Rice's depiction in 1931 of a Jew who exploits that most basic article of Jewish belief, the law, for selfish, even unscrupulous ends.

With the title borrowed from Isaiah and applied to urban life in the Great Depression, Clifford Odets's *Awake and Sing!* (1935) is a quintessential American Jewish play. Its depiction of the Bronx and its immigrant speech patterns stamp it with historical authenticity. The play marks the debut of characters who were to become staples (and ultimately, alas, stereotypes) on the American stage: three generations of male immigrants, bewildered by the values and demands of American life; discontented first-generation youths, avid for a life richer than their parents'; and the prototypical Jewish mother, compelled by circumstances to develop her extraordinary talent for effective, if insensitive, solutions to life's predicaments.

The genuineness of its plot and the depth of its characters stunned audiences when the Group Theatre premiered the play in 1935. Writer Alfred Kazin acclaimed the work's verisimilitude and its turning "blunt Jewish speech" into dialogue. Kazin marveled at "watching my mother and father and uncles and aunts occupying the stage . . . by as much right as if they were Hamlet and Lear."[26] It is striking how closely Kazin's appreciation of the play, which was written and produced under the aegis of the predominantly Jewish Group Theatre, echoes the words of Group co-founder Harold Clurman about the Yiddish theatre he loved, "Here the problems of [the immigrant audience's] life, past and present, could be given a voice. . . ."[27]

The Broome Street address in Sylvia Regan's *Morning Star* (1940) supplies a window on three decades of history. Personal events—two generations of bar mitzvahs and weddings—take place against the background of history, including the Russian Revolution, the First World War, and the Depression. The play's central event is the infamous Triangle Shirtwaist Factory fire of 1911, in which 147 women and 21 men perished in flames or in futile efforts to escape them by plunging from the building's top stories. The ambitious scope of the play is repeated in its large cast. Many of the characters are archetypal: the patient, amorous boarder, the angry radical, the angrily ambitious young woman, the wise and stalwart mater familias, the would-be artists. Judicious glimpses of the past—Becky Felderman's references to Old World deprivation, the boarder's account of his miserable passage to America, the unexpected fate of the Marxist who returns to Russia—provide perspective for the characters' adjustment to the inequities and disappointments in the New World. Despite tragedies and setbacks, these Jews demonstrate their appreciation of life in America; patriotism pervades the play, whose original title was *Spangled Banner*.

America is again saluted in Arthur Laurents's World War II play, *Home of the Brave* (1945). The work brings to the stage a phenomenon born of that war: the all-American platoon. This cross section of American youth, featured in numerous novels and in dramas like Edward Chodorov's *Common Ground,* Harry Brown's *The Sound of Hunting,* Moss Hart's *Winged Victory,* and Herman

Wouk's *The Caine Mutiny Court-Martial,* typically includes a Jew, whose behavior is frequently determined by unconditional love of country. Against the background of anti-Semitism that ran rampant in the military, these works show that the enforced intimacy of barracks and combat units promoted bonding between Jews and the men and women they otherwise might never have met—some of whom were encountering Jews for the first time. *Home of the Brave* concentrates on the dilemma such bonding creates for a young Jew. The sturdy defenses Peter Coen has built against anti-Semitism melt in his friendship with Arizonan Wally Finch. When that camaraderie is undermined by a misperceived slur, and ended by enemy fire, Coen is left totally vulnerable, literally immobilized by loss. He becomes a study in Jewish paranoia and survivor guilt. Laurents's play stands in the vanguard of a growing American preoccupation with psychological problems fostered by the breakdown of prevailing mores and by wartime experiences.

"Wartime rhetoric," writes historian C.W.E. Bigsby, commenting on the climate of postwar theatre, "had reinvented small-town America . . . where old values were preserved and celebrated, a world worth fighting for; now that was already fading into history. . . . Basic myths having to do with family and community, civility and responsibility, style and grace had dissolved."[28] As if in lonely but vigorous contradiction to Bigsby's assessment stands S. N. Behrman's *The Cold Wind and the Warm* (1958). Though Behrman's retrospective of his youth in Worcester, Massachusetts, during the first years of the century is gentle, it does not sentimentalize the hard edges of those "basic myths." The interest of this mood play derives largely from its Jewish community, an engaging mix of familiar and unusual characters. The former include the irrepressible matchmaker, the sage who lives by the wisdom of the Torah, the flighty but irresistible *belle Juive,* and the comically vulgar parvenu given to referring to himself in the third person. The Behrman persona's heroes are a fresher lot: a doctor who derives more consolation from playing the oboe than from practicing medicine, and a multitalented friend and mentor, tormented by unfocused aspirations and unrequited love. Finally, there is the Behrman character himself, an artist who learns that the considerable value of community lies in supplying not answers, but support and continuity. Despite its being set a half-century earlier, *The Cold Wind and the Warm* is clearly poised on the threshold of the 1960s' celebratory explorations of ethnic roots.

Both psychiatry and renewed ethnic awareness have their place in *The Tenth Man* (1959), but the matrix of Paddy Chayefsky's play is Anski's Yiddish classic, *The Dybbuk* (1914). The exorcism of a troublesome spirit that inhabits the soul of a living person supplies the spectacular *coup de théâtre* of both plays. But the solemn ritual staged by ten Hasidim in the East European *shtetl* synagogue in Anski's work contrasts starkly with the ceremony conducted by the disparate affiliates of a storefront synagogue in Mineola, Long Island. The poles of opposition in Anski's play, where two young lovers set themselves at odds with a homogeneous, hermetic community, are fragmented in the American work into a variety of conflicts affecting Jewish lives in an open, secular society. The sexton's daily search to round up ten men for a minyan becomes metaphoric of each character's struggle for enough meaning to get through the day. The past does not meld easily into the present here, and the future is threatening. Widowers joke heartbreakingly about their daughters-in-law's inhospitality and visit their own cemetery plots. A young lawyer's disenchantment with life is driving him to dependence on alcohol and psychoanalysis; a rabbi's dedication to spiritual leadership is being eroded by the worldlier demands of his congregants. To these dilemmas the play proposes a common approach: the restoration of the faith that fosters love. While the exorcism provides that answer, the play itself poses other questions. By making comparisons with *The Dybbuk* inevitable, Chayefsky's play invites us to assess the modifications necessary to adapt the givens of Jewish life in the East European *shtetl* to those of present-day Long Island. Of these, perhaps the most significant is the way in which the tenets that supported and inspirited the Old Jewish World survive to sustain the New.

—Ellen Schiff

NOTES

1. Tyrone Guthrie, preface, in *The Hebrew Theatre,* by Mendel Kohansky (New York: KTAV, 1969), v.

2. John Higham, "American Anti-Semitism Historically Reconsidered," in *Jews in the Mind of America,* ed. Charles Herbert Stember (New York: Basic Books, 1966), 240.

3. Between 1881 and 1924, almost two million Jews emigrated to the United States. In 1880, the beginning of the mass migration from Eastern Europe, 230,000 Jews constituted 0.5 percent of the total U.S. population; by 1927, America's 4,228,000 Jews represented 3.6 percent of her population. Sidney Goldstein, "American Jewry, 1970: A Demographic Profile," in *The Jew in American Society,* ed. Marshall Sklare (New York: Behrman House, 1974), 100–01.

4. Higham, 248.

5. Gilbert Seldes, "Jewish Plays and Jew Plays in New York," *The Menorah Journal* 8 (April 1922), 240.

6. Russell Lynes, *The Lively Audience: A Social History of the Visual and Performing Arts in America, 1890–1950* (New York: Harper and Row, 1985), 31.

7. Howard M. Sachar, *A History of the Jews in America* (New York: Knopf, 1991), 356.

8. *They Too Arise,* also known as *No Villain,* can be read in manuscript at the New York Public Library for the Performing Arts at Lincoln Center. Mr. Miller declined its inclusion in this collection.

9. Arthur Miller, *Timebends* (New York: Harper and Row, 1987). See pp. 62–63, 70, 73, 81–83, 105–106, 166–67, 314, 409–10.

10. Robert Alter, "The Jew Who Didn't Get Away: On the Possibility of an American Jewish Culture," in *The American Jewish Experience,* ed. Jonathan D. Sarna (New York and London: Holmes and Meier, 1986), 277.

11. For example, the preponderance of critical studies of American Jewish literature are, in fact, devoted almost

entirely to fiction. It is shorter and certainly more useful to list comprehensive works that include drama rather than attempting to list those that do not: Sarah Blacher Cohen, ed., *From Hester Street to Hollywood* (Bloomington: Indiana Univ. Press, 1983); Cathy N. Davidson and Linda Wagner-Martin, eds., *The Oxford Companion to Women's Writing in the United States* (New York: Oxford Univ. Press, 1994); Lewis Fried, ed., *Handbook of American-Jewish Literature* (New York: Greenwood, 1988); Louis Harap, *Dramatic Encounters* (New York: Greenwood, 1987); Sanford Pinsker and Jack Fischel, eds., *Jewish American History and Culture* (New York: Garland, 1991); Ann R. Shapiro, ed., *Jewish American Women Writers* (New York: Greenwood, 1994).

12. Quoted in Lynes, p. 168.

13. Moshe Davis, "The Jewish People in Metamorphosis," in *Tradition and Change in Jewish Experience,* ed. A. Leland Jamison (Syracuse: Syracuse Univ. Press, 1978), 7.

14. Joseph C. Landis, ed. and trans., *Three Great Jewish Plays* (New York: Applause, 1986).

15. Irving Howe, *World of Our Fathers* (New York: Schocken, 1989), 492.

16. Francine Prose, "Protecting the Dead," in *Testimony,* ed. David Rosenberg (New York: Times Books, 1989), 113.

17. Nahma Sandrow, *Vagabond Stars: A World History of Yiddish Theater* (New York: Harper and Row, 1977), 405–06.

18. *Chicago Tribune,* 26 September, 1920.

19. Alfred Kazin, "The Jew As Modern Writer," in *The Ghetto and Beyond,* ed. Peter I. Rose (New York: Random House, 1969), 423.

20. Leslie Fiedler, "What Can We Do About Fagin?: The Jew-Villain in Western Tradition," *Commentary* (May 1949), 418.

21. Richard F. Shepard, "Genesis, Yiddish Version," The *New York Times,* 24 Jan., 1989.

22. Nahma Sandrow concludes her essay "Yiddish Theater and American Theater" by observing, "It is . . . not surprising that many of the passionate reformers of the twentieth-century American theater, so many critics, so many sponsors and patrons, so many experimenters, came out of the Yiddish theater." In Cohen, ed., *From Hester Street to Hollywood,* 27.

23. Sandrow points out, "Chekhov's *Uncle Vanya,* Strindberg's *The Father,* Romain Rolland's *Wolves,* Schnitzler's *Professor Bernardi*—all were performed in Yiddish translation before they were performed in English. Ibsen's *A Doll's House* and *An Enemy of the People* were staples in the serious Yiddish repertories. . . ." In Cohen, ed., *From Hester Street to Hollywood,* 26 (see n. 11).

24. Quoted by Charles E. Silberman, foreword, in *American Modernity and Jewish Identity* by Stephen M. Cohen (New York: Tavistock, 1983), x.

25. Steven M. Cohen, *American Modernity and Jewish Identity*, 25.

26. Quoted in Margaret Brenman-Gibson, *Clifford Odets, American Playwright* (New York: Atheneum, 1982), 324.

27. Harold Clurman, *The Fervent Years* (New York: Hill and Wang, 1945), 4.

28. C.W.E. Bigsby, *Modern American Drama, 1945–1990,* (New York: Cambridge Univ. Press, 1992), 32.

WELCOME STRANGER

A COMEDY IN FOUR ACTS

by

Aaron Hoffman

Aaron Hoffman pioneered the trail from vaudeville to the legitimate stage. Born in St. Louis in 1880, he developed his gifts for theatre as a student at the University of Chicago. At twenty-one he went to New York, where he promptly established himself as a versatile and prolific writer, turning out material for musical comedies, Ziegfield productions, and the vaudeville stage. Among the many popular entertainers who performed his monologues, sketches, and routines were Nora Bayes (née Dora Goldberg), Joe Weber and Lew Fields (né Shanfield), and their rivals, the Rogers Brothers (Max and Gus Solomon). At Hoffman's death in 1924, *The New York Times* called him "one of the most prolific writers for the American stage," and noted that "few vaudeville programs are altogether lacking in Hoffman material."

Although most of Hoffman's creative energies were devoted to the theatre, he was successful as well in a foray into journalism. For a time he contributed a half-page of topical humor to the Sunday *New York American.*

The comic spirit animated Hoffman's life too. The press regularly reported his antics, which frequently involved searching for talent in unusual places. Once, for instance, looking to add authentic color to a Turkish act, he approached three young dancers in a Turkish café on Rector Street. Their animated conversation was misinterpreted by the café's owner, the women's father, who called the police. Hoffman narrowly escaped arrest, and had an even closer brush with the law when he was taken to court by an annoyed neighbor protesting the writer's nocturnal activities. Hoffman allegedly wrote through the dead of night on a typewriter that he otherwise kept in the refrigerator. He was given to rousing his family periodically—evidently, also waking the neighbors—to try out Ziegfield material. The judge found for Hoffman, persuaded by his plea that comedy was, for him, "a deed of darkness."

Hoffman understood comedy's powerful appeal to the intelligence. His playlet, *The Son of Solomon* (1912), depicts the rift between orthodox immigrant parents and their Americanized children, who discard religious customs and traditions. Headlining an Orpheum bill, the work won critical praise as "a faithful portrayal of Jewish life," which turned its back on the prevailing burlesque and caricatured stage Jews.

Hoffman's experience in vaudeville served him well in choosing appealing subjects for the full-length plays he wrote in the last years of his short life. He collaborated several times with Samuel Shipman (né Shiffman), most successfully on *Friendly Enemies* (1918). Hailed for its "fidelity to life" and "knowledge of human nature," *Friendly Enemies,* which ran for 440 performances, shows how the bonds between two German-born Americans were tested by their conflicting allegiances during World War I. On his own, Hoffman wrote *Two Blocks Away* (1921), where well-liked Nathan Pomerantz, a Lower East Side cobbler, inherits a fortune, moves to Fifth Avenue, but eventually returns to the friends, neighborhood, and values he had spurned. *Give and Take* (1923) is a comedy about labor problems. The scenes between its factory owner and his antagonistic foreman reminded one reviewer of a Potash and Perlmutter sketch. Hoffman's other plays, written between 1918 and 1924, include *Nothing But Lies, The Good Old Days, Welcome Stranger,* and *Good for Nothing Jones.*

In *Welcome Stranger* (1920), Hoffman builds on the innovations in characterization he introduced in *Son of Solomon.* With its portrayal of strongly contrasting, lifelike types, the play breaks new ground in the American theatre's representation of the Jew. It opens with a sketch of the "typically up-to-date Jew," who can't get out of the boondocks and back to New York fast enough. It ends with the regeneration of a self-hating Jew who thought he could avoid prejudice by falsifying his identity and becoming the town's most rabid anti-Semite. The best developed characterization is, of course, Isidor Solomon's, the titular stranger. His assertion of Jewish pride, his keen awareness of Jewish history, and his confidence in his rights as an American do not blind him to the faults to which he and his co-religionists are inclined. His Act IV scene with the erstwhile bigot, now unmasked as a Jew, amounts to an astonishingly objective self-assessment. Yet for all his wisdom, this Solomon bumbles and jokes, winning supporters by his candor and warm humanity. It is easy to understand why theatre critic Percy Hammond praised *Welcome Stranger* for countering "all the platitudinous and obsolete indictments of the Jew" by representing both his "lowliest and noblest aspects." In *The Oxford Companion to American Theatre* Gerald Bordman recognizes *Welcome Stranger* as "one of the earliest attempts to confront American anti-Semitism."

Welcome Stranger was produced by Sam H. Harris at the Cohan and Harris Theatre, New York, on September 13, 1920, with the following cast:

DAVID FRANKEL	*David Adler*
BIJE WARNER	*John Adair, Jr.*
CLEM BEEMIS	*David Higgins*
GIDEON TYLER	*Ben Johnson*
SETH TRIMBLE	*Edward L. Snader*
EB HOOKER	*Charles I. Schofield*
ICHABOD WHITSON	*Edmund Breeze*
ISIDOR SOLOMON	*George Sidney*
GRACE WHITSON	*Valerie Hickerson*
NED TYLER	*Frank Herbert*
MRS. TRIMBLE	*Isadora Martin*
MARY CLARK	*Margaret Mower*
ESTHER SOLOMON	*Mary Brandon*
DONEGAN	*Percival Lennon*
SAM	*Jules J. Bennet*

SYNOPSIS OF SCENES

The scenes are laid in a little town in New Hampshire.

ACT I

Lobby of the Grand Hotel.
New Year's Eve—1918.

ACT II

Clem's home.
A few weeks later.

ACT III

Office.
The following Spring.

ACT IV

Lobby of the Grand Hotel.
New Year's Eve—1919.

ACT I

SCENE: *Lobby of the Grand Hotel.*

TIME: *About ten p.m., New Year's Eve,* 1918.

An old-fashioned hotel, office and lobby L.C., *at back is door opening to street,* L. *of door, large window frosted by the cold. Counter downstage* L. *Safe below counter. Door above counter* L. *On counter is rack containing Christian Science literature, containing full stock of monitors, journals, pamphlets, etc.* R.C. *is stove and chairs. On* R. *side is a window downstage—in this window is one cracked pane of glass—above this window to the* R. *is a door leading to hotel dining room. At back* R.C. *is stairway leading to rooms of hotel. On landing of this stairway is a practical door—heavy bolt or lock on back of door, so that when bolt is shot later in act, it is heard distinctly throughout auditorium. On floor at door* C. *is a mat upon which is inscription in large letters: "Welcome."*

NOTE: *Wind storm and snow effects are highly important for this act.*

Arrange set of Act I so that it matches with brilliant set required for Act IV.

AT RISE: *Discovered:* BIJE *behind counter* L., *writing.* FRANKEL, *a typical New York drummer, Jewish, about thirty years of age—well-dressed, but should be typically up-to-date Jew. He is sitting at stove, overcoat collar turned up. He is a picture of misery. At rise a moment of silence, gale of wind, snowstorm effect.*

FRANKEL: *(Shivering—looks at his watch in despair.)* Fine burg to spend New Year's Eve in. There must be some way to get out. Can I get a rig—a sleigh—a haywagon?

BIJE: No.

CLEM: *(Enters* C. *door with some mail, packages and snow shovel.)* Train for Edendale, Sarah's Corners, Nashua connecting with Main line for New York.

FRANKEL: *(Picks up grip.)* Thank God!

CLEM: Is four hours late. *(Puts shovel up* L., *mail, etc., on counter.)*

FRANKEL: *(Crosses to* CLEM L. *Throws down grip in disgust and speaks. Drops grip in position for* TRIMBLE *to fall over it on his entrance*—R. *of table.)* Say, porter—

CLEM: I'm no porter.

FRANKEL: What are you?

CLEM: The town electrician.

FRANKEL: Where's the electricity? *(Looking about.)*

CLEM: Got none in the town yet—except in my house.

FRANKEL: Well, electrical supplies is my line. Maybe I can sell you some machinery?

CLEM: Sell *me* machinery? No, sir; invent all my own—got plans and models—whole shooting match—water power, generator, dynamo.

FRANKEL: Where?

CLEM: At home—in the kitchen sink—got it attached to the water faucet and it works like a charm.

FRANKEL: Oh, your electrical plant is in the sink. *(Takes New York newspaper from pocket—laughs.)*

CLEM: Oh, you can laugh—they laughed at Edison, too, but all I need is the capital.

FRANKEL: Maybe you can interest J. P. Morgan—here's a New York newspaper. *(Offers the paper to* CLEM.*)* You'll find his address on the financial page.

CLEM: Thanks. I'll look him up as soon as I'm not so busy. *(Exits* R.U.*)*

*(*FRANKEL *laughs and crosses down and sits in small chair* L. *of stove.)*

TYLER: *(Enters from dining room* R. *upper.)* My hands are stiff. *(Crosses down* R. *of stove.)*

*(*TRIMBLE *follows* TYLER *on stage. He goes downstage* L. *of stove.)*

TRIMBLE: Well, you can't go back on this. Gid, you owe me. *(*FRANKEL *rises.* TRIMBLE *stumbles over grip. Bus. angry.)** You here yet? *(Kicks grip upstage a bit and goes down to chair* FRANKEL *has left.)*

FRANKEL: *(Goes for grip, puts grip above table* C.*)* This is mine. *(Taking hold of chair.)*

TRIMBLE: 'Tain't neither—you ain't stopping here. *(*TRIMBLE *pulls chair away from* FRANKEL.*)*

(Enter WHITSON *door* C. FRANKEL *goes around stove to* R.*)*

WHITSON: Br-r-r. Evening, boys. *(Comes down* L.C.*)*

BIJE: Evening, Mr. Whitson.

(General greeting from others. TRIMBLE *and* TYLER *go up to table ad lib.)*

WHITSON: Happy New Year.

*(*CLEM *enters* R.U. *with jug of cider and two glasses.)*

CLEM: Here's your cider.

WHITSON: *(*CLEM *places jug on table.* WHITSON *and* TYLER *around table.)* Get another glass. *(*CLEM *exits* R.U.*)*

FRANKEL: *(*R. *Taking drinking cup out of pocket.)* It's all right—I got one—sanitary. *(Cup is collapsible drinking cup. As* FRANKEL *takes it from pocket, he opens it and comes downstage—to others.)*

TRIMBLE: *(Crosses down to* FRANKEL, *front stove.)* Oh, you get the hell out of here. *(Hits cup, closing it.)*

FRANKEL: Easy with that rough stuff—you big rube.

TRIMBLE: Oh, you go back to Jerusalem, where you belong. *(*TYLER *turns* TRIMBLE *upstage.)*

*Stage business. Hoffman may have been prompted by the importance of facial and body language on the vaudeville stage to include this frequently repeated indication that actors are to engage in appropriate looks and gestures.

WHITSON: *(L.C. Notices* FRANKEL *and that he is a Jew.)* How did you get in here?

FRANKEL: Waiting for my connection—train's snowbound. *(Crosses* L. *to* WHITSON.*)*

WHITSON: *(To* BIJE.*)* Didn't give him accommodation, did you? *(Removes coat, hat.* BIJE *takes same across to rack up* R.*)*

BIJE: I should say not.

WHITSON: Well, then, see here—you're not a guest here. Mr. Tyler owns this hotel and I'm the Mayor of this town and you'd better behave yourself or I'll send you to the lock-up. *(Crosses* R. *to stove.)*

TRIMBLE: *(Up* R.C.*)* You New York smart aleck.

FRANKEL: *(*L.C.*)* Oh, my nose is bleeding. *(Puts hand to nose.)*

WHITSON: Then keep it out where it isn't wanted.

TRIMBLE: Your kind of nose ain't wanted at all in this town.

FRANKEL: *(To* BIJE, *who is crossing around back to desk.)* Oh, I see. That's why you wouldn't give me a room, so I could rest up between trains. *(Enter* CLEM. CLEM *brings glass to table.* FRANKEL *speaks to* CLEM.*)* Say—you look like a decent fellow; can't you tell me how I can get out of this hole?

CLEM: Well, I'll tell you. There's the eleven-ten from Rocksboro. That stops at the watertank about twelve-thirty. That'll get over to Sour Lake and from there you can catch the accommodation which will get you into Greenfield Junction about eight-thirty in the morning—if the train's on time.

FRANKEL. Sounds like a nice, pleasant trip. *(Picks up grip. Opens door wide. Others have business of turning up their collars, etc.)* Well, it's better than spending New Year's Eve in this town. Good night, gentlemen, and I hope the New Year brings all that I wish you—*mackus.**

TRIMBLE: Oh, shut the door. *(Goes back of table.* FRANKEL *exits upstage door, going off* L. CLEM *shuts door.)*

WHITSON: *(*R.*)* That's the way we've got to handle them,

*Usually *makkes:* nothing. Leo Rosten traces *makkes* to the Hebrew *makot:* "plagues, blows, visitations." *The Joys of Yiddish,* p. 222.

or the first thing you know the town will be full of them. *(Crosses to table.)*

CLEM: But, Ichabod, if they make up their minds to come, you can't keep them out legally.

TRIMBLE: Legal or not, we've done it so far.

*(*CLEM *crosses over to desk under window* R. *and reads paper* FRANKEL *has given him.)*

TYLER: It's about time the young folks were coming home from the party. *(Crosses down, sits* R. *in front of fire.)*

WHITSON: Oh, let them have their fun, New Year's Eve—and it's the first time my Grace and your Ned have been out together for some time. I'm kind of hoping that Ned will pop the question tonight. *(Sits* R. *on* TYLER'S L.*)*

TYLER: Nothing would please me better. You know that your daughter Grace is a fine girl and I'm sure she'll make him a fine wife.

TRIMBLE: *(Bringing two glasses of cider to them, which he has poured, and keeps glass.)* Do you think Ned and Grace are going to make a match of it? I'd like to know, because I've got a fine line of wedding presents left over from the holidays.

WHITSON: Hadn't you better speak to Ned? He seems kind of backward.

TYLER: I think I will. I believe in folks getting married young, don't you, Eb?

BIJE: *(Comes downstage* L.*)* I don't think a young girl ought to be dictated to. She ought to be allowed to choose for herself.

WHITSON: Who asked for your opinion?

BIJE: Nobody.

WHITSON: Then keep it to yourself.

BIJE: Excuse me. *(Goes upstage—looks out of window.)*

TRIMBLE: Well—here's to the young folks.

TYLER: *(All have a glass of cider, standing and facing front.)* And here's to the old folks.

CLEM: *(Seated at writing desk—reading the paper.)* Better drink your liquor while you can, 'cause I'm just reading in this New York paper that by 1920 they're going to do away with alcohol in every shape and form.

TRIMBLE: Well, maybe they will, but I don't know, anyhow, that that'll stop *cider* from *fermenting*.

TYLER: Let's have a look at that paper, Clem. I haven't seen a New York paper in an age.

CLEM. *(Rises. Gives paper to* TYLER, *tears out a piece of paper.)* You can have it.

TYLER: What are you tearing out?

CLEM: Nothing that would interest you. *(Crosses front of others to* C., *takes glasses in passing.)* Just concerns me and J. P. Morgan.

WHITSON: Expect him to back you?

CLEM: Oh, you can laugh. You've laughed at me for twenty years, but I tell you you're stagnating, when you've got enough power in these falls to make this one of the most prosperous towns in New Hampshire.

TYLER: He's wound up again.

CLEM: All right—you'll find out some day. I've got inventions—I've got the franchise and I'll get the falls. I'm just setting back—that's all I'm doing—just setting back.

WHITSON: And all you want is a little money?

CLEM: Yes.

WHITSON: So you can set *us* back. *(All laugh.)*

CLEM: Oh, what's the use? Seems as if nobody's ever takin' me serious in this town. *(Takes glasses and puts them on small table upstage and exits* L. *above desk, taking jug with him.)*

WHITSON: Anything interesting, Gideon?

TYLER: *(Joshing* TRIMBLE.*)* Here's something that'll interest Seth.

TRIMBLE: What is it?

TYLER: About the Zion movement.

TRIMBLE: I'm in favor of it—send 'em all back—but give me the page with the ads. Want to see what's going on in the New York stores. *(*WHITSON *takes page of paper from* TYLER.*)*

WHITSON: Here's a big sale at Sterns.

TRIMBLE: Sterns! *(Takes paper from* WHITSON.*)* Bet it's a fake. Here's another one at Saks. Look at 'em—all in a row—Altman, Abraham and Strauss, Gimbel, Franklin Simon, Moe Levy— *(In rage—tears and throws paper on floor under stove.)*

TYLER: Seth—it certainly looks as if your Hebrew friends own New York City.

WHITSON: And there's a big lesson for us in those ads. Keep them out.

(At this point storm reaches its climax of violence. ISIDOR SOLOMON *appears at door at back. He manages to open the door—effect of wind and snow blow him in. Out of breath,* ISIDOR *staggers in.* ISIDOR *stands swaying and puffing. As* SOLOMON *comes down* L.C. *at entrance,* BIJE *comes from desk to* L. *of* SOLOMON.*)*

BIJE: A guest!

TRIMBLE: *(Crossing to* R. *of* SOLOMON.*)* Welcome, stranger! Bije, take his coat— *(*BIJE *does so.)* —and gloves— *(*BIJE *takes gloves and crosses up back to hat rack up* R. *Hangs up coat and puts gloves above on shelf.* TRIMBLE *continues as* SOLOMON *unwraps muffler.)* We'll make you nice and comfortable here—

(At this point SOLOMON *gets muffler off and speaks. During greeting business* TYLER *gets up* C. *behind table.)*

ISIDOR: Hello—Happy New Year. *(All recognize he is Jewish.)*

TRIMBLE: Another one—by the ever living jumping Moses.

ISIDOR: No, not Moses—Solomon—Isidor Solomon. Glad to meet you, boys. Excuse me while I get acquainted with the stove. *(Crosses to fire, tries to get warm, goes upstage and puts hat and scarf on hat rack.* BIJE *crosses at back to desk.)*

WHITSON: *(Shows he recognizes* ISIDOR. *To* BIJE.*)* Don't you put him up. *(Crosses* L., *meeting* BIJE *at desk.* BIJE *shakes his head.)*

ISIDOR: Maybe it ain't too late to get a bite to eat?

WHITSON: *(With sarcasm.)* Oh, I guess the cook would be tickled to death to get out of a nice warm bed just to wait on you.

ISIDOR: *(*R.C.*)* No, no, that's putting you to too much trouble.

TYLER: *(Behind table.)* Of course, if he's satisfied with a little snack, we could all go out and shoot him a brace of quail.

TRIMBLE: *(L. of* TYLER.*)* Maybe he don't like quail.

ISIDOR: *(Crosses to grip, which* BIJE *has left front of desk in front of counter* L.*)* Never mind; I got a couple of sandwiches in my grip. Look out, you'll spoil me the first night I'm in your town.

(General move here; TRIMBLE *sits in chair* R. *front of stove.* TYLER *upstage behind table and* WHITSON *crosses to chair* L. *of table.)*

WHITSON: *(Suggesting anxiety.)* How long do you expect to stay here?

ISIDOR: *(L. of desk.)* The rest of my life maybe.

WHITSON: You mean you're going to try and settle down here? *(Sits in chair* L. *of table.)*

ISIDOR. *(L.C.)* Why not? If I find the right location—with nice people, cheap rent—why, the way you treat me, already I feel at home. Where I come from I lived in one neighborhood for fifteen years and not once did anyone go out in the middle of the night and bring me quail. I feel like we're well acquainted—old friends—don't feel like I'm in a strange town at all. In fact, I got a long distance relative that lives some place around here. Maybe you know him? His name is Ike—

WHITSON: We don't know him. There are no Ikes in this town.

ISIDOR: So much the better for the town. Such a loafer. It's only for his mother's sake I'm looking for him. For his own sake I hope I never find him. *(To* WHITSON—*directly.)* Oh, Mr.—Mr.—

WHITSON: *(Intensely, but quietly.)* My name is Whitson—I'm the Mayor of this town.

ISIDOR: *(Turns to* BIJE *behind desk.)* Mayor! Is he really? *Turns back to* WHITSON—*bows.)*

BIJE: Sure he is.

ISIDOR: Well, what do you think of that? The first man I meet and wants to make friends with me, who is he? The Mayor! Well, really, this is an honor. Ain't you got a lawyer for me to meet?

BIJE: Sure, we have. Mr. Hooker! He handles insurance and is tax collector for a living. You'll meet him.

WHITSON: What brings you here anyway?

ISIDOR: Well, I had this place in my mind a long time. Years ago, before I opened my little shebang in Boston, I used to peddle through the mountain towns around here and many a time I used to look down on you in the valley, and everything here looked so nice and peaceful and friendly, the grass looked so green, the waterfalls lying there like pure silver. Many a time I wished I could come here and settle down. I love the country—in Boston I was never happy.

TRIMBLE: Oh, Boston wasn't good enough for you.

ISIDOR: Oh, Boston is a nice city all right.

WHITSON: Well, what did you leave it for?

ISIDOR: I got a good *reason.* I don't *like* to say it; you wouldn't believe it, but it's true. I left there because in Boston they don't *like* Jews. *(Laughs.)* Can you *beat that*? *(Bus. for others. Exchange quizzical glances.)*

TRIMBLE: What makes you think they like them here?

ISIDOR: Oh, in a small town it's different. It's more like a big family. People ain't so narrow-minded.

TYLER: Don't you think you're making a mistake, coming to a little town, giving up a going business in a big city?

ISIDOR: That's what it was—a going business—nobody coming.

TRIMBLE: What line of business do you think you're going to start?

ISIDOR: My plans are to open up a big general store on the Main Street. I'll have a grand opening. A big band of music. I'll slaughter the prices to bring the men—and to attract the ladies, I'll stand in front of the store myself. *(Chuckles.)* I'll give away candy to the children—not too much, so they won't get sick.

TRIMBLE: *(Going toward* ISIDOR. *Between* SOLOMON *and* WHITSON.*)* Now you listen to me—I'm running the general store here; there ain't room for two, and if you take my advice you won't waste no more time figuring on opening up here at all.

WHITSON: If you'll listen to us, you'll move on to some other town this very night. I'm quite sure you'll start a much happier New Year elsewhere.

ISIDOR: I appreciate your advice, coming from the Mayor.

I know you want to be friends and are trying to help me out.

WHITSON: Oh, yes—we're going to help you—out.

ISIDOR: Thank you. If you'll excuse me—I want to write a letter to my little daughter Essie. Have you got any writing paper here that don't cost nothing? Oh, here's some—right here—maybe I'd better register first and take up my grip. *(Bus. of* WHITSON *shaking head "No" to* BIJE.*)*

BIJE: No use registering. We ain't got any room for you.

ISIDOR: No room? I'm glad your hotel is doing such a nice business. *(To* TRIMBLE.*)* You see? It is a live town. If the hotels do business it's a good sign for everybody. Maybe you can put an extra cot in the hall for me?

BIJE: *(*WHITSON *repeats business. Shakes head.)* Got no extra cot for you, either.

ISIDOR: You won't get mad if I go to another hotel.

WHITSON: No—go ahead.

ISIDOR: *(Picks up grip—starts toward door—just a start.)* Where is the nearest one?

BIJE: In the next town. *(All laugh. Quietly.)*

ISIDOR: Oh, you mean there ain't no other hotel? That's a good joke on me. I was going to look for it and there ain't none. *(All snicker.)* Jolly people—well, I got to stay here, then. *(Goes to register. All turn and look at* ISIDOR.*)*

BIJE: But we ain't got no place ter put you.

ISIDOR: Oh, say, you'll find a place to put me all right. I don't take up much room—lengthwise. I'll write my letter and you figure it out where to put me. Anything at all suits me. Anything at all. *(Takes writing paper, goes over to desk* R.*, starts to write.)*

(Others stand watching him—pen scratches loudly. Tack small piece of sandpaper on desk to get this effect. TYLER *up* R.C. TRIMBLE *up* C. WHITSON L. *of table.)*

WHITSON: *(Rises, crosses to* BIJE*, who is behind counter.)* Get him out of here.

BIJE: You mean to throw him out?

WHITSON: If necessary—call Clem. *(*BIJE *rings tap bell for* CLEM.*)*

ISIDOR: This is a regular hotel all right—regular hotel pen. *(Sleigh bells in distance.* ISIDOR *resumes writing.)*

*(*CLEM *enters* L. *above desk, carrying shovel and broom, which he leaves by* C. *door when* WHITSON *calls him.)*

WHITSON: Clem! Come here. *(*CLEM *does so.* L. *to* WHITSON.*)*
CLEM: What's'a matter?
WHITSON: See that fellow over there. I want you and Bije to throw him out of here. *(Pantomimes to* CLEM *to throw* ISIDOR *out.)*
CLEM: It won't hurt to let him stay one night.
WHITSON: Don't argue.
TRIMBLE: *(Up* C.*)* If you're so tender-hearted, you can sleep him in the lock-up.

(In distance sleigh bells are heard. Bell and voices coming nearer to the hotel.)

TYLER: Here come the young folks. *(Crosses up to window up* L.*)*
CLEM: He don't look to be such a bad fellow. *(Crosses above table.)*
WHITSON: *(Follows* CLEM.*)* See here, Clem Beemis, you obey orders if you know what's good for you.
CLEM: *(Back of table.)* All right. I'll get him out quietly when everybody's gone. No use creating a disturbance.

(Sleigh has drawn near. Voices of party offstage—"Happy New Year," etc. Enter GRACE C. *door.)*

GRACE: *(*WHITSON *follows* TRIMBLE *to* R.C.*)* Hello, everybody. *(All respond.)* Happy New Year, Father dear.
WHITSON: *(To* GRACE.*)* You're cold.

*(*GRACE *crosses to* BIJE *at counter. As* GRACE *crosses to counter to* BIJE, NED *enters center and greets* TYLER, *who is* L. *of door.)*

NED: Happy New Year, Dad. *(Shakes hands.* TYLER *puts arm around son, taking him down toward table.)*

TYLER: Same to you, my boy.

NED: *(To* CLEM, *who drops down behind table.)* Happy New Year, Clem.

CLEM: How d'y, Ned.

NED: *(To* WHITSON, *who drops in* R. *of* CLEM.*)* Happy New Year, Mr. Whitson!

WHITSON: Happy New Year, Ned.

NED: *(To* TRIMBLE, *who drops in* R. *of* WHITSON.*)* Same to you, Mr. Trimble.

*(*TRIMBLE *bows in acknowledgement, but before he can answer* ISIDOR, *who has risen and come* R. *of* TRIMBLE, *butts in.)*

ISIDOR: *(Bowing.)* Happy New Year. Same to you! *(All turn and freeze* ISIDOR. TRIMBLE, *in disgust, thrusts hands in pockets and goes up.* TYLER *and* WHITSON *turn to each other behind table and* CLEM *goes up to center door and shows* NED *piece he tore from paper.* ISIDOR *returns to desk* R.*)*

BIJE: *(In undertone to* GRACE.*)* I've been thinking of you all night, Gracie.

GRACE: Well, I haven't been thinking of you; you're just as mean as you can be. *(Almost in tears.)*

BIJE: But I couldn't get away. Your father wouldn't let me off.

GRACE: It's mean— *(Looks around)* —that's what it is. He's just doing everything to keep us apart.

BIJE: Yes—and to bring you and Ned together. How do you suppose I feel when I see you and him—

GRACE: *(*TRIMBLE *is cold and goes to stove.* ISIDOR *sees this move and goes toward him.)* Now, Bije, you know very well that— *(Continues conversation in whispers.)*

ISIDOR: If you feel cold, I got a little something in my grip that'll warm you up better than the stove.

TRIMBLE: Don't want nothin' from you. *(Turns away, goes up.)*

*(*ISIDOR, *repulsed by* TRIMBLE, *looks around and tries to talk to others. All ignore him and he gets way over to desk right when* TYLER *calls "Ned!"* NED, *busy with* CLEM, *does not answer and* ISIDOR *calls. This business is during dialogue up to point mentioned.)*

BIJE: *(Bashfully.)* I've got something to show you, Gracie.

GRACE: What is it?

BIJE: I made it up all by myself. Took me almost a week!

WHITSON: *(*GRACE *sits in chair at end of counter downstage.* WHITSON *sees them.)* Hadn't you better speak to Ned? *(*BIJE *hands* GRACE *paper with poem on it.)*

GRACE: Why, it's poetry.

BIJE: Gee, I hope it is. *(Bus. between* GRACE *and* BIJE.*)*

TYLER: *(Indicating* GRACE *and* BIJE.*)* Seeing what's going on over there—I think I'd best speak to him immediately. Ned! Ned! Oh, Ned!

ISIDOR: Ned! Ned! *(All turn.)*

NED: Yes, Father.

*(*WHITSON *turns upstage, but eavesdrops on the conversation. Voices offstage: "Hurry up in there—we're freezing"—blow horns—exit* CLEM *with snow shovel.* TYLER *takes* NED *in front of table.* SOLOMON *up, looking in cigar case till* MRS. TRIMBLE *enters, when he rushes up to open door for her.)*

TYLER: You haven't spoken to Grace yet, have you?

NED: *(Reluctantly.)* No, Dad, not yet. Grace is an awfully sweet girl, but she doesn't seem to be crazy about me.

TYLER: Now, Ned. A nice girl isn't going to throw herself at you, until you say something. You can't expect her to propose to you. Now I don't want to rush matters, but my heart's set on this match and—

NED: Now, Dad. I'd rather not—at least, not yet.

CLEM: Mrs. Trimble's out there, Seth, and says for you to hurry.

MRS. TRIMBLE: *(Speaks outside.)* I'll get 'em. *(*SOLOMON *opens door* L. *and drops down* R.C., *bowing. Enter* MRS. TRIMBLE.*)* Well, I'm nearly frozen. *Down* L.C.*)*

WHITSON: *(Closing door.)* Happy New Year, Mrs. Trimble.

MRS. TRIMBLE: Wish you the same.

ISIDOR: Happy New Year. *(*MRS. TRIMBLE *pays no attention.)*

TYLER: Happy New Year, Martha.

MRS. TRIMBLE: Happy New Year, Gideon and Mr. Whitson. Come, Ned and Gracie—if those young folks ever expect me to chaperone them again they'll have to get home at a reasonable hour. It's almost eleven o'clock. Seth, get your coat.

TRIMBLE: I'm coming, Martha. *(Gets coat.)*

*(*WHITSON *and* TYLER *go to rack and get coats.* NED *helps* TYLER *on with his coat, etc.)*

ISIDOR: *(Meeting* MRS. TRIMBLE *front of table* C.*)* Excuse me, is that your husband? I'm glad to meet you.

MRS. TRIMBLE: *(Looks at him in surprise—recognizes he is Jewish.)* I beg your pardon. *(Says this haughtily.)*

ISIDOR: My name is Solomon. Isidor Solomon. I'm in the same line of business you and your husband are. I expect to open a new store here and he's a little bit worried.

MRS. TRIMBLE: Oh, there's not the slightest reason to worry about *you* opening a *store* here, not the *slightest.*

ISIDOR: That's nice. Thank you, Martha. *(*TRIMBLE *is struggling getting into his overcoat—*ISIDOR *helps him on with it—business.* TRIMBLE *turns—sees it is* ISIDOR *and pulls away.)* Say—you lost your sleeve.

TRIMBLE: Oh, let go. *(Goes* L. ISIDOR *starts up and works up to window* L.*)*

(Voices offstage: "Hurry up." CLEM *enters with snow shovel.)*

CLEM: The folks say they're freezing to death out there and want you to hurry up.

MRS. TRIMBLE: Ready, Seth? *(She goes up.)*

*(*TRIMBLE *crosses to* C. *He is stopped by* WHITSON *and* TYLER*—they call him in pantomime over* R. *by stove.)*

TRIMBLE: All right. Good night, Bije.

ISIDOR: Good night.

NED: Coming, Grace? *(*GRACE *pays no attention.)* Oh, excuse me. *(Turns to* TYLER.*)* Coming, Dad?

TYLER: We'll be right along, Ned.

NED: Good night, Clem. *(*CLEM *is in conversation with the others.)*

CLEM: I understand.

ISIDOR: Good night. Happy New Year. *(Opens door for* NED.*)*

NED: Same to you.

ISIDOR: Thanks. Don't slip now.

WHITSON: *(To* CLEM.*)* Well, it's up to you, if you don't think you need any help.

CLEM: Oh, me and Bije can handle him.

TRIMBLE: But he's got to go.

MRS. TRIMBLE: *(Off.)* Hurry up, Seth.

ISIDOR: *(To* SETH.*)* You better hurry up. It's your wife.

TRIMBLE: Bah! *(*TYLER, CLEM *and* TRIMBLE *exit.)*

WHITSON: Grace, come on. *(*BIJE *and* GRACE *still talking.)* Say, what are you two talking about?

GRACE: Why, we were just— Why, nothing, Papa. *(Hides poem.)*

WHITSON: Bije—you and Clem have enough to do with the business on hand. *(Referring to* ISIDOR.*)* Come on, Grace. *Starts for door.)*

ISIDOR: Nice girl, your daughter. I got one, too.

BIJE: *(Sadly.)* Good night, Grace.

GRACE: *(Tearfully.)* Good night, Bije.

WHITSON: Grace!! *(*ISIDOR *opens door for them. To* GRACE.*)* Good night. Happy New Year. *(*GRACE *crying—exits.)*

ISIDOR: Happy New Year. Good night to you.

WHITSON: Good bye to you. *(Exits.)*

(Sleigh bells, singing, etc., going off in the distance. ISIDOR *and* BIJE *at window back, waving farewell to the departing sleigh.)*

ISIDOR: *(Crosses down back of table.)* She likes you, that girl. You know, that's nice.

BIJE: I've got as much chance of getting her as you have of getting a store in this town.

ISIDOR: Then your chances look pretty good because I'm in right already. Listen—I want you to hear what I'm writing to my little daughter Essie. She lives with relatives now until I get settled. I tell you that girl loves her father—well, no wonder—for twelve years I've been her mother. *(Reads from letter.* BIJE *sits at table* L., *paying no attention to* ISIDOR.*)* Now, listen! "My dear darling, little sweetheart daughter Essie: Here I am stopping at the finest hotel in Valley Falls. See that? I think this town is the spot for us as there is no opposition hardly. The owner of the general store here looks like a Shlamiel. Give Aunt Mania my love and tell her to be sure and send me Ike's latest picture. Don't lose the storage receipt. I'll telegraph you when to ship the stock. Bushels of love and kisses from your loving papa—Mr. Solomon." *(To* BIJE.*)* Where's the mailbox?

BIJE: I'll attend to it. *(Takes letter and puts it in mailbox on counter.)*

ISIDOR: Oh, Bije, did you decide where to put me?

BIJE: Oh, yes, we've decided where to put you.

ISIDOR: Thank you, that's fine.

BIJE: I'm going to lock up. *(*BIJE *exits.)*

*(*ISIDOR, *left alone, looks about—gets grip and takes it to chair. Enter* CLEM—R. *at desk.)*

CLEM: Whew! It's cold. *(Goes to fire, shakes fire.)*

ISIDOR: I've got something that will warm you up. *(Takes out flask of whiskey—holds it toward* CLEM.*)*

CLEM: *(Looks at flask, about to reach for it, turns away, looks at flask again.)* Yeh? Considering what I've got to do—I don't think it would be right to take any.

ISIDOR: Oh, go on. A little drink won't hurt you.

CLEM: Gosh—I don't know what to do. *(Hesitates.)* You ain't never been in our town lock-up, have you?

ISIDOR: I ain't never been in any lock-up. Don't bother; I'll be comfortable here.

CLEM: But they ain't got any room for you here.

ISIDOR: Oh, yes, they have—Bije said he'd decided where he's going to put me.

CLEM: Well, I'm glad you got it fixed with Bije. *(Grabs flask.)* Relieves me of a mighty disagreeable job. *(Drinks from flask.)*

ISIDOR: Good, eh?

CLEM: You bet it's good—good and scarce. *(Goes to stove—turning damper, etc.)*

ISIDOR: I suppose it keeps you busy running this hotel, day and night?

CLEM: Oh, this ain't my profession. It's just a job.

ISIDOR: Is that so! What's your regular business?

CLEM: Town electrician.

ISIDOR: Where is it? *(Looks at lamps around room.)*

CLEM: Got it right here in my pocket. *(Takes out franchise and spreads it on the table.)*

ISIDOR: *(Reads—ad lib. Latin phrases—Anno Domini, etc. After ad lib. Latin.)* Thereafter—hereafter—heretofore—whereas— What is it in English?

CLEM: That's a franchise for laying mains, poles, tracks and everything appertaining to electric heat, light and power in the village of Valley Falls.

ISIDOR: You own all that?

CLEM: Every bit. Cost me a dollar a year.

ISIDOR: That's awful cheap, ain't it? *(Sits* L. *of table, pulls franchise toward him, reads.)*

CLEM: *(Sits* R. *of table.)* Cheap? I should say it is; it's the biggest snap that was every known in the history of hydraulic electricity. There it is made out in my name—there's the seal of the town—for and in consideration of one dollar a year—there's the signature of old Judge Stebbin. He was Mayor then. The Judge always felt he owed me something ever since he was took down with a paralytic stroke—couldn't walk and I made him a present of an electric wheel chair . . . my own invention—and at my own expense. He showed his gratitude by giving me this franchise—in perpetualis for the electric privileges of Valley Falls.

ISIDOR: Now you see, that was a case of throwing your loaf of bread on the waters and it came back sandwiches.

CLEM: Of course the franchise always was a sort of a joke to the Judge, same as it is to everybody else in this town, but it's the dream of my life, and I've kept on paying that franchise fee for the last fifteen years and developing my ideas of the plant and now all I need is the capital to put it through.

ISIDOR: Oh, you need capital. For what?

CLEM: To buy the land and build the plant.

ISIDOR: I thought you had it all working.

CLEM: I have—in my head.

ISIDOR: Oh, I see. I thought a dollar a year was too big a cinch.

CLEM: There never was a bigger cinch—with the waterfalls and my duplex turbine water motor patented—why, it's a mint.

ISIDOR: You mean to say with a little capital you could start up a mint?

CLEM: Yes, sir—just imagine every house in town paying for light. Then there's a half dozen towns within a radius of twenty-five miles that ain't got no connecting trolleys—short hauls, cheap juice—why, I wouldn't trade it for half a dozen gold mines. *(*ISIDOR *picks up franchise, looks at it—pause.)* It's the chance of a lifetime.

ISIDOR: Say, it's a wonderful business all right; of course for anybody that understands it.

CLEM: I'll guarantee that the man who'll put a little money into this will be a millionaire over night. And, of course, if you put up your money, I'd expect you to demand fifty percent.

ISIDOR: Yes—and you'd have a right to expect it. Of course, it's a new kind of a trade for me—it ain't like the clothing business.

CLEM: It's better—it's progress—it's bringing comforts to people that never had them and it's almost all clear profit.

ISIDOR: *(Picks up franchise again—looks at it.)* Almost all clear profit. I'd be proud to be in such a business. Say, a town like this ought to have electricity. Now what's the least—the very least amount of money you'd have to start things going?

CLEM: First thing is to clinch the water rights to the Falls. Now for five hundred dollars we could buy— *(*ISIDOR *turns away in his seat.)* Well, for three hundred we could— *(*ISIDOR *pays no attention—yawns.)* Well, for a hundred and fifty we could— *(*ISIDOR *now all attention)* —get an option on the property. We don't need much land. You see, here's where the river runs through the old Eastman farm— *(Shows* ISIDOR *blue print or diagram.)* —now all we need is a strip of about an acre on both sides of the Falls . . .

ISIDOR: To shut out competition— You're smart. *(Looking at diagram.)* And you get acres for a hundred and fifty dollars?

CLEM: You mean you're thinking of coming in with me?

ISIDOR: Yes, I'm thinking—a hundred and fifty dollars—

I'm thinking hard— Well, say, it might be the chance of a lifetime.

CLEM: You ain't joking with me now?

ISIDOR: Joking? I should joke a man with millions in his mind. I got the biggest respect for you—you're full of ideas.

CLEM: Yes—but do you think they're any good except to laugh at?

ISIDOR: Of course they are! They're wonderful, Clem—you shouldn't talk that way. You just haven't been appreciated, that's all—just like me in Boston—but you can't tell, it's never too late—we're far from being a couple of old foggys yet—you and I are still in the middle ages.

CLEM: If you'd go with me, Mr.—Mr.—

ISIDOR: Solomon.

CLEM: *(With deep feeling.)* I'd make good for you. You're the first man that's ever taken me serious in this whole blamed town, Mr. Solomon. *(Almost in tears.)*

ISIDOR: You can call me Izzie.

CLEM: Izzie!

ISIDOR: Cheer up, Clem—this is happy New Year.

CLEM: I can't help it. It is the first time anybody has given me a little encouragement and it just broke me all up.

ISIDOR: Let's get back to your electrical business. You say it'll cost only one hundred and fifty dollars to start up the mint—but when does it begin to julip. *(*CLEM *is puzzled.)* I mean how much more to put in before we take out.

CLEM: Let me see. Temporary building—necessary machinery— We'd have to have five thousand dollars in cash.

ISIDOR: *Oi*—five thousand dollars in cash—that's the obstikle.

CLEM: I thought maybe you'd put it up.

ISIDOR: I'd be glad to—if you'll tell me where I can get it.

CLEM: I thought you was a man of means?

ISIDOR: Well, I ain't altogether broke either, you know. I got—I can tell you—I got in the neighborhood of—let me see—three thousand—maybe four.

CLEM: Well, we could skimp along on four thousand in cash.

ISIDOR: Well, it ain't exactly in cash.

CLEM: In what then?

ISIDOR: In ladies' corsets—socks—lingerie—furniture—bedsteads—clothing, new and secondhand—mostly stickers out of date, but for this town they'll be the same as Lady Tough Gordon.

CLEM: But you can't build an electric plant with corsets, socks and lingerie, you got to have cash.

ISIDOR: That shouldn't be so hard to get—you're well known in this town.

CLEM: Yes—

ISIDOR: How *is* your credit at the local bank?

CLEM: No good at all.

ISIDOR: Oi, gevaldt—no credit—no money—all you got is ideas.

CLEM: Well, I've got a little property.

ISIDOR: Yes. How much can you realize on it, do you think?

CLEM: Oh, it's just a little old dwelling in fair condition, with a good-sized barn, but it's falling to pieces. I can't sell it any way because the mortgage is overdue and I owe seven years' back taxes.

ISIDOR: You'd make a fine partner for me.

CLEM: So, you don't want to come in with me? All right, I'm used to disappointments—

ISIDOR: Wait a minute—I haven't said *"No"* yet. Everything about the scheme sounds great—except putting in the money. But I believe in it. Collecting electric light bills and car fares would be a great sideline for me. I'll tell you what I'll do. I'll send for my stock—I'll open up a store here—but first so nobody gets ahead of us—we'll at least tie up the waterfalls. I'll put up the money.

CLEM: Then you will come in with me and back me up?

ISIDOR: Yes—for the present—up to and not exceeding a hundred and fifty dollars. Now, you see, you talked me into the waterfalls business—well—if it's no good for electricity we can use it for swimming. But anyhow from now on you got something to look forward to.

CLEM: We'll show 'em. *(Picks up Isidor's grip—enter*

BIJE—CLEM *goes upstage to him.)* Bije—what room have you assigned to Mr. Solomon?

BIJE: *(Puts out lamp in window upstage.)* He can't stop here.

CLEM: You told him you were going to take care of him.

BIJE: Yes—in the lock-up.

CLEM: Lock-up nothing—freezing people to death ain't in my line of business, so you go ahead and give him a room.

BIJE: Can't do it—they're all filled. *(First lamp out. Closes dining room door, locks it. Crosses to* R. *to window and puts out lamp.)*

CLEM: Well, if it's as you say—he can have my cot.

ISIDOR: No! No! I wouldn't have that—I wouldn't put nobody out, I can be nice and comfortable right here by the stove.

BIJE: No, you can't do that either—it's against the orders.

CLEM: I'll take the blame, but he's going to stay right here.

BIJE: Alright! Alright! But remember, in case of trouble, I ain't got nothing to do with it. *(He lowers light above table* C.*)*

ISIDOR: There ain't going to be no trouble. I ain't going to complain. I like it down here—in case of fire I'm almost on the outside already.

CLEM: I'd take you over to my house only it's all nailed up, no coal, pipes froze, 'tain't in fit condition to go into.

ISIDOR: Don't worry about me—I'll be all right here.

CLEM: Darned old square heads—it's a shame. *(Starts to go toward upstage.)*

BIJE: *(Goes behind counter. To* ISIDOR.*)* You got to pay in advance.

CLEM: Pay? What for?

BIJE: Lodging.

ISIDOR: How much?

BIJE: Two dollars.

CLEM: Why, you only charge one dollar for a *room.*

ISIDOR: The price is all right. *(Gives* BIJE *money—two bills.)* He only charges a dollar for an ordinary room and for two dollars I get the whole lobby.

CLEM: Are you sure you're going to be comfortable here? *(*BIJE *puts out lamp over counter.)*

ISIDOR: Why not? Don't bother about me. Good night—happy New Year.

CLEM: Same to you and many of them. Good night, partner. *(Shakes hands.)*

ISIDOR: Good night, Clem.

CLEM: Good night, Izzie. Partner—partner. *(Exit* CLEM *up steps.)*

ISIDOR: I couldn't get a room, but I got a partner.

*(*BIJE *looks at* ISIDOR *suspiciously—shows distrust of him, starts to put articles of value into the safe—even the slightest he puts away, showing by his manner that it is* ISIDOR *he is afraid of.* ISIDOR *notices this business, but fails to understand that these precautions are taken against him. He helps* BIJE *to gather up the things to put away for safekeeping. They put away the bell, matches, keys, so forth.* ISIDOR *takes the cigar lighter and tries to hand it to* BIJE, *but finds that it is chained to the counter. As* BIJE *is about to lock the safe,* ISIDOR *hands him his money—a roll of bills. During above business* BIJE *is on knees at safe and as he puts each thing away he turns and finds* ISIDOR *with another—till lamp bus.)*

ISIDOR: Oh, Bije, will you please take care of this money for me until tomorrow? Maybe there is thieves in this town. *(*BIJE *looks at him suspiciously—takes the money and places it in safe, then locks safe. Crosses to go to steps.)* Thank you, Bije, for your kindness.

BIJE: What kindness? *(He gets up on stool to blow lamp out, lifting globe off.)*

ISIDOR: I know. You even went against the rules to make me nice and comfortable. You're a nice boy, Bije, and she's a nice girl, and a nice boy has always got a chance with a nice girl. Good night, Bije. *(*BIJE *starts for steps—turns.)*

BIJE: Do you think so?

ISIDOR: Sure. *(*BIJE *blows out light* C. *and comes down.)* Good night, Bije.

BIJE: Good night, Mr.—Mr.— *(Goes to stairs, stops, thinks.)*

ISIDOR: Solomon.

BIJE: Mr. Solomon—I'd like to give you better accommodations, but I can't—I'd lose my job.

ISIDOR: That's all right, Bije. I understand.

BIJE: I'm awfully sorry—but— *(Takes out money—offers bill to* ISIDOR.*)* Anyhow, here's a dollar back.

ISIDOR: What's that for?

BIJE: Two dollars is too much.

ISIDOR: Here, now, keep that for yourself.

BIJE: That's what I was going to do, but I can't now.

ISIDOR: I told you, you was a nice boy.

BIJE: Good night—Happy New Year. *(Goes up steps—stops in door.)* Oh, if you want anything to read, over in that rack you'll find some reading matter.

ISIDOR: No, thanks—it's a little too dark to read. *(Looks at* BIJE.*)*

BIJE: It's free.

ISIDOR: Yes? Well, maybe I'll look at it after awhile. What is it about?

BIJE: Christian Science. *(Exits.)*

*(Wind and storm increase—*ISIDOR *shows he is cold—opens grip, takes out flask of whiskey and sets it on the table, gets pitcher of water and brings it to table. Wind howls again.* ISIDOR *realizes he is not going to get much sleep—looks about, goes to Christian Science rack and takes all the papers and magazines in it and comes down to table, sits at table* R. *and reads from* Christian Science Monthly.*)*

ISIDOR: "Hope all things—endure all things—expect every good to come, and come soon, and as we deserve it, God will make it so." That sounds sensible. *(Wind—climax of howling—cracked pane of glass breaks and falls into room—*ISIDOR *shivers—takes* Christian Science Monitor *and puts it in broken window. Wind dies down.* ISIDOR *looks at window and smiles.)* Science! *(*MARY *appears at door—tries to open it.* ISIDOR *is about to take a drink from flask when door bell rings—he rushes up to door, opens it and grabs* MARY *as she is about to fall in—shuts door.)* My goodness! *(*MARY *leans heavily on* ISIDOR*; he takes her to chair* L. *of table.)* Oh, you poor little thing, you're colder than ice. Here, sit down. *(He suddenly remembers whiskey.)*

I'll fix you up—here—take a little drink. *(He gives her drink of whiskey, which apparently has no effect on her—he offers her some more—she refuses.)* Did you get lost from the party? *(*MARY *does not answer.)* Oh, I see, your brains is froze. *(He chafes her hands.)* In a couple of minutes you'll get warm, then I'll take you home.

MARY: Home! *(Starts to cry—puts her head on arm on table.)*

ISIDOR: That's right—that's right—have a good cry, then afterwards you'll feel fine. *(*MARY *feels for handkerchief. Can't find one.* ISIDOR *reaches into grip and gets a fresh handkerchief, which he gives to her. She puts it to her nose.)* Wait a minute, I got one right here. *(Business.)* Go on, blow hard. *(After business.)* You feel better now, eh?

MARY: Are you the clerk?

ISIDOR: No, I don't work here—if I did I'd be in bed already. Anything I can do for you?

MARY: Can I get a room?

ISIDOR: Oh, then you don't live in this town? *(She shakes her head "No.")* Where do you come from?

MARY: From—from Portland.

ISIDOR: Why, there's no train from Portland tonight.

MARY: Oh, I mean Portsmouth.

ISIDOR: Sure which town you came from?

MARY: Oh, yes—I'm sure.

ISIDOR: From Portland?

MARY: Yes—no—from Portsmouth.

ISIDOR: Well, now that you are here, you ought to be glad. Oh, I didn't say it—Happy New Year.

MARY: Thank you. *(Looks around tearfully.)* Happy—Happy—New Ye— *(Starts to sob and cry—puts head on arms on table.)*

ISIDOR: That's no way to start the New Year. I see, last year wasn't so happy for you, but that won't come back again.

MARY: What town is this?

ISIDOR: You don't mean to tell me you don't know where you are at? How did you get here, if you didn't know where you was going?

MARY: I—I walked.

ISIDOR: From Portland?

MARY: No—from the train. It's snowbound out there—a mile or so.

ISIDOR: What train were you on? Where were you going?

MARY: I don't know. All I thought of was to get away.

ISIDOR: From Portsmouth.

MARY: No—from Portland.

ISIDOR: *(Places chair by stove.)* I thought you just said you came from Portsmouth?

MARY: Oh, please don't question me. *(Crosses to chair* R. *by stove and sits.)*

ISIDOR: But I got to look out for you. You don't know where you came from or where you are going to—*(Sits her down in chair, front stove.)*

MARY: I don't know and I don't care. All I thought of was to get away and end it all.

ISIDOR: End it all? A young girl like you? Shame on you. On a night like this with the river full of ice. You're liable to slip and hurt yourself. I'll make you comfortable. Now just put your feet up on this chair. *(Puts her feet on chair in front of her.)* I know what's the matter—you're hungry. What time did you have dinner? *(*MARY *smiles.)* I'll fix that. I got a couple of nice sandwiches; my daughter Essie made them up for me for the train, and I don't want them; why should I eat them? I'm fat enough—you eat them. See—you feel better already. Now what kind of a sandwich would you like to have?

MARY: Ham!

ISIDOR: *(Looks at* MARY.*)* Here's corn beef. *He hands her sandwich, which she eats ravenously—*ISIDOR *is about to eat the other one when he looks at her. She has already finished hers—he hands her the other sandwich and she eats about half if it—stops, looks at him.)*

MARY: Why, I'm eating your lunch—aren't you hungry?

ISIDOR: No, that's all right. I just *had* two sandwiches. *(*MARY *has been getting drowsy and closes her eyes—*ISIDOR *sees this.)* You poor thing—you need sleep. Maybe I can wake them up and get a room for you. I'll see. *(Starts for stairway.)* No, on second thought, I better keep my mouth shut; they're funny people here. If I wake them up now they're liable to change their mind and chuck us both out. Besides, it would look suspicious—you wouldn't know how to register anyhow—whether you came from Portland or Portsmouth or Puerto Rico; it's better that they think you came here with me. *(By this time she is fast asleep.)* Besides, a girl that talks so silly—she wants to end it all. I better keep my eye on you tonight. There's plenty of room here. We'll go partners; we'll go halves. From the stove over to there is your half and from the stove over to there is my half. You'll have a good sleep—the first thing you know it'll be morning. The sun will come out, everything'll look brighter, and oh, yes—I was just reading something I saved to remember—it'll do you good to listen. *(Reads from* Christian Science Monthly.*)* "Hope all things—endure all things—" *(Sees that she has fallen asleep, looks at her for a moment sympathetically, puts his fingers to his lips and tiptoes away quietly. The moonlight shining through window reflected by the snow lights up the room dimly.* Isidor *goes to* Mary *and looks at her to make sure she is asleep. She shivers slightly, apparently she is cold. He looks into stove—wind blows paper out of window—he puts it back. The fire is out. He goes upstage, gets his overcoat, about to put it on, takes it off and goes to* Mary, *covers her with it and tucks her in. He puts on his cap and sits down on chair preparatory to going to sleep, but it is cold—he gets up and looks around for something to cover himself with and finally sees the door mat upstage. He goes up and gets it and drags it downstage—he sits on both chairs and stretching his legs he places mat across him in such a position that the audience can see in large red letters—WELCOME—which is the inscription on the mat. He dozes off to sleep—the storm increases, the paper blows out of the window, but* Isidor *and* Mary *are both asleep and they do not heed it.)*

CURTAIN

ACT II

SCENE: *Clem's home.*

TIME: *About seven p.m. Five weeks later.*

Door up R. *of* C.*—window* C.*—another window* L., *through which may be seen in the distance, with window lighted, the barn. Under the window* C. *is a kitchen sink on which is a crude generator which is run by a water motor fastened to the sink faucet. Wires run from the generator under sink, to the switchboard leading to various parts of the room. Wires also running to the various lamps around the room. The switchboard is a homemade affair, with several small switches painted black. In* C. *is the main switch. In the door up* R. *of* C. *is a movable panel which is electrically controlled by a switch in switchboard—when the switch is pushed in the panel rises, and drops when the switch is released. Light effects must be consistent with this arrangement. Another door* R. *leads into other parts of the house. Practical clock* C. *at back wall. About the room are a number of* CLEM'S *electrical inventions.*

AT RISE: *Discovered:* ISIDOR *and* MARY. ISIDOR *is seated at table* C.L. *of table, buried deep in thought with a copy of* Science and Health; *however, he is paying no attention to it.* MARY *is seated* R. *of table* C., *reading Bible—she has copy of* Science Quarterly *also. Reads from Bible as curtain rises.*

MARY: "Whosoever shall say unto this Mountain, be thou removed, and be thou cast into the sea" . . . *(Turns, looks over and sees that* Isidor *is not paying attention.)* . . . why, you're not paying attention.

Isidor: Huh! Oh, yes, I was—I was only thinking about my poor little Essie—coming all the way from Boston alone—I tell you I'm worried.

Mary: But you mustn't worry—worry is fear, and you know what we've just been reading: "I will trust and not be afraid, for the Lord Jehovah is my strength and my song."

Isidor: But maybe an accident will happen to the train?

Mary: That isn't Science—why, you've just been reading that there's no such thing as an accident. Haven't you any faith in the Lord?

Isidor: Plenty—but I got absolutely none in the New York, New Haven and Hartford. *(Turns, looks at clock up* c. *wall.)* Don't you think we ought to go down to the train?

Mary: There's plenty of time. You might as well be patient until Ned Tyler calls for *us*.

Isidor: *Us*—he's going to call for us. I think he's got his eye on us—he's a fine young man—and if he asks us, don't you think we ought to marry him?

Mary: Now we have no time for gossip. You know we must go to the meeting tonight just the same as usual.

Isidor: Do you think it's right to drag that poor little girl Essie to a Science Meeting after she's all tired out from traveling?

Mary: But the meeting will do her good. This is Wednesday night, you know, and she'll enjoy the testimonials.

Isidor: That's right. Now, there's one thing I like. Those testimonials. There's no doubt this thing must be doing some good. I'm glad I got you interested in it, and it was certainly nice of Ned Tyler to give you this book. It's done *you* a lot of good.

Mary: Yes, it has—even though I don't quite understand it yet.

Isidor: Maybe it will do Essie good—she won't understand it either. Well, let's finish the lesson; I want to get down to the train.

Mary: *(Reading from Bible.)* "Let your light so shine before men that they may see your good works."

Isidor: You see, right in the Bible it says we should go in the electric business and give light.

MARY: You mustn't talk business while we're doing the lesson. Now it's your turn—page five seventy-eight.

ISIDOR: *(Reading.)* "Yea though I walk through the valley of the shadow of death I shall fear no evil, for love is with me"—

MARY: That simply means that you mustn't be afraid of anything, because in ways we do not always understand, everything happens for the best and if you remember that you can never be unhappy.

ISIDOR: I'm never unhappy—you're the one. Remember the first night you came here and wanted to— *(Bus. with hands like diving.)* In the river. Now ain't you ashamed? *(She bows her head.)* Mary, ain't you ever going to tell me who you are and where you came from?

MARY: I can't.

ISIDOR: All right. If you can't—then don't. And nobody in this town is going to know any different from what I told them—that you're my confidential girl and I brought you here to help me open up a store. What happened before is nobody's business and as far as I'm concerned, you were born the night I met you and you're five weeks old today. *(Goes toward sink to get a drink of water.)*

MARY: *(Rises and goes towards* ISIDOR.*)* Oh, you mustn't disconnect the water faucet—it will stop the electric generator.

ISIDOR: By golly, every time I want a drink he's got the water turned on to make his electricity. Well, we mustn't interrupt Clem while he's making his experiments out in the barn. That's what's going to get us the millions—maybe. Only he's got my whole stock stored out there all mixed in with his electrical wires; that's something else I got to worry about.

MARY: Worrier! Read line ten.

ISIDOR: For a man that can't get a store and hasn't got a nickel—line ten is gonna do me a lot of good.

CLEM: *(Rushes in from entrance* L. *all out of breath—excited—rushes up to switch and throws it off main switch.)* Och, good gracious.

ISIDOR: What's the matter?

CLEM: Short circuit in the barn—turned it off just in time. Had a small blaze. *(Goes down* L.*)*

ISIDOR: Oi—is the fire out? *(Runs to window.)*

CLEM: Yes—but for Heaven's sake, don't let anybody throw on that switch.

ISIDOR: Clem, please be careful with your electrical experiments in the barn—remember, our whole future is out there and I ain't got a cent of insurance. *(Down* L.C.*)*

CLEM: Why, you told me you was fully insured.

ISIDOR: That was a couple of weeks back—I had a floating policy by the month for four thousand dollars and it ran out two days ago. I got this notification from Mr. Hooker. *(Takes bill from pocket.)* Twenty-eight dollars and forty cents. And all my cash is tied up in those waterfalls. No money—no credit— *(Looks at* MARY.*)* —read line ten. *(Throws bill into basket on table.)*

CLEM: It's mighty risky keeping four thousand dollars' worth of stock out in that barn—do you know that?

ISIDOR: Well? Can I hold it in my hand—do I know? *(Starts for arch* L.*)* Bring a lantern. I want to see if you left any sparks laying around. I tell you fire is a terrible thing when you don't expect it. *(Exits* L. *into kitchen.)*

(Doorbell rings. MARY *starts for the door* R.U.*)*

CLEM: Wait a minute, Mary—see who it is. *(He pushes switch—panel in door opens, disclosing* NED TYLER *on the outside.)* Friend or foe?

NED: Ned Tyler.

CLEM: Friend?

NED: You bet I am. *(*CLEM *releases switch and panel closes—presses another switch and buzzer is heard opening door, which opens and admits* NED, *then closes after* NED'S *entrance.)* Gee! That's a great idea, Clem.

CLEM: Chock full of them. Who do you want to see?

NED: Miss Clark. *(*CLEM *throws on switch which works lamp on lower* R. *switch shelf* R., *revealing* MARY *standing at mantel. Lamp on. Lights lantern which he carries and as he exits into kitchen* L.*)* Good evening. I hope I'm not late?

MARY: Oh, no—we have plenty of time. Mr. Solomon will be right in. I'll call him. *(Crosses to* L.C.*)*

NED: No—no, please don't. There's something you ought to know. I don't want to hurt anybody's feelings and I think it's best to tell you first. Mr. Whitson called a meeting of the leading townspeople today and I'm afraid they're going to make it very unpleasant for Clem.

MARY: Why?

NED: Well, they object to him harboring an undesirable person.

MARY: Well, I'm not afraid of them—I'm under the protection of Mr. Solomon.

NED: That's just the point. *He's* the *one* they don't want in the town.

MARY: Why not?

NED: *(Half-ashamed.)* On account of—prejudice.

MARY: Oh, I see! Against his race—isn't it shameful! *(Sits* L. *of table.)*

NED: It certainly is—and I suppose if he goes—you'll go? *(Crosses up behind table.)*

MARY: Oh, of course.

NED: Then what am I going to do?

MARY: Just go along—the same as you did before you heard of us.

NED: But everything's different now. I can't go along the way I used to. I'm dissatisfied—I hate my routine job in that dinky little bank. Now I've got an incentive—I want to do things—big things to make her proud of me.

MARY: And I'm sure *Grace* will be proud of you.

NED: Grace!!

MARY: Why, yes, you're engaged, aren't you?

NED: Oh, no—that's only friendship. That isn't anything like love and I've found out the difference since I met you.

MARY: But you mustn't.

NED: I can't help it. Don't you—I—like me just a little?

MARY: Yes—I do—of course.

NED: Gee, I'm glad. Because if you like me a little now, maybe you'll like me a whole lot better after awhile and then that little old homestead my mother left me will come in kinda handy.

MARY: But it would be wrong for me to encourage you—because it will only bring you disappointment— *(Almost a tear.)* —and humiliation. *(Crying.)*

NED: I don't believe it. I won't let anyone say anything about you—not even yourself.

(Enter ISIDOR L.*)*

ISIDOR: Oh, *us* is here. *(*MARY *exits* R., *crying.)* What's the matter? What's she crying about? *(Crosses* R. *to door* R.2.*)*

NED: I don't know. I didn't think I was saying anything to make her cry.

ISIDOR: That's all right, Ned. I know how it is with women—if they don't have at least one good cry a day—something's the matter with them. *(Crosses down to fireplace* R.*)*

NED: Where's Clem? *(Sits* R. *of table.)*

ISIDOR: Out in his laboratory—in the stable. *(Standing in front of the fireplace* R.*)*

NED: How is he getting along with his experiments?

ISIDOR: Oh, fine—he nearly burned up his barn and my stock with it.

NED: Did you rent a store yet?

ISIDOR: No! I can't seem to get one; maybe it's because I haven't got enough money to pay my rent in advance. If I could only get a store for a short time—I'd turn my stock into cash—and then we'd be okay.

NED: You still have your hearts set on that electrical business?

ISIDOR: I should say so. Look, I'm a living electricity. I get volts for breakfast—amperes for dinner and for supper I get—currents. Already I got an option on the waterfalls—

NED: You have?

ISIDOR: Yes, it's in Mary's name.

NED: But why?

ISIDOR: Well, for some reason with me they wouldn't do business at all; in Clem's name we couldn't put it, because he owes everybody in the town; he owes the town seven years' back taxes and they could jump on the property and take it away; so quietly I sent Mary—she's got a business head—and in her own name, she got it almost as cheap as I could have.

NED: But it's a big undertaking, Mr. Solomon. Where are you going to get the capital?

ISIDOR: Oh, by next summer we'll have enough to start in a small way—we'll buy the machinery so much down and the balance—let them worry.

NED: But it won't pay on a small scale.

ISIDOR: No?

NED: The overhead would eat you up.

ISIDOR: It'll be all on the one floor—there'll be no overhead.

NED: I mean cost of operation and equipment—it's bound to be enormous.

ISIDOR: Then you don't think much of the proposition?

NED: Yes, I do. It's a great industry—needed in this section, but what you must have is sound financial backing—

ISIDOR: Choochum*—wise guy—smart feller.

NED: You can't raise it here—you'd have to get outside capital.

ISIDOR: Say, you got a good business head. Maybe you can go outside and get it for us. Saturday afternoons you ain't working.

NED: Maybe I can help later on. Gee, I'd like to—you deserve to succeed.

ISIDOR: Of course, for me it's a new business, but it don't take me long to learn. Let me show you something—Don't you think it's a little dark in here?

NED: No! Oh, yes, it's kind of.

ISIDOR: Now I'll fix it. *(Goes to switchboard, throws off switch, upper* R. *switch, and light in table lamp goes out on center table.)* Oh, I made a little mistake. *(*C. *switch on again.)* Well, that's liable to happen. But, now watch—look at that lamp over there. *(Indicates lamp on console.)* Don't watch me—watch the lamp. *(By mistake he throws on main switch, lamp does not light and* ISIDOR *goes to see what's wrong with it.)* Maybe the globe is burnt out. *(Turns and sees that the main switch is on—the light flashes outside.)* Oh, it's the barn. Do you see anything burning? Do you smell anything? I'd better leave the damn thing alone—that's Clem's department.

(Enter MARY R. CLEM *enters* L.*)*

CLEM: Who's been fooling with that switch?

ISIDOR: Nobody.

*Usually *chuchem*. Solomon translates his Yiddish compliment for Ned.

CLEM: That's funny. *(Comes down from switchboard, sucking his finger.)* Say—what's good for a burnt finger?

ISIDOR: Here—sit down and read this book.

*(*CLEM *sits and reads* Science and Health—MARY *is dressed for the street and has* ISIDOR'S *coat—she stands waiting for him.)*

MARY: We'll be late for Essie.

ISIDOR: Oh, my Essie—that poor little child. She's waiting for us.

CLEM: Got your key?

ISIDOR: Yes. Hurry, hurry. *(*NED *and* MARY *exit* L.2.*)*

CLEM: Say, Isidor—I'm afraid this book won't do me any good.

ISIDOR: Say, Clem—you never can tell what's liable to happen—look at a herring. He goes to sleep in the middle of the ocean and wakes up in a delicatessen store. *(*ISIDOR *exits.)*

(Doorbell rings. CLEM *goes up to switchboard and throws switch, opening panel, which discloses* HOOKER *on the outside—works switch and panel drops, then works switches for door.)*

CLEM: Evening, Hooker—come in.

*(*HOOKER *enters and watches working of door. Hangs up hat and coat on rack upstage. Comes down* R. *and sits.)*

HOOKER: Quite a contrivance. How's the electrical business?

CLEM: So, so. How's the law business?

HOOKER: I've got a case.

CLEM: I'm glad to hear it.

HOOKER: Well, I'm kind of sorry. It's the case of Valley Falls Township versus Clem Beemis.

CLEM: What's the use dunning me for them back taxes? You know I ain't got a cent.

(Doorbell rings—same bus. with switches and door. WHITSON'S *face appears, with* TYLER *and* TRIMBLE *behind*

him—door opens and they enter. WHITSON *crosses extreme* L. TYLER *behind table* C. TRIMBLE R. *of table.* HOOKER *down to fireplace.)*

WHITSON: Evening, Clem.

CLEM: Evening, Gid.

WHITSON: Where's Solomon?

CLEM: Down to the depot to meet his family. *(*CLEM, *at switchboard, turns on lamps.)*

WHITSON: Oh, his whole family coming?

CLEM: Yep.

TYLER: Clem, where's Ned?

CLEM: He's with Mr. Solomon.

WHITSON: We've got to take action immediately. *(Removes coat, puts on sofa* R. TRIMBLE *hangs his up* C.*)*

CLEM: What's the idea of meeting here? Ain't the town hall big enough for you?

WHITSON: This meeting concerns you and the members of this household.

CLEM: I know what you're driving at, but it ain't going to do any good—what goes on in this house is none of anybody's business—Mr. Solomon is my friend.

TYLER: You've known him only five weeks—and we've been your friends life long.

CLEM: I want to keep your friendship.

TYLER: Then all you've got to do is listen to reason.

CLEM: I don't call prejudice reason. And I think it's a darn shame—trying to squeeze out a good worthy citizen—men like him make a town prosperous.

TRIMBLE: Oh, we ain't saying he won't be prosperous. Jews are always successful—they've got tricks.

CLEM: I don't suppose us Yanks have got any at all.

TRIMBLE: Well—we ain't foreigners. *(*CLEM *sits at table* L.*)*

WHITSON: Look how he got the waterfalls property; they wouldn't sell it to him, so he went and got it in the name of Mary Clark.

TYLER: Who is this Mary Clark anyway? Where does she come from? What business has she got running after my boy, Ned?

WHITSON: I've got an idea that she's no better than she should be—

CLEM: *(Slamming book down on table—rises.)* If that's the way you're going to talk about her, this meeting might as well adjourn. You ain't going to come into my house and pick on Mary—she's as nice a girl as there is in this town.

WHITSON: Is that so? Well, I'm going to investigate that young lady.

HOOKER: *(Standing in front of fireplace.)* Clem's right—it's not the business of this committee to attack the character of Miss Clark.

TRIMBLE: We ain't worried so much about her—it's Solomon we've got to get rid of—when he goes she'll follow automatic.

WHITSON: And he's got to go.

CLEM: Aw, don't be so narrow, Ichabod—one Jew ain't going to ruin the town.

WHITSON: We're setting a precedent.

TYLER: If we let one in and he makes money, he'll bring in a lot more.

WHITSON: Naturally—he'll write to Jacob and Jacob will write to Isaac—and he'll write to Moses—then Moses will write to Aaron, then we'll get Rachels and Beckies and Ikies and Abies and Izzies and Sadies—and the first thing you know this town will be as bad as New York.

TRIMBLE: You lost your job at the hotel on account of him.

WHITSON: You can't afford to fight his battles; you haven't got a cent. You can't even pay your taxes—haven't paid 'em for years—and you've got to get rid of him.

CLEM: I can't throw him on the street.

TRIMBLE: Why not?

TYLER: All you have to do is to tell him that you can't put him up any longer and it's best for all concerned if he takes his goods and chattels, including Mary Clark, and locate elsewhere. *(Goes up* R.C.*)*

WHITSON: And you've got to tell him this very night—if you don't, Eb will attach this property tomorrow and it will be sold over your head. Well—

CLEM: I can't help it—I just can't do it.

WHITSON: Then we'll do it—we'll see that he goes and

you'll go with him. *(*WHITSON *crosses up to* TYLER *and* TRIMBLE *goes to* WHITSON'S L.*)*

Enter ISIDOR, L., *followed by* ESTHER, *who is a short, plump Jewish girl about eighteen years old—she is all smiles as she enters.* ISIDOR *carries her suitcase and parcels. He sees the company and is pleased.* CLEM *has crossed extreme* L.*)*

ISIDOR: Hello, everybody. Look, Essie, we got company. Well, this is an honor we didn't expect. Essie—first I want you to meet Mr. Beemis—you know—Clem.

ESSIE: With Mr. Beemis I'm well acquainted—I met you before I knew you—in papa's letters. *(Crosses* L. *to* CLEM, *followed by* ISIDOR.*)*

(As ISIDOR *and* ESSIE *cross* L. *to* CLEM, WHITSON *drops down behind table.* TYLER *about three feet to right and above* WHITSON. TRIMBLE *to upper end of fireplace.* HOOKER *lower end of fireplace. Must be in these positions for introduction.)*

CLEM: So this is little Essie. Well, well.

ISIDOR: *(Proudly.)* That's my baby, Clem—don't monopolize Clem—Essie, say "Glad to meet you" to Mr. Whitson—Mayor—

ESSIE: Glad to meet you, Mr. *Meyer. (Offers her hand which he refuses and goes up* C.*)*

ISIDOR: Not Meyer—*Mayor. (Going to* TYLER.*)* And this is Mr. Tyler—Neddie's papa . . . *(*ESSIE *hangs back on account of her cold treatment from* WHITSON—*they all treat her coldly.)* Come on—say "Glad to meet you"—he's the richest man in town.

ESSIE: I'm glad. *(*TYLER *joins* WHITSON *up* C.*)*

ISIDOR: *(Turns to* TRIMBLE; *does not see the cold treatment afforded* ESSIE.*)* And this is Mr. Trimble—my coming competitor— *(*TRIMBLE *and* HOOKER *simply ignore her. Bus. for* ESSIE—ISIDOR *turns to* EB.*)* And this is Mr. Hooker—lawyer, tax collector, insurance agent— *(*ESSIE *begins to cry and crosses to* CLEM.*)*

ESSIE: Oh, Papa—

ISIDOR: *(Coming quickly to* ESSIE.*)* What's the matter,

Essie? *(Turns and looks at the others.)* She's tired from the train. Sit down, Essie. *(She sits on couch or sofa* L.*)*

ESSIE: I'm sorry I came.

ISIDOR: Shame! And everybody's here to welcome you.

(Door opens and NED *and* MARY *enter* L.2. *They are laughing gaily.* NED *is carrying a bag—some bundles, same being the baggage of* ESSIE*—on seeing the others they both stop laughing—embarrassed.* TYLER *and* WHITSON *show displeasure and rage at* NED'S *being with* MARY.*)*

NED: Oh, hello, Father.

TYLER: Fine company you're keeping.

*(*MARY *haughtily crosses to* ESSIE*—comforts her.)*

NED: I don't see anything wrong with it. *(Crosses to* MARY *and* ESSIE.*)*

WHITSON: What did I tell you? This is what's going on behind your back.

TYLER: I'll soon put a stop to it. Ned, I want you to drive me home. I've got something to say to you and it can't wait.

NED: Very well—if it's as important as that—

TYLER: It is.

NED: Well, good night, folks. Good night, Clem. Good night, Mr. Solomon. Good night, Miss Solomon. I hope you'll be very happy here—anything I can do for you at any time will be a great pleasure.

TYLER: I'm waiting.

NED: *(To* MARY.*)* Good night.

MARY: Thank you—so much. *(Shakes hands with* NED.*)* Good night.

TYLER: Hurry up!

NED: I'm ready.

TYLER: About time.

ISIDOR: Thank you for calling, Mr. Tyler—come again—good night. *(Crosses* C. TYLER *and* NED *exit.* ESSIE *crying.)*

MARY: What's the matter, dear?

ESSIE: They don't like me.

ISIDOR: Are you foolish? Wait till you're here a couple of

days—then they'll like you the same as they like me. Did you have your supper?

ESSIE: I should say so—on the train—they charged me a dollar and a half.

ISIDOR: For only one supper?

ESSIE: But I got even—ooh—did I eat.

ISIDOR: I'll betcha.

ESSIE: Yeh.

ISIDOR: Oh, Essie—I just happen to think—you know that picture I wrote you about—from Aunt Mania—

ESSIE: She said she'd mail it right away.

WHITSON: Now, Solomon— *(Advances front table.)*

ISIDOR: Wait a minute. Mary, take Essie in and show her where to wash the train off her face.

MARY: Then we'll take her to the testimonal meeting. *(*MARY *and* ESSIE *exit door* R.U., *carrying traveling bag.)*

WHITSON: *(Crosses extreme* L.*)* Solomon. We want to see you privately—on a matter of business.

ISIDOR: Me? Private?

WHITSON: Yes—you.

ISIDOR: Clem—you take in the things for the girls—the Mayor wants to talk to me alone. *(*CLEM *exits door* R.U., *carrying umbrella, bundles, etc.* ISIDOR *pleased, looks around, satisfied with himself.* TRIMBLE *crosses and sits* L. *of table.)* Well, at last I got my whole family under the same roof—I tell you it's grand, Mr. Hooker. I wouldn't have a single worry if you would only renew the policy on my stock. Can't you see your way clear to take my note for twenty-eight dollars and forty cents?

WHITSON: We didn't come here to do you favors.

ISIDOR: No? What then?

TRIMBLE: We came here to tell you that you don't get a store in this town.

ISIDOR: Ain't you a little bit pessimistical?

WHITSON: *(Shows document.)* I've got an agreement here signed by the property owners wherein they bind themselves not to rent you anything at all.

ISIDOR: But what have you got against me?

WHITSON: The leading citizens of this town have decided that they don't want you here—they don't like you.

ISIDOR: But why?

HOOKER: Well—they have a feeling that you're—eh—undesirable because they're afraid that you are the—eh—the nucleus—

ISIDOR: *(Puzzled.)* I'm a nucleus— You're a mistaken—I'm a K.P.,* a B'nai B'rith, a Sons of Benjamin—

WHITSON: You're the nucleus of something we don't want in this town.

ISIDOR: What's that?

WHITSON: A Ghetto.

ISIDOR: Oh, I see—you mean they don't like me because I'm a Yahooda— Oh, say—that'll wear off—I've been in places before where they didn't like 'em at first and then after a while they got used to them—and when they ain't around they miss them.

TRIMBLE: Well, this is one place you'll never be missed.

WHITSON: You're not going to be here long enough to get used to.

ISIDOR: Now just wait a minute. *(Crosses behind table to* WHITSON.*)* You know I've got something to say, too, about me. You know very well you can't put me out of the town if I don't want to go.

WHITSON: I'm speaking for the town—and as Mayor I order you to get out.

ISIDOR: You ain't got no right to give such orders.

WHITSON: *I'm* running this town and my word's law.

ISIDOR: Well, law I don't know nothing much about—but I'm not altogether ignorant—a few things I know and it just happens that I've read the Constitution of the United States where it says that you can't deprive a man of his rights on account of his race, color, or creed, and you want to remember that the Constitution is bigger than Congress—bigger than the President, and one sure thing—it's bigger than the Mayor of Valley Falls. *(*HOOKER *sits.)*

TRIMBLE: Well, if you don't go voluntarily, you'll only starve here—we've got it fixed so you can't get a store. *(*WHITSON *takes agreement from pocket.)*

ISIDOR: That agreement don't worry me any, because if you try to put it through it's conspiracy—and for that I can go to Court and collect damages—and I can take

*Knights of Pythias, a fraternal organization open to all religions and devoted to charitable works, established in Washington, D.C., in 1864.

away your store— *(Indicating* TRIMBLE.*)* —your bank— *(Indicating* WHITSON.*)* —and even your rolltop desk, Mr. Hooker.

HOOKER: *(Seated* R.*)* Now, Mr. Solomon—perhaps we are a little narrow here—but isn't that all the more reason for you to try and locate somewhere else, where the atmosphere is more congenial, where your people are welcome and where this feeling does not exist?

ISIDOR: Where can you find such a place? I don't want to go to Heaven yet. I like this town. I got good prospects here and just because I'm a Jew is no reason I should be chased out like I was contagious. I'm a man just the same like anybody else—I got the same eyes, the same ears, the same mouth—nose a little different—

TRIMBLE: Now let me tell you something—you and your kind can't come here and take away my bread and butter—I'm giving you fair warning—I'm going to wipe you out.

ISIDOR: And let me tell you something, Mr. Trimble—for thousands of years better men than you have been trying to wipe us out and crush us and annihilate us—you can go all the way back to Pharaoh—but they can't do it—and why? Because for some particular reason God wants us to live and prosper and—what the Hell are you going to do about it?

(Enter MARY, ESSIE *and* CLEM *from* R. ESSIE *all smiles.)*

ESSIE: I'm ready, Papa.

ISIDOR: Feel better, darling, feel better?

ESSIE: Fine—I'm going to like this town—such nice people.

ISIDOR: Yes—fine people. Well, we better go to the meeting. I want to get seats way down front so I can hear every testimonial.

*(*MARY *and* ESSIE *exit.* WHITSON, TRIMBLE *and* HOOKER *conferring at sofa* L. TRIMBLE *stands with his foot on the sofa.)*

CLEM: Shall I go with you?

ISIDOR: No, Clem, you better stay here and see that nobody puts their feet on the sofa. *(Bus. and exits.* TRIMBLE *takes foot off sofa.)*

HOOKER: *(To* WHITSON *and* TRIMBLE.*)* I told you we were going too far.

TRIMBLE: Can he hold us for conspiracy?

HOOKER: Absolutely.

TRIMBLE: Better tear up that agreement.

WHITSON: Yes. We'll have to find some other way.

(Bell. CLEM *switch bus. down* R.C. *Enter* NED *excitedly* R.U. *exit.)*

NED: I want to see you, Clem. *(To* WHITSON.*)* I've just had a talk with my father and I've heard the details of your contemptible scheme against Mr. Solomon.

WHITSON: Everything I've done has been with your father's approval and I don't see that it's any of your affairs.

NED: I'm going to make it my affair. Solomon is going to have a chance.

CLEM: But the property owners have signed an agreement not to rent him a store.

NED: I didn't sign any such agreement and he's going to have one. That old dwelling on Main Street is my property and can be remodeled for very little money—it's a fine location.

CLEM: Ideal . . . Right opposite your store, Trimble.

TRIMBLE: So, you're going to try to ruin me, eh? *(Crosses* C. *behind table.)* I know why—all on account of that girl—a girl no decent woman in this town will have anything to do with.

NED: If you ever say a word against that girl—I'll just half kill you. *(Grabs* TRIMBLE *by the coat—*WHITSON *stops him, coming between.)*

WHITSON: Your father shall hear of this.

NED: I'm of age, Mr. Whitson.

TRIMBLE: Solomon ain't going to open no store here.

*(*HOOKER*, in disgust, crosses to rack by door to get coat, etc.)*

NED: Mr. Hooker, will you do me a favor?

HOOKER: What is it, my boy.

NED: Let's go right over to your office, and draw up that lease immediately.

TRIMBLE: Don't you dare do it, Eb.

HOOKER: Here's the key, Ned, I'll be right over. *(Exit* NED TYLER *exterior.)*

WHITSON: Eb Hooker—while you're drawing up that lease you might as well write out your resignation as tax collector.

HOOKER: Any time the Board demands my resignation they can have it, but that won't change my opinion in this matter. I'm ashamed of having had anything to do with it. I've learned a little lesson in this house tonight even if you gentlemen haven't. Good night. *(*HOOKER *exits.)*

CLEM: Good night, Eb.

TRIMBLE: Ned Tyler will know that I mean business before I get through with him. *(Crosses front table to door to get coat.)*

CLEM: If I was you, Seth—I'd leave him alone. *(*CLEM *goes to switchboard and puts out the lamp on organ.)*

TRIMBLE: Do you think I'm going to stand idly by and let this Solomon open a store here—undersell me and ruin my business? That would just suit you.

CLEM: I didn't put him up to open a store here—in fact, I'd rather he wouldn't. He feels the same way about it. Running a store in this town ain't the ambition of his life.

TRIMBLE: Then what's he doing it for?

CLEM: To get the money so we could start the electric plant.

WHITSON: Now, Clem, for once in your life be practical.

TRIMBLE: Get rid of this Solomon.

WHITSON: Take the advice of old friends.

CLEM: Old friends—that wouldn't go good for thirty-one dollars and sixty cents to save the roof over my head—and here's Solomon—a new friend, put up his last dollar 'cause he had faith in me and stands ready to back me up with everything he's got in the world.

WHITSON: Back you up— *(Picks up insurance bill from table. Bus. with paper.)* Why, he hasn't even got twenty-eight dollars and forty cents to pay the insurance on his stock.

CLEM: *(Taking bill from* WHITSON.*)* Oh, you see everything, don't you?

WHITSON: I saw that his policy expired last Monday and that he hasn't got a cent of insurance this minute.

CLEM: *(Starts up. Goes to switchboard, gets lantern.)* That just reminds me—

WHITSON: Where are you going?

CLEM: Get my tools. I got a short circuit in the barn and I'll have to disconnect those wires from this main switch. *Gets hat from organ, comes down back of sofa.)*

WHITSON: What's your hurry?

CLEM: Got to fix it before I go to bed, in case of accident—don't want my barn to burn down.

TRIMBLE: Come on.

CLEM: Going?

TRIMBLE: Yes.

CLEM: Don't forget to shut the door. *(*WHITSON *deep in thought—*CLEM *exits.)*

TRIMBLE: Come on—we've got to go over to Gideon's and tell him what the boy's up to.

WHITSON: Wait a minute. *(Door Slam. Door slams in kitchen off* L.*)* We can handle this ourselves. Right here—now.

TRIMBLE: *(Impressed by* WHITSON's *manner.)* And get rid of Solomon? *(*WHITSON *nods)* How?

WHITSON: You heard him—the main switch—this big one. *(Goes to switchboard.)*

TRIMBLE: The barn. *(*WHITSON *nods.)* I'll do most anything to get rid of him. But—suppose it spreads over towards my house?

WHITSON: We won't give it a chance, I'll ring the alarm at the square the minute it starts—it'll be over before you know it. Will you do it?

TRIMBLE: It's risky.

(Pantomime how to be done by TRIMBLE *going out, opening window and throwing switch.)*

WHITSON: Not at all. I'll show you. *(Opens latch on window. Bus.)* From the outside—it'll seem like an accident. They're all out except Clem—we'll have to get rid of him before he has a chance to fix them wires.

TRIMBLE: How'll we do it?

WHITSON: We'll send him over to pay his taxes.

TRIMBLE: He hasn't any money.

WHITSON: We'll give it to him. *(Door slams—*WHITSON *takes out cigar. Enter* CLEM.*)*

CLEM: Thought you'd gone.

WHITSON: No—we've been talking things over, Clem, and Seth and I feel kind of sorry for you.

CLEM: Is that so?

WHITSON: Sure—have a cigar?

CLEM: Thanks—I'll smoke it after a while.

WHITSON: You see—Clem—our fight is not against you. Of course we feel kind of hurt that you've taken sides with a stranger against us, but we don't think it's exactly right that we should take your home away from you.

CLEM: That would be kind of hard—I've lived here all my life and it's going to hurt to lose the old place for the lack of thirty-one dollars and sixty cents.

WHITSON: We understand. And that's why we decided to lend you the money to pay your taxes.

CLEM: You will? *(*WHITSON *and* TRIMBLE *nod their heads.)* That takes a load off my mind. When do I get it?

TRIMBLE: We're going to give it to you right now. *(Bus. with money.)*

WHITSON: But you must run right over to Eb Hooker's office and pay him.

CLEM: I'm only too glad to do that.

WHITSON: Here it is—thirty-one dollars—and—eh— *(Gives* CLEM *some bills.)*

TRIMBLE: And sixty cents. *(Gives* CLEM *some change.)*

CLEM: Now giving me this money ain't going to influence me to do anything against Mr. Solomon.

WHITSON: Oh, no, no, it's got nothing to do with Solomon at all.

TRIMBLE: It's just between ourselves.

WHITSON: For old time's sake.

CLEM: Well, it's mighty nice of you. Just shows there's some good in everybody.

WHITSON: Now you run right over to Hooker's office— because if you don't he's liable to sell your property right over your head.

*(*CLEM *goes to switchboard—throws off switches, extinguishing all the lights in room, leaving only the glow that comes from fireplace, and small blue spot in border to cover clock—picks up lantern and lights it—speaks as he exits exterior door.)*

CLEM: Don't worry, that money will be used for the proper purpose. I'm going right over to Eb's office now.
TRIMBLE: Good.
WHITSON: That's right.
CLEM: *(Outside.)* Good night.
WHITSON *and* TRIMBLE: Good night.

*(*CLEM *and lantern can be seen passing window and going* L. *Moonlight effect offstage. Then* TRIMBLE'S *form appears in the window* C. *at back—opens it and reaches in to switchboard. He throws on the main switch and a couple of flashes can be seen off* L. *Curtain thirty seconds, then up. Fire glows briefly, dims to fading blue light, showing clock before blackout. Fire alarm rings. Lights up to show effects of fire and illuminate face of clock. A half hour has passed.* ISIDOR, MARY *and* ESSIE *can be seen running from* L.2 *and enter through door* L.2. ISIDOR *is all in.* MARY *and* ESSIE *try to support him and lead him to chair* C.*)*

ISIDOR: Oi, my stock—everything I've got is gone!
MARY: *(Goes to switchboard—sees main switch on—puts in switch, lighting lamp on table.)* Look, the switch!!
ISIDOR: Yes, they succeeded—they wiped me out. *(Goes downstage, sits in chair* L. *of table.* MARY *and* ESSIE *put their arms around him.)*
ESSIE: Oh, Papa—Papa—
MARY: Now who's forgetting what they learned from the testimonials?
ISIDOR: Yes, testimonials—meetings—science—what good is it? Look!

(Enter CLEM *door* L.*)*

CLEM: What's the matter? Anything wrong?

ISIDOR: Anything wrong? Can't you see? The barn is burned to the ground—our electrical business is busted.

CLEM: No, it ain't. Instead of just starting in next summer—we'll be in full operation.

ISIDOR: What are we going to start with—ashes?

CLEM: No—your insurance.

ISIDOR: I got insurance—the policy expired.

CLEM: But I renewed it—tonight. *(Takes insurance out of pocket and gives it to* ISIDOR.*)*

ISIDOR: Where did you get the money?

CLEM: I got it from Whitson. *(Everybody jumping gleefully and ad lib.)*

ISIDOR: Clem—what a wonderful partner I got. Where's my hat? Where's my coat—?

MARY: You've got it on.

ISIDOR: Why didn't you tell me? Hurry—hurry!

CLEM: Where are you going?

ISIDOR: I'm going back to the meeting—I'm going to give them a testimonial that'll shake the building. *(*ISIDOR, MARY *and* ESSIE *exit.)*

*(*CLEM *comes downstage* C., *smoking cigar and very much satisfied with himself.)*

CURTAIN

ACT III

SCENE: *The office. Several months later.*

TIME: *About four p.m.*

Entrance door from the outside down L. *opening on stage. Door up* L. *to* MARY'S *office. Another door at* R. *leading into Power House. Modern office furniture and appointments, with inventions of* CLEM'S. *Dictaphone lying on flat top desk—clothes rack up* R. *Letter cabinet at back; electrical cigar lighter in desk which is operated by a button; dome light above desk. Cabinet holding model city under picture of Thomas Edison.*

AT RISE: ISIDOR'S *hat and coat hanging on rack.*

Bare stage.

ESSIE *enters from* L. *lower entrance. She is the bookkeeper now—eyeshade—pen in her hair, carries the afternoon mail, which includes letters of various kinds, circulars in different shade envelopes, quite a number of magazines, trade journals, etc. A number of bills, advertising cards and blotters of different sizes. Goes to desk and starts to assort the mail. With the mail that* ESSIE *brings in there must be a large envelope with letter and picture of* WHITSON *taken twenty years ago, with writing across the back.* ISIDOR *enters from power house* R., *very busy, carries a long paper, expense bill. As he opens door dynamo is heard humming busily; as soon as door is closed, this effect ceases.)*

ISIDOR: *(Looking at expense account angrily—both stand behind desk.)* Expense—expense—expense. Essie, watch that petty cash with a microscope.

ESSIE: Don't worry, Papa—the afternoon mail is in; maybe there's checks.

ISIDOR: Yes. Maybe—that's what we're living on—maybes and might be's and hope so's and if's— A letter from Aunt Mania. *(Opens it and extracts contents.)*

ESSIE: Did she send the picture?

ISIDOR: *(Takes photograph out of envelope and shows it to* ESSIE.*)* Yes!

ESSIE: *(Looks at photo, recognizes* WHITSON, *is greatly surprised.)* Why, Papa—it's the—

ISIDOR: *(Takes photo from* ESSIE.*)* Ssh! Not a word to a soul—living or dead. *(*ESSIE *exits door* L. ISIDOR *glances at letter, looks at photo, turns it over, looks at writing on back, sits in thought, then carefully places letter and photo in inside coat pocket. Turns on Beemisphone switch and listens. Presses buzzer for* MARY*—she enters from her office—she is bright and cheerful.)* Mary, what's the matter with the Beemisphone? It don't work.

MARY: *(Crosses to* R. *of* ISIDOR *at desk.)* Did you put the switch on?

ISIDOR: Sure; do you think I don't know anything about electricity?

MARY: Well, did you put in a record?

ISIDOR: Wait, I'll see! Empty! Get one, Mary, please.

MARY: *(Goes to record cabinet up* L.*)* Long or short letter?

ISIDOR: Long—it's to a creditor. *(As* MARY *is getting record,* ISIDOR *is looking over mail again.)* Bills, circulars, advertisements, blotters, more blotters—for nothing—well, if money don't come in soon, at least we can go in the blotter business.

MARY: *(Puts record in Beemisphone—in middle drawer.)* There you are.

ISIDOR: Thanks. *(Turns switch and starts to dictate—in very loud voice.)* Westinghouse Electric Company, New York City.

MARY: You don't have to yell at it, Mr. Solomon.

ISIDOR: No?

MARY: Certainly not. That's the great advantage of the Beemisphone—it is so sensitized that you can walk around the room and it will record everything you say.

ISIDOR: But I'm all mixed up with these switches.

MARY: *(Explaining.)* I'll show you again. Number one— *(Points to switches, indicating first switch.)* —is for recording—and number two is for repeating.

ISIDOR: I see. *(*MARY *exits* U.L. ISIDOR *dictates, stands behind desk.)* Westinghouse Electric Company, New York City. My dear Mr. Westinghouse: Enclosed please find check for two thousand dollars in full payment of our account. *(Slight pause—resumes dictating.)* The above is the way I would like to start this letter if we had the money; however, we expect to be booming very soon, so don't worry. Hoping that business is good with you and with kindest regards to Mrs. Westinghouse and all the folks, I am sincerely yours, Beemis Electric Company, per Isidor Solomon, President. *(Stops record, thinks. Turns switch, dictates in confidential tone of voice—much lower—sitting at desk.)* This is to Aunt Mania. It's confidential. Mrs. Mania Rochliah Wolfson, Fourteen Salem Street, Boston, Massachusetts. My dear Aunt Mania: I got your letter; the picture is all right. It is as clear as if it was taken yesterday, so please don't worry because in my next letter I might be able to say something. Being very busy, with no money coming in, I must close, with love to you and Aunt Yetta and love to your husband and love to Jake and his wife and love to Moisha and love to Schmule and Mrs. Schmule, and don't forget Essie puts in her love with mine. Your loving distant relation, Beemis Electric Company, Isidor Solomon, President. Now, we'll see. *(Adjusts Beemisphone, works switch, listens.)*

BEEMISPHONE. *(This effect is worked offstage.)* Westinghouse Electric Company, New York City. My dear Mr. Westinghouse: Enclosed please find check for two thousand dollars. *(*ISIDOR *throws off switch—stops it.)*

(Enter MARY *with letters and envelopes she has typed, places them on desk.)*

ISIDOR: Mary, take out the record—it works fine. *(She takes record out of drawer. He looks at typed letters.)* Nice work, Mary; that experience comes in handy that you had in Portsmouth—or was it—Portland?

MARY: Does it matter? I don't even want to think about

what happened before I came here. *(Crosses* L. *to desk.)*

ISIDOR: *(Stamping and signing letters.)* That's right, forget it. That's where your science comes in. Don't you remember what you read this morning in that pamphlet where it said—"Yesterday is gone—today is now—tomorrow ain't here yet—the past is behind—the present you got—the future is coming"— Anyhow, putting the whole thing together it means—the Hell with yesterday. You are happy here—ain't you?

MARY: Yes, I am—thanks to you. *(Pats him on the shoulder.)*

ISIDOR: Yes—me! Ned Tyler is me.

MARY: *(Turns, drops her head.)* Now, Mr. Solomon.

ISIDOR: Never mind. I know what's going on. When I go to bed at night—early, on purpose—and you and Ned are sitting on the porch, don't think that I'm asleep.

MARY: But please—

ISIDOR: I know what goes on in your little office. I know you've been writing him letters twice a day ever since he's been in Hartford—Essie counts every stamp. What does he say in his letters? Oh, it's none of my business—

MARY: Oh, nothing much—all about the business—how anxious he is to make the company a success.

ISIDOR: He has our future in his hands. If he comes back with the Phoenix Bank behind him, I wouldn't even fight him about his expense account.

*(*MARY *exits* L.U., *takes up small record as she does so. Enter* CLEM *from power house. He is dressed in engineer's clothes, grease on hands, etc., indicating hard work—as he opens door, dynamo is heard singing.)*

CLEM: Hasn't Eb Hooker come back yet? *(Crosses to* R. *of desk and stands.)*

ISIDOR: No—and I'm worried.

CLEM: Eb will handle those Selectmen all right—smart fellow.

ISIDOR: And who should get credit for hiring such a smart fellow? *(Signing stock certificates.)* Isidor Solomon, President.

CLEM: What did he say when you didn't pay him his salary this morning?

ISIDOR: I did pay him.

CLEM: With what?

ISIDOR: Stock.

CLEM: In the Beemis Electric Company?

ISIDOR: Yes.

CLEM: What did you do with the rest of the bills?

ISIDOR: Some I promised—some I paid.

CLEM: With stock?

ISIDOR: What else? How do you suppose I've been getting coal and groceries, and steaks and chops and even squabs once in a while.

CLEM: So that's how we've been living on the fat of the land?

ISIDOR: *(Tears off stock certificates.)* Sure. Nearly every storekeeper in this town has a hoping interest in this company.

CLEM: Well, from now on you can show the practicability of our plans. I just finished wiring the model. All I got to do is to hook it up. *(Enter* HOOKER *down* L., *angry, walks up and down, stands* L.*)* Well, Eb, what luck?

HOOKER: The Selectmen wouldn't give me a hearing.

ISIDOR: What kind of a lawyer is that—he can't even get a hearing?

HOOKER: But Whitson claims that the franchise is defective and that the town isn't bound.

ISIDOR: That franchise is all right—ain't it?

HOOKER: Absolutely. It was drawn up by old Judge Stebbins himself, who was one of the keenest legal minds in the country, and I'm willing and eager to take it to any Court.

ISIDOR: But we can't afford to have any Court business. It'll frighten capital off.

HOOKER: Whitson knows that—that's why he's so arbitrary. *(Sits* L. *of desk.)*

CLEM: And as long as he is Mayor—we're going to be in hot water.

ISIDOR: Maybe he'll be defeated at the next election? The people in this town want electricity and if we could get a good honest candidate to come out on an electric platform—he could win hands up. And for a man like that we don't have to look far. *(Indicates* HOOKER.*)*

CLEM: Best liked man in town.

HOOKER: *(Rising.)* Me?

CLEM: Ever since you quit being tax collector, you've become very popular.

ISIDOR: I don't see any reason why he shouldn't run.

CLEM: And win, too.

HOOKER: But that's impossible as long as Whitson has Gideon's support. Tyler owns half the town.

CLEM: *(Sits* R. *of desk.)* No doubt that Tyler's got the power—if there was only some way to win Tyler over.

ISIDOR: *(Sits in chair behind desk.)* If—if—I had an appointment with him this afternoon—but he didn't come.

CLEM: Tyler ought to be with us—Ned being connected here.

HOOKER: Hardly—Ned's leaving the bank is what has embittered him more than ever.

ISIDOR: But there was no future for Ned in that bank—here at least he's got a chance to get out and do something—he's been in Hartford now for five weeks and I hope and pray he's done something.

CLEM: Don't worry about that boy—he'll come home and bring you the bacon.

ISIDOR: He'd better bring me something else besides bacon.

(Enter ESSIE L. *lower door.)*

ESSIE: Papa—Mr. Gideon Tyler is outside—waiting—he's been sitting there I don't know how long.

ISIDOR: *(All rise—*HOOKER *crosses to* R. *of desk.)* Oi, Mr. Tyler she keeps waiting—what kind of an office boy are you? *(Quietly)* Open the door—quietly—quietly. *(*ESSIE *opens door, then* ISIDOR, *very loud.)* What do you mean by keeping a man like Mr. Tyler waiting?

ESSIE: *(Very loud.)* I couldn't help it, Papa. The cash box is outside and I hate to leave it alone with strangers.

ISIDOR: *(Bus. of holding head, etc.)* Get out of here. *(*ESSIE *exits down* L. CLEM *exits* R. ISIDOR *goes to chair and sits;* HOOKER R. *of desk, busy with papers, etc. Enter* TYLER *from* L. HOOKER *and* ISIDOR *pretend not to see him.)* I know Edendale needs electricity—so does Valley Falls. If Mr. Whitson isn't big enough to see the advantages our company will bring to this town, there is one man here who is big enough and that's—Mr. Tyler— How do you do? *(Rises.)*

TYLER: Oh, you're busy.

ISIDOR: *(Standing.)* No, no. I'm through.

HOOKER: I'll run right over to Edendale now. *(Crosses* L. *to door* L. *downstage.)*

ISIDOR: No, don't run; just hold their offer in abeyance till we see what transpires here.

HOOKER: Very well. Good afternoon, Gideon—afternoon, Mr. Solomon. *(At door* L.*)* I'll drop around to the house tonight after supper.

ISIDOR: No, come to supper—it's Friday—Essie's making gefilte fish.

HOOKER: I won't miss that.

ISIDOR: Be sure and come.

HOOKER: Sure.

ISIDOR: And bring along an opener. *(*HOOKER *exits* L.*)*

TYLER: *(Crosses to* R. *of desk and sits.)* Mr. Solomon—there's something I want to talk to you about.

ISIDOR: *(Standing behind desk—eagerly.)* About this franchise?

TYLER: No, no, I've got nothing to do with that.

ISIDOR: You've got everything to do with it.

TYLER: Whitson has his own plans for the best interests of the community.

ISIDOR: What he's doing isn't for the benefit of the town—it's for personal reasons against me.

TYLER: Well, you can't very well blame him.

ISIDOR: What did I do?

TYLER: Whitson had his heart set on his daughter Grace and my boy Ned making a match of it and you interfered.

ISIDOR: How did I interfere? Did I go to your boy and say: "Ned, you've got to like this girl?" Did I go to her and say: "Mary, you've got to like this boy?" I made them love—chickens lay eggs, is that my fault?

TYLER: But Ned is all I've got in the world—and I want to make sure that he doesn't make a mistake. I want you to tell me something about this Mary Clark—where does she come from?

ISIDOR: Portland—er—Portsmouth.

TYLER: How long have you known her?

ISIDOR: Long enough to know that she's as good as gold.

TYLER: But *is* she?

ISIDOR: Now, Mr. Tyler—that makes me mad. Ain't she living in the same house with my daughter?

TYLER: Mr. Solomon—it's my duty— *(Rises.)*

*(*MARY *enters with record and two typewritten letters and envelopes up* L.*)*

MARY: Oh, excuse me— *(Puts record in cabinet, comes down behind desk with letters, puts them on desk.)*

TYLER: *(*R.C.*)* Oh, that's all right—we were just talking about you. You see, on account of certain conditions, we haven't got as well acquainted as we might, however, my boy being interested in you—

MARY: In me?

ISIDOR: You see? *(Bus.)*

TYLER: Naturally—I'm interested too. Want to know all about you—where you came from—where was it—Portland or Portsmouth?

MARY: *(Very nervous during this scene.)* I came from Manchester. *(Bus. for* ISIDOR*—first time he has heard this. Looks at* MARY*—puzzled.)*

ISIDOR: That's right—my mistake.

TYLER: Did you live there with your folks?

MARY: They are dead.

TYLER: I'm sorry—had to work for a living?

MARY: Yes, sir.

TYLER: What did you work at in Manchester?

MARY: Public stenographer.

TYLER: M'h'm! Manchester's a pretty lively, prosperous town, isn't it?

MARY: Yes, sir.

TYLER: You did well there—had lots of friends, I suppose?

MARY: A few—yes, sir.

TYLER: I was just wondering what made you leave there and come to a little out of the way place like this. *(*MARY *does not answer—turns—exits* L.U. *quickly.)* I thought there was something.

ISIDOR: I don't blame her for not answering—you talk to her like you was a judge getting ready to give her thirty days.

TYLER: But she ought to be glad of the chance to give a clear account of herself—unless she's got something to hide.

ISIDOR: She's got nothing at all to be ashamed of.

TYLER: Then why didn't she answer?

ISIDOR: I can answer for her.

TYLER: Then you know all about her?

ISIDOR: I ought to—she's been working for me for a long time. Smart girl. Fine family.

TYLER: But I never heard of the Clarks of Manchester.

ISIDOR: Surely you've heard of the big Clarks—prominent people.

TYLER: Which ones?

ISIDOR: O.N.T.* *(Sits behind desk.)*

TYLER: Oh, yes: old friends of my family. *(*ISIDOR *seems to be caught in a trap.)*

ISIDOR: She's only slightly related to the cotton people—you see, she's from a different spool of the family.

TYLER: What Clarks do you refer to?

ISIDOR: You surely remember the Clarks in the Revolution?

TYLER: I know there were lots of them in it.

ISIDOR: Say, she had so many relatives in the Revolution—if it wasn't for them I don't think it would have been a success.

TYLER: Then why did she refuse to give me that information?

ISIDOR: Well, a girl like that from a fine family—you ask her a lot of questions like you were a police station—she felt insulted.

TYLER: Well, if what you say is true—I'm sorry. *(Rises.)*

ISIDOR: That's all right—I'll get her to excuse you. *(Rises—*TYLER *is about to go.)* Have a cigar? *(Takes box of cigars out of desk drawer—offers box.)*

TYLER: Thanks.

ISIDOR: They're clear of Havana. They ain't so good, but I want you should try our new patent cigar lighter. Clem's invention.

TYLER: Where is it?

ISIDOR: Right over there. Just push that button.

*Brand name of yarns manufactured by the Clark Thread Company, Newark, NJ.

TYLER: *(Pushes.)* Quite an invention.

ISIDOR: See—when you want it, it's there. And when you don't, it ain't. *(Pushes light back.)* I'd send one over to your house complimentary—for nothing—but you ain't got no electricity—so you can see the comforts you're missing.

TYLER: Maybe there's something in this enterprise after all.

ISIDOR: If there wasn't, do you think a smart boy like Ned would give up his job in the bank and come in with us? It seems to me that your own son being interested—that you would use your influence to get the Mayor to okay our plans and let us start up and begin to get in some money.

TYLER: Mayor Whitson is only carrying out what he feels is the will of the majority of the people of this town.

ISIDOR: But he won't even give us a hearing—is that fair?

TYLER: Perhaps not—but—well—you know the prejudice that exists against you.

ISIDOR: Now ain't that silly? To mix up religion with electricity? They won't have electric lights because I'm an Israelite.

TYLER: Now see here, Solomon, I'll be frank with you, your people are tricky, you're too smart and I don't mind admitting to you that we're afraid of you in a small community like this.

ISIDOR: *(Long pause.)* Mr. Tyler, that's all foolishness. We ain't half as tricky and we ain't half as smart as a lot of people give us credit for. I want to ask you something, if you think we're so smart—who is the head of Standard Oil? Mr. Rockfeller. Is he a Jew? Oh, no. Who are the heads of the railroads? The Vanderbilts, the Goulds. Are they Jews? Oh, no. Who are the heads of the Steel Industry, Mr. Schwab, Mr. Gary. Who are the heads of the coal industry? Mr. Burns, Mr. Farrell. Who controls the telegraphs and the cables? Mr. Mackay. Are they Jews? Oh, no. Who is the big financial gun in America? Mr. Morgan. Is he a Jew? Oh, no. Believe me, we ain't half as smart as a lot of people think we are.

TYLER: That may be true, Mr. Solomon—but how about such names as Julius Rosenwald, Nathan Strauss, Jacob

Schiff, Barney Baruch, Henry Morgenthau and the Rothschilds, eh?

ISIDOR: Of course—we ain't altogether damn fools either.

TYLER: *(Rises.)* Hardly. Nobody has ever accused you of that. *(Gets hat—about to go—enter* CLEM *from* R.*)*

CLEM: *(Crosses* L.C.*)* Going, Gideon?

TYLER: Yes.

ISIDOR: Just wait a minute, Mr. Tyler. I want to show you this model.

TYLER: Model of what?

CLEM: Miniature City—showing the Beemis system of illumination.

TYLER: Well, I'd like to see it. *(*ISIDOR L. *of model—*TYLER L.C. CLEM R. *of model.)*

CLEM: I'll give you an idea of how Valley Falls would look if the plans were approved and we were allowed to carry out our ideas. *(*ISIDOR *and* CLEM *pull down shades.* ISIDOR L. CLEM R.*)* Now I'll show you what was in my head all the time that you were laughing at me. *(Shades down—lights out—stage dark—*ISIDOR *works electric switches.)* It's evening, this is the way Valley Falls looks now—you can't see your hand in front of your face. Sundown—the houses begin to light up—

ISIDOR: You see, Mr. Tyler—look at your house—don't it look nice?

CLEM: Then the stores—

ISIDOR: You can keep open all night. Now watch the street lamps and the public square as it should be. Now we're going to show you Main Street and the Public Square—you see we furnish them almost free—you only have to pay once a month.

TYLER: Looks as pretty as the World's Fair.

CLEM: Prettier.

ISIDOR: And don't forget—cheaper. Now keep your eyes open for Edendale. Edendale is begging us to move our plant there—they've got a smart Mayor.

CLEM: Now comes Sarah's Corners.

ISIDOR: Look! Sarah's Corners! You can see every corner she's got.

TYLER: Amazing! Beyond description! *(Lights up.* ISIDOR *and* CLEM *raise window shades. Lights come up full.)*

CLEM: That's the way we'd make things look around here if you gave us a Mayor that knew his business.

ISIDOR: And it won't cost the town a cent either, Mr. Tyler.

TYLER: Well—all I can say is you've opened my eyes. You've given me food for thought. I'll go right over and take it up with the Mayor.

*(*TYLER *exits down* L. ISIDOR *and* CLEM *show great joy—dance around and hug each other.)*

CLEM: Didn't we knock him a twister? *(Both downstage in front of desk.* ISIDOR L. CLEM R.*)*

ISIDOR: Did you see him? We got him—we got him hooked—we got the big fish. We got everything we need—except the money.

CLEM: We'll get that. We're going to be the two biggest men in this town; in my mind's eye I can see the big stores—the hotels—I can see the trolleys running. *(Both looking front.)* A great big electric park—and right in the middle of the park, a great big fountain—and right in the middle of the fountain a great big statue of Isidor Solomon—

ISIDOR: No, no—Clem. The statue is going to be of Clem Beemis—I ain't got a shape for a statue.

CLEM: I won't have anybody standing up in the middle of that fountain but you.

ISIDOR: All right. But you got to be with me. We'll have twin statues—you and me with the water running out of our mouths. *(Both stand facing front with their mouths open. Statue business.)*

(Enter NED.*)*

NED: *(*L.I. *Very happy—laughing.)* Hello, Mr. Solomon—hello, Clem. Gee, I'm glad to get back.

ISIDOR: Look! Look! Here is Ned. *(Shakes hand.)* Did you bring the bank with you?

NED: The money is all right. The Phoenix Bank of Hartford has accepted our proposition to finance us. *(All embrace each other in ecstasy.)*

ISIDOR: We got the capital—oh, what a relief. *(All embrace each other again.)*

NED: Everything is all fixed and here are the contracts

ready for your signature. *(Takes contracts out of pocket—gives them to* ISIDOR.*)*

ISIDOR: I don't sign anything without my lawyer. You run right over and get Eb Hooker. *(Takes* NED *by the arm, leads him to door down* L.*)*

NED: Just a minute. I want to see Mary first. *(Pulls back a little.)*

ISIDOR: Never mind—Mary'll keep. You go over and get Eb Hooker—business before loving.

NED: Yes—but—

ISIDOR: Now, I'll tell you what I'll do. Come over to the house tonight and from eight o'clock on I'll see that you have the parlor all to yourself and you can stay till the milkman comes and let in the cat. *(Exit* NED *down* L.*, laughing.)* Clem, we're made! We got the backing—now, Mr. Edison, look out. *(Shakes finger at picture of Edison which is on top of model. Crosses upstage behind desk.* CLEM *stands* R. *of desk. Enter* ESSIE *down* L.*)* What's the matter?

ESSIE: The Mayor is outside.

ISIDOR: *(Standing beside desk.)* Why don't you show him in?

ESSIE: He wants to see Mary.

ISIDOR: Let the Mayor in. *(*ESSIE *exits.)* Excuse me, Clem. I want to have a little talk with Mr. Whitson all by myself. *(Goes up and gets record and puts in drawer.)*

CLEM: If you need any help, call for me; I'll be waiting outside with a monkey wrench in my hand.

ISIDOR: Never mind. I can handle him. *(*CLEM *exits* R.*)*

*(*NOTE: *Since dictating of letters in early part of act, the horn of Beemisphone has been left standing up.* ISIDOR *sits at desk—pretends to be busy with papers; enter* WHITSON L.*, stands looking.* WHITSON *notices that* MARY *is not in the room, looks offstage and speaks off.)*

WHITSON: *(Crosses* L. *of desk—very angry—to* ISIDOR.*)* See here, Solomon—what do you mean by trying to undermine me with Mr. Tyler?

ISIDOR: *(Standing beside desk.)* I only told the truth. That you wouldn't let Mr. Hooker in at the meeting to state our case.

WHITSON: You've got no case. Your franchise was never

anything but a practical joke played by old Judge Stebbins, on Clem Beemis, the town fool.

ISIDOR: Still for fifteen years the town took his consideration of a dollar a year and I tell you to get fifteen dollars out of anybody in this town is no joke. But we don't want to hold you to the exact terms of that franchise—we are willing to modify.

WHITSON: That franchise is never going to get by me in any form, so you might as well give it up and go about your business.

ISIDOR: But this is my business.

WHITSON: Oh, well, of course. I'll see that you get back every cent that you put into it.

ISIDOR: You mean the town would really be kind enough?

WHITSON: I'm not talking for the town—you understand? *(Looks around room to give* ISIDOR *a chance to throw on switch on Beemisphone.)*

ISIDOR: Oh—I think I do. *(Puts on Beemisphone switch.)*

WHITSON: I'm speaking as an individual.

ISIDOR: Oh, for yourself?

WHITSON: Yes—you can make better terms with me than you can with the town. Interested? *(Sits* L. *of desk.)*

ISIDOR: Very much.

WHITSON: *(Feels for pencil—*ISIDOR *gives him a gold pencil out of his pocket. Bus. of figuring with pencil on pad.)* Now the way I figure it—all you put into this originally was twenty-eight dollars and forty cents. That was the premium you paid for your insurance.

ISIDOR: *(Sits behind desk.)* Oh, yes—and it was your money—I never had a chance to thank you for the loan.

WHITSON: We won't speak of that.

ISIDOR: I would never say a word to anybody, but you brought it up.

WHITSON: Say you did put in four thousand dollars—I'm willing to give you six. That's fifty percent profit. *(Puts* ISIDOR'S *pencil in his pocket.)* Well?

ISIDOR: Give me back my pencil.

WHITSON: *(Gives back pencil.)* What do you say?

ISIDOR: It's ridiculous. How about the water rights and the land?

WHITSON: You can't sell me that.

ISIDOR: Why not?

WHITSON: It's in the name of Mary Clark and it's never been transferred to you.

ISIDOR: Don't be silly—that's a detail.

WHITSON: Oh, then it's still in her name?

ISIDOR: Yes—but Mary's the same like my own daughter.

WHITSON: Well, to come down to brass tacks, I'll give you ten thousand dollars if you'll sell out and clear out.

ISIDOR: You're wasting time, Mr. Whitson—we won't sell.

WHITSON: *(Rises.)* Then you can't put it through. Now, then, Solomon. I warn you, if you don't sell out to me, you haven't got a chance. You can't string a wire or raise a pole until your plans are approved by me—and as long as I'm Mayor, they're never going to be. *(Turns* L.*)*

ISIDOR: I can see what a chance I got as long as you are Mayor. *(*ISIDOR *throws off switch.)*

WHITSON: *(Walks back to desk* L.*)* And let me tell you this—I'm going to keep on being Mayor.

ISIDOR: *(Rises.)* You can't tell—it's a month between now and election. *(Pushes buzzer for* MARY. *Calls.)* You know how it is in politics—one day you're in office—the next day you're in jail. *(*MARY *enters.)* Oh, Mary—I just got a proposition from Mr. Whitson—first-class grafter—and I want— *(Indicates Beemisphone.* MARY *goes to it and starts to open drawer.)*

WHITSON: *(To* MARY.*)* What's your real name? *(*MARY, *shock of fear, stops, catches her breath and runs for power house door* R.*)* Wait a minute, Miss.

ISIDOR: Don't be afraid, Mary. You don't have to run away. *(He says this to* MARY. *Then to* WHITSON.*)* Say, don't get so fresh—you wait a minute.

WHITSON: *(To* MARY.*)* What's your real name?

ISIDOR: It's Mary Clark!

WHITSON: It's Mary Grey.

ISIDOR: You're crazy—she's Mary Clark.

WHITSON: I know who she is.

ISIDOR: *(To* WHITSON.*)* What's it your business?

WHITSON: This girl has misrepresented herself. *(Shows paper.)* I received this today from a private detective I employed. I've been investigating her for some time.

MARY: *(Facing* WHITSON.*)* Well, what if I am Mary Grey?

ISIDOR: Yes—what of it?

WHITSON: Then I have something to say to her of a private nature. Don't you think so, Miss Grey?

MARY: Will you leave us alone for a few minutes?

ISIDOR: Leave you alone with a—

MARY: Please!

ISIDOR: Are you sure it's all right?

MARY: Sure.

(ISIDOR starts to exit—goes to door R., stops as if to listen.)

WHITSON: Now, then, Miss Grey— *(Sees ISIDOR and stops.)*

ISIDOR: Oh, excuse me. I forgot something. *(Opens drawer and takes out record, then picks up box of cigars from desk and exits into power house.)*

WHITSON: Now, then, Miss Grey—I know all about you. I've got it right here. *(Crosses to L. of desk downstage—indicates large envelope.)*

MARY: *(Comes to R. of desk—downstage.)* But I did nothing wrong.

WHITSON: Your friends didn't think so—these Manchester papers didn't think so and you'll never make anybody believe in your innocence.

MARY: I know that. That's why I ran away. What have I done to you? Why should you do this?

WHITSON: Now don't be alarmed—I'm going to keep your secret. *(MARY is puzzled.)* On one condition—the property this plant stands on is still in your name—

MARY: Yes—but I don't own that property.

WHITSON: As long as it's in your name—legally you own it.

MARY: Oh, I see—and you think I would ruin them to save myself?

WHITSON: But you won't ruin them; they can never put this business through. They'll lose every dollar and it's up to somebody who has their interests at heart to force them to act like sane, human beings for their own good. You can do it. Turn over the property rights to me and I'll take over the plant and hand them ten thousand dollars in cash. *(MARY looks at him in indignation.)* Now you're not hurting anybody if you agree to do it. You'll be saving yourself, your friends will make a large profit—you know what you've got at stake. You will have to run away from here the same as you did from Manchester. Wherever you go it will follow you—now you've got the chance to stop it right here. Get married and settle down—I'll keep my mouth shut!

MARY: I won't do it, Mr. Whitson—I won't.

WHITSON: Very well, then—I'll expose you and see that you're driven out of *this* town. *(Crosses* R.*)*

(Enter ISIDOR, *followed by* CLEM.*)*

ISIDOR: Shall I stay out yet?

WHITSON: That's all I've got to say.

ISIDOR: Good.

WHITSON: Good afternoon—*Miss Grey. (Exits door* L.*)*

*(*MARY *breaks down, cries;* ISIDOR *and* CLEM *go to her.)*

CLEM: Now, Mary—

ISIDOR: We don't care what happened before—you got good friends now. And no matter what trouble you got—you ain't going to stand alone.

MARY: I know—I know. But through me he's trying to ruin you. My stay here is only making your struggle all the harder—and—and I'm going.

ISIDOR *and* CLEM: *(Following* MARY *to door* U.L.*)* No, no, no.

CLEM: We ain't going to let you.

ISIDOR: You're all excited—cool yourself down. Now go home and take a good rest, then when Ned calls tonight—

MARY: He sha'n't ruin you and I'm not going to drag Ned into this. *(Turns and exits* L.U., *crying.)*

ISIDOR: *(Downhearted—comes down to* L. *of desk.)* That Whitson—I tell you, Clem—I can't stand it any longer. He's starting in on Mary—I got it up to here— *(Indicates his neck.)* —now I'm going to start in on him. I don't care if he is the Mayor—I wouldn't care if he was the Chief of Police—

*(*TYLER *enters—taps* ISIDOR *on the shoulder.* TYLER *has the same large envelope that* WHITSON *had, with newspapers and clippings in it.)*

TYLER: You!!! *(*ISIDOR *wheels sharply with raised hand as though to strike back, thinking it is* WHITSON, *sees* TYLER, *apologetic.)* You lied to me about that girl.

ISIDOR: No, I didn't. I only lied about her family. I told you the truth about the girl—she's all right.

TYLER: I know better—Whitson has given me all the facts.

CLEM: Who are you talking about—Mary Clark?

TYLER: Clark—that isn't even her right name—she's a—

ISIDOR: Look out, Mr. Tyler—I'm excited. Be careful what you say about Mary.

TYLER: Her record speaks for itself and here it is in the Manchester newspaper of six months ago. Mary Grey—named as co-respondent in a notorious divorce scandal— There's the story with all its disgraceful details—she was even afraid to face trial. No wonder she ran away and hid herself. Well?

ISIDOR: I don't care what it says. I know that girl is sweet and good—and nothing is going to make me believe she's any different than the way I know her. All right—you bring me newspapers from Whitson—how do I know he didn't have them printed himself? Don't you see, Mr. Tyler—he's trying to drive our Mary away—he's trying to come between her and Ned—and why is he doing this? Just to take his mean spite out on me—he's got no use for me—that you know—but the worst you don't know—he's not only mean but crooked.

TYLER: You'll have to prove that, Solomon.

*(*CLEM *has moved up behind desk in position for business of pulling* ISIDOR'S *sleeve.)*

ISIDOR: I'll be much obliged for the chance. I'm going to start in right now. I'm going to show you that as soon as he thought we were going to make a fortune with this electrical business he tried to use his power as Mayor to get the plant—not for the town—not for the people—but for himself, and when he found he couldn't steal our business away and he couldn't win his fight with men—that robber—he started in on the women— *(*CLEM *pulls* ISIDOR'S *sleeve to attract his attention to the fact that* WHITSON *has entered* L. *down-*

stage during the above speech and stands listening.) I see him, but don't stop me now—I got a good start.

WHITSON: Well—what's all this about? *(Stands at door* L. *downstage.)*

ISIDOR: Clem, give me that record. *(*CLEM *hands* ISIDOR *record from desk.)*

TYLER: Solomon has just been making serious charges against you of malfeasance in office.

ISIDOR: I got the whole proposition— *(Crosses to* WHITSON L.*)*

WHITSON: I never made you any proposition . . .

ISIDOR: It's on the Beemisphone record. Would you like to hear it, Mr. Tyler?

TYLER: Might as well.

ISIDOR: Clem, put this in the Beemisphone.

(As ISIDOR *turns to give record to* CLEM, WHITSON *grabs record from his hand.)*

WHITSON: It's all nonsense—you've got nothing. *(Smashes record on arm of chair* L. ISIDOR *heartbroken.)*

ISIDOR: That's the kind of a man he is. He can't stand to hear the truth and he smashes it. A fine man you picked out to be Mayor of the town. But from now on you'll find out it ain't so easy to get elected. Before I get through with you, I'll show you, Mr.—Whitson—

WHITSON: And before I get through with you, I'll run you out of town, you little Kike.

ISIDOR: Kike. That's the first time I heard that word since I left Boston. *(Takes photo and letter out of inside pocket.)* I got something from Boston today that will be of great interest to you and the voters when it's printed in the *Valley Falls Gazette*. *(Showing photo to* TYLER.*)* Here's his picture taken twenty years ago and here's his signature—his right name across the back.

TYLER: *(Taking photo from* ISIDOR.*)* His right name?

WHITSON: My name is Ichabod Whitson.

ISIDOR: Yoh. Ichabod Whitson. Here's his own handwriting. *(*TYLER *compares photo with* WHITSON.*)*

TYLER: Why, it's incredible.

WHITSON: Of course—just a cheap trick to discredit me—why, it's ridiculous.

ISIDOR: Oh, is it? Well, here's something that ain't ridiculous. *(Shows* WHITSON *the letter.)* Do you remember the handwriting? *(*WHITSON *looks at it—shows recognition.)* Oh, it comes back to you, huh? Twenty years ago—the way you left your people that brought you up and loved you. Just when they needed you—they were too much responsibility, they were in the way—the old folks. You see, Mr. Tyler, he can't make a liar out of this letter. Want to read it? *(To* WHITSON.*)*

TYLER: Well, why don't you read it—Whitson—or whatever your name is?

ISIDOR: It's from his mother. He's her only son. Read it for yourself. This letter will prove everything I've said. *(Hands letter to* TYLER—TYLER *puzzled.)* Excuse me—I'll read it, and this letter will prove everything I've said. *(Reads from letter.) "Mein taierer Itzkele—ich shich dere in dame briefe—"* (Etc. Reads letter in Yiddish.)*

CURTAIN

*My dear Itzkele, I'm sending you in this letter . . .

ACT IV

SCENE: *Lobby of the Grand Hotel*—1919.

The hotel has been remodeled and is now a modern, bright, attractive place. Curtains, chandeliers, grand staircase, ballroom, cloakroom L. *Reception room* L.C. *at back. Amen Corner* where stove was in Act I. Marble counter, writing desk, up-to-the-minute paraphernalia of hotel. Behind desk, electric sign indicating elevator off* L., *same direction as coatroom. Music offstage* R. *Punch bowl setting off-stage* R. *When swinging door of ballroom opens, music can be heard—when it swings shut, music ceases.*

NOTE: *Taboret has a shelf underneath, on which is large ash receiver—nickel. Something in the form of a cuspidor, only slightly different—sort of an urn for cigar ashes. Early in the act, as they are smoking, the characters seated in Amen Corner drop their ashes and matches in the urn.*

Everybody in evening dress, not grotesque.

NOTE: *Back drop is replica of model in Act III, showing hills and villages in the distance—lit up—trolley, etc.*

AT RISE: *Discovered:* BIJE *at desk, disconsolate.*

Singing and music offstage R. *Telephone rings at desk.* BIJE *answers it. Street car passes windows and doors upstage in distance.*

*Hoffman probably intends a long wooden bench; the script subsequently refers to it as a settee. The original production used a horseshoe-shaped bench with seat cushions.

BIJE: Grand Hotel . . . No, I'm not the clerk; I'm the manager . . . Oh . . .

(Enter HOOKER, CLEM *and* TRIMBLE *from ballroom* L.U. TRIMBLE *very slightly under the influence of the punch bowl. Not jagged—just feeling good.)*

HOOKER: We'll have a little drink out here.
BIJE: *(Still speaking into phone.)* No telegram . . . no, sir . . . I'll tell Mr. Beemis . . . Good bye. *(Hangs up receiver.)*
CLEM: Who was it, Bije?
BIJE: Mr. Solomon. He said not to start the supper until he arrives.
TRIMBLE: What's keeping Isidor?

*(Positions. Settee—*TRIMBLE L. HOOKER *upstage on settee.* CLEM R. BIJE *passes a box of cigars to men; after they take cigars he returns box.)*

BIJE: Here you are, gentlemen.
HOOKER, CLEM *and* TRIMBLE: *(Drink.)* Happy New Year. *(Ad lib.)*
TRIMBLE: Certainly has a good old-fashioned kick in it.
HOOKER: Where did you *get* all the liquor, Clem?
CLEM: I didn't get it—it was Isidor's idea. *(Music stops.)*
TRIMBLE: He's certainly done big things for the town.

(Car passes the window upstage in the distance.)

CLEM: Well, here we are—the Beemis Electric Company in a fair way to become one of the biggest public utilities in New England.
TRIMBLE: And we all got stock in it. *(Bus. all sit.)*
HOOKER: And when you look back and think—remember what we were doing last New Year's Eve? *(Sits back on settee.)*
CLEM: You were just setting back—letting the falls go to waste—laughing at me and roasting the Jews—we didn't realize that we all came from the same Adam—the same Eve and the same apple.
TRIMBLE: Sure enough. We're all one family and it's

against nature to persecute our own on account of their beliefs—and to burn 'em at the stake.

CLEM: Yes. Or to burn up their stock.

TRIMBLE: Now, Clem, let up on that— *(Looks anxiously at others.)* You know it was Ichabod Whitson who got me to—who stirred up all the feeling against Isidor.

HOOKER: Not Ichabod Whitson, but Isaac Wolfson; he's got a lot to answer for. If it wasn't for him, Mary wouldn't have run away.

TRIMBLE: How long has she been gone now?

HOOKER: She disappeared the day that Whitson came to the office and threatened to expose her.

(Enter TYLER, *main door upstage* L.C. *He is in evening dress—worried and sad.* BIJE *helps him off with coat. Ad lib. greetings between all. All rise and go to* TYLER *and shake hands.)*

BIJE: *(Back behind counter.)* Happy New Year.

CLEM: Evening, Gideon—you're a little late.

TYLER: *(To settee.)* Well, I'm not exactly in a mood for hilarity. If I didn't consider it my duty on account of my friendship for Mr. Solomon, I wouldn't be here at all. *(Goes to settee and sits upstage.* HOOKER *stands behind settee,* TRIMBLE *sits* L., CLEM *stands* R.*)*

HOOKER: Don't worry about Ned.

TYLER: How can I help it?

HOOKER: The boy'll be all right.

TYLER: He's been away a month this time. Every little rumor or clue, he's packed and gone. Don't suppose he'll ever settle down until he finds that girl.

HOOKER: Mr. Solomon is leaving no stone unturned to find her.

TRIMBLE: Ever find out the truth about her connection with the Kimball divorce case?

TYLER: Yes—went down to Manchester and made a personal investigation. It seems that Mary was employed as a stenographer in the hotel where Mr. Kimball was stopping. He and his wife were living apart on account of Mrs. Kimball's violent jealousy. Kimball was taken ill and confined to his bed. Had a lot of correspondence. Mary went to his room in her capacity as hotel stenographer. Mrs. Kimball had detectives watching him—they broke into the room. To a suspicious wife Mary's presence in Kimball's room was evidence enough to start a divorce suit, naming Mary as co-respondent.

HOOKER: Mary was entirely innocent?

TYLER: Absolutely.

TRIMBLE: Then why didn't she stay there and fight it out?

CLEM: Just because our poor little Mary is not the fighting kind.

HOOKER: Certainly not the kind that could go into Court and brazen out a charge of that nature. She was alone in the world and didn't have proper advice.

TYLER: Besides—you know a girl in that situation—guilty until proven innocent—the whole town—all her friends—turned against her.

TRIMBLE: Yes—I've heard how narrow they are in them small towns—thank the Lord we're bigger and broader.

CLEM: And it's all Isidor's idea. *(To others.)* Nice fellow.

TRIMBLE: You bet—I took a great liking to him from the very first. *(Drinks.)*

(Enter MRS. TRIMBLE *from* R.U.*)*

MRS. TRIMBLE: You've been smoking long enough. It's high time us girls broke up this stag party. Seth, Clem, Eb, come, gentlemen—I have partners for you all. *(Music starts. Exit* MRS. TRIMBLE, HOOKER *and* TRIMBLE *to ballroom* R.*)*

ISIDOR: *(Offstage* L.U.*)* Tell my chauffeur to wait. *(*ISIDOR *enters main door upstage—with fur coat, silk hat and dress suit.)*

CLEM: Well, Isidor—any news?

ISIDOR: Nothing.

CLEM: Well, cheer up, Isidor. *(Takes* ISIDOR *by arm and goes* R.*)* I've got a surprise for you. *(Reaches ballroom. Bus. Stops music.)* Stop the music. Committee on Presentation, step this way. Mr. Solomon has arrived. *(All cheer and applaud—exit* ISIDOR *and* CLEM *into ballroom. General greetings by all heard offstage* R.*)*

(Enter WHITSON *from door back up* L.C. *Stands listening to speech coming from ballroom, downcast.)*

HOOKER: *(Offstage.)* Ladies and gentlemen—and our genial host— *(Applause.)* —Mr. Solomon—it is my pleasant duty this evening to convey to you the feeling of esteem and regard in which you are held in this community and to extend to you greetings and best wishes for prosperity and happiness for the coming year. *(Applause.)* Moreover—on behalf of your associates and fellow citizens—in gratitude and appreciation—allow me to present to you this little token. *(Cheers, applause, voices.)*

VOICE: *(Offstage.)* Speech from Mr. Solomon.

ISIDOR: *(Ad lib.—offstage.)* I can't make a speech—I don't want to make a speech—want to make a fool out of me? *(Etc.)* Leave me alone. *(Etc. Others insist—mob comes on stage with* ISIDOR, *who enters backwards—dragging others who try to get away. He carries silver loving cup in his hand, protesting against speech making—they get him up on settee.* WHITSON *exits* L.*—into writing room.* TYLER *remains upstage.)*

VOICE: Speech—speech—

ISIDOR: Friends, relatives, and consumers. I'd like to tell you in beautiful language how much I appreciate this grand, wonderful, magnificent, brand new shaving mug. *(Cheers, applause, laughter.)*

ESSIE: Papa!

ISIDOR: Never mind, I know what it is. *(Looks at tag on cup.)* Happy New Year. Say—that's nice. Same to you.

CROWD: Thank you, Mr. Solomon.

ISIDOR: And me, too. *(Looks at other side of tag.)* Nineteen twenty-one. Say—that's cheap. I don't know what else I can say except that I hope that during the coming year that your houses will be brighter and brighter—because the brighter they get the more light you use, and there's no reason for your lives to be gloomy or dark, or your streets either, because we furnish the lamps and fixtures at cost price—and all we ask is a small deposit on new accounts. I thank you.

(Music starts. All applaud. Everybody exits—but ESSIE, ISIDOR, TYLER *and* TRIMBLE*—to ballroom.*

ESSIE: *(Comes down to* ISIDOR.*)* Oh, Papa—isn't it wonderful?

ISIDOR: It's just simply— Get away—you're taking the shine off. *(Blows breath on cup and polishes it—sees* TYLER *is downhearted—crosses to him*—ESSIE *upstage in pantomime with* TRIMBLE.*)* Now, Mr. Tyler—I know how you feel. You're missing Ned and I'm missing Mary, but maybe the New Year will bring us what we're wishing for if we greet it with a smile. You know we got to have faith and understanding. Did you ever read *Science and Health*?

TYLER: *(Smiling.)* Have you become a Christian Scientist?

ISIDOR: Not exactly—I'm a Jewish Scientist. I take the best out of everything.

ESSIE: *(Coming down to* ISIDOR.*)* Oh, Papa!

ISIDOR: Say, why don't you ask Mr. Tyler for a dance?

ESSIE: I've just been waiting for him to ask me.

TYLER: *(Offers his arm to* ESSIE*—they exit ballroom* R.*)* Well, nothing would please me better.

ISIDOR: Look at you. You make a nice couple—either one of you. *(*TRIMBLE *comes down to* ISIDOR*—smokes.)*

TRIMBLE: *(Downstage* R.—ISIDOR L.*—front of settee.)* Mr. Solomon—I've been waiting to have a word with you. *Lights cigar—throws match into loving cup unconsciously*—ISIDOR *looks daggers at him for this. Takes cup, empties it, brushes it, sets it back.)* It's been on my mind a long time—but if you was to send me to the lock-up the next minute, I couldn't hold it any longer.

ISIDOR: Why should I send you to the lock-up? You're one of our best customers.

TRIMBLE: Well—I'm just throwing myself on your mercy—to do with as you will. *(Flicks ashes from cigar into cup—same bus. for* ISIDOR.*)*

ISIDOR: What are you talking about? What did you do?

TRIMBLE: You remember Clem's barn—your stock? Set on purpose by an enemy.

ISIDOR: Who was the enemy?

TRIMBLE: Me.

ISIDOR: And you call that being an enemy? Why, you kept me out of the clothing business and no man can do more for another than that.

TRIMBLE: Gee, I'm glad you feel that way about it. *(Throws ashes and cigar into cup again—same bus.)*

ISIDOR: But you know the Insurance Company lost four thousand dollars by the transaction?

TRIMBLE: Yes, but I don't know what to do about that. I can't tell them.

ISIDOR: You don't have to. Every Insurance Company has got what they call a "Conscience Account" and all you got to do is to send them the money anonymous.

TRIMBLE: I'll send them the money tomorrow.

ISIDOR: You don't have to. Send it to me; I sent it to them already.

TRIMBLE: I tell you it's a great relief to me. Makes me feel like a new man and I'm starting the New Year right. *(*ISIDOR *takes* TRIMBLE *by the arm and pushes him off into the ballroom, talking as he does so.)* But— *(*TRIMBLE *exits* R.*)*

ISIDOR: That's all right—I'm glad you don't chew tobacco. *(Music stops. Takes cup and wipes it tenderly with handkerchief.* WHITSON *enters* L.U.*—stands.)* Happy New Year.

WHITSON: *(*L. *of settee—*ISIDOR R. *downstage.)* Same to you, Mr. Solomon.

ISIDOR: Thank you, Mr. Whitson.

WHITSON: My name is Wolfson—Isaac Wolfson.

ISIDOR: Pardon me—but I didn't know what name you decided on.

WHITSON: I want to thank you for your invitation.

ISIDOR: Oh, that's all right. How's Gracie? Is she having a good time in there?

WHITSON: She asked me to thank you, but she doesn't go to parties any more.

ISIDOR: Now that spoils my whole party. I had it all figured out—tonight was the night I was going to bring her and Bije together.

WHITSON: Grace doesn't talk to Bije—they quarreled on account of me.

ISIDOR: Well, ain't you going to take off your coat and stay a while?

WHITSON: I'm not wanted here. Nobody in town has a kind word for me. The first I've received has been from you. I want to tell you that I'm sorry for everything I've done against you, but they won't give me a second chance.

ISIDOR: Now that makes me tired. Everybody in the world

gets a second chance. Bryan* had three chances. *(Walks to settee—motions* WHITSON *to come over.)* Now what do you want me to do?

WHITSON: Show that you are letting by-gones be by-gones and the rest of the town will follow your example. All you've got to do is to reinstate me in the bank. Oh, I'm not speaking for myself—it's for my daughter. On account of me her friends avoid her and I owe it to her to right myself in this town.

ISIDOR: Well—we'll see; maybe I can fix it.

WHITSON: But Gideon is very bitter against me. *(Sits* L. *on settee.)*

ISIDOR: Never mind—with Gideon anything I say is K. O. and besides, tonight I'm giving him a surprise that will— Well, anyhow—you'll get your second chance—you're reinstated.

WHITSON: You will do this for me?

ISIDOR: *(Sits on settee.)* That's settled. Now we can talk as man to man. Once again you are going to be placed in a position of trust. You are going to make a new start. I want you to start right—I want you to remember that from now on you and I represent the entire Jewish race in this town. It's a big responsibility.

WHITSON: My great fault was—that I was overambitious.

ISIDOR: That's the main fault with us—anything to get ahead of somebody else—we got to have the noisiest automobiles—we got to wear the biggest diamonds—others buy them by the karat—we must buy them by the quarts. Anything to show off just to make a big splash.

WHITSON: But I've never done those things—I've always been discreet—and until you came here no one ever suspected my origin.

ISIDOR: Yeh. But look how you stand now. What you did is the worst thing about us—pretending we are richer than we are—pretending we are smarter than we are—pretending we ain't what we are.

WHITSON: *(Rises.)* I did it because I thought I had to in order to succeed. I thought it was the easiest way to avoid the handicap of prejudice that exists against us.

*William Jennings Bryan was the unsuccessful Democratic candidate for President of the United States in 1896, 1900, and 1908.

ISIDOR: *(Rises.)* That's the old story—prejudice. If a fellow gets fired from a job that he didn't make good in—he calls it rishus. You know what rishus is?

WHITSON: Prejudice.

ISIDOR: Somebody steps on your foot by accident—prejudice. If you put a penny in the gum-slot and it don't work—rishus. No matter what a man is—no matter where he goes—he can make himself liked if he behaves himself and thinks of other people besides himself. If he is honest and kind and straightforward, he don't have to push himself in anywheres—they'll ask him in and be glad to have him. You can say all you want about prejudice. Yes—there is prejudice, but whether it's going to be against you or in your favor is entirely up to yourself.

WHITSON: I see it clearly enough now.

ISIDOR: And in the future—

WHITSON: Well, I'm not saying what I'm going to do, Mr. Solomon, but let me tell you one thing. I'm never going to forget what you've done for me tonight and that comes right from here.

ISIDOR: Now won't you go in and join the folks and enjoy yourself?

WHITSON: No, thank you. I'm going home to my little girl and tell her the good news.

ISIDOR: Well, maybe that will be better.

WHITSON: Good night—God bless you and bring you a Happy New Year. *(Shakes hands. Exit* WHITSON L.U.*)*

ISIDOR: *(Calling after him.)* Happy New Year. *(*BIJE *enters, disconsolate, up* L.U.*)* Oh, Bije, any telegrams for me since I phoned?

BIJE: No—Mr. Solomon.

ISIDOR: You don't feel so good—huh?

BIJE: No, I don't.

ISIDOR: I know what's the matter. Will you do something for me?

BIJE: Glad to.

ISIDOR: I want you to get your hat and coat and run over to Mr. Whitson's house. Tell him I sent you.

BIJE: Well, what do you want me to do there?

ISIDOR: Well, first you walk in the parlor and ask to see Grace.

BIJE: Grace doesn't speak to me any more.

ISIDOR: Don't you worry about her. You just do as I tell you.
BIJE: Yes?
ISIDOR: And when you see her—
BIJE: Yes?
ISIDOR: Turn down the light, and then sit down on the sofa with her.
BIJE: Yes—and then—?
ISIDOR: And then, if you don't know what to do—telephone me. *(Pushes* BIJE *off*—BIJE *exits* L.U. *Phone rings.* ISIDOR *goes to phone.)* Hello . . . Is it you? . . . Honest? . . . Where? . . . Hold the wire . . . I'm coming right over.

(Enter ESSIE, R., *from ballroom, crosses to* ISIDOR, L.*)*

ESSIE: Oh, isn't it a beautiful party, Papa?
ISIDOR: You're having a good time, eh?
ESSIE: Fine—only Mary and Ned are missing. *(Starts to cry.)*
ISIDOR: Now stop crying. You'll spoil your face for the party.
ESSIE: Where are you going?
ISIDOR: I won't be long—look out for the company; don't let them start to eat until I get back. *(Exit* ESSIE *into other room,* L.U. ISIDOR *exits* L.U.*)*

(Enter NED *arch* L.—*dress clothes, downhearted. Enter* CLEM *from ballroom.)*

CLEM: *(Coming down stage* R. *to* R. *lower*—NED L.*)* Well—if it ain't . . . *(Goes to* NED *and shakes hands with him.)*
NED: Clem— Gee! But I'm glad to see you.
CLEM: I can see, Ned, you haven't found Mary.
NED: Not a trace, Clem. Haven't you heard from her?
CLEM: No.
NED: Then why that urgent wire to come home at once?
CLEM: I don't know, Ned—that was Isidor's idea.

(Enter ISIDOR, *out of breath, main entrance upstage* L.U.*)*

ISIDOR: Ned! Ned!

NED: Oh, Mr. Solomon—

CLEM: *(Crosses to* R.*)* Your father's in there; hadn't you better go in there and see him? *(Means ballroom.* NED *walks toward ballroom.)*

ISIDOR: Wait a minute—I got a better idea. *(Runs upstage, exits, comes right back, leading* MARY L.U.*)*

NED: *(Turns, sees* MARY. ISIDOR *grabs* CLEM *and rushes off with him into ballroom off* R. NED *goes to* MARY.*)* Mary—dear—why did you leave us?

MARY: Because I was afraid—afraid of shadows.

NED: And now?

MARY: Do you remember that little book you gave me?

NED: What book?

MARY: That little book that comforts the sorrowing; has taught me how wrong it is to be afraid—just think—I thought I was running away from sorrow and I was running away from happiness. *(They embrace.)*

*(*TYLER, ISIDOR *and* CLEM *enter from ballroom.)*

TYLER: To bring my boy back to me on New Year's Eve—and to bring back to him the girl that he loves—why, it's the hand of the Lord.

CLEM: Maybe—but it was Isidor's idea.

CURTAIN DESCENDS

COUNSELLOR-AT-LAW

A PLAY IN THREE ACTS

by

Elmer Rice

With the sole exception of Eugene O'Neill, with whom he was often compared, no playwright experimented more boldly or fostered the maturation of the American theatre more enthusiastically than Elmer Rice (1892–1967). A native New Yorker, he dropped out of high school, then took evening courses at New York Law School, from which he graduated cum laude in 1912. He clerked in a Manhattan law office while writing his first plays, which he signed Elmer L. Reizenstein. Intrigued by the notion of unraveling a plot backwards, he introduced the filmic technique of flashback to the theatre in *On Trial* (1914). The innovation was a sensational success. It ensured *On Trial* an extended run and subsequent life in film and radio drama. It also enabled Rice to leave his fifteen-dollar-a-week job to study drama at Columbia and write plays. Henceforth, he signed them Elmer Rice because, he explained, that name was easier to say, spell, and remember.

Although he confessed that after *On Trial* he never again subordinated plot and characters to exploit a technical device, he continued to experiment. To dramatize the tragedy of Mr. Zero, a victim of the mechanized world in *The Adding Machine* (1923), Rice used expressionistic devices; interchangeable characters, distorted exteriors, and staccato dialogue reveal the inner life of Zero and his co-workers. Next Rice tried a drastically different stage style, domesticating the naturalism he had admired in Europe's playhouses. In *Street Scene* (1929), he recreated the life of a New York tenement neighborhood, representing its multicultural population with seventy-five characters.

The enormous scope and technical demands of *Street*

Scene bore unanticipated consequences. Having barely succeeded in attracting a producer, the play was abandoned in midcasting by its director. Rice stepped forward, undaunted by his lack of professional experience. *Street Scene* won the 1929 Pulitzer Prize, and launched its author on a parallel career. Henceforth, he directed his own plays.

Much of this directing was done with the Playwrights Company, a producing group which Rice founded in 1938 with S. N. Behrman, Maxwell Anderson, Robert E. Sherwood, and Sidney Howard. Later the principals included Kurt Weill, a refugee from Hitler's Europe, who in 1947 collaborated with Rice and Langston Hughes to turn *Street Scene* into a critically heralded opera. Playwrights, which lasted until 1960, gave Rice the opportunity he often seized to promote the work of other theatre people. Well informed about the history of the American stage and deeply concerned with its future, he forcefully expressed his views on the theatre in his collection of essays, *The Living Theatre* (1959), where he proposed reforms and practices, many of which have since been instituted.

Rice was an outspoken champion of liberal causes and human rights, a position he associated with his Jewishness. "The minority man I have always been is just a grown-up minority boy," he remarked. Along with Clifford Odets, S. N. Behrman, and Lillian Hellman, he figured among the few American dramatists who spoke out against the rise of fascism in Europe. His first warnings were voiced in *Judgment Day* (1934), a play based on the trial that followed the Reichstag Fire, an arson the Nazis imputed to the communists. That the play addressed an incredulous or indifferent public can be seen in Burns Mantle's *New York Daily News* review: "It matters very little that Mr. Rice can bring into court evidence to prove that he has not . . . overstated the case of Hitler. . . . The audience does not believe it humanly possible for so vicious and brazen a travesty of justice to have taken place in any civilized state. . . ."

Then Rice wrote a pair of works about a menace closer to home. *American Landscape* (1938) tells of the attempt of a Bund group to construct a training camp in Connecticut and casts a critical eye on American isolationism and commercialism. *Flight to the West* (1940) depicts the gamut of political attitudes toward Nazi Germany that prevailed in this country just prior to its entering World War II. One of *Flight*'s characters is a young Jew who abandons pacifism to oppose Hitlerism; another is a Jewish refugee from Nazi Europe. While *Flight* is not one of Rice's finer works, it stands as one of the few prewar American plays that dared confront Nazi anti-Semitism.

Rice's commitment to society as well as to the arts asserted itself in his brief tenure as New York regional director of the Federal Theatre Project. He had been instrumental in the organization of this program of the Works Progress Administration, which, between 1935 and 1939, kept thousands of theatre professionals employed, providing welcome diversion to dispirited Americans. Rice vigorously advocated one of the FTP's projects, the Living Newspaper, which used documentary materials to dramatize current issues. When State Department censors interfered with the first of these docudramas, an outraged Rice resigned in protest. Such vigorous expression of his principles became Rice's signature. Firmly opposed to the judging of art and artists by political standards, he withdrew *Counsellor-at-Law* from a TV production in 1951 because John Garfield, who was to play the title role, was blacklisted.

Thus, *Counsellor-at-Law* asks to be viewed as the work of a man of cosmopolitan interests and passionate convictions. Rice's own energy and multiple talents seem to animate the play's protagonist, George Simon. *Counsellor* opened in New York in November 1931, on the heels of his *The Left Bank,* which had premiered just a month earlier. Both were well received, but the accomplished performance of Paul Muni as George Simon made *Counsellor* an "overnight success," as one reviewer put it. Brooks Atkinson of *The New York Times* praised Rice's "accuracy of observation [and] genius for dialogue," judging George Simon's characterization "the most significant as a fragment of New York." The play ran for 396 performances on Broadway, and sold out through its national tour with

Otto Kruger as Simon. One unusual critical notice merits particular attention. It was written by a wonderfully literate inmate, reviewing a performance at Sing Sing in 1932. Two thousand prisoners applauded thunderously, he wrote. They understood George Simon perfectly: "He fights our battles. He confirms our hates."*

So identified was Paul Muni with the role of Simon that when *Counsellor* was revived in 1942, Louis Kronenberger's *PM* review trumpeted, "Mr. Muni Resumes His Law Practice." Muni had come to the English-language theatre and film from a brilliant career on the Yiddish stage as Muni Weisenfreund. However, when *Counsellor* was filmed in 1933, the lead was played by John Barrymore, not because of Hollywood's well-documented penchant for deSemitizing Jewish characters, but because Muni declined the role. He was already actively in quest of the reputation he would earn as "the Man of Many Faces"—not all of them Jewish. The power of the character Rice created is apparent in the *New York Times* film reviewer's admiring comparison, "The mere fact that Mr. Muni is a Jew and that Mr. Barrymore is a Gentile makes little if any difference to the portrayal." Today we might see things differently. George Simon is first of all an unaccommodated Jew who never resolves his struggle with ingrained Jewish values.

*This perceptive reception anticipates by some twenty-five years the San Quentin prisoners' appreciation in 1957 of *Waiting for Godot*, which had mystified more sophisticated audiences all over the world.

Counsellor-at-Law was presented at the Plymouth Theatre, New York, November 6, 1931, staged by Elmer Rice, settings by Raymond Sovey, with the following cast:

Bessie Green	*Constance McKay*
Henry Susskind	*Lester Salkow*
Sarah Becker	*Malka Kornstein*
A Tall Man	*Victor Wolfson*
A Stout Man	*Jack Collins*
A Postman	*Ned Glass*
Zedorah Chapman	*Gladys Feldman*
Goldie Rindskopf	*Angela Jacobs*
Charles McFadden	*J. Hammond Dailey*
John P. Tedesco	*Sam Bonnell*
A Bootblack	*William Vaughn*
Regina Gordon	*Anna Kostant*
Herbert Howard Weinberg	*Marvin Kline*
Arthur Sandler	*Conway Washburne*
Lillian Larue	*Dorothy Dodge*
An Errand Boy	*Buddy Proctor*
Roy Darwin	*Jack Leslie*
George Simon	*Paul Muni*
Cora Simon	*Louise Prussing*
A Woman	*Jane Hamilton*
Lena Simon	*Jennie Moscowitz*
Peter J. Malone	*T. H. Manning*
Johann Breitstein	*John M. Qualen*
David Simon	*Ned Glass*
Harry Becker	*Martin Wolfson*
Richard Dwight, Jr.	*David Vivian*
Dorothy Dwight	*June Cox*
Francis Clark Baird	*Elmer Brown*

SYNOPSIS OF SCENES

The action is laid in a suite of law offices in the midtown section in New York.

Act I

A morning in Spring.

Scene 1. The reception room.
Scene 2. George Simon's private office.
Scene 3. The reception room.
Scene 4. Simon's office.

Act II

The next morning.

Scene 1. Simon's office.
Scene 2. The reception room.
Scene 3. Simon's office.

Act III

A week later.

Scene 1. Simon's office.
Scene 2. The reception room.

ACT I

Scene 1

The reception room of a suite of law offices, high up in a skyscraper, in the midtown section of New York. Two large windows, in the rear wall, look westward upon a view which includes several tall buildings in the middle distance, and the Hudson River and New Jersey shore in the background. Between the windows is a comfortable sofa. In the right wall are two doors. The one downstage is the entrance door to the offices from the public corridor. Upon the opaque glass panel of the door is seen in reverse the following: "Law Offices of Simon and Tedesco." Immediately below this, are the names "George Simon" and "John P. Tedesco," then a line and below it, in smaller letters, "Herbert Howard Weinberg" and "Arthur Sandler." The upstage door bears the legend "Mr. Simon" and opens upon a private corridor, leading to the offices of Simon and his secretary. Against the wall, between the doors, is the telephone switchboard, so that the operator sits facing the entrance door. In the upstage right corner, is a small revolving bookstand filled with a miscellany of books and periodicals. In the left wall are two doors, both well upstage. The upper is labeled "Mr. Tedesco," the lower "Library," "Mr. Weinberg," "Mr. Sandler." Below the doors against the left wall is another sofa. In the middle of the room is a rectangular table, with several chairs around it. On the table are scattered law reviews and periodicals.

AT RISE: *At the rise of the curtain,* BESSIE GREEN, *the telephone operator, is at the switchboard. She is young and pretty. Several sets of wires are plugged in, and throughout, she reads a popular movie magazine, with half an eye on the switchboard.* Henry Susskind, *the office boy, an ungainly youth of fifteen, is seated at the center table, filling out some legal forms and whistling softly. Across the table from him, a* Tall Man *is inattentively reading an Italian newspaper. On the sofa, at the left, a stout, swarthy* Man *is seated, busily covering the back of an envelope with figures. On the sofa, between the windows,* Sarah Becker *is seated. She is small, poorly clad and prematurely old. She is obviously frightened and in awe of her surroundings. Every time a door opens, the two men and* Mrs. Becker *look towards it. There is a buzz and* Bessie, *scarcely looking up from her magazine, disconnects one of the completed calls. Then an incoming call buzzes.*

Bessie: *(Plugging in.)* Simon and Tedesco— Who is calling, please? Mr. McGee?— Mr. McKee? K like in Kitty? One moment, please— *(Plugging in another wire.)* Mr. McKee of Bartlett, Bartlett and McKee calling Mr. Simon— *(Completing the connection.)* All rightee, go ahead. *(She resumes her magazine. A middle-aged* Postman *enters from the public corridor.)*

The Postman: Mornin', dearie. Here's a bunch o' love letters for you. *(He slaps down a stack of letters on the switchboard.)*

Bessie: Don't get so funny.

The Postman: What's the matter? Get out o' bed the wrong side, this mornin'?

Bessie: What do you care if I did? An' never mind about that dearie stuff, either.

The Postman: The voice wit' the smile wins. *(He laughs and exits.)*

Bessie: Fresh egg! *(An incoming call buzzes)* Simon and Tedesco— Who is calling, please?— He's not in, yet. Do you want to talk to Miss Gordon? Well, just a minute, she's on another wire— All right, here she is now— Mr. Simon's brother calling— All rightee, go ahead. *(Turning.)* Mail, Henry.

Henry: Aw, gee, I gotta get out these notices of trial.

Bessie: All right. But you know what Mr. Tedesco said, yesterday, about lettin' the mail lay around.

Henry: Aw, for God's sake! *(Going over and getting the*

mail) Can't you even sort it? You're not doing anything.

BESSIE: Say, listen, how many people's work do you think I'm goin' to do around here? *(An incoming call.* HENRY *goes to the table and sorts the mail.)* Simon and Tedesco— Oh, it's you, is it?— Why, I thought you was dead and buried— No, I don't look so good in black— Yeah, sure I missed you: like Booth missed Lincoln— Well, what do you think I've been doing: sittin' home embroiderin' doilies? Gee, I'm glad I'm wearin' long sleeves, so's I can laugh in 'em— All right, now I'll tell one— *(A buzz.)* Wait a minute— Simon and Tedesco— Mr. Tedesco hasn't come in yet— Any minute— What is the name, please?— How do you spell that?— Napoli Importing Company?— All rightee, I'll tell him— Hello— Yeah, I had another call— No, I can't tonight— I can't, I'm tellin' you— I got another date— Ask me no questions and you'll hear no lies— How do you know I want to break it?— Say, you must have your hats made in a barrel factory—

HENRY: *(Taking some letters into* SIMON's *office.)* Is that Louis or Jack?

BESSIE: *(As* HENRY *exits.)* Mind your own business, you!— Oh, just a fresh kid in the office, here— No, an' I don't want to see it; I'm sick of gangsters— Wait a minute— All rightee— *(She dials a number.)* Hello— I don't know if I do or not— Yeah? Go on, tell me some more— You know all the answers, don't you?— Wait a minute— Simon and Tedesco— Mr. Weinberg?— One moment, please— Hello, National Security Company?— Mr. Welford, please— Mr. George Simon's secretary— Here's Mr. Welford, Miss Gordon— Hello— *(As the entrance door opens and* MRS. ZEDORAH CHAPMAN *enters.)* Say, you better call me back later. I'm busy now. *(Effusively.)* Well, good morning, Mrs. Chapman!

MRS. CHAPMAN: Good morning, Bessie. *(She is an elaborately dressed brunette, in the early thirties.)*

BESSIE: Well, you sure must be feeling good, this mornin'.

(The two Men *who are waiting listen with great interest.)*

Mrs. Chapman: *(Conscious of the sensation she is making.)* I feel just like a new woman, that's how I feel.

Bessie: Yes, I'll bet you do. After all you've been through. Excuse me— Simon and Tedesco— No, he hasn't come in yet, Mr. Bellini— All rightee, I'll tell him.

(Meanwhile, Goldie Rindskopf, *a middle-aged, unattractive stenographer, has entered from the library and crossed to* Mrs. Chapman.*)*

Goldie: *(Effusively.)* Well, good morning, Mrs. Chapman. Congratulations!

Mrs. Chapman: Well, thanks, Goldie. I'm sure glad it's over. You can't imagine what I went through while that jury was out.

Goldie: I never could have lived through it. Well, anyhow, all's well that ends well.

Mrs. Chapman: Of course, after Mr. Simon talked to the jury, I had a feeling that everything was going to be all right. Were you there?

Goldie: No.

Bessie: We never can get away durin' office hours. But I read all about it this mornin'. It must have been wonderful.

Mrs. Chapman: It was simply marvelous. You certainly missed something worth while. Why, do you know, I just sat there and cried like a baby. And I noticed that some of the jury were crying, too.

Bessie: Tt! Gee, I wish I could have heard it.

Goldie: I guess you're pretty glad you had Mr. Simon.

Mrs. Chapman: Well, of course, I *was* innocent. It was a clear case of self-defense, just like Mr. Simon told them. Still, that's not saying he wasn't marvelous.

Henry: *(Entering from* Simon's *office.)* Hello, Mrs. Chapman. Well, how does it feel to be walking around again?

Mrs. Chapman: It feels wonderful, Henry. It's just as though I suddenly woke up from a bad dream.

Henry: There's a bunch of mail here for you.

MRS. CHAPMAN: Oh thanks, Henry. You should have seen the stack that came this morning. Proposals of marriage and goodness knows what all. And the flowers! Why, my apartment looks like a regular conservatory.

BESSIE: It must be beautiful.

GOLDIE: You ought to take a nice little trip somewhere, now that it's all over.

MRS. CHAPMAN: Yes, I think that's just what I'll do, Goldie. I feel as if I was entitled to a rest, after what I've been through.

BESSIE: You sure are.

GOLDIE: Well, take good care of yourself, Mrs. Chapman.

MRS. CHAPMAN: Thanks, Goldie. *(GOLDIE exits to the corridor. HENRY enters the library with more letters.)* Is Mr. Simon in?

BESSIE: No, he isn't. But I'll tell Miss Gordon that you're here— Mrs. Chapman is here, Miss Gordon— All rightee— What number?— All rightee— She says she's not sure just when Mr. Simon will be in, but if you want to wait—

MRS. CHAPMAN: Well, I think I'll just sit down and read my letters.

BESSIE: Yes, sure; just sit down and make yourself comfortable.

(She dials a number. MRS. CHAPMAN crosses to the sofa at the left. The STOUT MAN rises, with a courtly flourish.)

MRS. CHAPMAN: *(Sweetly.)* Oh, don't get up, please. There's plenty of room.

(She seats herself and the STOUT MAN sits down beside her. She begins to read her letters.)

BESSIE: Hello, Gilbert and Gilbert? One moment, please— Here's Gilbert and Gilbert, Miss Gordon— All rightee, go ahead. *(CHARLES MCFADDEN, the firm's process server, comes in at the entrance door. He is a small, middle-aged man.)* Miss Gordon wants you, right away, Charlie. She's got some papers for you to serve.

MCFADDEN: Okay. Good mornin', Mrs. Chapman.

MRS. CHAPMAN: *(Looking up.)* Oh, good morning, Mr. McFadden.

McFadden: Well, you're up bright an' early, this mornin'. I thought you'd be sleepin' the clock around, today.

Mrs. Chapman: Well, so did I. But the telephone started at seven.

McFadden: *(Producing a newspaper.)* Have you seen the *Mirror*?

Mrs. Chapman: No, I haven't. It wasn't out, when I left home.

McFadden: *(Handing her the paper.)* There's a whole page o' pictures.

Mrs. Chapman: Oh, thank you.

McFadden: An' I got a whole pack o' letters for you, one of the keepers at the Tombs give me.

Mrs. Chapman: Goodness, more letters! I don't know how I'm ever going to read them all.

McFadden: Well, that's what happens when you're famous. But did you ever hear anythin' more heartbreakin' than that summin'-up speech of Mr. Simon's?

Mrs. Chapman: It was simply wonderful.

McFadden: You know, I just sat there an' bawled like a kid. An' I been through a dozen murder trials with him, too. I tell you, there's nobody can come within a mile of him.

(He exits to Simon's *office.* Henry *comes out of the library and enters* Tedesco's *office.)*

Bessie: Simon and Tedesco— Oh, hello, Gracie; I was jus' goin' to call you— I'm not feelin' so good, today— I don't know. My stomach don' feel so good. Must be somethin' I ate— Oh, I hate takin' that stuff— Well, maybe I will take a little tonight, before I go to bed— Listen, Fred just called me up— Sure, you do; the one we met on the Iron Steamboat— Yeah, that's the one— Well, so did I, but he says he's been out west— Wait a minute— Simon and Tedesco— One moment, please, I'll connect you with his secretary— Mr. Hawthorn of the Chase National Bank calling Mr. Simon— All rightee, go ahead—

*(*Henry *has come out of* Tedesco's *office and resumed his work at the table.* McFadden *comes out of* Simon's

office and goes toward the entrance door. MRS. CHAPMAN *drops a letter and the* STOUT MAN *picks it up.)*

MRS. CHAPMAN: *(Smiling sweetly.)* Oh, thanks ever so much.

BESSIE: Charlie, wait a minute.

MCFADDEN: I can't. I gotta go right down to Wall Street for Miss Gordon.

BESSIE: Well, listen, get me some lunch on the way back, will you?

MCFADDEN: All right. What do you want? Make it quick.

BESSIE: *(Taking a quarter out of her purse.)* I want a tongue on rye and a chocolate malted. Here. *(As he hurries out.)* And tell him I want a lot of Russian dressin'.

MCFADDEN: Okay. *(He exits.)*

BESSIE: Hello, Gracie?— I was just orderin' my lunch— No, I don't think I'll go out today, on account of my stomach— Well, listen, I started to tell you. Fred wants me to go out with him, tonight— *(As the door opens and* TEDESCO *enters.)* I'm busy, now, I'll call you back.

*(*TEDESCO *is a small, dark Italian of American birth. He is in the late thirties.)*

HENRY *and* BESSIE: Good morning, Mr. Tedesco.

TEDESCO: Good morning. *(Both* MEN *who are waiting rise. To the* STOUT MAN.*)* Hello, Moretti. I'm sorry to keep you waiting.

THE STOUT MAN: Oh, that's all right, counsellor.

TEDESCO: Go right in my office.

(The STOUT MAN *smiles and bows to* MRS. CHAPMAN, *then enters* TEDESCO's *office.)*

TEDESCO: Any messages for me?

BESSIE: *(Giving him several slips of paper.)* Yes, sir. Mr. Bellini called twice. He says it's important.

TEDESCO: All right. Has G.S. come in?

BESSIE: No sir, not yet.

THE TALL MAN: *(Timidly.) Buon giorno, signor.*

TEDESCO: I haven't heard from those people yet. Come in next week. *Lunedi.*

THE TALL MAN: All right, signor. Sure. *(He goes out slowly.)*

MRS. CHAPMAN: *(As* TEDESCO *crosses to his office.)* Good morning, Mr. Tedesco.

TEDESCO: Oh, good morning, Mrs. Chapman. Well, G.S. got you out of it, all right, didn't he?

MRS. CHAPMAN: Yes, he was wonderful. But, of course, it was a clear case of self-defense.

TEDESCO: Oh, yes, sure; we all knew that. But you always have to convince the jury, you know. Well, excuse me, I got a client waiting. Tell Goldie I want her, Bessie.

BESSIE: She just stepped outside, Mr. Tedesco.

TEDESCO: Well, as soon as she comes in. And let me know when G.S. comes in.

BESSIE: Yes sir. *(*TEDESCO *exits to his office.)* Simon and Tedesco— Who's calling, please?— One moment, please— Wilson and Devore calling Mr. Simon— All rightee, go ahead— Simon and Tedesco— Mr. Weinberg?— Go ahead.

MRS. CHAPMAN: What time do you think he'll be in?

BESSIE: I don't know. He's in the Supreme Court. *(*HENRY *exits to the library.)* Simon and Tedesco— Oh, good morning, Mrs. Simon— No ma'am, he hasn't come in yet— No ma'am, he's in court— Miss Gordon is talking on another wire. Do you want to wait?— Yes ma'am— Yes ma'am— Yes ma'am, I'll tell him— Yes ma'am, and he can reach you at the Colony Club— All right, Mrs. Simon— Good-bye. *(To* MRS. CHAPMAN.*)* That was Mrs. Simon.

MRS. CHAPMAN: Does she come around here a lot?

BESSIE: Well, not so much. They live up in Westchester. She's one of the four hundred, you know. Her father used to be the governor of some state—Connecticut, I guess it was.

MRS. CHAPMAN: Yes, I've seen her picture in the Sunday sections.

BESSIE: Didn't you ever meet her?

MRS. CHAPMAN: No. I guess she must be kind of ritzy, isn't she?

BESSIE: Well, you know the way all these society dames are, sort of proud and haughty. They kind of have a way of lookin' at you, as if they didn't see you.

MRS. CHAPMAN: Yes, they think they're so much better

than anybody else, just because they get their names in the paper. Well, I guess I've had my name in the paper as much as any of them.

BESSIE: She can be very nice, though, when she wants to. *(An Italian* BOOTBLACK *enters.)* He's not in yet. Come back later.

THE BOOTBLACK: Okay. *(He exits.)*

BESSIE: You ought to see the clothes she wears. Wait a minute. Yes sir— Yes sir— *(She dials a number.)* I've never seen her wear the same dress twice.

MRS. CHAPMAN: The way he talks about her, you'd think she was a queen or goodness knows what.

BESSIE: He worships the ground she walks on. Hello— Is this the Italian counsellate?— Mr. Bellini, please— Hello, Mr. Bellini?— Mr. Tedesco calling— Here's Mr. Bellini, Mr. Tedesco— All rightee, go ahead. He got her her divorce from her first husband and then they ran away and got married.

MRS. CHAPMAN: Yes, I know. The matron in the Tombs was telling me.

BESSIE: She's got two children, too. You know, from her first marriage. An' talk about spoiled kids—

(She stops abruptly as REGINA GORDON *enters from* SIMON'S *office.* REGINA *is in her late twenties; an attractive girl, but in her official hours rather severe in dress and manner.)*

REGINA: Where is Mr. Sandler?

BESSIE: He hasn't come back from the courthouse yet.

REGINA: Well, I want to see him as soon as he comes in.

BESSIE: All right, Miss Gordon, I'll tell him. Mrs. Simon called up while you were on the other wire. She wants Mr. Simon to call her, at the Colony Club.

REGINA: Very well.

MRS. CHAPMAN: How do, Miss Gordon? When do you expect Mr. Simon?

REGINA: In a little while. Did he know you were coming in, Mrs. Chapman?

MRS. CHAPMAN: Well, not exactly—

REGINA: He has a very busy day. Isn't there anything I can do?

MRS. CHAPMAN: No. I've got some things to talk over with Mr. Simon.

REGINA: All right, if you want to wait—

MRS. CHAPMAN: Yes, of course, I'll wait.

MRS. BECKER: *(Who has risen timidly.)* Excuse me, lady—

REGINA: Mr. Simon hasn't come in yet.

MRS. BECKER: Please, he's coming soon, now?

REGINA: Yes, I expect him soon.

MRS. BECKER: Please, lady: mine boy—they took him in the police station—

REGINA: Yes, I know. But I can't do anything about it until Mr. Simon gets here. You'll have to wait.

MRS. BECKER: Thank you, lady.

(She resumes her seat. HERBERT HOWARD WEINBERG *enters. He is a slender, young intellectual.)*

WEINBERG: Oh, Miss Gordon—

REGINA: *(Turning.)* Mr. Weinberg, Wilson and Devore called me up again about that stipulation in Rosenblatt against the Baltimore and Ohio. They were supposed to have it by ten o'clock.

WEINBERG: I told Arthur to be sure to get it over there. *(To Bessie.)* Where is Mr. Sandler?

BESSIE: He's down at the courthouse. Hello— What number?— Yes sir— *(She dials a number.)*

REGINA: Mr. Simon promised them that they would surely have it this morning.

WEINBERG: Well, I'll get it out, myself. G.S. wanted that memorandum of law in the Pickford case. That's why I asked Arthur to do it.

REGINA: Well, will you please see that they get it right away?

WEINBERG: Yes, I will.

BESSIE: Hello, Napoli Importing Company?— One moment, please. All right, Mr. Tedesco, go ahead.

WEINBERG: *(As* REGINA *is about to go.)* Oh, Miss Gordon. *(She stops.)* A friend has just offered me two tickets for the Boston Symphony Orchestra tonight. Would you care to go with me?

REGINA: No, thank you, very much, Mr. Weinberg. I really don't care to go.

WEINBERG: It's a very fine program: the Brahms First and the Beethoven Violin Concerto, with Heifetz as soloist. I thought perhaps you would have dinner with me somewhere first—

REGINA: No, thanks; I really can't tonight.

WEINBERG: I'm sure you'd enjoy it. If you decide later in the day—

REGINA: I've decided already. I really don't care to go. *(As* ARTHUR SANDLER, *a law clerk of twenty-two, enters.)* Arthur, why didn't you get out that stipulation in Rosenblatt against the Baltimore and Ohio?

WEINBERG: I told you that G.S. wanted Wilson and Devore to have it, this morning.

SANDLER: I had to answer the calendar in Part Three, didn't I? And then I had to go to the Surrogate's Court for Mr. Tedesco.

REGINA: When Mr. Simon promises something, he likes it to be there on time.

SANDLER: All right; I'll get it out right away. Arrow against the Radio Corporation was marked ready and passed. It may be reached Monday.

REGINA: It doesn't matter. Mr. Simon is going to settle it today.

BESSIE: Simon and Tedesco— Yes, who's calling?— Senator Wells? One moment, please— *(To* REGINA.*)* Senator Wells calling from Washington.

REGINA: All right. *(To* SANDLER.*)* Arthur, please get that stipulation right out.

SANDLER: All right.

*(*REGINA *exits.)*

BESSIE: One moment, please.

SANDLER: Hello, Mrs. Chapman.

MRS. CHAPMAN: Good morning, Mr. Sandler.

SANDLER: Well, I'll bet you're feeling pretty good this morning.

MRS. CHAPMAN: Yes, indeed, I am.

WEINBERG: *(To* BESSIE.*)* Please get me Wilson and Devore.

BESSIE: I'll give you a wire. *(*WEINBERG *starts to protest, then changes his mind and exits to the library.)* Simon and Tedesco— Mr. Simon's secretary is busy on another wire— All rightee—

SANDLER: Where's Goldie?

BESSIE: She'll be back in a minute. But Mr. Tedesco wants her.

SANDLER: God, I have to do everything myself, around here. *(He exits to the library.)*

BESSIE: Simon and Tedesco— Yes. Who is this: Jack?— Oh, not so good, Jack— I don' know; I just feel kind of punk— Is that so? Well, if you want to know, I haven't had a drink in a week: not enough to hurt me, anyhow— wait a minute— No, Mr. Tedesco, she hasn't come back yet— Yes, sir— Hello— No, she's still busy— Hello, Jack— Yeah, I had another call— No, I can't tonight, Jack— No, honest I can't— I got another date— With Gracie— Yeah, you know Gracie; Gracie Ferguson— No, I couldn't do that— Why she'd be sore at me, that's why— Yes, sure, I'd like to, but I can't tonight— All rightee; give me a ring tomorrow— Bye-bye— Hello— Here's Mr. Simon's secretary now.

(The STOUT MAN *comes out of* TEDESCO'S *office. As he passes* MRS. CHAPMAN, *he smiles and tips his hat. She smiles sweetly at him. He crosses to go to the entrance door, and as he opens it* LILLIAN LARUE, *a young, bleached blonde, flashily dressed, enters. He holds the door open, gallantly, for her, then exits.)*

LILLIAN: I'm Miss Lillian Larue. I got an appointment to see Mr. Simon.

BESSIE: He hasn't come in yet. Take a seat, won't you?

LILLIAN: Yeah. Sure.

BESSIE: I'll tell his secretary you're here?

LILLIAN: *(Seating herself beside* MRS. BECKER.*)* Yeah, will you? Miss Lillian Larue.

*(*HENRY *enters and seats himself at the table.)*

BESSIE: Miss Lillian Larue is here to see Mr. Simon. *(To* LILLIAN.*)* He's expected any minute, Miss Larue.

LILLIAN: Okay.

(She lights a cigarette, meanwhile staring curiously at MRS. CHAPMAN. *An* ERRAND BOY *enters and slaps some papers down before* BESSIE.*)*

THE BOY: Admission of service.

BESSIE: Don't you even know how to say please? (THE BOY *stares at her.*) Here, Henry.

(HENRY *takes the papers and goes into the library.*)

BESSIE: (*To* THE BOY.) Wait. And don't stand right in the doorway, either. Simon and Tedesco— One moment, please— *New York Times* calling Mr. Simon— All rightee, go ahead.

MRS. CHAPMAN: (*Eagerly.*) Is that the *New York Times*?

BESSIE: Yes, ma'am.

MRS. CHAPMAN: I wonder if they want to know anything—

BESSIE: I don't think so— Wait a minute, I'll find out. (*She listens in.*)

MRS. CHAPMAN: Is It?

BESSIE: No, it's just about some bankruptcy case.

MRS. CHAPMAN: (*Disappointed.*) Oh.

HENRY: (*Entering from the library; to the waiting* BOY.) He'll be out in a minute.

THE BOY: Okay. (*He starts to whistle.*)

BESSIE: No whistlin' allowed here. (THE BOY *stops.*)

LILLIAN: (*Rising and going towards* MRS. CHAPMAN.) Pardon me. Aren't you Mrs. Zedorah Chapman?

MRS. CHAPMAN: Why yes, I am.

LILLIAN: (*Seating herself at the table.*) Well, I thought it was you, the minute I came in. You look a lot like your picture.

MRS. CHAPMAN: Well, some of them have been pretty good. The one in the *News* this morning was a dandy one.

LILLIAN: Yeah, that's just the one I saw. Well, it certainly is a coincidence to walk in and see you sittin' right here. I wanted to come down to the trial but we've been havin' rehearsals nearly every day.

MRS. CHAPMAN: Oh, are you on the stage?

LILLIAN: Yeah, I'm with the Scandals. I been with Mr. White three years now. He's gonna give me a bit in a black-out in his new show.

MRS. CHAPMAN: I've been thinking maybe I'd like to go on the stage.

LILLIAN: Well, say, it'll be a cinch for you to get a break, with your name.

BESSIE: You oughta ask Mr. Simon to give you some introductions. He knows lots of theatrical people.

MRS. CHAPMAN: Yes, I think maybe I will.

LILLIAN: Say, I wonder if you'd do me a favor? I wonder if you'd write out your autograph for me?

MRS. CHAPMAN: Why, certainly, I'd be glad to. *(They both fumble in their handbags.)*

LILLIAN: I don't think I've got a piece of paper with me. Gee, I wish I'd of known you was gonna be here. I'd of brought my little book.

BESSIE: Here's some paper if you want it.

MRS. CHAPMAN: Never mind, I'll put it on the back of one of my cards. Oh, but I haven't got a pen.

HENRY: Here's a pen, Mrs. Chapman.

MRS. CHAPMAN: Oh, thank you.

(She takes the pen from HENRY *and seats herself at the table.* SANDLER *enters from the library and crosses to the waiting* BOY.*)*

SANDLER: I can't give you admission on this. It was due yesterday. You'll have to leave a copy and make an affidavit of service.

THE BOY: *(Stolidly.)* He told me to get admission of service.

SANDLER: I don't care what he told you. It's a day late. Go ahead; I'll call up your office.

*(*THE BOY *hesitates, then goes, with a final look at* MRS. CHAPMAN.*)*

MRS. CHAPMAN: *(With a little laugh.)* I never know just what to write.

LILLIAN: Oh, just write anything. It's just the idea of the thing.

SANDLER: *(To* BESSIE.*)* Say, that's some run you've got in your stocking, kid.

BESSIE: Where? Oh, God, wouldn't that give you a pain! An' I just put them on clean this mornin'.

SANDLER: I'll buy you a new pair, if you let me put them on for you.

BESSIE: Say, listen, one more crack like that out of you and you'll get a good smack in the face.

SANDLER: Get hot. Get hot.

BESSIE: Well, you just remember, that's all. Hello— No, she hasn't, Mr. Tedesco— Yes, sir. *(As the door opens and* GOLDIE *enters.)* Goldie, go right in to Mr. Tedesco. He's been askin' for you, two or three times.

*(*GOLDIE *nods majestically and, without quickening her pace, crosses to* TEDESCO'S *office.)*

SANDLER: *(Crossing to the library.)* Did you have a nice weekend?

GOLDIE: Shut your mouth, you!

(She exits to TEDESCO'S *office.* SANDLER *laughs and exits to the library.)*

MRS. CHAPMAN: Is this all right? To my friend, Miss Larue, from yours sincerely, Mrs. Zedorah Chapman.

LILLIAN: Yeah, that's lovely. Thanks ever so much. It's just sort of a hobby of mine. I got a whole book full, home—lots of famous people, too. I got Legs Diamond and Babe Ruth and Belle Livingston—and, oh, I forget who all. And, of course, I got a lot of people in the profession, too. Eddie Cantor gave me one of his pictures. Only after what he wrote on it, I can't show it to nobody.

(The door opens and ROY DARWIN *enters: a handsome, well-dressed man of forty.)*

BESSIE: Yes sir?

DARWIN: Will you please tell Mr. Simon that Mr. Roy Darwin would like to see him?

BESSIE: Mr. Simon hasn't come in yet. Have you an appointment?

DARWIN: Why no, I haven't. Just when do you expect him?

BESSIE: Wait a minute— Simon and Tedesco— One moment, please— District attorney's office calling Mr. Simon. And Mr. Roy Darwin is here to see Mr. Simon— All rightee— All rightee, district attorney's office, go ahead. *(To* DARWIN.*)* Mr. Simon ought to be here, any moment, if you care to wait.

DARWIN: Very well; I'll wait.

(He crosses to the sofa, and sits beside MRS. BECKER, *glancing curiously at* MRS. CHAPMAN. *A Western Union* MESSENGER *enters.)*

THE MESSENGER: Simon?

BESSIE: Yes. *(She signs the receipt.)* Here, Henry. *(*HENRY *takes the telegram into* SIMON'S *office.* THE MESSENGER *exits.)*

MRS. CHAPMAN: Mr. Simon is certainly a busy man.

LILLIAN: Well, I guess he's just about the biggest lawyer in New York, isn't he?

MRS. CHAPMAN: *(With a laugh.)* Well, naturally, I think so.

*(*BESSIE *dials a number.)*

LILLIAN: Say, if you wouldn't, who would?

BESSIE: Hello: Gracie?— Yeah— Say, listen, about tonight— I told you about Fred callin' up, didn't I?— Well, listen, if you happen to see Jack and he asks you about tonight, I was out with you, see?— Yeah, I know, but in case you do— Well, listen, tell him—

HENRY: *(Entering.)* G.S. is in.

BESSIE: I'm busy now, Gracie. I'll call you back.

REGINA: *(Entering.)* Get Senator Wells at the Hotel Shoreham, in Washington, and then get these other numbers. *(She hands* BESSIE *several slips of paper.* BESSIE *dials.)* Mr. Simon will see you in just a minute, Miss Larue.

LILLIAN: All rightee.

BESSIE: Hello, long distance? I want Washington, D. C.— That's right— Hotel Shoreham— No, Shoreham—

REGINA: I'll tell Mr. Simon you're here, Mr. Darwin. But it may be a half-hour before he can see you.

DARWIN: That's quite all right. I don't mind waiting.

BESSIE: *(As* REGINA *exits.)* Shoreham— S like in Sammy, H like in Howard, O like in Oscar, R like in Robert, E like in Eddie, H like in Henry, A like in Albert, M like in Max. That's right.

(The scene blacks out.)

CURTAIN

Scene 2

The inner office. A large room, simply furnished in modernistic style. Two windows in the rear wall face south, affording a panoramic view of lower Manhattan. In the right wall are two doors, the one downstage leading to the corridor which communicates with the outer office: the other leading to REGINA*'s office.* SIMON*'s large flat-top desk faces the entrance door. Above the desk is a comfortable chair. In the middle of the room is a large sofa. Between the windows is a small desk and a chair.* SIMON*'s desk is equipped with a telephone, an interoffice phone and a handsome desk set. There is also a cigarette box, containing several kinds of cigarettes, a cigar box of fine wood, and a photograph of Cora Simon in a leather frame. On the smaller desk are a telephone equipped with a Hushaphone, writing materials and so on.*

As the lights go up on the scene, GEORGE SIMON *is seated at his desk, making a connection on the interoffice phone. He is forty, clean-shaven, rather good-looking and well-dressed.*

SIMON: Hello, John, do you want me?— Yes— Yes— Yes, sure I'll see him— All right, let me know when he gets here— All right— Oh say, didn't I tell you I'd get an acquittal in the Chapman case?— Well, I never had any doubt about it— Not after that bunch of buttonhole makers on the jury got a good look at her— Well, maybe I can fix it up for you, John— No, those days are over for me— All right, John. *(He disconnects.* REGINA *has entered, during the preceding conversation, and has stood waiting, unable to conceal her embarrassment.)* Did you get Senator Wells?

REGINA: She's getting him, now. Mr. Darwin is outside.

SIMON: Roy Darwin?

REGINA: Yes sir.

SIMON: What does he want?

REGINA: Shall I ask him?

SIMON: No. But tell him he'll have to wait.

REGINA: I did tell him.

SIMON: And as soon as I'm through with Senator Wells, I want to talk to Mrs. Simon.

REGINA: Yes sir.

SIMON: *(Looking through his mail.)* Take a letter to Judge Wiley. Dear Clarence. I am in receipt of yours of the ninth, inviting me to be a speaker at the testimonial dinner to be given for Luther Ridgeway, in honor of his appointment as Minister to Austria. Nothing would give me greater pleasure than to do honor to Luther, whom I love and esteem. The fact is, however, that I am leaving next week for a little trip abroad with Cora. We will be married five years on the eighteenth and I have decided to break away, for once in my life, and make a real celebration of it. Please convey— *(The telephone rings.)* See if that's Wells.

*(*REGINA *goes to her desk and speaks into the Hushaphone.)*

REGINA: Yes sir.

SIMON: Take this down. *(He lifts the receiver of the telephone on his desk.* REGINA *listens in on the other telephone and makes stenographic notes.)* Hello, Senator, how are you?— I'm fine, thanks— Oh, thanks very much— Well, that's all there is in these murder cases: a lot of publicity and damn little money— Yes— Yes, I did— I was instructed to do so by my clients— I understand that, Senator, but as I explained to you, a decrease of two cents a pound is going to put my clients out of business— Now, now, wait a minute, Senator. Don't get excited— Well, what of it? There's nothing illegal about lobbying. If there were, they'd have to lock up half the population of Washington— We're living under a democratic form of government, Senator, and even a corporation has a right to be heard— No, I don't want to block the whole bill. I'm simply acting in what I believe to be the best interests of my client, just as you're acting in what you believe to be the best interests of the people of Montana— Sure, I'm always willing to listen to reason— Well, why not hop on the midnight sleeper and have lunch with me tomorrow?— All right, twelve-thirty tomorrow, at the Lawyers' Club— Fine. And give my regards to that charming daughter of yours— Good-bye. *(To* REGINA.*)* Make a transcript of that, and send it around to Colonel Adolph Wertheimer, Chairman of the Board of the International Metal Refineries. Oh, you'd better leave out the part about the murder cases. And take this letter to go with it. Dear Colonel Wertheimer. I enclose stenographic transcript of a long-distance conversation with Senator Wells. After you have read and digested it, please communicate with me. Personally, I do not think we have anything to worry about. That's all. You'd better let me see that transcript before it goes out.

REGINA: Yes sir.

SIMON: Is she getting Mrs. Simon for me?

REGINA: I'll remind her. *(She speaks into the Hushaphone.)* She's calling her, now.

SIMON: All right. I'll see that blonde bedroom artist now. What's her name?

REGINA: Lillian Larue.

SIMON: I'll bet she wasn't born Lillian Larue. Well, let her come in. And get me Mr. Vandenbogen of Woodbridge, McCormick, Vandenbogen and Delancey. *(*REGINA *talks into the Hushaphone.* SIMON *takes a box of chocolates from the top drawer and helps himself to them, while he continues to look through his mail. Reading a letter.)* Here, I don't want this. Take a letter to that Mrs. Moran, you know the one I mean.

REGINA: Yes sir.

SIMON: Dear Mrs. Moran. I am returning herewith your money order for fifty dollars, as I was actuated— No, strike that out: she won't understand it. As I handled your daughter's case only because of our old friendship and because of my interest in you and your family. I am sorry that it was impossible— *(As* LILLIAN *enters.)*

Good morning, Miss Larue. Just take a seat, won't you?

LILLIAN: Yeah, thanks.

SIMON: I'll be right with you, as soon as I've finished this letter.

LILLIAN: Oh, that's all right; go ahead.

REGINA: I am sorry that it was impossible—

SIMON: Impossible to obtain a larger settlement, but inasmuch as there was no liability on the part of the defendant— No, strike that out. But owing to the fact that the trucking company was not to blame, I could not do any better. I hope that Helen will soon be able to walk. Give her my love. All right, that's all. *(*REGINA *exits upstage.)* There's a pathetic case. This young girl, Helen Moran, and a beautiful girl, too. She was in a hurry to get home and crossed against the traffic lights and a truck ran her down.

LILLIAN: God, it's awful! Was she hurt bad?

SIMON: She'll be lame all her life. I managed to get her a few hundred dollars from the trucking company, but that doesn't give her back the use of her legs. Her mother runs a grocery store on Second Avenue. I've known them all my life.

LILLIAN: I guess you must hear plenty of people's troubles. I should think it would make you feel kinda goofy.

SIMON: Well, being a lawyer is like being a doctor. You see a lot and you hear a lot, but you can't take it too much to heart. Will you have a chocolate cream? They're very good.

LILLIAN: N-n. I'm on a diet. But if you've got a cigarette—

SIMON: Oh, excuse me. Here, help yourself. Turkish, Virginia, whatever you want. I don't know one from the other, myself.

LILLIAN: I'll try one of these with the gold tip.

SIMON: I'm getting that lawyer on the phone, now.

REGINA: *(Entering.)* Mrs. Simon is on the phone.

SIMON: Oh yes. *(To* LILLIAN.*)* Excuse me. *(*REGINA *exits.)* Hello, darling— Yes, I just got in. How are you?— That's good. Sorry I couldn't get home last night, but the jury didn't come in until after midnight, and by the time I got through with the reporters and all, it was nearly two— What is it, darling?— Well, why don't you have lunch with me?— All right, you can tell me, then— Can you pick me up here?— All right, darling, whenever you want— Good-bye, sweetheart. *(To* LILLIAN.*)* What a wonderful woman that is! *(Taking up the photograph.)* There she is. My wife.

LILLIAN: Yeah, you showed it to me last time. She sure looks like a winner. *(She produces lipstick and powder puff.)*

SIMON: It's not only her looks. That's the least important part of it. In every respect, she's a wonderful woman.

REGINA: *(Entering.)* Mr. Vandenbogen on the phone.

SIMON: Here's Schuyler's lawyer, now. *(He takes up the receiver as* REGINA *exits.)* Good morning, Mr. Vandenbogen, how are you today?— That's fine. Well, have you got any word for me, about the little lady in the breach of promise case?— Is that so— Well, I don't think that ten thousand would be acceptable to my client—

LILLIAN: Well, I should say not!

SIMON: *(Motioning her to be silent.)* Well, frankly, Mr. Vandenbogen, I don't think I could conscientiously advise her to take it— I don't agree with you— Well, I've had a good deal of experience with juries, Mr. Vandenbogen, and I know that they are inclined to be extremely sympathetic to a young girl who has entered into an intimate relationship with a man, upon his explicit promise of marriage, especially when the young man is a millionaire and the young lady is obliged to earn her own living— *(*LILLIAN, *who is busily powdering her face, nods emphatically.)* Not at all. As a matter of fact, she's sitting right here in my office and I don't mind telling you that she's taking this thing pretty much to heart— Well, now, don't you think that's a little strong?— But Schuyler met her at a nightclub, not in a convent— Well, this is my position, Mr. Vandenbogen. As a courtesy to you and to the Schuyler family, I've held off bringing suit, because I know it would be very embarrassing to them if those letters— Two days? Yes, I'll wait two days— All right— All right— Thank *you*— Good-bye. Mr. Vandenbogen, remember me to Mr. Woodbridge.

LILLIAN: Ten thousand? Is that what he expects me to take?

SIMON: He came up to fifteen. But I think they'll go twenty-five. It may take a few days, though. *(He rises.)* Call me up in about three days.

LILLIAN: *(Rising.)* The dirty little tightwad. Tryin' to jew me down a few thousand dollars after all the pearls and Rolls-Royces he was goin' to buy me.

SIMON: They seem to think that you had been a little indiscreet before you met Schuyler.

LILLIAN: Well, for God's sake, what do they expect for fifteen thousand dollars: a virgin?

SIMON: I think they'll pay twenty-five. Call me up in three or four days.

LILLIAN: I won't take a cent less. Why, there's words in some of those letters that I wouldn't use in front of my colored maid. Is this the way out?

REGINA: *(Who has entered.)* Yes.

LILLIAN: All right, I'll give you a ring.

SIMON: That's right. Good-bye.

LILLIAN: Good-bye. *(She exits.)*

SIMON: Now that's my idea of a nice, sweet, little girl.

REGINA: How can a woman make herself so cheap?

SIMON: Well, Rexie, when you come right down to it, she's not as bad as that young loafer that buys her diamonds and takes her to Florida on the millions his grandfather made by looting the Pennsylvania Traction Company. Let the good-for-nothing pay. Is that Chapman woman still waiting?

REGINA: Yes. And Mrs. Becker, too.

SIMON: Oh yes. Well, let's get rid of Chapman first.

(REGINA's phone rings. She answers it.)

REGINA: Do you want to talk to Mr. Crayfield?

SIMON: Yes. Hello, Mr. Crayfield— Yes, I read them very carefully— Well, I think you have a very good case— Yes, I'm quite sure that we can break the will— Yes. I'd like to talk to you about it— Well, how soon can you get over?— All right— All right— Good-bye, Have Mrs. Chapman come in. No, wait a minute: first get me Mrs. Richter.

*(*REGINA *calls the number on her phone.)*

REGINA: You didn't finish the letter to Judge Wiley.
SIMON: Wiley? Oh yes, about the dinner to Ridgeway. What did I say?
REGINA: You said— Oh well, it's just the end. I'll finish it up.
SIMON: All right. And on the day of the dinner, send Ridgeway something from me, with a nice card in it. Something that looks pretty good.
REGINA: How much do you want to spend?
SIMON: Oh, a hundred or a hundred and fifty.

*(*REGINA*'s phone rings.)*

REGINA: Mrs. Richter.
SIMON: Hello, Mrs. Richter— I'm fine, thanks. How's yourself?— How's the baby's cough?— Well, that's fine; I'm glad to hear it— Well, I've got some good news for you— Yes, I had a nice long talk with your husband, last night— Well, I told him that since you had agreed to disagree, I felt it was up to him to see that you and the baby were well provided for— How much do you think?— No, I did better than that— A thousand a week— Well, I thought you'd be pleased— Frankly, it's much more than any court would have given you— Oh, that's all right, don't mention it— Can you come in tomorrow at four to sign the papers?— All right— Not at all. I'm glad I was able to get it for you— Good-bye. *(To* REGINA.*)* Tomorrow at four for the closing of the separation agreement in Richter against Richter. Notify Klein and Davis to have their client here. Now I'll see that Chapman woman. And then tell Weinberg I want to see him. *(*REGINA *gives these instructions over the Hushaphone.)* How much of a retainer did we get from Mrs. Richter?
REGINA: Twenty-five hundred dollars.
SIMON: As soon as the separation agreement is signed, send her a bill for five thousand. I want her to get it, while she's still grateful. *(As* MRS. CHAPMAN *enters.)* Hello, Zedorah. Sit down.
MRS. CHAPMAN: Hello, George darling. Well, my good-

ness, I thought you were never going to see me. *(*Regina *throws her a quick look and exits.)*

Simon: I'm pretty busy, today. What's on your mind: anything special?

Mrs. Chapman: No, nothing special. I just dropped in to tell you how wonderful it feels to be a free woman again, and to have a little chat. We really haven't had a chance to talk about anything but that horrible case.

Simon: I've got quite a lot of clients waiting for me—

Mrs. Chapman: Oh well, let them wait. I want to have a chance to thank you and to tell you how much it all means to me. *(Putting her hand on his arm.)* George darling, how can I ever thank you enough?

Simon: *(Withdrawing his arm.)* You thanked me last night. It's my business to help people when they get into trouble. If you'll take my advice, you'll go away somewhere for a while and forget about it. And, hereafter, don't keep any firearms around the house. It might not turn out so well next time.

Mrs. Chapman: Oh, George, you were so wonderful when you talked to the jury. All those beautiful things you said about me. It made me feel that you were the first man that ever really understood me.

Simon: Well, anyhow, I understand juries. *(Rising and extending his hand.)* It was very nice of you to come in. Any time I can—

Mrs. Chapman: *(Rising.)* Why are you so cold to me, George? Don't you know how fond of you I am? Oh, George dear, I've learned to grow so fond of you. *(She throws her arms around his neck and kisses him.)*

Simon: *(Disengaging himself.)* For God's sake! What do you call this, anyhow? Listen, Mrs. Chapman, I was engaged to defend you on the charge of murdering your husband. There's nothing in the retainer that requires me to sleep with you.

Mrs. Chapman: Shut up your mouth, you!

Simon: That's the way out!

Mrs. Chapman: Go to hell. *(She exits as* Regina *enters with a telegram.)*

Simon: Why do you leave me alone with that woman?

Regina: I thought it might be something personal.

Simon: Personal! *(He rubs his lips with his hand.)* Pfui! So help me God, that's the last one of those goddam female murder cases I'll ever handle. Excuse me, Rexie. What have you got there?

REGINA: It's from Washington. All it says is "Yes," and it's just signed "X. Y. Z."

SIMON: Aha! Let's see it. *(He looks at the telegram.)* Get me Fishman and Company, right away. I want to talk to Joe Fishman, personally.

*(*REGINA *gives these instructions on the Hushaphone and exits as* WEINBERG *enters.* SIMON *tears up telegram.)*

Listen, Weinberg, I want you to get out that Richter separation agreement right away. He's to pay her a thousand a week for the support and maintenance of herself and child. The other clauses you know about, don't you?

WEINBERG: Yes. Shall I let the memorandum of law in the Pickford case wait?

SIMON: Yes. They're coming in at four tomorrow to sign the Richter agreement. Then, I want— *(The interoffice phone buzzes.)* Yes, John— Is he there now?— All right, I'll be in right away— Oh, John— Say, Weinberg, will you wait outside for just a minute?

WEINBERG: Certainly. *(He exits.)*

SIMON: Say, John, listen. I just got a hot tip from Washington that the Supreme Court is reversing the lower court and dismissing the complaint in the Gulf Coast Utilities case— No, neither did I— Yes, I'm going to take a little flier in the stock. Do you want to go fifty-fifty with me— Five thousand shares?— All right, I'll be in as soon as I've talked to Joe Fishman— All right.

REGINA: *(Entering.)* Mr. Fishman. *(She exits.)*

SIMON: Hello, Joe— Fine, how are you?— Say, Joe, what's the last Gulf Coast Utilities?— Well, I want you to buy me ten thousand shares at the market— I know it's a lousy stock, but I've got a hunch it's due for a little whirl— No, I haven't any information; just a hunch, that's all— Well, that's all right, if I lose, I'll have only myself to blame— All right, and say, don't buy it all in one block— All right, Joe— Good-bye. Come in, Weinberg. *(*WEINBERG *enters.)* Listen, I've been retained by the Crayfield family to oppose the probate of Edward Crayfield's will. They have unquestionable proof that the child is illegitimate. Look these over and then run down a line of cases for me.

WEINBERG: Very well. *(*REGINA *enters.)*

SIMON: I'm going into Mr. Tedesco's office for a minute.

REGINA: That Mrs. Becker has been waiting since nine o'clock.

SIMON: All right, have her come in. I'll see her in a few minutes. *(He exits.)*

WEINBERG: *(As* REGINA *goes towards the telephone.)* Miss Gordon.

REGINA: Well?

WEINBERG: Won't you change your mind about going to the concert tonight?

REGINA: I've told you I don't care to go, Mr. Weinberg. Did that stipulation go over to Wilson and Devore?

WEINBERG: Yes; the boy is on his way now. Why is my society so distasteful to you?

REGINA: It's not a question of that, Mr. Weinberg. I just don't care to go, that's all. *(At* SIMON's *phone.)* Have Mrs. Becker come in, please.

WEINBERG: Will you go to the theatre with me Saturday night?

REGINA: No, thanks. I'm going to my sister's for dinner.

WEINBERG: You always have some excuse, haven't you?

REGINA: Then why do you keep on asking me?

WEINBERG: I suppose if the great G.S. asked you, you wouldn't refuse.

REGINA: Please keep your remarks to yourself. I don't care to listen to them and what's more, I don't have to.

WEINBERG: What have I ever done to you, to make you treat me like this?

REGINA: Then don't make personal remarks.

WEINBERG: I'm not accustomed to being treated like an office boy; to be ordered out of the room, while my employer has a telephone conversation.

REGINA: You're not the first Harvard Law School man we've had in the office, Mr. Weinberg. You ought to be grateful for the opportunity to get your training from a brilliant man like Mr. Simon.

WEINBERG: It's not difficult to be brilliant, when you make capital of other people's brains.

REGINA: Then, if I were you, I'd take my wonderful brains where they're appreciated more.

WEINBERG: Thank you. I'm glad to know what your sentiments towards me are.

REGINA: I think you're a very ungrateful boy, that's what I think. If I were in your place— Yes, Mrs. Becker, come right in.

MRS. BECKER: I wait here, yes?

REGINA: No, it's all right; come right in. Sit down here. Mr. Simon will be right back. *(*MRS. BECKER *seats herself, timidly.)* I wish you'd let me know, Mr. Weinberg, when that stipulation comes back from Wilson and Devore. *(*SIMON *enters before* WEINBERG *can reply.)*

SIMON: Make a note, Rexie, that I'm having lunch on Tuesday at one-thirty at the Sherry-Netherlands with Mr. Tedesco and Mr. Ferraro.

REGINA: Yes sir.

SIMON: Want to see me, Weinberg?

WEINBERG: No. *(He exits.)*

SIMON: *(Calling after him.)* Get busy on that separation agreement, will you? *(Shaking hands with* MRS. BECKER, *who has risen.)* Well, hello, Mrs. Becker. I'm glad to see you.

MRS. BECKER: Good morning, counsellor. *(*REGINA *exits to her office.)*

SIMON: Sit down. Sit down. How's your husband?

MRS. BECKER: You don't hoid? He's already dead six years.

SIMON: No! Why, he was always a big, healthy fellow.

MRS. BECKER: Yes, big. But not healthy. He's got in de stomach a cancer.

SIMON: You don't say! Tt! That's terrible. Why I remember him, since I was that high. I used to watch his pushcart when he had to go upstairs for a minute.

MRS. BECKER: *(Weeping.)* Yes. Yes.

SIMON: You've had your share of trouble, hm? Who looks after you now?

MRS BECKER: I got by the sev'ty-seven street station a newspaper stand.

SIMON: And do you get along all right?

MRS. BECKER: W'en my boy Harry is woikin' is everything oll right.

SIMON: Is Harry old enough to work? Why, last time I saw him, he was in a baby carriage.

MRS. BECKER: He's already twenty.

SIMON: No! My God, I can't realize it. Well, how is he? Is he a good boy?

MRS. BECKER: He's a good boy. Only oll the time he's getting in trouble.

SIMON: What do you mean trouble? What kind of trouble? With girls?

MRS. BECKER: No, no, counsellor! Mine Harry is a good boy. Only oll the time he's making speeches there should be yet in America a revolution.

SIMON: What do you mean? Harry goes around making Communist speeches?

MRS. BECKER: Oll the time. And from this he is losing oll the time his job. And now they put him in the police station.

SIMON: He's been arrested?

MRS. BECKER: Yes, counsellor. The whole night I don't sleep. So I don't know what I'm going to do. So I'm coming here because you know from the old times mine husband. Oi, counsellor, what I'm going to do, if they're putting my boy in preeson?

SIMON: Don't worry, we won't let them put him in prison. When did this happen: yesterday?

MRS. BECKER: Yes. He's making in Union Square a speech and a policeman comes and hits him with such a club on the head. So they're taking him to the station house. On the whole head, he's got bandages. Counsellor, you wouldn't let them send mine boy to preeson?

SIMON: No, I won't. Don't worry about it. Just leave it to me. You go home and get some sleep and leave everything to me. *(He presses the call button on his desk.)*

MRS. BECKER: Oi, counsellor, every night I'm going to say for you a prayer. *(She covers his hand with kisses.)*

SIMON: *(Patting her head.)* That's all right, Mama Becker. We're old friends. *(Thrusting a bill into her hand.)* Here, take this. *(*REGINA *enters.)*

MRS. BECKER: No, no. I wouldn't take it.

SIMON: Yes, you take it. Buy yourself some groceries.

MRS. BECKER: Tenks, counsellor, tenks.

REGINA: *(Kindly; taking her by the arm.)* This way, Mrs. Becker.

MRS. BECKER: Tenk you, lady. *(She stops, takes a pocketbook out of a pocket in her petticoat and offers* REGINA *a ten-cent piece.)*

REGINA: No, thanks, I really don't—

MRS. BECKER: Please, please, you take—

REGINA: Well, thank you very much. *(She leads* MRS. BECKER *into the corridor.* SIMON *blows his nose.* REGINA *reenters, wiping her eyes.)* Poor old thing.

SIMON: I used to live in the same house with them. That's a fine joke, that is. The police beat up a kid, who's making a speech, and then they arrest him for disorderly conduct.

REGINA: It's terrible the way some of those rough-neck cops treat people.

SIMON: Well, that's the way it is with a lot of those fellows. You take a fellow that's come up from the gutter and you put a club in his hands and, as likely as not, he'll turn around and use it on his own kind. Listen, this is what I want you to do. Find out where this Becker boy is being held and get me a transcript of the police blotter. Then call up the surety company and arrange for bail. I'll go bail for him, personally. Do that right away.

REGINA: Yes sir. Do you want to see Mr. Darwin now?

SIMON: Yes, let him come in. Oh, and find out the name of the assistant district attorney in charge.

*(*REGINA *phones these instructions on the Hushaphone.)*

REGINA: Mr. Walter Littlefield is on the wire.

SIMON: All right. Hello, Mr. Littlefield— I'm fine, thanks— Yes— Yes— Yes, I'm very familiar with it— Well, I'm afraid I can't do that— *(As* DARWIN *enters.)* Sit down, Mr. Darwin.

DARWIN: *(Seating himself.)* Thanks.

SIMON: *(Resuming his telephone conversation.)* Well, I can't— Because my partner happens to be the receiver— Yes, I understand; but you can't expect me to represent the principal creditor in a proceeding in which my partner is the receiver— Because that isn't the way I practice law, Mr. Littlefield— I don't care who says it's all right. I know what's right and what's wrong, without asking anybody's opinion— No, I don't have to think it over; I'm telling you right now that I won't have anything to do with it— So am I— Good-bye. Sorry to keep you waiting, Mr. Darwin.

DARWIN: Oh, that's perfectly all right. I'm not in a great hurry.

REGINA: *(Entering.)* Excuse me, but Mr. Crayfield is here.

SIMON: I'll see him in a few minutes.

*(*REGINA *exits.)*

DARWIN: Excuse me, but is that Rigby Crayfield?

SIMON: Yes, it is.

DARWIN: I don't mean to be impertinent. But that's really one of the things I wanted to see you about.

SIMON: Oh, is that so?

DARWIN: Yes. I heard that the Crayfield family was thinking of retaining you for the purpose of breaking Edward's will.

SIMON: I'm very sorry, Mr. Darwin, but I can't discuss—

DARWIN: Oh, of course, I understand perfectly. I shouldn't think of asking you to violate any professional confidences. But you see, Wilma Crayfield, Edward's widow, happens to be a first cousin of mine.

SIMON: Yes, I know.

DARWIN: And I understand that this will contest would involve her in a rather painful scandal. So, I'd rather hoped that because of your friendship for Wilma—

SIMON: I scarcely know Mrs. Crayfield.

DARWIN: Well, I mean to say, she's dined at your home, and all that.

SIMON: Once, I believe. And three years ago—

DARWIN: Still—

SIMON: An attorney can't let such considerations stand in the way of his practice, Mr. Darwin.

DARWIN: Well, of course, I can't very well hope to persuade you. Of course, she's a friend of Cora's, too.

SIMON: My wife would be the last person in the world, Mr. Darwin, to ask me to give up an important case because she happens to be socially acquainted with one of the interested parties.

DARWIN: *(Rising.)* Well, I don't want to take up any more of your time.

SIMON: *(Rising.)* I'm sorry I can't oblige you.

DARWIN: Well, if you can't, you can't. Oh, by the way, I wonder if you could help me out of a temporary embarrassment?

SIMON: Why, I'd be glad to do anything that's—

DARWIN: Well, you see, I'm a rather heavy holder of Amalgamated Zinc, and now I've just learned that the miserable beggars have gone and passed their quarterly dividend. So, for the moment, that leaves me rather up against it. I was wondering if—

SIMON: How much do you need?

DARWIN: Oh, a couple thousand or so. I'll only need it until July. I've quite a bit of money coming in then.

SIMON: Well, I guess I can manage that.

DARWIN: Well, thanks very much, old man. I'll be glad to give you my note, of course.

SIMON: All right. Can you drop in tomorrow morning?

DARWIN: I'll be delighted. About eleven?

SIMON: Yes. Any time in the morning. My secretary will have the check and the note ready for you.

REGINA: *(Entering.)* Excuse me. But Mrs. Simon is outside.

SIMON: Oh, ask her please to wait in your office, while I see Mr. Crayfield. And have Mr. Crayfield come in.

*(*REGINA *telephones on the Hushaphone.)*

DARWIN: Well, so long, old man. And thanks ever so much.

SIMON: Not a bit. You can get out this way.

DARWIN: Why, thanks. I think I'll just say hello to Cora, on the way out. Good day.

SIMON: Good-bye. *(*DARWIN *exits.)* Draw a check for two thousand dollars on my personal account to the order of Roy Darwin. And a promissory note payable in three months. He'll be in tomorrow morning.

REGINA: Yes sir.

SIMON: Oh, and how much did I tell you to send a bill to Mrs. Richter for?

REGINA: Five thousand.

SIMON: Better make it seventy-five hundred.

REGINA: Yes sir. Come right in, Mr. Crayfield.

(The scene blacks out.)

CURTAIN

Scene 3

The outer office. Bessie *is at the switchboard. A small dark* Woman *is seated on the sofa between the windows.* Cora Simon *is seated on the sofa, downstage left. She is an attractive woman in the late thirties, tastefully and expensively dressed. As the lights go up,* Darwin *comes out of the door of* Simon*'s office and crosses to* Cora.

Darwin: Hello, Cora.

Cora: Why, hello, Roy! What are you doing here? *(They shake hands very cordially.)*

Darwin: Why, there was something I wanted to talk over with George.

Cora: Tell me, wasn't that Rigby Crayfield who just went into George's office?

Darwin: Yes, it was. That's why I'm here.

Regina: *(Coming out of* Simon's *office.)* Good morning, Mrs. Simon.

Cora: *(Cooly.)* Good morning, Miss Gordon.

Regina: Mr. Simon will be busy with a client for about fifteen minutes. Do you mind waiting in my office?

Cora: Thank you. I want to have a word with Mr. Darwin first.

Bessie: Simon and Tedesco— Who's calling?— One moment, please— *(To* Regina.*)* Clerk of the Surrogate's Court calling you.

Regina: I'll take it in my office. *(She exits.)*

Bessie: One moment please, I'm getting her for you— All rightee, go ahead.

Darwin: She's a bustling creature, isn't she?

Cora: Oh yes, very. But George finds her indispensable.

Well, Wilma Crayfield called me up this morning. The poor thing is in a terrible state. She's heard that the Crayfield family is engaging George to contest the will. Have you spoken to George about it?

DARWIN: Yes, I have. He's absolutely firm about it.

CORA: Oh, but Roy, he mustn't! Think how awful it would be for poor Wilma.

DARWIN: Well, perhaps you can persuade him. He wouldn't listen to me. *(Lowering his voice.)* Tell me, Cora, is it definitely settled that George is going to Europe with you?

CORA: Yes.

DARWIN: Well, that's that. When am I going to see you?

CORA: Well—I don't know, exactly.

DARWIN: Are you free for lunch?

CORA: No, I'm lunching with George.

DARWIN: Oh. How about tea?

CORA: Why yes, I can make it for tea. I have an appointment for a fitting, but I can change that.

DARWIN: Shall we say four at the Plaza?

CORA: Yes.

DARWIN: Au revoir, then.

CORA: Au revoir. *(He exits.* BESSIE *dials a number.* CORA *rises and crosses towards the door to* SIMON's *office.)* Bessie, I'm going to wait in Miss Gordon's office. Will you get me Miss Williams at Bergdorf-Goodman, please?

*(*HENRY *enters and, seating himself at the table, begins to solve a crossword puzzle.)*

BESSIE: Yes, ma'am.

CORA: Thank you. *(She exits.)*

BESSIE: Hello. District attorney's office?— One moment please— Here's the district attorney's office— All rightee, go ahead. *(She looks through the telephone directory.* CHARLIE MCFADDEN *enters with a paper bag.)*

MCFADDEN: Here's your tongue on rye and chocolate malted.

BESSIE: Thanks, Charlie. Did you tell him to put a lot of Russian dressing on it?

McFadden: Yeah; he smeared it on thick.

(He crosses to the library and exits. Bessie *dials a number.)*

Bessie: Hello— Hello, Arthur— Will you take the board now? I want to get my lunch.— He can't. He has to go right out for Mr. Tedesco— Hello— Bergdorf-Goodman?— Miss Williams, please— Hello, Miss Williams?— One moment, please. Here's Miss Williams, Mrs. Simon— All rightee, go ahead—

*(*Weinberg *enters from the library and crosses to the entrance door.)*

Weinberg: I'm going to lunch. I'll be back in a half-hour.
Bessie: All rightee.

*(*Weinberg *exits.* Bessie *rises and takes a towel from the drawer of the switchboard.* Sandler *enters from the library.)*

Sandler: *(To* Henry.*)* Hey, kid, do you know what became of volume M to S of Stoddard's Digest?
Henry: I'll look around for it. *(He exits to the library.)*
Sandler: *(To* Bessie.*)* All right, peaches and vinegar.
Bessie: This lady is waiting to see Mr. Tedesco. And G.S. has someone with him. And Mr. Weinberg will be back from lunch in a half an hour.
Sandler: You wouldn't fool me, would you? *(*Bessie *exits to the corridor. A* Woman *comes out of* Tedesco's *office and exits.)* Hello?— Yes sir— *(To the* Woman *who is waiting.)* Are you Mrs. Gardi?
The Woman: Yes.
Sandler: All right. Mr. Tedesco will see you now. *(The* Woman *goes into* Tedesco's *office.)* Hello— The passenger department of the French Line?— Who is this, please— Oh, all right, Mrs. Simon, I'll get it right away— Don't mention it.

(He looks up a number in the directory. Henry *enters carrying a law book.)*

HENRY: Here it is. It was on the wrong shelf.

SANDLER: Oh, it was, was it? What are you doing: reading up on rape cases again?

HENRY: I was not.

SANDLER: You ought to know them all by heart, by now.

(He dials a number. GOLDIE *appears at the door of* TEDESCO*'s office with a letter.)*

GOLDIE: Here, Henry, take this right around to the Napoli Importing Company. *(*HENRY *takes the letter from her.)* Mr. Tedesco wants it delivered right away. *(*HENRY *goes to the revolving bookstand and takes his cap from behind it.)* Don't delay now. It's very important.

HENRY: All right. All right. Can't you see I'm going?

GOLDIE: Don't be impudent to me, please.

*(*HENRY *goes out the entrance door.* GOLDIE *exits to the library.)*

SANDLER: Hello, French Line?— Passenger department, please— Hold the wire a minute— Here's the French Line for Mrs. Simon— Go ahead. *(While he is speaking,* MRS. LENA SIMON *has entered. She is a quiet little woman in her sixties.)* Who do you wish to see, madam?

MRS. SIMON: Is Mr. Simon busy, please?

SANDLER: Yes, he is. Will anybody else do?

MRS. SIMON: I'll wait for him.

SANDLER: He may be busy for quite a while.

MRS. SIMON: Oh, that's nothing. I got plenty time.

SANDLER: All right. Take a seat.

MRS. SIMON: Thank you. *(She sits on the sofa between the windows.)*

SANDLER: Hello— What number?— All right— *(He dials a number.* GOLDIE *enters from the library and crosses to the entrance door.)*

GOLDIE: *(Importantly.)* I'm going to lunch.

SANDLER: All right, beautiful. Can you be reached at the Automat?

GOLDIE: You're very funny—I don't think! *(She exits.)*

SANDLER: Hello— 4979?— Go ahead.

(He becomes absorbed in his law book. McFADDEN *comes out of the library and is about to enter* TEDESCO*'s office when he stops and looks curiously at* MRS. SIMON.*)*

McFADDEN: Excuse me, ma'am, but ain't you Mr. Simon's mother?
MRS. SIMON: Yes.
McFADDEN: I thought I recognized you. I guess you don't remember me.
MRS. SIMON: Well, I think I saw you somewhere before.
McFADDEN: I'm Charlie McFadden, that used to be the helper to Barney O'Rourke, the plumber, on Third Avenue.
MRS. SIMON: Oh, of course! When we were living on Eighty-second Street.
McFADDEN: That's right. An' I was livin' right across the street in number 319. That's many a long day ago.
MRS. SIMON: I should say so. Well, well, what do you think of that!
McFADDEN: Well, say, you're lookin' great. Why you don't look a day older than the last time I saw you.
MRS. SIMON: Yes, sure; you expect me to believe that, you jollier? Next month, I'll be sixty-four.
McFADDEN: Well, you sure don't look it.
MRS. SIMON: Well, I have my health, thank God. And my boy gives me every comfort. Why shouldn't I look well?
McFADDEN: You've sure got reason to be proud of your son, Mrs. Simon He's a prince among men, that's what he is.
MRS. SIMON: Yes, that's just what he is, Mr. McFadden.
McFADDEN: An' ain't I the one to know it, too. I guess you know what he done for me, don't you?
MRS. SIMON: *(Shaking her head.)* No. I know how to mind my own business, Mr. McFadden. He doesn't tell me anything and I don't ask any questions.
McFADDEN: Well, he gave me a new start in life, that's what he did. You know I was nothin' but a jailbird.
MRS. SIMON: Tt! Tt!
McFADDEN: Yes, sure. I did a couple good long stretches for burglary; and I guess that's where I'd of ended my days if I hadn't happened to meet him on the street one day. Well, it seems he'd heard all about me, so he says

to me: "Charlie," he says, "if you'll go straight, I'll give you a job in the office." "On the level," says I. "Sure," says he. "For old time's sake," says he. So I took him at his word and here I've been ever since.

MRS. SIMON: You're working here for George?

MCFADDEN: Yep. Nearly four years now. Process server. And now and again I do a little private detective work. You see, I got ways of findin' things out.

MRS. SIMON: What do you think of that!

MCFADDEN: It's made a new man o' me, Mrs. Simon. I got a good steady job here and I meet lots of fine people and I know all the boys around the courthouse. And it's all his doin'.

MRS. SIMON: He's a good, good man, my Georgie.

MCFADDEN: I'd cut off my right hand for him, that's what I'd do. Well, it's mighty nice to be seein' you again, Mrs. Simon. *(He shakes hands with her.)*

MRS. SIMON: I've been very happy to see you, Mr. McFadden.

MCFADDEN: God bless you!

(He enters TEDESCO*'s office.* PETER J. MALONE *enters from the corridor. He is a plump politician of fifty-five, fastidiously dressed.)*

MALONE: County Clerk Peter J. Malone to see Mr. Simon.

SANDLER: Yes sir. Just take a seat, Mr. Malone, and I'll tell him you're here.

MALONE: All right.

SANDLER: County Clerk Malone to see Mr. Simon— Just a few minutes, Mr. Malone.

MALONE: Okay.

MRS. SIMON: What's the matter, Mr. Malone, don't you remember your old friends?

MALONE: What? Well, will you look who's sittin' there! Why, I didn't see you at all. *(He goes over to her and shakes hands with her.)*

MRS. SIMON: What's the matter? Did I shrink so much that you couldn't see me?

MALONE: Why, no. I thought it was a young girl sittin' there. You know, one of them expensive Park Avenue divorce cases of George's.

MRS. SIMON: Yes, you're a fine one, you are. If anybody believed everything that you say!

MALONE: *(Sitting beside her.)* Well, you're a sight for sore eyes, you are. Why, I ain't seen you since the Dewey Parade. How are you, anyhow?

MRS. SIMON: I'm fine. And you! I don't have to ask you. *(She indicates his bulk.)*

MALONE: Yeah, quite a bay window. But when a fellow gets to be my age, you know.

MRS. SIMON: What are you talking about! Why, you're only a spring chicken.

MALONE: *(Behind his hand.)* Fifty-six. But don't tell anybody. Well, a lot o' water has flowed under the bridge since the old days in Yorkville.

MRS. SIMON: Yes, we're all a little better off than in those days.

MALONE: I'll say we are. Me drivin' a truck and you runnin' a little bakery and George sellin' papers. Well, you ought to be mighty proud of your son, Mrs. Simon.

SANDLER: *(Nervously.)* Excuse me, madam. Are you Mr. Simon's mother?

MRS. SIMON: Yes.

SANDLER: Oh, I'll tell him you're here. I didn't know who you were.

MRS. SIMON: Oh, that's all right. I got plenty time.

*(*SIMON *enters from his office with a middle-aged* MAN.*)*

SIMON: All right, Mr. Crayfield. I'll phone you in the morning.

THE MAN: Very well. *(He exits.)*

SIMON: Hello, Pete.

MALONE: *(Rising.)* Hello, George.

SIMON: Hello, Mama. I didn't know you were here. *(He goes over and kisses her affectionately.)*

MRS. SIMON: Hello, Georgie.

SIMON: Have you been here long? *(To* SANDLER.*)* Why didn't you tell me my mother was waiting?

MRS. SIMON: It's only five minutes, Georgie.

SANDLER: I'm very sorry, Mr. Simon. I didn't know the lady was your mother.

SIMON: What do you mean, you didn't know? Don't you ask people who they are when they come in?

MRS SIMON: Georgie, please!

SANDLER: I'm very sorry, Mr. Simon.

SIMON: You're going up for your bar examination and you can't even announce a caller.

MRS. SIMON: Georgie, be a good boy.

SIMON: The next time my mother calls, I want her announced immediately, do you understand?

SANDLER: Yes, Mr. Simon.

SIMON: Come in, Mama. Come in, Pete.

MALONE: Say, I can wait.

SIMON: No, no. Come in, both of you. *(They exit to* SIMON's *office.)*

SANDLER: Hello— Yes— Who's calling?— Wait a minute, I'll see if he's in—

(The scene blacks out.)

CURTAIN

Scene 4

The inner office. REGINA *is at* SIMON*'s desk, telephoning.*

REGINA: I'll see if I can find him— Wait, I think he's coming now. Hold the wire.

(SIMON, MRS. SIMON *and* MALONE *enter, downstage.)*

SIMON: Did you have your lunch, Mama?
MRS. SIMON: Yes, of course. A long time ago already.
REGINA: Mr. Fishman on the phone.
SIMON: All right, I'll talk to him. Sit down, Mama. Sit down, Pete.
REGINA: Here he is now, Mr. Fishman.
SIMON: Hello, Joe— That's fine— Well, maybe you're right— No, don't do anything— All right— All right, I'll tell you when to sell— All right— Good bye, Joe.
REGINA: *(Meanwhile.)* How are you, Mrs. Simon. *(She shakes hands cordially with her.)* You're looking very well.
MRS. SIMON: Oh, I can't complain. I don't get any younger, but otherwise I'm fine.
MALONE: Hello, Rexie. How are you?
REGINA: Oh, I'm all right, thanks, Mr. Malone.
MALONE: I guess George is keeping you pretty busy, ain't he?
REGINA: Oh, I don't mind that. If there's one thing I don't like, it's being idle.
SIMON: *(Hanging up the receiver.)* Where's Mrs. Simon?
REGINA: She's in my office. I think she's telephoning.
SIMON: *(Opening the door of* REGINA's *office.)* Hello, darling.

CORA: *(Offstage.)* Hello, George. I still have another call to make.

SIMON: All right, sweetheart. Come in whenever you're through. *(He closes the door and goes to his desk.)*

MRS. SIMON: George, I'm going to wait outside and you talk with Mr. Malone.

MALONE: No, no, you stay right where you are. I've got to call up Albany. Where's a phone I can use?

SIMON: In the library. Rexie, show Mr. Malone—

REGINA: Yes sir.

MALONE: Never mind, Rexie. I know the way.

SIMON: Go ahead with him, Rexie, and if there's anybody in the library, chase 'em out till Mr. Malone is through. And listen, see that he gets his number. That fat-head at the switchboard doesn't know his ear from his elbow.

REGINA: Yes sir.

MALONE:. Thanks. I'll see you later.

SIMON: Yes, come back, as soon as you're through.

(MALONE exits.)

REGINA: That Becker boy is being held on two thousand dollars bail on a felonious assault charge. I'm arranging the bail and the district attorney's office is going to call me back to let me know who's handling the case.

SIMON: All right. Have the boy come in to see me.

REGINA: Yes sir. *(She exits.)*

MRS. SIMON: That's a nice girl, George, that Miss Gordon.

SIMON: She's a wonderful secretary. I couldn't get along without her. Mama, have a piece of candy.

MRS. SIMON: No, thanks, Georgie.

SIMON: *(Taking several pieces.)* They're very good.

MRS. SIMON: You'll spoil your lunch, Georgie, nasching like that.

SIMON: Nonsense! Why should a piece of candy spoil my lunch?

MRS. SIMON: Georgie, how is it a nice girl like Miss Gordon doesn't find herself a husband?

SIMON: I don't know. I don't think she's interested in men. Mama, do you remember Sarah Becker from Second Avenue?

MRS. SIMON: Becker? No, I don't remember any Becker.

SIMON: Certainly you do. Her husband used to sell neckties from a pushcart. A great big fellow.

MRS. SIMON: Oh yes, of course, of course! It must be twenty years ago. She had a little baby with red curls—little Harry.

SIMON: That's the one. Well, little Harry has been making Communist speeches in Union Square and getting into trouble with the police.

MRS. SIMON: What, that little baby! I can't believe it.

SIMON: He hasn't stayed a little baby all these years, Mama.

MRS. SIMON: But you're going to do something for him, George?

SIMON: Yes, I guess I can get him out of it, all right. His mother was in this morning. Becker died of cancer a few years ago, and I think she's been having a pretty hard time of it.

MRS. SIMON: Ach, the poor thing. I think I'll go and pay her a little visit.

SIMON: Yes, why don't you do that? Rexie will give you her address. And take her a little fruit or something. The poor thing looks as though she didn't have enough to eat. And I guess she's too proud to go to the charities.

MRS. SIMON: Yes, the charities! Don't talk to me about those charities! It's better to starve.

SIMON: Well, Mama, I've decided to go to Europe with Cora next week.

MRS. SIMON: That's good, Georgie. You need a good rest. You work too hard.

SIMON: Oh, I don't need any rest. Hard work is good for me. But I made up my mind that we'd celebrate our fifth anniversary by taking a trip together. You know, I haven't really had a chance to be alone with Cora since we eloped together.

MRS. SIMON: Yes, that's just what you should do, Georgie. A man and wife should be just as close together as they can.

SIMON: Especially when a man has a wife like Cora. She's a wonderful, wonderful woman, Mama.

MRS. SIMON: Well, she has a good husband, in you, too, Georgie.

SIMON: Oh yes, of course. According to you, nobody would be good enough for me. It's a wonder the King of England never asked me to become his son-in-law.

MRS. SIMON: Well, I'm sure his daughters couldn't do any better.

SIMON: What a *naar** you are, Mama.

MRS. SIMON: All right, laugh. It doesn't change my opinion.

SIMON: Well, anyhow, I wish I deserved a wife like Cora.

MRS. SIMON: Georgie, listen, I want to talk to you.

SIMON: Is anything wrong? Are you feeling all right?

MRS. SIMON: Of course, I'm feeling all right, Georgie. You mustn't worry about me.

SIMON: Well, what's the matter, then? What do you look so serious about?

MRS. SIMON: Georgie, you mustn't be angry with me—

SIMON: I'm not going to be angry. What is it?

MRS. SIMON: Georgie, Davie called me up this morning—

SIMON: Well?

MRS. SIMON: You told me you wouldn't be angry.

SIMON: I'm not angry. Go ahead.

MRS. SIMON: He needs a little money.

SIMON: Money? What does he need money for this time?

MRS. SIMON: A check came back from the bank.

SIMON: You mean he gave somebody a bum check?

MRS. SIMON: He made a little mistake in his balance.

SIMON: The hell he made a little mistake in his balance. He's a goddam crook, that's what he is.

MRS. SIMON: Georgie, is that a way to talk about your brother?

SIMON: Yes, brother. A fine brother he is. All he does is one dirty, crooked thing after another. I no sooner get him out of one thing then he gets himself into another. But I'm through with him. He can get himself out of this one.

MRS. SIMON: Georgie, please—

SIMON: No, to hell with him. Let him go to jail. That's where he belongs, anyhow.

MRS. SIMON: Georgie, be a good boy. It's the last time. He won't do anything again.

SIMON: Yes! How many times have I heard that one be-

*Silly.

fore, too? I'm through with him, I tell you. That *lausbub** has given me more headaches than my whole practice put together. I'm supposed to be an important lawyer around here. I'm mixed up in more front-page cases than any lawyer in New York. People from old families come in and think I'm doing them a favor if I accept their retainers. If I don't happen to like a millionaire's looks, I throw him out of the office. It's fine for me, isn't it, to have a brother going around getting himself pinched in gambling raids and annoying women in the subway and handing out rubber checks? It's great, isn't it?

MRS. SIMON: It won't happen again, Georgie.

SIMON: No, I've done all I'm going to do. Let him shift for himself.

MRS. SIMON: Georgie, please. For me, do it; not for him.

SIMON: No.

MRS. SIMON: I don't often ask you for something, Georgie—

CORA: *(Entering.)* May I come in? Oh, I'm sorry. I didn't know you were busy.

SIMON: It's all right, darling. Come right in.

CORA: *(Shaking hands with* MRS. SIMON.*)* How do you do, Mrs. Simon?

MRS. SIMON: I'm very well, thank you. And you?

CORA: Quite well, thanks.

MRS. SIMON: That's good. You got a little thinner since the last time I saw you.

CORA: Have I? I don't think so.

REGINA: *(Entering.)* Excuse me, Mr. Simon. Mr. Hirschberg is outside. He has an appointment with you.

SIMON: Oh yes, I forgot about him.

CORA: Shall I clear out?

SIMON: No, stay right here. I'll see him in one of the other offices. Mama, are you sure you won't have a little lunch with us?

MRS. SIMON: No, I must go now.

SIMON: *(Kissing her.)* Well, good bye, Mama. Take a taxi uptown.

*While the context makes clear Simon's annoyance with his brother, *lausbub* remains elusive. It could be a corruption of the Yiddish *shlub* (*zhlub*), oaf, or even the Polish *Łobus,* scoundrel.

MRS. SIMON: The bus is good enough, Georgie, don't forget.

SIMON: I'll think it over and call you up tonight. I won't be five minutes, darling. Oh, Rexie, write down that Mrs. Becker's address for my mother.

REGINA: Yes sir.

*(*SIMON *exits to the corridor,* REGINA *to her office.)*

CORA: Lovely spring weather we're having, isn't it?

MRS. SIMON: Yes, today it's beautiful. I'm always glad when the winter is over.

CORA: Yes, I prefer warm weather, too.

(A moment of silence.)

MRS. SIMON: And your children: are they well, too?

CORA: Yes, very well, thank you.

MRS. SIMON: They must be getting big now.

CORA: Yes, Richard is fourteen and Dorothy twelve.

MRS. SIMON: Tt! Tt! Before you know it, they're grown up. It seems like yesterday since Georgie was a little boy.

CORA: I know. They do grow up awfully fast.

MRS. SIMON: They don't mind that you go to Europe and leave them?

CORA: Oh, no! They're quite accustomed to being left. They're very fond of their governess.

MRS. SIMON: Well, I'm glad Georgie is going to have a little vacation. He works so hard.

CORA: Yes, he does work hard. Too hard, in fact.

MRS. SIMON: He always worked hard. Since he was a little boy, he's been working hard. Always working and studying and trying to better himself. That's how he made his success.

CORA: Yes, of course. But now that he's achieved success, there's really no longer any necessity for it.

MRS. SIMON: It's his nature. You can't change his nature.

CORA: Yes, I think perhaps you're right. Marvelous view from here, isn't it?

MRS. SIMON: Yes, it's beautiful.

CORA: *(Looking at her watch.)* Heavens, it's half-past one already.

REGINA: *(Entering.)* Here's the address, Mrs. Simon.

MRS. SIMON: Oh, thank you. Thank you, very much. Well, I think I'll go now.

REGINA: Shall I tell Mr. Simon you're going?

MRS. SIMON: No, no, don't disturb him. *(Extending her hand to* CORA.*)* Well, good-bye.

CORA: *(Shaking hands.)* Good-bye. Awfully nice to have seen you again.

MRS. SIMON: Maybe I'll see you again before you go to Europe.

CORA: Oh, I hope so.

MRS. SIMON: But in case I don't, I hope you have a wonderful trip and that you come back safe and sound.

CORA: Thanks, very much.

MRS. SIMON: And take good care of my Georgie.

CORA: I'll do my best.

MRS. SIMON: Good-bye, Miss Gordon.

REGINA: Good-bye, Mrs. Simon. Shall I show you the way?

MRS. SIMON: No, no. I know the way.

REGINA: I'm going to come and pay you a little visit soon.

MRS. SIMON: Oh, that will be very nice. Come any time: I don't go out very much. Well, good-bye.

REGINA: Good-bye, Mrs. Simon.

CORA: Good-bye. *(*MRS. SIMON *exits.* REGINA *is about to go to her office.)* Oh, Miss Gordon!

REGINA: Yes, Mrs. Simon.

CORA: I'd like you to do something for me.

REGINA: Certainly.

CORA: I'd like you, between three and four this afternoon, to call up the French Line and ask for Mr. Morell—M-O-R-E-double L. You'd better write it down, hadn't you?

REGINA: I'll remember it. *(Nevertheless, she takes up a piece of paper and makes some notes.)*

CORA: I want to make sure that our suite on the *Paris* has a serving pantry. I forgot to ask him this morning.

REGINA: And if it hasn't?

CORA: Well, if it hasn't, you'd better— No, never mind. In that case, I'll take it up with him, myself. I'm almost certain it has, but I want to make sure. Also I wish you'd ask him to arrange to have a steward named

Marcel Lebon— Have you got that?— Lebon— L-E-B-O-N.

REGINA: Yes, I have it.

CORA: I want him assigned to our suite. He's served me several times before, and I prefer to have someone who is familiar with my requirements. You'll attend to that, will you?

REGINA: Yes, ma'am, is that all?

CORA: Yes, thank you. I think that's all. Oh, you'd better phone me about the pantry this evening, at dinner time.

REGINA: I can tell Mr. Simon.

CORA: He's likely to forget. I'd rather you phoned me.

REGINA: Very well.

CORA: Thank you. *(As* REGINA *is about to go.)* Oh, I wonder if you'd mind giving me a cigarette. I seem to have run out of them.

REGINA: Certainly. *(She takes the cigarette box over to* CORA.*)*

CORA: Thanks. Heavens, I seem to be out of matches, too. *(*REGINA, *without a word, strikes a match and offers* CORA *a light.)* Thanks very much.

SIMON: *(Entering.)* I'm sorry to keep you waiting, darling.

CORA: It doesn't matter.

SIMON: *(To* REGINA, *who is about to exit.)* Rexie, you'd better go get your lunch.

REGINA: I'm in no hurry. *(She exits abruptly.)*

SIMON: That girl's a human dynamo. Why, it's half-past one already! You must be starved, darling.

CORA: Well, I am rather hungry. I had an early breakfast and I've been running errands all morning.

SIMON: Well, sweetheart, I've got to see Peter Malone for a few minutes. Why don't you go ahead and start your lunch and I'll join you in ten or fifteen minutes?

CORA: Perhaps I'll do that. I've lots of things to attend to after lunch. But there's something I must talk to you about, first.

SIMON: *(Sitting on the sofa beside her.)* All right, honey. Nothing's wrong, is it?

CORA: It's about Wilma Crayfield.

SIMON: Oh! Your friend Mr. Darwin has been talking to me about that, too.

CORA: Yes, so he told me. George, you're really not thinking seriously of trying to break that will, are you?

SIMON: Yes, darling, very seriously. In fact, Rigby Crayfield was in here this morning and engaged me to represent the Crayfield family.

CORA: But George, you can't do that!

SIMON: Why, darling?

CORA: Why, it's a scandalous case!

SIMON: It certainly is! Do you know the facts?

CORA: No, I don't.

SIMON: Well, in a couple of words, it turns out that Madame Wilma played a pretty dirty trick on her husband and that the child to whom he left the bulk of the estate isn't his child after all.

CORA: Why, I don't believe it! It's preposterous.

SIMON: I've got the proofs right here, darling. You don't think I'd take the case, do you, unless I were convinced of the facts?

CORA: I can't understand why you would want to have anything to do with such a case.

SIMON: There's a hundred thousand dollar fee in it, if I win. The estate will come to over four million.

CORA: You don't need the money. Especially money that you get by such means.

SIMON: By such means? I don't understand you, darling.

CORA: Think of what this is going to do to Wilma!

SIMON: But think of what she did to Crayfield!

CORA: Well, he's dead and buried and none the worse off for it.

SIMON: I really don't follow your logic, sweetheart. I don't see that there's much reason for sympathizing with a woman who's palmed off a bastard on her husband and then gets found out.

CORA: We all make mistakes and do foolish things that we regret. Anyhow, there's no reason why *you* should have anything to do with the nasty mess.

SIMON: As an attorney, I owe it to myself to take a lucrative and important case when it's offered me. And as a member of the bar, I owe it to the community to see substantial justice done. You don't think Edward Crayfield would have made that will, do you, if he'd known the child wasn't his?

CORA: I don't know anything about it. I do know that Wilma Crayfield is a friend of mine and has been for years. Why, you know her, too, George. She's dined at our house.

SIMON: But so have hundreds of other people, darling. Does that mean that I can't appear in any case in which their interests are involved? It's a pretty high price to pay for having people to dinner.

CORA: You know I don't mean that. This is a very special case. It's a friend's reputation that's involved.

SIMON: Her reputation can't be saved, anyhow. If I didn't take the case, a hundred other lawyers would be glad to.

CORA: Well, at least, you would have made a magnanimous gesture.

SIMON: I should say so! A hundred thousand dollars! That's not the way law is practiced, darling.

CORA: I don't see why it isn't possible to practice law, like a gentleman.

SIMON: *(Rising and walking away.)* I never laid any claims to being a gentleman, dear. The last time I crossed the Atlantic, it was in the steerage.

CORA: I didn't mean it in that way, George. Heavens, nobody admires you more than I for the handicaps you've overcome. I couldn't have given any better demonstration of it, could I, than making a runaway marriage with you, after divorcing the man I'd been married to for eleven years?

SIMON: Well, we've been pretty happy together, haven't we?

CORA: Yes, of course we have.

SIMON: The old saying about marrying in haste and repenting at leisure hasn't held good with us. I know I haven't lived up to all your expectations of me. I told you from the start I wasn't good enough for you. But I've tried my best.

CORA: I'm not complaining, George.

SIMON: I know you're not. You're very sweet to me. But I know there are lots of ways in which I don't measure up to your standards.

CORA: Well, it's only that I feel that now that you've made your success, you should try to disassociate yourself from all these unsavory *affaires de scandale*. Like that awful murder case, for example—

SIMON: I know: the Chapman case. Yes, I'm through with

cases of that sort. What do you think, sweetheart, she was in here this morning and tied to steal me away from you!

CORA: What an awful person she must be!

SIMON: Fine chance she had, huh? *(He tries to kiss her.)*

CORA: My mouth, George! I just put it on.

SIMON: I used to be quite a lady-killer, in the old days, too. But that was before I knew you, darling.

CORA: You see it's a little embarrassing for me to have your name constantly associated with these sensational cases. After all, it's my name now, too, you know. And the sort of people I've always known can't help thinking it's a little strange.

SIMON: Sweetheart, the last thing in the world I want to do is cause you any embarrassment. My one object in life is to make you happy and give you everything you want.

CORA: Oh. I didn't mean to imply for a minute that it's been intentional. Only—

SIMON: I don't even want it to be unintentional. Listen, darling, would it make you any happier if I dropped this Crayfield case?

CORA: It would make me feel that I was married to a man who recognizes the value of the social amenities.

SIMON: Okay. *(He pushes the call button on his desk. Almost instantly,* REGINA *enters.)* Take a letter to Rigby Crayfield, Rexie. Dear Mr. Crayfield, I regret to inform you that it will be impossible for me to represent you in the matter of the probate of the will of Edward Crayfield. My reasons for withdrawing from the case have nothing to do with the merits of your claims, but are of a personal nature, the details of which I shall not burden you with. I am enclosing herewith all the papers in the matter, of which kindly acknowledge receipt. Regretting any inconvenience I may have caused you, I am, et cetera. Get that right out and send it around by messenger. And get the papers from Weinberg.

REGINA: Yes sir. *(She throws a swift look at* CORA *and exits.)*

CORA: Thank you, George dear.

SIMON: Feel better, now?

CORA: Yes, much better.

SIMON: Don't I rate a kiss? *(*CORA *holds up her face. He*

kisses her on the lips.) You'll make a gentleman of me, yet.

CORA: I'm sure you've ruined my beautiful mouth. Yes, you have. *(She busies herself with her lipstick.)*

MALONE: *(Appearing in the doorway.)* Am I intrudin'?

SIMON: No, I was just kissing my wife.

MALONE: Well, I'm glad there's some that still do.

SIMON: Darling, this is Pete Malone, who makes governors and presidents.

MALONE: *(Shaking hands with* CORA.*)* And assemblymen, George. Don't forget the assemblymen.

CORA: How do you do, Mr. Malone?

MALONE: I had the pleasure of meetin' you in Washington, before you and George were married.

CORA: *(Rising.)* Oh yes, of course. Well, George, I think I'll go on to lunch now.

SIMON: All right, darling. Where will you be?

CORA: At the Marguery.

SIMON: I'll be there in fifteen minutes.

MALONE: I won't keep him long.

CORA: All right. Au revoir, George. Good bye, Mr. Malone. Awfully nice to have seen you again.

MALONE: Thank you, ma'am, it was a great pleasure to see you again, too.

*(*CORA *exits.* MALONE *seats himself upstage of the desk.)*

SIMON: *(Sitting on sofa.)* God, what a woman that is, Pete! I can't realize, half the time, that I'm really married to her.

MALONE: *(Taking a cigar from the box on the desk.)* Well, you sure are hittin' the high places, George. In the old days, when you were peddlin' papers in the rain and your toes comin' through your boots, it was a million to one, and no takers, that I'd live to see you ridin' around in a Hispano-whaddya-call-it with a Daughter of the American Revolution.

SIMON: Well, you haven't done so badly by yourself, either, Pete.

MALONE: Oh, I'm not complainin'. Only you're on the front page defendin' the beautiful Flossie McFloosie, whilst I'm back amongst the editorials, in a long tail an' stripes, makin' a hearty meal of Civic Virtue.

SIMON: Pete, there's something I want to talk to you about. Matter of fact, I meant to give you a ring. I think John Tedesco's got a Supreme Court nomination coming to him.

MALONE: Well, I don't know, George.

SIMON: Why not? He's worked mighty hard for the organization, John has.

MALONE: Oh yeah, sure, that part of it's all right.

SIMON: And there's not a lawyer in the whole judicial department that stands in stronger with the Italian voters than John does.

MALONE: I guess that's right, too. The wops have got another judgeship coming to them. And I don't think anybody's got anything on John. His record's all right.

SIMON: Why, certainly his record's all right. Listen, John and I grew up together. I tell you there's not a whiter man on the face of the earth.

MALONE: Oh, I'm not sayin' anythin' against John. It's just a question if he's big enough for the Supreme Court.

SIMON: What do you mean, big enough? What about some of those horse's piazzas that are decorating the bench now? What about Edgar Thayer?

MALONE: Oh, sure. The trouble is John's father don't happen to be a railroad president. Anyhow, that's what I'm drivin' at. We gotta keep up the standard of the judiciary. There's been an awful lot of bellyachin' lately about keepin' the bench out of politics. We gotta get A-1 men. Now if it was you, George—

SIMON: Nothing doing, Pete. What the hell do I want to be a judge for? I'd get locomotor ataxia sitting up there all day on my fanny doing nothing but looking important. Anyhow, I can't afford it. It costs me a hundred thousand a year to live.

MALONE: A hundred grand would of gone a long way on Second Avenue, George.

SIMON: Sure, it's crazy. I know that just as well as you do. But when you've got that kind of a set-up what can you do about it?

MALONE: John ain't so hot on the legal end, is he?

SIMON: Oh, he knows his law, all right. I don't say he's a

Blackstone. But hell, neither am I. I've got a young Harvard boy in the office here, named Weinberg, that John can have for his secretary. Believe me, he'll hand down opinions that will give the Court of Appeals an inferiority complex.

MALONE: All right, George, I'll think it over. I'd like to do it for you, if I can, and I think maybe we can work it.

SIMON: I wish you would, Pete. It would mean an awful lot to John.

MALONE: Okay. Tell you why I came in, George. You know my brother Ed, the warden up at Elmira?

SIMON: Yes, sure I know him. How's he getting along up there?

MALONE: Oh, he's getting along all right. Well, he tipped me off to something that I think you oughta know.

SIMON: All right.

MALONE: Do you ever remember handling a case for some fellow named— Wait a minute, till I think of his name. It's some Dutch or Hebrew name, something-or-other-stein. Wait, I think I wrote it down somewhere. Yeah, here it is. Breitstein, Jo-hann Breitstein. Remember him?

SIMON: Yes, I remember. Johann Breitstein, a German boy. I defended him on a larceny charge, about eight or nine years ago, and got him an acquittal. What about it?

MALONE: Was there something about an alibi?

SIMON: Yes, he had an airtight alibi. That's why the jury acquitted him.

MALONE: Yeah. Well, it seems there was a guy named Whitey Cushman who was mixed up in the case. Is that right?

SIMON: Yes. He established the alibi for Breitstein.

MALONE: That's it. Well, this bird Cushman is doin' a stretch up at Elmira and it seems he had a session with your friend Francis Clark Baird, who's a member of the Parole Board.

SIMON: Yes? well? What about it?

MALONE: Well, this Cushman has been givin' Francis Clark Baird some song-and-dance about the alibi in the Breitstein case bein' framed up.

SIMON: What do you mean framed up?

MALONE: I'm just tellin' you what Ed told me over the phone last night. Is this guy Baird on the grievance committee of the Bar Association, too?

SIMON: Yes, I think so.

MALONE: That's what Ed said. He says he's got a hunch that Baird would like to get something on you. And I guess that's right, too, ain't it?

SIMON: Yes, sure he would. I've licked him to a fare-you-well in half a dozen cases.

MALONE: Yeah. I know you have. Well, accordin' to Ed, Baird thinks he can cook up some kind of a disbarment proceedin' against you out of this Breitstein case. Any-how, he's havin' Cushman brought down to New York next week, to take his deposition.

SIMON: Oh he is, is he? Well, let him! What the hell do I care? He's got nothing on me.

MALONE: Well, that's what I told Ed. "There's nothin' to it, Ed," I says. "George is too smart a boy," I says, "to let himself get mixed up with anything like that." Only I thought I'd better tip you off.

SIMON: Francis Clark Baird: To hell with Francis Clark Baird: He's got nothing on me. I've been practicing law for eighteen years and my record is an open book. It's not the first time this Baird and the rest of those silk-stocking babies in the Bar Association have tried to get me. They've been gunning for me for years. But they haven't got anything on me, yet. No, and they never will. So they're going to disbar me on a crook's deposition, are they? Ho, that's a laugh, that is! Just let Mr. Francis Clark Baird try it, and he'll find himself holding the dirty end of the stick. Jesus Christ! Some lousy little crook makes a play for a parole and they think they're going to pin something on me. That's funny, that is!

MALONE: That's what Ed said. He says this Cushman is a bad egg and a trouble maker: A guy that throws fits and all that. Well, don't worry about it, George. I guess nothin' much will come of it. I just wanted to give you the lowdown, that's all.

SIMON: Thanks, Pete. It was damn nice of you to let me know. What do you think of those S.O.B.s trying to pull a thing like that on me!

MALONE: Well, you know how it is, George. These guys

that came over on the *Mayflower* don't like to see the boys from Second Avenue sittin' in the high places. We're just a lot of riffraff to them. They've had their knives out for me, for a long time, too, but, hell, it's me that has the laugh when the votes are counted. Well, I got to be gettin' back to the office. And I guess the missis is gettin' tried of keepin' the filly de bee's wax warm for you. So long, George. Come around to the club, some night.

SIMON: Yes, I will, Pete. And thanks for the steer.

MALONE: Keep the change. Well, *Scholem aleichem.*

(He exits. The moment he has gone, SIMON *slumps down in his chair and stares fixedly ahead of him. Then he suddenly raises both fists and brings them down on the desk.)*

SIMON: Goddam it to hell!

(He springs to his feet and walks swiftly up and down the office, pounding his palm with his fist. Then he goes to the desk and pushes a button. REGINA *enters, almost instantly.)*

Listen, Rexie. About eight or nine years ago, I defended a fellow named Johann Breitstein in General Sessions. I want to get hold of Breitstein right away. I met him three or four years ago and at that time he was working as an usher in one of the Warner Brothers' Theatres. Call up Warner Brothers and see if you can trace him and have him come in here as soon as possible. Get McFadden or anybody else to help you, if necessary. Let everything else go until you locate him. Understand?

REGINA: Yes sir.

SIMON: Then get me all the papers out of the files and have them here for me when I get back from lunch. People against Johann Breitstein. Then send up to General Sessions and order a transcript of the stenographer's minutes of the trial. No, wait a minute! You'd better not do that. No, never mind that. Just get me the papers out of the files. And locate Brietstein; that's the important thing.

REGINA: Yes sir.

SIMON: Get right on the job, will you? I'm going around to the Marguery to join Mrs. Simon at lunch, and I'll be back in three-quarters of an hour.

(He exits. REGINA *sits at* SIMON*'s desk and takes up the telephone receiver.)*

REGINA: Hello— Get me Warner Brothers' Picture Corporation, please— Yes, that's right.

(She hangs up the receiver and sits staring at CORA*'s picture. Then with a sudden gesture, she sweeps the photograph off the desk.)*

CURTAIN

Act II

Scene 1

The inner office. Bessie *lies stretched out upon the sofa, in the corner, her eyes closed. Her shoes are on the floor beside the sofa.* Regina *enters quickly, with a glass in her hand, and crosses to* Bessie.

Regina: Here, Bessie, drink this.
Bessie: *(Opening her eyes.)* What is it?
Regina: It's just some bromides to quiet your nerves. Drink it.
Bessie: *(Sitting up.)* Does it taste bad?
Regina: No, no, it's nothing at all. Take it; it will make you feel better.
Bessie: I hate taking stuff. *(She closes her eyes, shudders and drains the glass.)*
Regina: In a little while, you'll feel much better. How do you feel now?
Bessie: I still feel kinda funny inside.
Regina: You'd better lie down again.
Bessie: No, I don't want to. I'm sick o' layin' down.
Regina: I'll tell you what I'm going to do. I'm going to send you home in a taxi.
Bessie: No, I don't want to go home, honest I don't. I'll only start thinkin' if I go home.
Regina: Are you sure?
Bessie: Yes, I'll be all right in a minute. I think I'll go back to the board. *(As* Simon *enters.)* Look, here's Mr. Simon. I better get out. *(She gets up, quickly, and puts her shoes on.)*
Simon: What's the matter? Anything wrong?
Regina: It's nothing. Bessie had a little shock this morning and it upset her. But she's all right again.

SIMON: You'd better jump into a cab, Bessie, and go home.

BESSIE: No, I'm all right, again, Mr. Simon, honest I am. I'm goin' back to the board now.

SIMON: Well, listen, if you're not feeling all right, I want you to go home.

BESSIE: I'm all right, Mr. Simon. Thanks ever so much, Miss Gordon. *(She exits.)*

SIMON: What's the matter with her?

REGINA: She saw somebody jump out of the window of an office building and it gave her a bad shock.

SIMON: God, that's awful! Where was it?

REGINA: I don't know exactly where. Somewhere on Fifth Avenue.

SIMON: It's terrible! Imagine a fellow doing a thing like that.

REGINA: Well, I suppose if you're tired of living, it's as good a way as any to end it.

SIMON: What, jumping out of a window like that?

REGINA: Why not? A few seconds and it's all over. I guess people don't do it unless they have a pretty good reason.

SIMON: What the hell are *you* so morbid about?

REGINA: I'm not morbid. Only, we don't ask to be brought into the world, and if we feel like leaving it, I don't see that it's anybody's business but our own.

SIMON: What's the matter? Don't you feel well or something?

REGINA: Yes, of course! I'm just talking a lot of nonsense, that's all. I haven't been able to get Mrs. Simon yet. She left home early this morning, with the children. I've left messages at half-a-dozen places. She's sure to get one of them.

SIMON: Is Breitstein here?

REGINA: Yes sir; he's waiting outside.

SIMON: I'll see him right away. Wait a minute. See if you can get me Francis Clark Baird.

*(*REGINA *calls on her telephone.)*

SIMON: Is there anything important in the mail?

REGINA: There's a letter from Mr. Upjohn, confirming the terms of settlement in Arrow against the Radio Corporation. And there's a transcript of the minutes of the directors' meeting of the International Metal Refineries.

SIMON: Anything else?

REGINA: Nothing of importance. A check came in from the Murray Packing Company.

SIMON: How much?

REGINA: Ten thousand, plus two hundred and some odd dollars for disbursements. I forget the exact amount.

SIMON: Never mind it. *(*REGINA's *phone rings.)* See if that's Baird.

*(*REGINA *answers the phone.)*

REGINA: Mr. Baird is not in.

SIMON: Oh! When is he expected? Wait a minute! Is that his secretary?

REGINA: Yes sir.

SIMON: I'll talk to her, myself. Hello— Is this Mr. Baird's secretary?— This is Mr. Simon speaking; Mr. George Simon— Do you know when Mr. Baird will be in?— Oh, I see— Well, do you know where he can be reached?— Well, he's in town, isn't he?— Oh, I see; you don't know that, either— Do you think you're likely to hear from him during the day?— Yes, it's all pretty indefinite, isn't it?— Well, if you do hear from him, will you tell him that I called and ask him if he'll be good enough to call me? Thank you very much— Good-bye. *(He hangs up the receiver.)* You'd think that Baird could afford to employ a more convincing liar than that. All right, I'll see Breitstein now. *(*REGINA's *telephone rings.)* See if that's Mrs. Simon.

REGINA: *(After answering the phone.)* It's Mrs. Schwarzfeld.

SIMON: I'm in court and may not be back today. She can get me in the morning. *(*REGINA *relays this message.)* Is Breitstein coming in?

REGINA: Yes sir.

SIMON: All right. And I don't want to be disturbed. Have I any engagements?

REGINA: Lunch at twelve-thirty with Senator Wells.

SIMON: Yes, I must keep that. Anybody else?

REGINA: I've put off all the others. Except that Becker boy. I couldn't reach him.

SIMON: What Becker boy?

REGINA: You know, that young Communist—

SIMON: Oh yes. Well, that's not important. All right, Breitstein, come right in.

*(*JOHANN BREITSTEIN *enters, a fair German in the early thirties.)*

SIMON: Rexie, see that I'm not disturbed, will you?

REGINA: Yes sir. *(She exits.)*

SIMON: Hello, Breitstein. Glad to see you again.

BREITSTEIN: I'm very glad to see you, Mr. Simon.

SIMON: Sit down. How have you been?

BREITSTEIN: I been fine, Mr. Simon. I got a good job, now.

SIMON: You have? What are you doing?

BREITSTEIN: I'm assistant cameraman for the Pathé newsreel.

SIMON: Is that so? Well, that's great!

BREITSTEIN: I don't need to ask you how you are, Mr. Simon. I read about you in the papers almost every day.

SIMON: Yes, I manage to keep busy. Listen, Breitstein, I'll tell you why I asked you to come in. Oh, have a cigarette, will you? Or a cigar.

BREITSTEIN: Thanks, I'll take a cigarette.

SIMON: Breitstein, has anybody been talking to you lately about that case of yours?

BREITSTEIN: Why no, Mr. Simon, they haven't.

SIMON: Nobody's approached you or asked you any questions?

BREITSTEIN: No sir. Why, is there anything—

SIMON: Well, the reason I've sent for you is that I want to put you on your guard. There's a complication that's come up and you've got to be prepared to answer a lot of questions.

BREITSTEIN: What kind of a complication, Mr. Simon?

SIMON: Well, it seems that this fellow Whitey Cushman has been doing some talking.

BREITSTEIN: Why he's up in Elmira, doing twenty years for manslaughter.

SIMON: I know it; but he's been telling some people that we cooked up that alibi.

BREITSTEIN: Holy Moses, Mr. Simon, does that mean that they're going to come after me again?

SIMON: Yes, they're likely to.

BREITSTEIN: Holy smoke, Mr. Simon. What am I going to do?

SIMON: Now don't get excited, Breitstein. I think maybe everything will be all right, if you just do what I tell you to.

BREITSTEIN: Well, sure I will, Mr. Simon. Gee whiz, I got a wife and family now. I don't know what I'd do if—

SIMON: What you've got to do is stick by that alibi story, understand?

BREITSTEIN: Yes sure, Mr. Simon, whatever you say. And you think—

SIMON: I'll do the best I can for you. And I guess between us, we can fix it up all right. But we've got to stick together, Breitstein. You know it just might happen that somebody would try to make trouble for me, too.

BREITSTEIN: For you, Mr. Simon?

SIMON: Yes. You know I took an awful chance in order to get you out of that jam you were in. And if this thing were to get up before the Bar Association, there might be a nasty stink about it.

BREITSTEIN: Well, gosh, Mr. Simon, I wouldn't want you to get into trouble on account of me. Why, everything I got, I owe to you. Jiminy, if it wasn't for you, I'd be in for life. I'd go through fire and water for you.

SIMON: *(Rising.)* All right, Breitstein, thanks. I knew I could count on you. Just keep all this under your hat, and if anybody questions you, just stick to your story and act dumb. And let me know, if you're approached.

BREITSTEIN: You betcha. And you think everything's going to be all right?

SIMON: Well, I hope it is. Why, don't you?

BREITSTEIN: Oh yes, sure. Only I was just thinking—

SIMON: What?

BREITSTEIN: Well, I was thinking in case they should look up the hospital records.

SIMON: What hospital records?

BREITSTEIN: The hospital records of Whitey Cushman.

SIMON: What hospital records of Whitey Cushman. What the hell are you talking about?

BREITSTEIN: Well, you know the day it happened, the day he said I was in his house, he was in the hospital.

SIMON: You mean to say that the day you robbed the bath-house, Whitey Cushman was in the hospital?

BREITSTEIN: Yes. He used to have fits—what do you call them?— epileptic fits; and they took him to the hospital.

SIMON: Holy—! Are you sure of this, Breitstein?

BREITSTEIN: Yes, sure. That's why I had to pay him two hundred dollars to testify. He was afraid they'd find out about him being in the hospital that day. I thought you knew all about it, Mr. Simon.

SIMON: It's the first I ever heard of it. What hospital was it, do you know?

BREITSTEIN: I think it was the Polyclinic. Mr. Simon—

SIMON: All right, Breitstein, I've got to think about this. I may ask you to come in again, in a day or two. Good-bye.

BREITSTEIN: Good-bye, Mr. Simon. I hope everything's going to be all right.

SIMON: Yes, so do I.

*(*BREITSTEIN *exits.* SIMON *sits biting his lips and pounding the desk with his fists. Then he pushes the call button, and rising, walks about the office.* REGINA *enters.)*

SIMON: What is it, Rexie?

REGINA: You rang.

SIMON: Did I? Well, I forget what I wanted.

REGINA: Your brother is outside.

SIMON: Oh, he is, is he? Well, I don't want to see him. No, wait a minute. Let him wait.

REGINA: Yes sir. *(She exits.)*

SIMON: *(On the interoffice phone.)* Hello— Say, John, I want to talk to you about something— Oh. Well, come in when you're through, will you?— All right. *(He pushes the call button.* REGINA *enters.)* Have my brother come in.

REGINA: Yes sir.

(She exits. SIMON *goes to the window and looks out.* DAVID SIMON *enters; a slovenly, shifty fellow, some years younger than* GEORGE.*)*

DAVID: Morning, Georgie.

SIMON: *(Turning.)* What? Oh, it's you, is it? Well, what the hell do you want?

DAVID: Well, I just came in to—

SIMON: Oh, you just came in, did you? Well, you can just get out again. I don't want to see your dirty mug around here.

DAVID: Geez, Georgie, don't get sore. I just wanted to tell you—

SIMON: I don't care what you wanted to tell me, you lousy bum. You think I've got time to listen to anything you've got to say? What the hell do you mean by passing around bum checks, you heel?

DAVID: Well, that's what I was goin' to tell you, Georgie. You see, I happened to get into a little crap game—

SIMON: What do you mean, you happened to get into a little crap game? What the hell are you, anyhow, a Pullman porter?

DAVID: Geez, Georgie, just give me a chance and I'll—

SIMON: Shut up, you louse! I'm the one that does the talking around here. You listen to what I got to say, do you hear me?

DAVID: Sure, I'll listen, Georgie.

SIMON: You'd better listen, if you know what's good for you. Well, this is what I got to say—and this time I mean it. It's the last time you're going to get anything out of me. Have you got that through your thick head?

DAVID: I certainly appreciate you helpin' me out, Georgie. I wouldn't of asked you, only—

SIMON: Do you think I'd do anything for you, you cockroach? I wouldn't lift my little finger to save you from the electric chair. I only did it because Mama asked me to, that's the only reason.

DAVID: It's the last time, Georgie. I swear to God it is.

SIMON: It better be. The next time you can go to jail, that's what you can do. And what's more, I'll have myself appointed special prosecutor, so that you'll be sure of getting a good, long term. If you haven't got any respect for me, you ought to have some for Mama.

DAVID: Geez, Georgie, everybody can make a mistake, once in a while.

SIMON: Yes? Is that so? Well, I guess you're one of God's mistakes. All right, that's all I got to say to you.

REGINA: *(Entering.)* Mrs. Simon is on the phone.

SIMON: All right; I'll talk to her right away. *(*REGINA *exits.)*

DAVID: Mama tells me you got a swell-lookin' wife, Georgie. Well, give her my regards, even though I guess she never heard of me.

SIMON: All right. Get out, now. And here. *(Tossing him a bill.)* Buy yourself a hat. You look like one of Coxey's army.*

DAVID: Thanks, Georgie. I hope you have a nice trip to Europe. *(He exits.)*

SIMON: Hello, darling— Sorry to keep you waiting— You're not angry, are you, sweetheart, that I couldn't get home last night? Listen, dear, I've got a little bad news for you— Well, I'm afraid we'll have to postpone the trip to Europe— Something of the utmost importance has come up and I can't get away.— Well, I can't over the telephone. Where are you?— Well, why don't you come in?— That's all right. Bring them along— All right; as soon as you can get here— All right— Good-bye, sweetheart.

(He hangs up the receiver and sit motionless for a moment. Then he pushes the call button. REGINA *enters.)*

SIMON: Rexie, I've changed my plans about going to Europe. *(She looks at him in silence.)* Something has come up and I won't be able to get away for a while.

REGINA: That's a shame.

SIMON: Well, it can't be helped. Just keep it under your hat for the present, will you?

REGINA: Yes sir. *(She stands looking at him.)*

SIMON: All right; that's all for just now. *(*REGINA *exits.* TEDESCO *enters.)*

TEDESCO: I couldn't get rid of that woman, George.

SIMON: It's all right, John. Sit down. I want to talk to you.

*(*TEDESCO *seats himself.* SIMON *paces the room.)*

*A body of jobless men who, led by social reformer Jacob Sechler Coxey, marched on Washington after the Panic of 1893 to petition Congress for relief measures.

SIMON: *(At length.)* Listen, John, I'm in a hell of a bad spot. *(TEDESCO looks at him, attentively.)* I'll tell you what it is. You know Francis Clark Baird, don't you? The cornerstone of the Union League Club and the right-hand man of the Lord God Jehovah?

TEDESCO: Yes.

SIMON: Well, he's got something on me; and he's going to break me.

TEDESCO: What do you mean, he's got something on you?

SIMON: Well, you'll think I'm crazy when you hear this, and maybe you're right. But I once helped a fellow out of a jam by putting over a fake alibi.

TEDESCO: For God's sake! Subornation of perjury!

SIMON: They can't get me on a criminal charge. The statute of limitations has run. But what the hell's the difference? They can disbar me, and they will!

TEDESCO: But, George, how did you ever get yourself mixed up in anything like that?

SIMON: Don't ask me! I was just a goddam fool, that's all. I'll tell you how it happened. A kid by the name of Breitstein had stolen twelve dollars out of a locker in a bathhouse. Well, I advised him to plead guilty and get off with a few months, and then I discovered that he was a fourth offender and that a conviction meant a life sentence. Well, I didn't know what the hell to do about it. So, finally, Breitstein said that he could get a fellow named Whitey Cushman to swear that Breitstein was in his house in Jamaica the day the robbery was committed. I couldn't refuse, John. I'd known the kid and his family since God knows when. I knew he'd go straight if I got him off—and he has, too! I just couldn't see that kid get a life sentence. So, like a sucker, I went into it. And now, the chickens are coming home to roost.

TEDESCO: But has this fellow Breitstein been squealing?

SIMON: No, Cushman. He's doing twenty years in Elmira and now I guess he's decided to make a play for a parole. And, of course, Francis Clark Baird has to be on the Parole Board. It's funny, in a way. For years, that Yankee has been trying to get something on me, and every time he's drawn a blank. And now, this one thing that was dead and buried and forgotten, falls right into his lap, and it's as good as if I'd misappropriated a million dollars.

TEDESCO: But can't you bluff it through, George?

SIMON: Well, maybe yes and maybe no. Breitstein was just here. They can't do anything to him, of course, but I've thrown a scare into him and I guess I can rely upon him. The trouble is that the case won't bear any investigating. I've been over the record and it's phoney as hell right on its face. And now I've just learned from Breitstein that Cushman was in the hospital on the day of the robbery. That sews it up for me, good and proper.

TEDESCO: God! *(He springs to his feet and paces the room.)*

SIMON: What am I going to do, John? They're going to disbar me, as sure as God made little green apples. It's rich, isn't it?

TEDESCO: I guess there's not much use going to Francis Clark Baird with the whole story?

SIMON: That's a laugh, John. You might just as well throw a biscuit to a man-eating tiger. Anyhow, I've been trying to make an appointment with him and he's been dodging me. I could hear him sharpening his knife, over the phone.

TEDESCO: I know some ways that you could get him that would put an end to his funny business forever.

SIMON: John, listen. *(Seizing him by the arms.)* We're a long way from Sicily, boy. Put it out of your mind, for God's sake. You'll make me sorry that I told you, in a minute.

TEDESCO: Well, what good is a rat like that? He's out after *our* scalps, isn't he? And why? Because we came from the streets and our parents talk with an accent.

SIMON: What's the good of talking about all that? He's technically right and he's doing his duty, as a member of the grievance committee. The rest is off the record and not worth a hoot in hell.

TEDESCO: Well, we've got to get you out of it, that's all. Give me some time to think about it.

SIMON: Yes, that's what I want you to do, John. I'm not licked yet. But it's going to take some headwork to get me out of this. I'll pull all the wires I can, or do any goddam thing, so long as I get out of it. God, disbarment! After all these years, and all I've sweated through to get where I am. I don't think I could face it, John.

TEDESCO: George, I don't need to tell you—

SIMON: No, you don't, John. I know I can count on you to the last drop of blood. That's the one bright spot in the picture. I've got you and one or two other friends that'll stick to the finish. And a wife that's one hundred percent. That's the tough part, now, John. I've got to break it to Cora.

TEDESCO: Why do you have to tell her?

SIMON: Oh, I've got to. She's entitled to know. Everything's always been open and above-board between us. Anyhow, I've got to call off this European trip and she has to know why. *(Looking at his watch.)* I'm going around to the Polyclinic Hospital now, to look up those records. *(Extending his hand.)* Thanks, John.

TEDESCO: *(Grasping* SIMON's *hand.)* George—!

SIMON: I know, boy.

TEDESCO: Don't worry about it, George.

SIMON: Well, it's something to worry about. *(*REGINA *enters.)* I'm going out for a few minutes. I won't be long.

REGINA: Yes sir. That Becker boy is here.

SIMON: He'll have to wait until I get back. And if Mrs. Simon comes, let her wait in here for me.

REGINA: Yes sir.

*(*SIMON *exits.* TEDESCO *stands looking out of the window.)*

REGINA: *(After considerable hesitation.)* Mr. Tedesco.

TEDESCO: *(Turning.)* What?

REGINA: I don't want to be inquisitive, but I have a feeling that Mr. Simon is in some kind of trouble. Is he?

TEDESCO: Trouble? No, he's not in any trouble.

REGINA: Well, I know it's none of my business and I shouldn't have asked. But I just wanted to tell you that if there's anything that I can do, it doesn't matter what, you can count on me.

TEDESCO: All right, Rexie; I guess Mr. Simon knows that. But there's nothing to worry about.

(He exits. REGINA *remains, troubled and deep in thought.)*

WEINBERG: *(Entering.)* Oh, isn't G.S. in?

REGINA: No.

WEINBERG: Here's that Richter separation agreement. He wants to look it over.

REGINA: All right. I'll give it to him when he comes in.

WEINBERG: Thank you. *(Looking at her.)* Aren't you feeling well today?

REGINA: Yes, of course.

WEINBERG: You don't look very well.

REGINA: I wish you wouldn't worry so much about me, Mr. Weinberg. I'd really prefer it if you didn't.

WEINBERG: You might at least be civil to me. Everywhere else I go, people treat me with civility. Everywhere but here.

REGINA: I try to be civil to everybody, Mr. Weinberg. But you seem to think that because you work in the same office with somebody, that you have to get personal right away.

WEINBERG: All I did was to inquire about your health. I can't see that there's anything in that to take offense at.

REGINA: I'm not taking offense, only— *(Impatiently.)* Oh, well, what's the difference! I'll have to ask you to excuse me, Mr. Weinberg. I have a lot of work to do. *(She goes towards her office.)*

WEINBERG: Miss Gordon.

REGINA: *(Turning.)* What?

WEINBERG: Will you have lunch with me today?

REGINA: No, I can't. I have some shopping to do.

WEINBERG: You don't think up very clever excuses.

REGINA: We can't all be clever, Mr. Weinberg.

WEINBERG: It isn't necessary to be sarcastic, Miss Gordon. I know what your opinion of me is.

REGINA: I'm sorry, but I really can't stand here all day, talking about nothing. Excuse me. *(She exits to her office and closes the door.)*

WEINBERG: *(Despairingly.)* Regina, I—

(He turns and exits abruptly. The scene blacks out.)

CURTAIN

Scene 2

The outer office. Bessie *is at the switchboard. Between the windows,* Mrs. Becker *and* Harry Becker *are seated.* Becker *is a boy of twenty, shabbily dressed. His head is entirely swathed in bandages.*

Bessie: Simon and Tedesco— Who's calling, please?— One moment, please— Colonel Wertheimer calling Mr. Simon— Yes, thanks, Miss Gordon, I'm feeling much better— No, I'm all right, honest I am— Hello, here's Mr. Simon's secretary. Go ahead.

(While she is talking, Weinberg *comes out of the door to* Simon*'s office and crosses to the library.)*

Weinberg: *(Stopping.)* Oh, Bessie, get me the County Lawyers' Association, will you please?
Bessie: I'll give you a wire.

*(*Weinberg *is about to protest, then goes into the library.)*

Mrs. Becker: Harry, you got bad pains?
Becker: I tell you it's nothing. Forget about it, can't you?
Bessie: Hello— Yes sir—

(She dials a number. Goldie *comes out of the library, humming softly, and crossing to the entrance door, exits.)*

Bessie: Simon and Tedesco— Oh, hello, Gracie— I was jus' gonna call you— Wait a minute— Hello, is Mr. Bellini there? Mr. Tedesco calling— Hello, Mr. Bellini?— One moment, please— Here's Mr. Bellini, Mr. Tedesco— All rightee, go ahead— Hello, Gracie— Say, listen, can you imagine what happened to me this morning?— Well, I was on my way to the office, see, and a man jumps out of about a twelfth-story window almost right in front of my eyes— I'll say it is. It makes me sick to my stomach just to think about it— Wait a minute— Simon and Tedesco— Mr. Weinberg? One moment, please— Hello, Gracie— Oh God, don't talk about it! It was awful— Yeah, it's a wonder I didn't faint—

*(*SANDLER*, meanwhile, has crossed from the library to the entrance door.)*

SANDLER: I'm going to Special Term Part II, the Surrogate's Court and lunch. Did you hear what I said, Greta Garbo?

BESSIE: Yes, I heard you. I heard you. Go ahead.

SANDLER: I can hardly bear to tear myself away from you. Here's a little present for you. *(He puts a paper clip down her back.)*

BESSIE: Say, quit it, will you! *(She strikes at him.)*

SANDLER: *(His hand to his heart, sings.)* Give me something to remember you by. *(He exits.)*

BESSIE: Fresh egg! *(She reaches down her back for the paper clip.)* What?— Oh, a fresh mugg in the office, putting things down my back— Yeah, I know, they never can keep their hands to themselves— Wait a minute— Hello— Why, she just stepped outside for a minute, Mr. Tedesco— All right, sir, I'll tell her as soon as she comes in— Hello, Gracie— No, I don't think I'll go out to lunch today— Yeah, I know, but I think I better give my stomach a rest— Well, I'll just send out for a chocolate malted or something— Wait a minute— Simon and Tedesco— Who's calling, please?— One moment, please— Your sister, Miss Gordon— All rightee, go ahead— Say, Gracie, listen. I was out with Fred last night— Well, it all ended up in an awful fight— Well, wait till I tell you about it— *(As the door opens and* CORA *and her* CHILDREN *enter.)* Listen, I'm busy now. I'll call you back this afternoon— How do, Mrs. Simon? Why, hello, Richard. Hello, Dorothy.

THE CHILDREN: *(Distantly.)* Hello.

CORA: Tell Mr. Simon I'm here, please.

BESSIE: He's not in right now, Mrs. Simon.

CORA: Are you sure? Why, he's expecting me.

BESSIE: I think he'll be back soon. I'll ask Miss Gordon as soon as she's through talking on this wire.

CORA: Well, we may as well sit down, children. I don't understand his not being here. *(They all seat themselves.)*

BESSIE: I don't think he'll be long.

*(*MCFADDEN *enters.)*

MCFADDEN: Good morning, Mrs. Simon.

CORA: Good morning.

MCFADDEN: Good morning, Miss. Good morning, young man.

THE CHILDREN: Good morning.

MCFADDEN: Well, you sure are growin' up, the two of you. *(To* CORA.*)* Why, the last time I saw them, ma'am, they were little bits of shavers.

CORA: Really! *(To* BESSIE.*)* Are you sure Mr. Simon didn't leave a message for me.

BESSIE: He probably did with Miss Gordon. She'll be through in just a minute, now.

*(*MCFADDEN *hesitates a moment, then goes into the library.)*

DOROTHY: Who's that man?

CORA: He's one of the employees in the office, here.

RICHARD: People always make such original remarks about how big you're getting. What do they expect you to do, get smaller?

DOROTHY: Look at the man with his head all bandaged, mother.

CORA: Don't make remarks about people, Dorothy.

BESSIE: Simon and Tedesco— Who's calling, please?— One moment, please: the wire's busy— She's through now— Miss Gordon, Mrs. Simon and the children are here. And Mr. Vandenbogen is on the other wire— All rightee, Mr. Vandenbogen, go ahead— *(To* CORA.*)* Miss Gordon will be out, just as soon as she's taken this call.

CORA: Well, really—

TEDESCO: *(Coming out of his office.)* Bessie, hasn't Goldie come in, yet?

BESSIE: Not yet, Mr. Tedesco.

TEDESCO: Oh, how do you do, Mrs. Simon?

CORA: How do you do, Mr. Tedesco?

TEDESCO: Are these your children? I don't think I've ever met them, before.

CORA: Haven't you really? Richard, Dorothy, this is Mr. Tedesco.

TEDESCO: *(Shaking hands with them.)* Hello, Richard. Hello, Dorothy.

THE CHILDREN: Hello.

TEDESCO: Well, young man, are we going to have you here in the office, some day?

RICHARD: No.

CORA: My father wants Richard to enter the diplomatic service.

TEDESCO: Well, that's too bad. We could use a bright young fellow around here. Does George know you're here?

CORA: He doesn't seem to be in. I can't understand it. He knew I was coming.

TEDESCO: Oh yes, that's right. He had to go out for a few minutes on a very important matter. He'll be back soon. Well, if you'll excuse me—

CORA: Certainly.

TEDESCO: Good-bye, Richard. Good-bye, Dorothy. I'm glad to have met you.

THE CHILDREN: Good-bye.

TEDESCO: *(To* CORA.*)* I didn't expect them to be so grown up. *(*THE CHILDREN *exchange a look.)*

TEDESCO: *(To* BESSIE.*)* I want Goldie, as soon as she comes in.

BESSIE: Yes sir.

*(*TEDESCO *exits to the library.* REGINA *enters from* SIMON*'s office.)*

REGINA: Good morning, Mrs. Simon.

CORA: Good morning, Miss Gordon. I've been waiting quite a while.

REGINA: I'm very sorry. I've been on the telephone. Hello, Richard. Hello, Dorothy.

THE CHILDREN: Hello.

CORA: Isn't Mr. Simon in?

REGINA: No ma'am. But he'll be back in a few minutes. He left word for you to wait in his office.

CORA: I have a thousand things to do this morning. Well, I suppose there's nothing to do but wait.

(She rises and THE CHILDREN *rise, too.)*

REGINA: He'll only be a few minutes.

CORA: I think you'd better wait out here, Richard and Dorothy.

*(*THE CHILDREN *sit down again.)*

RICHARD: Are you going to be long?

CORA: No, I can't stay long. I have too many things to do. *(She exits.)*

REGINA: *(To* THE CHILDREN.*)* There's a wonderful view from the windows.

RICHARD: We've been up the Chrysler Building and the Empire State.

DOROTHY: And the Woolworth.

RICHARD: The Chrysler and the Empire State are bigger.

DOROTHY: I know it.

REGINA: *(Going to bookcase.)* I'll see if I can find you a magazine to read. I don't know if there's anything that will interest you. Yes, here's the *National Geographic.*

RICHARD: I don't care to read it, thank you.

DOROTHY: Neither do I.

*(*REGINA *puts the magazine back on the bookcase.)*

BESSIE: Simon and Tedesco— One moment, please— Devore and Wilson calling, Miss Gordon.

REGINA: I'll take it in my office. *(She exits.)*

BESSIE: One moment, please— *(*GOLDIE *enters.)* Goldie, Mr. Tedesco wants you right away. He's in the library. All rightee, go ahead.

GOLDIE: Goodness! Are these the little Simon children?

RICHARD: I'm Richard Dwight, Jr.

DOROTHY: And I'm Dorothy Dwight.

GOLDIE: *(To* BESSIE.*)* I guess they still keep their father's name. Goodness, haven't they grown, though! Well, you're both very nice-looking children. Good-bye. *(She pats the cheek of each, then exits to the library.)*

DOROTHY: Who's that awful person?

RICHARD: Oh, some old stenographer or something. How many more people do we have to talk to?

DOROTHY: Yes, that's what I say.

BESSIE: Hello, Bank of America?— Mr. Riccordi, please— Well, leave word for him to call Mr. Tedesco, please— That's right. Thank you— *(To* THE CHILDREN.*)* Well, I suppose you'll be having lunch with your father today.

RICHARD: Our father lives in Washington.

BESSIE: I mean Mr. Simon.

RICHARD: He's not our father.

DOROTHY: Our father's name is Richard Dwight. He's in the Apartment of State.

RICHARD: *De*partment.

DOROTHY: *De*partment of State.

BESSIE: Oh, I know Mr. Simon isn't your real father. But being married to your mother makes him your father in a way.

RICHARD: No, it doesn't.

MCFADDEN: *(Entering from the library.)* Well, are you learnin' all about the inside of a law office?

*(*THE CHILDREN *do not answer.)*

MCFADDEN: *(To* BESSIE.*)* I'm going to 535 Fifth Avenue for Mr. Tedesco— *(Sotto voce.)* They're high and mighty little beggars, ain't they?

BESSIE: I'll say they are. Oh, Charlie, will you get me a chocolate malted and a tongue on rye on the way back?

MCFADDEN: All right.

BESSIE: *(Giving him money.)* And don't forget: lots of Russian dressing.

*(*MCFADDEN *exits.)*

BESSIE: *(Taking a box of chocolates out of the drawer.)* Want some chocolates?

RICHARD: No, thank you.

BESSIE: Dorothy, how about you?

DOROTHY: *(After a look at* RICHARD.*)* No, thank you.

BESSIE: They're good. Chocolate caramels. Sure you don't want any? *(She eats one.)*

RICHARD: No, thank you.

DOROTHY: No, thank you.

BESSIE: Simon and Tedesco— Who's calling, please— One moment, please— Mrs. Axelrod calling Mr. Simon— All rightee, go ahead— *(She listens in on the conversation.)*

DOROTHY: Who is Mr Tedesco?

RICHARD: He's his partner. Don't you see the name on the door there? Simon and Tedesco.

DOROTHY: Where?

RICHARD: Right there on the door.

DOROTHY: Oh, I see where you mean. Why is it written backwards?

RICHARD: It isn't backwards. You're just seeing it through the glass, that's all.

DOROTHY: But the others don't look like that.

RICHARD: Of course, they don't. You're looking at them from the front, aren't you?

DOROTHY: Oh. But I thought a partner was somebody on your side in a game: like tennis or bridge.

RICHARD: Don't be stupid. It means anybody you're in partnership with.

DOROTHY: Oh. Is he a Jew, too?

RICHARD: No, of course not.

DOROTHY: He has a funny way of talking.

RICHARD: Well, he's some kind of a foreigner. An Italian or something like that. Gosh, I wonder how long we have to sit here. I want to go to a matinée this afternoon.

DOROTHY: I have an appointment with the hairdresser at two.

*(*HENRY *enters from the corridor, wearing his cap.)*

HENRY: Is Mr. Tedesco in?

BESSIE: What? Yes, he's in the library.

(HENRY *puts his cap in his pocket and crosses to the library.)*

DOROTHY: Who's that?
RICHARD: Oh, just some errand boy or office boy.
DOROTHY: Would you like to be an errand boy?
RICHARD: Of course, I wouldn't! Don't ask so many silly questions.

(HARRY BECKER *suddenly stands up.)*

MRS. BECKER: *(Nervously.)* What's the matter, Harry? Don't you feel good?
BECKER: I'm not going to wait around here all day.
MRS. BECKER: Harry, please, be a good boy. He's coming soon.

(BECKER *silently resumes his seat.)*

DOROTHY: *(Sotto voce.)* Who's he, Richard?
RICHARD: Oh, some gangster, probably, that got into a fight.
DOROTHY: Maybe he's a murderer.
RICHARD: Of course not.
DOROTHY: How do you know he isn't?
RICHARD: Don't be silly. He'd be in prison, wouldn't he, if he were a murderer?
DOROTHY: Maybe he escaped.
RICHARD: As though an escaped murderer would be sitting around in an office.
DOROTHY: Sh! He can hear us.
BESSIE: Hello— Yes sir— *(She dials a number.)*
RICHARD: Well, we may as well look at that *National Geographic* as just sit here.

(He is about to go over and get it when HENRY *comes out of the library.)*

RICHARD: Oh, would you mind handing me that magazine, please?

(HENRY *looks at him a moment, then goes over to the bookcase.)*

HENRY: This?

RICHARD: Yes, please. *(HENRY takes it over to him.)* Thank you.

(HENRY goes to the table and begins filling out some forms, every now and then glancing at RICHARD and DOROTHY, who are looking at the magazine.)

BESSIE: Hello— Goldie, tell Mr. Tedesco that that number don't answer, will you?

RICHARD: Look, this is the kind of a movie camera I want. Albert Adams has one and it's three times as good as that old, cheap one that I have.

DOROTHY: Why don't you ask mother to buy one for you?

RICHARD: I will.

DARWIN: *(Entering.)* Mr. Roy Darwin to see Mr. Simon, please.

BESSIE: Yes sir.

DARWIN: Why, hello, Richard. Hello, Dorothy.

RICHARD: Hello, Roy.

DOROTHY: Hello, Roy.

(They both get up to greet him. He shakes hands with RICHARD and kisses DOROTHY.)

BESSIE: Mr. Roy Darwin to see Mr. Simon— All rightee— Mr. Simon's secretary will be right out, Mr. Darwin.

DARWIN: Thank you. Well, what are you fellows doing here?

DOROTHY: We came with mother.

DARWIN: Oh, really, is your mother here?

RICHARD: Yes, she's in his office, waiting for him.

REGINA: *(Entering.)* Those papers are ready for you, Mr. Darwin, if you'll just step in.

DARWIN: Yes. Thank you. Well, I'll see you later, old dears.

(He precedes REGINA into SIMON's office. HARRY BECKER rises but REGINA has gone before he can speak to her.)

MRS. BECKER: Hev a little patience, Harry.

*(*BECKER *resumes his seat.* THE CHILDREN *seat themselves again.)*

DOROTHY: Roy is nice.
RICHARD: Yes, he's a good old scout.

(The scene blacks out.)

CURTAIN

Scene 3

The inner office. CORA *is walking up and down the office impatiently, smoking a cigarette. After a moment, there is a knock at the door of* REGINA*'s office.*

CORA: *(Turning.)* Yes?

DARWIN: *(Opening the door and entering.)* Is it all right? May I come in?

CORA: Hello, Roy. I seem always to be running into you here.

DARWIN: Well, I've had a tiresome business matter to dispose of. And little Miss—the little secretary—said you were in here. So I thought I'd say hello. *(He is about to close the door.)*

CORA: No, don't.

DARWIN: What? Oh, I see what you mean. Little pitchers have big eyes, eh? *(He comes over and kisses her hand.)* How are you, today? You look a little *distrait. (He puts his hat and stick on the table upstage.)*

CORA: I'm more than a little *distrait.* I'm quite provoked.

DARWIN: Anything wrong? Or isn't it any of my business?

CORA: George tells me now that he can't go to Europe.

DARWIN: Oh, really! He's not going to Europe?

CORA: So he told me a little while ago, over the telephone. Some business matter or something has come up.

DARWIN: Well, that's rather disturbing, isn't it, after all your plans are made?

CORA: Yes, it's most disturbing. But that's George for you. He's so impulsive, so impetuous—one never quite knows what to expect next. He has a way of carrying things by storm, of sweeping you off your feet. You know, he carried me off and married me almost before I knew what was happening. It's rather exciting in a way but— *(Breaking off.)* Well, heavens, I seem to be telling you all my troubles.

DARWIN: You know I'm interested.

CORA: Yes, I do, Roy.

DARWIN: Does this change in plans mean that you won't go to Europe, either?

CORA: I don't know. I haven't had time to think about it. I don't know what to do. I've made all my arrangements here, about the house and the children and all. And I've bought my clothes. And I'm meeting people in London and on the Continent. It's really most upsetting.

DARWIN: It does seem a shame to have to give it all up, now.

CORA: Well, I'll see. Goodness, I wish George would get back. I have a thousand things to do.

DARWIN: Can I help?

CORA: No, thanks, Roy. I'll just have to wait now and hear what George has to say.

DARWIN: Well, if I *can* be of any help—

CORA: Thanks, Roy; you're very sweet. That was a lovely tea yesterday.

DARWIN: *You* were lovely; not that that's anything out of the ordinary.

CORA: I don't feel a bit lovely this morning. I feel horrid.

DARWIN: Will you have a cigarette?

CORA: Yes, thanks; I will.

(He gives her a cigarette and a light.)

REGINA: *(Knocking and entering.)* Excuse me.

(She hurries to SIMON*'s desk, finds a paper and goes out, at the downstage door.* CORA *watches her exit.* DARWIN *walks over to chair upstage of the desk.)*

DARWIN: Talk about the way of Martha*! She's a human beehive. But damned little honey, if you ask me.

*In medieval Christian literature, Jesus' friend Martha represents the active life, as contrasted with the contemplative.

CORA: What a vulgar little person!
DARWIN: Was that just the common or secretarial knock, or was it—?
CORA: Yes, it was!
DARWIN: Oh!

(A moment of silence.)

DARWIN: Funny, you know, I've been thinking of going to Europe myself.
CORA: Have you, Roy?
DARWIN: Yes. Chiefly in the hope of running into you somewhere, I confess.
CORA: That would have been nice.
DARWIN: And, now, you're probably not going at all! Well, *c'est la guerre.*
CORA: I wish I knew *what* to do.

(A moment of silence.)

DARWIN: Have you ever been to La Baule?
CORA: Yes, I adore it.
DARWIN: Everyone tells me it's charming.
CORA: You'll love it there.
DARWIN: Well, I don't know what to do, either.
CORA: When would you be sailing, if you did go?
DARWIN: Oh, I don't know. In a week or ten days. I've nothing to keep me here. That is—
CORA: If you go to La Baule, be sure to motor over to Dinard and St. Malo.
DARWIN: I probably shan't be going. *(He rises and walks over to get his hat and stick.)* Am I going to see you soon, Cora?
CORA: Yes, if you want to.
DARWIN: You know I want to. Tea today?
CORA: I can't today; I have Dorothy on my hands.
DARWIN: Tomorrow?
CORA: I wasn't coming in tomorrow. Why don't you drive out and have lunch with me? It's lovely in the country now.
DARWIN: I'd be delighted to. Is it all right?
CORA: Yes, I think so.
DARWIN: About one?

CORA: Yes.
DARWIN: Fine.

(They shake hands. DARWIN *starts to exit.)*

SIMON: *(Offstage.)* Are you there, sweetheart?
CORA: Yes.
SIMON: I saw the car downstairs. I'm sorry— Oh, hello, Mr. Darwin.
DARWIN: Hello, George. I've just been keeping Cora company, until you got back.
SIMON: Yes, I had to go out. I'm sorry to keep you waiting, darling.
CORA: Well, it's all right now that you're here.
DARWIN: Well, I'm going along. Good-bye, George.
SIMON: Good-bye, Mr. Darwin. Did my secretary fix you up all right?
DARWIN: Yes, thanks very much.
SIMON: Don't mention it.
DARWIN: Good-bye, Cora.
CORA: Good-bye, Roy. Oh, I'll tell you what you can do for me, if you're not terribly busy.
DARWIN: Anything you like. I haven't a thing to do for the rest of the day.
CORA: Well, I wish you'd take the children to lunch.
DARWIN: Certainly, I'd like nothing better.
CORA: I don't like them sitting out there so long. I don't think it's a particularly good atmosphere for Dorothy.
SIMON: Oh, are they outside?
CORA: Yes, I didn't know you'd be so long.
DARWIN: I'll take them to the Biltmore, shall I?
CORA: Yes, and I'll join you as soon as I leave here.
SIMON: Wait, I'll have them come in.
CORA: Don't bother, George. Roy can pick them up on the way out.
DARWIN: Yes, of course.
SIMON: Well, I thought I'd like to say hello to them. I haven't seen them for three or four days.
CORA: Well, just as you like.
SIMON: *(At the telephone.)* Have my son and daughter come in.— Oh, and is Charlie McFadden in?— Well, I want to see him, as soon as he gets in. *(To* DARWIN.*)* I

don't have as much time to spend with the children as I'd like to.

REGINA: *(Offstage.)* This way, children. Right in here.

*(*THE CHILDREN *enter, followed by* REGINA, *who goes into her own office.)*

SIMON: Well, hello, strangers. I haven't seen you in a month of Sundays.

THE CHILDREN: *(Indifferently.)* Hello.

*(*SIMON *shakes hands with* RICHARD.*)*

SIMON: And how's my young lady, today?

DOROTHY: I'm all right.

(He attempts to kiss her, but she averts her head.)

RICHARD: Mother, look, this is the kind of a movie camera I want.

CORA: I haven't time now, Richard. Roy is going to take you to lunch now.

DOROTHY: Oh, goody! Are we going to the Ritz?

CORA: No, to the Biltmore.

DOROTHY: Ah, why not to the Ritz? I like the Ritz better.

RICHARD: So do I.

DARWIN: I can take them to the Ritz just as easily, if they prefer it.

CORA: All right, then, make it the Ritz. I'll join you in a few minutes.

SIMON: I'm sorry I can't come along, but I have an important business engagement.

DARWIN: All right, old dears, come along.

(He links an arm through each of theirs.)

SIMON: Good-bye.

THE CHILDREN: Good-bye.

SIMON: Wait, you can get out this way; right through my secretary's office.

*(*DARWIN *and* THE CHILDREN *exit.)*

SIMON: They get along very well with Mr. Darwin, don't they?

CORA: Yes, they're very fond of Roy.

REGINA: *(Entering.)* Excuse me, Mr. Simon.

SIMON: Yes? What is it, Rexie?

REGINA: Mr. Vandenbogen called and will call you again this afternoon. And Colonel Wertheimer would like to know the result of your conference with Senator Wells.

SIMON: All right. I'd like not to be disturbed now.

REGINA: Yes sir.

SIMON: Close both doors, will you please?

REGINA: Yes sir.

(She closes the downstage door, then exits to her office, closing the door behind her.)

SIMON: *(Sitting beside* CORA *on the sofa.)* Well, darling, I'm afraid the European trip is off.

CORA: So you said over the telephone.

SIMON: I know it's a big disappointment to you. And I assure you it is to me, too. I never in my life looked forward so much to anything. But something has come up and I can't get away.

CORA: You were so certain, no longer ago than yesterday, that nothing could keep you from going.

SIMON: Yes, I know it. That's the funny part of it. I would have sworn yesterday that nothing in the world could have made me call off the trip—barring something happening to Mama. And then this thing had to come up.

CORA: What is it: another hundred thousand dollar fee?

SIMON: Why, darling, you don't think a hundred thousand or five hundred thousand would make me call off our little honeymoon trip, do you? I wouldn't have called it off for a retainer from the United States Steel Corporation.

CORA: Then it's not business that's detaining you?

SIMON: Well, it is and it isn't. I don't know just how to tell you.

CORA: Don't tell me, if you don't want to. I didn't mean to be prying.

SIMON: Why, darling, of course I want to. You don't think I'd have any secrets from you, do you? It's just a little hard to explain, that's all. I'm afraid it's going to upset you a little.

CORA: Well, tell me, George, what it is. It doesn't help matters to pile up the suspense.

SIMON: *(Rising.)* No, I guess you're right. *(With a great effort.)* Well, darling, I'm in trouble: the worst trouble I've ever been in in my whole life. *(He pauses.)*

CORA: Well, tell me.

SIMON: Well, I'm threatened with disbarment.

CORA: Oh, how perfectly awful!

SIMON: I knew it would be a shock to you. That's why it took me so long to get it out. And it's been a shock to me, I can tell you. I didn't know anybody could go through such hell as I've been going through these last twenty-four hours.

CORA: But I don't understand it. Disbarment! Why, I thought—

SIMON: Of all the things that could have happened to me! God, you never know from one day till the next.

CORA: But doesn't disbarment imply—?

SIMON: Yes, it does more than imply. It establishes that a man is guilty of conduct which makes him unworthy to practice his profession. That's what I'm faced with this very minute.

CORA: Then—I mean—I'm quite bewildered—

SIMON: Eighteen years I've been a full-fledged lawyer. Eighteen years and nobody's ever had anything on me. And then this one thing, this one, little thing, that was dead and buried, comes up—and bing, out I go like a candle. God, I can't believe it.

CORA: But, what was it that you did, George?

SIMON: Wait until you hear. Then you'll understand the irony of the whole thing. Once, mind you, once in eighteen years—yes, and with a thousand opportunities to get away with murder—once I overstepped the mark and then it was to save a poor devil from going to prison for life. Do you know what it means to frame up an alibi?

CORA: Yes, I think I do. Getting someone to testify falsely—

SIMON: Yes, that's it. I had a hand in framing up an alibi, so that a kid who had committed a number of petty crimes wouldn't have to spend the rest of his life in prison.

CORA: I don't know much about these things. But wasn't that a dishonest thing to do?

SIMON: *(Seating himself at his desk.)* It was conniving at a lie, to prevent a conviction that nobody wanted, not the judge, nor the district attorney, nor the jury; but that the law made inevitable.

CORA: *(Rising.)* Why do you have anything to do with such people; thieves, criminals?

SIMON: I'm a lawyer, darling.

CORA: All lawyers don't have dealings with such people.

SIMON: Somebody's got to defend people who are accused of crime.

CORA: This boy was guilty.

SIMON: Guilty of stealing a few dollars, yes. I'd known the boy since he was a baby. Why, I never would have had a night's sleep if I'd let that boy go up the river for life.

CORA: And now someone has found out and they are going to disbar you, is that it?

SIMON: Yes, someone has found out. And it's just my luck that it happens to be a man who's had it in for me for years: a gentleman by the name of Francis Clark Baird.

CORA: Francis Clark Baird. Why, he's a very eminent lawyer, isn't he? I think I've heard father speak of him. Isn't he one of the Connecticut Bairds?

SIMON: He may be, for all I know. But that doesn't mean much to me. All that I know is that he's got the drop on me and he's going to make me pay through the nose.

CORA: Why do you always put things on a personal basis, George? Isn't it the duty of a man like Mr. Baird?

SIMON: No man has to break another man, unless he wants to. I've locked horns with this Baird a good many times, and he's always come out on the short end. He doesn't like taking that from a nobody, from an East Side boy that started in the police court.

CORA: Is a person who began in the police court necessarily superior to one who grew up in an atmosphere of culture and refinement?

SIMON: Why, darling, you're not siding with Baird, are you?

CORA: It isn't a matter of siding with anyone. But I can't help resenting a little the constant implication that there's some peculiar merit in having a humble origin.

SIMON: I'm not implying that, darling. You ought to know me better than that. I realize my shortcomings. Especially when I compare myself with you. I know that you sacrificed a lot to marry me, and that you've had to put up with a lot of things that you didn't like. And it's because you've been so sweet and understanding about it that I'm putting all my cards on the table: telling you just where I stand and what I'm up against. It's because I know I can count on you to help me through this thing.

CORA: I don't see how I can help you, George.

SIMON: I don't mean that I want you to do anything, sweetheart. I'm going to do whatever can be done. I'm in a tough spot, but I'm going to take an awful lot of licking before I throw up the sponge. It's just having you with me and knowing that you're standing by me that's going to make all the difference to me. Because in you I've got something worth fighting for.

CORA: *(Seating herself.)* I really don't know what to say, George. It's most distressing.

SIMON: Yes, it's just about as bad as anything that could have happened. But there's nothing to do but face it. Maybe something will break for me, who can tell? I've got lots of loyal friends, and when you've got your back to the wall, you can do an awful lot of fighting.

CORA: Yes, that's all very well, George. I understand thoroughly how you must feel about it. And, of course, I'm quite willing to accept your explanation of the whole thing.

SIMON: I knew you would, Cora.

CORA: I know how you've had to struggle and work and it's all very admirable. But it's made it possible for you to accept things that are rather difficult for me to accept.

SIMON: What things, darling?

CORA: Oh, I don't know. There's something distasteful—frankly, something rather repellent—about the whole atmosphere of the thing. This association with thieves and perjurers, and all the intrigue and conniving that goes with it. And now this scandal—it will be a scandal, I'm sure—newspaper publicity and all that.

SIMON: Yes, no doubt about it.

CORA: It's a horrible prospect. I suppose I'll have my picture in the papers, too. And reporters knocking at my door.

SIMON: I'll try to spare you all I can, darling.

CORA: And what are my friends going to say? How am I going to face them?

SIMON: Do they mean more to you than I do?

CORA: That isn't the point. It's something deeply vital to you: your career, your reputation, all the rest of it. But what am I to do? Flutter about pathetically in the background, in an atmosphere of scandal and recrimination? *(She rises.)* No, I can't. The best thing for me to do is to go to Europe as I had planned. If this thing blows over—and let's hope it will—you can join me abroad later. If it doesn't, well, then there's time enough to think about that.

SIMON: You mean you're going to walk out on me?

CORA: That's a very crude way of putting it. And very unfair to me, too. It implies that I'm deserting you when you need me. You know that isn't fair. It isn't as though I could do anything to help you. If there were, I'd be glad to stay. But you've said yourself that there isn't, haven't you now?

SIMON: Yes, I guess I did. It was just that at a time like this, I thought I'd like to have you around, that's all.

CORA: But isn't that just a little selfish, George: to ask me to stay and be subjected to all that miserable business, because it would give you a little satisfaction to have me here?

SIMON: Yes, I guess you're right. I guess it is selfish. I hadn't looked at it in that way. I just thought that maybe you'd want to stay.

CORA: *(Going to him and putting her hand on his shoulder.)* Please don't misunderstand me, George. Please don't think I'm unsympathetic. I assure you I'm terribly upset about this thing. If there were anything I could do, I should be only too happy to do it. Would you like me to ask father to intercede with Mr. Baird?

SIMON: No, I wish you wouldn't do that. *(He goes to his desk.)*

CORA: *(Following him.)* Well, just whatever you say. I do hope sincerely that everything will turn out for the best. And I give you my word, George, that if I could see how giving up my trip could possibly help you out of this difficulty, I'd give it up in a minute. But you know it couldn't.

SIMON: Yes, sure. Just forget about it, darling. It was just a foolish idea of mine. But you're perfectly right. I've got to fight this thing out, myself, and there really isn't anybody that can help me.

CORA: If you think of any way at all in which I can be helpful—

SIMON: I'll let you know. Thanks, sweetheart.

CORA: I've really got to run now. Both Dorothy and I must be at the hairdresser's at two. Will you be coming out to the country tonight?

SIMON: I don't know whether I'll be able to make it or not. I'll phone you, if I can't.

CORA: Yes, do. *(She puts her hand on his.)* Au revoir, George, and I do hope that everything is going to be all right.

SIMON: *(Patting her hand.)* Well, we'll see. Good-bye, sweetheart. Here, you can go out through Rexie's office.

CORA: Don't bother. I know the way. *(She exits.)*

(SIMON seats himself slowly at his desk, his hands stretched out before him. He looks straight ahead of him. Then his eyes wander to CORA's photograph, and taking it up, he holds it before him, in both hands, and stares at it. There is a knock at the downstage door. SIMON, startled, puts down the photograph hastily.)

SIMON: Well? What is it? Come in.

(The door opens and MCFADDEN enters.)

MCFADDEN: Excuse me, chief, but Bessie said you was askin' for me.

SIMON: Yes. Yes. I was asking for you. Sit down. *(MCFADDEN seats himself.)* Listen, Charlie, there's something I'd like you to do for me.

MCFADDEN: Okay, chief.

SIMON: There's a lawyer by the name of Francis Clark Baird—

MCFADDEN: The one that was attorney for Mr. DeWitt in that alienation case?

SIMON: Yes, that's the one.

MCFADDEN: Sure, I know him. He's right across the street in the French Building.

SIMON: Yes. Well, what I'd like you to do, Charlie, is to see what you can find out about him.

MCFADDEN: You want him shadowed, is that it?

SIMON: Yes. I want to know how he spends his time and who his friends are and where he goes nights.

MCFADDEN: I get you.

SIMON: But you've got to go about it carefully, Charlie. I don't want anybody to get on to it, do you understand?

MCFADDEN: Oh, don't worry about that, chief. I shadowed that singer—what was his name? Gerchy or Goochy, or somethin' like that—for a whole month nearly I shadowed him, and he wasn't any the wiser. Don't you remember, we finally caught him in that little hotel way out on Long Island, with that red-headed jane?

SIMON: Yes, I remember. Well, get on the job now, right away. Let everything else go for the present, understand?

MCFADDEN: *(Rising.)* You bet, chief.

SIMON: And give me a daily report of everything he does.

MCFADDEN: Leave it to me, chief. I got lots of ways of finding things out.

SIMON: Never mind the expense. Spend whatever is necessary. And whatever you do, keep it under your hat.

MCFADDEN: Sure, I got you, chief. Mum's the word.

(A knock at the door.)

SIMON: Well? See who it is, Charlie.

*(*MCFADDEN *opens the door and the* BOOTBLACK *enters.)*

SIMON: No, not now, Joe.

JOE: All right, boss. After lunch?

SIMON: Yes. Come back after lunch. Well, no, wait a minute. You'd better shine 'em up now, I guess.

JOE: Sure, boss.

(He kneels at SIMON*'s feet and begins to shine his shoes.)*

SIMON: All right, Charlie, that's all.
MCFADDEN: Yes, sir.

(He exits. SIMON *presses the call button.* REGINA *enters.)*

SIMON: I've put Charlie McFadden on a job that will probably keep him busy for several days. I don't want him interfered with. So, if necessary, take on somebody else temporarily to do his work.
REGINA: Yes sir. Do you want to see Mrs. Becker and her son?
SIMON: Oh, are they still waiting? Tell them to come back tomorrow.
REGINA: They've been waiting a long time.
SIMON: All right, I'll see them. No, wait a minute. Just have the boy come in. I can talk to him better if he hasn't got his mother here to sympathize with him.
REGINA: Yes sir. *(She exits.)*
JOE: Well, boss, I hear you gonna take a nice little trip.
SIMON: What's that? Oh yes, sure.
JOE: You gonna take da missis along, too?
SIMON: Yes, I guess so. Make it snappy, will you, Joe? I'm busy.
JOE: Yes, sure, boss.
REGINA: *(Ushering in* BECKER.*)* Go right in.

*(*BECKER *enters.* REGINA *goes to her office.)*

SIMON: Sit down, Becker.

*(*BECKER *seats himself.)*

SIMON: Now, listen, to what I got to say— *(He breaks off.)* God, they did beat you up, didn't they? Are you badly hurt?
BECKER: I'm all right.
SIMON: You don't look all right. Well, maybe this will be a lesson to you. Maybe in the future, you'll keep your

mouth shut. Now, listen, and I'll tell you what I've done for you. But first I want you to get this straight. The reason I've done it is not because I have any sympathy for you. I think you're just a goddam silly kid. But I've known your mother since you were wearing diapers. She's a good, honest, hard-working woman, and she's had troubles enough in her life, without a young smart aleck like you making more trouble. That's why I'm doing this, do you understand? What's the matter, can't you talk? You seem to be doing a hell of a lot of talking in Union Square.

BECKER: I can talk when there's any need to talk.

SIMON: Well, I'm glad to hear it. Now, listen, and I'll tell you what I've done for you. I've got quite a lot of influence with the district attorney's office and the assistant in charge of this case happens to be a boy who used to work for me. So, I explained to him that you're just a crazy kid that likes to hear himself talk and he's agreed to accept a plea of guilty and to ask the court to give you a suspended sentence. That means that you're all right, as long as you behave yourself and keep your mouth shut. And if you ask me, you're damned lucky to get off so easily.

BECKER: I won't plead guilty and I won't keep my mouth shut.

SIMON: Oh, you won't, won't you? Well, listen, kid, as long as I'm representing you, you're going to be guided by my advice, do you understand?

BECKER: I never asked you to represent me.

SIMON: Well, that's a nice way to talk to me, isn't it, when I'm trying to help you out of a jam. Do you know that I put up the bail for you out of my own pocket?

BECKER: What do I care? Keep your charity for your parasites.

SIMON: Say, listen to me, boy— All right, Joe, that'll do.

JOE: All right, boss. Good-bye, boss. *(He exits.)*

SIMON: Good-bye. All right, now that you haven't got an audience, let's cut out the soapbox stuff and get down to cases. I'm used to making grandstand plays to juries, and I know just how you feel about it. But you've got to promise me that hereafter you're going to keep quiet with the Communist stuff.

BECKER: Listen, Simon, you can't make me keep quiet and neither can anybody else. If the Cossacks want to beat me up, let them do it. They killed my grandfather and my uncle, and the only way they can keep me quiet is to kill me, too.

SIMON: What do you mean, Cossacks? What the hell are you talking about? This is America, not Russia.

BECKER: It's worse than Russia ever was under the Czar.

SIMON: Don't talk so foolish. What do you know about Russia under the Czar? Were you ever there?

BECKER: I was born in the steerage.

SIMON: Yes? Well, anyhow, you had better meals coming over than I had. You know what's the matter with you? I'll tell you what's the matter with you. You're very young—

BECKER: Is it a crime to be young, too?

SIMON: You're very young and you've got a lot of crazy ideas. But I think you've got some good stuff in you, otherwise I wouldn't be wasting my time talking to you. I'm pretty nearly old enough to be your father and I'm going to give you some good, practical advice—

BECKER: Who wants your advice? I don't want your advice or your help or your friendship. You and I have nothing in common. I'm on one side of the class war and you're on the other.

SIMON: Get some sense into your head, will you, and stop talking like a goddam idiot. Class war, my backside. You're going to tell me about class wars, are you? You're going to explain to me about the working class, is that it? Do you think I was born with a silver spoon in my mouth? I started working before I was through shedding my milk teeth. I began life in the same gutter that you did. If I were to tell you what I had to go through to get where I am, it would take me a week. Why, you wouldn't have the guts to go through one-tenth of it, you and your Cossacks and your class wars. Do you think I don't know what it is to sweat and to freeze and to go hungry? You're barking up the wrong tree this time, son. I can give you cards and spades and beat you at your own game. Don't come around me with any of your goddam half-baked Communistic bull and expect me to fall for it.

BECKER: Do you think it's to your credit that you started

in the working class? You ought to be ashamed of it. You ought to be ashamed to admit that you're a traitor to your class.

SIMON: Oh, so I'm a traitor to my class, am I? Why you, little—

BECKER: Yes, a traitor. A dirty traitor and a renegade, that's what you are.

SIMON: All right, I don't want to hear any more out of you.

BECKER: *(Rising.)* Shut up, Simon. I'm going to do the talking here. How did you get where you are? I'll tell you. By betraying your own class, that's how. By climbing on the backs of the working class, that's how. Getting in right with crooked bourgeois politicians and pimping for corporations that feed on the blood and sweat of the workers.

SIMON: That's enough, do you hear?

BECKER: No, it's not enough. I'm going to tell you what you are, Counsellor Simon, sitting here in your Fifth Avenue office, with a bootblack at your feet and a lot of white-collar slaves running your errands for you. You're a cheap prostitute, that's what you are, you and your cars and your country estate and your kept parasite of a wife.

SIMON: *(Rising.)* Shut up, goddam you!

BECKER: No, I won't shut up. I'll say it again. Your kept parasite of a wife, the daughter of capitalists and slave drivers and her two pampered brats.

SIMON: If you don't stop, I'll—

BECKER: Go ahead. Hit me. Beat me up. I'm used to it. I like it. I'd like to be beaten up by Comrade Simon of the working class, who sits rolling in wealth and luxury, while millions of his brothers starve.

SIMON: Get out.

BECKER: Aren't you going to beat me up? Why not? You've got everything and I've got nothing, so why don't you beat me up? Why don't you be true to the traditions of your class, of the capitalistic class?

*(*SIMON *points silently to the door.)*

BECKER: You dirty traitor, you!

(He spits venomously on the floor and exits. Simon *slinks down into his chair. His hand taps the desk, idly.)*

Regina: *(Entering.)* It's time to leave for your luncheon appointment with Senator Wells.
Simon: What? Oh yes. Is it time to leave?
Regina: Yes sir.

*(*Simon *rises and goes towards the door.)*

Regina: Excuse me, Mr. Simon.
Simon: Well?
Regina: Is there anything wrong?
Simon: Of course not. Why should there be anything wrong?
Regina: Because if there were anything I could do—
Simon: You can mind your own business, that's what you can do.

(He exits quickly. Regina *stands looking after him.)*

CURTAIN

ACT III

Scene 1

The inner office. REGINA *is seated at* SIMON'S *desk, telephoning.*

REGINA: Well, I don't know. It's almost five now, you'd better call him in the morning about eleven. You'll be sure to get him, then— All right. Good-bye. *(She hangs up the receiver. The phone rings again almost instantly.)* Hello—all right, I'll speak to her. *(*MCFADDEN *thrusts his head into the door.)* Not yet, Charlie. *(*MCFADDEN *exits.)* Hello— Good afternoon, Mrs. Simon— No ma'am, he hasn't returned from Washington yet— Are you at the pier, now?— Oh, well, he may have gone from Pennsylvania Station to the pier— No, I haven't heard from him all day; but I know he's planning to see you off— How soon will you be at the pier?— All right— All right— Yes ma'am— Yes ma'am— All right, I will— Good-bye, I hope you have a pleasant trip. *(She hangs up the receiver.)* I hope you fall overboard.

*(*WEINBERG *enters, with some papers.* REGINA *ostentatiously picks up a letter from the desk and reads it.* WEINBERG *looks at her, then puts the papers on the desk. She ignores his presence. He looks at her again, is about to speak, then changes his mind and goes out hastily, almost colliding with* TEDESCO, *who is entering.)*

WEINBERG: I'm sorry.
TEDESCO: Oh, did you get that answer out?
WEINBERG: I'm going to dictate it now. *(He exits.)*
TEDESCO: G.S. isn't back yet?

REGINA: No sir, not yet.

TEDESCO: It's almost five. Maybe he won't come in at all, today.

REGINA: I think he may have gone right to the French Line pier. Mrs. Simon's boat sails at six.

TEDESCO: Yes, I guess he did. Oh, I forgot to send her a telegram.

REGINA: There's still plenty of time.

TEDESCO: I guess it's too late for a basket of fruit or some flowers, isn't it?

REGINA: Not for flowers. Do you want me to take care of it for you?

TEDESCO: Yes, if you don't mind.

REGINA: I'll be glad to. How much do you want to spend—about five dollars?

TEDESCO: Yes, I guess so. No, you'd better make it ten.

REGINA: All right. I'll attend to it, right away. Oh, here's Mr. Simon now.

SIMON: *(Entering and seating himself on the sofa.)* Hello, Rexie. Hello, John. *(He is weary and dispirited.)*

REGINA: Good afternoon, Mr. Simon.

TEDESCO: Hello, George.

REGINA: Mrs. Simon just called up about five minutes ago.

SIMON: Oh, did she? Well, get her for me.

REGINA: Why, I don't think I can get her now. She's on her way to the steamer, I don't think she'll be there for about a half-hour yet. I didn't know whether you'd be back or not.

SIMON: Well, call up the pier— No, never mind. I'll go down there in a few minutes. What time does the boat sail—six?

REGINA: Yes sir.

SIMON: Well, have a taxi ready for me, in about fifteen minutes.

REGINA: Yes sir. *(She starts to exit.)*

SIMON: Oh, did you arrange about the books and flowers?

REGINA: Yes sir.

SIMON: Fresh flowers every day, do they understand that?

REGINA: Yes sir, it's all taken care of.

SIMON: All right. And make a note to remind me to send a radiogram every day.

REGINA: Yes sir. Is that all?

SIMON: Yes, that's all. *(REGINA exits.)* Well, John, Pete Malone and I just got back from Washington.

TEDESCO: Well?

SIMON: Well, we might just as well have saved ourselves the trip.

TEDESCO: Didn't you see him?

SIMON: Oh, yes, sure. We saw him. We were with him nearly an hour.

TEDESCO: What did he say?

SIMON: Oh, he handed out the usual line of bull, about what a great guy I am, and how he loves me like a brother, and about what a tough break it is that this thing had to come up.

TEDESCO: Yes, well, is he going to do something about it?

SIMON: He's not going to do a goddam thing about it, John. Pete tried to get him to make a personal appeal to Baird, but it wasn't a bit of use.

TEDESCO: You mean he refused to do it?

SIMON: Well, of course, he wouldn't have the face to refuse right off the bat. He hasn't got the guts to do that. He just talked all around it. You know, he's going to think it over and all that. He can't abuse the power of his office and he can't take advantage of the fact that Baird is his brother-in-law; and this and that. It was pitiable to sit there and watch him crawl. It nearly made me puke.

TEDESCO: The yellow mutt! Why didn't you tell him that if it hadn't been for you, he never would have got the nomination?

SIMON: What's the use? If he doesn't know it already, it's because he doesn't want to know it. I could have told him too about the stumping I did for him, and about the twenty-five thousand I contributed to his campaign fund.

TEDESCO: Well, why the hell didn't you?

SIMON: I tell you it's no use, John. Didn't you know that when you give somebody a helping hand, he always turns around and kicks you in the pants? You see, John, the little fellow's getting ambitious. He's a statesman now. He dreams about the White House and I hear he's having himself measured for a laurel wreath and a toga. You can't expect a big shot who's headed for the Hall of Fame to get himself mixed up with a little shyster who's been up to some funny business. God, it is to laugh!

TEDESCO: I don't blame you for being good and sore: the dirty little sneak.

SIMON: Well, what the hell, John! What did you expect? This is a cut-throat game we're in, and it's every man for himself. Well, I'm about at the end of my rope! Tomorrow the grievance committee meets and once it gets before them I can kiss my career good-bye.

TEDESCO: They haven't got you licked yet, George. You've got some pretty good friends in the Appellate Division.

SIMON: That's not going to help me, John. There's not a thing in the world they can do but disbar me. It's an open and shut case. Technically, I'm as guilty as hell, and any judge that didn't say so wouldn't be fit to be on the bench. No, I don't believe in kidding myself, John. As long as there was a chance of keeping this thing from getting before the Grievance Committee, why maybe I had an out. But I've shot my last bolt. Between us, we've tried everything that could be tried, and now I'm licked. I'm finished—through—kaput.

TEDESCO: The hell you are! We're going to fight and we're going to get you out of it.

SIMON: John, there's not a chance, I tell you. I'm about ready to quit now. Why the hell shouldn't I? *(He rises and paces the room.)* Why shouldn't I thumb my nose at the whole lot of them and walk right out on them?

TEDESCO: You're crazy!

SIMON: Why? Why am I crazy? Let them disbar me. What the hell do I care? I'll go and get on a boat somewhere and spend the rest of my life enjoying myself. Why shouldn't I? I've been working like a horse ever since I'm eight years old. Why shouldn't I quit and see the world and have a good time? Why, this thing may turn out to be a godsend to me: a chance to get out of harness and live a life of leisure, instead of working myself into an early grave.

TEDESCO: You'd get sick of it in a year, just the same as I would.

SIMON: I don't know about that. Why would I? The world's a big place. There's a lot to see and a lot to do. And when I got tired of sightseeing, I could settle down somewhere and get out into the sun a lot. I could take up golf, maybe. Probably be the best thing in the world for me: I'm beginning to put on a little weight. I could— *(He sits down at his desk.)* Jesus, you're right, John. A year! God, I'd go nuts in six months.

TEDESCO: Forget all about that, will you, George? Just make up your mind that you're going to fight this thing and win out.

SIMON: What am I going to do, John? How am I going to spend the rest of my life? How am I going to face the people I know, the people who think I'm the cat's whiskers? How am I going to put in my time? What am I going to do every morning and every afternoon and every evening? I'm no golf player, John. And I don't know an ace from a king. I don't even know how to get drunk. All I know is work. Take work away from me and what the hell am I: a car without a motor, a living corpse.

TEDESCO: Listen, take my advice, and get some sleep tonight. I guess you haven't been sleeping much, have you?

SIMON: No, not much.

TEDESCO: Well, that's what you need, a good sleep. Why don't you lie down and take a nap now?

SIMON: No, I've got to go down to the boat to say goodbye to Cora. I guess it's time to go. *(He rings the bell.)* This is pretty hard on her, John. A woman with her background married to a lawyer who gets himself kicked out of his profession. *(*REGINA *enters.)* Is it time for me to go?

REGINA: You still have a few minutes. I don't think Mrs. Simon will be there yet. Mr. Uccello is on the phone for you, Mr. Tedesco.

TEDESCO: All right, I'll take it in my office. George, will you have dinner with me tonight at the club?

SIMON: Yes, all right. I'll meet you there at six-thirty.

TEDESCO: Okay. *(He exits.)*

REGINA: Do you want to go over your mail?

SIMON: No, let it wait.

REGINA: Mr. Fishman called up and said that he had sold your Gulf Coast Utilities at an average price of 28¼.

SIMON: 28¼? Let's see, what did I pay for it? About 24.

That's four points profit. About forty thousand dollars. What the hell good does it do me?

REGINA: Sir?

SIMON: Nothing. Tell Mr. Tedesco he made twenty thousand dollars profit on the Gulf Coast Utilities deal.

REGINA: Yes sir. *(She is about to go, then stops.)* Oh, I called the Bellevue Hospital a little while ago to inquire about Harry Becker.

SIMON: Yes. Well, how is he getting along?

REGINA: He died early this morning of a cerebral hemorrhage.

SIMON: What? He died?

REGINA: Yes sir. It's terrible, isn't it?

SIMON: It's awful.

REGINA: Think of his poor mother.

SIMON: It's terrible. Listen, I'll tell you what I want you to do. Arrange to have me pay for the funeral expenses. If necessary, buy a little plot somewhere so they don't bury him in Potter's Field. And then, send his mother a check for five hundred dollars. Remind me tomorrow to write her a nice letter. What do you think of that—dead!

REGINA: A young boy like that!

SIMON: Well, maybe he's better off. His troubles are over and, in his own eyes, he died a hero and a martyr to a cause. That's better than living to be old and ending your days in disgrace. Yes, after all, it's not such a bad thing to die at twenty, believing in the millennium and the brotherhood of man. *(*REGINA *wipes her eyes.)* What are you crying about?

REGINA: Nothing.

SIMON: He's better off where he is.

REGINA: I'm not crying about him.

SIMON: No? Then what are you crying about?

REGINA: It's nothing. Nothing at all. Do you—

SIMON: *(Going over to her.)* What's the matter with you, lately?

REGINA: There's nothing the matter with me.

SIMON: Don't you feel well?

REGINA: Yes, of course.

SIMON: Maybe you've been working too hard. Maybe you ought to have a little vacation.

REGINA: No, I don't want any vacation.

SIMON: *(Turning away from her and going back to his desk.)* Maybe I'll be going away myself, soon. Then you can get a good rest.
REGINA: I don't want a rest. I'll get a cab for you, now.

(She exits. SIMON *sits staring ahead of him. Then, suddenly, he rises, goes to the window, throws it open, and looks down. He draws back, with a shudder, and covers his eyes. Then, as he closes the window,* REGINA *enters.)*

SIMON: *(Sharply.)* Well?
REGINA: I forgot to tell you. Charlie McFadden wants to see you about something.
SIMON: It can wait until tomorrow. Are you getting me a cab?
REGINA: Yes sir. Right away.

(She throws him a quick look, then exits. There is a knock at the downstage door.)

SIMON: Well?
MCFADDEN: *(Entering.)* Excuse me, chief. Can I see you for a minute?
SIMON: Not now. I've got to go down to the boat to see Mrs. Simon off.
MCFADDEN: I've got some news for you.
SIMON: What kind of news?
MCFADDEN: About our friend across the way.
SIMON: Who? Baird?
MCFADDEN: That's him.
SIMON: You've found out something about him?
MCFADDEN: I'll say I have.
SIMON: Well, what is it?
MCFADDEN: *(Looking about.)* He's leadin' a double life.
SIMON: What do you mean he's leading a double life?
MCFADDEN: Wait, till I tell you, chief. Remember my tellin' you the other day how I found out that's he always makin' business trips to Philydelphy?
SIMON: Yes, well?
MCFADDEN: *(Seating himself on the sofa.)* Well, yesterday off he goes to Pennsylvania Station and boards a train for Philly, with me right behind him.
SIMON: Well?

McFADDEN: Well, he gets out of the station and hops a taxi, but on account of the noise and bein' afraid of gettin' too close to him, all I can hear him say is "Germantown." So I grabs another hack and tells the driver to folly him.

SIMON: Yes. Go on.

McFADDEN: Well, we're goin' along great, when all of a sudden we gets into a traffic jam and by the time it gets straightened out, we loses him.

SIMON: Well, is that all?

McFADDEN: Lord, no. That's jus' the beginnin'.

SIMON: All right, go on.

McFADDEN: Well, I tells the boy to go ahead out to Germantown, thinkin' we might find the cab around somewhere. But, geez, this Germantown is a hell of a big place.

SIMON: Go ahead.

McFADDEN: Well, after cruisin' around for a couple of hours with the old meter clickin' away, I had to give it up, so I goes back to the station and hangs around waitin' to see if the other taxi is gonna come back. Well, after waitin' about three hours, sure enough back it comes—

SIMON: Was Baird in it?

McFADDEN: No, sir, he wasn't.

SIMON: Go on.

McFADDEN: Well, I gets talkin' to the driver and asks him if he remembers takin' a party out to Germantown. He says he does and he thinks it was Sycamore Drive, but he can't remember the number. So I gets in, and tells him to take me out there—

REGINA: *(Entering.)* Oh, excuse me. The taxi is ready for you.

SIMON: All right. Let it wait a minute. *(REGINA exits.)* Go ahead.

McFADDEN: Well, he takes me out to this Sycamore Drive, but he can't remember just which house it is. So I gets out, and kinda looks in through the windows of the houses, thinkin' maybe I'll see Baird. But I don't see no sign of him.

SIMON: Yes? Well?

McFADDEN: So I begins gettin' acquainted and askin' a few questions around from the feller in the service station and another guy that's got a little tobacco store. It's a kind of a quiet, family neighborhood, with mostly one and two-family houses.

SIMON: Well, what did you find out?

MCFADDEN: Well, I asked if there was any gentleman that came aroun' callin' answerin' to the description of our friend Mr. Baird. At first, nobody seemed to know, but after a while the feller in the tobacco store says: "Why, yes, that sounds like the uncle of little Mrs. Allen, over at 1217." So I gets him talkin' about this Mrs. Allen, and accordin' to this feller she's a poor little widow woman, an' her husband was killed in an automobile accident when the baby was only two months old. So with the insurance money, she bought this little house in Germantown, and she and the baby have been livin' there now for eight years.

SIMON: She lives there all alone?

MCFADDEN: Yes sir: just her and the kid.

SIMON: Well? What else?

MCFADDEN: Well, says the feller in the tobacco store, it's a shame about this young widow woman, and all the kith or kin she has in the whole world is this old uncle from Pittsburgh, that comes to see her once in a while.

SIMON: Pittsburgh?

MCFADDEN: Accordin' to this feller.

SIMON: All right. Go on.

MCFADDEN: So I strolls over to 1217 and it's dark by now, so I looks in the window, and there is the little widow havin' supper with the kid—a pretty, little youngster, too.

SIMON: Was Baird there?

MCFADDEN: No sir, he wasn't.

SIMON: Well, what the hell is all this? What proof have you got that he ever was there?

MCFADDEN: Wait a minute, chief. I ain't done yet. I says to myself: "That little lady don't look like no niece to me, an' as for the kid, he's the spitten image of old man Baird."

SIMON: Jesus Christ, is that what you call evidence?

MCFADDEN: No sir.

SIMON: Go on.

MCFADDEN: Well, I hangs aroun' a little while, but there's nothin' to do till everybody's in bed. So I goes away and has a feed an' takes in a movie, an' along about two o'clock, I goes back to 1217 an' takes a look into the house.

SIMON: What do you mean: you broke into the house?

MCFADDEN: I wouldn't want to admit that, chief. I'd be li'ble to arrest an' imprisonment if I did.

SIMON: Are you crazy? What the hell did you do a thing like that for?

MCFADDEN: Don't worry about it, chief. It was an easy job an' I ain't as much out of practice, as I thought I'd be. I was back in New York before anybody was the wiser.

SIMON: Well, what did you find out?

MCFADDEN: Well, I figgered there'd be letters from him—an' there was.

SIMON: You found letters from Baird to this woman?

MCFADDEN: Yes sir. A whole stack of 'em.

SIMON: Where are they? What do they say?

MCFADDEN: *(Giving* SIMON *a packet.)* Right here, chief. They're all about how much he loves her, an' about how she don't have to worry about her future an' the kid's future, if she'll just keep mum. An'—

SIMON: *(Who has been reading the letters.)* Good God! This is a clear admission of the paternity of the child!

MCFADDEN: Yes sir. An' here's his picture an' the kid's picture. They were both in a frame, on her dresser. I didn't think you'd want the frame: it was a kind of a big leather one. But you can see the kid's the spitten image of him.

SIMON: *(Absorbed in the letters.)* "Your Frankie" huh? So that's the way the Pilgrim Fathers sign their love letters, is it? I suppose we can verify the handwriting easily enough.

MCFADDEN: I've done it, chief. I went through the files in that DeWitt alienation case an' there's three or four letters signed by Mr. Francis Clark Baird. Anybody can see it's the same handwritin'.

SIMON: Well, what do you know about that? So that's what this old boy has been up to, is it?

MCFADDEN: I hope it's what you wanted, chief.

SIMON: Listen, Charlie, these letters are worth a million dollars to me. You don't know what you've done for me. Only you were a goddam fool to go breaking into that house.

McFadden: Well, it's the least I could do, chief, after all you've done for me.

Regina: *(Entering.)* You really should go now, Mr. Simon.

Simon: What? No, not now. I can't leave now. Get me Francis Clark Baird on the phone right away.

Regina: Yes sir. *(She goes to her desk and calls the number.)*

McFadden: Well, if you're not needin' me now, chief, I think maybe I'll go home. I didn't get much sleep last night.

Simon: Come in to see me in the morning, Charlie.

McFadden: Yes sir.

Simon: Wait a minute. What is that address: Sycamore Drive?

McFadden: Yes sir. 1217.

Simon: All right. And Charlie—! *(He puts his finger to his lips.* McFadden *nods and exits.)*

Regina: Mr. Baird is busy and can't be disturbed.

Simon: Oh, he is, is he? Who is that—his secretary?

Regina: Yes sir.

Simon: I'll talk to her. Hello, this is Mr. Simon speaking; Mr. George Simon— You say Mr. Baird can't be disturbed? Well, it's extremely important.— Oh, I see. Well, will you take a message for Mr. Baird?— Thank you. Tell him, please, that a client of mine is interested in the property at 1217 Sycamore Drive, Germantown— No, Germantown, Germantown, Pennsylvania.— Yes, that's right— And tell him I'll be here for another half-hour, in case he wants to call me back— Thank you. Listen, Rexie, as soon as Baird calls back, put him right on.

Regina: It's quarter past five, and the boat sails at six.

Simon: All right, listen. Call up the French Line pier and have them connect you with the steamer. If Mrs. Simon is there, I want to talk to her right away. If she hasn't arrived yet, I want her to call me as soon as she arrives. Tell them it's of the utmost importance. No, wait a minute. Take this note. Darling. Don't sail. Get right off the boat. I think that everything is going to be all right and that I'll be able to go with you in a few weeks. Phone me the instant you get this and have your baggage taken off the boat. Hastily and happily. Get that right out and send a messenger down by taxi. No, wait. Get McFadden and have him take it down. Tell him to give it to Mrs. Simon personally, and then to help her to get her baggage off the boat. Hurry up; you haven't much time.

REGINA: Yes sir.

(She hurries out. SIMON *picks up the letters, and reads them over, laughing and chuckling to himself. Then he walks up and down the office, swinging his arms wildly about and clapping his hands together. Then he goes to his desk and makes a connection on the interoffice phone.)*

SIMON: John, come in, will you?— I've got some hot news.— All right, come in, right away. *(He disconnects and begins pacing the office again.)*

REGINA: *(Entering.)* Do you want to sign this?

SIMON: Yes. Did you tell McFadden?

REGINA: Yes sir; he's waiting.

SIMON: All right. Tell him to take a taxi and get there as quick as he can. And he's to give this to Mrs. Simon, personally.

REGINA: Yes sir.

SIMON: And as soon as Mr. Baird phones, I want to talk to him.

REGINA: Yes sir. *(She exits as* TEDESCO *enters.)*

SIMON: Well, John, I've got that son-of-a-bitch where I want him, at last. Read those.

CURTAIN

Scene 2

The outer office. BESSIE *is at the switchboard.* MCFADDEN *is waiting, with his hat on.*

BESSIE: Simon and Tedesco— Mr. Weinberg? All rightee. Go ahead.

*(*REGINA *enters from* SIMON'S *office.)*

REGINA: Here, Charlie. Take a taxi and get right down to the French Line pier with this. And give it to Mrs. Simon personally.
MCFADDEN: Okay.
REGINA: *(As he exits.)* There's very little time.
MCFADDEN: I'll make it, all right.

*(*REGINA *exits.)*

BESSIE: Simon and Tedesco— Oh, hello, Gracie— Gee, I'm glad you called up. I been tryin' to get you all day— Where you been? Oh. Well, listen, Gracie, there's something I want to ask you— *(She looks about to make sure that she is alone.)* Listen, I want to get the name of that doctor— You know the one I mean— Yeah, that's the one— Wait a minute— *(*HENRY *comes out of the library, whistling, and carrying a stack of letters to be mailed. He crosses the room and exits to the corridor.)* Hello, Gracie. Somebody was just here— Yeah, you bet I'm worried— Yeah, yeah, I didn't sleep a wink all last night— I feel like the wrath o' God— Yeah, I think I'd better. Gee, I'm scared to death— What is it? P like in Paul?— Yeah, I got it— An' what's the address?— Gee, that's way downtown, ain't it?— Six to seven? Well, I better leave right away, then— Wait a minute, Gracie. *(As* HENRY *re-enters.)* Say, listen, Henry, will you do me a favor?

HENRY: What?

BESSIE: Will you take the board, like a nice boy? I got some shoppin' to do before the stores close.

HENRY: Say, don't you think I wanna get home, too?

BESSIE: Ah, come on, Henry, be nice. They'll all be goin' home in a few minutes. I'll do somethin' nice for you some day.

HENRY: Aw, all right.

BESSIE: Thanks, Henry, you're a nice kid.

HENRY: I'll be back in a minute. *(He goes to the library.)*

BESSIE: Hello, Gracie— Yeah, I was gettin' the office boy to take the board, so's I can get away— No, they never go home around here— Yeah, I'm goin' right away— Listen, do you have to be known or anythin'?— Suppose he asks me who I am?— Well, I hope so. God, I'm shakin' like a leaf— Yeah, I'll call you up tonight— Well, I don't know. I'll have to go out to call you. Gee, if my family was ever to find out— Yeah, well, don't mention it to nobody, will you, Gracie?— What?— There's somebody comin' now. I'll call you tonight— Good-bye.

(The outer door opens and a middle-aged MAN *of dignified bearing enters.)*

THE MAN: I'd like to see Mr. Simon, please. Mr. Baird calling. Mr. Francis Clark Baird.

BESSIE: Just a minute, Mr. Baird. I'll see if Mr. Simon is in.

BAIRD: I'm sure he's in. He telephoned my office just a few minutes ago.

BESSIE: He may have gone out again. Just a moment, please. Hello— Mr. Francis Clark Baird is here to see Mr. Simon, Miss Gordon— No, he's right out here, in the office— All rightee— Just a moment, Mr. Baird— Hello— All rightee— Mr. Simon is busy, Mr. Baird, but if you care to sit down and wait, he'll see you in a little while.

BAIRD: Well—is he likely to be long?

BESSIE: She didn't say. But I don't think he'll be very long.

BAIRD: Very well; I'll wait.

(BAIRD walks to the window and looks out. BESSIE begins putting her things away for the day. GOLDIE comes out of the library, dressed for the street. BAIRD turns as he hears the door open.)

GOLDIE: I'm going for the day. Good night.

BESSIE: Good night, Goldie.

(GOLDIE exits. REGINA comes out of SIMON's office. BAIRD turns again.)

REGINA: Bessie, if Mrs. Simon or Charlie McFadden calls up, connect them with Mr. Simon right away.

BESSIE: All rightee.

REGINA: Are you leaving now?

BESSIE: I gotta get some medicine made up for my mother on the way home. She needs it very bad. Henry's gonna take the board.

REGINA: Well, it's all right, as long as someone is at the board. Be sure to tell him—

BESSIE: Oh, yes, sure, Miss Gordon.

REGINA: And if anyone else calls, he's gone for the day.

BESSIE: All rightee.

(REGINA crosses to the library.)

BAIRD: Excuse me. Do you think Mr. Simon is likely to be busy long?

REGINA: I don't think very long, Mr. Baird. Why don't you just sit down and make yourself comfortable?

BAIRD: Thank you. I don't care to sit down.

REGINA: I'm sure he won't be very long. I know he tried to get you a little while ago.

BAIRD: Yes. Thank you.

(REGINA exits to the library. TEDESCO enters from SIMON's office.)

TEDESCO: Tell Goldie I want her, please.

BESSIE: She's gone for the day, Mr. Tedesco.

TEDESCO: Has she? *(He looks at his watch.)* Oh, I didn't know it was so late. Well, never mind. *(He starts to cross to his office, then stops.)* How do, Mr. Baird?

BAIRD: Oh, how do you do?

TEDESCO: I guess you don't remember me. I'm John Tedesco, Mr. Simon's partner.

BAIRD: Oh yes, of course.

TEDESCO: We met in Trial Term, Part Eight, during the trial of DeWitt against Carter.

BAIRD: Yes, I remember. Do you think Mr. Simon will be free soon?

TEDESCO: Well, I really couldn't say. Does he know you're here?

BAIRD: Yes, he does. That is, I assume he does.

BESSIE: Yes, he does, Mr. Tedesco.

TEDESCO: Oh. *(As* REGINA *enters.)* Rexie, will you remind Mr. Simon that Mr. Baird is waiting?

REGINA: He said he'd see Mr. Baird in just a few minutes.

TEDESCO: Well, remind him again, will you?

REGINA: Yes sir. *(She exits to* SIMON's *office.)*

BAIRD: Thank you.

TEDESCO: Well, I was glad to see you again, Mr. Baird. I hope we meet soon again. *(He shakes hands with* BAIRD.*)*

BAIRD: Thank you.

TEDESCO: Good night.

BAIRD: Good night.

*(*TEDESCO *enters his office.* HENRY *enters from the library.)*

BESSIE: All right, Henry. Come ahead, will you? I gotta go.

HENRY: Yeah? An' what about me? When do I get home?

BESSIE: They won't be long. Listen, if Mrs. Simon calls up, or Charlie—

HENRY: I know. I know. Miss Gordon tol' me all about it.

BESSIE: An' this gentleman is waitin' to see Mr. Simon.

HENRY: All right. All right. Go ahead. Beat it.

BESSIE: *(Going towards the library.)* Oh, there's some chocolates there, if you want some.

HENRY: I don' want no choc'lates.

*(*BESSIE *enters the library.)*

REGINA: *(Entering from* SIMON'S *office.)* Mr. Simon will see you now, Mr. Baird.
BAIRD: Thank you.
REGINA: Right in this way. It's the first door to your right.
BAIRD: Thank you. *(He exits to* SIMON'S *office.)*
REGINA: If Mrs. Simon calls while Mr. Baird is in there, put her on my wire.
HENRY: Okay.

*(*WEINBERG *enters from library, wearing his hat, as* REGINA *is about to exit to* SIMON'S *office.)*

WEINBERG: Miss Gordon. *(*REGINA *turns without answering.)* Are you going up on the el* tonight?
REGINA: No, I'm not. *(She exits abruptly.)*
WEINBERG: Well—good night.

(But she has already gone. WEINBERG *goes toward the entrance door.)*

HENRY: Going for the day, Mr. Weinberg?
WEINBERG: Yes.

(He exits. BESSIE *comes out of the library, dressed for the street).*

SANDLER: *(Coming out of the library.)* Wait a minute, Cleopatra.
BESSIE: I'm can't; I'm in a hurry.
SANDLER: Well, can't my chauffeur drop you somewhere?

(He links his arm through hers. HENRY *is highly amused.)*

BESSIE: *(Freeing her arm.)* Say, quit it, will you? Can't you keep your hands to yourself? *(She pushes him away and exits.)*
SANDLER: *(Tossing an imaginary petal in the air.)* She loves me not.

*Elevated train, part of New York City's public transportation system.

(HENRY *laughs.)*

SANDLER: *(To* HENRY.*)* Good night, Oswald. If Peggy Joyce calls me, I can be reached in my box at the Opera.

HENRY: *(Laughing.)* All right. *(*SANDLER *exits.* HENRY *takes the box of chocolates out of the drawer and begins to eat them. Then he dials a number.)* Hello. Sporting Department, please— Have you got the final score of the Yankees' game?— Gee, they did. Oh, boy! An' what about the Robins— All right. Thanks. *(*MRS. LENA SIMON *enters from the corridor.)* Good evenin', Mrs. Simon.

MRS. SIMON: Good evening. Is my son still here?

HENRY: I think there's somebody in there with him.

MRS. SIMON: *(Seating herself to the right of the table.)* It's all right. I'll wait. I got plenty time.

HENRY: I'll tell Miss Gordon you're here.

MRS. SIMON: So you're a telephone operator, too.

HENRY: Oh, I'm jus' takin' Bessie's place. Mr. Simon's mother is here, Miss Gordon. Okay. Miss Gordon will be right out.

MRS. SIMON: It's no hurry. What time do you close the office?

HENRY: Well, we're supposed to close at five, but it's all accordin' if Mr. Simon or Mr. Tedesco stays later or not.

MRS. SIMON: You're going to be a lawyer, too?

HENRY: I don' know.

MRS. SIMON: My son began just like you. When he was thirteen years old, he was office boy for Hirsch and Rosenthal, for four dollars a week.

HENRY: Four dollars! Gee, I started with nine, an' I'm gettin' ten now.

MRS. SIMON: Yes, four dollars he started with. And today, he's the biggest lawyer in New York.

REGINA: *(Entering.)* Hello, Mrs. Simon. How are you today? *(She goes over to her and shakes hands.)*

MRS. SIMON: Oh, I can't complain. And you?

REGINA: I'm all right, thanks. I can't disturb Mr. Simon now. There's someone with him. But I don't think he'll be very long.

MRS. SIMON: I can wait. Miss Gordon, he's feeling all right, is he?

REGINA: Yes, as far as I know. Why?

MRS. SIMON: I don't know. Every day when he calls me up, he sounds so blue.

REGINA: Well, if there's anything wrong, he hasn't told me.

(The door to SIMON*'s office opens.)*

SIMON: No, after you.

BAIRD: Thank you.

(He enters, followed by SIMON.*)*

SIMON: Hello, Mama. What are you doing here?

MRS. SIMON: Hello, Georgie.

SIMON: Mr. Baird, I want you to meet my mother.

BAIRD: How do you do, Mrs. Simon?

MRS. SIMON: How do you do?

SIMON: She's a regular old shrew. If I don't behave myself, she comes after me with a rolling pin.

MRS. SIMON: Georgie, how can you talk such foolishness?

BAIRD: I'm afraid I really must be going.

SIMON: All right, Mr. Baird. Thanks for coming in. Why don't you drop in some day and have lunch with me?

BAIRD: Thank you very much. Good day, Mrs. Simon.

MRS. SIMON: Good-bye.

*(*BAIRD *exits.)*

SIMON: That's my pal, Francis Clark Baird. He's one of the finest, handsomest, blue-blooded stuffed shirts I ever met.

MRS. SIMON: What's the matter with you, Georgie?

SIMON: With me? There's nothing the matter with me! Why should there be something the matter with me? I'm just feeling good, that's all. Can't I feel good if I want to?

MRS. SIMON: I'm glad you're feeling good, Georgie.

SIMON: I'm feeling fine, Mama. I never felt so fine in my

life. How about a little dance? Come on, Lena, give me a dance. *(He seizes her and whirls her around.)*

MRS. SIMON: Georgie, are you *verruckt*? (Pushing him away.)*

SIMON: You're a fine dancer, you are. I'll have to give you a few lessons. Come on, I'll give you a lesson right now.

MRS. SIMON: Georgie, be a good boy! Now.

SIMON: That's a beautiful hat you have on, Mama. Is that a new hat?

MRS. SIMON: Yes, of course. Two years ago, it was new.

SIMON: I never saw it before. *(He takes a roll of bills out of his pocket and gives her one.)* Here, buy yourself a new hat.

MRS. SIMON: I don't want a new hat, Georgie.

SIMON: I want you to buy yourself a new hat. Take it.

MRS. SIMON: Georgie! *(She indicates* HENRY, *who is grinning with merriment.)*

SIMON: What? *(He turns.)* Go home, kid. I don't need you any more.

REGINA: You're expecting Mrs. Simon to call.

SIMON: That's all right. I'll take the call, myself. Go on, kid. Beat it.

HENRY: *(Getting his cap.)* Yes sir.

SIMON: *(Giving him a bill.)* And here, treat yourself to the ball game Sunday.

HENRY: Gee, thanks, Mr. Simon. Good night.

THE OTHERS: Good night.

*(*HENRY *exits.)*

SIMON: I used to be a lummox like that, too.

MRS. SIMON: You were no lummox, Georgie.

SIMON: A lot you know about lummoxes. Rexie, go home.

REGINA: I'm in no hurry.

SIMON: Go home, I tell you. Don't you know there's a law against night work for women?

(He takes her by the shoulder and pushes her towards the door of his office.)

*Crazy.

REGINA: Are you sure you don't need me?

SIMON: Listen, if you don't go right away, I'll drop you out of the window. Go on, run along.

REGINA: Well, good night, Mrs. Simon.

MRS. SIMON: Good night, Miss Gordon.

*(*REGINA *exits to* SIMON*'s office.)*

MRS. SIMON: George, why do you act like crazy?

SIMON: I'm just feeling good, that's all. Don't you like to see me feeling good?

MRS. SIMON: I didn't think you were feeling good, Georgie. That's why I came in to see you. It's a whole week since I saw you, and over the telephone you sounded so blue. I was worried about you.

SIMON: There's nothing to worry about, Mama. I've been busy, that's all. And I had one or two important things on my mind. That's why I haven't been to see you. But everything is all right now. And I feel great.

MRS. SIMON: I knew there was something wrong.

SIMON: It's all over now, I tell you, Mama— *(The telephone buzzes.)* Wait a minute. That must be Cora. *(He goes to the switchboard and plugs in.)* Hello— Yes, darling, this is me speaking— Listen, sweetheart, I've got some wonderful news for you— Yes, listen, everything is all right— You know, the Baird matter— Yes, it's all fixed up and it's going to be all right and there's nothing to worry about— I knew you would be. Where are you now?— Well, listen, darling, get right off. You've only got ten minutes— Why, didn't you get my note?— Yes, but I told you I thought I'd be able to go with you, in two or three weeks— But you've still got time to get off. We'll have a little celebration tonight. Just the two of us— But, darling, it's only postponing it two or three weeks— But nothing could interfere now. Everything is all right, now— Oh, oh— You mean you don't want to— I see— Yes— Yes— Yes, sure. I wouldn't want you to do anything unreasonable— Yes, I see— No, it's all right— No— No— Thanks— Well, have a wonderful trip— Goodbye.

(He disconnects and sits motionless at the switchboard. MRS. SIMON *watches him anxiously. Then, after a moment, she goes over to him.)*

MRS. SIMON: *(Putting her hand on his shoulder.)* Georgie!

SIMON: *(Startled.)* What's the matter, Mama? What do you want?

MRS. SIMON: Georgie, is something wrong? Tell Mama.

SIMON: There's nothing wrong, Mama. Didn't I tell you there's nothing wrong?

MRS. SIMON: Why don't you tell me, Georgie?

SIMON: Let me alone, Mama. Can't you let me alone?

MRS. SIMON: Yes, Georgie. Only if I can help you—

SIMON: I don't want any help. You can help me by going home, that's how you can help me.

MRS. SIMON: All right, Georgie, if you want me to go, I'll go.

SIMON: Yes, I wish you would. I—I have some work to do.

MRS. SIMON: Good-bye, Georgie. Please take care of yourself.

SIMON: Good-bye, Mama. And stop worrying about me. I'm all right. *(She looks at him, silently, then exits.* SIMON *puts his hand across his eyes, then rises and walks slowly up and down the office. Then, suddenly, he hurries to the switchboard, takes down the telephone directory and looks up a number. Then he seats himself and begins dialing, when* REGINA *enters.* SIMON *abruptly stops dialing.)* I thought you went home.

REGINA: I just wanted to make sure there was nothing else you wanted.

SIMON: No, there isn't. I want you to go home, that's all I want.

REGINA: Yes sir. Good night.

SIMON: Good night. *(*REGINA *exits.* SIMON *waits to make sure that she has gone, then begins dialing.)* Goddam it! *(He has forgotten the number. He takes down the book and looks it up again, then dials it.)* Hello— 9246?— I'd like to speak to Mr. Roy Darwin, please— Oh, is that so? When did he sail?— At six this evening, you mean?— I see— Oh, hello— Do you happen to know the boat he's sailing on?— Thank you.

(He disconnects and clasps both temples with his hands. It is beginning to grow quite dark. TEDESCO *comes out of his office.)*

TEDESCO: Oh, hello, George! Well, is everything all right? What's the matter?

SIMON: Nothing. I just thought everybody had gone. Yes, everything's all right.

TEDESCO: Well, thank God! Boy, but I'm happy about it. *(Wringing* SIMON's *hand.)* Well, you must feel like a new man.

SIMON: Yes, I do. I feel fine.

TEDESCO: Well, what happened, tell me? Did he try to throw a bluff?

SIMON: No, he— Listen, John—I'll tell you about it tomorrow. I'm pretty tired now.

TEDESCO: How about dinner?

SIMON: I think I'll have to call it off, John. I'm pretty tired tonight.

TEDESCO. Well, hell, that's only natural. You've been under an awful strain.

SIMON: Yes, I guess that must be it.

TEDESCO: Well, as long as it turned out all right. A good rest tonight will fix you up.

SIMON: Yes, that's what I need: a good rest.

TEDESCO: Oh, what about Cora? Did you get her?

SIMON: No, I couldn't get her.

TEDESCO: Oh, then she sailed! That's too bad.

SIMON: Yes, she sailed. I couldn't get her.

TEDESCO: Well, you can send her a radiogram.

SIMON: Yes, sure. That's just what I'm going to do: send her a radiogram.

TEDESCO: You look all in, George. Come on, let me take you home.

SIMON: No, I'm all right, John. I've got—I've got one or two things to do before I go.

TEDESCO: Well, good night. I'll see you in the morning.

SIMON: Yes, sure. Good night, John.

TEDESCO: I'm sure glad it's all over.

SIMON: Yes, so am I.

TEDESCO: You know all I wish you, George.

SIMON: Thanks, John.

Tedesco: Good night.

Simon: Good night. *(*Tedesco *exits. It has grown quite dark.* Simon *gets up slowly and walks to the window. He stands there, looking out. Then suddenly, he throws the sash wide open, and climbing up on the sofa, stands upright on the windowsill. Then, holding the sash with both hands, he leans out. The entrance door opens and* Regina *enters. She sees* Simon *and smothers a scream with her hand.* Simon *turns and sees her. Hoarsely.)* What do you want? What the hell do you want? *(*Regina *does not answer. She stands looking at him, paralyzed with terror.* Simon *jumps to the floor.)* What do you want here? Didn't I tell you to go home? What's the matter, can't you talk?

Regina: I—I was in the ladies' room.

Simon: In the ladies' room? What the hell were you doing in the ladies' room? You've been hanging around spying on me—that's what you've been doing.

Regina: No, I haven't—honest, I haven't—I—

Simon: Don't lie to me. You've been spying on me. What the hell do you mean by spying on me?

Regina: I met Mr. Tedesco in the hall—he said you were still here—I was so worried— *(Suddenly beginning to sob.)* Oh, my God!

Simon: Shut up! Shut up, do you hear me, or I'll break every goddam bone in your body. *(He makes a step towards her, then collapses into the sofa. They remain without speaking,* Regina *standing near the door, trying to control her sobs,* Simon *trembling from head to foot. The telephone signal begins to buzz and goes on buzzing. At length.)* Answer that goddam thing. Can't you even answer the telephone?

*(*Regina *goes to the switchboard.)*

Regina: Hello— Yes— Yes— I'll see if he's still here. Who's calling, please? It's Mr. Theodore Wingdale, the president of the American Steel Company.

Simon: Tell him to go to hell.

Regina: Shall I say you're not in?

Simon: I don't give a damn what you say.

Regina: I'm afraid he's gone. Mr. Wingdale— Is there

anything I can do? This is his secretary speaking— No, I don't—well, just one moment— He says it's a matter of life and death.

SIMON: What do I care? Tell him— Is that Wingdale himself?

REGINA: Yes sir.

SIMON: Well, tell him— Wait a minute, I'll talk to him myself. Let me get there. *(He takes* REGINA'S *place at switchboard.)* Hello, Mr. Wingdale— Yes, this is George Simon talking— Yes, she got me just as I was getting into the elevator. It's after office hours, you know— Yes— Well, what's the trouble?— Oh, I see— Is that so? Yes— Yes— Have the police been there?— I see— Well, you haven't made any statement, have you?— No, that's right, don't say anything— And don't let the boy say anything either— Yes— I'll be there within an hour— Wait a minute, until I get the address— *(He fumbles around in the drawer of the desk. To* REGINA.*)* Put up the lights. *(*REGINA *switches on the lights.)* One moment, Mr. Wingdale. *(He takes the box of chocolates from the drawer, then a memorandum pad.)* All right, go ahead— Yes— Yes— All right, I've got it— Yes, I'll be there before eight— One moment. You haven't consulted any other lawyer, have you?— All right— All right— Don't mention it— Good-bye. *(He disconnects. To* REGINA.*)* Wingdale of the American Steel Company. His twenty-seven-year-old son had a quarrel with his wife this afternoon and shot her dead.

REGINA: How awful!

SIMON: *(Nibbling a chocolate.)* They've only been married two years. And you know who she is, don't you? The daughter of one of the richest oil men in Texas. Can you imagine what a case that's going to be? We've got to get right on the job. Come on!

REGINA: Yes sir.

SIMON: I've got to get my hat.

REGINA: I'll get it for you.

SIMON: Never mind. We'll go out the other way. I'll bet he hasn't got a scrap of defense. Those millionaire's sons: they're a lot of good-for-nothings, that's what they are. Well, we'll have to see what we can dope out. Are you ready?

REGINA: Yes sir.

SIMON: All right, come on. We'll grab a sandwich on the way up.

(They exit.)

CURTAIN

AWAKE AND SING!

by

Clifford Odets

By 1938, when he was featured on the cover of *Time,* Clifford Odets had already been lionized as "the country's most promising playwright," "the proletarian Jesus," and "the poet of the Jewish middle class." Born in Philadelphia in 1906, Odets grew up in the Bronx, which he would dramatize so vividly. Less interested in formal education than in literature, movies, and the stage, he quit high school to become an actor. In 1931, he was playing bit parts with the Theatre Guild when he was invited to join those who broke away from the Guild to become charter members of the Group Theatre. The association reaped mutual benefits: the Group's major contributions to the American theatre are inseparable from its distinguished productions of half of Odets's dozen plays.

Though Odets joined the Group as an actor, the company hardly exploited his performing talents. As an understudy waiting in vain to replace Luther Adler as the Jewish careerist in John Howard Lawson's *Success Story* (1932), a "sore" Odets wrote a script called *I Got the Blues.* Despite the success of the second act with audiences at Green Mansions, an adult camp, the Group was reluctant to mount the entire work. However, some of its actors did stage Odets's one-act play about the genesis of a taxi drivers' strike. *Waiting for Lefty*'s sensational success was instant and unanticipated. It has since become the very definition of an agitprop play, its revolutionary statement earning it international popularity. And the thunderous reception that greeted *Lefty* in 1935 changed the Group's mind about Odets the playwright. The company prepared to stage *I Got the Blues,* newly retitled *Awake and Sing!*

The year 1935 was eventful for Odets. *Lefty,* which premiered in January, was followed a month later by *Awake and Sing!,* rocketing their author to acclaim. In March, Odets's anti-Nazi play, *Till the Day I Die,* opened in New York, inspiring productions across the country, though the play was banned in seven cities and its Los Angeles producer was beaten by Nazi sympathizers. In May, Group actor Morris Carnovsky performed "I Can't Sleep," a powerful monologue by a worker who has betrayed his fellows. Meantime, Odets's championing of proletarian causes and human rights kept him busy offstage. A member of the Communist Party for eight months, he headed an ill-fated mission to Cuba in the summer of 1935. The year ended on another disappointment—the failure in December of *Paradise Lost,* a play about the dashed aspirations of the members of two Bronx Jewish families. Small wonder that by early 1936, Odets was ready to accept one of Hollywood's extravagant offers. He got off to a slow start. His first script, *The General Died at Dawn,* provoked critic Frank Nugent's famous gibe, "Odets, where is thy sting?"

However, by 1938, when he became the subject of the *Time* cover story, Odets had redeemed himself in Hollywood and returned to the Broadway stage with *Golden Boy* (1937). Here, as in *The Big Knife* (1949), he developed a theme he had introduced in the earlier, Jewish plays: artistic, sensitive individuals whose quest for self-actualization conflicts with their desire for material success. Almost until his death in 1963, Odets himself lived this tension, alternating between the commercial certainty of screenwriting and the chancier artistry of the theatre.

After *Awake and Sing!* and *Paradise Lost,* Odets did not focus on Jews again until his last play, *The Flowering Peach* (1954). Drawing on family figures rather than on Scripture, he made Jews of the Noah clan. The story of the Flood functions as a metaphor for contemporary life threatened by atomic obliteration and a context for the playwright's exploration of the limits of human responsibility. Sadly, many of the fresh Jewish characters Odets had developed two decades before emerge in *Peach* as parodies of themselves. Reviewers of the original production generously accepted Odets's recasting of the powerful material from Genesis as a Jewish family comedy. Although several critics faulted the "repetitious family wranglings," and "petty quarrels," and one was "embarrassed" by the "wise-cracking burlesque," all praised Menasha Skulnik's performance as Noah. The play, which also became a Richard Rodgers musical, *Two by Two,* is occasionally revived, though its 1994 production by New York's National Actors Theatre, for example, evoked little enthusiasm. *Peach*'s timeless legend and the universal questions it raises are not well served by its cast of largely stereotyped characters. Among them, however, Noah's youngest son, Japheth, stands out for his stubborn self-sufficiency. Japheth's fierce struggle for independence from parental control echoes Ralph Berger's in *Awake and Sing!* His unshakable belief in humankind, much more focused than Ralph's, provides reassurance that at least one of Odets's memorable early Jewish characters could mature without fading into a stock type.

The Group had been initially reluctant to stage *Awake and Sing!* because it objected to the play's "small horizon" and "messiness," that is, its preoccupation with the assorted miseries of the Bergers. As Odets biographer Margaret Brenman-Gibson has shown, these woes and discontents translate many of Odets's own. The work, in John Gassner's words, had to "emerge out of its private chrysalis"—an evolution explicit in the revised title. To bring the play squarely into alignment with the Group's proletarian view of its times, Odets emphasized conflicting ideologies and the climate of the Depression as forces aggravating tensions in the Berger household. Ironically, in making his work more stageworthy for his predominantly Jewish colleagues, Odets stripped away much of its original Jewish explicitness. Since *Awake and Sing!* remains a profoundly Jewish play, it is interesting to see what was accomplished in the rewriting.

The early drafts of *I Got the Blues* are laden with Yiddish expressions, and Odets reconsidered them judiciously. Sometimes he just translated them (Morty originally said Bessie's cooking *"schmekt gitt"* rather than "smells good"). A few changes simplified the plot (Bessie first opposed Ralph's girlfriend not as "a girl with no parents" [named Miss Hirsch in the final script], but "a *shiksa*!"). A number of such astute modifications helped to make the language of *Awake and Sing!* one of its most notable features. Among its other admirable qualities (vigor, insightful non-sequiturs, and authentic cadences), it represents the Yiddishized English of countless American Jews, making their idiom available to those who, like critic Grenville Vernon, appreciated "dialogue not created by the dramatist, but inherited by him from the speech of his people."

In rewriting dialogue, Odets eliminated numerous specifically Jewish allusions, making characterizations contribute more pointedly to the plot. For instance, Jacob's earlier stream of references to "the Jew Bible" are replaced by repeated socialist sentiments ("It needs a new world"). Such statements reorient his objections to the values prevailing in his daughter's house ("In my day the propaganda was for God. Now it's for success") and make clearer his legacy to Ralph ("DO!").

Odets eliminated some superb material that fleshed out characterizations without contributing to the forward motion of the play. Morty, harassed by agitation at his shop, originally reflected bitterly on its organizers: "I see even the Jews are changing in modern America—a people who hung together for thousands of years like bananas on a bunch. Who sits shivah nowadays for the dead—to sit seven days on a soap box? Now they talk from the boxes and make strikes. Kikes in Union Square who yell no equality in the country. Crazy!" However wonderful this speech, it came from the mouth of a man who expresses little awareness of Jewishness, his own or others'. Similarly out of character was another beautiful line omitted by Odets: The cynical Moe's extravagant promises to Hennie originally included the kind of ecstasy experienced by "the kid who stood in the synagogue while the Rabbi sang sad songs."

The transformation of the matriarch of *Blues* warrants fuller examination. According to Brenman-Gibson, she embodies the resentment Odets felt for his father. Seizing the opportunity to disdain the object of his wrath, Odets at first gave the offending parent no name other than "Mrs." One excised incident vividly dramatizes behavior that Odets found reprehensible. Ralph brings a tramp home for a meal, only to have Mrs. turn him out ("He should eat off our dishes and make germs?"), to which

Ralph responds by giving the man his own next day's lunch money—both deeds unmistakable acts of *tsedakah* (charity). Mean-spirited Mrs. has an astonishing speech in which she disparages the men in her life ("mice from the kitchen"), proclaims herself at fifty ready to "handle two more husbands yet," and vows to "step into the street a free woman." It is easier to view Mrs. as a caricature of an angry feminist *avant la lettre* than as the prototype of Bessie Berger, one of Clifford Odets's most memorable characters. In reworking his play, Odets added a dimension to the mother that, by contrast with the emendations noted above, makes the play more explicitly Jewish.

When Mrs. breaks Jacob's Caruso records in *Blues,* she is energized by the malice that inspires her behavior throughout. The Bessie of *Awake and Sing!,* however controlling and insensitive, is not nasty. Other motives explain her one act of violence, and they are not hard to find. The record-smashing scene shows the cost to Bessie of being a dreambuster and the reliable dispenser of workable, if unsavory, solutions. She finally vents her frustrations as a daughter exasperated with her father's ineffectuality; as a wife, disillusioned by the "paradiso" promised in Caruso's arias, but unrealizable in her marriage to a man who never stopped believing the Messiah would come in the form of a hair restorative or a winning sweepstakes ticket; and as a mother who saw her children had what they needed, not what they asked for, or even what she might have liked to give. Bessie Berger may be one of strongest representations of the Odetsian struggle between idealism and pragmatism. By developing his materfamilias from a personification of spite to a fully dimensional human being, Odets makes her represent countless first-generation American Jewish women who, by instinct or from Old World experience, understood "when one lives in the jungle one must look out for the wild life."

Nor does this masterful characterization stand alone. As revised, *Awake and Sing!* launched the stage career of a half-dozen carefully drawn types: the restless *belle juive,* the mild husband bewildered by "life in America," the sybaritic moneyman, the socialist grandfather, the bitter racketeer, and the sensitive, discontented young hero. They have had long stage lives, not always (as *The Flow-*

ering Peach demonstrates) retaining the sap and dimension with which Odets endowed them in the extraordinary descriptions that precede the play.

The work itself, well received in 1935, was quickly translated into Yiddish, understandably becoming a favorite production of Yiddish units of the Federal Theatre Project. The continuing worldwide popularity of the play belies its grounding in America of the 30s. Writing of the 1992 Chicago production, critic John Lahr saw untarnished the play's "quirky blend of deep Jewish pessimism and a very American desire to shine."

Awake and Sing! was presented by the Group Theatre at the Belasco Theatre on the evening of February 19th, 1935, with the following members of the Group Theatre Acting Company:

MYRON BERGER	*Art Smith*
BESSIE BERGER	*Stella Adler*
JACOB	*Morris Carnovsky*
HENNIE BERGER	*Phoebe Brand*
RALPH BERGER	*Jules Garfield*
SCHLOSSER	*Roman Bohnen*
MOE AXELROD	*Luther Adler*
UNCLE MORTY	*J.E. Bromberg*
SAM FEINSCHREIBER	*Sanford Meisner*

The entire action takes place in an apartment in the Bronx, New York City.

The production was directed by HAROLD CLURMAN
The setting was designed by BORIS ARONSON

THE CHARACTERS OF THE PLAY

All of the characters in *Awake and Sing!* share a fundamental activity: a struggle for life amidst petty conditions.

BESSIE BERGER, *as she herself states, is not only the mother in this home but also the father. She is constantly arranging and taking care of her family. She loves life, likes to laugh, has great resourcefulness and enjoys living from day to day. A high degree of energy accounts for her quick exasperation at ineptitude. She is a shrewd judge of realistic qualities in people in the sense of being able to gauge quickly their effectiveness. In her eyes all of the people in the house are equal. She is naïve and quick in emotional response. She is afraid of utter poverty. She is proper according to her own standards, which are fairly close to those of most middle-class families. She knows that when one lives in the jungle one must look out for the wild life.*

MYRON, *her husband, is a born follower. He would like to be a leader. He would like to make a million dollars. He is not sad or ever depressed. Life is an even sweet event to him, but the "old days" were sweeter yet. He has a dignified sense of himself. He likes people. He likes everything. But he is heartbroken without being aware of it.*

HENNIE *is a girl who has had few friends, male or female. She is proud of her body. She won't ask favors. She travels alone. She is fatalistic about being trapped, but will escape if possible. She is self-reliant in the best sense. Till the day she dies she will be faithful to a loved man. She inherits her mother's sense of humor and energy.*

RALPH *is a boy with a clean spirit. He wants to know, wants to learn. He is ardent, he is romantic, he is sensitive. He is naïve too. He is trying to find why so much dirt must be cleared away before it is possible to "get to first base."*

JACOB, *too, is trying to find a right path for himself and the others. He is aware of justice, of dignity. He is an observer of the others, compares their activities with his real and ideal sense of life. This produces a reflective nature. In this home he is a constant boarder. He is a sentimental idealist with no power to turn ideal to action.*

With physical facts—such as housework—he putters. But as a barber he demonstrates the flair of an artist. He is an old Jew with living eyes in his tired face.

UNCLE MORTY *is a successful American businessman with five good senses. Something sinister comes out of the fact that the lives of others seldom touch him deeply. He holds to his own line of life. When he is generous he wants others to be aware of it. He is pleased by attention—a rich relative to the* BERGER *family. He is a shrewd judge of material values. He will die unmarried. Two and two make four, never five with him. He can blink in the sun for hours, a fat tomcat. Tickle him, he laughs. He lives in a penthouse with a real Japanese butler to serve him. He sleeps with dress models, but not from his own showrooms. He plays cards for hours on end. He smokes expensive cigars. He sees every Mickey Mouse cartoon that appears. He is a 32-degree Mason. He is really deeply intolerant finally.*

MOE AXELROD *lost a leg in the war. He seldom forgets that fact. He has killed two men in extra-martial activity. He is mordant, bitter. Life has taught him a disbelief in everything, but he will fight his way through. He seldom shows his feelings: fights against his own sensitivity. He has been everywhere and seen everything. All he wants is* HENNIE. *He is very proud. He scorns the inability of others to make their way in life, but he likes people for whatever good qualities they possess. His passionate outbursts come from a strong but contained emotional mechanism.*

SAM FEINSCHREIBER *wants to find a home. He is a lonely man, a foreigner in a strange land, hypersensitive about this fact, conditioned by the humiliation of not making his way alone. He has a sense of others laughing at him. At night he gets up and sits alone in the dark. He hears acutely all the small sounds of life. He might have been a poet in another time and place. He approaches his wife as if he were always offering her a delicate flower. Life is a high chill wind weaving itself around his head.*

SCHLOSSER, *the janitor, is an overworked German whose wife ran away with another man and left him with a young daughter who in turn ran away and joined a burlesque show as chorus girl. The man suffers rheumatic pains. He has lost his identity twenty years before.*

THE SCENE

Exposed on the stage are the dining room and adjoining front room of the BERGER *apartment. These two rooms are typically furnished. There is a curtain between them. A small door off the front room leads to* JACOB'S *room. When his door is open one sees a picture of* SACCO *and* VANZETTI *on the wall and several shelves of books. Stage left of this door presents the entrance to the foyer hall of the apartment. The two other bedrooms of the apartment are off this hall, but not necessarily shown.*

Stage left of the dining room presents a swinging door which opens on the kitchen.

Awake and sing, ye that dwell in dust:

ISAIAH *26:19*

ACT I

TIME: *The present; the family finishing supper.*

PLACE: *An apartment in the Bronx, New York City.*

RALPH: Where's advancement down the place? Work like crazy! Think they see it? You'd drop dead first.
MYRON: Never mind, son, merit never goes unrewarded. Teddy Roosevelt used to say—
HENNIE: It rewarded you—thirty years a haberdashery clerk!

(JACOB *laughs.)*

RALPH: All I want's a chance to get to first base!
HENNIE: That's all?
RALPH: Stuck down in that joint on Fourth Avenue—a stock clerk in a silk house! Just look at Eddie. I'm as good as he is—pulling in two-fifty a week for forty-eight minutes a day. A headliner, his name in all the papers.
JACOB: That's what you want, Ralphie? Your name in the paper?
RALPH: I wanna make up my own mind about things . . . be something! Didn't I want to take up tap dancing, too?
BESSIE: So take lessons. Who stopped you?
RALPH: On what?
BESSIE: On what? Save money.
RALPH: Sure, five dollars a week for expenses and the rest in the house. I can't save even for shoelaces.

BESSIE: You mean we shouldn't have food in the house, but you'll make a jig on the street corner?

RALPH: I mean something.

BESSIE: You also mean something when you studied on the drum, Mr. Smartie!

RALPH: I don't know. . . . Every other day to sit around with the blues and mud in your mouth.

MYRON: That's how it is—life is like that—a cake walk.

RALPH: What's it get you?

HENNIE: A four-car funeral.

RALPH: What's it for?

JACOB: What's it for? If this life leads to a revolution it's a good life. Otherwise it's for nothing.

BESSIE: Never mind, Pop! Pass me the salt.

RALPH: It's crazy—all my life I want a pair of black and white shoes and can't get them. It's crazy!

BESSIE: In a minute I'll get up from the table. I can't take a bite in my mouth no more.

MYRON: *(Restraining her.)* Now, Momma, just don't excite yourself—

BESSIE: I'm so nervous I can't hold a knife in my hand.

MYRON: Is that a way to talk, Ralphie? Don't Momma work hard enough all day? *(*BESSIE *allows herself to be reseated.)*

BESSIE: On my feet twenty-four hours?

MYRON: On her feet—

RALPH *(Jumps up.)* What do I do—go to nightclubs with Greta Garbo? Then when I come home can't even have my own room? Sleep on a day bed in the front room! *(Choked, he exits to front room.)*

BESSIE: He's starting up that stuff again. *(Shouts to him.)* When Hennie here marries you'll have her room—I should only live to see the day.

HENNIE: Me, too. *(They settle down to serious eating.)*

MYRON: This morning the sink was full of ants. Where they come from I just don't know. I thought it was coffee grounds . . . and then they began moving.

BESSIE: You gave the dog eat?

JACOB: I gave the dog eat. *(*HENNIE *drops a knife and picks it up again.)*

BESSIE: You got dropsy tonight.

HENNIE: Company's coming.

MYRON: You can buy a ticket for fifty cents and win fortunes. A man came in the store—it's the Irish Sweepstakes.

BESSIE: What?

MYRON: Like a raffle, only different. A man came in—

BESSIE: Who spends fifty-cent pieces for Irish raffles? They threw out a family on Dawson Street today. All the furniture on the sidewalk. A fine old woman with gray hair.

JACOB: Come eat, Ralph.

MYRON: A butcher on Beck Street won eighty thousand dollars.

BESSIE: Eighty thousand dollars! You'll excuse my expression, you're bughouse!

MYRON: I seen it in the paper—on one ticket—765 Beck Street.

BESSIE: Impossible!

MYRON: He did . . . yes he did. He says he'll take his old mother to Europe . . . an Austrian—

HENNIE: Europe . . .

MYRON: Six percent on eighty thousand—forty-eight hundred a year.

BESSIE: I'll give you money. Buy a ticket in Hennie's name. Say, you can't tell—lightning never struck us yet. If they win on Beck Street we could win on Longwood Avenue.

JACOB *(Ironically.)* If it rained pearls—who would work?

BESSIE: Another county heard from. *(*RALPH *enters and silently seats himself.)*

MYRON: I forgot, Beauty—Sam Feinschreiber sent you a present. Since I brought him for supper he just can't stop talking about you.

HENNIE: What's that "mockie"* bothering about? Who needs him?

MYRON: He's a very lonely boy.

HENNIE: So I'll sit down and bust out crying " 'cause he's lonely."

BESSIE: *(Opening candy.)* He'd marry you one two three.

HENNIE: Too bad about him.

BESSIE: *(Naively delighted.)* Chocolate peanuts.

HENNIE: Loft's weekend special, two for thirty-nine.

BESSIE: You could think about it. It wouldn't hurt.

*Greenhorn.

HENNIE: *(Laughing.)* To quote Moe Axelrod, "Don't make me laugh."

BESSIE: Never mind laughing. It's time you already had in your head a serious thought. A girl twenty-six don't grow younger. When I was your age it was already a big family with responsibilities.

HENNIE: *(Laughing.)* Maybe that's what ails you, Mom.

BESSIE: Don't you feel well?

HENNIE: 'Cause I'm laughing? I feel fine. It's just funny—that poor guy sending me presents 'cause he loves me.

BESSIE: I think it's very, very nice.

HENNIE: Sure . . . swell!

BESSIE: Mrs. Marcus' Rose is engaged to a Brooklyn boy, a dentist. He came in his car today. A little dope should get such a boy. *(Finished with the meal,* BESSIE, MYRON *and* JACOB *rise. Both* HENNIE *and* RALPH *sits silently at the table, he eating. Suddenly she rises.)*

HENNIE: Tell you what, Mom. I saved for a new dress, but I'll take you and Pop to the Franklin. Don't need a dress. From now on I'm planning to stay in nights. Hold everything!

BESSIE: What's the matter—a bedbug bit you suddenly?

HENNIE: It's a good bill—Belle Baker. Maybe she'll sing "Eli, Eli."

BESSIE: We was going to a movie.

HENNIE: Forget it. Let's go.

MYRON: I see in the papers *(as he picks his teeth)* Sophie Tucker took off twenty-six pounds. Fearful business with Japan.

HENNIE: Write a book, Pop! Come on, we'll go early for good seats.

MYRON: Moe said you had a date with him for tonight.

BESSIE: Axelrod?

HENNIE: I told him no, but he don't believe it. I'll tell him no for the next hundred years, too.

MYRON: Don't break appointments, Beauty, and hurt people's feelings. *(*BESSIE *exits.)*

HENNIE: His hands got free-wheeling. *(She exits.)*

MYRON: I don't know . . . people ain't the same. N-O- The whole world's changing right under our eyes. Presto! No manners. Like the great Italian lover in the movies. What was his name? The Sheik. . . . No one remembers? *(Exits, shaking his head.)*

RALPH: *(Unmoving at the table.)* Jake . . .

JACOB: Noo?

RALPH: I can't stand it.

JACOB: There's an expression—"strong as iron you must be."

RALPH: It's a cock-eyed world.

JACOB: Boys like you could fix it some day. Look on the world, not on yourself so much. Every country with starving millions, no? In Germany and Poland a Jew couldn't walk in the street. Everybody hates, nobody loves.

RALPH: I don't get all that.

JACOB: For years, I watched you grow up. Wait! You'll graduate from my university. *(The others enter, dressed.)*

MYRON: *(Lighting.)* Good cigars now for a nickel.

BESSIE: *(To* JACOB.*)* After take Tootsie on the roof. *(To* RALPH*)*: What'll you do?

RALPH: Don't know.

BESSIE: You'll see the boys around the block?

RALPH: I'll stay home every night!

MYRON: Momma don't mean for you—

RALPH: I'm flying to Hollywood by plane, that's what I'm doing. *(Doorbell rings.* MYRON *answers it.)*

BESSIE: I don't like my boy to be seen with those tramps on the corner.

MYRON: *(Without.)* Schlosser's here, Momma, with the garbage can.

BESSIE: Come in here, Schlosser. *(Sotto voce.)* Wait, I'll give him a piece of my mind. *(*MYRON *ushers in* SCHLOSSER, *who carries a garbage can in each hand.)* What's the matter, the dumbwaiter's broken again?

SCHLOSSER: Mr. Wimmer sends new ropes next week. I got a sore arm.

BESSIE: He should live so long, your Mr. Wimmer. For seven years already he's sending new ropes. No dumbwaiter, no hot water, no steam— In a respectable house, they don't allow such conditions.

SCHLOSSER: In a decent house, dogs are not running to make dirty the hallway.

BESSIE: Tootsie's making dirty? Our Tootsie's making dirty in the hall?

SCHLOSSER *(To* JACOB*)* I tell you yesterday again. You must not leave her—

BESSIE: *(Indignantly.)* Excuse me! Please don't yell on an old man. He's got more brains in his finger than you got—I don't know where. Did you ever see—he should talk to you an old man?

MYRON: Awful.

BESSIE: From now on we don't walk up the stairs no more. You keep it so clean we'll fly in the windows.

SCHLOSSER: I speak to Mr. Wimmer.

BESSIE: Speak! Speak. Tootsie walks behind me like a lady any time, any place. So good-bye . . . good-bye, Mr. Schlosser.

SCHLOSSER: I tell you dot—I verk verry hard here. My arms is. . . . *(Exits in confusion.)*

BESSIE: Tootsie should lay all day in the kitchen maybe. Give him back if he yells on you. What's funny?

JACOB: *(Laughing.)* Nothing.

BESSIE: Come. *(Exits.)*

JACOB: Hennie, take care. . . .

HENNIE: Sure.

JACOB: Bye-bye. *(*HENNIE *exits.* MYRON *pops head back in door.)*

MYRON: Valentino! That's the one! *(He exits.)*

RALPH: I never in my life even had a birthday party. Every time I went and cried in the toilet when my birthday came.

JACOB. *(Seeing* RALPH *remove his tie.)* You're going to bed?

RALPH: No, I'm putting on a clean shirt.

JACOB: Why?

RALPH: I got a girl. . . . Don't laugh!

JACOB: Who laughs? Since when?

RALPH: Three weeks. She lives in Yorkville with an aunt and uncle. A bunch of relatives, but no parents.

JACOB: An orphan girl—tch, tch.

RALPH: But she's got me! Boy, I'm telling you I could sing! Jake, she's like stars. She's so beautiful, you look at her and cry! She's like French words! We went to the park the other night. Heard the last band concert.

JACOB: Music. . . .

RALPH: *(Stuffing shirt in trousers.)* It got cold and I gave her my coat to wear. We just walked along like that, see, without a word, see. I never was so happy in all my life. It got late . . . we just sat there. She looked at me—you know what I mean, how a girl looks at you—right in the eyes? "I love you," she says, "Ralph." I took her home. . . . I wanted to cry. That's how I felt!

JACOB: It's a beautiful feeling.

RALPH: You said a mouthful!

JACOB: Her name is—

RALPH: Blanche.

JACOB: A fine name. Bring her sometimes here.

RALPH: She's scared to meet Mom.

JACOB: Why?

RALPH: You know Mom's not letting my sixteen bucks out of the house if she can help it. She'd take one look at Blanche and insult her in a minute—a kid who's got nothing.

JACOB: Boychick!

RALPH: What's the diff?

JACOB: It's no difference—a plain bourgeois prejudice—but when they find out a poor girl—it ain't so kosher.

RALPH: They don't have to know I've got a girl.

JACOB: What's in the end?

RALPH: Out I go! I don't mean maybe!

JACOB: And then what?

RALPH: Life begins.

JACOB: What life?

RALPH: Life with my girl. Boy, I could sing when I think about it! Her and me together—that's a new life!

JACOB: Don't make a mistake! A new death!

RALPH: What's the idea?

JACOB: Me, I'm the idea! Once I had in *my* heart a dream, a vision, but came marriage and then you forget. Children come and you forget because—

RALPH: Don't worry, Jake.

JACOB: Remember, a woman insults a man's soul like no other thing in the whole world!

RALPH: Why get so excited? No one—

JACOB: Boychick, wake up! Be something! Make your life something good. For the love of an old man who sees in your young days his new life, for such love take the world in your two hands and make it like new. Go out and fight so life shouldn't be printed on dollar bills. A woman waits.

RALPH: Say, I'm no fool!

JACOB: From my heart I hope not. In the meantime— *(Bell rings.)*

RALPH: See who it is, will you? *(Stands off.)* Don't want Mom to catch me with a clean shirt.

JACOB: *(Calls.)* Come in. *(Sotto voce.)* Moe Axelrod. *(*MOE *enters.)*

MOE: Hello girls, how's your whiskers? *(To* RALPH.*)* All dolled up. What's it, the weekly visit to the cat house?

RALPH: Please mind your business.

MOE: Okay, sweetheart.

RALPH: *(Taking a hidden dollar from a book.)* If Mom asks where I went—

JACOB: I know. Enjoy yourself.

RALPH: Bye-bye. *(He exits.)*

JACOB: Bye-bye.

MOE: Who's home?

JACOB: Me.

MOE: Good. I'll stick around a few minutes. Where's Hennie?

JACOB: She went with Bessie and Myron to a show.

MOE: She what?!

JACOB: You had a date?

MOE: *(Hiding his feelings.)* Here—I brought you some halavah.

JACOB: Halavah? Thanks. I'll eat a piece after.

MOE: So Ralph's got a dame? Hot stuff—a kid can't even play a card game.

JACOB: Moe, you're a no-good, a bum of the first water. To your dying day you won't change.

MOE: Where'd you get that stuff, a no-good?

JACOB: But I like you.

MOE: Didn't I go fight in France for democracy? Didn't I get my goddam leg shot off in that war the day before the armistice? Uncle Sam give me the Order of the Purple Heart, didn't he? What'd you mean, a no-good?

JACOB: Excuse me.

MOE: If you got an orange I'll eat an orange.

JACOB: No orange. An apple.

MOE: No oranges, huh? What a dump!

JACOB: Bessie hears you once talking like this she'll knock your head off.

MOE: Hennie went with, huh? She wantsa see me squirm, only I don't squirm for dames.

JACOB: You came to see her?

MOE: What for? I got a present for our boy friend, Myron. He'll drop dead when I tell him his gentle horse galloped in fifteen to one. He'll die.

JACOB: It really won? The first time I remember.

MOE: Where'd they go?

JACOB: A vaudeville by the Franklin.

MOE: What's special tonight?

JACOB: Someone tells a few jokes . . . and they forget the street is filled with starving beggars.

MOE: What'll they do—start a war?

JACOB: I don't know.

MOE: You oughta know. What the hell you got all the books for?

JACOB: It needs a new world.

MOE: That's why they had the big war—to make a new world, they said—safe for democracy. Sure every big general laying up in a Paris hotel with a half dozen broads pinned on his mustache. Democracy! I learned a lesson.

JACOB: An imperial war. You know what this means?

MOE: Sure, I know everything!

JACOB: By money men the interests must be protected. Who gave you such a rotten haircut? Please *(Fishing in his vest pocket),* give me for a cent a cigarette. I didn't have since yesterday—

MOE: *(Giving one.)* Don't make me laugh. *(A cent passes back and forth between them,* MOE *finally throwing it over his shoulder.)* Don't look so tired all the time. You're a wow—always sore about something.

JACOB: And you?

MOE: You got one thing—you can play pinochle. I'll take you over in a game. Then you'll have something to be sore on.

JACOB: Who'll wash dishes? *(*MOE *takes deck from buffet drawer.)*

MOE: Do 'em after. Ten cents a deal.

JACOB: Who's got ten cents?

MOE: I got ten cents. I'll lend it to you.

JACOB: Commence.

MOE: *(Shaking cards.)* The first time I had my hands on a pack in two days. Lemme shake up these cards. I'll make 'em talk. *(*JACOB *goes to his room, where he puts on a Caruso record.)*

JACOB: You should live so long.

MOE: Ever see oranges grow? I know a certain place— One summer I laid under a tree and let them fall right in my mouth.

JACOB: *(Off, the music is playing, the card game begins.)* From "L'Africana" . . . a big explorer comes on a new land—"O Paradiso." From act four this piece. Caruso stands on the ship and looks on a Utopia. You hear? "Oh paradise! Oh paradise on earth! Oh blue sky, oh fragrant air—"

MOE: Ask him does he see any oranges?

*(*BESSIE, MYRON *and* HENNIE *enter.)*

JACOB: You came back so soon?

BESSIE: Hennie got sick on the way.

MYRON: Hello, Moe. . . . *(*MOE *puts cards back in pocket.)*

BESSIE: Take off the phonograph, Pop. *(To* HENNIE.*)* Lay down . . . I'll call the doctor. You should see how she got sick on Prospect Avenue. Two weeks already she don't feel right.

MYRON: Moe . . .?

BESSIE: Go to bed, Hennie.

HENNIE: I'll sit here.

BESSIE: Such a girl I never saw! Now you'll be stubborn?

MYRON: It's for your own good, Beauty. Influenza—

HENNIE: I'll sit here.

BESSIE: You ever seen a girl should say no to everything. She can't stand on her feet, so—

HENNIE: Don't yell in my ears. I hear. Nothing's wrong. I ate tuna fish for lunch.

MYRON: Canned goods. . . .

BESSIE: Last week you also ate tuna fish?

HENNIE: Yeah, I'm funny for tuna fish. Go to the show—have a good time.

BESSIE: I don't understand what I did to God He blessed me with such children. From the whole world—

MOE: *(Coming to aid of* HENNIE.*)* For Chris' sake, don't kibitz so much!

BESSIE: You don't like it?

MOE: *(Aping.)* No, I don't like it.

BESSIE: That's too bad, Axelrod. Maybe it's better by your cigar-store friends. Here we're different people.

MOE: Don't gimme that cigar-store line, Bessie. I walked up five flights—

BESSIE: To take out Hennie. But my daughter ain't in your class, Axelrod.

MOE: To see Myron.

MYRON: Did he, did he, Moe?

MOE: Did he what?

MYRON: "Sky Rocket"?

BESSIE: You bet on a horse!

MOE: Paid twelve and a half to one.

MYRON: There! You hear that, Momma? Our horse came in. You see, it happens, and twelve and a half to one. Just look at that!

MOE: What the hell, a sure thing. I told you.

BESSIE: If Moe said a sure thing, you couldn't bet a few dollars instead of fifty cents?

JACOB: *(Laughs.)* "Aie, aie, aie."

MOE: *(At his wallet.)* I'm carrying six hundred "plunks" in big denominations.

BESSIE: A banker!

MOE: Uncle Sam sends me ninety a month.

BESSIE: So you save it?

MOE: Run it up, Run-it-up-Axelrod, that's me.

BESSIE: The police should know how.

MOE: *(Shutting her up.)* All right, all right— Change twenty, sweetheart.

MYRON: Can you make change?

BESSIE: Don't be crazy.

MOE: I'll meet a guy in Goldman's restaurant. I'll meet 'im and come back with change.

MYRON: *(Figuring on paper.)* You can give it to me tomorrow in the store.

BESSIE: *(Acquisitive.)* He'll come back, he'll come back!

MOE: Lucky I bet some bucks myself. *(In derision, to* HENNIE.*)* Let's step out tomorrow night, Par-a-dise. *(Thumbs his nose at her, laughs mordantly and exits.)*

MYRON: Oh, that's big percentage. If I picked a winner every day . . .

BESSIE: Poppa, did you take Tootsie on the roof?

JACOB: All right.

MYRON: Just look at that—a cake walk. We can make—

BESSIE: It's enough talk. I got a splitting headache. Hennie, go in bed. I'll call Dr. Cantor.

HENNIE: I'll sit here . . . and don't call that old Ignatz 'cause I won't see him.

MYRON: If you get sick Momma can't nurse you. You don't want to go to a hospital.

JACOB: She don't look sick, Bessie, it's a fact.

BESSIE: She's got fever. I see in her eyes, so he tells me no. Myron, call Dr. Cantor. *(*MYRON *picks up phone, but* HENNIE *grabs it from him.)*

HENNIE: I don't want any doctor. I ain't sick. Leave me alone.

MYRON: Beauty, it's for your own sake.

HENNIE: Day in and day out pestering. Why are you always right and no one else can say a word?

BESSIE: When you have your own children—

HENNIE: I'm not sick! Hear what I say? I'm not sick! Nothing's the matter with me! I don't want a doctor. *(*BESSIE *is watching her with slow progressive understanding.)*

BESSIE: What's the matter?

HENNIE: Nothing, I told you!

BESSIE: You told me, but— *(A long pause of examination follows.)*

HENNIE: See much?

BESSIE: Myron, put down the . . . the. . . . *(He slowly puts the phone down.)* Tell me what happened. . . .

HENNIE: Brooklyn Bridge fell down.

BESSIE: *(Approaching.)* I'm asking a question. . . .

MYRON: What's happened, Momma?

BESSIE: Listen to me!

HENNIE: What the hell are you talking?

BESSIE: Poppa—take Tootsie on the roof.

HENNIE: *(Holding* JACOB *back.)* If he wants, he can stay here.

MYRON: What's wrong, Momma?

BESSIE: *(Her voice quivering slightly.)* Myron, your fine Beauty's in trouble. Our society lady . . .

MYRON: Trouble? I don't under—is it—?

BESSIE: Look in her face. *(He looks, understands and slowly sits in a chair, utterly crushed.)* Who's the man?

HENNIE: The Prince of Wales.

BESSIE: My gall is busting in me. In two seconds—

HENNIE: *(In a violent outburst.)* Shut up! Shut up! I'll jump out the window in a minute! Shut up! *(Finally she gains control of herself, says in a low, hard voice)* You don't know him.

JACOB: Bessie. . . .

BESSIE: He's a Bronx boy?

HENNIE: From out of town.

BESSIE: What do you mean?

HENNIE: From out of town!

BESSIE: A long time you know him? You were sleeping by a girl from the office Saturday nights? You slept good, my lovely lady. You'll go to him . . . he'll marry you.

HENNIE: That's what you say.

BESSIE: That's what I say! He'll do it, take *my* word he'll do it!

HENNIE: Where? *(To* JACOB*)* Give her the letter. *(*JACOB *does so.)*

BESSIE: What? *(Reads.)* "Dear sir: In reply to your request of the 14th inst., we can state that no Mr. Ben Grossman has ever been connected with our organization . . ." You don't know where he is?

HENNIE: No.

BESSIE: *(Walks back and forth.)* Stop crying like a baby, Myron.

MYRON: It's like a play on the stage. . . .

BESSIE: To a mother you couldn't say something before. I'm old-fashioned—like your friends I'm not smart—I don't eat chop suey and run around Coney Island with tramps. *(She walks reflectively to buffet, picks up a box of candy, puts it down, says to* MYRON*)* Tomorrow night bring Sam Feinschreiber for supper.

HENNIE: I won't do it.

BESSIE: You'll do it, my fine beauty, you'll do it!

HENNIE: I'm not marrying a poor foreigner like him. Can't even speak an English word. Not me! I'll go to my grave without a husband.

BESSIE: You don't say! We'll find for you somewhere a

millionaire with a pleasure boat. He's going to night school, Sam. For a boy only three years in the country he speaks very nice. In three years he put enough in the bank, a good living.

JACOB: This is serious?

BESSIE: What then? I'm talking for my health? He'll come tomorrow night for supper. By Saturday they're engaged.

JACOB: Such a thing you can't do.

BESSIE: Who asked your advice?

JACOB: Such a thing—

BESSIE: Never mind!

JACOB: The lowest from the low!

BESSIE: Don't talk! I'm warning you! A man who don't believe in God—with crazy ideas—

JACOB: So bad I never imagined you could be.

BESSIE: Maybe if you didn't talk so much it wouldn't happen like this. You with your ideas—I'm a mother. I raise a family they should have respect.

JACOB: Respect? *(Spits.)* Respect! For the neighbors' opinion! You insult me, Bessie!

BESSIE: Go in your room, Papa. Every job he ever had he lost because he's got a big mouth. He opens his mouth and the whole Bronx could fall in. Everybody said it—

MYRON: Momma, they'll hear you down the dumbwaiter.

BESSIE: A good barber not to hold a job a week. Maybe you never heard charity starts at home. You never heard it, Pop?

JACOB: All you know, I heard, and more yet. But Ralph you don't make like you. Before you do it, I'll die first. He'll find a girl. He'll go in a fresh world with her. This is a house? Marx said it—abolish such families.

BESSIE: Go in your room, Papa.

JACOB: Ralph you don't make like you!

BESSIE: Go lay in your room with Caruso and the books together.

JACOB: All right!

BESSIE: Go in the room!

JACOB: Some day I'll come out I'll— *(Unable to continue, he turns, looks at* HENNIE, *goes to his door and there says with an attempt at humor)* Bessie, some day you'll talk to me so fresh . . . I'll leave the house for good! *(He exits.)*

BESSIE: *(Crying.)* You ever in your life seen it? He should dare! He should just dare say in the house another word. Your gall could bust from such a man. *(Bell rings,* MYRON *goes.)* Go to sleep now. It won't hurt.

HENNIE: Yeah? *(*MOE *enters, a box in his hand.* MYRON *follows and sits down.)*

MOE: *(Looks around first—putting box on table.)* Cake. *(About to give* MYRON *the money, he turns instead to* BESSIE.*)* Six-fifty, four bits change . . . come on, hand over half a buck. *(She does so. Of* MYRON*)* Who bit him?

BESSIE: We're soon losing our Hennie, Moe.

MOE: Why? What's the matter?

BESSIE: She made her engagement.

MOE: Zat so?

BESSIE: Today it happened . . . he asked her.

MOE: Did he? Who? Who's the corpse?

BESSIE: It's a secret.

MOE: In the bag, huh?

HENNIE: Yeah. . . .

BESSIE: When a mother gives away an only daughter it's no joke. Wait, when you'll get married you'll know. . . .

MOE: *(Bitterly.)* Don't make me laugh—when I get married! What I think a women? Take 'em all, cut 'em in little pieces like a herring in Greek salad. A guy in France had the right idea—dropped his wife in a bathtub fulla acid. *(Whistles.)* Sss, down the pipe! Pfft—not even a corset button left!

MYRON: Corsets don't have buttons.

MOE: *(To* HENNIE.*)* What's the great idea? Gone big time, Paradise? Christ, it's suicide! Sure, kids you'll have, gold teeth, get fat, big in the tangerines—

HENNIE: Shut your face!

MOE: Who's it—some dope pullin' down twenty bucks a week? Cut your throat, sweetheart. Save time.

BESSIE: Never mind your two cents, Axelrod.

MOE: I say what I think—that's me!

HENNIE: That's you—a lousy fourflusher who'd steal the glasses off a blind man.

MOE: Get hot!

HENNIE: My God, do I need it—to listen to this mutt shoot his mouth off?

MYRON: Please. . . .

MOE: Now wait a minute, sweetheart, wait a minute. I don't have to take that from you.

BESSIE: Don't yell at her!

HENNIE: For two cents I'd spit in your eye.

MOE: *(Throwing coin to table.)* Here's two bits. *(*HENNIE *looks at him and then starts across the room.)*

BESSIE: Where are you going?

HENNIE: *(Crying.)* For my beauty nap, Mussolini. Wake me up when it's apple blossom time in Normandy. *(Exits.)*

MOE: Pretty, pretty—a sweet gal, your Hennie. See the look in her eyes?

BESSIE: She don't feel well. . . .

MYRON: Canned goods. . . .

BESSIE: So don't start with her.

MOE: Like a battleship she's got it. Not like other dames—shove 'em and they lay. Not her. I got a yen for her and I don't mean a Chinee coin.

BESSIE: Listen, Axelrod, in my house you don't talk this way. Either have respect or get out.

MOE: When I think about it . . . maybe I'd marry her myself.

BESSIE: *(Suddenly aware of* MOE*)* You could— What do you mean, Moe?

MOE: You ain't sunburnt—you heard me.

BESSIE: Why don't you, Moe? An old friend of the family like you. It would be a blessing on all of us.

MOE: You said she's engaged.

BESSIE: But maybe she don't know her own mind. Say, it's—

MOE: I need a wife like a hole in the head. . . . What's to know about women, I know. Even if I asked her. She won't do it! A guy with one leg—it gives her the heebie-jeebies. I know what she's looking for. An arrow-collar guy, a hero, but with a wad of jack. Only the two don't go together. But I got what it takes . . . plenty, and more where it comes from. . . . *(Breaks off, snorts and rubs his knee. A pause. In his room* JACOB *puts on Caruso singing the lament from "The Pearl Fishers.")*

BESSIE: It's right—she wants a millionaire with a mansion on Riverside Drive. So go fight City Hall. Cake?

MOE: Cake.

BESSIE: I'll make tea. But one thing—she's got a fine boy with a business brain. Caruso! *(Exits into the front room and stands in the dark, at the window.)*

MOE: No wet smack . . . a fine girl. . . . She'll burn that guy out in a month. *(*MOE *retrieves the quarter and spins it on the table.)*

MYRON: I remember that song . . . beautiful. Nora Bayes sang it at the old Proctor's Twenty-third Street—"When It's Apple Blossom Time in Normandy." . . .

MOE: She wantsa see me crawl—my head on a plate she wants! A snowball in hell's got a better chance. *(Out of sheer fury he spins the quarter in his fingers.)*

MYRON: *(as his eyes slowly fill with tears)*: Beautiful . . .

MOE: Match you for a quarter. Match you for any goddam thing you got. *(Spins the coin viciously.)* What the hell kind of house is this it ain't got an orange!!

SLOW CURTAIN

ACT II

Scene 1

One year later, a Sunday afternoon. The front room. JACOB *is giving his son* MORDECAI *(*UNCLE MORTY*) a haircut, newspapers spread around the base of the chair.* MOE *is reading a newspaper, leg propped on a chair.* RALPH, *in another chair, is spasmodically reading a paper.* UNCLE MORTY *reads colored jokes. Silence, then* BESSIE *enters.*

BESSIE: Dinner's in half an hour, Morty.

MORTY: *(Still reading jokes.)* I got time.

BESSIE: A duck. Don't get hair on the rug, Pop. *(Goes to the window and pulls down shade.)* What's the matter the shade's up to the ceiling?

JACOB: *(Pulling it up again.)* Since when do I give a haircut in the dark? *(He mimics her tone.)*

BESSIE: When you're finished, pull it down. I like my house to look respectable. Ralphie, bring up two bottles seltzer from Weiss.

RALPH: I'm reading the paper.

BESSIE: Uncle Morty likes a little seltzer.

RALPH: I'm expecting a phone call.

BESSIE: Noo, if it comes you'll be back. What's the matter? *(Gives him money from apron pocket.)* Take down the old bottles.

RALPH: *(To* JACOB.*)* Get that call if it comes. Say I'll be right back. *(*JACOB *nods assent.)*

MORTY: *(Giving change from vest.)* Get grandpa some cigarettes.

RALPH: Okay. *(Exits.)*

JACOB: What's new in the paper, Moe?

MOE: Still jumping off the high buildings like flies—the big shots who lost all their cocoanuts. Pfft!

JACOB: Suicides?

MOE: Plenty can't take it—good in the break, but can't take the whip in the stretch.

MORTY: *(Without looking up.)* I saw it happen Monday in my building. My hair stood up how they shoveled him together—like a pancake—a bankrupt manufacturer.

MOE: No brains.

MORTY: Enough . . . all over the sidewalk.

JACOB: If someone said five, ten years ago I couldn't make for myself a living, I wouldn't believe—

MORTY: Duck for dinner?

BESSIE: The best Long Island duck.

MORTY: I like goose.

BESSIE: A duck is just like a goose, only better.

MORTY: I like a goose.

BESSIE: The next time you'll be for Sunday dinner I'll make a goose.

MORTY: *(Sniffs deeply.)* Smells good. I'm a great boy for smells.

BESSIE: Ain't you ashamed? Once in a blue moon he should come to an only sister's house.

MORTY: Bessie, leave me live.

BESSIE: You should be ashamed!

MORTY: Quack quack!

BESSIE: No, better to lay around Mecca Temple playing cards with the Masons.

MORTY: *(With good nature.)* Bessie, don't you see Pop's giving me a haircut?

BESSIE: You don't need no haircut. Look, two hairs he took off.

MORTY: Pop likes to give me a haircut. If I said no he don't forget for a year, do you, Pop? An old man's like that.

JACOB: I still do an A-1 job.

MORTY: *(Winking.)* Pop cuts hair to fit the face, don't you, Pop?

JACOB: For sure, Morty. To each face a different haircut. Custom-built, no ready-made. A round face needs special—

BESSIE: *(Cutting him short.)* A Graduate from the B.M.T. *(Going.)* Don't forget the shade. *(The phone rings. She beats* JACOB *to it.)* Hello? Who is it, please? . . . Who is it please? . . . Miss Hirsch? No, he ain't here. . . . No, I couldn't say when. *(Hangs up sharply.)*

JACOB: For Ralph?

BESSIE: A wrong number. *(*JACOB *looks at her and goes back to his job.)*

JACOB: Excuse me!

BESSIE: *(To* MORTY.*)* Ralphie took another cut down the place yesterday.

MORTY: Business is bad. I saw his boss Harry Glicksman Thursday. I bought some velvets . . . they're coming in again.

BESSIE: Do something for Ralphie down there.

MORTY: What can I do? I mentioned it to Glicksman. He told me they squeezed out half the people. . . . *(*MYRON *enters dressed in apron.)*

BESSIE: What's gonna be the end? Myron's working only three days a week now.

MYRON: It's conditions.

BESSIE: Hennie's married with a baby . . . money just don't come in. I never saw conditions should be so bad.

MORTY: Times'll change.

MOE: The only thing'll change is my underwear.

MORTY: These last few years I got my share of gray hairs. *(Still reading jokes without having looked up once.)* Ha, ha, ha— Popeye the sailor ate spinach and knocked out four bums.

MYRON: I'll tell you the way I see it. The country needs a great man now—a regular Teddy Roosevelt.

MOE: What this country needs is a good five-cent earthquake.

JACOB: So long labor lives it should increase private gain—

BESSIE: *(To* JACOB.*)* Listen, Poppa, go talk on the street corner. The government'll give you free board the rest of your life.

MORTY: I'm surprised. Don't I send a five-dollar check for Pop every week?

BESSIE: You could afford a couple more and not miss it.

MORTY: Tell me jokes. Business is so rotten I could just as soon lay all day in the Turkish bath.

MYRON: Why'd I come in here? *(Puzzled, he exits.)*

MORTY: *(To* MOE.*)* I hear the bootleggers still do business, Moe.

MOE: Wake up! I kissed bootlegging bye-bye two years back.

MORTY: For a fact? What kind of racket is it now?

MOE: If I told you, you'd know something. *(*HENNIE *comes from bedroom.)*

HENNIE: Where's Sam?

BESSIE: Sam? In the kitchen.

HENNIE: *(Calls.)* Sam. Come take the diaper.

MORTY: How's the Mickey Louse? Ha, ha, ha. . . .

HENNIE: Sleeping.

MORTY: Ah, that's life to a baby. He sleeps—gets it in the mouth—sleeps some more. To raise a family nowadays you must be a damn fool.

BESSIE: Never mind, never mind, a woman who don't raise a family—a girl—should jump overboard. What's she good for? *(To* MOE*—to change the subject.)* Your leg bothers you bad?

MOE: It's okay, sweetheart.

BESSIE: *(To* MORTY.*)* It hurts him every time it's cold out. He's got four legs in the closet.

MORTY: Four wooden legs?

MOE: Three.

MORTY: What's the big idea?

MOE: Why not? Uncle Sam gives them out free.

MORTY: Say, maybe if Uncle Sam gave out less legs we could balance the budget.

JACOB: Or not have a war so they wouldn't have to give out legs.

MORTY: Shame on you, Pop. Everybody knows war is necessary.

MOE: Don't make me laugh. Ask me—the first time you pick up a dead one in the trench—then you learn war ain't so damn necessary.

MORTY: Say, you should kick. The rest of your life Uncle Sam pays you ninety a month. Look, not a worry in the world.

MOE: Don't make me laugh. Uncle Sam can take his *seventy* bucks and— *(Finishes with a gesture.)* Nothing good hurts. *(He rubs his stump.)*

HENNIE: Use a crutch, Axelrod. Give the stump a rest.

MOE: Mind your business, Feinschreiber.

BESSIE: It's a sensible idea.

MOE: Who asked you?

BESSIE: Look, he's ashamed.

MOE: So's your Aunt Fanny.

BESSIE: *(Naïvely.)* Who's got an Aunt Fanny? *(She cleans a rubber plant's leaves with her apron.)*

MORTY: It's a joke!

MOE: I don't want my paper creased before I read it. I want it fresh. Fifty times I said that.

BESSIE: Don't get so excited for a five-cent paper—our star boarder.

MOE: And I don't want no one using my razor either. Get it straight. I'm not buying ten blades a week for the Berger family. *(Furious, he limps out.)*

BESSIE: Maybe I'm using his razor too.

HENNIE: Proud!

BESSIE: You need luck with plants. I didn't clean off the leaves in a month.

MORTY: You keep the house like a pin and I like your cooking. Any time Myron fires you, come to me, Bessie. I'll let the butler go and you'll be my housekeeper. I don't like Japs so much—sneaky.

BESSIE: Say, you can't tell. Maybe any day I'm coming to stay. *(HENNIE exits.)*

JACOB: Finished.

MORTY: How much, Ed. Pinaud? *(Disengages self from chair.)*

JACOB: Five cents.

MORTY: Still five cents for a haircut to fit the face?

JACOB: Prices don't change by me. *(Takes a dollar.)* I can't change—

MORTY: Keep it. Buy yourself a Packard. Ha, ha, ha.

JACOB: *(Taking large envelope from pocket.)* Please, you'll keep this for me. Put it away.

MORTY: What is it?

JACOB: My insurance policy. I don't like it should lay around where something could happen.

MORTY: What could happen?

JACOB: Who knows, robbers, fire . . . they took next door. Fifty dollars from O'Reilly.

MORTY: Say, lucky a Berger didn't lose it.

JACOB: Put it downtown in the safe. Bessie don't have to know.

MORTY: It's made out to Bessie?

JACOB: No, to Ralph.

MORTY: To Ralph?

JACOB: He don't know. Some day he'll get three thousand.

MORTY: You got good years ahead.

JACOB: Behind. *(*RALPH *enters.)*

RALPH: Cigarettes. Did a call come?

JACOB: A few minutes. She don't let me answer it.

RALPH: Did Mom say I was coming back?

JACOB: No. *(*MORTY *is back at new jokes.)*

RALPH: She starting that stuff again? *(*BESSIE *enters.)* A call come for me?

BESSIE: *(Waters pot from milk bottle.)* A wrong number.

JACOB: Don't say a lie, Bessie.

RALPH: Blanche said she'd call me at two—was it her?

BESSIE: I said a wrong number.

RALPH: Please, Mom, if it was her tell me.

BESSIE: You call me a liar next. You got no shame—to start a scene in front of Uncle Morty. Once in a blue moon he comes—

RALPH: What's the shame? If my girl calls, I wanna know it.

BESSIE: You made enough mish mosh with her until now.

MORTY: I'm surprised, Bessie. For the love of Mike tell him yes or no.

BESSIE: I didn't tell him? No!

MORTY: *(To* RALPH.*)* No! *(*RALPH *goes to a window and looks out.)*

BESSIE: Morty, I didn't say before—he runs around steady with a girl.

MORTY: Terrible. Should he run around with a foxie-woxie?

BESSIE: A girl with no parents.

MORTY: An orphan?

BESSIE: I could die from shame. A year already he runs around with her. He brought her once for supper. Believe me, she didn't come again, no!

RALPH: Don't think I didn't ask her.

BESSIE: You hear? You raise them and what's in the end for all your trouble?

JACOB: When you'll lay in a grave, no more trouble. *(Exits.)*

MORTY: Quack quack!

BESSIE: A girl like that he wants to marry. A skinny consumptive-looking . . . six months already she's not working—taking charity from an aunt. You should see her. In a year she's dead on his hands.

RALPH: You'd cut her throat if you could.

BESSIE: That's right! Before she'd ruin a nice boy's life I would first go to prison. Miss Nobody should step in the picture and I'll stand by with my mouth shut.

RALPH: Miss Nobody! Who am I? Al Jolson?

BESSIE: Fix your tie!

RALPH: I'll take care of my own life.

BESSIE: You'll take care? Excuse my expression, you can't even wipe your nose yet! He'll take care!

MORTY: *(To* BESSIE.*)* I'm surprised. Don't worry so much, Bessie. When it's time to settle down he won't marry a poor girl, will you? In the long run common sense is thicker than love. I'm a great boy for live and let live.

BESSIE: Sure, it's easy to say. In the meantime he eats out my heart. You know I'm not strong.

MORTY: I know . . . a pussy cat . . . ha, ha, ha.

BESSIE: You got money and money talks. But without the dollar who sleeps at night?

RALPH: I been working for years, bringing in money here—putting it in your hand like a kid. All right, I can't get my teeth fixed. All right, that a new suit's like trying to buy the Chrysler Building. You never in your life bought me a pair of skates even—things I died for when I was a kid. I don't care about that stuff, see. Only just remember I pay some of the bills around here, just a few . . . and if my girl calls me on the phone I'll talk to her any time I please. *(He exits.* HENNIE *applauds.)*

BESSIE: Don't be so smart, Miss America! *(To* MORTY.*)* He didn't have skates! But when he got sick, a twelve-year-old boy, who called a big specialist for the last $25 in the house? Skates!

JACOB: *(Just in. Adjusts window shade.)* It looks like snow today.

MORTY: It's about time—winter.

BESSIE: Poppa here could talk like Samuel Webster, too, but it's just talk. He should try to buy a two-cent pickle in the Burland Market without money.

MORTY: I'm getting an appetite.

BESSIE: Right away we'll eat. I made chopped liver for you.

MORTY: My specialty!

BESSIE: Ralph should only be a success like you, Morty. I should only live to see the day when he rides up to the door in a big car with a chauffeur and a radio. I could die happy, believe me.

MORTY: Success she says. She should see how we spend thousands of dollars making up a winter line and winter don't come—summer in January. Can you beat it?

JACOB: Don't live, just make success.

MORTY: Chopped liver—ha!

JACOB: Ha! *(Exits.)*

MORTY: When they start arguing, I don't hear. Suddenly I'm deaf. I'm a great boy for the practical side. *(He looks over to* HENNIE, *who sits rubbing her hands with lotion.)*

HENNIE: Hands like a raw potato.

MORTY: What's the matter? You don't look so well . . . no pep.

HENNIE: I'm swell.

MORTY: You used to be such a pretty girl.

HENNIE: Maybe I got the blues. You can't tell.

MORTY: You could stand a new dress.

HENNIE: That's not all I could stand.

MORTY: Come down to the place tomorrow and pick out a couple from the "eleven-eighty" line. Only don't sing me the blues.

HENNIE: Thanks. I need some new clothes.

MORTY: I got two thousand pieces of merchandise waiting in the stock room for winter.

HENNIE: I never had anything from life. Sam don't help.

MORTY: He's crazy about the kid.

HENNIE: Crazy is right. Twenty-one a week he brings in—a nigger don't have it so hard. I wore my fingers off on an Underwood for six years. For what? Now I wash baby diapers. Sure, I'm crazy about the kid too. But half the night the kid's up. Try to sleep. You don't know how it is, Uncle Morty.

MORTY: No, I don't know. I was born yesterday. Ha, ha, ha. Some day I'll leave you a little nest egg. You like eggs? Ha?

HENNIE: When? When I'm dead and buried?

MORTY: No, when *I'm* dead and buried. Ha, ha, ha.

HENNIE: You should know what I'm thinking.

MORTY: Ha, ha, ha, I know. *(*MYRON *enters.)*

MYRON: I never take a drink. I'm just surprised at myself, I—

MORTY: I got a pain. Maybe I'm hungry.

MYRON: Come inside, Morty. Bessie's got some schnapps.

MORTY: I'll take a drink. Yesterday I missed the Turkish bath.

MYRON: I get so bitter when I take a drink, it just surprises me.

MORTY: Look how fat. Say, you live once. . . . Quack, quack. *(Both exit.* MOE *stands silently in the doorway.)*

SAM: *(Entering.)* I'll make Leon's bottle now!

HENNIE: No, let him sleep, Sam. Take away the diaper. *(He does. Exits.)*

MOE: *(Advancing into the room.)* That your husband?

HENNIE: Don't you know?

MOE: Maybe he's a nurse you hired for the kid—it looks it—how he tends it. A guy comes howling to your old lady every time you look cock-eyed. Does he sleep with you?

HENNIE: Don't be so wise!

MOE: *(Indicating newspaper.)* Here's a dame strangled her hubby with wire. Claimed she didn't like him. Why don't you brain Sam with an axe some night?

HENNIE: Why don't you lay an egg, Axelrod?

MOE: I laid a few in my day, Feinschreiber. Hard-boiled ones too.

HENNIE: Yeah?

MOE: Yeah. You wanna know what I see when I look in your eyes?

HENNIE: No.

MOE: Ted Lewis playing the clarinet—some of those high crazy notes! Christ, you coulda had a guy with some guts instead of a cluck stands around boilin' baby nipples.

HENNIE: Meaning you?

MOE: Meaning me, sweetheart.

HENNIE: Think you're pretty good.

MOE: You'd know if I slept with you again.

HENNIE: I'll smack your face in a minute.

MOE: You do and I'll break your arm. *(Holds up paper.)* Take a look. *(Reads.)* "Ten-day luxury cruise to Havana." That's the stuff you coulda had. Put up at ritzy hotels, frenchie soap, champagne. Now you're tied down to "Snake-Eye" here. What for? What's it get you? . . . A 2 × 4 flat on 108th Street . . . a pain in the bustle it gets you.

HENNIE: What's it to you?

MOE: I know you from the old days. How you like to spend it! What I mean! Lizard-skin shoes, perfume behind the ears. . . . You're in a mess, Paradise! Paradise—that's a hot one—yah, crazy to eat a knish at your own wedding.

HENNIE: I get it—you're jealous. You can't get me.

MOE: Don't make me laugh.

HENNIE: Kid Jailbird's been trying to make me for years. You'd give your other leg. I'm hooked? Maybe, but you're in the same boat. Only it's worse for you. I don't give a damn no more, but you gotta yen makes you—

MOE: Don't make me laugh.

HENNIE: Compared to you I'm sittin' on top of the world.

MOE: You're losing your looks. A dame don't stay young forever.

HENNIE: You're a liar. I'm only twenty-four.

MOE: When you comin' home to stay?

HENNIE: Wouldn't you like to know?

MOE: I'll get you again.

HENNIE: Think so?

MOE: Sure, whatever goes up comes down. You're easy—you remember—two for a nickel—a pushover! *(Suddenly she slaps him. They both seem stunned.)* What's the idea?

HENNIE: Go on . . . break my arm.

MOE: *(As if saying "I love you.")* Listen, lousy.

HENNIE: Go on, do something!

MOE: Listen—

HENNIE: You're so damn tough!

MOE: You like me. *(He takes her.)*

HENNIE: Take your hand off! *(Pushes him away.)* Come around when it's a flood again and they put you in the ark with the animals. Not even then—if you was the last man!

MOE: Baby, if you had a dog I'd love the dog.

HENNIE: Gorilla! *(Exits.* RALPH *enters.)*

RALPH: Were you here before?

MOE: *(Sits.)* What?

RALPH: When the call came for me?

MOE: What?

RALPH: The call came. *(*JACOB *enters.)*

MOE: *(Rubbing his leg.)* No.

JACOB: Don't worry, Ralphie, she'll call back.

RALPH: Maybe not. I think somethin's the matter.

JACOB: What?

RALPH: I don't know. I took her home from the movie last night. She asked me what I'd think if she went away.

JACOB: Don't worry, she'll call again.

RALPH: Maybe not, if Mom insulted her. She gets it on both ends, the poor kid. Lived in an orphan asylum most of her life. They shove her around like an empty freight train.

JACOB: After dinner go see her.

RALPH: Twice they kicked me down the stairs.

JACOB: Life should have some dignity.

RALPH: Every time I go near the place I get heart failure. The uncle drives a bus. You oughta see him—like Babe Ruth.

MOE: Use your brains. Stop acting like a kid who still wets the bed. Hire a room somewhere—a club room for two members.

RALPH: Not that kind of proposition, Moe.

MOE: Don't be a bush leaguer all your life.

RALPH: Cut it out!

MOE: *(On a sudden upsurge of emotion.)* Ever sleep with one? Look at 'im blush.

RALPH: You don't know her.

MOE: I seen her—the kind no one sees undressed till the undertaker works on her.

RALPH: Why give me the needles all the time? What'd I ever do to you?

MOE: Not a thing. You're a nice kid. But grow up! In life there's two kinds—the men that's sure of themselves and the ones who ain't! It's time you quit being a selling plater* and got in the first class.

*A mediocre horse, unlikely to win a race.

JACOB: And you, Axelrod?

MOE: *(To* JACOB.*)* Scratch your whiskers! *(To* RALPH.*)* Get independent. Get what-it-takes and be yourself. Do what you like.

RALPH: Got a suggestion?

*(*MORTY *enters, eating.)*

MOE: Sure, pick out a racket. Shake down the cocoanuts. See what that does.

MORTY: We know what it does—puts a pudding on your nose! Sing Sing! Easy money's against the law. Against the law don't win. A racket is illegitimate, no?

MOE: It's all a racket—from horse racing down. Marriage, politics, big business—everybody plays cops and robbers. You, you're a racketeer yourself.

MORTY: Who? Me? Personally I manufacture dresses.

MOE: Horse feathers!

MORTY: *(Seriously.)* Don't make such remarks to me without proof. I'm a great one for proof. That's why I made a success in business. Proof—put up or shut up, like a game of cards. I heard this remark before—a rich man's a crook who steals from the poor. Personally, I don't like it. It's a big lie!

MOE: If you don't like it, buy yourself a fife and drum—and go fight your own war.

MORTY: Sweatshop talk. Every Jew and Wop in the shop eats my bread and behind my back says, "a sonofabitch." I started from a poor boy who worked on an ice wagon for two dollars a week. Pop's right here—he'll tell you. I made it honest. In the whole industry nobody's got a better name.

JACOB: It's an exception, such success.

MORTY: Ralph can't do the same thing?

JACOB: No, Morty, I don't think. In a house like this he don't realize even the possibilities of life. Economics comes down like a ton of coal on the head.

MOE: Red rover, red rover, let Jacob come over!

JACOB: In my day the propaganda was for God. Now it's for success. A boy don't turn around without having shoved in him he should make success.

MORTY: Pop, you're a comedian, a regular Charlie Chaplin.

JACOB: He dreams all night of fortunes. Why not? Don't it say in the movies he should have a personal steamship, pyjamas for fifty dollars a pair and a toilet like a monument? But in the morning he wakes up and for ten dollars he can't fix the teeth. And millions more worse off in the mills of the South—starvation wages. The blood from the worker's heart. *(*MORTY *laughs loud and long.)* Laugh, laugh . . . tomorrow not.

MORTY: A real, a real Boob McNutt* you're getting to be.

JACOB: Laugh, my son. . . .

MORTY: Here is the North, Pop.

JACOB: North, south, it's one country.

MORTY: The country's all right. A duck quacks in every pot!

JACOB: You never heard how they shoot down men and women which ask a better wage? Kentucky 1932?

MORTY: That's a pile of chopped liver, Pop.

*(*BESSIE *and others enter.)*

JACOB: Pittsburgh, Passaic, Illinois—slavery—it begins where success begins in a competitive system.

*(*MORTY *howls with delight.)*

MORTY: Oh Pop, what are you bothering? Why? Tell me why? Ha ha ha. I bought you a phonograph . . . stick to Caruso.

BESSIE: He's starting up again.

MORTY: Don't bother with Kentucky. It's full of moonshiners.

JACOB: Sure, sure—

MORTY: You don't know practical affairs. Stay home and cut hair to fit the face.

JACOB: It says in the Bible how the Red Sea opened and the Egyptians went in and the sea rolled over them. *(Quotes two lines of Hebrew.)* In this boy's life a Red Sea will happen again. I see it!

MORTY: I'm getting sore, Pop, with all this sweatshop talk.

*A character in the "colored jokes" (comic strips) Morty reads.

BESSIE: He don't stop a minute. The whole day, like a phonograph.

MORTY: I'm surprised. Without a rich man you don't have a roof over your head. You don't know it?

MYRON: Now you can't bite the hand that feeds you.

RALPH: Let him alone—he's right!

BESSIE: Another county heard from.

RALPH: It's the truth. It's—

MORTY: Keep quiet, snotnose!

JACOB: For sure, charity, a bone for an old dog. But in Russia an old man don't take charity so his eyes turn black in his head. In Russia they got Marx.

MORTY: *(Scoffingly.)* Who's Marx?

MOE: An outfielder for the Yanks. *(*MORTY *howls with delight.)*

MORTY: Ha ha ha, it's better than the jokes. I'm telling you. This is Uncle Sam's country. Put it in your pipe and smoke it.

BESSIE: Russia, he says! Read the papers.

SAM: Here is opportunity.

MYRON: People can't believe in God in Russia. The papers tell the truth, they do.

JACOB: So you believe in God . . . you got something for it? You! You worked for all the capitalists. You harvested the fruit from your labor? You got God! But the past comforts you? The present smiles on you, yes? It promises you the future something? Did you found a piece of earth where you could live like a human being and die with the sun on your face? Tell me, yes, tell me. I would like to know myself. But on these questions, on this theme—the struggle for existence—you can't make an answer. The answer I see in your face . . . the answer is your mouth can't talk. In this dark corner you sit and you die. But abolish private property!

BESSIE: *(Settling the issue.)* Noo, go fight City Hall!

MORTY: He's drunk!

JACOB: I'm studying from books a whole lifetime.

MORTY: That's what it is—he's drunk. What the hell does all that mean?

JACOB: If you don't know, why should I tell you.

MORTY: *(Triumphant at last.)* You see? Hear him? Like all those nuts, don't know what they're saying.

JACOB: I know, I know.

MORTY: Like Boob McNutt you know! Don't go in the park, Pop—the squirrels'll get you. Ha, ha, ha. . . .

BESSIE: Save your appetite, Morty. *(To* MYRON.*)* Don't drop the duck.

MYRON: We're ready to eat, Momma.

MORTY: *(To* JACOB.*)* Shame on you. It's your second childhood.

(Now they file out, MYRON *first with the duck, the others behind him.)*

BESSIE: Come eat. We had enough for one day. *(Exits.)*

MORTY: Ha, ha, ha. Quack, quack. *(Exits.)*

*(*JACOB *sits there trembling and deeply humiliated.* MOE *approaches him and thumbs the old man's nose in the direction of the dining room.)*

MOE: Give 'em five. *(Takes his hand away.)* They got you pasted on the wall like a picture, Jake. *(He limps out to seat himself at the table in the next room.)*

JACOB: Go eat, boychick. *(*RALPH *comes to him.)* He gives me eat, so I'll climb in a needle. One time I saw an old horse in summer . . . he wore a straw hat . . . the ears stuck out on top. An old horse for hire. Give me back my young days . . . give me fresh blood . . . arms . . . give me— *(The telephone rings. Quickly* RALPH *goes to it.* JACOB *pulls the curtains and stands there, a sentry on guard.)*

RALPH: Hello? . . . Yeah, I went to the store and came right back, right after you called. *(Looks at* JACOB.*)*

JACOB: Speak, speak. Don't be afraid they'll hear.

RALPH: I'm sorry if Mom said something. You know how excitable Mom is . . . Sure! What? . . . Sure, I'm listening. . . . Put on the radio, Jake. *(*JACOB *does so. Music comes in and up, a tango, grating with an insistent nostalgic pulse. Under the cover of the music* RALPH *speaks more freely.)* Yes . . . yes . . . What's the matter? Why're you crying? What happened? *(To* JACOB.*)* She's putting her uncle on. Yes? . . . Listen, Mr. Hirsch, what're you trying to do? What's the big idea? Honest to God. I'm in no mood for joking! Lemme talk to her! Gimme Blanche! *(Waits.)* Blanche? What's this? Is this a joke? Is that true? I'm coming right down! I know, but— You wanna do that? . . . I know, but— I'm coming down . . . tonight! Nine o'clock . . . sure . . . sure . . . sure. . . . *(Hangs up.)*

JACOB: What happened?

MORTY: *(Enters.)* Listen, Pop. I'm surprised you didn't— *(He howls, shakes his head in mock despair, exits.)*

JACOB: Boychick, what?

RALPH: I don't get it straight. *(To* JACOB.*)* She's leaving . . .

JACOB: Where?

RALPH: Out West— To Cleveland.

JACOB: Cleveland?

RALPH: . . . In a week or two. Can you picture it? It's a put-up job. But they can't get away with that.

JACOB: We'll find something.

RALPH: Sure, the angels of heaven'll come down on her uncle's cab and whisper in his ear.

JACOB: Come eat. . . . We'll find something.

RALPH: I'm meeting her tonight, but I know— *(*BESSIE *throws open the curtain between the two rooms and enters.)*

BESSIE: Maybe we'll serve you for a special blue plate supper in the garden?

JACOB: All right, all right. *(*BESSIE *goes over to the window, levels the shade and on her way out, clicks off the radio.)*

MORTY: *(Within.)* Leave the music, Bessie. *(She clicks it on again, looks at them, exits.)*

RALPH: I know . . .

JACOB: Don't cry, boychick. *(Goes over to* RALPH.*)* Why should you make like this? Tell me why you should cry, just tell me. . . . *(*JACOB *takes* RALPH *in his arms and both, trying to keep back the tears, trying fearfully not to be heard by the others in the dining room, begin crying.)* You mustn't cry. . . .

(The tango twists on. Inside, the clatter of dishes and the clash of cutlery sound. MORTY *begins to howl with laughter.)*

CURTAIN

Scene 2

That night. The dark dining room.

AT RISE: JACOB *is heard in his lighted room, reading from a sheet, declaiming aloud as if to an audience.*

JACOB: They are there to remind us of the horrors—under those crosses lie hundreds of thousands of workers and farmers who murdered each other in uniform for the greater glory of capitalism. *(Comes out of his room.)* The new imperialist war will send millions to their death, will bring prosperity to the pockets of the capitalist—aie, Morty—and will bring only greater hunger and misery to the masses of workers and farmers. The memories of the last world slaughter are still vivid in our minds. *(Hearing a noise he quickly retreats to his room.* RALPH *comes in from the street. He sits with hat and coat on.* JACOB *tentatively opens door and asks)* Ralphie?

RALPH: It's getting pretty cold out.

JACOB: *(Enters room fully, cleaning hair clippers.)* We should have steam till twelve instead of ten. Go complain to the Board of Health.

RALPH: It might snow.

JACOB: It don't hurt . . . extra work for men.

RALPH: When I was a kid I laid awake at nights and heard the sounds of trains . . . faraway lonesome sounds . . . boats going up and down the river. I used to think of all kinds of things I wanted to do. What was it, Jake? Just a bunch of noise in my head?

JACOB: *(Waiting for news of the girl.)* You wanted to make for yourself a certain kind of world.

RALPH: I guess I didn't. I'm feeling pretty, pretty low.

JACOB: You're a young boy and for you life is all in front like a big mountain. You got feet to climb.

RALPH: I don't know how.

JACOB: So you'll find out. Never a young man had such opportunity like today. He could make history.

RALPH: Ten P.M. and all is well. Where's everybody?

JACOB: They went.

RALPH: Uncle Morty too?

JACOB: Hennie and Sam he drove down.

RALPH: I saw her.

JACOB: *(Alert and eager.)* Yes, yes, tell me.

RALPH: I waited in Mount Morris Park till she came out. So cold I did a buck'n wing to keep warm. She's scared to death.

JACOB: They made her?

RALPH: Sure. She wants to go. They keep yelling at her—they want her to marry a millionaire, too.

JACOB: You told her you love her?

RALPH: Sure. "Marry me," I said. "Marry me tomorrow." On sixteen bucks a week. On top of that I had to admit Mom'd have Uncle Morty get me fired in a second. . . . Two can starve as cheap as one!

JACOB: So what happened?

RALPH: I made her promise to meet me tomorrow.

JACOB: Now she'll go in the West?

RALPH: I'd fight the whole goddam world with her, but not her. No guts. The hell with her. If she wantsa go—all right—I'll get along.

JACOB: For sure, there's more important things than girls. . . .

RALPH: You said a mouthful . . . and maybe I don't see it. She'll see what I can do. No one stops me when I get going. . . .

(Near to tears, he has to stop. JACOB *examines his clippers very closely.)*

JACOB: Electric clippers never do a job like by hand.

RALPH: Why won't Mom let us live here?

JACOB: Why? Why? Because in a society like this, today people don't love. Hate!

RALPH: Gee, I'm no bum who hangs around pool parlors. I got the stuff to go ahead. I don't know what to do.

JACOB: Look on me and learn what to do, boychick. Here sits an old man polishing tools. You think maybe I'll use them again! Look on this failure and see for seventy years he talked with good ideas, but only in the head. It's enough for me now I should see your happiness. This is why I tell you—DO! Do what is in your heart and you carry in yourself a revolution. But you should act. Not like me. A man who had golden opportunities but drank instead a glass tea. No. . . .

(A pause of silence.)

RALPH: *(Listening.)* Hear it? The Boston airmail plane. Ten minutes late. I get a kick the way it cuts across the Bronx every night.

(The bell rings. SAM, *excited, disheveled, enters.)*

JACOB: You came back so soon?

SAM: Where's Mom?

JACOB: Mom? Look on the chandelier.

SAM: Nobody's home?

JACOB: Sit down. Right away they're coming. You went in the street without a tie?

SAM: Maybe it's a crime.

JACOB: Excuse me.

RALPH: You had a fight with Hennie again?

SAM: She'll fight once . . . some day. . . . *(Lapses into silence.)*

JACOB: In my day the daughter came home. Now comes the son-in-law.

SAM: Once too often she'll fight with me, Hennie. I mean it. I mean it like anything. I'm a person with a bad heart. I sit quiet, but inside I got a—

RALPH: What happened?

SAM: I'll talk to Mom. I'll see Mom.

JACOB: Take an apple.

SAM: Please . . . he tells me apples.

RALPH: Why hop around like a billiard ball?

SAM: Even in a joke she should dare say it.

JACOB: My grandchild said something?

SAM: To my father in the old country they did a joke . . . I'll tell you: One day in Odessa he talked to another Jew on the street. They didn't like it, they jumped on him like a wild wolf.

RALPH: Who?

SAM: Cossacks. They cut off his beard. A Jew without a beard! He came home—I remember like yesterday how he came home and went in bed for two days. He put like this the cover on his face. No one should see. The third morning he died.

RALPH: From what?

SAM: From a broken heart. . . . Some people are like this. Me too. I could die like this from shame.

JACOB: Hennie told you something?

SAM: Straight out she said it—like a lightning from the sky. The baby ain't mine. She said it.

RALPH: Don't be a dope.

JACOB: For sure, a joke.

RALPH: She's kidding you.

SAM: She should kid a policeman, not Sam Feinschreiber. Please . . . you don't know her like me. I wake up in the nighttime and she sits watching me like I don't know what. I make a nice living from the store. But it's no use—she looks for a star in the sky. I'm afraid like anything. You could go crazy from less even. What I shall do I'll ask Mom.

JACOB: "Go home and sleep," she'll say. "It's a bad dream."

SAM: It don't satisfy me more, such remarks, when Hennie could kill in the bed. *(*JACOB *laughs.)* Don't laugh. I'm so nervous—look, two times I weighed myself on the subway station. *(Throws small cards to table.)*

JACOB: *(Examining one.)* One hundred and thirty-eight—also a fortune. *(Turns it and reads)* "You are inclined to deep thinking, and have a high admiration for intellectual excellence and inclined to be very exclusive in the selection of friends." Correct! I think maybe you got mixed up in the wrong family, Sam.

*(*MYRON *and* BESSIE *now enter.)*

BESSIE: Look, a guest! What's the matter? Something wrong with the baby? *(Waits.)*

SAM: No.

BESSIE: Noo?

SAM: *(In a burst.)* I wash my hands from everything.

BESSIE: Take off your coat and hat. Have a seat. Excitement don't help. Myron, make tea. You'll have a glass tea. We'll talk like civilized people. *(*MYRON *goes.)* What is it, Ralph, you're all dressed up for a party? *(He looks at her silently and exits. To* SAM.*)* We saw a very good movie, with Wallace Beery. He acts like life, very good.

MYRON: *(Within.)* Polly Moran too.

BESSIE: Polly Moran too—a woman with a nose from here to Hunts Point, but a fine player. Poppa, take away the tools and the books.

JACOB: All right. *(Exits to his room.)*

BESSIE: Noo, Sam, why do you look like a funeral?

SAM: I can't stand it. . . .

BESSIE: Wait. *(Yells.)* You took up Tootsie on the roof.

JACOB: *(Within.)* In a minute.

BESSIE: What can't you stand?

SAM: She said I'm a second fiddle in my own house.

BESSIE: Who?

SAM: Hennie. In the second place, it ain't my baby, she said.

BESSIE: What? What are you talking? *(*MYRON *enters with dishes.)*

SAM: From her own mouth. It went like a knife in my heart.

BESSIE: Sam, what're you saying?

SAM: Please, I'm making a story? I fell in the chair like a dead.

BESSIE: Such a story you believe?

SAM: I don't know.

BESSIE: How you don't know?

SAM: She told me even the man.

BESSIE: Impossible!

SAM: I can't believe myself. But she said it. I'm a second fiddle, she said. She made such a yell everybody heard for ten miles.

BESSIE: Such a thing Hennie should say—impossible!

SAM: What should I do? With my bad heart such a remark kills.

MYRON: Hennie don't feel well, Sam. You see, she—

BESSIE: What then?—a sick girl. Believe me, a mother knows. Nerves. Our Hennie's got a bad temper. You'll let her she says anything. She takes after me—nervous. *(To* MYRON.*)* You ever heard such a remark in all your life? She should make such a statement! Bughouse.

MYRON: The little one's been sick all these months. Hennie needs a rest. No doubt.

BESSIE: Sam don't think she means it—

MYRON: Oh, I know he don't, of course—

BESSIE: I'll say the truth, Sam. We didn't half the time understand her ourselves. A girl with her own mind. When she makes it up, wild horses wouldn't change her.

SAM: She don't love me.

BESSIE: This is sensible, Sam?

SAM: Not for a nickel.

BESSIE: What do you think? She married you for your money? For your looks? You ain't no John Barrymore, Sam. No, she liked you.

SAM: Please, not for a nickel. *(*JACOB *stands in the doorway.)*

BESSIE: We stood right here the first time she said it. "Sam Feinschreiber's a nice boy," she said it, "a boy he's got good common sense, with a business head." Right here she said it, in this room. You sent her two boxes of candy together, you remember?

MYRON: Loft's candy.

BESSIE: This is when she said it. What do you think?

MYRON: You were just the only boy she cared for.

BESSIE: So she married you. Such a world . . . plenty of boy friends she had, believe me!

JACOB: A popular girl. . . .

MYRON: Y-e-s.

BESSIE: I'll say it plain out—Moe Axelrod offered her plenty—a servant, a house . . . she don't have to pick up a hand.

MYRON: Oh, Moe? Just wild about her. . . .

SAM: Moe Axelrod? He wanted to—

BESSIE: But she didn't care. A girl like Hennie you don't

buy. I should never live to see another day if I'm telling a lie.

SAM: She was kidding me.

BESSIE: What then? You shouldn't be foolish.

SAM: The baby looks like my family. He's got Feinschreiber eyes.

BESSIE: A blind man could see it.

JACOB: Sure . . . sure. . . .

SAM: The baby looks like me. Yes. . . .

BESSIE: You could believe me.

JACOB: Any day. . . .

SAM: But she tells me the man. She made up his name too?

BESSIE: Sam, Sam, look in the phone book—a million names.

MYRON: Tom, Dick and Harry. *(*JACOB *laughs quietly, soberly.)*

BESSIE: Don't stand around, Poppa. Take Tootsie on the roof. And you don't let her go under the water tank.

JACOB: Schmah Yisroeal. Behold! *(Quietly laughing, he goes back into his room, closing the door behind him.)*

SAM: I won't stand he should make insults. A man eats out his—

BESSIE: No, no, he's an old man—a second childhood. Myron, bring in the tea. Open a jar of raspberry jelly. *(*MYRON *exits.)*

SAM: Mom, you think—?

BESSIE: I'll talk to Hennie. It's all right.

SAM: Tomorrow, I'll take her by the doctor. *(*RALPH *enters.)*

BESSIE: Stay for a little tea.

SAM: No, I'll go home. I'm tired. Already I caught a cold in such weather. *(Blows his nose.)*

MYRON: *(Entering with stuffs.)* Going home?

SAM: I'll go in bed. I caught a cold.

MYRON: Teddy Roosevelt used to say, "When you have a problem, sleep on it."

BESSIE: My Sam is no problem.

MYRON: I don't mean . . . I mean he said—

BESSIE: Call me tomorrow, Sam.

SAM: I'll phone suppertime. Sometime I think there's something funny about me. *(*MYRON *sees him out. In the following pause, Caruso is heard singing within.)*

BESSIE: A bargain! Second fiddle. By me he don't even play in the orchestra—a man like a mouse. Maybe she'll lay down and die 'cause he makes a living?

RALPH: Can I talk to you about something?

BESSIE: What's the matter—I'm biting you?

RALPH: It's something about Blanche.

BESSIE: Don't tell me.

RALPH: Listen now—

BESSIE: I don't wanna know.

RALPH: She's got no place to go.

BESSIE: I don't want to know.

RALPH: Mom, I love this girl. . . .

BESSIE: So go knock your head against the wall.

RALPH: I want her to come here. Listen, Mom, I want you to let her live here for a while.

BESSIE: You got funny ideas, my son.

RALPH: I'm as good as anyone else. Don't I have some rights in the world? Listen, Mom, if I don't do something, she's going away. Why don't you do it? Why don't you let her stay here for a few weeks? Things'll pick up. Then we can—

BESSIE: Sure, sure. I'll keep her fresh on ice for a wedding day. That's what you want?

RALPH: No, I mean you should—

BESSIE: Or maybe you'll sleep here in the same bed without marriage. *(JACOB stands in his doorway, dressed.)*

RALPH: Don't say that, Mom. I only mean. . . .

BESSIE: What you mean, I know . . . and what I mean I also know. Make up your mind. For your own good, Ralphie. If she dropped in the ocean I don't lift a finger.

RALPH: That's all, I suppose.

BESSIE: With me it's one thing—a boy should have respect for his own future. Go to sleep, you look tired. In the morning you'll forget.

JACOB: "Awake and sing, ye that dwell in dust, and the earth shall cast out the dead." It's cold out?

MYRON: Oh, yes.

JACOB: I'll take up Tootsie now.

MYRON: *(Eating bread and jam.)* He come on us like the wild man of Borneo, Sam. I don't think Hennie was fool enough to tell him the truth like that.

BESSIE: Myron! *(A deep pause.)*

RALPH: What did he say?
BESSIE: Never mind.
RALPH: I heard him. I heard him. You don't needa tell me.
BESSIE: Never mind.
RALPH: You trapped that guy.
BESSIE: Don't say another word.
RALPH: Just have respect? That's the idea?
BESSIE: Don't say another word. I'm boiling over ten times inside.
RALPH: You won't let Blanche here, huh. I'm not sure I want her. You put one over on that little shrimp. The cat's whiskers, Mom?
BESSIE: I'm telling you something!
RALPH: I got the whole idea. I get it so quick my head's swimming. Boy, what a laugh! I suppose you know about this, Jake?
JACOB: Yes.
RALPH: Why didn't you do something?
JACOB: I'm an old man.
RALPH: What's that got to do with the price of bonds? Sits around and lets a thing like that happen! You make me sick too.
MYRON: *(After a pause.)* Let me say something, son.
RALPH: Take your hand away! Sit in a corner and wag your tail. Keep on boasting you went to law school for two years.
MYRON: I want to tell you—
RALPH: You never in your life had a thing to tell me.
BESSIE: *(Bitterly.)* Don't say a word. Let him, let him run and tell Sam. Publish in the papers, give a broadcast on the radio. To him it don't matter nothing his family sits with tears pouring from the eyes. *(To* JACOB.*)* What are you waiting for? I didn't tell you twice already about the dog? You'll stand around with Caruso and make a bughouse. It ain't enough all day long. Fifty times I told you I'll break every record in the house. *(She brushes past him, breaks the records, comes out.)* The next time I say something you'll maybe believe it. Now maybe you learned a lesson. *(Pause.)*
JACOB: *(Quietly.)* Bessie, new lessons . . . not for an old dog.

*(*MOE *enters.)*

MYRON: You didn't have to do it, Momma.

BESSIE: Talk better to your son, Mr. Berger! Me, I don't lay down and die for him and Poppa no more. I'll work like a nigger? For what? Wait, the day comes when you'll be punished. When it's too late you'll remember how you sucked away a mother's life. Talk to him, tell him how I don't sleep at night. *(Bursts into tears and exits.)*

MOE: *(Sings.)* "Good by to all your sorrows. You never hear them talk about the war, in the land of Yama Yama. . . ."

MYRON: Yes, Momma's a sick woman, Ralphie.

RALPH: Yeah?

MOE: We'll be out of the trenches by Christmas. Putt, putt, putt . . . here, stinker. . . . *(Picks up Tootsie, a small, white poodle that just then enters from the hall.)* If there's reincarnation in the next life I wanna be a dog and lay in a fat lady's lap. Barrage over? How 'bout a little pinochle, Pop?

JACOB: Nnno.

RALPH: *(Taking dog.)* I'll take her up. *(Conciliatory.)*

JACOB: No, I'll do it. *(Takes dog.)*

RALPH: *(Ashamed.)* It's cold out.

JACOB: I was cold before in my life. A man sixty-seven. . . . *(Strokes the dog.)* Tootsie is my favorite lady in the house. *(He slowly passes across the room and exits. A settling pause.)*

MYRON: She cried all last night—Tootsie—I heard her in the kitchen like a young girl.

MOE: Tonight I could do something. I got a yen . . . I don't know.

MYRON: *(Rubbing his head.)* My scalp is impoverished.

RALPH: Mom bust all his records.

MYRON: She didn't have to do it.

MOE: Tough tit! Now I can sleep in the morning. Who the hell wantsa hear a wop air his tonsils all day long!

RALPH: *(Handling the fragment of a record.)* "O Paradiso!"

MOE: *(Gets cards.)* It's snowing out, girls.

MYRON: There's no more big snows like in the old days. I think the whole world's changing. I see it, right under our very eyes. No one hardly remembers any more when we used to have gaslight and all the dishes had little fishes on them.

MOE: It's the system, girls.

MYRON: I was a little boy when it happened—the Great Blizzard. It snowed three days without a stop that time. Yes, and the horse cars stopped. A silence of death was on the city and little babies got no milk . . . they say a lot of people died that year.

MOE: *(Singing as he deals himself cards.)*

"Lights are blinking while you're drinking,
That's the place where the good fellows go.
Good-bye to all your sorrows,
You never hear them talk about the war,
In the land of Yama Yama
Funicalee, funicala, funicalo. . . ."

MYRON: What can I say to you, Big Boy?

RALPH: Not a damn word.

MOE: *(Goes "ta ra ta ra" throughout.)*

MYRON: I know how you feel about all those things, I know.

RALPH: Forget it.

MYRON: And your girl. . . .

RALPH: Don't soft soap me all of a sudden.

MYRON: I'm not foreign-born. I'm an American, and yet I never got close to you. It's an American father's duty to be his son's friend.

RALPH: Who said that—Teddy R.?

MOE: *(Dealing cards.)* You're breaking his heart, "Litvak."

MYRON: It just happened the other day. The moment I began losing my hair I just knew I was destined to be a failure in life . . . and when I grew bald I was. Now isn't that funny, Big Boy?

MOE: It's a pisscutter!

MYRON: I believe in Destiny.

MOE: You get what-it-takes. Then they don't catch you with your pants down. *(Sings out)*: Eight of clubs. . . .

MYRON: I really don't know. I sold jewelry on the road before I married. It's one thing to— Now here's a thing the druggist gave me. *(Reads)* "The Marvel Cosmetic Girl of Hollywood is going on the air. Give this charming little radio singer a name and win five thousand dollars. If you will send—"

MOE: Your old man still believes in Santy Claus.

MYRON: Someone's got to win. The government isn't gonna allow everything to be a fake.

MOE: It's a fake. There ain't no prizes. It's a fake.

MYRON: It says—

RALPH: *(Snatching it.)* For Christ's sake, Pop, forget it. Grow up. Jake's right—everybody's crazy. It's like a zoo in this house. I'm going to bed.

MOE: In the land of Yama Yama. . . . *(Goes on with ta ra.)*

MYRON: Don't think life's easy with Momma. No, but she means for your good all the time. I tell you she does, she—

RALPH: Maybe, but I'm going to bed.

(Downstairs, doorbell rings violently.)

MOE: *(Ring.)* Enemy barrage begins on sector eight seventy-five.

RALPH: That's downstairs.

MYRON: We ain't expecting anyone this hour of the night.

MOE: "Lights are blinking while you're drinking, that's the place where the good fellows go. Good-bye to ta ra tara ra," etc.

RALPH: I better see who it is.

MYRON: I'll tick the button.

(As he starts, the apartment doorbell begins ringing, followed by large knocking. MYRON *goes out.)*

RALPH: Who's ever ringing means it.

(A loud excited voice outside.)

MOE: "In the land of Yama Yama, Funicalee, funicalo, funic—"

*(*MYRON *enters, followed by* SCHLOSSER *the janitor.* BESSIE *cuts in from the other side.)*

BESSIE: Who's ringing like a lunatic?

RALPH: What's the matter?

MYRON: Momma. . . .
BESSIE: Noo, what's the matter?

(Downstairs bell continues.)

RALPH: What's the matter?
BESSIE: Well, well . . . ?
MYRON: Poppa. . . .
BESSIE: What happened?
SCHLOSSER: He shlipped maybe in de snow.
RALPH: Who?
SCHLOSSER: *(To* BESSIE.*)* Your fadder fall off de roof. . . . Ja. *(A dead pause.* RALPH *then runs out.)*
BESSIE: *(Dazed.)* Myron. . . . Call Morty on the phone . . . call him. *(*MYRON *starts for phone.)* No. I'll do it myself. I'll . . . do it. *(*MYRON *exits.)*
SCHLOSSER: *(Standing stupidly.)* Since I was in dis country . . . I was pudding out de ash can . . . The snow is vet. . . .
MOE: *(To* SCHLOSSER.*)* Scram. *(*SCHLOSSER *exits.)*

*(*BESSIE *goes blindly to the phone, fumbles and gets it.* MOE *sits quietly, slowly turning cards over, but watching her.)*

BESSIE: He slipped . . .
MOE: *(Deeply moved.)* Slipped?
BESSIE: I can't see the numbers. Make it, Moe, make it. . . .
MOE: Make it yourself. *(He looks at her and slowly goes back to his game of cards with shaking hands.)*
BESSIE: Riverside 7— . . .

(Unable to talk, she dials slowly. The dial whizzes on.)

MOE: Don't . . . make me laugh. . . . *(He turns over cards.)*

CURTAIN

ACT III

A week later in the dining room. Morty, Bessie *and* Myron *eating. Sitting in the front room is* Moe, *marking a "dope sheet," but really listening to the others.*

Bessie: You're sure he'll come tonight—the insurance man?

Morty: Why not? I shtupped him a ten-dollar bill. Everything's hot delicatessen.

Bessie: Why must he come so soon?

Morty: Because you had a big expense. You'll settle once and for all. I'm a great boy for making hay while the sun shines.

Bessie: Stay till he'll come, Morty. . . .

Morty: No, I got a strike downtown. Business don't stop for personal life. Two times already in the past week those bastards threw stink bombs in the showroom. Wait! We'll give them strikes—in the kishkas we'll give them. . . .

Bessie: I'm a woman. I don't know about policies. Stay till he comes.

Morty: Bessie—sweetheart, leave me live.

Bessie: I'm afraid, Morty.

Morty: Be practical. They made an investigation. Everybody knows Pop had an accident. Now we'll collect.

Myron: Ralphie don't know Papa left the insurance in his name.

Morty: It's not his business. And I'll tell him.

Bessie: The way he feels. *(Enter* Ralph *into front room.)* He'll do something crazy. He thinks Poppa jumped off the roof.

MORTY: Be practical, Bessie. Ralphie will sign when I tell him. Everything is peaches and cream.

BESSIE: Wait for a few minutes. . . .

MORTY: Look, I'll show you in black on white what the policy says. *For God's sake, leave me live! (Angrily exits to kitchen. In parlor,* MOE *speaks to* RALPH, *who is reading a letter.)*

MOE: What's the letter say?

RALPH: Blanche won't see me no more, she says. I couldn't care very much, she says. If I didn't come like I said. . . . She'll phone before she leaves.

MOE: She don't know about Pop?

RALPH: She won't ever forget me, she says. Look what she sends me . . . a little locket on a chain . . . if she calls I'm out.

MOE: You mean it?

RALPH: For a week I'm trying to go in his room. I guess he'd like me to have it, but I can't. . . .

MOE: Wait a minute! *(Crosses over.)* They're trying to rook you—a freeze-out.

RALPH: Who?

MOE: That bunch stuffin' their gut with hot pastrami. Morty in particular. Jake left the insurance—three thousand dollars—for you.

RALPH: For me?

MOE: Now you got wings, kid. Pop figured you could use it. That's why. . . .

RALPH: That's why what?

MOE: It ain't the only reason he done it.

RALPH: He done it?

MOE: You think a breeze blew him off?

*(*HENNIE *enters and sits.)*

RALPH: I'm not sure what I think.

MOE: The insurance guy's coming tonight. Morty "shtupped" him.

RALPH: Yeah?

MOE: I'll back you up. You're dead on your feet. Grab a sleep for yourself.

RALPH: No!

MOE: Go on! *(Pushes boy into room.)*

SAM: *(Whom* MORTY *has sent in for the paper.)* Morty wants the paper.

HENNIE: So?

SAM: You're sitting on it. *(Gets paper.)* We could go home now, Hennie! Leon is alone by Mrs. Strasberg a whole day.

HENNIE: Go on home if you're so anxious. A full tub of diapers is waiting.

SAM: Why should you act this way?

HENNIE: 'Cause there's no bones in ice cream. Don't touch me.

SAM: Please, what's the matter. . . .

MOE: She don't like you. Plain as the face on your nose. . . .

SAM: To me, my friend, you talk a foreign language.

MOE: A quarter you're lousy. *(*SAM *exits.)* Gimme a buck, I'll run it up to ten.

HENNIE: Don't do me no favors.

MOE: Take a chance. *(Stopping her as she crosses to doorway.)*

HENNIE: I'm a pushover.

MOE: I say lotsa things. You don't know me.

HENNIE: I know you—when you knock 'em down you're through.

MOE: *(Sadly.)* You still don't know me.

HENNIE: I know what goes in your wise-guy head.

MOE: Don't run away. . . . I ain't got hydrophobia. Wait. I want to tell you. . . . I'm leaving.

HENNIE: Leaving?

MOE: Tonight. Already packed.

HENNIE: Where?

MORTY: *(As he enters followed by the others.)* My car goes through snow like a dose of salts.

BESSIE: Hennie, go eat. . . .

MORTY: Where's Ralphie?

MOE: In his new room. *(Moves into dining room.)*

MORTY: I didn't have a piece of hot pastrami in my mouth for years.

BESSIE: Take a sandwich, Hennie. You didn't eat all day. . . . *(At window.)* A whole week it rained cats and dogs.

MYRON: Rain, rain, go away. Come again some other day. *(Puts shawl on her.)*

MORTY: Where's my gloves?
SAM: *(Sits on stool.)* I'm sorry the old man lays in the rain.
MORTY: Personally, Pop was a fine man. But I'm a great boy for an honest opinion. He had enough crazy ideas for a regiment.
MYRON: Poppa never had a doctor in his whole life. . . . *(Enter* RALPH.*)*
MORTY: He had Caruso. Who's got more from life?
BESSIE: Who's got more? . . .
MYRON: And Marx he had.

*(*MYRON *and* BESSIE *sit on sofa.)*

MORTY: Marx! Some say Marx is the new God today. Maybe I'm wrong. Ha ha ha. . . . Personally I counted my ten million last night. . . . I'm sixteen cents short. So tomorrow I'll go to Union Square and yell no equality in the country! Ah, it's a new generation.
RALPH: You said it!
MORTY: What's the matter, Ralphie? What are you looking funny?
RALPH: I hear I'm left insurance and the man's coming tonight.
MORTY: Poppa didn't leave no insurance for you.
RALPH: What?
MORTY: In your name he left it—but not for you.
RALPH: It's my name on the paper.
MORTY: Who said so?
RALPH: *(To his mother.)* The insurance man's coming tonight?
MORTY: What's the matter?
RALPH: I'm not talking to you. *(To his mother.)* Why?
BESSIE: I don't know why.
RALPH: He don't come in this house tonight.
MORTY: That's what *you* say.
RALPH: I'm not talking to you, Uncle Morty, but I'll tell you, too, he don't come here tonight when there's still mud on a grave. *(To his mother.)* Couldn't you give the house a chance to cool off?
MORTY: Is this a way to talk to your mother?
RALPH: Was that a way to talk to your father?
MORTY: Don't be so smart with me, Mr. Ralph Berger!

RALPH: Don't be so smart with *me*.

MORTY: What'll you do? I say he's coming tonight. Who says no?

MOE: *(Suddenly, from the background.)* Me.

MORTY: Take a back seat, Axelrod. When you're in the family—

MOE: I got a little document here. *(Produces paper.)* I found it under his pillow that night. A guy who slips off a roof don't leave a note before he does it.

MORTY: *(Starting for* MOE *after a horrified silence.)* Let me see this note.

BESSIE: Morty, don't touch it!

MOE: Not if you crawled.

MORTY: It's a fake. Poppa wouldn't—

MOE: Get the insurance guy here and we'll see how— *(The bell rings.)* Speak of the devil. . . . Answer it, see what happens. *(*MORTY *starts for the ticker.)*

BESSIE: Morty, don't!

MORTY: *(Stopping.)* Be practical, Bessie.

MOE: Sometimes you don't collect on suicides if they know about it.

MORTY: You should let. . . . You should let him. . . . *(A pause in which* ALL *seem dazed. Bell rings insistently.)*

MOE: Well, we're waiting.

MORTY: Give me the note.

MOE: I'll give you the head off your shoulders.

MORTY: Bessie, you'll stand for this? *(Points to* RALPH.*)* Pull down his pants and give him with a strap.

RALPH: *(As bell rings again.)* How about it?

BESSIE: Don't be crazy. It's not my fault. Morty said he should come tonight. It's not nice so soon. I didn't—

MORTY: I said it? Me?

BESSIE: Who then?

MORTY: You didn't sing a song in my ear a whole week to settle quick?

BESSIE: I'm surprised. Morty, you're a big liar.

MYRON: Momma's telling the truth, she is!

MORTY: Lissen. In two shakes of a lamb's tail, we'll start a real fight and then nobody won't like nobody. Where's my fur gloves? I'm going downtown. *(To* SAM.*)* You coming? I'll drive you down.

HENNIE: *(To* SAM, *who looks questioningly at her.)* Don't look at me. Go home if you want.

SAM: If you're coming soon, I'll wait.

HENNIE: Don't do me any favors. Night and day he pesters me.

MORTY: You made a cushion—sleep!

SAM: I'll go home. I know . . . to my worst enemy I don't wish such a life—

HENNIE: Sam, keep quiet.

SAM: *(Quietly, sadly.)* No more free speech in America? *(Gets his hat and coat.)* I'm a lonely person. Nobody likes me.

MYRON: I like you, Sam.

HENNIE: *(Going to him gently, sensing the end.)* Please go home, Sam. I'll sleep here. . . . I'm tired and nervous. Tomorrow I'll come home. I love you . . . I mean it. *(She kisses him with real feeling.)*

SAM: I would die for you. . . . *(*SAM *looks at her. Tries to say something, but his voice chokes up with a mingled feeling. He turns and leaves the room.)*

MORTY: A bird in the hand is worth two in the bush. Remember I said it. Good night. *(Exits after* SAM.*)*

*(*HENNIE *sits depressed.* BESSIE *goes up and looks at the picture calendar again.* MYRON *finally breaks the silence.)*

MYRON: Yesterday a man wanted to sell me a saxophone with pearl buttons. But I—

BESSIE: It's a beautiful picture. In this land, nobody works. . . . Nobody worries. . . . Come to bed, Myron. *(Stops at the door, and says to* RALPH*)* Please don't have foolish ideas about the money.

RALPH: Let's call it a day.

BESSIE: It belongs for the whole family. You'll get your teeth fixed—

RALPH: And a pair of black and white shoes?

BESSIE: Hennie needs a vacation. She'll take two weeks in the mountains and I'll mind the baby.

RALPH: I'll take care of my own affairs.

BESSIE: A family needs for a rainy day. Times is getting worse. Prospect Avenue, Dawson, Beck Street—every day furniture's on the sidewalk.

RALPH: Forget it, Mom.

BESSIE: Ralphie, I worked too hard all my years to be

treated like dirt. It's no law we should be stuck together like Siamese twins. Summer shoes you didn't have, skates you never had, but I bought a new dress every week. A lover I kept—Mr. Gigolo! Did I ever play a game of cards like Mrs. Marcus? Or was Bessie Berger's children always the cleanest on the block?! Here I'm not only the mother, but also the father. The first two years I worked in a stocking factory for six dollars while Myron Berger went to law school. If I didn't worry about the family who would? On the calendar it's a different place, but here without a dollar you don't look the world in the eye. Talk from now to next year—this is life in America.

RALPH: Then it's wrong. It don't make sense. If life made you this way, then it's wrong!

BESSIE: Maybe you wanted me to give up twenty years ago. Where would you be now? You'll excuse my expression—a bum in the park!

RALPH: I'm not blaming you, Mom. Sink or swim—I see it. But it can't stay like this.

BESSIE: My foolish boy. . . .

RALPH: No, I see every house lousy with lies and hate. He said it, Grandpa— Brooklyn hates the Bronx. Smacked on the nose twice a day. But boys and girls can get ahead like that, Mom. We don't want life printed on dollar bills, Mom!

BESSIE: So go out and change the world if you don't like it.

RALPH: I will! And why? 'Cause life's different in my head. Gimme the earth in two hands. I'm strong. There . . . hear him? The airmail off to Boston. Day or night, he flies away, a job to do. That's us and it's no time to die.

(The airplane sound fades off as MYRON *gives alarm clock to* BESSIE, *which she begins to wind.)*

BESSIE: "Mom, what does she know? She's old-fashioned!" But I'll tell you a big secret: My whole life I wanted to go away too, but with children a woman stays home. A fire burned in *my* heart too, but now it's too late. I'm no spring chicken. The clock goes and Bessie goes. Only my machinery can't be fixed. *(She lifts a button: the alarm rings on the clock; she stops it, says "Good night" and exits.)*

MYRON: I guess I'm no prize bag. . . .

BESSIE: *(From within.)* Come to bed, Myron.

MYRON: *(Tears page off calendar.)* Hmmm. . . . *(Exits to her.)*

RALPH: Look at him, draggin' after her like an old shoe.

MOE: Punch drunk. *(Phone rings.)* That's for me. *(At phone.)* Yeah? . . . Just a minute. *(To* RALPH.*)* Your girl . . .

RALPH: Jeez, I don't know what to say to her.

MOE: Hang up? *(*RALPH *slowly takes phone.)*

RALPH: Hello. . . . Blanche, I wish. . . . I don't know what to say. . . . Yes . . . Hello? . . . *(Puts phone down.)* She hung up on me . . .

MOE: Sorry?

RALPH: No girl means anything to me until. . . .

MOE: Till when?

RALPH: Till I can take care of her. Till we don't look out on an airshaft. Till we can take the world in two hands and polish off the dirt.

MOE: That's a big order.

RALPH: Once upon a time I thought I'd drown to death in bolts of silk and velour. But I grew up these last few weeks. Jake said a lot.

MOE: Your memory's okay?

RALPH: But take a look at this. *(Brings armful of books from* JACOB*'s room—dumps them on table.)* His books, I got them too—the pages ain't cut in half of them.

MOE: Perfect.

RALPH: Does it prove something? Damn tootin'! A ten-cent nail file cuts them. Uptown, downtown, I'll read them on the way. Get a big lamp over the bed. *(Picks up one.)* My eyes are good. *(Puts book in pocket.)* Sure, inventory tomorrow. Coletti to Driscoll to Berger—that's how we work. It's a team down the warehouse. Driscoll's a show-off, a wiseguy, and Joe talks pigeons day and night. But they're like me, looking for a chance to get to first base too. Joe razzed me about my girl. But he don't know why. I'll tell him. Hell, he might tell me something I don't know. Get teams together all over. Spit on your hands and get to work. And with enough teams together maybe we'll get steam in the warehouse so our fingers don't freeze off. Maybe we'll fix it so life won't be printed on dollar bills.

MOE: Graduation Day.

RALPH: *(Starts for door of his room, stops.)* Can I have . . . Grandpa's note?

MOE: Sure you want it?

RALPH: Please— *(*MOE *gives it.)* It's blank!

MOE: *(Taking note back and tearing it up.)* That's right.

RALPH: Thanks! *(Exits.)*

MOE: The kid's a fighter! *(To* HENNIE.*)* Why are you crying?

HENNIE: I never cried in my life. *(She is now.)*

MOE: *(Starts for door. Stops.)* You told Sam you love him. . . .

HENNIE: If I'm sore on life, why take it out on him?

MOE: You won't forget me to your dyin' day—I was the first guy. Part of your insides. You won't forget. I wrote my name on you—indelible ink!

HENNIE: One thing I won't forget—how you left me crying on the bed like I was two for a cent!

MOE: Listen, do you think—

HENNIE: Sure. Waits till the family goes to the open-air movie. He brings me perfume. . . . He grabs my arms—

MOE: You won't forget me!

HENNIE: How you left the next week?

MOE: So I made a mistake. For Chris' sake, don't act like the Queen of Romania!

HENNIE: Don't make me laugh!

MOE: What the hell do you want, my head on a plate?! Was my life so happy? Chris', my old man was a bum. I supported the whole damn family—five kids and Mom. When they grew up they beat it the hell away like rabbits. Mom died. I went to the war; got clapped down like a bedbug; woke up in a room without a leg. What the hell do you think, anyone's got it better than you? I never had a home either. I'm lookin' too!

HENNIE: So what?

MOE: So you're it—you're home for me, a place to live! That's the whole parade, sickness, eating out your heart! Sometimes you meet a girl—she stops it—that's love. . . . So take a chance! Be with me, Paradise. What's to lose?

HENNIE: My pride!

MOE: *(Grabbing her.)* What do you want? Say the word—I'll tango on a dime. Don't gimme ice when your heart's on fire!

HENNIE: Let me go! *(He stops her.)*

MOE: WHERE?!!

HENNIE: What do you want, Moe, what do you want?

MOE: You!

HENNIE: You'll be sorry you ever started—

MOE: You!

HENNIE: Moe, lemme go— *(Trying to leave.)* I'm getting up early—lemme go.

MOE: No! . . . I got enough fever to blow the whole damn town to hell. *(He suddenly releases her and half stumbles backwards. Forces himself to quiet down.)* You wanna go back to him? Say the word. I'll know what to do. . . .

HENNIE: *(Helplessly.)* Moe, I don't know what to say.

MOE: Listen to me.

HENNIE: What?

MOE: Come away. A certain place where it's moonlight and roses. We'll lay down, count stars. Hear the big ocean making noise. You lay under the trees. Champagne flows like— *(Phone rings.* MOE *finally answers the telephone.)* Hello? . . . Just a minute. *(Looks at* HENNIE.*)*

HENNIE: Who is it?

MOE: Sam.

HENNIE: *(Starts for phone, but changes her mind.)* I'm sleeping. . . .

MOE: *(In phone.)* She's sleeping. . . . *(Hangs up. Watches* HENNIE, *who slowly sits.)* He wants you to know he got home okay. . . . What's on your mind?

HENNIE: Nothing.

MOE: Sam?

HENNIE: They say it's a palace on those Havana boats.

MOE: What's on your mind?

HENNIE: *(Trying to escape.)* Moe, I don't care for Sam—I never loved him—

MOE: But your kid—?

HENNIE: All my life I waited for this minute.

MOE: *(Holding her.)* Me too. Made believe I was talkin'

just bedroom golf, but you and me forever was what I meant! Christ, baby, there's one life to live! Live it!

HENNIE: Leave the baby?

MOE: Yeah!

HENNIE: I can't. . . .

MOE: You can!

HENNIE: No. . . .

MOE: But you're not sure!

HENNIE: I don't know.

MOE: Make a break or spend the rest of your life in a coffin.

HENNIE: Oh God, I don't know where I stand.

MOE: Don't look up there. Paradise, you're on a big boat headed south. No more pins and needles in your heart, no snake juice squirted in your arm. The whole world's green grass and when you cry it's because you're happy.

HENNIE: Moe, I don't know. . . .

MOE: Nobody knows, but you do it and find out. When you're scared the answer's zero.

HENNIE: You're hurting my arm.

MOE: The doctor said it—cut off your leg to save your life! And they done it—one thing to get another. *(Enter* RALPH.*)*

RALPH: I didn't hear a word, but do it, Hennie, do it!

MOE: Mom can mind the kid. She'll go on forever, Mom. We'll send money back, and Easter eggs.

RALPH: I'll be here.

MOE: Get your coat . . . get it.

HENNIE: Moe!

MOE: I know . . . but get your coat and hat and kiss the house good bye.

HENNIE: The man I love. . . . *(*MYRON *entering.)* I left my coat in Mom's room. *(Exits.)*

MYRON: Don't wake her up, Beauty. Momma fell asleep as soon as her head hit the pillow. I can't sleep. It was a long day. Hmmm. *(Examines his tongue in buffet mirror.)* I was reading the other day a person with a thick tongue is feeble-minded. I can do anything with my tongue. Make it thick, flat. No fruit in the house lately. Just a lone apple. *(He gets apple and paring knife and starts paring.)* Must be something wrong with me—I say I won't eat but I eat. *(*HENNIE *enters dressed to go out.)* Where you going, little Red Riding Hood?

HENNIE: Nobody knows, Peter Rabbit.

MYRON: You're looking very pretty tonight. You were a beautiful baby too. 1910, that was the year you was born. The same year Teddy Roosevelt come back from Africa.

HENNIE: Gee, Pop; you're such a funny guy.

MYRON: He was a boisterous man, Teddy. Good night. *(He exits, paring apple.)*

RALPH: When I look at him, I'm sad. Let me die like a dog, if I can't get more from life.

HENNIE: Where?

RALPH: Right here in the house! My days won't be for nothing. Let Mom have the dough. I'm twenty-two and kickin'! I'll get along. Did Jake die for us to fight about nickels? No! "Awake and sing," he said. Right here he stood and said it. The night he died, I saw it like a thunderbolt! I saw he was dead and I was born! I swear to God, I'm one week old! I want the whole city to hear it—fresh blood, arms. We got 'em. We're glad we're living.

MOE: I wouldn't trade you for two pitchers and an outfielder. Hold the fort!

RALPH: So long.

MOE: So long.

(They go, and RALPH *stands full and strong in the doorway, seeing them off as the curtain slowly falls.)*

CURTAIN

MORNING STAR

A PLAY IN THREE ACTS

by

Sylvia Regan

Sylvia Regan (née Hoffenberg) came to playwriting after early demonstrating a number of other theatrical aptitudes. A native New Yorker, she studied at the American Academy of Dramatic Arts. In 1926, at the age of eighteen, she made her professional stage debut in Milton Herbert Gropper and Max Siegel's *We Americans,* the work in which Paul Muni played his first English-language role. Still in her teens, Regan assisted the social director at Camp Tamamint, an adult resort whose entertainment programs became famous as a training ground for future headliners. She ran the weekly Saturday night shows, casting them and contributing costumes, choreography, and her own acting talents. Turning next to theatrical publicity and public relations, she worked for the Theatre Union and for Orson Welles and John Houseman's Mercury Theatre, where her job was to "upholster seats with backsides." Then, immobilized by a severe sunburn during the summer of 1937, she transformed into a dramatic script a story she had been told by her childhood friend, Clifford Odets. Though *Every Day But Friday* was not produced, Sylvia Regan had found her métier.

Regan's subsequent plays include *A Hundred Million Nickles, Morning Star, Safe Harbor, 44 West, The Twelfth Hour,* and *Zelda*. Her biggest commercial success came in 1953 with *The Fifth Season,* which ran for 654 performances. It is a work about the vicissitudes of the garment industry, which insiders claim responds to five seasons: winter, spring, summer, fall, and slack. Menasha Skulnik, renowned comedian of the Yiddish stage, made his English-language debut, earning critical raves for himself ("one of the funniest men who ever lived") and for the play ("irresistible fun"). A musical version of *The Fifth*

Season, adapted by Luba Kadison into Yiddish and English, had a run of 122 performances in 1975.

In 1940, Regan married composer Abraham Ellstein, who, with lyricist Robert Sour, had provided the songs for *Morning Star*. Regan and Ellstein collaborated on two musicals, *Marianne* and *Great to Be Alive*. Together they wrote an adaptation of *The Golem,* commissioned by the Ford Foundation and produced in 1962 by the New York City Opera under the direction of Julius Rudel. Though Regan no longer writes for the theatre, she is working on a novel.

The inspiration for *Morning Star,* Regan's first produced play, grew out of an early memory. As a three-year-old, she had stood across the street from what had been the Triangle Shirtwaist Factory listening to her mother tell a friend about the disaster. Had the fire not broken out on Saturday, whose sanctity her grandfather insisted his daughters observe, Regan's mother and aunts would have been at work in the building. Regan made this historic event the literal and metaphorical center of her script. She set the play in a milieu she knew intimately. Though the characters are fictionalized composites, there is a life drawing in the importunate Brownstein: he is modeled on a Marxist who bedeviled Regan's father, proprietor of a tobacco shop. The marvelous petticoat scene which opens the play had its origins in Regan's mother's family home, where there were four daughters.

Morning Star made a promising start. Regan's agent sold it almost immediately to producer George Kondolf. Brilliantly cast, with Joseph Buloff as the admiring boarder, fifteen-year-old Sidney Lumet as the bar mitzvah boy, and Molly Picon as a diminutive contrast to the more typically ample Jewish mother, it opened on Broadway on April 16, 1940. Three weeks later, the devastating news from Europe—Luxembourg and the Netherlands had rapidly fallen before Nazi Germany's war machine—dampened New York's enthusiasm for theatre. The run ended despite the active efforts of producer John Golden and writer and director Rose Franken.*

*Franken was the creator of the extremely popular "Claudia" short story series and the author of a half dozen successful plays, of which one, *Outrageous Fortune* (1943), has significant Jewish content.

Then *Morning Star*'s fortunes changed again. As the second script to be published by the newly formed Dramatists Play Service, Regan's play was promptly launched into a long career in stock and amateur productions. Wee and Leventhal made it part of New York's Subway Circuit, in which productions toured the city's five boroughs. The play subsequently earned enthusiastic reviews off-Broadway and across the country. In a 1963 Los Angeles production, retitled *In Mama's House,* sixteen-year-old Richard Dreyfuss played the bar mitzvah boy.

Although *Morning Star* encapsulates the American Jewish experience, the play's international successes testify to its universal appeal. It made its European debut in Scotland in 1946, and has been mounted there regularly ever since in the repertoire of Glasgow's Jewish Institute Players. In Hempstead, England, retitled *The Golden Door,* it sold out for nearly a year, and took first prize as an amateur entry in the British Drama Festival in the early 1950s. A few years later, *Morning Star* was produced in Hebrew by Tel Aviv's Ohel Theatre. In the mid-1950s, it was done in Buenos Aires both in Spanish and in Yiddish, starring Bertha Gerstein and Jacob Ben Ami. In 1972, it played to packed houses in South Wales, Australia. A Yiddish adaptation by Miriam Kressyn, titled *Broome Street, America,* was presented in 1985 at the Folksbiene. That production impressed one New York reviewer as "as fine a piece of theatre as can be found anywhere on Broadway or off."

Morning Star was produced for the first time by George Kondolf at the Longacre Theatre, New York, April 16, 1940, with the following cast:

FANNY	*Jeanne Greene*
BECKY FELDERMAN	*Molly Picon*
AARON GREENSPAN	*Joseph Buloff*
ESTHER	*Cecilia Evans*
HYMIE *(as a boy)*	*Kenneth LeRoy*
HARRY ENGEL	*Martin Blaine*
SADIE	*Ruth Yorke*
IRVING TASHMAN	*David Morris*
BENJAMIN BROWNSTEIN	*Harold J. Stone*
MYRON ENGEL	*Henry Sharp*
HYMIE *(as a young man)*	*Ross Elliott*
PANSY	*Georgette Harvey*
HYMIE TASHMAN	*Sidney Lumet*

SYNOPSIS OF SCENES

The action takes place in Becky Felderman's home, on the lower East Side of New York.

ACT I

SCENE 1. A December afternoon, 1910.
SCENE 2. A month later.

ACT II

SCENE 1. Early morning, March 25th, 1911.
(During this scene the curtain will be lowered twice to denote a passage of time.)
SCENE 2. Early April, six years later.
SCENE 3. Eighteen months later.

ACT III

Thirteen years later, November, 1931.

AUTHOR'S NOTE

Since the language of the play is rich in Jewish idiom and speech color, there is a danger of caricaturing the lines should the accent be used. Therefore, with the possible exception of Aaron's speech, it is suggested that no other accent be used throughout.

NOTE: The songs "We'll Bring the Rue de la Paix" and "Under a Painted Smile," by Abraham Ellstein and Robert Sour, are reprinted by permission of Sylvia Regan (Mrs. Abraham Ellstein).

ACT I

Scene 1

Late afternoon in December, 1910. The scene is the combination living room-dining room of the Felderman household, on the lower East Side, New York. A door up L. *leads to hall. Two doors at* R. *lead to bedrooms. Door* L. *leads to kitchen and door up* L. *to bathroom. There is a neatly curtained window up* R., *which faces on the street. An old leather couch stands downstage* R. *A round table* C., *several hideous straight-backed chairs and a heavy buffet at upstage wall. An old upright piano, the one note of luxury, stands down* L. *At the moment, a dressmaker's form stands in front of window. The fancy calendar of the type given away free by tradesmen, bric-a-brac, and other decoration may be left to the discretion of the director.*

AT RISE: *A general feeling of disorder. It is ironing day. A number of freshly ironed petticoats of the period, stiff with starch, stand around the room as though on legs, and take up all the available floor space between table and chairs.*

ESTHER FELDERMAN *is at ironing board. She is a frail girl, no more than sixteen. Enormous eyes set off her thin, fair-complexioned face.* BECKY FELDERMAN, *her mother, is at dressmaker's form, working on a much-flowered dress.* BECKY *is about thirty-seven, with a girlish alive quality.*

FANNY FELDERMAN, *her second daughter, is at piano, hammering out a tune with one finger. She is a little over seventeen, a dark, buxom peasant beauty, with a vivacious and excitable manner.* AARON GREENSPAN, *the boarder, a man of about forty, is stretched out on couch, sleeping the sleep of the dead, snoring occasionally.* Becky *hums as she works.*

Fanny: *(Looking up. Good-naturedly.)* Mama, those aren't the words.
Becky: *(Singing off-key.)* Ta-ta-ta—ta-ta-ta— It's just like you sing it, no?
Fanny: No, Mama. It goes like this— Ta-ta-ta-ta—ta-ta—

*(*Becky *joins in. By this time they are making a terrific racket.)*

Aaron: *(Sits up.)* In Grand Central Station it's more quiet!
Becky: In Grand Central they take in boarders?
Fanny: *(Of the song she has been playing.)* Is this new song beautiful! *(Laughing.)* In "Alma, Where Do You Live?" the man in the music store told me Kitty Gordon takes off all her clothes when she sings it!
Becky: Such a song you are singing?
Fanny: Mama, please—don't get excited—
Becky: To ruin your life singing in the Apollo Nickelette every night—
Fanny: If that's how you felt, why'd you have to go to the contest with me?
Becky: Because I didn't think you could win—
Fanny: What!
Becky: To sing in a place where they throw on the actors eggs—
Fanny: *(Cutting in hotly.)* On me they throw eggs? They *love* me—
Becky: Every night I am taking you from the theatre, a dozen bums standing by the back door. Even to me, an old woman, they are making "Hello, baby." That's *love*? That's *respect*?
Fanny: *(As she starts to exit.)* You make me so nervous, I can't even practice! *(She is gone.)*
Aaron: Aye, Becky, Becky, you need a *man* in the house.
Esther: *(Accidentally dropping the iron onto the board.)* Ouch!
Becky: You burned yourself?
Aaron: You can't wear it without pressing? Who sees it?

BECKY: And if, God forbid, an accident, you get run down from a horse-car—they take you to the hospital, it looks nice the petticoat should be with wrinkles?
AARON: The trouble is, Becky, you are a *pessimist.*
BECKY: What?
AARON: You can only see from everything the *bad* side!
ESTHER: Mama is always making us feel good when *we* are seeing the bad side—
AARON: All right! She is always seeing the *good* side! You are satisfied? So, if you'll excuse me!

(The picture of AARON *treading gingerly between the petticoats as he exits into bathroom is too much for* BECKY *and* ESTHER. *They start to laugh.)*

ESTHER: *(Picking up the much-flowered dress.)* For what Mrs. Smith is paying, without seam binding would be good enough. In Sadie's shop they never sew a piece of seam binding.
BECKY: What can you expect in ready-made? *(A clock strikes.)* Hymie is late from school—
ESTHER: *(Hesitating.)* Mama, please, can I go with Sadie tomorrow?
BECKY: Where?
ESTHER: To the Triangle Shop.
BECKY: Again you ask me? Esther—
ESTHER: When Fanny was in the shop you didn't mind. Sadie, you don't mind. Only me—
BECKY: You're too young.
ESTHER: Mrs. O'Shaughnessy's Annie is only fifteen.
BECKY: Mrs. O'Shaughnessy has also cockroaches in the sink!
ESTHER: Six, seven dollars a week—
BECKY: Esther, what did I tell you yesterday?
ESTHER: You told me "no"—
BECKY: And the day before?
ESTHER: "No" also—
BECKY: And this morning?
ESTHER: "No"—
BECKY: So?
ESTHER: *(Eagerly.)* So I can?
BECKY: No! *(*BECKY *gets up, starts to take away ironing board.)*

ESTHER: But, Mama, Sadie says to work gives a girl independence.

BECKY: What?

ESTHER: You have money in your pocket, you are the boss!

BECKY: The boss is not the boss? *You* are the boss?

ESTHER: Over yourself, Mama! You don't need to go to anybody for something! *(Inspired.)* You are free!

BECKY: *(Settling the matter.)* In America everybody is free! Something is on your mind, Esther. Mama can tell—

ESTHER: Mama, please—sometimes I would like to have a pair of lisle stockings! Not cotton—

BECKY: *(Smiling.)* That's all? So I'll buy you a pair of lisle stockings— *(Touching* ESTHER*'s face, as though seeking the source of her apparent upset.)* Will that make you happier?

*(*BECKY *exits into kitchen with ironing board.* ESTHER *looks after her a moment, then starts to gather petticoats together, placing one over the other on dressmaker's form.* AARON *enters.* ESTHER *looks away, embarrassed, but he calmly goes on pulling up his suspenders.)*

ESTHER: Aaron, please, try to remember, *women* live in this house!

AARON: It's my fault conditions is crowded? I'm not exactly complaining, but a boarder has some rights, too! I pay my rent, no?

ESTHER: No!

AARON: *(Abashed.)* Well—it is my *intention* to pay! It's my fault I'm a millinery worker on straw and the season is late this year? A man can suddenly get hard up! *(*ESTHER *stares at him skeptically.)* If you have to know, little lady, right this minute, I could be in the millinery business for myself, a boss—if I wanted!

ESTHER: *(Still skeptical.)* It doesn't cost money to go into business?

AARON: Who says no? My friend Van Brett the blocker—*he* has the money. He begs me! With his thousand dollars and my brains, the sky is the limitation!

ESTHER: So what stops you?

AARON: Because I have a conscience! On one side of me, Van Brett! He says to me, "Become a boss, make a million. It's America—one, two, three."

ESTHER: Then why don't you do it?

AARON: Because on the other side of me is my friend Brownstein the radical. He says to me, "Exploiter! On the backs of the workers you don't climb to success." Can I help it if I have a conscience? I'm completely confused.

ESTHER: *(Impressed.)* Please don't tell Mama I said anything about—the rent. I apologize.

AARON: *(Grandly.)* I accept— *(*BECKY *enters.)*

BECKY: I didn't study the lesson for today—and Mr. Engel will be here any minute— *(She takes a book from buffet, starts to glance through it.)*

AARON: The whole house English lessons! Does a woman have to vote for the President? What does she need citizna papers for?

BECKY: My children and I should have a place in the world. To belong here.

AARON: Listen, Becky, why should you bother with examinations, lessons? If you would listen to my proposition—after all—I'm a citizen and in America the law is—

BECKY: You're starting up again?

AARON: What's the use, Becky, you need a man in the house!

BECKY: *(Playfully.)* So you live here, no?

AARON: A boarder ain't the same thing! *(*BECKY *stares at him.)* All right! I'm not starting up again! But a man can put in a good word for himself?

BECKY: You're not ashamed in front of the world—

ESTHER: *(Giggling.)* Should I go into the kitchen, Mama?

AARON: What I have to say to your mother, I'm not ashamed the world to hear! *(To* BECKY*, directly.)* Nu? *(*BECKY *laughs.)* You ever saw such a woman? Can you tell me please, one objection you could have to me? I'm an honest man, I don't drink, I don't gamble. Thank God, I make a good living— *(He breaks off, embarrassed by this obvious overstatement.)* When I'm working— *(Pause.)* Becky, say the word, I go into partnership with Van Brett, in no time I could dress you up in Hudson sealskin from head to toe! *(*BECKY *pays no attention.)* You are exactly my type.

BECKY: Aaron, please—

AARON: A beautiful woman like you—a woman full of life. To live out your days without a husband, ain't—ain't natural!

BECKY: Aaron, please, once and for all—to me it's natural a woman should know her responsibility to her four children—

AARON: Children! You can't fool me, Becky! It's Jacob. Jacob Felderman. A man is dead so many years, but in your heart he's lucky! He'll live forever! *(*BECKY *continues to read her book. A pause.* AARON *sits on couch dejectedly. Suddenly he jumps up, goes to door, puts on his overcoat and hat.)* Ask me where I'm going? *(He exits.)*

BECKY: *(To* ESTHER.*)* So—where was I?

ESTHER: You're on Columbus, Mama.

BECKY: That's right—Columbus— *(Turning over pages.)* In 1492 Columbus discovered America. *(A knock at door.* ESTHER *remains at table, trying to contain her excitement.* HARRY ENGEL *enters. He is about twenty-three, a slender young man with a gentle scholarly manner.)* Hello, Mr. Engel. Come in—

HARRY: How do you do? And Miss Esther?

ESTHER: Very, very fine, thank you—

BECKY: I'm ashamed of myself. I didn't hardly study the lesson today. *(They get settled,* HARRY *and* BECKY *at table,* ESTHER *on couch where she follows his every movement. Occasionally he glances in her direction.* BECKY *puts on spectacles.)* This minute I was looking up when did Columbus discover America. Oy! *(Giggles.)* I forgot it already. Wait! Don't tell me—fourteen, fourteen is right, yes?

HARRY: That's right. Fourteen what?

BECKY: You have to give the exact *minute* when they ask you?

HARRY: I think they'll want to know the year. Shall I tell you?

BECKY: What can I do?

HARRY: Mrs. Felderman, I'll tell you and when I do, you'll never forget it again. Listen—

"In fourteen hundred and ninety-two
Columbus sailed the ocean blue."

BECKY:

"In fourteen hundred and ninety-two
Columbus sailed the ocean blue."

That's wonderful. I'll never forget it. *(Pause.)* I better write it down. *(Writing laboriously, she looks up.)* Mr. Engel, what do you think? Am I passing for my "citizna papers"?

HARRY: It means a lot to you, doesn't it?

BECKY: The world. *(She laughs.)* I could die laughing when I think how many times they caught us by the border. My Sadie used to say, "Mama, there is no America. It's only a dream in your head." But the dream came true. Mr. Engel, I could kiss George Washington's feet for chopping down the cherry tree, we should be free.

ESTHER: *(Laughing.)* Mama, he chopped it down and didn't tell a lie.

BECKY: Mr. Engel knows what I mean—

HARRY: Now tell me, when was the Declaration of Independence signed?

BECKY: July the fourth, 1776!

HARRY: Good!

BECKY: I should say it's good! In Russia when my brother Abraham used to say "Revolution," I laughed, but now I have different ideas—if a Revolution could make a country like this, maybe Abraham was right? *(*HARRY *looks doubtful.)* Was he?

HARRY: *(With a smile.)* Not exactly, Mrs. Felderman. It's never war that makes a country great. It's the work of her people during peace times—

BECKY: You explain things so good—please don't be mad on me, Mr. Engel, but I have to thank you for what you're doing.

HARRY: Mrs. Felderman, it's nothing—

BECKY: Free lessons to Sadie and Esther and me is nothing?

HARRY: I couldn't take money from you. It would be like taking it from my own family—

BECKY: Yes?

HARRY: *(Afraid he has said too much.)* It's good experience for me, too. I'm taking an examination myself in a few weeks. To teach school—

BECKY: That's wonderful—

HARRY: I think so. To me, it's the most important job in the whole world— *(With some enthusiasm.)* Matter of fact, I intend to specialize in American History.

BECKY: Columbus and Lincoln?

HARRY: That's right. *(Enthusiastically.)* Some day I expect to write a textbook for children. A new kind of history book that doesn't glorify "war"!

BECKY: You're so smart, Mr. Engel. Your mother must be proud of you.

HARRY: I have only my father. I think he's proud of me, but not to my face— *(*HYMIE FELDERMAN *enters. He is not quite thirteen—a thin kid with a sensitive face.)*

HYMIE: *(Going directly to* BECKY *at table.)* Hello, Mama—

BECKY: You're late from school!

HYMIE: The teacher kept us— *(Hesitating.)* Mama, could you come now with me to the Rabbi, to get my speech?

BECKY: My Hymie is being Bar Mitzvah next month, Mr. Engel. I would be very happy if you and your papa could come—

HARRY: Thank you very much—

HYMIE: Mama, could you come now?

BECKY: Mr. Engel, would you please excuse me—I've been promising him for a week already—

HARRY: Certainly—of course— *(Glancing toward* ESTHER.*)* We'll give Miss Esther a little more time for her lesson.

BECKY: *(Putting on a shawl.)* Well, good bye and thank you, Mr. Engel. I'll be back soon, Esther— *(Calling out.)* Fanny, get dressed!

HARRY: And, Mrs. Felderman, WHEN did Columbus discover America?

BECKY: *(Delightedly.)*

"In fourteen hundred and ninety-two
Columbus sailed the blue ocean."

*(*BECKY *and* HYMIE *exit. The moment they are gone,* HARRY *and* ESTHER *quickly go toward one another. His manner changes from the pedantic school teacher of the moment before to a young boy in love. They are about to embrace, think better of it as* ESTHER *reminds him by gestures of* FANNY*'s presence in next room. They stare at one another for a moment.)*

HARRY: Esther, darling—

ESTHER: You were five minutes late—

HARRY: I ran all the way from Canal Street. Can you meet me tonight? Delancey Park, near the fence, like yesterday?

ESTHER: *(Giggling.)* Mama can't understand why I'm always wanting to go down for a walk after supper!

HARRY: The minute I pass my examination, we'll tell them— *(Tenderly.)* So sweet—

ESTHER: Harry, do you think Mama will be mad when we tell her? I'm the youngest. A mother always likes it better when the *oldest* gets married first.

HARRY: *(Upset.)* But you told me yourself your mother was only sixteen and three months when Sadie was born, so how can she be mad? Please, Esther, maybe we ought to tell her right away—

ESTHER: Oh, no—please—it wouldn't look nice. We don't know each other so long—

HARRY: You mean you're not sure? *(They draw apart quickly as* FANNY *enters, still in her kimono. She makes a beeline for bathroom.)* As I was saying— *(Discovering* FANNY.*)* Oh—how do you do, Miss Fanny?

FANNY: *(Wrapping kimono around her modestly.)* Very fine, thank you. *(With exaggerated politeness.)* Pardon the appearance— *(She is gone, banging door behind her.)*

HARRY: *(When* FANNY *has gone.)* You didn't answer me. Aren't you sure? About us?

ESTHER: Please, Harry, I'm sure—I—I would die for you, so sure I am—

HARRY: Gosh, for a minute you had me scared— *(Glancing around.)* If—if I kissed you somebody might see. Look at me. *(Pause.)* I have just kissed you.

ESTHER: *(Slowly.)* I felt it— *(Giggling.)* This is a fine English lesson—

HARRY: *(Laughing happily.)* And did you hear your mother invite us to the Bar Mitzvah? Like being in the family already!

ESTHER: I was holding my breath!

HARRY: I can hardly wait for my father to meet you. I have already told him about you.

ESTHER: *(Frightened.)* Oh—what did he say?

HARRY: He said, "If you love her, I love her." According to my father we could get married tomorrow.

ESTHER: *(Frightened again.)* So soon?

HARRY: In one month I'll be able to support a wife—

ESTHER: Mama'll be so mad on me—

HARRY: Then we better tell her right away—

ESTHER: Oh, Harry, please—no— *(*SADIE FELDERMAN *enters. She is about nineteen, thin and sallow-complexioned, with a forceful drive in her manner that belies her slight frame.)*

SADIE: *(Pleased to see him.)* Oh—how do you do, Mr. Engel—?

HARRY: Very well. And you?

SADIE: Simply exhausted. The last minute they brought in a hundred and fifty new waists to finish up! Please pardon my appearance—I must look a sight— *(As she goes toward bedroom.)* I'll be back in a moment— *(She exits into bedroom.)*

ESTHER: Harry, please, maybe you better go—

HARRY: But we didn't settle anything. About when we are getting married.

ESTHER: Please, Harry, we can't talk about it now—somebody'll hear.

HARRY: You'll have to meet me tonight so we can talk.

ESTHER: Maybe Mama won't let me go out—

HARRY: *(Adamant.)* I'll wait for you. Same time tonight.

ESTHER: I'll try my best. Good-bye—

HARRY: Until tonight—darling— *(He is at door.)* Mrs. Engel— *(He is gone.* ESTHER *runs to window.)*

FANNY: *(Calling out.)* Esther! He's gone?

ESTHER: Yes—

FANNY: *(Entering, comes toward* ESTHER.*)* Esther, I—I couldn't help myself, honest, but I heard what you and your boy friend were talking about.

ESTHER: Oh—

FANNY: Don't get scared. I won't tell anyone, darling. Can you keep a secret?

ESTHER: Surely— *(FANNY nods her head vigorously.)* You mean *you,* too?

FANNY: That's right.

ESTHER: Oh, Fanny, Fanny—both of us— *(The girls embrace, giggling happily.)* Is he nice?

FANNY: He's *wonderful*! The way he dresses—you should just see him!

ESTHER: I'm thinking what Mama will say—

FANNY: She'll have to get used to it. We ain't babies! *(Excitedly.)* He's an usher in the Apollo, where I work. But he's only doing it *temporary*. He writes songs!

ESTHER: No!

FANNY: Honest! He's writing a song for me to sing—

ESTHER: Oh, Fanny, please, let's have a double wedding.

FANNY: He didn't *ask* me yet!

ESTHER: Oh— *(Cheerily.)* But don't worry! Harry didn't *really* ask me right away! Maybe he's bashful?

FANNY: *(Laughing.)* Him bashful? He wouldn't be bashful to tell President William Howard Taft to go to the dickens—

ESTHER: Fanny—

FANNY: I mean it. He's got some mouth on him!

ESTHER: What's his name?

FANNY: Irving. Irving Tashman. I'll be *Mrs.* Irving Tashman—if he asks me—

ESTHER: Oh—he will—how could he help it? You're so beautiful. And you sing so beautiful—

FANNY: *(Pleased.)* Go on— *(She surveys herself in mirror over buffet, wrapping kimono tightly about her.)* Maybe you're right. I don't know— *(Trying to be modest and hardly succeeding.)* Everybody tells me I'm beautiful. And when I sing everybody *whistles*! *(As though telling a great secret.)* I'm going to tell you something I wouldn't tell a soul— *(AARON enters, disconsolately. The girls draw apart quickly.)*

AARON: *(As he goes toward couch.)* A man can go crazy when he's not working. Sit in the house, it's on your nerves. Take a walk—so where are you going? Aye, confusion! *(He lies full-length on couch.)*

FANNY: *(Whispering to ESTHER.)* Tonight, he's taking me to a *restaurant*!

ESTHER: Mama won't let you go— *(*BECKY *enters with* HYMIE.*)*

BECKY: *(To* FANNY.*)* You're not dressed yet?

FANNY: I'm getting dressed now— *(She exits, making gesture for secrecy to* ESTHER.*)*

BECKY: Mr. Engel is gone already?

ESTHER: He had to leave— *(*HYMIE *goes into kitchen.* SADIE *enters.)*

SADIE: *(Looking around disappointed.)* Mr. Engel is gone already?

ESTHER: He had to leave—

SADIE: *(Disappointed, she takes it out on* AARON, *now lying on couch.)* You have to use the living room for a bedroom even in the daytime?

AARON: *(Sitting up.)* Oh, *you're* here.

SADIE: Mama, I asked you—

BECKY: But the living room *is* his bedroom—

SADIE: Even when he don't pay rent weeks already?

BECKY: Sadie!

AARON: Never mind, Miss Smarty.— These humiliations! Why do I stand for it? These—these insults! If I had money you would speak to me with kid gloves! I ask you, would Brownstein be such a Socialist, if he had my opportunity to go into business and be treated like a gentleman?

SADIE: And hereafter on a Wednesday night, be so kind as to take a walk for yourself! Last night when I'm taking my lesson, he lays there on the couch talking to himself the whole time!

AARON: Engel doesn't care if I sit here. Who do I hurt?

SADIE: I care! Like living in the middle of Castle Garden,* this house! *(She exits lower bedroom.)*

AARON: What did I come to America for? To be insulted I could have stayed in Russia.

BECKY: Don't be mad on her, Aaron. She can't help it—she's the nervous type.

AARON: How is it *you* ain't the nervous type? I know those skinny women already!

BECKY: In her heart is something which pushes her—to build herself up—to improve her life—

*Huge, busy reception center for immigrants arriving in the port of New York.

AARON: She should learn first to improve her temper!

*(*FANNY *enters, wearing an evening dress, obviously home-made, but very becoming.* SADIE *follows her in.)*

SADIE: Mama, look at Fanny—
BECKY: The stage dress for eating supper in the kitchen?
FANNY: *(Excitedly.)* Mama, please don't get excited—tonight I am not eating supper home. I am eating in a restaurant.
BECKY: A restaurant?
FANNY: *(Anxious.)* I was invited!
BECKY: *(Quietly.)* Who invited you?
FANNY: *(Almost hysterical now.)* Mr. Irving Tashman, he invited me!
BECKY: Who?
FANNY: Mama, please, don't get excited! He's a Jewish boy!
BECKY: All day you're home you couldn't tell me—
FANNY: I was afraid to tell you, you might say "no."
BECKY: It's still not too late to say "no."
FANNY: *(Screaming.)* Mama!
SADIE: And who is this Mr. Tashman?
FANNY: He works in my theatre and he's a very nice fellow!
SADIE: An actor?
FANNY: An usher. His Uncle Abe owns the place. And the usher is only *temporary— (Anxiously to* BECKY.*)* Mama, please, he's taking me to a French restaurant!
BECKY: French? American ain't good enough?
AARON: Aye, Becky, if you had a man in the house!
FANNY: *(To* AARON.*)* Your two cents, too? The company I am keeping is plenty good enough.
SADIE: Fine company! With tramps!
FANNY: It's *my* life! I should give a care what you think! When I'm a big star, you'll be kissing my feet! *(To* BECKY.*)* Gee, Mom—you got to get used to it. In America a girl don't wait till the *Shotchun** comes. Here we gotta meet our own fellows, or how are we going to get a husband?

*Or *shadchen,* a professional matchmaker.

BECKY: From husbands you are thinking already? *(Doorbell rings.)*

FANNY: It's him! *(The house is suddenly galvanized into action.* FANNY *runs to window, opens it, calling out.)* Yoo-hoo—I'll be right down!

BECKY: He's not coming upstairs?

FANNY: Mama, please—

BECKY: You don't go with him one step unless he comes upstairs first. Mama should take a look at him! *(*HYMIE *has entered a moment before.)*

FANNY: *(Tearfully.)* In this dump? What will he think of me?

BECKY: *(Pointing to window, sternly.)* Upstairs first!

FANNY: *(Reluctantly calling down again.)* Irving! Mr. Tashman! Please come upstairs, will you! *(She comes away from window unhappily, spots* AARON *on couch.)* Aaron, please—

AARON: *(Sitting up.)* All right, all right! It's not so terrible he should find me on the couch!

ESTHER: Maybe I'll go into the bedroom, the house won't be so crowded?

FANNY: *(Gently.)* Please stay, Esther. I want *you* to meet him. *(They all stand around in stiff, expectant attitudes, waiting for* IRVING TASHMAN'S *arrival. There is a knock at door.* IRVING *enters. A slender fellow, with a breezy manner. His clothes are sporty and perhaps a little too colorful, his hat a little too cocked to one side.)* Hello. This—this is my family. And Mr. Greenspan—a *friend.*

IRVING: Pleased to meet ya—everybody— *(Looking around.)* Nice little place you got here.

FANNY: It's not fancy exactly.

IRVING: But it's home. No place like home, I always say— *(Spotting piano.)* Say, you didn't tell me you had a piano in the house.

BECKY: You play the piano?

IRVING: *(Trying to be modest.)* Do I play? Tell her.

FANNY: Like Paderewski—

IRVING: *(About to demonstrate.)* Would you like me to show you something I just knocked out—it's a beaut—

FANNY: *(Drawing his attention away from piano.)* Irving—I'm all ready—

IRVING: Ready for the big time? Taking her out big-time tonight. Didja tell 'em?

BECKY: A *French* place. She told us—

IRVING: Best place in town. I always say, you gonna take a girl out? Then take her to the best! That's my motto.

FANNY: And, Mama, tonight it's not necessary for you to take me home from the Apollo.

BECKY: I'll let you go home alone, Jack the Ripper should catch you?

FANNY: *(Looking at* IRVING *shyly.)* Mr. Tashman is escorting me home tonight.

IRVING: Don't you worry, Mom—I'll take good care of your little girl. Wouldn't let anything happen to her for the world—

FANNY: Irving, are we going?

IRVING: *(Breezily.)* Well—glad to 'a' metya—everybody— *(To* AARON.*)* Have a cigar. Havana. Have 'em made up special for me—

AARON: Thanks. It's a pleasure.

IRVING: Don't even mention it— *(He and* FANNY *exit.)*

SADIE: Cigars made special for him! Two for three cents, I betcha. Candy-store sport! *(*HYMIE *exits into kitchen.* AARON *has lighted cigar and now inhales the aroma.)*

AARON: If you have to know, Miss Smarty, this cigar costs at least ten cents!

SADIE: And how would you know?

BECKY: I like him. He's a nice boy. A little bit fresh, but nice!

SADIE: *(Laughing.)* Mama, you meet a fellow two minutes, and you know already he's nice?

BECKY: One look and I can tell. He's a good boy.

ESTHER: *(As she exits into kitchen.)* I think he is very nice.

SADIE: Another party heard from—

AARON: Well, in my opinion—

SADIE: *(Nastily.)* Oh! So you have an opinion, too—

AARON: Well, that settles it! *(Jumps up and starts to put on his coat.)*

BECKY: Where are you going?

AARON: I'm taking myself for a walk to the Bronx to see Van Brett! And believe me, I'm going to tell it to Brownstein. To hell with my conscience! *(He exits, banging door.* SADIE *remains behind, absorbed.)*

SADIE: *(After a pause, quietly.)* Mama, he was here again today—and again I didn't get a chance to talk to him.

(Bursting out passionately.) If I could only have more time with him alone!

BECKY: He's bashful—

SADIE: What could *any* man say with Aaron on the couch, people walking in and out— *(Pause—then quietly.)* All week I wait on pins till Wednesday when he comes to give me the lesson. I have figured out what I am going to say—how I am going to say it— *(Ruefully.)* Comes the time—I sit, shivering, afraid to open my mouth.

BECKY: He said something today, makes me wonder—

SADIE: What?

BECKY: I was thanking him for what he was doing, lessons for nothing, so he said, money he couldn't take, like from his own family.

SADIE: He really said that?

BECKY: It's a good sign—

SADIE: *(Throwing her arms around* BECKY.*)* Oh, Mama—

BECKY: *(Smiling.)* So maybe now you'll feel better?

SADIE: *(Gaily.)* I should say so. What's for supper, Mama?

*(*SADIE *exits. Clock strikes six.* BECKY *steps on a chair, about to turn on gas.* ESTHER *enters.)*

ESTHER: Mama, I don't feel so hungry. I—I think I'll take a little walk—

BECKY: Now?

ESTHER: I was in the house all day. I need a little air—

BECKY: So take a walk. Don't stay long. *(*ESTHER *quickly takes her coat from rack and exits.* BECKY *lights gas. A warm glow of light suffuses the room.* BECKY *steps down, glances at book on table. Reciting, half to herself.)*

"In fourteen hundred and ninety-two
Columbus sailed the ocean blue—"

(She exits into kitchen as)

CURTAIN

Scene 2

The same. A month later. The house has a festive air. There are candles in the brass candelabra on buffet. Table is covered with a white cloth and there are new curtains at window.

AT RISE: IRVING TASHMAN *is at piano, playing. He is in his shirtsleeves, and is by now completely "at home."* BECKY *and* FANNY, *in new silk dresses, are busy setting table.* HYMIE, *in a stiff new suit, is on floor studying a paper in his hand.*

HYMIE: *(Half to himself.)* "My dear mama and sisters and brother-in-law and—friends— Today I yam a man. I—I—" *(His nose is back in paper.)*

FANNY: Mama, you're putting the knives on the wrong side.

BECKY: What's the difference? A person can tell it's a knife.

HYMIE: *(Laughing.)* Oh boy, was the Rabbi sore when I told him I'm makin' the speech in English!

BECKY: I told him to tell the Rabbi he shouldn't be mad. After all, God can understand English and in America you have to do like the Romans do. *(To* FANNY.*)* Oh, I forgot! We have to make another setting. I told Aaron to invite his friend Brownstein.

FANNY: Him? Tonight? Gee, Mom—why?

BECKY: The poor man— God knows when he gets something homemade to eat—

FANNY: So we have to listen a whole night to his politics? Hymie, get out of the way!

BECKY: Hymie, your new suit—

*(*HYMIE *exits into upper bedroom, holding paper behind his back, muttering.)*

IRVING: *(As he plays.)* What's it sound like to you, Mom?

BECKY: Beautiful—

IRVING: *(To* FANNY.*)* C'mon, Kiddo, let's sing the chorus for Mom. *(*FANNY *and* IRVING *sing as he plays, "Under a Painted Smile." They finish song with great aplomb.)*

BECKY: Beautiful—

IRVING: And whose little sweetheart am I writing it for?

FANNY: *(Giggling.)* Yours!

IRVING: And what's her name?

FANNY: Mrs. Fanny Tashman!

BECKY: For that I am not forgiving you so easy!

IRVING: *(Getting up, playfully putting his arms around her.)* Whatsa matter, Mom! Still sore? I didn't wanna elope. Fanny made me. She took one look at the way I look at you and she got jealous—

BECKY: *(Fighting him off good-naturedly.)* Go away, you loafer, you! I'll go with the broom to you!

FANNY: Irv, let's fix up the cake like you said— *(They exit into kitchen, laughing.* SADIE *and* ESTHER *enter from street.)*

ESTHER: *(Excitedly, as they remove their wraps.)* We ran all the way home!

SADIE: We tried to get off a few minutes early, so the foreman wouldn't let us—

ESTHER: *(Laughing.)* I went up to him and I said, "We don't feel so good—we're sick"—so he says, "Only one of you is allowed to be sick at one time. Make up your mind—" *(*ESTHER *exits into lower bedroom.* SADIE *goes to window, looks out pensively.)*

BECKY: *(Noticing* SADIE*'s absorption.)* Last night he didn't say anything? *(*SADIE *shakes her head despondently.)* You'll see. He will—

SADIE: What's the use—? *(She turns suddenly.)* All he knows is, I'm a shop girl and he's a school teacher—Why should he even look at me?

BECKY: He's a bashful type boy—

SADIE: I bet if I was a secretary or a bookkeeper—he would look at me then, all right. *(Directly.)* Is Mrs. Gold's Dora smarter than me, Mama?

BECKY: I should say not—

SADIE: That's all I want to know— *(Pause.)* Mama, help me—I want to quit the shop and go to secretary school. I know it's a lot of money, but if you give me thirty dollars I'll pay you back—

BECKY: Why not? Of course I'll give it to you—

SADIE: Oh, Mama, Mama, thank you! And the minute I get a job in an office, have I got plans! The first thing I'm going to do is—throw out that couch—I'm ashamed every time he walks into the house—it's so homely—

BECKY: I don't think it makes a difference to Mr. Engel. He's a very plain boy. He don't expect to get rich.

SADIE: Don't be foolish, Mama. Everybody cares about getting rich. You should see the way people live uptown. You should see what they eat and the way they dress— *(Giggling.)* Honest, Mama, I think he's afraid of girls. He's so polite he still calls me "Miss" Sadie. I'm afraid a boy like him you have to *push* into saying something.

BECKY: *(Smiling.)* So—you want Mama to give him a push for you? *(A knock at door.* BECKY *goes to answer it.* SADIE *exits.* BENJAMIN BROWNSTEIN *enters. He is a large man with a bald head and enormous mustachios. His clothes are those of a poor working man, and he has made no concessions in dress to the occasion.)* Come in, Mr. Brownstein. *(*HYMIE *enters.)*

BENJAMIN: *(Looking around.)* Greenspan is not home yet?

BECKY: Any minute. Take off your coat.

BENJAMIN: *(Removing coat, he finds a place on couch.)* He told me six o'clock we're eating.

HYMIE: Hello, Mr. Brownstein.

BENJAMIN: *(To* HYMIE, *whom he favors.)* How are you, my boy? *(*IRVING *and* FANNY *enter.)*

IRVING: *(Holding cake under* BECKY'S *nose.)* Rector's* comes to Broome Street! *(Placing cake on buffet.)* How'ya, Brownstein—

*(*IRVING *goes back to piano, starts to play.)*

BENJAMIN: Excuse me if I am insulting you, Mrs. Felderman, but this celebration, to me, it's a barbaric

*A high-class restaurant.

bourgeois custom! Gefilte fish and kugel on a boy's thirteenth birthday does not make a man!

HYMIE: *(Listening with all ears.)* What's a bourgeois, Mr. Brownstein?

BENJAMIN: *(About to hold forth.)* A bourgeois—

FANNY: Mr. Brownstein, if it is not too much trouble, *tonight* could we live without a discussion of politics?

BENJAMIN: *(To* HYMIE.*)* You see, Hymie? That's a bourgeois!

HYMIE: *(Puzzled.)* I see—

FANNY: Honest, I betcha this song sells a million copies!

IRVING: And when it does, you and me'll be living on Riverside Drive and Mama'll be living with us—with a colored cook!

BECKY: I would starve first!

BENJAMIN: Ambitions! To lay a head on a pillow on Riverside Drive when millions ain't got straw to sleep on.

IRVING: That's my fault? Listen to him! I say a man's got one life to live. Make your mark and live it easy. That's my motto.

BENJAMIN: Aye, boychick, boychick, comes the Revolution, ideas like yours will not be popular. *(*ESTHER *enters, wearing new dress.)*

ESTHER: *(Pirouetting.)* So—how do I look?

BECKY: Even if I made it myself, it looks good!

IRVING: Now *that's* what I call class—

FANNY: Like a doll! I could get you a job in my theatre any time—

IRVING: Seeing as how you don't work there any more?

FANNY: *(Petulantly.)* It's just *temporary*—

BECKY: When did this happen?

IRVING: Yesterday. And it's as permanent as Christmas!

FANNY: Ish kabibble,* what you say! Monday I'll go see Mr. Shubert and ask him to try me out for the new Winter Garden—

IRVING: You'll see Shubert over my dead body—

FANNY: You make me sick! The way you carry on, you'd think I was undressing in front of the audience—

IRVING: You don't have to undress in front of them! Those guys out front are doin' it for you!

*Comic character whose name became synonymous with "I should worry."

FANNY: You just want to ruin my life! All I want is to give pleasure to people—

BECKY: You have it in your heart to sing, so sing for Irving's pleasure—for mine— *(*BECKY *exits into kitchen.)*

FANNY: You and Irving are going to make a star outta me? *(Dramatically.)* Can I help it if I have it in my nature to be loved and admired by the world? Do you know what it means to sing for an *audience*? To hear them *whistling* for you?

IRVING: Aw, cut it out, Sarah Bernhardt—I'll whistle for you any time—

FANNY: Go away from me—you—you— *(She sniffles unhappily.* SADIE *enters, goes to window, looks out anxiously.)*

IRVING: *(Taking* FANNY *in his arms.)* If it will make you feel better Uncle Abe fired me, too.

FANNY: What?

IRVING: That's right. I ain't workin' for him any more—

FANNY: Why didn't you tell me?

BENJAMIN: Aha! I told you, workers of the world unite!

IRVING: So I'm *united* with Fanny. So we both lost our jobs! *(*BECKY *enters with a challis bread wrapped in napkin.)*

FANNY: Did you hear, Mama? Irving lost his job, too!

BECKY: That's terrible. How did it happen?

IRVING: Uncle Abe is selling the Apollo to Jack Greenfal—so he had to fire us on account Greenfal will have to hire *his own* relatives.

BECKY: He's selling the theatre?

IRVING: *(Laughing skeptically.)* To go to California to make those moving pictures!

FANNY: Gee—Irv—maybe he'll take us with him?

IRVING: You looney? Go all the way out there, we should have to walk back?

FANNY: In the meantime we'll starve—

BECKY: What are you talking about? Tomorrow you move out of the furnished room into the house—

SADIE: *(Who has been listening, all ears, unhappier by the moment.)* The house isn't already overstuffed?

BECKY: *(Firmly.)* We'll find room. Tomorrow you move in—

IRVING: Gee, thanks. You'll get it back. With interest. See

if you don't. *(*AARON *enters from street, dressed in what he considers the well-dressed businessman should wear.)*

SADIE: *(Disappointed.)* Oh—it's you.

AARON: Hello. Hello. Mazeltuff! And how is my friend Brownstein?

BENJAMIN: You said six o'clock—we're eating— *(*ESTHER *sticks her head through door.)*

ESTHER: *(Disappointed.)* Oh—it's you—

AARON: What is this? They are expecting the King of England and it's only me? *(He hands* HYMIE *a package, ostentatiously.)* For you, Hymie. On the occasion of your thirteenth birthday! That's why I was late!

BECKY: Aaron—you shouldn't—

AARON: *(Grandly.)* Why not? I can afford it!

HYMIE: *(Fingering package shyly.)* Should I open it up now? *(*SADIE *and* ESTHER *exit lower bedroom.)*

BECKY: Why not? *(All eyes are on him as he opens package. It contains a large white silk handkerchief.)*

AARON: I asked the fellow, "For the Bar Mitzvah of a boy who is playing the violin, what would be suitable?" So he said, "For under the chin when you play violin, a white silk handkerchief is very suitable."

HYMIE: Gee—thanks—

BENJAMIN: *(Reluctantly taking package from his coat pocket.)* You might as well take this, too.

HYMIE: *(Opening it quickly.)* Thank you, Mr. Brownstein—

BECKY: You shouldn't—

BENJAMIN: *(Angrily.)* Why not? From *him* is all right and not from me? *(*HYMIE *opens package.)*

BECKY: A book!

BENJAMIN: *(Looking directly at* AARON.*)* I asked *myself,* for the Bar Mitzvah of a boy who wants to be a *man*! Take a look, Mr. Greenspan! *The Writings of Karl Marx*—by Marx! *(*AARON *takes a large envelope from his pocket, nonchalantly throws it on table.)*

AARON: And *furthermore*—open this up, Mrs. Felderman, mine darling, and get yourself an excitement.

BECKY: What is this?

AARON: Open it up!

BECKY: *(Opening envelope, takes out sheaf of money.)* I'm

dying! Look what he throws on the table like a newspaper!

AARON: *(Pompously to* BENJAMIN.*)* Seventy-five dollars, cash money! *(Sorting bills, hands* BECKY *several.)* And this, mine sweet Becky, is yours. In full payment of my just debts!

BENJAMIN: *(Bursting out violently.)* Blood money!

BECKY: *(Disregarding* BENJAMIN*'s outburst. She fingers bills, worried.)* That means you're moving out?

AARON: Who said? Even if the couch is not so comfortable, the landlady is one in a million! For the rest of my life, you can count on me! *(*BENJAMIN *continues to glare at* AARON.*)* And out of next month's profits, the first thing I am going to buy is a new couch. A comfortable bed is a good investment. *(To* BECKY *pointedly.)* Unless, Mrs. Becky, you are changing your mind. Mine proposition is still good! *(*BECKY *glares at him.)* All right! All right! Forget I said it! *(*ESTHER *and* SADIE *enter.* SADIE *carries small package, which she gives to* HYMIE.*)*

SADIE: Hymie!

HYMIE: *(Overwhelmed.)* I'm getting a present from you, too? *(Hastily opens package, takes out a small watch.)*

SADIE: From Esther and Mama and me—

HYMIE: *(Putting it to his ear.)* It ticks! Mama—it ticks!

BECKY: *(Proudly.)* Sure it ticks. *(*HYMIE *swallows hard, trying to contain his emotion and pleasure. He gathers his bundles together and runs into bedroom.)*

ESTHER: *(Laughing, exiting after him.)* Hymie! Don't cry! You have to laugh, not cry! *(*SADIE, FANNY *and* ESTHER *exit after him, laughing.)*

BECKY: *(Sniffing.)* The fish! *(She exits into kitchen. A moment's pause.* BENJAMIN *glares at* AARON.*)*

BENJAMIN: *(Unable to contain himself.)* Exploiter!

AARON: Please! You are starting up again? Don't confuse me now! A man is entitled to make a living!

BENJAMIN: Five hundred percent profit is a *living* for you and a *dying* for the man on the machine who does all the work!

IRVING: Don't you guys ever get tired? *(He exits into kitchen.)*

AARON: Don't exaggerate! Five hundred percent profit I'm not making—yet! And even if I was, who is stopping anybody from doing the same? You'll excuse me, it's a free country!

BENJAMIN: A free country, you'll excuse *me,* to starve!

AARON: You're starving? You been working steady in a bakery since the first day you came here!

BENJAMIN: Fourteen hours a day in a dirty bakery cellar—Five men side by side in a room half like this. No windows. Every five minutes somebody mops the floor. Water? No! Sweat! Sweat I said? Blood! The blood of the workers is in every piece of bread you eat!

AARON: I don't taste it!

BENJAMIN: *(Almost apoplectic.)* You will! *(A knock on door.* BECKY *enters to answer it.)*

BECKY: Aaron—Mr. Brownstein—please, the company! *(She opens door.* HARRY ENGEL *and his father,* MYRON *enter.* MYRON ENGEL *is a fifty-year-old edition of his son. Quiet, pedantic, scholarly.)*

HARRY: Papa, this is Mrs. Felderman. And this is my father, Myron Engel.

MYRON: How do you do?

BECKY: I'm glad you came— *(Calling out.)* Girls! Sadie! The company is here! *(*HYMIE *and the girls enter.* IRVING *comes out of kitchen.)* Meet my family. This is Mr. Engel's father—and this is my Fanny's husband, Mr. Tashman—and Mr. Greenspan and Benjamin Brownstein—

HYMIE: How about me? It's my birthday—

BECKY: The most important one we forgot—this is my Hymie— *(Laughing.)* If you'll excuse me, I have to see to the dinner— Fanny! Esther! *(*BECKY *exits.* ESTHER *glances at* HARRY *shyly, then she and* FANNY *follow their mother into kitchen.)*

SADIE: *(Trying to gain* HARRY*'s attention.)* Won't you be seated, Mr. Engel? *(To* MYRON.*)* And you, Mr. Engel—won't you make yourself comfortable?

MYRON: *(As he sits.)* Thank you.

AARON: What line are you in, Mr. Engel?

MYRON: You might call it the *hospital* line.

AARON: A doctor?

MYRON: I am in what you might call the cleaning up line in the hospital. *(With a smile.)* Not exactly a professional man—but my son, Harry, is— *(Proudly.)* He has just passed his examination to teach public school.

SADIE: Congratulations!

HARRY: Thank you.

BENJAMIN: A worthy profession, teaching. But, unfortunately, the school system is a tool of the bosses!

AARON: My friend is slightly inclined toward the Socialistic system— *(*BECKY *enters.* FANNY *and* ESTHER *follow her in, carrying plates of food.)*

BECKY: It's ready, gentlemen. The dinner.

MYRON: A pleasure to sit at the table with such a nice family—

IRVING: C'mon, folks! Let's dig in!

MYRON: Everything looks delicious. *(*HARRY *whispers into* ESTHER*'s ear.)*

SADIE: Secrets, Mr. Engel?

ESTHER: You're going to tell them now?

HARRY: You said tonight at the Bar Mitzvah—

ESTHER: *(Looking around embarrassed, then suddenly.)* All right—now.

HARRY: *(He clears his throat nervously.)* My dear friends—

AARON: Hear! Hear! He's going to make a speech!

HARRY: I—we—that is to say—Esther and I—well—well—I can't make a speech, but Esther and I—well—

MYRON: *(Beaming.)* Don't be nervous, son— *(*HARRY *looks around tongue-tied.)* They are engaged!

HARRY: Thank you, Papa, for telling it for me. *(*SADIE *stares straight ahead, trying to contain herself during following.)*

(Simultaneously.)

FANNY: *(Screaming happily.)* I knew it all the time, but I didn't tell. Not even to Irving!

BECKY: *(Her voice choked.)* It's a great surprise—

AARON: Those quiet fellows certainly put it over on us.

FANNY: *(Embracing* IRVING.*)* They'll love married life, won't they, Irving?

ESTHER: *(To* BECKY.*)* You're not mad we kept it a secret?

BECKY: How could I be mad?— He's a fine boy—

MYRON: *(Shaking* BECKY*'s hand, solemnly.)* Your daughter is a lovely girl. My son is lucky.

BECKY: *(Glancing toward* SADIE, *words do not come easily.)* My daughter is lucky too.

HARRY: *(To* SADIE.*)* I can't thank you enough for bringing me into the house to teach you, Miss Sadie.

SADIE: *(Dryly.)* You can call me Sadie now, without the *Miss*—

MYRON: You have settled on a day for wedding? *(*HARRY *and* ESTHER *nod vigorously.)*

ESTHER: *(Shyly.)* Harry wants it soon.

HARRY: And you are all invited to the wedding!

AARON: Right away is the best. Once I was engaged to a girl, I found out so much about her, I didn't marry her! *(General congratulations and laughter.)* So kiss the bride!

(They all tap on glasses with silverware. The tinkling sound continues as HARRY *kisses her tenderly. Everyone applauds.)*

MYRON: Aren't you forgetting something, my son?

HARRY: Oh, for goodness' sakes! In my pocket— *(He tenderly extracts a small box, taking out ring.)* It's for you— *(He puts it on* ESTHER*'s finger.)*

ESTHER: Oh, Harry—you shouldn't—

HARRY: My father went with me to pick it out.

ESTHER: It must have cost so much—

HARRY: In Greenhut's they have inaugurated a new system. If you are reliable, they give it to you for a dollar a week for two years!

FANNY: Listen to that—

AARON: The man who thought it up will make a million. They charge ten percent interest— *(*HYMIE, *completely neglected, has been watching proceedings with great interest.)*

HYMIE: Don't anybody want to hear my speech? *(No one pays any attention to him.)*

ESTHER: Sadie, isn't the ring wonderful! You didn't say anything!

SADIE: I—I wish you everything.

ESTHER: I can't tell you how happy I am—

SADIE: *(Dryly.)* You should be!

MYRON: *(Getting up.)* Let us drink a toast to the bride-to-be— *(Holding up his glass.)* To Esther, my future daughter. A long life and a happy one! *(They all drink, exclaim happily.)*

FANNY: Now you, Mama—you make a toast!

BECKY: Me?

IRVING: C'mon, Mom—it ain't hard—

MYRON: Just say what's in your heart, Mrs. Felderman.

BECKY: *(Getting up.)* I—I don't know what— *(She clears her throat.)*

AARON: *(Applauding.)* Hear! Hear! *(They are seated now, as follows:* BECKY, *table* R., AARON, FANNY, IRVING, *from* R. *to* L., *backs facing audience,* HYMIE *at table* L., MYRON, SADIE, HARRY, ESTHER *and* BENJAMIN *from* R. *to* L., *facing audience.)*

BECKY: A lifetime it would take to say what's in my heart— *(They are quiet now.* BECKY *looks from one to other, then last at* SADIE. *In an effort to give* SADIE *courage,* BECKY *decides to make speech. Quietly.)* I look around this table and I see: My Fanny has a good husband who loves her— *(*FANNY *takes* IRVING*'s hand.)* For my Esther and her Harry . . . life is just beginning— *(Pause.)* Then I see my Hymie sitting in the place where his father would be sitting—and I think, today he is a man. I remember, where we came from was chances only for a man to die—and here—here they beg you to take the chances for living— *(She pauses, then fixes her gaze on* SADIE, *who sits, head bowed.)* Then I look at my Sadie, and for her, too, my heart is happy. *(*SADIE *looks up sharply.)* Oh, yes! She also has an important announcement surprise. My Sadie is going to give up working in the shop and will go to a school to become a secretary! *(General exclamation, "A secretary"—"That's wonderful!" etc.)* Oh, yes! My Sadie knows in America are chances for everybody to be somebody! *(She lifts her glass.)* So, if it is allowed we should drink, not to a person, but to a place—then please—to America! *(Pause.)* Because we know only good can come to us here! *(She looks around.)* Now should we drink?

(They are all visibly affected by BECKY*'s speech.* BENJAMIN *has taken out his handkerchief and chooses at this point to blow his nose vigorously. The spell is broken.*

They begin to drink and eat, all except Sadie, *who continues to stare straight ahead, as though in a trance.)*

Hymie: *(Suddenly.)* Mama! Please! *Now* can I make my speech? *(He gets up.)* My dear mother and sisters and brother-in-law and friends! Today I yam a man— *(As)*

CURTAIN

ACT II

Scene 1

The same. Early morning of Saturday, March 25, 1911. AARON*'s couch is disheveled, sheets thrown in a lump, etc.* SADIE *is at window, wan and dispirited.* BECKY *enters from kitchen. She goes to upper bedroom door and knocks.*

BECKY: Fanny!

FANNY: *(Off.)* I'm up! *(Yelling.)* Irving! Get up—

BECKY: Let him sleep.

FANNY: *(Entering.)* If I can get up at six, he can get up at six! *(*BECKY, *folding* AARON*'s sheets, watches* SADIE *in deep concern.* FANNY *making a beeline for bathroom.)* I'm first— *(She is gone.)*

BECKY: *(To* SADIE.*)* Maybe you won't go to the *shop* today?

SADIE: *(Wearily.)* I'm all right.

BECKY: Sadie, please, do me a favor, don't go.

SADIE: Why shouldn't I go? It's *my* wedding? Tell her to stay home. She's the bride! *(A pause.)* I know. You're afraid I'll say something—

BECKY: Did I say it?

SADIE: That's what you're thinking, isn't it? *(Getting up wearily.)* Don't worry, I won't say anything. *(Passionately.)* But you can't stop a person's *thoughts*! Today I'll be sitting at the machine, biting my tongue to keep from running to the window and throwing myself out of it!

BECKY: You don't go to the shop today! I'll tie you with ropes to the bed—

SADIE: Don't worry. They say when a person talks about it, he doesn't do it.

BECKY: Sadie—please—I'll give you breakfast.

SADIE: I'm not hungry.

BECKY: You're killing yourself! A whole month not to eat—

SADIE: I don't know what you want from me.— Leave me alone— *(She exits into bedroom.* BECKY *stares unhappily at her retreating form.)*

FANNY: *(Entering.)* I'm out! Who's next? *(She stops when she sees* BECKY*'s expression.)* What's the matter? *(*BECKY *nods toward door.)* Sadie? She'll get over it.

BECKY: It's easy for somebody else to say it.

FANNY: *(Calling out as she exits into upper bedroom.)* Irving! Get up! *(*BECKY *continues to fold sheets as* ESTHER *enters. She is half dressed.)*

ESTHER: Sadie is sick?

BECKY: She didn't sleep so good—

ESTHER: *(She laughs.)* I guess I made her nervous. Pinching myself all night— *(With a sigh.)* Today, the last day in the shop. Tomorrow I'm getting married. Me! *(Pause.)* Mama, could I ask you a question?

BECKY: Why not?

ESTHER: Were you scared, Mama—when the time came? *(She runs to* BECKY*.)* Last night when Harry was here, I got so frightened, I wanted to say, "Please excuse me, but I can't do it." I wanted to run away— Is that how you felt?

BECKY: *(Smiling gently.)* If you want to know, I *did* run away. I got up early in the morning and I ran into the fields. I buried my head in the grass and I said to myself, no—no—I wouldn't go back! *(Laughing.)* An hour later, I got hungry, I went back.

ESTHER: *(Laughing, incredulous.)* No!

BECKY: That evening I married Papa—

ESTHER: Mama, Mama, I'm so nervous, I wish it were tomorrow already!

BECKY: Hurry up, get dressed; you'll be late!

ESTHER: *(Gaily, as she exits into bathroom.)* If I'm late today, the foreman can fire me! *(*BECKY *looks after her a moment, then at door where* SADIE *is. With a sigh she exits into kitchen.* FANNY *enters dressed for street.)*

FANNY: *(In high agitation.)* You'll see if I'll stand for it!

IRVING: *(Coming to door, in his bathrobe.)* Give me one good reason why I have to get up at six-thirty?

FANNY: It's the principle!

IRVING: What principle? Six-thirty you have to hand me four-syllable words?

FANNY: All right—I don't mind working in the shop again. I know it's only *temporary*. But when my back is breaking over the machine, I feel ten times worse if I know you're laying in bed!

IRVING: Have a heart—darling. I'm dead on my feet.

FANNY: The thing that tears me up—this minute I could be turning over on the other side! If you'd only let me go back on the stage . . . Milton Glaser, the agent, came looking for me—

IRVING: *(Angrily.)* All over again? Half the night wasn't enough? I'm a mild man, Fanny, but—

FANNY: Go ahead! Hit me, why don't you!

IRVING: *(Falling into chair, half asleep.)* I'm too tired—

FANNY: If I knew I'd have to give up my career when I married you, I wouldn't— *(breaking off hotly.)* Irving! You're not listening!

IRVING: *(Wearily.)* I'm listening.

FANNY: That man will drive me wild! *(*IRVING *gets up.)* Where are you going?

IRVING: Back to sleep.

FANNY: That's all the appreciation—

IRVING: Look, baby, I know we're having a hard time. But, honey—look at me—c'mon—look at me— *(His arms on her shoulders.)* Do I look like the kinda fellow that likes his wife to work for him? Do I?

FANNY: *(Reluctantly.)* No—

IRVING: You know it's only *temporary*— *(Reasoning with her.)* And if I go to a publishing house early, I gotta buy lunch outside and lunch means a quarter. So you think I'm gonna spend your hard-earned quarters buying myself lunch? See the point? *(Pause.)*

FANNY: I see it—

IRVING: *(Sitting next to her, arm about her.)* Now you're talking! You know it's just a question of minutes! Kitty Gordon is *positively* trying out my song at the new Roseland Palace! It's as good as published already—

FANNY: *(Jumping up. Tearfully.)* And you wrote that song for me!

IRVING: *(Whistling impatiently.)* Sure I did. And I'm even gonna make 'em print it on the sheet! "For My

Wife"—just like that! Gee, baby, don't cry— *(Holding her close.)* I'm crazy about you—

FANNY: *(Through her tears.)* Are you?

IRVING: You've got the most beautiful nose in the whole world! *(Kisses her nose.)*

FANNY: Have I?

IRVING: I'll kill anybody says "no"— *(Pause, as he and* FANNY *embrace.)* As if I don't appreciate what you're doin'—and never, *never* throwin' it up to me— *(He breaks off.)* Well—hardly ever. And, baby, will I make it up to you! You'll have so many dresses hangin' in your closet, it'll take you an hour to make up your mind which one to wear.

FANNY: Oh, Irving— *(They embrace again.)*

IRVING: Now can I go back to sleep?

FANNY: *(Tenderly.)* Go back to sleep, Poppy— *(Pause as she watches him go toward door.)* Today is pay day. Should I bring you home something, darling? *(*ESTHER *enters, dressed for street.)*

IRVING: *(Yawning.)* Cuppla Havana Burns Specials— Am I sleepy— *(He is gone.)*

BECKY: *(Calling out from kitchen.)* Girls, come eat breakfast—

ESTHER: Come on, Fanny, we'll be late—

FANNY: *(Still filled with spell of* IRVING*'s presence.)* Married life is wonderful! It's so legitimate! *(*SADIE *enters.)*

ESTHER: Are you feeling any better, Sadie?

SADIE: This is a wonderful day for you—

ESTHER: I feel—like on air— Fanny, did you feel that way?

FANNY: To tell you the truth, I don't remember *how* I felt! I was so scared Mama would be mad—

ESTHER: I—I feel so empty—

SADIE: *(Quietly.)* *You* feel empty—?

ESTHER: *(Gaily.)* Wouldn't you? *(She is about to exit into kitchen.)* I don't know how I'll live through this day—

SADIE: You don't know how *you'll* live through this day— *(Forcing* ESTHER*'s attention to her.)* And how do you think *I'll* live through this day? And tomorrow? And for days and days and years after that? For the rest of my life! *(*ESTHER *stares at her, still uncomprehending.)* That's right! Stand there looking at me as if I were crazy! *(Her voice reaching a wild crescendo.)*

You took him away from me! I brought him into the house! He would have married *me!* You took him away from me, do you hear me?—I hate you! I wish you were dead! *(*BECKY *has entered at sounds of* SADIE*'s hysteria.)*

BECKY: Sadie! No! No! *(*ESTHER *has been staring at* SADIE*—the full implication of her words dawning gradually. Suddenly, with a cry of deep hurt, she runs from the house.* FANNY *looks at* SADIE *as if she could strike her, quickly takes* ESTHER*'s wraps and her own from rack, exits after* ESTHER*.)*

SADIE: *(Falling into chair.)* Mama, please—do something—help me! I can't stand it— *(She weeps—dry hacking sobs escaping her.* BECKY *looks on—bewildered and unhappy—as—the curtain is lowered to show the lapse of several hours.)*

TIME: *Four-thirty same afternoon.*

BECKY *is at table, kneading dough.* AARON *watches her.* HYMIE *is at piano, playing "Here Comes the Bride" on his violin.*

AARON: Cakes! Wedding! One by one they'll get married and leave you alone. *(*BECKY *looks at him, sharply.)* All right! All right! I didn't say it. *(He goes to couch, sits down.)* A double wedding we could make it. They would even put it in the *Forwartz*. Mother and daughter marry on the same day. *(*BECKY *continues her work, not looking at him. He lies full-length on couch.)*

BECKY: Hymie! Go downstairs and play! What are you doing, hanging around the house on such a nice day?

HYMIE: I was practicing for tomorrow, I shouldn't make a mistake.

BECKY: If you make one little mistake, who will notice? *(*HYMIE *puts away violin and exits.* IRVING enters, yawning.)

IRVING: To the "Wedding March" I was dreaming. You know, Mom, the kid's got a nice touch. *(*SADIE *enters from street as* IRVING *nears bathroom.)*

SADIE: Good morning, Mr. Tashman! Sleep till four-thirty in the afternoon with his wife slaving in the shop! *(As she goes toward bedroom.)* If I had a man like you, I would throw him out of the window. *(She exits.)*

IRVING: *(As he exits into bathroom.)* I believe you! In your house murder would be an everyday occurrence! *(He is gone.* AARON *starts fussing with baking utensils on table.)*

BECKY: Aaron! What are you doing?

AARON: Why not? Somebody else helps you around this house?

BECKY: It's very nice of you.

AARON: Becky, Becky, if you would only let me . . . *(*BECKY *does not answer. He changes his tack.)* Listen, Mrs. Felderman—lately, since I am doing business with the outside world, I am subject to *embarrassment*! How can I explain to my friends that I'm not married? Am I twenty-one? A schoolboy? They think there's something the matter with me.

BECKY: Maybe your friends are right, Aaron. A man like you should be married. . . .

AARON: So?

BECKY: Take my advice, look around. You'll find a good woman who can give you a heart one hundred percent for yourself! *(She looks around at doors of her house in concern.)*

AARON: Tell me the truth—if I took your advice, you mean to say you wouldn't miss me? *(A knock at door.)*

BECKY: Answer the door, Aaron. *(*AARON *opens door.* BENJAMIN *enters, greatly perturbed.)*

BENJAMIN: *(Banging on a newspaper.)* What did I tell you American justice? Hello, Mrs. Felderman— On the side of the bosses!

AARON: Brownstein, do you ever give yourself a minute's peace?

BENJAMIN: In war how can there be peace?

AARON: What war?

BENJAMIN: *(Banging on paper again.)* They're not ashamed to print the decision in the paper! The New York State ten-hour-a-day legislation for bakers is unconstitutional! Mr. Justice Peckham! The *Supreme* Court! *(Snorting.)* That's justice?

AARON: I don't know about you, Brownstein, but I'm hungry.

BENJAMIN: Don't change the subject.

AARON: It's easier to change the subject than to change the world. The only thing a sensible man can do is take care of himself. *(*BENJAMIN *glares at him.)* That makes me a criminal? Brownstein, I wouldn't hurt a fly.

BENJAMIN: *(Angrily.)* Boss of a nonunion sweat shop, and he wouldn't hurt a fly!

AARON: Tell them to get a union, and I'll have a union! I'm stopping them? *(*BENJAMIN *looks at* AARON, *unable to face force of his logic.)* The trouble is, Brownstein, you are not looking for a system. You are looking for a Heaven! *(*BECKY *has been listening, all ears.)*

BECKY: Mr. Brownstein! My three girls work in the Triangle Shop, and they are not complaining and I am not complaining, so why should you? *(Suddenly.)* Tell me, where you and I came from did we have even a *chance* to work? If you ask me, in America it's a "Paradise" for the workingman.

BENJAMIN: *(Almost apoplectic.)* Paradise! Excuse me for insulting you, but you're crazy! *(Watching her as she kneads dough.)* Furthermore, you make me nervous. With the fingers you don't do it! With the hands—the *palms* of the hands— *(He goes at dough.* BECKY *pushes him away.)*

BECKY: Wash your hands first!

BENJAMIN: *(Examining his hands.)* To hell with it! *(He walks away, brooding.* SADIE *enters.)*

AARON: I'm still hungry.

BENJAMIN: I could eat myself.

BECKY: *(Good-naturedly.)* Two grown men, you can't help yourself? The icebox is full.

AARON: Come, Brownstein, I'll make you a sandwich like in Delmonico's Restaurant.

BENJAMIN: It doesn't have to be so fancy— *(*AARON *and* BENJAMIN *exit into kitchen. A moment of pause. From street we hear dimly sounds of fire engines and bells.)*

SADIE: Well, why don't you say something?

BECKY: What should I say?

SADIE: Haven't you any curiosity? Don't you want to know where I went in such a rush?

BECKY: I'm hoping in my heart you went to the shop to apologize to your sister Esther for what you did this morning.

SADIE: If you have to know, I took myself for a walk to

the secretary school! I enrolled! *(*Becky *does not answer.)* Nobody in this world will ever have the satisfaction of seeing Sadie Felderman crying her eyes out over a man! From now on, it's something else in my life! You said in America are chances for everybody to be somebody! Well, I'm going to be somebody! And I won't stop at secretary school, either! That's just the beginning! I'll show them! I'll show— *(She breaks completely, dropping into a chair, weeping.)*

Becky: *(Gently, going to her.) Kind, kind,* as if I don't know how you're feeling. Don't I know what it means for a woman to lose the man she loves? I lived with Papa for ten years—and when I lost him, I wanted to die— *(Sounds of engines, sirens and bells playing a strange counterpoint to her voice.)* But I remembered I had other things to live for. I said to myself, "I cannot take out on my innocent children what I feel." Sadie, Sadie, a family is something you have to hold on to with all your strength! You don't tear it to pieces because you lost a man you never had!

Sadie: Didn't I try? Did I say something all month? But when I see you making preparations, wedding cake, wedding dresses—a stone couldn't stand it!

Becky: *Kind, kind,* what is the trick in being strong when everything is going your way? *(Firmly.)* Be a *mensch,* Sadie!

(Door bursts open. Hymie *is there gesticulating, wildly, breathlessly.)*

Hymie: Mama—Mama— *(His voice trails off in a wail. Finding his voice, he screams the words.)* The shop—the Triangle Shop—Mama—it's on fire—

Sadie: *(Screaming the word.)* No!

*(*Irving *has entered from bathroom, face covered with shaving lather.)*

Hymie: *(Hysterically.)* It's burning—

(They stand shocked, unable to believe their ears.)

Becky: The girls!

(Following action happens simultaneously: IRVING *grabs his coat from rack, wiping his face with it as he rushes out of door, followed by* BECKY. HYMIE, *breathless, stands staring at* SADIE, *then quickly exits after them hurriedly.* SADIE *stands alone, looking at open door, not daring to move as—the curtain is lowered to show the lapse of several hours.)*

TIME: *Midnight.*
SADIE *is at table, her head buried in her arms.*
HYMIE *is at window. Restlessly, he looks out.*

HYMIE: Sadie, please, can't I go downstairs?

SADIE: Hymie, I asked you not to— *(From outside we hear sounds of wailing.)* It's Mrs. O'Shaughnessy—her Annie, she worked in the shop—

HYMIE: *(Frightened.)* I don't care. I'm gonna go. I'm going downstairs to look for Mama— *(He exits quickly.)*

SADIE: *(Calling after him.)* Hymie! Come back— *(Exhausted, she sits, head in arms again. A moment's pause.* IRVING *enters, grimy, disheveled.)* No news? *(*IRVING *shakes his head. He sits, suddenly doubles up as if in physical pain. She goes toward him.)* Maybe no news is good news—

IRVING: If they're all right, why aren't they *home*? *(The horror pouring out of him.)* Maybe they jumped! The way I seen 'em jump. Cracking the sidewalks! At the windows screaming at you. All you could do was watch 'em burn up in front of your eyes— *(He weeps dryly, silently.)* This morning I held her in my arms—she was laughing—

SADIE: Stop it—

IRVING: *One* fire escape for eight hundred people. It broke in the middle—with twenty—thirty people on it—

(A pause, both SADIE *and* IRVING *lost in their own grief. Door opens.* FANNY *is there. She stands still, half demented, her clothes hanging about her, wildly.* IRVING *throws his arms around her, hardly believing she is there.)*

FANNY: *(In a dull flat tone, almost unrecognizable.)* Where's Esther?

IRVING: Fanny—Fanny— *(He kisses her hands over and over again.)*

SADIE: She'll be home right away— Didn't you come home? Irving—go quick—find Mama—tell her Fanny is home—

IRVING: *(Shaking her, trying to impress his words on her.)* Fanny—listen to me—I'm going to look for Mama—tell her you're here— *(He suddenly begins to laugh hysterically.)* Fanny—you're home—you're home, darling—laugh! Laugh, Fanny! *(He continues to laugh, his hysteria mounting.)*

FANNY: Where's Esther?

SADIE: *(Breaking.)* We don't know where she is!

FANNY: *(Quietly, after pause.)* I am downstairs. Walking, walking—I ask everybody, where is Esther? Nobody knows. *(She notices* SADIE.*)*

IRVING: Sadie, please, I'll stay here with her. Go try to find Mama—please—

FANNY: *(Suddenly, pointing to* SADIE.*)* *She* did it—she put the curse on her! I heard you! This morning you said to her, "I wish you were dead—"

*(*SADIE, *frightened, runs to door, exits quickly.* IRVING *holds* FANNY *close, quieting her.)*

IRVING: Look, Fanny—it's me, Irving. Remember Irving? Just like yesterday and the day before—your piece of candy—

FANNY: *(Quietly.)* I forgot—the pay envelope. Here— *(She takes small envelope out of her pocket, miraculously safe. Suddenly rational.)* The bell is ringing. Everybody talking and laughing. We are going home. Then—we are running—like crazy we are running—screaming. I am near a wall and somebody is pushing me up a ladder. *(Her voice trails off.)* Who is pushing me— Oh, yes— Piney—

IRVING: *(Weeping unashamedly.)* I'm going to kiss Piney for that, you'll see, I'll kiss him for pushing you—

FANNY: *(Suddenly she breaks away from* IRVING *and starts running around, pushing* IRVING *aside as though he were in the way. She starts screaming.)* I gotta get out! Out—out—help—out—Esther—Esther—

*(*IRVING *picks her up, carries her into upper bedroom, where her moans resound for a moment.* AARON *and* BECKY *enter.* BECKY *is near collapse.* SADIE *follows them in.)*

BECKY: Oh— *(She quickly exits into upper bedroom.* AARON *sits, exhausted.* MYRON *enters.)*

AARON: *(Looking up.)* Fanny is home—

MYRON: Thank God!

AARON: We left Harry in our place in the line—thousands waiting to get into the morgue. All of them had relatives or friends? No. Curiosity seekers. At a time like this, curiosity seekers!

MYRON: *(Quietly.)* They'll know soon enough. The morgue has no secrets. Tomorrow the whole East Side will be in mourning— *(Pause.* SADIE *enters.)* For eight hours I have been making the rounds of the hospitals. After what I saw the first five minutes I prayed in my heart I would not find them—better off dead. Better off— *(A pause. The men look at one another.)* You have to hope. Fanny came home.

AARON: A child—a baby. *(*BECKY *enters from bedroom.)*

BECKY: Asleep. It's good she can sleep—

AARON: *(Placating, to* BECKY.*)* Becky, where was Fanny all day? Maybe Esther is also walking around like Fanny. They'll find her—they'll bring her home—

BECKY: *(In a daze.)* She *got* to come home—tomorrow is the wedding—everything is ready— *(Looking around.)* I didn't finish the challis— *(She touches dough, still resting on table where she left it.)* Mrs. O'Shaughnessy's Annie. They found her there— *(Looking around suddenly.)* Where's Hymie?

SADIE: He went downstairs—I'll go find him. *(She exits quickly.)*

BECKY: *(Dazed.)* Mrs. Pomerantz's two boys and her husband— *(Suddenly she runs to rack, grabs her shawl.)*

AARON: *(Gently taking her arm.)* Where are you going?

BECKY: Esther is there—somewhere—I have to find her—

AARON: *(Gently drawing her away from door.)* Please, you have to wait—

BECKY: *(To* MYRON *as she walks toward table.)* I have to wait—wait— *(Dropping into chair, exhausted.)* Wait— *(A pause. A moment later door opens and* HARRY *enters. He is too quiet. They all look at him with pleading eyes.* HARRY *goes toward* BECKY. *Taking her hand, he opens it, placing* ESTHER*'s ring in it.* HARRY *turns away, goes to buffet quietly, his back to them. He suddenly doubles up in a spasm of dry, hacking sobs.* BECKY *continues to stare at ring in her hand. Quietly, dazed, unbelieving.)* A dollar a week for two years— *(Her voice breaks as)*

CURTAIN

Scene 2

The same. Early April, 1917. Six years later. Late afternoon. The set is changed only in so far as six years of living in one place will bring about the inevitable changes of a different set of curtains, a new calendar, perhaps a new chair or two. The old couch has been exchanged for a new sofa in the best Grand Rapids manner of the period. Otherwise everything remains the same.

AT RISE: HYMIE *and* HARRY *in heated discussion.* HARRY *is now close to thirty, he wears glasses and has developed a more scholarly manner.* HYMIE *is now nineteen, a good-looking young man with a vivacious excitable manner.*

HYMIE: I tell you it's any minute now, Harry. Did you see where we handed the German Ambassador his walking papers?

HARRY: *(Unnerved.)* Severing of diplomatic relations doesn't necessarily mean war! *(*HYMIE *takes up violin and plays a bar of scales.)* The *Illinois*'s not the first ship that went down. They can still send a note of regret.

HYMIE: Not this time. She told us six weeks ago she's starting unrestricted submarine warfare! They're calling National Guardsmen up for Federal Service already!

(A knock at door. HYMIE *answers it.* BENJAMIN *enters. The years have made little change in his appearance.)*

BENJAMIN: Greenspan is home?

HYMIE: Not yet—

BENJAMIN: *(Ill at ease, not in his usual manner.)* If it's all right with you, I'll wait.

HYMIE: How'ya, Brownstein?

BENJAMIN: *(Absorbed in his own thoughts.)* All right—

HYMIE: *(With a laugh.)* You *should* be all right! Kerensky and your boyfriends sure fixed the Czar!

BENJAMIN: Kerensky! When I think of him, with my two hands I could— *(He makes gesture of choking.)*

HYMIE: You're complaining?

BENJAMIN: The workers made a Revolution to reestablish the old order? No! *(He gets up, agitated.)* Any minute they'll start sweeping again—they'll sweep him out with the rest of the dirt!

HARRY: *(Suddenly, out of his own absorption.)* Benjamin, do you think America will enter the war?

BENJAMIN: Wall Street, you should excuse me, will sit on its fat behind, and let Germany win? And lose their investment in the Allies?

HYMIE: *(Laughing.)* Speech! Speech! *(*BECKY *enters from kitchen.)*

BENJAMIN: Go ahead! Make fun! The propaganda presses will start rolling, before you know it you'll be sporting a uniform and acting like it was your own idea! You give your life. Wall Street gets back its money! Fifty-fifty! Fine America! *(He spits disgustedly.)*

BECKY: Mr. Brownstein! This is a free country, but about America please don't spit in my house!

BENJAMIN: What did I tell you? Propaganda presses!

HARRY: *(More and more disturbed.)* I'll never go to war. I'll go to jail first!

HYMIE: *(Laughing.)* I think I'll give up the violin and start playing the bugle!

BECKY: Nothing is settled yet, so Hymie is playing the bugle and Harry is sitting in jail already!

BENJAMIN: *(Quietly.)* And I am on my way to Russia.

BECKY: Russia?

BENJAMIN: Saturday I am sailing.

BECKY: *(Concerned.)* Why should you go to Russia? You're an American citizen—

BENJAMIN: *(Solemnly.)* They *need* me.

BECKY: Without you they made it— How about a bite supper with us, Mr. Brownstein?

BENJAMIN: *(Getting up instantly, follows* BECKY *into*

kitchen.) Supper? I wouldn't care if I did. *(They are gone.* HARRY, *greatly upset, continues to read paper, anxiously.)*

HYMIE: *(Putting violin back into case. Noticing* HARRY*'s absorption.)* Got you worried, hasn't it—

HARRY: *(Picking up newspaper.)* Seven thousand dead—like they were describing a baseball game— Everything I've tried to teach, all being destroyed in front of my eyes! *(Pleading suddenly.)* Wilson was re-elected because he kept us out of it— He can't suddenly turn turkey on us—

HYMIE: He'll do what he has to do! *(Pause as he sees* HARRY*'s expression.)* They're fighting our battle, Harry. How can we avoid it? This is a war to end war!

HARRY: War to end war? Man! There's no such thing!

HYMIE: *(After a pause.)* Well—I'm enlisting—

HARRY: Hymie, my God—why?

HYMIE: Sh—Mom doesn't know yet—

HARRY: Do you mean to say you could go out and kill a man?

HYMIE: About such things you have to be strictly impersonal—

HARRY: What's impersonal about killing a man who wants to live as much as you do?

HYMIE: I don't like that part of it any more than you do! But fellows like you take too much for granted! Freedom, Democracy—just words in a dictionary to you! When I think of that guy and what he's doing over there—I see red!

HARRY: Listen to me, Hymie—you're not going to preserve Freedom and Democracy by killing! You're going to *destroy* it! Just look at your history books—even the rotten books they gave you to read. The books I've had to teach all my life— *(Breaks off.)* Maybe it's my fault. Maybe if I and others like me had done our parts better—maybe if I had *fought* for the things I stood for— *(Pause.)* But I lost interest— *(Pause.)* Do I talk this way because I'm afraid to die? God knows I've thought of death often enough, as a way out—

HYMIE: *(Quietly.)* Harry, don't talk like a fool—

HARRY: Don't do it, Hymie.

HYMIE: *(Quietly.)* Please, I've made up my mind—a man's gotta do what he has to do—

HARRY: *(After pause.)* All right. We see things differently. You want to go—I can't stop you. But I won't go, because I don't believe in it! I have no faith in violence as a means of settling anything.

BECKY: *(Calling out from kitchen.)* Boys! Come eat supper—

*(*HARRY *exits into kitchen.* HYMIE *remains behind absorbed in thought.* AARON *enters. The six years have dealt kindly with him. A few gray hairs add distinction to his appearance.)*

HYMIE: Hello, Mr. Greenspan—

BECKY: *(Calling out again.)* That's you, Aaron?

AARON: Who else?

BECKY: *(Through kitchen door.)* Mr. Brownstein, Aaron is here—

AARON: *(To* HYMIE.*)* Some warm day for this time of year— *(*HYMIE *grabs his hat, and exits suddenly.)* Where are you going in such a hurry? *(*BENJAMIN *enters. To* BENJAMIN.*)* And how is the world treating you, Brownstein?

BENJAMIN: *(Coming to point.)* Greenspan, I won't waste your time and my time with preliminaries! You can answer "yes" or "no" and I won't be insulted. Last week I told you I am going to Russia. Well—there is a small matter of two hundred dollars for expenses. I need a loan. *(*AARON *is taken by surprise. Suddenly implication of* BENJAMIN*'s words dawns on him.* AARON *starts to laugh.)* What's the joke?

AARON: *(Laughing heartily.)* You are asking *me,* the dirtiest capitalist exploiter in America, by your own words, to lend you the money to go to Russia to fight a revolution?

BENJAMIN: I thought you wouldn't see it my way. Never mind—

AARON: Wait a minute! Did I say "no"? *(*BENJAMIN *stops in his tracks.)* Give a man at least a good laugh for his two hundred dollar investment?

BENJAMIN: Please—I don't see the joke!

AARON: Aye, Brownstein, one reason I like you is because you can always be depended on *not* to see the joke!

BENJAMIN: Greenspan, yes or no, do I get the money?

AARON: *(With a smile.)* I'll lend you the money, on *one* condition—

BENJAMIN: *(Almost apoplectic.)* Conditions?

AARON: Yes. On condition that— *(Pretending to be serious.)* comes the Revolution in America, when they are putting me against the wall, you'll tell them, if it weren't for *me*—you would never—

BENJAMIN: *(Cutting in.)* Never! You can't buy your immunity with two hundred dollars, Greenspan.

AARON: *(Laughing.)* Brownstein, Brownstein, you are worth the price of an admission! *(Suddenly serious.)* You want to know the *truth*? Comes the Revolution in America— *(Forcefully.)* they can line me against the wall and to hell with your immunity!

BENJAMIN: So? *(*AARON *takes out checkbook, makes out check.)*

AARON: *(As he writes.)* Believe it or not, I will miss you, Brownstein.

BENJAMIN: A man must go where his principles send him. *(Ostentatiously, blows his nose. It is evident that* AARON*'s generosity has touched him.* AARON *solemnly hands check to* BENJAMIN.*)*

AARON: *(Holding out his hand.)* Will I see you again in my life?

BENJAMIN: Where I am going, a man can't make plans for the future.

AARON: So it's good-bye— *(They shake hands.)*

BENJAMIN: Well— *(He fingers check, then shoves it into his pocket, and goes toward kitchen door.)* On good-byes and thank-yous, I'm not so good— *(Pause.)* You tell her— *(*BENJAMIN *is gone.)*

BECKY: *(Entering.)* Aaron, supper is ready—where's Brownstein? *(*AARON *looks after him a moment.)*

AARON: He went to Russia— Becky, would you call me a fool? I gave him two hundred dollars to go there.

BECKY: Oh— *(Slowly, after a moment.)* I think if a man believes in something so strong he's willing to give up his life for it— *(Shaking her head.)* a person shouldn't stand in his way.

AARON: *(Gently.)* That's what I thought, too. *(They smile at each other, a look of understanding passing between them.* HARRY *enters from kitchen, goes to window, pensively.)* What's for supper, mine dear lady? *(*AARON *exits.* BECKY *remains behind, watching* HARRY. *She is about to exit into kitchen when* FANNY *and* IRVING *enter from street.)*

BECKY: How was the picture?

IRVING: I never saw such trash—

FANNY: Maybe it's trash, but in the meantime your Uncle Abe is in California making thousands out of it, and you're starving to death!

IRVING: I'm starving?

FANNY: That's right! Take me literal—

IRVING: *(As they go toward kitchen.)* The public wants live shows! Movies are a novelty. There's no *future* in it!

FANNY: I suppose there's a big future for you in a forty-cent table de hote restaurant! Singing for *tips*! *(She is gone.)*

IRVING: If you don't stop nagging me, I'll go out of the house, I won't come back! What's for supper? *(He exits after her.)*

BECKY: *(Smiling gently.)* They talk like they mean it— *(Going to window, she opens it, sniffing the air.)* It's spring on Broome Street already, Harry— *(*BECKY *comes away from window, humming.)* "I didn't raise my boy to be a soldier. I raised him up to be my pride and—" *(She stops short, alarm in her voice.)* Harry!

HARRY: *(Out of his absorption.)* Yes?

BECKY: If—if they declare war—will my Hymie have to go? *(*HARRY *does not answer.* BECKY *is suddenly filled with the realization that War is the personal business of one's son going.)* Of course he'll have to go. Mrs. Strong's boy is only eighteen and he's a sailor— *(Pause.)* I'm so mixed up, Harry. When I took out my papers I swore to hold up the Constitution—to give my life—my life—gladly—but—but Hymie— *(She breaks off, tries to throw off her mood, hardly succeeding.)* You know what I am? Aaron calls me a pessimist. A Calamity Jane—that's me. *(Pleading with* HARRY *for confirmation.)* I bet in a few days the whole thing is over and I'm worrying about Hymie—

HARRY: We stayed out of it so far—there's not a chance in the world— *(Pause.)*

BECKY: *(Seeing* HARRY*'s absorption.)* After all these years, Harry—I think of you as if you were my own—

HARRY: *(Looks up, caught by her tone.)* Yes?

BECKY: *(Shaking her head.)* It's no good—Harry—what you have made of your life. *(With some force.)* A man mustn't dig a hole in the ground beside the loved one and lie down in it for the rest of his life! No! Six years of death for the living is a sin!

HARRY: When she died the life went out of me—as if I were blinded—

BECKY: Maybe it's because you have eyes in your head but you won't see what's right under your nose— *(She breaks off, looks closely at him.)* Sadie.

HARRY: You mean Sadie—and me? *(*BECKY *nods gently. Disquieted.)* But—I never thought of Sadie that way—I—

BECKY: Maybe if you did think about? *(*HARRY *turns away.)* I worry about you, Harry. I think what you were like, six, seven years ago! You were going to *do* so much! The world was yours—I look at you today, I get frightened. A young man and you never smile. Sitting for hours with your nose in a book, looking for companionship with people who aren't real. Who never lived— Tell me, is that a way for a man to live? Is it healthy? What will become of you? *(Pause.)* My Sadie—I can see how she buries her feelings in the *job.* Why? Because she has to have something to fill up her life—it's no way for a woman to live, either! *(Quietly.)* Believe me, Harry, there is still time for you to make a life for yourself. But you can't do it alone. I think to myself—two fine young people—if they were *together,* they would be living for each other, and they would both be happy— *(She breaks off.)* Harry—if you can't do what I said—please forget I said it—

(Door opens and SADIE *enters. In six years she has gained a successful, satisfied look. She is well-dressed and her manner is brisk.)*

SADIE: Good evening.

HARRY: How are you?

SADIE: *(Taking off wraps.)* Same as I was last evening and the evening before. Exhausted!

BECKY: The shop is still going overtime? Aaron is home a while already— *(She exits to kitchen.)*

SADIE: He can leave. He's the boss— *(*AARON *comes to door.)*

AARON: Where's the ketchup?

SADIE: *(Laughing.)* Did you see today's papers, Greenspan? The shop'll be going overtime plenty.

AARON: *(Pompously.)* We're equipped!

SADIE: Aaron, please, put me in charge of production. I'll make a fortune for you! Don't leave me rotting behind that cage!

AARON: What will I do with Van Brett?

SADIE: Get rid of him. What do you need him for?

AARON: *(Angrily.)* What are you talking about—? *(To no one in particular.)* Did you ever see such a hard-boiled—I'm in partners with a man—my friend—

SADIE: *(Cutting in.)* He'll still be your friend when he bankrupts you? *(Sarcastically.)* Production manager! Buys ribbons when they wear feathers, and feathers when they wear flowers and flowers when they want ribbons, and when you ask him *why,* he says he *likes* it!

AARON: We're making enough for a few mistakes. He's an old man— By the way, make a note, I gave Benjamin Brownstein two hundred dollars. A loan.

SADIE: What?

AARON: Don't get excited! I shouldn't have told you.

SADIE: I'm the bookkeeper so I wouldn't find out? Of course, the three hundred dollars you owe me—

AARON: *(Angrily.)* You don't trust me? I'm going to skip town with it?

SADIE: Aaron, Aaron—sometimes, if you weren't my boss I would lose my temper.

AARON: That stops you? *(He exits into kitchen, ketchup bottle in his hand.* HARRY *is at window again, his back to* SADIE. *Her manner softens. We sense her old feeling for this man is still an active part of her.)*

SADIE: *(As she takes some silver out of buffet drawer and sets a place for herself at table.)* Do you think I'm hard-boiled? When all I'm doing is protecting his interests. In business you have to follow the rules of *good* business.

HARRY: I don't understand much about such things—

SADIE: *(After pause.)* Did you have your supper?

HARRY: Yes, thanks. Earlier—

SADIE: And how is the teaching business?

HARRY: It's all right— *(Awkward pause.* HARRY *suddenly looks at* SADIE *as though seeing her for the first time. Pointing to her dress.)* Is that what they call violet color?

SADIE: *(Pleased.)* More on the purple side. Do you like it? I got it wholesale. *(She laughs.)* For as many years as I know you, never once did you remark on something I wore. You surprise me.

HARRY: Sadie—I was wondering if you— *(He breaks off.)*

SADIE: *(Starting to eat, newspaper by her side, she glances through it.)* Yes?

HARRY: I—I wanted to ask you something—

SADIE: *(After pause.)* You were saying—?

HARRY: In—in all the years I have been practically living in the house—you know—eating here every night since Papa died—well—what I'd like to know is— *(Suddenly.)* What do you think of me—that is to say—if you think of me at all? *(From street we hear the faint call of newsboys shouting "Extry"—"Extry." The two pay no attention.)*

SADIE: That's a funny question. We think of you as *belonging* in the house. Like a fixture—

HARRY: I see. *(Simply.)* I guess I feel that way, too. *(Rationalizing, more for his own benefit than hers.)* This is my home. The only home I've known for a long time. I—I guess somehow I've attached myself to the family— *(Clears his throat.)* I feel very close to *all* of you. *(Pause.)* Do I make myself clear?

(We now make out cries of "Extry, Extry" as being quite close.)

SADIE: Harry Engel, what are you trying to say to me?

*(*AARON *enters.)*

AARON: They're calling "Extra"—

*(*BECKY, FANNY, *and* IRVING *have now entered, rush to window excitedly.)*

IRVING: Wait a minute—

AARON: *(To* IRVING.*)* Run down and get a paper.

BECKY: *(Frightened.)* What could the Extra say? *(*IRVING *is at door, about to exit.* HYMIE *bursts into room. He carries a newspaper. They crowd around him.)* What is the Extra?

HYMIE: *(Throwing paper on table.)* Listen, everybody! Wilson just called another session of Congress—

*(*HARRY *has picked paper up, scans it anxiously.)*

AARON: An emergency?

HYMIE: Just wants to talk a few things over with them.

SADIE: I thought for a minute war was declared—

IRVING: This means war, sure as there's hair on my head—

AARON: Why should you care? You're a married man—

*(*FANNY, IRVING, *and* AARON *exit into kitchen, chattering excitedly.)*

HARRY: Sadie—how—how would you like to take a walk—

SADIE: *(Pleased.)* Why—that would be very nice. *(She goes toward rack, taking her jacket.* BECKY *has picked up newspaper which* HARRY *has dropped.)*

HARRY: *(Pointedly, as he helps* SADIE *on with her coat.)* We'll be back in a little while, Mama—

*(*BECKY *looks up, torn between her realization that war is imminent and her pleasure that* HARRY *has asked* SADIE *to take a walk, perhaps more may come of it.* HARRY *and* SADIE *exit.)*

BECKY: Come, I'll give you supper, Hymie—

HYMIE: Mom—

BECKY: Yes—

HYMIE: First—I—I—gotta tell you something. *(Goes toward her, takes her hand in his, looking at her.)* Now, Mom, please don't be mad on me—

BECKY: *(A frightened tone in her voice.)* Wait! Don't tell me— *(She glances at paper on table, then quietly.)* I know—

CURTAIN

Scene 3

The same. A year and a half later. November, 1918. About six-thirty in the evening.

AT RISE: FANNY *and* BECKY *enter from street. They take off their wraps, put their bundles down.*

FANNY: *(Calling out.)* Irving! We're home! I don't feel my feet any more. *(She waits for his response.)* Asleep! Sometimes I get so mad at that man I could— *(She goes to bedroom door.)* Irving! He's not home. *(*FANNY *sits disconsolately.)*

BECKY: He said he was going to see Mr. Strauss, the publisher—

FANNY: That's what he tells you. How—how do I know he's not with some—some—?

BECKY: You're not ashamed to think such a thing? What's got into you—?

FANNY: I could swear—lately, he's *different*. Mama, I'm going crazy—

BECKY: Foolish girl—he loves you like—I don't know what— *(Sternly.)* You know why he's never in the house? It's because you are making his life miserable, nagging and picking on him— *(Shaking head.)* All because he didn't make a million dollars—

FANNY: *(Defensively.)* Who wants a *million*—just a living—

BECKY: *(Gently.)* Fanny, Fanny, in your condition, a woman always imagines things ten times worse—

FANNY: I'm giving him one last chance! If something doesn't happen by the time the baby comes, we're packing up! *(Pacing nervously.)* Right this minute he could be making fifty dollars a week with his Uncle Abe! Has he the right to bring a third person into the world when he can't take care of himself?

BECKY: The boy hasn't luck—

FANNY: If he found a horseshoe in front of the door, it would be his luck to trip on it, and break his neck!

BECKY: *(Knocking on wood.)* God forbid! *(*FANNY *sits, exhausted by her tirade. Pause.)* Fanny—

FANNY: Yes, Mama?

BECKY: I believe in Irving. *(Simply.)* When he plays me one of his songs, I sing it in my head for a week. And if I could sing it—somebody else will—

FANNY: *(Suddenly bitter again.)* Mama, Mama—I get so discouraged sometimes—I—I could die!

BECKY: Sh! Don't say it. Never. Even if you feel it, *don't* say it. *(Gently patting* FANNY*'s head.)*

FANNY: *(After pause.)* Mama, are my feet *supposed* to hurt—?

*(*FANNY *gets up. She kisses her mother gently, then exits into bedroom.* BECKY *remains behind looking after her.* BECKY *goes to window, raises shade. The raised shade discloses a service flag with a single gold star on it. A moment's pause.* BECKY *goes to buffet and takes a small watch from drawer. She winds it, puts it to her ear. After a moment, a knock at door. Hastily she puts it back into drawer—runs to open door.* HARRY *and* SADIE *enter. A year and a half of marriage has given* SADIE *added confidence in herself. Her manner is brisk, poised.* HARRY, *by contrast, is quieter than ever.)*

SADIE: *(Pecking* BECKY*'s cheek.)* How are you, Mom?

BECKY: All right. Hello, Harry.

HARRY: Hello, Mama—

SADIE: *(As she takes off her wraps.)* I'm starved. So busy today, I didn't eat lunch. *(As she comes down* C.*)* How's Fanny?

BECKY: Fine. She's resting now.

SADIE: Some people can *afford* to have babies. *(Pause.)* Well, Mama—we have wonderful news!

BECKY: Yes?

SADIE: We are going into business for ourselves! Today we settled everything! *(*HARRY *does not look particu-*

larly happy about this, but he nods when BECKY *looks in his direction.)*

BECKY: You're quitting Aaron?

SADIE: That's right.

BECKY: Now is a good time to go into business? Everybody says the war will be over any minute—

SADIE: So the millinery business will be better than ever. The girls will be so happy the boys are coming home, they'll be dressed to kill!

BECKY: What did Aaron say?

SADIE: I didn't ask his opinion! *(Gaily to* HARRY.*)* And Harry is going to be my sales manager—

BECKY: Harry? *(She turns toward him.)* You're giving up teaching?

SADIE: Foolish to pay a stranger sixty a week when we can keep it in the family— *(*BECKY *looks at* HARRY, *searchingly, aware how painful this business must be to him.)* And, Mama—speaking of keeping it in the family, how much money do you have?

BECKY: You know what I have— *(A catch in her throat.)* Hymie's—the college money—

SADIE: Well, I'm borrowing two hundred—

HARRY: *(Cutting in.)* Sadie, I asked you not to—

SADIE: She's using it? I'll pay her back with interest! We need cash, don't we? Come on—let's eat—

*(*SADIE *and* HARRY *exit into kitchen.* BECKY *is about to exit.* AARON *enters from street, visibly shaken.* BECKY *follows his every movement, deeply concerned. He walks to couch, sits down, buries face in his hands.)*

BECKY: Aaron—what's the matter?

AARON: Mrs. Felderman, you see before you a man at the end of his senses. That daughter of yours, Sadie—if—if I am arrested for committing murder on her, please, you should excuse me, but I am *entitled* to it!

BECKY: What are you talking about?

AARON: With her own hands to stick the knife in my back— *(Mops his brow.)* Today she quit Van Brett and Greenspan. A woman has a *right* to quit— *(Quietly, a catch in his throat.)* Just now I find out why she quit! To open a millinery factory next door!

BECKY: *(Softly.)* Oh—

AARON: Would you call that ethical? A woman works for us seven years—gets on friendly terms with all our customers—gets them all in the bag—and quits us to open up next door! *(Pause.)* To take away our business. For myself, to hell with it! But Van Brett—over sixty years old—a man with a wife and four children— *(SADIE comes to door.)* Oh! There you are!

BECKY: *(To SADIE forcibly.)* Sadie! Is he telling me the truth?

SADIE: *(Coldly, without emotion.)* Did you also tell her why I haven't a cent in cash? How much money you owe me in five and ten dollar bills, out of my salary every other week—six hundred dollars! *(Directly to AARON.)* Would you like it better if I put you into bankruptcy? I am entitled to it! But I am simply going into legitimate competition with you!

AARON: Competition to ruin our business?

SADIE: A man like you doesn't have the *right* to be in business! You're an old fool! Now I can tell it to you!

AARON: *(Almost apoplectic.)* I'm a fool? What I forgot about the millinery business, you don't have in your little finger! *(To BECKY.)* You know what she can't stand? Because I have a *union* in my shop!

SADIE: To be the *only* manufacturer on Grand Street with a union shop is to be in the charity business, not the millinery business!

AARON: In my shop I don't want to be ashamed my workingmen should look me in the face! *(HARRY is at door watching proceedings with distaste. AARON, in a daze.)* You know what this will do to Van Brett? It will kill him. *(Pleading.)* Please, so I owe you a few cents. *(Pause.)* A man has a season's hard luck. Notes I'll give you—with my life's blood, I'll pay you back—

SADIE: Hard luck? To lose a fortune in a boom period? If you have to know, you're the laughing stock in the whole trade!

AARON: *(Screaming.)* What I forgot about the millinery business—

SADIE: *(Cutting in.)* In my little finger—I know! *(Laughing.)* You shouldn't be afraid of a little competition! It's the life and spirit of American business! On that principle, my dear man, there is room for everybody! I am quoting you, Mr. Greenspan!

*(*SADIE *exits into kitchen.* HARRY *and* BECKY *remain behind, watching* AARON. *He takes a much-battered suitcase from behind couch, opens buffet drawer and starts to throw his clothes into it.)*

BECKY: What are you doing?

AARON: How will I face Van Brett! *(Paying no attention. Pursues his own train of thought. He throws more clothes into suitcase.)* Van Brett never liked her. But I said to him, "Let's hire her. She's not so good-natured, but she's smart. And she's the daughter of my best friend." So we hired her. *(Goes to bedroom door, takes two suits which hang behind it, packs them into suitcase through the next.)* How can I tell him we had behind our cage a snake in the grass! *(Addressing* HARRY *and* BECKY *directly.)* You heard her! "Room for everybody." Me she was quoting! My own words come home to slap me in the face! *(He continues to pack. Quietly, with resignation.)* America I wanted. In a potato barrel I escaped to come here. For five days and five nights it rained. When they pulled me out on the other side of the border, I was half drowned. *(He laughs, a thin laugh, with no mirth in it.)* You know what, Mrs. Felderman, my darling? I *should* have drowned.

BECKY: *(A frightened strain in her voice.)* You're moving out—

AARON: *(Gently.)* I'll visit you, Becky. She's your daughter. You can't refuse her the house. To meet her accidentally, ten years from now, would be too soon— *(Picks up his suitcase. With nod to* HARRY *and gentle look in* BECKY*'s direction, he exits.* BECKY *looks at* HARRY, *then in direction of kitchen door, as though making up her mind. Suddenly calls out, a forceful dominant quality in her voice.)*

BECKY: Sadie!

SADIE: *(Coming to door.)* He's gone?

BECKY: You didn't tell me going into business would mean this—

SADIE: Mama, please, take care of your own life. And I'll take care of mine! In business it's the survival of the *fittest*!

BECKY: With not one penny of mine! *(Pleading.)* Sadie,

Sadie, with such ideas—to go through life— *(*FANNY *enters from bedroom.)*

HARRY: *(Has been listening, now speaks suddenly, agitated.)* I never wanted to go into business, anyway!

SADIE: *(Sharply.)* I'll stay home and bake a cake waiting for your twenty-seven dollar pay envelope from the City of New York?

HARRY: But business is not in my nature—I like to teach school. It's useful, important work—

SADIE: Where *promotion* is something the *kids* get! You took the examination, they threw you into 5-B—to sit there till you rot! Well, I want something better from life than a three-room flat in the Bronx, even if it has got an elevator! *(*BECKY *turns away, the picture of* HARRY *at the mercy of* SADIE*'s bitter tongue too much for her.* SADIE *putting coat on, impatiently.)* I did all the arguing in one day I'm going to— *(To* HARRY.*)* Get your coat. We're going home. *(To* BECKY.*)* Never mind your money. I'll get what I need from the bank! *(*SADIE *is gone. A pause.)*

BECKY: *(Quietly, in self-castigation.)* I begged Aaron to give her the job. *(Pause, as she closes buffet drawer, breaks off.)* And worst of all, Harry, what did I do to you?

HARRY: Don't blame yourself, Mama. A man should be able to face his life like—like a *man. (Pause, then wryly.)* I guess I'm a pretty poor excuse for one— *(Taking his coat from rack. With a level glance in* BECKY*'s direction, he exits.)*

FANNY: *(When he is gone.)* Why does he stand for it? If I was him, I'd leave and I'd never come back! *(Torn,* BECKY *goes to window.* IRVING *enters, morose, his appearance has changed considerably. He looks tired, seedy.)*

IRVING: *(With no spirit.)* How'ya, Mom? Hello, honey— *(Managing a wry smile.)* Well—I saw Strauss today— *(*IRVING *looks at* FANNY.*)* You win, baby! We're packing for California the minute the kid comes!

BECKY: Something happened, Irving—I can tell—

IRVING: He told me the truth! He can't publish my stuff. And you wanna know why? Because they're *too* sad. They want happy songs! Optimistic songs! Songs that'll make 'em forget we're still fightin' a war— *(Breaking out.)* How in hell can I *write* happy, if I don't feel happy?

FANNY: *(Gently.)* You hate to leave New York, don't you?

IRVING: Like taking poison—

FANNY: Then we *don't* go! No! No! *(To* BECKY.*)* I'm not doing to my Irving what she's doing to Harry! No, sir! *(Going to* IRVING.*)* You want to stay here, you stay here, darling! Even if you don't make a million dollars, if *you're* happy, I'm happy! *(*BECKY *looks on, fighting tears. From outside we hear faint cries and a whistle blowing.)*

IRVING: *(Hugging* FANNY.*)* God! What a woman! What a woman!

FANNY: Irving, sweetheart, only one thing I'm going to ask you— Promise me, when you become a big songwriter, you'll let me sing your songs.

IRVING: *(Laughing affectionately.)* Okay, I swear! When I write my hit, you can sing it all you want.

FANNY: Oh, Irving—

IRVING: Except on the stage!

FANNY: You rotten thing! *(*BECKY *goes to window, opens it. Sounds from outside grow louder. She looks out.)*

BECKY: What's all the blowing, Irving? I can't see what—

IRVING: *(Going to window.)* Something in the street—

FANNY: *(She too is at window now. Excitedly.)* It's coming from across the way. Look! Mrs. Gold! She's going crazy! She's banging on the window with a pot!

BECKY: Mr. Sullivan is hanging with his head out yelling— *(Calling down.)* Mr. Sullivan! What's the noise? *(A pause as she listens for his answer.)* What? Did you hear him? It's over! IT'S OVER!

*(*BECKY, IRVING *and* FANNY, *now hysterical, hang over window yelling "Hooray"—"Hooray"—"It's over"—"It's over." Street noises, whistles, sirens, voices have grown to tremendous proportions. The three embrace for a moment, dancing around. Suddenly* BECKY *disengages herself, walks away, lost in her own grief.)*

FANNY: Irving! Quick! Let's go downstairs!

IRVING: *(Rushing to piano.)* Wait a minute! Wait a minute!

FANNY: The war is over and he's at the piano!

IRVING: *(Excitedly, plays something with a stirring mar-*

tial quality.) He said he wants it happy, didn't he? Didn't he?

FANNY: Irving, please, take me downstairs!

IRVING: *(Playing four bars over again.)* Just listen to this, will ya? The same tune I wrote last week. I change it from a major key to a minor key—and put it in four, four time! *(*FANNY *suddenly begins to double over with pain, a surprised look on her face.)* And what a title! "We'll Bring the Rue de la Paix Back to Old Broadway, and Make the Boys Forget Paree"— *(He repeats four bars, playing while he sings.)*

FANNY: *(Calling out suddenly.)* Irving! *(He pays no attention to her. Sounds of sirens, whistles are now joined by a brass band, filling room.* FANNY *screams again.)* Mama!

(In a moment BECKY*'s grief is forgotten in* FANNY*'s need of her.* BECKY *rushes to* FANNY*'s side.)*

BECKY: Irving! Quick! Run for the doctor! It's her time!

IRVING: *(Frightened.)* Oh, my God—

BECKY: Stop swearing and run for the doctor! You'll talk to God later— *(The room is filled with the sounds of Armistice as)*

CURTAIN

ACT III

NOTE ON SET DECORATION: *It is suggested that a simple change can be effected by the substitution of two wall-paper plugs, one at upstage wall and one at lower* L. *wall.*

SCENE: *Late afternoon, November, 1931. Thirteen years later. While the set remains the same, considerable change has taken place in its furnishings. The old furniture is gone and a heterogeneous assortment of modern and overstuffed pieces takes its place. The old upright piano has been exchanged for a radio. This is still* BECKY*'s home, however, so that the whole suggests a comfortable living atmosphere, in spite of* IRVING *and* FANNY*'s overgenerosity in the matter of "buying Mama a nice thing occasionally." The table* C. *is elaborately set with a complete service for seven, including shining glassware and silver.*

AT RISE: PANSY, *the Tashman's colored maid, finishing setting table. She is about fifty, inclined to fat, with a broad good-humored smile. She hums a tune. Goes to a drawer, takes some linen out of it.* SADIE *and* HARRY *enter. Both are now definitely middle-aged.* SADIE *is thinner, drier, her voice more carping than ever.* HARRY, *now forty-five, looks closer to fifty. The years have taken their toll of his health and spirit.*

SADIE: *(As they enter.)* I told Mama the minute I laid eyes on that fellow— *(Breaks off when she sees* PANSY.*)* What are you doing here?

PANSY: Mis' Fanny sent me. *(Pompously.)* I'm supposed

to be helpin' with the dinner for Mr. Hymie's birthday— *(Exits into kitchen.)*

HARRY: *(Coming down to couch.)* In spite of what the papers say—I never met a finer, more generous fellow than Irving—

SADIE: Why shouldn't he be? Mama didn't do enough for him? *(Laughing.)* Some generous. Carrying on with that Hope—Hope whatever-her-name-is—

HARRY: *(As he sits.)* Please, Sadie—

SADIE: All right! There's nobody around— *(Placing package on buffet which she has brought in with her.)* You think he deserves it, the fresh kid! Image of his father—

HARRY: For his Bar Mitzvah, you could have bought him something better than two shirts. There are a hundred things a boy would enjoy more—

SADIE: Let his father watch out for his son's enjoyment. Eighty-five dollar Erector sets, hundred dollar trains—if I spent my hard-earned money on foolishness like his father— *(*HARRY *looks at her. She goes to table, sits down.)* I hope Aaron shows up! It's our only chance. Four times I got him to the phone. When I tell him who it is, he hangs up—

HARRY: He can't do anything anyway—

SADIE: *(Getting up impatiently.)* He's influential in the union, isn't he? You'll have to talk to him, Harry—

HARRY: What could I say? He'd be on their side, not yours—

SADIE: Tell him, with thirty-two stores all canceling our orders because the union threatens to picket them, it absolutely ain't fair!

HARRY: They catch you where it hurts the most, so you have to sign with them—

SADIE: What I want to know is, what side are *you* on? *(*PANSY *enters with seltzer bottle, places it on table.)*

HARRY: *(Cutting in, patiently.)* Sadie, I've had a hard day. I don't feel well—I'm going to lie down. *(Exits up* R.*)*

SADIE: *(Following him in.)* I was in the office three hours before you came in—I can hardly stand on my feet—and you don't feel well—

(They are gone. A moment later BECKY *enters, carrying a number of bundles. Well preserved, nicely dressed, she still retains her youthful vivacity.)*

PANSY: Lordy, Lordy—what you got there? I thought you was jes' goin' 'cross the street to show Mrs. Gold your dress—

BECKY: *(Handing her bundles.)* A few extra things I figured we would need— *(Surveying herself happily.)* She says I look like a girl in it.

PANSY: Sure do! Cake's finished, ma'am. Stuck a straw in it. It come out clean, so I took it outta the stove—

BECKY: *(Smiling.)* On Broome Street you can *smell* a cake is done, Pansy.

PANSY: *(Near kitchen door.)* Miss Sadie and Mr. Harry, they're here—and Mr. Tashman, he brung the liquor— *(Whispering.)* And, ma'am—he gimme a note for you— (BECKY *takes it.)* He said nobody else was to see it—

*(*BECKY *reads note.* PANSY *exits into kitchen.* BECKY *goes to phone. She is about to make a call, when voices of* FANNY *and* YOUNG HYMIE *are heard in hall.* BECKY *puts down receiver, drops note in her pocket, opens door.* FANNY *and* YOUNG HYMIE *enter. She is now thirty-eight, smartly dressed, inclined to plumpness.* HYMIE *is thirteen—a cute, spoiled kid.)*

FANNY: I don't feel my feet any more.

BECKY: How was the parade, Hymie?

HYMIE: *(In a bored tone.)* It was all right—

FANNY: Every time I go, I vow never again! If it wasn't for the kid— *(She is sitting now and has removed one shoe.)* Everything is ready, Mama? Pansy was a help to you?

BECKY: *(Laughing.)* If somebody told me thirteen years ago Pansy would be making gefilte fish for Hymie's Bar Mitzvah—

FANNY: *(Rubbing the aching foot.)* With a bunch of dummies pushing you around like you were nothing! I don't know if it's from walking or because it's going to rain!

HYMIE: *(Speaking up.)* Not enough we gotta *watch* the parade, Mom makes us *follow* it from 34th Street to 59th Street—

FANNY: *(Defensively.)* What's the matter? Don't I do it for you?

HYMIE: *(Trying to be patient.)* Mom, in my whole life did I ever ask you to take me to a parade?

FANNY: Will you listen to that kid, Mama? That's all the appreciation—

HYMIE: Well, did I? *(*BECKY *starts to laugh.)* She's always saying we go to the parade on account of *me*. I don't even *like* parades. *She* likes them, that's why we go.

FANNY: *(Laughing.)* I'll kill that kid! You're not ashamed to embarrass me in front of Grandma? *(*FANNY *makes playful dash for him. He eludes her, laughing.)* Hurry up, take your bath—

HYMIE: Gee, I had a bath this morning, didn't I—?

FANNY: My hair is turning white—

HYMIE: Okay, okay.— *(As he walks toward kitchen door.)* Hey, Mom—do I have to make the speech tonight?

FANNY: I should say so!

HYMIE: Gee—it's so dumb—I don't wanna—

FANNY: What did I tell you out of respect for Grandma?

HYMIE: So can't I make it for her *alone*?

FANNY: You have to make it for everybody, or it's not good luck!

HYMIE: *(As he exits into kitchen.)* Today I yam a man! Crap!

FANNY: *(Laughing.)* I'll die with that kid! Where he picks up those words! *(*SADIE *enters.)* Hello.

BECKY: How is Harry feeling?

SADIE: I made him lay down a while.

BECKY: He saw the doctor last week?

SADIE: *(Sitting.)* If he were really sick, he'd run! *(Sighing.)* Mama—have I trouble—times are terrible. They've been picketing my place for three weeks already—

BECKY: I thought you were going to settle with them?

SADIE: They should live so, if I'll let a union dictate how my business should be run! I'll starve first!

FANNY: You won't starve.

SADIE: *(Sharply.)* What do you mean by that? *(Hotly.)* Every cent I have is frozen in real estate. Maybe you are not aware we are up to our ears in a depression, the worst in the history—

FANNY: People still pay you rent, or they'd get a dispossess. *(Laughing.)* I should know. Any minute I expect to find them sticking one under *my* door—

SADIE: You're certainly very cheerful about it—

FANNY: Why shouldn't I be cheerful? Even if Irving's royalties only came to a couple of hundred last month, a son's Bar Mitzvah doesn't happen every day in the week. *(Cheerfully rubbing the offending member.)* I bet I walked a hundred blocks today. Oh—those high heels. *(*HARRY *enters, stands at doorway, stretching.)*

SADIE: *(Relentlessly pursuing subject.)* For a man who's making so little money, he certainly allows himself expensive *pastimes*—

FANNY: *(Hotly.)* Well—we're not like *some* people! We like to live!

SADIE: Evidently you don't read the papers, or you wouldn't be so cheerful—

FANNY: *(Suddenly looking from one to other.)* Wait a minute. What was that remark? *(An embarrassed pause.)*

SADIE: It just struck me funny you don't read the newspapers.

FANNY: *(Beseechingly to* BECKY.*)* Mama, what is she talking about?

SADIE: *(Casually.)* Turn to page 26 in the *Graphic*—

FANNY: Where's the paper, Mama?

BECKY: I don't know—

SADIE: *(Pointing to table.)* I brought one in— *(*FANNY *grabs paper, hastily scans it.)*

HARRY: Did you have to tell her?

SADIE: *(Defensively.)* Better to hear it from her sister than her poker-playing girl friends!

*(*BECKY *looks on, fear growing in her expression.* FANNY *reads item, thrusts paper into* BECKY*'s hand. She exits quickly, lower* R.*, a sob escaping her.* BECKY *reads item quickly.)*

BECKY: *(Exiting after* FANNY*, calling out as she goes.)* Fanny! Don't believe it! It's not true—

HARRY: *(Too quietly.)* Well, I guess we can go home now.

SADIE: We're staying right here for our family obligations! *(We hear* FANNY*'s voice in hysterical weeping.)*

HARRY: Was that a family obligation, too?

SADIE: The *Graphic* has a circulation of a million, so she

wouldn't find out? *(*HARRY *stares at her a moment, turns on his heels.)* Where are you going?

HARRY: Home.

SADIE: You're staying right here to speak to Greenspan tonight!

HARRY: *(With quiet determination.)* This is as good a time as any to tell you, Monday morning won't see me in that shop again. I'm re-applying for my license to teach school, and I'm going back!

SADIE: *(Startled.)* The fact that I need you in the shop more than ever—

HARRY: *(Quietly, but with strange force.)* For my part, lock it up, throw the key in the river!

SADIE: This is my reward, my thanks for fighting to build up some security for our old age?

HARRY: I don't need security for my old age. I'm a sick man, Sadie. I want to live the last few years of my life in *peace*!

*(*BECKY *enters distracted and upset.)*

SADIE: Did you hear him, Mama? After all these years he wants to go back to 5-B again!

HARRY: *(Cutting in.)* Do we have to talk about it here?

SADIE: Anything I have to say to you, my mother can hear! *(With self-assurance.)* Make up your mind to it, Engel. Monday morning finds you in the office as usual!

HARRY: *(Quietly.)* I'll see you in hell first!

SADIE: *(Aghast.)* Who do you think you are, to talk to me—?

HARRY: *(With a new kind of determination.)* I'm a man! I know you don't think I'm much of a man—but *once* I had a heart and a spirit and a head! I didn't ask for much. A decent useful life with a woman—

SADIE: Well, you had it, so what do you want?

HARRY: No! No! Now I can say it! Never with you! Not for one minute— *(Pause.)* When I married you I was lost and I wanted to find myself again. I thought I could find myself with you! I wanted to love you! For fifteen years I tried! For fifteen years I've watched you violate every code of human behavior—putting money before human decency—playing one dirty trick after another on people who trusted you—what you did to Fanny just now—I just can't take it any longer! Ask me why I'm telling you now! I could have told you when you murdered Van Brett—

BECKY: Harry—no—

HARRY: *(Relentlessly pursuing subject.)* A coincidence—wasn't it, his jumping out of a window just thirteen years ago today! The Armistice bells were still ringing when we got the news! I didn't tell you then because I was afraid of your tongue. Afraid of that cyclone in you that goes through life tearing people up by the roots! Ask me why I'm telling you now! Why I'm no longer afraid— *(Pause.)* Because I'm dying, Sadie. As surely as I stand here.

BECKY: *(Taking step toward* HARRY, *horrified.)* It's not true—you'll see a doctor—

HARRY: It's no use, Mama. On Saturday I saw the best heart specialist in the country. At the most I've got one, maybe two years—

BECKY: *(Heartbroken.)* Harry—Harry—

HARRY: And I'm not sorry, Sadie. No. I deserved what I got. I gave in to you because it was easier than fighting with you. It took me all these years to learn that men who don't fight for the things they believe in deserve to die—

SADIE: *(Turning.)* I hope you're being paid back for what you did to me. You think you fooled me all these years? You think a woman doesn't know when she lives with a man who's in love with a memory? The joke is on me! Break my heart over a man for the best years of my life! I finally get him! What do I get? A weak—spineless—impotent—

(She breaks off. With look of complete contempt, HARRY *turns, takes his hat, exits without a backward glance.)*

BECKY: Harry, come back—

SADIE: He'll come back. *(After pause.)* Well, we put on a fine show for you, didn't we? Trying to scare me that way—

BECKY: *(Stonily.)* He was telling the truth—

SADIE: Oh, go on—

BECKY: I know Harry. Only if he were dying could he tell you the truth about yourself!

SADIE: That's right—go ahead—

BECKY: *(Flaring out.)* The outside world doesn't do enough to tear a family to pieces, you have to tear it apart from the *inside*! I ask you, can a string of tenement properties and a boxful of printed papers in a bank bring you an ounce of happiness, when there's not a human soul in the world cares if they never saw you again—

SADIE: *(Waving hand grandly.)* My sentiments are ditto for them—

BECKY: All these years watching what you did to Harry—every time I saw you together, my heart broke—*because I told him to marry you!* (SADIE *sits, stunned.)* I didn't have to tell you, but I did it so you would know how it feels to be hurt for no reason—the way you hurt Fanny just now! I should have recognized this terrible thing in you when you were a child! I should have *beat* it out of you! *When*—when will you learn there are other things in life besides building up a fortune! Decency—human decency—

SADIE: *(Going toward rack.)* If you think I'm going to stay here to be insulted!

BECKY: Oh, no, you don't! *(With authority.)* You will sit here tonight at this table, eating Hymie's Bar Mitzvah supper if it kills you. You will talk and be friendly like nothing happened— *(Quietly.)* When you go home tonight—you do not have to come back here again. Never. *(*SADIE *makes move toward door.* BECKY *shouts.)* You will do as I say!

(Reluctant and frightened, SADIE *drops into a chair, weeping.* BECKY *exits into kitchen, a tiny, unhappy figure, torn by her participation in the scene.* FANNY *enters, looks at* SADIE*. Unable to face her gaze,* SADIE *exits into upper bedroom.)*

FANNY: *(Calling out.)* Mama! *(*BECKY *enters.)* Well, Mama, I've made up my mind!

BECKY: *(Her voice choked.)* Yes?

FANNY: I'm leaving for Reno in the morning!

BECKY: *(Frightened.)* Reno? In the magazines where they get divorces?

FANNY: Not only in magazines. In real life too! *(Pause.)* Well, *say* something! You stand there like the Sphinx in Egypt!

BECKY: Don't do it, Fanny—

FANNY: Mama, Mama, I can't tell you how miserable I've been!

BECKY: Fanny, darling, don't believe it! It's not true—

FANNY: Mama, don't be naive! This isn't the first time! Three years ago when I read he was seen out with that dancer, I didn't believe it either! I let him get away with it. How long can I keep on closing my eyes—when Hope Robert's husband is suing her for divorce and naming Irving co-respondent?

BECKY: The man says in the column he only *thinks* so—

FANNY: He wouldn't dare to print it if it weren't true! He could be sued! *(Pause.)* Why should it happen to me? Am I ugly? Am I like some women married twenty years? I'm still beautiful, even if I do say so myself! *(Her voice breaks. Summoning her courage.)* Well, he won't get away with it! I'm leaving for Reno in the morning and he'll pay alimony through the nose!

BECKY: With what? No song in a show for two years—

FANNY: *(Heatedly.)* Right this minute he could be making three, four hundred a week in Hollywood with his Uncle Abe. *(Determined.)* Anyway, I don't need his money. I'm going back on the stage!

BECKY: Thirty-eight years old, you do not start a career—

FANNY: I'm thirty-seven.

BECKY: If a year could make a difference to your voice—Maybe if you *still* had a voice—

FANNY: All my friends think my voice is grand!

BECKY: *(Firmly.)* They don't *pay* to hear you— *(Sadly.)* It makes me sad to say it, but you sound, you should excuse me, like a duck. *(*FANNY *stares at* BECKY. *Suddenly she understands* BECKY *is telling her the truth. In a daze she sits, then crumples up, dissolved in tears.)* Fanny—Fanny—

FANNY: *(Miserably.)* Leave me alone—

BECKY: I'm sorry I had to be the one to tell you. *(Pause.)*

Hymie will not be so happy when he hears you are leaving Irving. *(No response from* FANNY.*)* I suppose he'll live through it. Children live through worse. *(*BECKY *has been making up her mind to say something. Now she finds courage to do so.)* You asked me before to say something— *(Quietly.)* What could I say? You see—once I came to my mother with a story— *(The words do not come easily.)* The *same* story—

FANNY: *(Incredulous.)* Our papa? You're lying— *(Heatedly.)* You always said he was the finest, the most wonderful—

BECKY: *(Cutting in.)* He *was*—the finest, the sweetest man a woman ever had— *(Quickly.)* But he was a *man*—

FANNY: A man can't be wonderful in one breath and a cheater in the other!

BECKY: *(Angrily.)* Don't you say such a thing about Papa!

FANNY: I can't understand it. All these years you talked about him like he was God—

BECKY: And he was! Even if he was dead he was alive enough in my heart to help me keep the family together— *(Pleading suddenly.)* Fanny, please, don't do it! I know he loves you— *(*FANNY *exits lower bedroom in tears. Pause. Torn,* BECKY *goes to phone. Consulting note, dials number. After a pause.)* Hello? Irving? It's Mama. I—just talked to Fanny. She—she didn't sound so—so encouraging. . . . Sure she knows. *(Pause.)* It's not exactly a *secret*. Irving, I know how you feel. Right now I don't feel so hot myself. But never mind that. It's Hymie's birthday. I think if you came down and brought his mother a little present—or even a *big* one— *(Pause.)* No, not over the telephone. You'll kiss my feet when you get here. *(*BECKY *hangs up. In a daze, she walks toward kitchen. Halfway she changes her mind. Goes toward buffet, examines bottle of liquor. Making up her mind quickly, she pours some rye into glass, adds seltzer from table.* PANSY *enters. When she notices* PANSY*'s expression.)* There is always a first time for everything. *(She takes sip, makes a wry face.)* People drink this for pleasure? *(Pause.)* It tastes terrible.

PANSY: My James says it feels mighty good after.

BECKY: *(Like a hurt child.)* That's what I want. To feel

good after. *(Pause.)* I think I'll sit a while. Have a seat, Pansy.

PANSY: Lordy, no, ma'am—I got work to do.

BECKY: Sit, sit—on Mr. Tashman's time you can take a little rest—maybe you'll have a drink?

PANSY: Lordy, no—not while I'm on the job, ma'am.

BECKY: *(Smiling gently.)* When I went to Paris, France, five years ago, I was the only Gold Star mother on the boat who didn't drink cocktails—

PANSY: You been that far, ma'am? To Paris, France?

BECKY: *(Proudly.)* Oh, yes. My son-in-law, Mr. Tashman, sent me— *(Breaking suddenly.)* Pansy, Pansy—I did a terrible thing tonight—

PANSY: You couldn't do anything terrible, Mis' Becky.

BECKY: *(Pause.)* Yes, I did. I told a lie—I spoiled Jacob's memory. The only thing I had left, and I spoiled it. *(She is weeping now, unashamedly. A strange new* BECKY, *for whom a first drink of hard liquor has meant a loosening of her tongue and her emotions as well.)* I'm afraid all the perfumes in Arabia won't wash away my sin. *(Pause.)* Lady Macbeth said it.

PANSY: *(Admiringly.)* I could lissen to you talkin' all day, Mis' Becky. You sure are powerful eddicated—

BECKY: Oh, yes, I am a high school graduate from Night School— *(Her mood changes.)* I went to Washington with my Night School Delegation. I shook hands with President Harding. Afterwards, they said he was a crook. But I never believed it. Such a fine looking man— *(Slightly tipsy now, she is in a reminiscent mood.)* In Washington they took us in buses to Arlington Cemetery. Beautiful. Like a park. Only instead of trees, millions of little crosses growing up from the ground. And flags! So many little American flags on the graves, and when the wind blows, they wave in the breeze like this— *(Waves hand in front of her dizzily. Suddenly getting up.)* I looked for my Hymie there. *(Staring straight ahead, her body erect.)* Then they showed us the place where one soldier is buried. And him they call the Unknown Soldier. And him they never leave alone. Always, day and night, two live soldiers are walking up and down—day and night— *(Breaks off, then simply.)* I think of this place, and I am glad they don't leave him alone. Please,

Pansy, don't tell anybody, but *that's* the place where my Hymie is! *(Pause.)* I lost my Esther in the Triangle Fire. After that the inspector came and made me take my plants off the fire escape. It was the law. And after that, the committee from the Garment Workers came to tell me that she didn't die for nothing. And after that—my Sadie got her husband—

PANSY: *(Incredulously.)* Lordy, Lordy— *(A pause.)*

BECKY: Tell me, Pansy, do *you* think everything in this world happens for the best?

PANSY: Hard to say for sure, ma'am—but if you believes it, it makes you feel mighty good when the bad is happenin'.

BECKY: I wanted my family to have *life*. That's why I brought them here. They sing about it. "The Land of the Free and the Home of the Brave." *(Pause.)* My Hymie was brave. The day before he went away he said to me, "Mama, don't be a Calamity Jane. Here's my watch. When you get lonely, just wind it. When it ticks, it'll be me, talking to you." Then he went away! *(Pause.)* What is left, Pansy? Nothing—not even Jacob's memory—

PANSY: *(After pause.)* You sure feel bad, don't you, Mis' Becky? *(*BECKY *looks up, tries to smile. The smile does not come.)* Down home the ole folks use'n to say, "The Morning Star, she always shines brighter after a real dark night." Yes, ma'am—guess as long as she's there every morning, the end a the world ain't come yet—

BECKY: *(Sitting suddenly, exhausted.)* Life is very hard, but life is wonderful, no?

PANSY: *(Wiping a tear from her eye.)* It sure is, Mis' Becky—

BECKY: *(Slowly as though this were a revelation.)* I guess a person has to have patience to live through history while they are making it— *(*IRVING *enters. Goes toward* BECKY *like a frightened child.)*

IRVING: Mama—what am I going to do?

*(*PANSY *exits into kitchen.)*

BECKY: Now you're asking? She's inside. Go—go in to her, look her straight in the eye and tell her he printed a lie. That you are going to *sue* him for it!

IRVING: But, Mama—

BECKY: I know it's true—but she'll believe you because she *wants* to believe you, and if she doesn't— *(Forcefully.)* Make her! Slap her face! Do something—anything—but if you let her get away, I'll never talk to you again as long as I live! You heard me?

IRVING: I heard you— *(Takes off coat, goes to rack, hangs it up.)*

BECKY: *(With great authority.)* And furthermore, tomorrow morning you will go downtown and buy yourself three tickets to Hollywood, California!

IRVING: *(Coming toward her.)* Me?

BECKY: *(Continuing firmly.)* Yes, you! You will take a job with your Uncle Abe once and for all. You will keep yourself so busy day and night writing songs for the all-singing pictures, you won't have time to get yourself in the papers— *(Winking.)* And if you live in California, how can you sue him in New York?

IRVING: Mom—the only brains in the family—thanks, Mom—

BECKY: I am not through yet— *(Roughly.)* Come here! *(*IRVING *goes toward her.* BECKY *slaps him sharply across face.)* That's for being a bad boy! *(She slaps him again.)* And *that's* in *advance*—if you ever hurt my Fanny again—I, myself, personally will— *(Breaks off, contrite.)* Did I hurt you?

IRVING: *(Throwing arms around* BECKY, *bursting with laughter.)* Mom, do I love you, do I love you— *(Pause.)* Becky Felderman! What in hell have you been drinking?

BECKY: A cocktail! What's wrong with it?

IRVING: *(Shouting with laughter.)* Where's my wife? *(Goes toward upper bedroom.)*

BECKY: Not in there. Sadie is in there.

*(*IRVING *exits lower* R. BECKY *looks after him, smiling, then looks at her* R. *hand, which has so gloriously told* IRVING *off. She salutes it, with a nod of her head.* YOUNG HYMIE *comes out of kitchen.)*

HYMIE: Did I hear my pop?

BECKY: Don't go in there now, Hymela—

(Her tone seems odd to Hymie. *He exits into kitchen, looking back at her with a puzzled expression.* Becky *goes to buffet, takes out a small package, placing it at head of table. A knock at door. Out of habit,* Becky *starts to answer it, but* Pansy *rushes through to door, from kitchen.* Aaron Greenspan *enters. He is now sixty, hair turned white, a tall, straight, boyish figure for his years. Takes off coat and hat, hangs them up.)*

Aaron: *(Coming toward* Becky, *hands outstretched.)* Becky, Becky, Mazeltuff—

Becky: Thanks, Aaron, thanks. You are looking very well.

Aaron: You don't look so bad yourself—

Becky: *(Laughing.)* Thank you—

Aaron: *(Touching couch.)* Aye, Becky—where is my old good friend— *(Pause.)* It's a great day for you, Becky—

Becky: *(Looking up meaningfully.)* They have an old saying, "Never say a man lived a happy life till he's dead." Anything could happen the last minute.

Aaron: *(Laughing.)* Aye, Becky, Becky—still the pessimist!

Becky: I'm a pessimist? If you have to know, I am the world's biggest optimist. If I wasn't, I would have been dead long ago— *(Pause.* Becky*'s manner softens.)* A fine way for me to treat a guest. Five minutes in the house, and I'm fighting with you—

Aaron: *(Feeling sorry for himself.)* It's all right. Fight all you want. Even a fight is a pleasure for a lonely old man— *(After pause.)* Oh—I knew I had to tell you something funny. The other night I went to a newsreel. I could swear, on my life, standing next to Stalin on the platform was—guess who?

Becky: Who?

Aaron: Benjamin Brownstein!

Becky: No! Time flies— *(Pause.)* And otherwise, how do you spend your time?

Aaron: Work all day. Comes the night, *again* to a movie or a pinochle. Some life for a man, yes? *(Stares at her. She turns away.)* Oh, yes—last night for a change, in Gold's house, we played guess what, a game! That's the style today—to play games. Well, in this game they ask you questions. So, they asked me, "Who would I rather be, in the whole world, if I could positively *not* be Aaron Greenspan?" *(Turning toward her.)* Should I tell you what I answered? *(Pause.)* I said, I would rather be Jacob Felderman.

BECKY: *(Breaking completely.)* Oh—Aaron—Aaron—

AARON: Becky, please—I didn't mean to hurt your feelings— *(Pause.)*

BECKY: *You*—you didn't hurt my feelings, Aaron.

AARON: So—what's wrong?

BECKY: Plenty! *(Slowly.)* Sadie—after tonight, she does not step foot in this house. Irving and Fanny and Hymie? To California. As they say, "New worlds to conquer"—and Harry— *(Shaking head.)* Harry is a sick boy—very sick— *(Pause.)* My world! The reason I lived and breathed. Finished—done—

AARON: Aye, Becky, still the Calamity Jane—

BECKY: *(Angrily.)* If a woman doesn't have the right to have heartache—

AARON: *(Going toward her.)* If it's a family you want— *(Suddenly angry.)* For years I have been waiting to be your family! As long as you had them—damned kids— *(*BECKY *looks at him sharply. Looks around, afraid he has been overheard.)* We—we could have such a fine, sweet life together. We talk a little—we laugh a little—all right—we *fight* a little— *(Pause.)* Well! Why don't you *say* something?

BECKY: I—I don't know what to say—

AARON: *(Incredulous.)* You mean, you didn't say "no"?

BECKY: Please—Aaron—I have to think—

AARON: If you didn't shut me up with "no"—it's—it's practically a declaration of love!

BECKY: Stop hollering—they'll hear—

AARON: Once in a lifetime a man is entitled to holler! *(Pause.)* Nu? *(A moment of pause.)*

BECKY: *(Quietly.)* Well, consider I said it. *(*AARON *stares at her, hardly believing his success. Completely overcome with emotion, takes out handkerchief.)*

AARON: All my life I pictured this moment and all I can do is blow my nose—Becky, Becky darling—

BECKY: *(Smiles gently.* AARON *goes toward her, kissing her hand.)* But first, I have a favor to ask—

AARON: Already?

BECKY: Tonight—*no* announcements!
AARON: Your slightest wish is my command, madam!

(Bows low, takes her hand in his, kissing it in cavalier fashion. Suddenly, as one person, they start to laugh. They are still laughing when PANSY *enters. She wears a fresh apron and cap and is beaming.)*

PANSY: Dinner's ready to serve now, Mis' Becky—
BECKY: Knock on the door and tell the others—

*(*PANSY *knocks on upper bedroom door, calling out, "Supper's ready."* IRVING, FANNY *and* YOUNG HYMIE *enter arm-in-arm, smiling happily.* PANSY *exits into kitchen.)*

FANNY: *(Showing* BECKY *a bracelet.)* Mama! Look at this! Hello, Aaron—
BECKY: It's beautiful—
FANNY: Irving, darling, you shouldn't have done it!
IRVING: What else have I got to do, except make you happy?

*(*SADIE *enters, slightly the worse for a crying fit, in which she has obviously been indulging.)*

FANNY: *(Throwing arms around* IRVING.*)* I wouldn't care if I never saw another bracelet in my life! It's you I love, not the bracelet! *(To* BECKY, *proudly.)* Irving is bringing suit first thing next week!
IRVING: *(With a wink toward* BECKY.*)* I should say so! For damages to my reputation and happiness! And, Mom—how'd you like to come to California to live?
FANNY: He's doing a musical for his Uncle Abe!
IRVING: He sold me a bill of goods this afternoon—*(Winking to* BECKY *again.)* I didn't want it, but you don't sneeze at five hundred a week!
AARON: *(Whistling.)* I wouldn't sneeze at it—
FANNY: *(To* SADIE.*)* You see, it doesn't pay to believe everything you read in the papers! *(Goes toward kitchen.)*
BECKY: *(Giving* HYMIE *small package.)* For you, Hymela— *(*HYMIE *opens package, takes out watch.)*
HYMIE: Gee, thanks, Grandma— *(Reading inscription.)*

"To Hymie, from Mama and Esther and Sadie"—was that Tanta Esther?

BECKY: Yes. Tanta Esther. The watch belonged to your Uncle Hymie.

*(*HARRY *has entered quietly through the last. Looks up at mention of* ESTHER*'s name, quietly takes his place near others. They gather around table. Speaking as they seat themselves in following order:* HYMIE*, head of table* L. BECKY*, head of table* R. AARON *and* SADIE *facing audience.* HARRY *next to* SADIE. FANNY *and* IRVING *with backs facing audience.)*

IRVING: Tonight Mama and Hymie sit at the heads. This is their night.

AARON: Believe me, Irving, judging from the talking moving pictures I seen lately, your mediocrity will be rewarded by great success—

IRVING: My what?

SADIE: And how are you, Greenspan?

AARON: I never felt better in my life!

SADIE: The world is having a depression, but on you evidently it doesn't make a dent!

AARON: Not even a pin scratch. The union scale is very good. That is, for *us*—but not for you, when you'll have to pay it!

SADIE: Never! I'll move to Jersey first!

*(*PANSY *enters with tray of food.)*

FANNY: You may serve now, Pansy—

PANSY: Ain't we gonna hear Mr. Hymie's speech first?

HYMIE: Aw, gee, didja have to remind her?

FANNY: Hymie! Remember what I said!

HYMIE: *(Getting up reluctantly, takes out crumpled paper, consults it.)* Well—dear Grandma and Mama and Papa and everything—I mean everybody— *(In a sing-song manner.)* Today I yam a man. I am thirteen years old. I promise to be a good boy, I mean man—and, well— *(Quickly.)* If it's true I'm a man, I guess I better be getting more than a dollar and a quarter a week spending money—

FANNY: *(Horrified.)* Hymie! That's not in the speech!

HYMIE: Well—I put it in— *(Continuing.)* And, dear God, we thank you for all the blessings—and please bless Grandma and my dear mother and my dear father— *(As the)*

CURTAIN SLOWLY DESCENDS

Under a Painted Smile

Lyrics by Robert Sour

Music by Abraham Ellstein

E♭ C7 (E bass) F7 B♭
Under a paint - ed smile there is a
B♭7 (A♭ bass) E♭ (G bass) A♭ A♭m
heart that's breaking Clothes of the lat - est
E♭ F7 B♭7
style tell of the step she's taking
E♭ E°7 F7 B♭
Powder and paint won't hide the tears that she's
Fm (A♭ bass) G7 A♭ F♯ °7
shed - ding the while For there is a heart that's
E♭ (G bass) C7 F7 B♭7 E♭
break - ing Un - der a paint - ed smile.

We'll Bring the Rue de la Paix!

Lyrics by Robert Sour

Music by Abraham Ellstein

G
We'll bring the Rue de la Paix ___ back to
A7 D7 G6
old Broadway ___ and make the boys for - get Pa - ree ___
Daug9 G (B bass) B♭ aug D (A bass) A7
___ We'll change the farm back home in - to the Place ___ Ven -
D (F♯ bass) A7 D7
dôme ___ And teach the girls to par - ley - voo that old ___ oui - oui
G
___ There'll be a plen - ty of jazz - - in' and ___
A7 D7 C7
razz - a - ma - tazz ___ when they come home from a - cross ___ the ___
B7 E7
sea ___ We'll bring the Rue de la Paix ___ back ___ to
A7 D D7 G
old Broadway ___ and make the soldierboys for - get Pa - ree. ___

HOME OF THE BRAVE

A PLAY IN THREE ACTS

by

Arthur Laurents

Arthur Laurents was born in Brooklyn in 1918. His father was a lawyer, his mother a teacher. After earning a bachelor's degree from Cornell University in 1937, he began writing plays for radio, contributing episodes to such popular shows of the late 1930s and 1940s as *Hollywood Playhouse* and *The Thin Man.* He continued to practice his dramatic skills in the Army, where he served from 1940 to 1945. One of his radio plays, *Assignment Home,* earned a citation from the Secretary of War and *Variety*'s Radio Award in 1945.

Laurents has proven himself master of every kind of dramatic writing. Beside ten dramas and the books for a half-dozen musical comedies, he has written for the large and small screens. He co-authored *The Snake Pit,* his first film, with Frank Partos and Millen Brand in 1948; his twelfth, *The Turning Point,* won Golden Globe, Screenwriters Guild, and National Board of Review awards in 1977. Among his Hollywood credits are films adapted from material he originally wrote for other genres. In addition to *Home of the Brave* (1949), on whose screenplay he worked with Carl Foreman, there are adaptations of the musicals *West Side Story* (1961) and *Gypsy* (1962), which he wrote with Ernest Lehman and Leonard Spigelgass, respectively. He adapted both his novels, *The Way We Were* (1973) and *The Turning Point,* as screenplays.

Home of the Brave (1945) inaugurated Laurents's impressively long career in the legitimate theatre. Fifty years later, he is working on a trilogy about America in the 1950s, 60s, and 70s. The first two plays, *Jolson Sings Again* and *Radical Chic* are scheduled for production in 1995.

Although he is not the only American writer of straight plays to contribute librettos to the musical stage—the group includes Elmer Rice *(Street Scene),* Lillian Hellman *(Candide),* S. N. Behrman *(Fanny),* William Gibson *(Golden Boy),* and Harvey Fierstein *(La Cage aux Folles)*—he has repeatedly made it a specialty. *West Side Story* (1957), on which he collaborated with Leonard Bernstein, Stephen Sondheim, and Jerome Robbins, was an enormous success. *Gypsy* (1959), a collaboration with Sondheim and Jule Styne, won praise as "one of the most carefully integrated musicals in the American theatre." Other hits include *Anyone Can Whistle* (1964), *Do I Hear a Waltz?* (1966, based on Laurents's *Time of the Cuckoo),* and the Tony Award–winning *Hallelujah Baby!* (1967).

Not all of Laurents's theatrical activities take place in a study. He initiated a much-honored career as a director with his own *Time of the Cuckoo* (1953). Three decades later, *La Cage aux Folles* (1984) earned both a Tony and a Sydney (Australia) Drama Critics Award for direction.

The scope of his accomplishments notwithstanding, Laurents's writing is marked by certain recurring themes and preoccupations. They stem from his interest in the fragility of the individual in an alien, often hostile world. It is interesting to speculate on the possible influence of earlier Jewish playwriting. For example, while the intentional analogies between *West Side Story* and *Romeo and Juliet* are apparent, there are also strong parallels between the book of the musical comedy and Elmer Rice's *Street Scene*. In both cases, characters are made wretched by their hunger for a place for themselves and for psychic comfort amid urban chaos. The people in both works yearn futilely to escape the biases and restricting mores of their ethnic groups. And in each case, audiences are led to an understanding of the displaced desperation that provokes violent death.

Some of *West Side Story*'s characters are modifications of types who populate Laurents's plays beginning with *Home of the Brave*. He depicts sensitive, insecure people who have difficulty entrusting themselves to relationships: the unhappy son in *The Bird Cage* (1950), the unmarried woman vainly seeking romance in *Time of the Cuckoo* (1952), and the self-conscious Jewish soldier in *Home of the Brave*. Counterbalancing them, often in active opposition, are aggressive individuals driven by their own demons to torment or brutalize the more vulnerable ones: the nightclub owner in *Bird Cage,* T.J. in *Home of the Brave,* and the stage mother in *Gypsy,* whose monomaniacal ambition makes her a fickle wife and a monstrous parent.

Home of the Brave, Laurents's first Broadway play, draws on important strands of the dramatist's own experiences. The wartime setting was a natural for a man who served in the military throughout America's involvement in World War II. The flashback scenes in which Captain Bitterger treats the paralyzed Coen draw on Laurents's experience with radio drama. And, according to W. David Sievers in *Freud on Broadway,* Laurents acknowledges the influence of his own psychotherapy in writing *Home of the Brave.*

The war, like mental illnesses and their treatment, dominated American novels and drama in the 1940s. *Home of the Brave* was one of the earliest plays to deal with the psychosomatic ravages of combat. Its protagonist, Peter Coen, has to be persuaded that the guilt that paralyzes him is a normal reaction to surviving action where comrades die. But Coen cannot think of himself in those terms. Scarred by years of anti-Semitism, he has accepted his tormenters' image of himself as different from everybody else, and less worthy. Coen's perception of being a Jew is the very antithesis of the pitiless but protective distinction voiced by the psychiatrist in Arthur Miller's *Incident at Vichy,* who defines a Jew as "the man whose death leaves you relieved that you are not him," having just observed that, "Each man has his Jew; it is the other. And the Jews have their Jews."

Home of the Brave earned Laurents critical recognition. John Chapman of the New York *Daily News* enthused that of all the World War II plays he had seen, *Home* "was the one I believe in most." Named one of the Ten Best Plays of the year in *The Best Plays* series, the work was co-winner of the Sidney Howard Memorial Award, and Laurents was awarded a National Institute of Arts and Letters grant.

The most significant component of the play is its frank depiction of the effects of anti-Semitic behavior. Yet it says a good deal about the perception of Jews in 1945 that, although reviewers clearly took Laurents's point, they saw Peter Coen's story as representative either of "the sensitive man in war, whether he is a Gentile or a Jew" *(New York Journal-American),* or of "all the plays we have had in the fight against race prejudice" *(New York World Telegram).*

When United Artists filmed *Home of the Brave,* it exploited that point of view: Peter Coen became Mossie, a Black. Reviewers acknowledged the switch nonchalantly. The film's favorable reception indicates that its message about intolerance and plea for self-respect and mutual understanding apply equally to other racial prejudices. One assumes that Laurents, involved with the filmscript, agreed.

However, the substitution of Black for Jew in the film made another, more disturbing statement about the perception of ethnics, at least on screen, at mid-century. It is disheartening to read *Life*'s report (23 May, 1949) of the film as contender in a race to break Hollywood's taboo against depicting America's "Negro problem." Even more troubling was *The New York Journal of Commerce*'s praise (17 May, 1949) for the wisdom of exchanging ethnic subjects, since the "original thesis has perhaps been overworked in the movies."

Home of the Brave was first presented by Lee Sabinson, in association with William R. Katzell, on December 27, 1945, at the Belasco Theatre, New York, with the following cast:

CAPT. HAROLD BITTERGER	*Eduard Franz*
MAJOR DENNIS ROBINSON, JR.	*Kendall Clark*
T.J.	*Russell Hardie*
CONEY	*Joseph Pevney*
FINCH	*Henry Barnard*
MINGO	*Alan Baxter*

Directed by MICHAEL GORDON
Production designed and lighted by RALPH ALSWANG

SYNOPSIS OF SCENES

ACT I

SCENE 1. Hospital Room. A Pacific Base.
SCENE 2. Office. The Pacific Base.
SCENE 3. A Clearing. A Pacific Island.

ACT II

SCENE 1. Hospital Room.
SCENE 2. Another Clearing. The Island.
SCENE 3. Hospital Room.

ACT III

SCENE 1. Hospital Room. Two weeks later.
SCENE 2. The Office. A few days later.

ACT I

Scene 1

SCENE: *Hospital Room. A Pacific Base. This is a small room, the office, really, of* CAPTAIN HAROLD BITTERGER, *a doctor. There is a window, rear, through which we might see tropical foliage and bright sunlight. Up* R. *in* R. *wall is a door, downstage of this, a desk heavy with official army papers and a chair behind the desk. Across the room, near the* L. *wall, is a made-up army cot. Near this is a small table on which is medical paraphernalia: some small bottles, a hypodermic case, cotton and, possibly, some charts. Also, a rubber tourniquet. There are two light chairs near the desk.*

Seated in one of these chairs is MAJOR DENNIS E. ROBINSON, JR. *He is about 26, a cigarette ad with a blond crew cut. He is self-conscious about his rank and position (and his shortcomings) and attempts to hide his natural boyishness by a stalwart military manner. In the other chair is* CORPORAL T. J. EVERITT, *a rather pompously good-looking Rotarian, about 35. He resents the Army, his position, almost everything. He has found it difficult to adjust himself to this new life and, therefore, seems and acts more pettish and mean than he actually is. Standing in front of the desk with a sheaf of papers in his hand is the* DOCTOR, CAPTAIN BITTERGER: *a stocky man with graying hair, about 43. He knows a good deal about men, particularly soldiers, is anxious to learn more, to have the world learn more. When curtain rises, there is silence.* DOCTOR *has apparently just asked a question.* MAJOR *and* T.J. *look at him uncomfortably for a second, then turn away.*

DOCTOR: *(Impatiently.)* Well? *(A slight wait.)*

MAJOR: I don't know, Doctor.

DOCTOR: *(Holding up sheaf of papers.)* This is the whole story?

MAJOR: All that we know.

DOCTOR: All the events, at any rate.

MAJOR: Yes, sir.

T.J.: Captain, maybe Sergeant Mingo—

DOCTOR: *(Brusquely.)* I've spoken to Sergeant Mingo. You *all* agree on the facts. Wonderful thing: facts. Wonderful word. Doesn't mean a goddam thing.

MAJOR: Doctor, if there's—

DOCTOR: They help. Facts help, Major. And I thank you for them. But they're not quite enough.

MAJOR: I hope you don't think, sir—

DOCTOR: Major, forgive me. I'm sorry about your feelings. And yours, Corporal. And Sergeant Mingo's. And the whole world's. But at this point, I'm only interested in one man. A patient. A Private First Class Peter Coen. *(Slight pause.)*

T.J.: Doctor—

DOCTOR: Yes?

T.J.: I just happened to remember. There was something else. There was a fight.

MAJOR: A fight? When?

DOCTOR: The last day you were on the island, wasn't it?

T.J.: Yes, sir.

MAJOR: I didn't know! Who had a fight?

DOCTOR: *(To* T.J.*)* You see, I did speak to Sergeant Mingo, Corporal.

T.J.: Well, I just happened to remember it now.

DOCTOR: Really?

T.J.: It didn't seem so important. I just forgot it.

DOCTOR: Everything's important with a case like this.

MAJOR: Coney's going to be all right, isn't he?

DOCTOR: I'm a psychiatrist, Major, not a clairvoyant. The boy suffered a traumatic shock. Now he has paralysis. Amnesia. Physical manifestations. They're curable—sometimes. And sometimes—

MAJOR: Can we see him?

DOCTOR: He won't recognize you.

MAJOR: I'd like to see him, though.

DOCTOR: He's due for a treatment now.

MAJOR: Just for a second, Captain.

DOCTOR: *(After a moment's hesitation—to* T.J.*)* Corporal, he's in the first ward to your left. Do you want to bring him in?

T.J.: Well—yes, sir. *(He goes out door* R.*)*

DOCTOR: *(During following, he prepares for amytal injection to follow. He breaks top off one of small bottles on table, inserts hypodermic needle in bottle and presumably fills it.)* Fine day. God's in His heaven and all's wrong with the world.

MAJOR: How are you treating him, Captain?

DOCTOR: Narcosynthesis, Major. *(Turns and looks at* MAJOR, *who obviously doesn't understand.)* Narcosynthesis. You administer a drug that acts as a release for the patient. Usually, he will relive the experiences immediately preceding shock if the doctor leads him. Usually one or two injections are enough for him to recover physically . . . I'm starting the treatment today.

MAJOR: You mean Coney'll be able to walk? He'll get his memory back?

DOCTOR: Maybe. I don't know. But suppose he can walk, suppose he can remember—that's only half the battle. There'll still be something in him—deep in him—that caused all this.

MAJOR: But can't this narcosynthesis—

DOCTOR: It's not perfect. It was started about fifteen years ago. We're still learning. But we've learned a great deal using it in this war. See? War has its uses.

MAJOR: I hope to God it works for Coney.

DOCTOR: His collapse wasn't your fault.

MAJOR: Well—he was my responsibility.

DOCTOR: The job was.

MAJOR: That's what I thought but—

DOCTOR: Major, how old are you? Twenty-five?

MAJOR: Twenty-six.

DOCTOR: Well, twenty-six. What do you know? Your job. Period. Let me tell you something, Major—Robinson?

MAJOR: That's right, sir.

DOCTOR: Look, Robinson. You were right. The job comes first. The men count. But they count second. How many were there on that mission? Five. But you were doing that job for hundreds, for thousands, for the whole goddam war. That's a little more important—

MAJOR: I know. But Coney's important, too.

DOCTOR: Sure. And maybe if you were smarter—but you're twenty-six. And hell! I'm not so smart. How the devil do I know that if you were smarter, you could have prevented this? Matter of fact, I doubt it. Maybe you're wrong, maybe I'm wrong—and God knows that's possible—too goddam possible—but that kid's crack-up goes back to a thousand million people being wrong.

MAJOR: What do you mean?

DOCTOR: They don't take a man for himself . . . for what he is.

MAJOR: I don't get it.

DOCTOR: *(Smiling.)* I didn't think you would. You probably never came face to face—

(Door opens and T.J. *brings in* CONEY, *who is in a wheelchair.* CONEY *is dressed in the dark-red hospital robe. He is slumped in the chair with a melancholic, frightened look on his face.)*

MAJOR: Hello, Coney!

T.J.: He didn't know me.

MAJOR: Coney . . . how do you feel, fellow?

CONEY: All right, sir.

DOCTOR: Coney . . . do you remember Major Robinson?

CONEY: *(Looks at* MAJOR *slowly, then back to* DOCTOR.*)* No, sir.

MAJOR: Coney, you remember. Don't you remember me? Don't you remember Mingo?

CONEY: Mingo? Mingo?

MAJOR: *(To* DOCTOR.*)* Does he remember about—Finch?

DOCTOR: Ask him.

CONEY: What? Who?

MAJOR: Coney . . . Coney . . . remember Finch?

CONEY: No, sir. No, sir. *(His voice cracks.)* Doctor—

DOCTOR: All right, son. All right. . . .

CONEY: Doctor—

DOCTOR: *(To* T.J.*)* Help me lift him on the bed, please. *(They do.)* Thanks. Chair. *(*T.J. *quickly brings him a chair. He sits in it and holds* CONEY*'s hand.)* I'm sorry.

MAJOR: Will you let us know?

DOCTOR: Yes.

MAJOR: Let's go. So long, Coney. Be seeing you. *(He waits a moment for an answer. But there is none. They walk out, closing door behind them.)*

DOCTOR: *(His manner changes now. He is soft, gentle, kind—a father to this boy.)* Don't be frightened, son. There's nothing to be frightened of. Nothing in the world. *(He gets up, as he continues, and pulls down shade. Room is in half light. As he talks, he moves small table with his instruments near bed.)* You know who I am, don't you, Coney?

CONEY: Doctor . . .

DOCTOR: Sure. I'm your doctor. And you know what doctors do, don't you? They make you well. And that's what I'm going to do. I'm going to make you well, Coney. I'm going to fix you up so you'll remember everything and be able to walk again. *(He is now rolling up* CONEY*'s sleeve and putting on a tourniquet.)* You'd like to walk again, wouldn't you?

CONEY: Yes, sir.

DOCTOR: Well, you will. You'll be fine. *(He begins to swab* CONEY*'s arm with a piece of cotton.)* Now, you mustn't be afraid. This isn't going to hurt. I'm your doctor. Doctors don't hurt, son. They make you better. *(Picks up hypodermic needle from table.)* All you'll feel will be a little prick with a needle. Just like when you stick yourself with a pin. That's all this is. Just a long pin. Do you understand?

CONEY: Yes, sir.

DOCTOR: All right. Now when I put the needle in, I want you to start counting backwards from one hundred. Backwards. 99, 98, 97. Like that. Is that clear?

CONEY: Yes, sir. *(A frightened cry.)* Doctor, I—

DOCTOR: This is going to make you feel fine, son. This is going to make you sleep without all those bad dreams . . . Now then. Just a little— *(He removes tourniquet and injects needle.)* sting—there. Now you start counting. 100, 99 . . .

CONEY: *(As he gets along in this counting, his speech gets slightly thicker and there is an occasional cough.)* 100—99—98—97—96—95—94—93—92—91—90—89—87—86—85—84—8—

DOCTOR: 83.

CONEY: 83—82—81—82—1— *(*DOCTOR *has been watch-*

ing needle in CONEY*'s arm. Now he looks up and leans forward deliberately.)*

DOCTOR: Who do you work for, Coney?

CONEY: Major Robinson. *(A second's pause.* DOCTOR *sits up and smiles.)*

DOCTOR: Is he a good C.O.?

CONEY: Oh, the Major's an all right guy. Darn decent. And he knows his stuff. He's decent, only . . .

DOCTOR: Only what?

CONEY: He's an all right guy. He's okay.

DOCTOR: Not as smart as Mingo, though, is he?

CONEY: Oh, he knows more about engineering, but Mingo's a sharp boy. He knows. He knows plenty. You know his wife writes poetry?

DOCTOR: She does?

CONEY: Yep. Real poetry. Sometimes, he's kind of touchy, though.

DOCTOR: Touchy? Like you?

CONEY: No . . . No, not like me. None of them are like me. I—I—

DOCTOR: You what, Coney?

CONEY: Mingo's sensitive about—well, about his wife. About how they treat him—us. Once . . . once I heard a poem. A poem Mingo's wife wrote. I heard that.

DOCTOR: Did he recite it to you?

CONEY: Once . . . Just once . . .

DOCTOR: Why shouldn't he recite it to you? You're his buddy.

CONEY: Oh, no. I'm not his buddy. He doesn't have a buddy. You can't get real close to Mingo.

DOCTOR: Who's your buddy, Coney? *(Pause.)* Who's your buddy? *(No answer.)* Finch? Finch is your buddy, isn't he? *(Withdraws needle, puts cotton over injection spot, and folds* CONEY*'s arm to keep cotton in place.)*

CONEY: Yes.

DOCTOR: He's been your buddy almost since you came in the Army.

CONEY: *(Low.)* Yes.

DOCTOR: Finch is an all right guy. He likes you. And you like him, don't you?

CONEY: Yes, I— *(Suddenly, loudly.)* No. No, I don't. He doesn't really like me! He's like all of them. He doesn't like me and I hate him! I hate him!

DOCTOR: You really hate Finch?

CONEY: Yes! *(Long pause. Then, very quietly.)* No. Finch is a sweet kid. He's my buddy, the dumb Arizona hayseed. Didn't know from nothing when he came into the outfit. But he's learning. He's a sweet kid. He doesn't seem like the others only—only I wonder if he is.

DOCTOR: If Finch is what?

CONEY: Like the others.

DOCTOR: What others?

CONEY: The ones who make the cracks.

DOCTOR: Who, Coney? Who makes the cracks?

CONEY: T.J. *(Venomously.)* Corporal T.J. Everitt. *(With slow fury.)* I hate his guts.

DOCTOR: What cracks does he make, Coney?

CONEY: Finch doesn't let him get away with them, though. Finch— *(Suddenly springs up to a sitting position. He is frightened.)* Finch! Where's Finch?

DOCTOR: He's all right.

CONEY: Where is he? Where's Finch?

DOCTOR: He's all right.

CONEY: Where is he?

DOCTOR: Don't worry about him.

CONEY: *(Calling.)* Finch? *(Frightened.)* Finch? *(He looks around frantically.)*

DOCTOR: *(Hesitates—then throws arm around* CONEY.*)* Hi, Coney.

CONEY: *(Cheerfully.)* Finch! Where the hell have you been? The Major wants us in his office.

(Lights start to dim down.)

DOCTOR: What for?

CONEY: How the hell would I know what for? Do they ever tell you anything in the Army? All I know is we got to get to the Major's office on the double. So come on. Let's take off!

(By now stage is blacked out. Through the darkness, we hear distant sound of a field phone ringing. Sound gets louder and louder gradually.)

Scene 2

SCENE: *An office. A Pacific Base. This is a section of a quonset hut. The hut serves as an army office building, wooden partitions separate one "room" from another. This one is an outer office. The spotted walls, the littered desks, the four or five posters—none of this really belies the temporary air that this room and the thousands like it invariably have. In center of rear wall is a door marked plainly with a wooden plaque: "*MAJOR ROBINSON.*" Up* R. *are a desk and a chair. Down* L. *in* L. *wall is another door which leads to the street outside. There are two or three chairs or crates serving as chairs. Each side wall has a small window through which the morning sun is boiling despite the tropical trees.*

AT RISE: *As lights come up phone is ringing and through screened street door we see two soldiers running up. First is* PFC. PETER COEN—"CONEY"—*and we now see that he is of medium height with a strong, solid body. His face is fairly nondescript until he smiles. Then his hard, tough manner washes away in warmth and good humor. He is about twenty-three and wears faded green coveralls. Second soldier looks a little younger and a little neater. He is a tall, bony kid named* FINCH—*a private. He is immediately likeable. He is rather simple, rather gentle and, at the moment, a little worried. It is apparent that neither of the boys knows what they are here for. They look about the empty room for a moment, then* CONEY *moves* C. *with a shrug.*

CONEY: Nobody's home.

FINCH: I thought you said the Major wanted us on the double.

(Phone stops ringing.)

CONEY: They always want you here two minutes ago, but they're never here when you're here.

FINCH: We could have cleaned up.

CONEY: *(Wandering around, snooping at papers on desks.)* What've you got to be clean for anyway? Short arm? The only thing we could pick up around here is mildew.

FINCH: Oh, that's charming.

CONEY: Delightful. *(Slight pause.)*

FINCH: Who else did he send for?

CONEY: *(Taking out cigarette.)* I don't know. Maybe he only wants us. Fresh young meat for the grinder.

FINCH: Oh! Great! *(*FINCH *refuses cigarette and walks over to window.)*

CONEY: *(Tenderly.)* Hey, jerk ... *(*FINCH *turns around.)* Hell, I'm no pipeline. It might be a furlough.

FINCH: *(Denying it.)* Yep, yep.

CONEY: It might be. We've been over two years plus and it says in the book—

FINCH: What book, Grimm's Fairy Tales?

CONEY: *(Quietly.)* I guess. *(Slight pause.)* Ah, come on, Finch. You think every time they send for you in the Army, it's for something bad.

FINCH: Isn't it?

CONEY: *(Trying hard to pick* FINCH *up.)* You know, if it is a furlough, we'll have a chance to look for a spot for that bar we're gonna have.

FINCH: I thought we decided.

CONEY: That whistle stop in Arizona?

FINCH: It's a nice town. And it's near home.

CONEY: Your home. Listen, did you tell her?

FINCH: Tell who?

CONEY: Your mother, jerk. About us going to own a bar together after the war.

FINCH: I told her it was going to be a restaurant.

CONEY: A restaurant!

FINCH: Mothers don't understand about bars. But I wrote

her about how I'm going to paint pictures on the walls and about how it's going to be the kind of place you said.

CONEY: Where a guy can bring his wife.

FINCH: She liked that.

CONEY: Sure. I know just how it should be run. Your mother'll like it fine. *(*FINCH *starts to whistle a tune called "Shoo, Fly," or some other similar folk melody.)* Finch . . .

FINCH: Huh?

CONEY: Does your mother know who I am?

FINCH: Of course.

CONEY: I mean, does she know my name?

FINCH: Well, sure she does!

CONEY: Oh.

FINCH: What did you think?

CONEY: I don't know. I just wondered.

FINCH: You can be an A-1 jerk sometimes. The whole family knows about you and Mom's so het up, I think she's got ideas about mating you and my sister.

CONEY: Yep, yep.

FINCH: What do you think she sends you all that food for? My sister cooks it.

CONEY: Ah, Finch . . .

FINCH: Ah, Finch, nothing! And all those letters telling me to be sure to bring you home when we get our furlough. . . .

CONEY: Nuts.

FINCH: There's plenty of room. It's only a ranch, of course—nothing fancy—

CONEY: Like a quonset hut.

FINCH: We'd have a helluva time.

CONEY: My mother wants to meet you but—Judas, I sleep on the couch.

FINCH: We wouldn't have enough time on a furlough to visit both— Gosh! You think it might be a furlough, Coney? You think it might be?

CONEY: *Quién sabe?*

FINCH: The orderly room said it was something special.

CONEY: Like a new kind of latrine duty.

FINCH: Oh, great! Make up your mind, will you? First you tell me no furlough; then you start me thinking maybe there will be one; then—

(During this, street door opens and, unseen by FINCH *or* CONEY, T/SGT. CARL MINGO *comes in. He is about twenty-seven, has dark red hair and looks taller than he is. He gives a feeling of strength, he's someone you want to know. He stands now at door for a moment, then knocks on sill and says.)*

MINGO: Is this the way to the powder room? *(He comes in, closing door behind him.)*
FINCH: Are you in on this, Mingo?
MINGO: In on what?
CONEY: Whatever it is.
FINCH: Don't you know?
MINGO: Gentlemen, I don't know from nothing.
CONEY: Yep, yep.
MINGO: I don't, Coney. So help me.
FINCH: We thought—well, we were kind of hoping that—well, it might be for a furlough. We've been over two years. You've been over longer. You've seen more action than anybody else. Maybe . . . *(Finishing lamely.)* Well, it could be a furlough.
MINGO: *(Kindly.)* Sure. It could be, kid. We could all do with a couple of weeks in a rest camp.
FINCH: Rest camp?
CONEY: Cut it out. The Arizona tumbleweed's homesick.
FINCH: Blow it, will ya?
MINGO: One week back there and I'll bet you'd really be homesick—for this joint.
CONEY: *(To* MINGO.*)* Hey, what's been eating you the last couple of days?
MINGO: Mosquitoes.
FINCH: Gee, I was sure you'd know what they wanted us for, Mingo.
MINGO: Why should I know?
CONEY: Didn't you learn anything at college?
MINGO: I only went a year. Write my wife. She's a big hot diploma girl.
CONEY: Yuk, yuk.
MINGO: Maybe we're moving out.
FINCH: Again?
MINGO: Maybe.
FINCH: Why?
MINGO: The General's restless.

FINCH: But where would we be going?
MINGO: Where the little men make with the big bullets.
CONEY: Now that's a real charming thought.
FINCH: Delightful. *(Slight pause.)* Remember that first time, Coney? When Major Robinson said: Men, you're going to have the excitement you've been itching for?
MINGO: Major Blueberry Pie.
FINCH: He was a captain then.
MINGO: Pardon me. Captain Blueberry Pie.
CONEY: Sometimes the Maj acts like war was a hot baseball game. Batter up! Sqush. Sub-stitute please!
FINCH: That's charming!
CONEY: I'm a charming fellow.
FINCH: You stink.

(Door to street opens and CORP. T. J. EVERITT *comes in. He, like the others, wears faded coveralls. But* T.J. *is in a temper.)*

T.J.: What the hell is this? They put me in charge of a detail, tell me I've got to finish that new road by noon—and then they yank me off with no explanation. What's going on around here?
MINGO: It is not for engineers to reason why.
CONEY: My Ouija board's on strike.
T.J.: I wasn't asking you, Coney.
MINGO: Your guess is as good as ours, T.J.
FINCH: I heard a rumor they were going to give you a commission, T.J.
CONEY: All of us.
FINCH: Only Coney and me are going to be captains.
CONEY: Majors.
FINCH: Colonels.
CONEY: What the hell—generals.
FINCH: Congratulations, General Coen.
CONEY: *Gracias,* Commander Finch.
T.J.: Oh, blow it, will you? *(To* MINGO.*)* You'd think that by now they'd have somebody mature enough to run an outfit.
FINCH: The Major's all right. I don't see you doing any better.
T.J.: If I couldn't do better with my eyes blindfolded, I'd resign.

CONEY: The Army's kind of touchy about resigning, T.J.
MINGO: Just what makes you such a hot blue-plate special, T.J.?
FINCH: Don't you know who he is, Mingo? Tell him, Coney.
CONEY: *(Exaggerated sotto voce.)* That's T. J. Everitt, former vice-president in charge of distribution for Universal Products, Inc.
FINCH: No!
CONEY: Yeah!
T.J.: Oh, Christ! Do we have to go through that again?
FINCH: Say, is he the Joe who used to make fifteen thousand a year?
CONEY: Oh, that was a bad year. He usually made sixteen thousand.
FINCH: No!
CONEY: Yeah!
FINCH: Think of his taxes!
CONEY: Rugged.
MINGO: Say, what's he doing now?
CONEY: Now? Oh, now he's a corporal making sixty-two bucks a month.
FINCH: No!
CONEY: Yeah!
FINCH: Tsk! Tsk! What won't they think of next!
T.J.: That's enough.
CONEY: Well, I heard just the—
T.J.: All right. That's enough—Jakie!
CONEY: *(Quietly.)* Hold your hats, boys.
FINCH: *(To* T.J.*)* Can that.
T.J.: *(To* FINCH.*)* Why don't you let your little friend—
FINCH: I said can it!
T.J.: I heard you.
MINGO: Well, then, can it and can it for good!
CONEY: Drop it, fellas. It isn't worth it.
T.J.: *(To* MINGO.*)* Oh, the firm has a new partner.
MINGO: Up your floo, Rockefeller. *(Rear door opens and* MAJ. ROBINSON *comes out of his office.)*
MAJOR: At ease, men. I'm sorry I had to keep you waiting. . . . You'd better make yourselves comfortable. We're in for a session. Sit if you want to. Smoke. But stay put and give me your attention. *(*CONEY *gestures*

"thumbs down" to FINCH. MAJOR, *brusquely.)* What's that for, Co-en?

CONEY: Oh, we . . . we thought maybe this was about furloughs, sir.

MAJOR: No. Sit down, Finch. I realize you men have furloughs coming to you. Particularly Mingo. And you ought to know that if I could get them for you, I would. However, we've got a job to do. Right, Mingo?

MINGO: *(With a wry smile.)* Yes, sir.

MAJOR: *(With charm.)* Well, maybe after this you'll get those furloughs. I certainly hope so. . . . Anybody been bothered with anything lately—anything physical, I mean?

T.J.: Well, Major, my back—

MAJOR: I know, T.J. Outside of that, though? *(He looks around at the men. No answer.)* All right. Now—before anything else, get this straight: everything you hear from now on is top secret. Whatever you do or don't do, it's secret. Running off at the mouth will get a court-martial. Understand? *(The men nod.)* Okay. . . . I'll get right to the point. You four men are the best engineers in the outfit. We need A-1 engineers for this job. *(*MINGO *smiles.)* What's the matter, Mingo?

MINGO: Nothing, sir.

MAJOR: I mean that. Seriously. Now, there's an island—never mind where—that we want to invade next. It's darned important that we take that island. It can shorten this whole bloody war. . . . But right now, there are fifteen thousand Japs on it. To take it and hold it—we'll need airstrips. And we'll need 'em quick. To fly supplies in and to have a base for fighters and bombers. Clear? . . . Well, I'm flying to that island tonight.

FINCH: With fifteen thousand Japs on it, sir?

MAJOR: Yes. I need a few men to go with me. One to sketch the terrain and draw maps— *(*CONEY *nudges* FINCH; *the others stare at* FINCH.*)* and three others to help survey. I suppose two more would really be enough but—well, it's a ticklish job, all right, and—What is it, T.J.?

T.J.: I was thinking about aerial photographs.

MAJOR: Leave the thinking to me and Headquarters, please. Aerial photos don't show what we want to find out. Too much foliage.

MINGO: Is there any intelligence on the Jap airstrips?

MAJOR: There's only one strip and it stinks. Besides, if we don't blow it up, they will. . . . Any other questions?

MINGO: Major . . .

MAJOR: Yes?

MINGO: Did you say you were flying to this island?

MAJOR: Yes. Natives'll pick us up offshore with canoes when we get there.

MINGO: How long do you figure the job will take?

MAJOR: Four days. Top. Then we get off the island the same way we got on.

MINGO: Canoes and then the plane.

MAJOR: Yes.

T.J.: Suppose something happens?

MAJOR: The Japs are only defending the side of the island facing us. We'll be working in back of them—on the part facing Japan. Actually, it shouldn't be too bad because we shouldn't ever run into them. *(With a smile.)* I say "we." Really, it's up to you.

CONEY: To us?

MAJOR: This is purely voluntary, fellows. Whether you come or not—that's up to each of you. *(Pause.)* I know how you feel. You've all been in plenty; you've done plenty. And I'm not going to try to kid you about this job: it's no picnic. But believe me, it's worth doing. And anyway, it's got to be done. *(Another pause. He walks around a bit.)* I wouldn't have asked you—particularly you, Mingo, except that I need the best men I have. That's the kind of job it is. But it's still up to each of you individually. If you say "no," there won't be any questions asked. I mean that. . . . Talk it over. Together or by yourselves. That's up to you. I'm sorry, but I can't give you more than— *(Looks at his watch.)* ten minutes but—it came up damn fast and—well, you men know the Army. *(He walks up to door to his office, starts to open it, then turns.)* Just remember it's damned important. Probably the least you'll get out of this will be a furlough. I can't promise, of course, that you'll get one but—that isn't the reason for going anyway. The reason is that you're the best men for the job. *(He exits into his office. Slight pause.)*

MINGO: *(Softly—with a wry smile.)* Oh, my aching back.

CONEY: What?
MINGO: That vaseline about volunteering.
FINCH: What do you mean?
T.J.: With a nice little bribe of furloughs.
CONEY: He didn't say he was promising us furloughs.
MINGO: Well—if he wanted to play fair and square with us, he would have called us in one at a time and not let us know who the others were. That's volunteering.
CONEY: Why?
MINGO: Because that way, if a man wants out, he can get out—and no one's the wiser. But this way! Well, who's going to chicken out in front of anyone else?
T.J.: What do you mean—chicken out?
MINGO: Are you going?
T.J.: Are you?
MINGO: I'm not making up your mind.
T.J.: I'm not asking you to!
MINGO: *(Lightly.)* Okay. *(Pause.)*
FINCH: Fifteen thousand Japs. *(Whistles softly.)*
CONEY: The first day I was inducted, some Joe said: Keep your eyes open, your mouth shut and never volunteer. No matter what it's for, it stinks.
MINGO: Well, who's gonna ride the broomstick to that island? That stinks, but good.
CONEY: If it's the way you said . . .
MINGO: What way?
CONEY: You know. That this is half-assed volunteering.
MINGO: Oh . . . It is.
CONEY: Then either we all go or we all don't go.
T.J.: Why?
MINGO: Because if one of us says "yes," nobody else can say, "Count me out, Major. I'm sitting home on my yellow butt."
T.J.: It doesn't mean you're yellow.
MINGO: Could you say "count me out"? *(*FINCH *whistles "Shoo, Fly." Slight pause.)*
CONEY: I wonder what would happen if we all said it. *(Slight pause.)*
FINCH: Maybe it won't be so tough. He said the Japs are all on the other side of the island.
T.J.: There's no law they have to stay there.
CONEY: The more times you go in, the less chance you have of coming out in one piece.

FINCH: That's a charming thought.

CONEY: Delightful. *(Pause, during which* FINCH *starts to whistle "Shoo, Fly.")*

FINCH: *(Sings.)* "Shoo, fly, don't bother me. For I'm in Company Q."

T.J.: Company G.

CONEY: Anybody can make it rhyme. *(Slight pause.)*

T.J.: Well, Christ! We ought to talk about it, anyway!

MINGO: About what? Japs? They have several ways of killing you. They can—

T.J.: Oh, put your head in a bowl, will you? *(Slight pause.)*

FINCH: How long did he say?

CONEY: Four days.

FINCH: No. I mean to decide.

CONEY: Ten minutes.

MINGO: What's the difference? It's either too much or too little. The dirtiest trick you can play on a man in war is to make him think.

FINCH: Well, what do you say, Coney?

CONEY: I don't know.

FINCH: Well, you say it.

T.J.: Oh, great. Let's play follow the leader.

FINCH: Mind your own business, T.J.!

MINGO: This *is* his business, Finch. It's kind of all our business.

FINCH: What do you mean?

MINGO: Whatever you two decide, we're stuck with it.

CONEY: Hey! Hey!

MINGO: It's perfectly okay by me, Coney.

T.J.: It's okay by you?

MINGO: Yeah.

T.J.: That's great! Well, maybe it's okay for the three of you, but what makes you think I'll string along?

MINGO: You haven't got the guts to do anything else.

FINCH: *(To* CONEY.*)* Come on, you jerk. What do you say?

CONEY: You know what I say? I say I think of four G.I.s going to an island crawling with fifteen thousand Japs, and I say they're crazy.

MINGO: Okay. Then we don't go. We don't have to.

CONEY: But the Major says we're the four best men. That it's important and it's winning the war.

T.J.: You mean you want to go?

CONEY: Nobody wants to go.

MINGO: You can say that again.

FINCH: Well, you say it, Coney. Somebody has to.

CONEY: No. I don't want to, Finch. This is tough enough for a guy to decide for himself, but to decide for three other guys—I don't want to.

MINGO: Seems like we're putting him on a big black spot marked X, Finch.

CONEY: Look, Mingo, going on a mission like this ain't kidding. When they tell you to do something, it's not so bad. You have to do it, so you do it. But this way. Well, what the hell! Let somebody else decide. *(Stops as rear door opens and* MAJOR *walks in.)*

MAJOR: Sorry, men. Time's up. . . . I want to say one thing again. If you've decided the job is too much for you, there'll be no questions asked. All you have to do is say "yes" or "no." . . . I—well, whatever you say, I want to thank you for your past work. *(He faces toward* MINGO *as though he were going to ask him first, changes his mind, looks at others, finally stops at* FINCH.*)* Well, Finch? Yes or no? *(*FINCH *looks at* MAJOR, *then directly at* CONEY. *Slight pause. Then* MAJOR *looks at* CONEY, *too. They all look at him now. He looks at* FINCH, *pauses, then turns slightly more to* MAJOR.*)*

CONEY: Yes, sir.

(Blackout. After a pause, through the darkness comes the sound of crickets, then, faintly at first, cries of jungle birds.)

Scene 3

SCENE: *Clearing. A Pacific Island. Before lights go up, we hear a jungle bird shriek. A few more birds shriek, then we hear* FINCH *whistling "Shoo, Fly." Slowly, scene fades in. We are looking at part of what must be a fairly large clearing in the midst of the jungle. It ends in a vague semicircle of bushes and trees. Vines drop from above and crawl over the rest of the cleared area. Hot, muggy sunlight slices down, but the general feeling is of some place dank, dark and unpleasant. This is not motion-picture jungle, it is not pretty.*

When lights go up, FINCH *is propped up, downstage, against a pile of equipment. He is completing a map, and has his sketching pad braced on his knees.* CONEY *is next to him, cleaning his rifle. Both have their guns next to them and, like all the men in this scene, wear jungle combat uniforms. A slight wait as* FINCH *works and whistles. Then a bird screeches again.*

CONEY: This place smells.
FINCH: It's not so bad.
CONEY: I don't mean stinks. I mean smells. Really. This kind of smells. *(He sniffs.)* Like a graveyard.
FINCH: When did you ever smell a graveyard?
CONEY: When we set foot on this trap four days ago. *(Bird screams again.)* Shut up! They make you jumpy, Finch?
FINCH: Some. Coyotes are worse.
CONEY: I never heard coyotes, but I'd like to. I'd like to be where I could hear 'em this minute.

FINCH: In Arizona.

CONEY: God knows you couldn't hear 'em in Pittsburgh.

FINCH: They're kind of scarey—if you wake up and hear them in the middle of the night.

CONEY: I remember waking up in the middle of the night and hearing something. I was ten years old.

FINCH: What'd you hear?

CONEY: A human coyote. *(Gets up.)* I've really got the jumps.

FINCH: We'll be out of here tonight. Why don't you relax? It's a fine day.

CONEY: Yep, yep.

FINCH: It is. I'd like to lie under a tree and have cocoanuts fall in my lap.

CONEY: I'd rather have a Polynesian babe fall in mine.

FINCH: Too much trouble. I'll take cocoanuts.

CONEY: You have to open cocoanuts.

FINCH and CONEY: *(Together.)* Yuk, yuk, yuk.

FINCH: Well—it may not be a good map, but it's a pretty one.

CONEY: You finished?

FINCH: Almost. They ought to be finished soon, too. They're just rechecking.

CONEY: Yeah. *(Bird scream.)* All right, sweetheart. We heard you the first time!

FINCH: Coney . . .

CONEY: Yeah?

FINCH: You think girls want it as much as fellas?

CONEY: More.

FINCH: But more girls are virgins.

CONEY: Enemy propaganda.

FINCH: I wonder if my sister is. Would you care?

CONEY: What?

FINCH: If the girl you married wasn't?

CONEY: Stop trying to cook up something between me and your sister.

FINCH: She's a good cook.

CONEY: I thought we were going to run a bar?

FINCH: A bar-restaurant.

CONEY: How's she on mixing drinks?

FINCH: She could learn.

CONEY: I wish she'd send up a stiff one now. I'm beginning to see Japs.

FINCH: They're on the other side of the island.

CONEY: It's not like Japs to stay there. *(Bird screams.)* Ah . . .

FINCH: Mingo's wife writes poetry.

CONEY: Yeah. I know.

FINCH: He ever let you read any of it?

CONEY: He never lets anybody read it. It probably stinks.

FINCH: I wonder what she's like.

CONEY: Not bad. From her picture. Did you ever see that picture of the Major's girl?

FINCH: Oh, my aching back!

CONEY: And I'll bet he's a virgin. Him and T.J.

FINCH: T.J.'s been married three times.

CONEY: He's still a virgin.

FINCH: How could he be?

CONEY: He's mean enough. *(Bird screams.)* And you too, you bitch.

FINCH: That's charming.

CONEY: Delightful. *(A rustling in the bushes.* CONEY *jerks for his gun, then lies back again as* T.J. *comes out.)*

T.J.: *(Perspiring heavily.)* You're certainly working yourselves into an early grave.

FINCH: I'm finishing the map.

T.J.: What's your friend doing? Posing for it?

CONEY: I'm thinking up interoffice memos.

T.J.: Don't rupture yourself.

CONEY: You guys finish?

T.J.: If you're so interested, go see for yourself.

CONEY: That's charming.

FINCH: Delightful.

T.J.: Screw off. *(Starts to sit.)* Christ, I'm dripping. *(Bird screams, he turns violently.)*

CONEY: Watch out for the birdie.

T.J.: Look, Coney, I've—

FINCH: *(Cutting in.)* What are they doing there anyway, T.J.?

T.J.: Oh, you know the boy Major. He's got to do things his way. Which makes it twice as long.

FINCH: We'll get off tonight on schedule, though.

T.J.: If I were running it, we'd have been through and left yesterday.

CONEY: Yep, yep.

T.J.: Yes! *(To* FINCH.*)* He wants the clinometer.

FINCH: Who does?

T.J.: The Major.

FINCH: You know where it is.

T.J.: Why don't you get the lead out of your can and do something for once?

CONEY: *(To* FINCH.*)* You finish your map.

FINCH: It's finished, Coney.

CONEY: Well, let T.J. Rockefeller do something besides blowing that tin horn.

T.J.: Look who's talking.

FINCH: *(Jumping up.)* Yeah, look! He stood guard two nights out of three while you snored your fat face off. The Major told him to take it easy today and you know it.

T.J.: *(To* FINCH.*)* The little kike lover.

FINCH: You always get around to that, don't you?

T.J.: Every time I see your friend's face.

CONEY: You son of a bitch.

T.J.: Watch your language or I'll ram it down your throat, Jew boy.

FINCH: You'll get yours rammed down your throat first.

T.J.: Not by him.

CONEY: Listen, T.J.—

T.J.: You listen to me, you lousy yellow Jew bastard! I'm going to— *(At this,* FINCH *steps forward and clips* T.J. T.J. *reels, but comes back at* FINCH.*)* You little— *(He swings,* FINCH *ducks and socks him again.* T.J. *hits back.* CONEY *tries to break it up but they are punching away as* MINGO *rushes in from down* R.*)*

MINGO: What the hell is this? Come on, break it up. *(He steps in.)* Why don't you jerks save it for the Japs?

T.J.: He's more interested in saving his yellow Jew friend. *(*CONEY *turns away sharply and walks a little up* R. *by a tree. Brief pause.)*

MINGO: *(Evenly.)* The Major wants the clinometer, T.J. *(*T.J. *just stands, looking at him.)* Go bring it to him! *(There is a slight wait. Then* T.J. *goes to pile of gear, fishes out clinometer and exits down* R.*)* We're practically through. *(*FINCH *doesn't answer.* CONEY *stands by tree, his back to audience.* MINGO *takes out cigarette and lights up.)*

FINCH: *(Low.)* That bastard.

MINGO: We've got plenty of time to pack up and get to

the beach. The plane isn't due till nightfall. . . . One thing you can say for the Major. He gets the job done.

FINCH: That bastard.

MINGO: All right.

FINCH: It's not all right.

MINGO: Well—the Major should have known, I guess, but—none of them bother to find out what a guy's like.

FINCH: What makes him such a bastard?

MINGO: Hell, the guy's thirty-five, thirty-six. He can't adjust himself to the Army so he winds up hating everything and resenting everybody. He's just a civilian in G.I. clothes.

FINCH: So am I, but he still stinks.

MINGO: Sure. He stinks from way back. The Army makes him worse. I'm not apologizing for him. I think he's a bastard, too. But you ought to try to understand him.

CONEY: *(Turning around sharply.)* You try to understand him! I haven't got time. *(Coming over to them.)* I'm too busy trying to understand all this crap about Jews.

FINCH: Coney . . .

CONEY: I told you I heard something in the middle of the night once. Some drunken bum across the hall from my aunt's yelling: Throw out the dirty sheenies! . . . That was us. But I just turned over and went back to sleep. I was used to it by then. What the hell! I was ten. That's old for a Jew. When I was six, my first week in school, I stayed out for the Jewish New Year. The next day a bunch of kids got around me and said: "Were you in school yesterday?" I smiled and said, "No." They wiped the smile off my face. They beat the hell out of me. I had to get beat up a coupla more times before I learned that if you're a Jew, you stink. You're not like other guys. You're—you're alone. You're—you're something—strange, different. *(Suddenly furious.)* Well, goddammit, you make us different, you dirty bastards! What the hell do you want us to do?

FINCH: Coney . . .

CONEY: Let me alone.

MINGO: Coney, listen—

CONEY: Tell your wife to write a poem about it.

MINGO: Screw me *and* my wife. You know damn well Finch at least doesn't feel like that.

CONEY: I don't know anything. I'm a lousy yellow Jew bastard.

(He turns and walks back to tree. FINCH *hesitates and then walks to him.)*

FINCH: Coney . . .

CONEY: Drop it.

FINCH: You know that doesn't go for me.

CONEY: I said drop it, Finch.

FINCH: Maybe I'm dumb. Maybe I'm an Arizona hayseed like you say. But I never met any Jewish boys till I got in the Army. I didn't even realize out loud that *you* were until somebody said something.

CONEY: I can imagine what.

FINCH: Yes. And I took a poke at him, too. Because I couldn't see any reason for it. And there isn't any. Okay. I'm a jerk, but to me—you like a guy or you don't. That's all there is to it. That's all there ever will be to it. . . . And you know that—don't you? *(Waits for an answer, but there is none. Takes a step back toward* MINGO, *then turns and moves swiftly to* CONEY, *puts arm around him.)* Aw heck, aren't we buddies?

CONEY: *(Turning—with a smile.)* You corny bastard.

FINCH: You stubborn jerk. *(Shot rings out from off* R. *The three on stage freeze.)*

CONEY: What the—

MINGO: Ssh! *(They stand and listen. Bird screams a few times.)*

FINCH: Maybe it was T.J. He's dumb enough.

MINGO: Not that dumb. A shot could bring the Japs—

CONEY: Listen! *(They hold for a moment, listening to* R.*)*

MINGO: Take cover. Quick!

(They pick up their guns and start for bushes upstage just as MAJOR *and* T.J. *run out from bushes,* R. *From here to curtain, the men speak in hushed tones.)*

MAJOR: Sniper took a pot shot and missed.

FINCH: Judas!

MAJOR: Grab the gear and let's beat it fast.

FINCH: Right.

MAJOR: *(To* MINGO.*)* You and Coney keep your rifles ready.

CONEY: Yes, sir.

MAJOR: Forget that sir! Japs love officers. *(*FINCH *and* T.J. *are hastily picking up gear. The* MAJOR *is picking up equipment.* CONEY *and* MINGO *put on their packs and helmets, always watching to* R.*)* Got the maps, Finch?

FINCH: All packed.

MAJOR: Good. Would happen the last day.

MINGO: Did you finish?

MAJOR: Yes. Watch there.

*(*MINGO *moves closer to bushes down* R. *with his rifle ready.* CONEY *is also facing in that direction but is nearer* C.*)*

CONEY: It's so damn dark in there.

T.J.: And we're out in the open.

MAJOR: Knock off, T.J. Get that talkie.

*(*FINCH *starts for it just as two sharp shots crack out from off* R. *The men flatten to the earth, except* MINGO, *who grabs his* R. *arm, dropping his rifle. Then he drops down. A moment's hesitation—then* CONEY *fires. A wait of a moment—then the sound of a body crashing through the trees.)*

CONEY: *(Softly.)* Got the bastard!

MAJOR: Stay down. There may be others. Finch—see if he's dead. *(*FINCH *starts to crawl toward spot where body crashed.)* If he isn't, use your knife. There's been enough shooting to bring the whole island down on us. . . . Anybody hit?

MINGO: Yes.

MAJOR: Where?

MINGO: Right arm.

MAJOR: Bad?

MINGO: Bad enough.

MAJOR: We've got to get out of here. I'll make a tourniquet.

(He starts to crawl toward MINGO. FINCH, *by this time, has reached the bushes and is on his knees, peering through at the body.)*

FINCH: Major, I don't think he— *(Bushes move slightly.)*
MAJOR: Make sure! *(*FINCH *turns slightly to look at him.)* Quick—goddammit—make sure!

*(*FINCH *turns back, then with a sharp movement, gets up, goes into bushes with his knife raised. Pause. Sound of* FINCH *rustling in bushes off* R. *Then he comes back.)*

FINCH: Okay.
MAJOR: *(Whipping out a handkerchief, which he makes into tourniquet for* MINGO.*)* If there was anybody else, we should have heard by now. Still— *(*FINCH *has walked up* R. *and now starts to retch. The* MAJOR *turns at the sound and sees* CONEY *move toward* FINCH.*)* Let him alone. Pick up the gear. We've got to beat it. *(A bird screams.)*
T.J.: Well, for Chrissakes, let's go.
MAJOR: All right. *(Getting up.)* We'll make for that clearing near the beach.
MINGO: *(Getting up.)* Thanks.
MAJOR: I'll do better later. Forget the pack.
MINGO: I can take it.

*(*MAJOR *puts his pack on, starts to pick up some equipment.* T.J. *stands impatiently near bushes,* L.*)*

T.J.: You never can tell about those slant-eyed bastards. Come on. Let's get out of here.
MAJOR: Take it easy. Who's got the maps?
CONEY: Finch.
FINCH: *(Coming downstage.)* I never can get used to it. I'm sorry.
MAJOR: Okay. Forget about it. You got the maps?
FINCH: Yes, sir.
MAJOR: Everybody set?
CONEY: I'll take care of Finch. *(*FINCH *shakes his head violently.)* What's the matter?
FINCH: I never can get used to it. I got the shakes.
MAJOR: Forget it.

FINCH: It was like killing a dead man.
MAJOR: If you didn't kill him, he would have killed us.
FINCH: I got the shakes, Coney.
CONEY: We all have, Finch. *(Bird screams.)*
T.J.: Christ!
MAJOR: Come on. Let's go. *(He plunges into brush.)*
T.J.: Come on, Mingo.
MINGO: *(To* FINCH.*)* So it stinks. Come on, kiddo.
T.J.: Mingo!
MINGO: All right. After you, feedbox.

(T.J. *goes into brush.* CONEY *picks up* FINCH*'s pack and helps him put it on.* MINGO *pauses at end of brush.)*

MINGO: Coney—
CONEY: We're coming. *(*MINGO *exits off* L. CONEY, *picking up his gear.)* Let's go, Finch. It ain't healthy around here. *(*FINCH *starts to wander around.)* Finch, listen—
FINCH: I'm all right, I'm all right. I just can't remember where I put the map case.
CONEY: O Judas!
FINCH: You go.
CONEY: Try to think.
FINCH: I had it just before I—
CONEY: This is a helluva time!
FINCH: I just had it.
CONEY: Maybe one of them has it.
FINCH: No. *(Bird screams. Both look feverishly for case.)*
CONEY: Listen, we'll lose them.
FINCH: We gotta have those maps.
CONEY: The maps won't do us any good if we get picked off!
FINCH: That's the only thing we came here for.
CONEY: Goddammit. Where the hell are they? *(Bird screams.)* Christ!
FINCH: Shut up.
CONEY: You'll get us both killed! You dumb Arizona bastard!
FINCH: I'm not asking you to stay, you lousy yellow— *(He cuts off. Both stand dead still, staring at each other.)* jerk! *(He turns and begins looking again for map case.* CONEY *waits a moment, his head bowed in hurt. Then turns swiftly and starts for bushes. Just as*

he gets there, FINCH *spots case.)* Here they are! I knew I— *(A shot smashes out. He clutches his belly and falls.* CONEY, *whose back is to* FINCH, *flattens out at sound of shot. Then he looks around.)*

CONEY: Finch!

FINCH: Okay.

CONEY: *(As he scrambles to him.)* You hit?

FINCH: Coney, I didn't mean—

CONEY: Never mind. Are you hit?

FINCH: Take the maps.

CONEY: Where'd they hit you?

FINCH: *(Thrusting map case at him.)* Take the maps.

CONEY: Finch—

FINCH: Take 'em!

CONEY: Give me your arm. *(*CONEY *tries to carry him.* FINCH *pushes* CONEY *down.)*

FINCH: I'm all right, you dumb bastard—

CONEY: You sure you—

FINCH: I'll follow. Go on. Quick! *(*CONEY *looks at him and then darts to bushes,* L. FINCH *watches him and when* CONEY *looks back, he starts crawling.)* I'm coming, I tell you! Go on, go on!

*(*CONEY *turns and disappears into brush. Immediately,* FINCH *stops crawling and lies flat. Then he gathers his strength and starts to crawl again. Suddenly he stops and listens. He swings his body around so that he is facing the jungle,* R. *Bushes,* R., *begin to rustle.* FINCH, *still holding his rifle, begins to inch his body downstage toward tree. When* FINCH *is out of sight downstage* L., *the bushes move.)*

CONEY: *(Calling softly, offstage.)* Finch! Where are you, Finch? Finch! *(Coming on.)* Finch, for Christ sake where are you? *(A shot rings out and* CONEY *hits the dirt. A pause.)* Finch? Finch? *(Looking around, he starts to back off upstage.)* Where are you, Finch? *(Bushes rustle off.* CONEY *is still calling softly as curtain falls.)*

CURTAIN

ACT II

Scene 1

SCENE: *Hospital Room. The Pacific Base.*

CONEY *is stretched out on the cot with his head buried in the pillow. He is in same position as in* ACT I. *The* DOCTOR *is sitting on the bed, patting his shoulder.*

DOCTOR: *(Gently.)* Coney . . . Coney.
CONEY: I shouldn't have left him. I shouldn't have left him. Mingo.
DOCTOR: What?
CONEY: *(Turning.)* I should have stayed with him.
DOCTOR: If you'd stayed with him the maps would be lost. The maps were your job and the job comes first.
CONEY: So to hell with Finch!
DOCTOR: Finch knew he had to get those maps. He told you to take them and go, didn't he? Didn't he, Coney?
CONEY: He's dead.
DOCTOR: Didn't he say: Take the maps and get out of here? *(Pause.)*
CONEY: I shouldn't have left him.
DOCTOR: Coney, take the maps and get out of here!
CONEY: No, Finch.
DOCTOR: Take them and beat it. Go on, will you?
CONEY: Finch—are you sure—
DOCTOR: Go on! *(A slight pause.* CONEY *slowly raises himself up on his arms.* DOCTOR *watches him tensely.* CONEY *moves as though to get off bed.)* Go on! *(*CONEY *starts to make effort to get off bed. Then slowly, he sinks back, shaking his head pitifully.)*
CONEY: *(Pathetically.)* I can't. I can't.
DOCTOR: Coney . . . go on!

CONEY: I can't, Doc. I'm sorry. *(A slight pause.* DOCTOR *takes a new tack now.)*

DOCTOR: Coney . . . remember when Finch was shot?

CONEY: Yeah. I remember.

DOCTOR: When you heard that shot and saw he was hit, what did you think of?

CONEY: I—I got a bad feeling.

DOCTOR: But what did you think of, Coney? At that moment, what went through your mind?

CONEY: I didn't want to leave him.

DOCTOR: What did you think of at that instant, Coney?

CONEY: He told me to leave him.

DOCTOR: Coney. Listen. A shot! You turn. *(Slaps his hands together sharply.)* You turn now. You see it's Finch.

CONEY: Finch!

DOCTOR: What are you thinking of, Coney? *(No answer.)* Coney, what just went through your mind?

CONEY: I . . . I . . .

DOCTOR: What?

CONEY: I didn't want to leave him.

DOCTOR: Coney—

CONEY: But he said to leave him! He said to take the maps and beat it. It wasn't because I was yellow. It was because he said to go. Finch said to go!

DOCTOR: You were right to go. You were right to go, Coney.

CONEY: They didn't think so.

DOCTOR: How do you know?

CONEY: I know. I could tell that T.J.—

DOCTOR: Did he say anything?

CONEY: No.

DOCTOR: Did the Major say anything? Did Mingo say anything?

CONEY: No.

DOCTOR: Of course not. Because you were right to leave. You did what you had to do: you saved the maps. That's what you had to do, Coney.

CONEY: *(Plaintively.)* Was it? Was it really?

DOCTOR: Of course it was, son. It was the only thing you could do.

(Pause.)

CONEY: We did come to get the maps.
DOCTOR: Sure.
CONEY: And I saved them.
DOCTOR: Yes.
CONEY: I saved them . . . But Finch made them and . . . and . . . now . . .
DOCTOR: Coney, you had to leave him, you know that.
CONEY: Yes.
DOCTOR: You can't blame yourself.
CONEY: No . . . Only . . .
DOCTOR: Only what?
CONEY: I still got that feeling.
DOCTOR: What feeling?
CONEY: I don't know. That—that bad feeling.
DOCTOR: Did you first get it when you heard that shot? When you saw it was Finch who was hit?
CONEY: I—I'm not sure.
DOCTOR: Did it come back stronger when you found you couldn't walk?
CONEY: I—think so.
DOCTOR: When was that, Coney? When did you find you couldn't walk?
CONEY: It was . . . It was . . . I don't know.
DOCTOR: Think.
CONEY: I'm trying to.
DOCTOR: Why did it happen? Why couldn't you walk?
CONEY: I—I can't remember.
DOCTOR: Why can't you walk now?
CONEY: I—I don't know. I just can't.
DOCTOR: Why?
CONEY: I don't know. I think it started when—when—
DOCTOR: When what, Coney?
CONEY: When—when—
DOCTOR: When what, Coney?
CONEY: Oh, gee, Doc, I'm afraid I'm gonna cry.
DOCTOR: Go on, son. Cry if you want to.
CONEY: But guys don't cry. You shouldn't cry.
DOCTOR: Let it out, son. Let it all out.
CONEY: No, no, I don't want to. I cried when Finch—
DOCTOR: When Finch what?
CONEY: When he—when . . .
DOCTOR: When you left him?

CONEY: No. No, it was after that. Long after that. I'd been waiting for him.

DOCTOR: Where? *(Lights start to fade.)*

CONEY: In the clearing. The clearing by the beach. We were all there. Waiting. Nothing to do but wait and listen to those lousy birds. And all the time, I was wondering about Finch, waiting for Finch, hoping that . . .

(The stage is dark now. Through the last, there have been the faint sounds of crickets and jungle birds.)

Scene 2

SCENE: *Another clearing. The Pacific Island. This clearing is smaller than the other, there is more of a feeling of being hemmed in. The trees, bushes and vines at the edge are thicker, closer, darker. At the rear, just* L. *of* C., *however, there is the suggestion of a path. This leads to the beach. It is late afternoon, but it is hot and quite dark. Before the lights come up, we again hear the screech of birds. This continues intermittently through the scene. Although the men reach a high excitement pitch in this scene, they never yell. Their voices are tight and tense, but they remain aware of where they are and of the danger.*

AT RISE: CONEY *is peering anxiously through trees,* R. T.J. *is sitting fairly near him, drinking from his canteen.* MINGO *is down* L. *sitting back against some equipment while the* MAJOR, *who kneels next to him, loosens tourniquet on his arm. All the men have removed their packs, but have their rifles ready.*

CONEY: We ought to be able to hear him coming.
T.J.: If we could hear him, the Japs could hear him. Finch isn't that dumb.

(MAJOR *takes out his knife and slashes* MINGO*'s sleeve.)*

MINGO: Bleeding pretty bad.
MAJOR: Not too bad.
T.J.: *(To* CONEY.*)* You make me hot just standing. Why

don't you sit down? *(No answer.)* Listen, if Finch is busy ducking them, it'll take him time to get here.

CONEY: *(Coldly.)* He was hit.

MINGO: How's it look, Major?

MAJOR: A little messy.

MINGO: *(Struggling to take his first-aid kit off his web belt with one hand.)* This damn first-aid kit is more—

MAJOR: Let me.

T.J.: *(To* CONEY.*)* You don't know how bad he was hit?

CONEY: No.

T.J.: Ah, come on and relax, Coney. *(Holds out his canteen.)* Have a drink.

CONEY: *(Reaching for his own canteen.)* I've got some. I wouldn't want you to catch anything, T.J. *(He drinks from his own canteen.* MAJOR *starts to sprinkle sulfa over* MINGO's *wound.* MINGO *turns his face and looks toward* CONEY.*)*

MINGO: *(To* CONEY.*)* Open mine for me, will you, kiddo?

CONEY: *(Holding out his own.)* Here.

MINGO: Thanks. *(He drinks.)*

MAJOR: *(Looking at* MINGO's *wound.)* I think you've got two slugs in there.

CONEY: How's it feel, Mingo?

MINGO: Fine. Ready to be lopped off.

CONEY: That's charming.

T.J.: Delightful. *(*CONEY *shoots him a look.)*

MINGO: *(To* CONEY.*)* Quit worrying, kiddo. Finch knows the way here.

MAJOR: Sure. He drew the maps. *(*MAJOR *starts to bandage* MINGO's *wound.)*

CONEY: He might think we're out there on the beach.

MAJOR: The beach is too open. He knows we wouldn't wait there.

MINGO: Anyway, he'd have to come through here to— *(He gasps.)*

MAJOR: Sorry.

MINGO: That's okay.

T.J.: I was just thinking. If the Japs spot Finch, they might let him go—thinking he'd lead them to us.

CONEY: Finch wouldn't lead any Japs to us.

T.J.: But if he didn't know.

CONEY: He'd know. And he'd never give us away! *(He turns and walks back to his watching position by trees.)*

T.J.: I didn't say he would deliberately. For Chrissake, you get so—

MINGO: Hang up, T.J.

MAJOR: And keep your voices down . . . How's that, Mingo?

MINGO: Feels okay. *(Attempt at lightness.)* It ought to do till they amputate.

MAJOR: Amputate?

MINGO: Just a bad joke, Major.

MAJOR: I'll say it is. That sulfa should prevent infection.

MINGO: Sure.

MAJOR: And if you loosen the tourniquet every twenty minutes—

MINGO: I know. I'm just building it up. *(Bird screams.)* On your way, vulture. No meat today.

MAJOR: The plane'll be here in about an hour, Mingo. You can be in the hospital tomorrow.

CONEY: *(Turning.)* Major—suppose Finch isn't here?

MAJOR: What?

CONEY: *(Coming closer.)* Suppose Finch isn't here when the plane comes?

MAJOR: He'll be here.

CONEY: But suppose he isn't?

MAJOR: We'll worry about that when the time comes.

MINGO: What would we do, though?

MAJOR: I said we'll worry about that when the time comes. *(Pause.)* Lord, it's sticky.

MINGO: *(To* CONEY.*)* He's got over an hour yet, Coney.

CONEY: You know darn well if he's going to get here, he'll turn up in the next few minutes or not at all. *(Pause.)*

T.J.: I don't need a shower. I'm giving myself one.

MINGO: That's part of the charm of the South Seas.

T.J.: I once took a cruise in these waters.

MINGO: I once set up a travel booklet about them. I was a linotyper after I had to quit college. You learn a lot of crap setting up type. I learned about the balmy blue Pacific. Come to the Heavenly Isles! An orchid on every bazoom—and two bazooms on every babe. I'd like to find the gent who wrote that booklet. I'd like to find him now and make him come to his goddam Heavenly Isles! *(Slight pause.)*

T.J.: You know—if they hit Finch bad . . .

MINGO: Shut up. *(He tests his arm, trying to see how well he can move it. He winces.)*
MAJOR: It'll be all right, Mingo.
MINGO: I wonder how a one-armed linotyper would make out.
CONEY: Major . . . I gotta go look for him.
MAJOR: Finch knows the path, Coney.
CONEY: Yeah, but maybe he—

(He cuts off as T.J., *who is looking off* R., *suddenly brings up his gun. Others grab theirs and wait tensely, watching* T.J. *He holds for a moment, staring into trees, then a bird screams. He lowers his gun.)*

T.J.: Sorry.
MAJOR: What was it?
T.J.: Animal, bird, something. I don't know. Since I came up with that cheerful idea of Japs following Finch—sorry.
MAJOR: Forget it. It's better to be over-alert than to be caught napping.
MINGO: I wonder if the squints know how many of us there are.
MAJOR: Not yet. And I don't think they know where we are, either. *(Walks over to* CONEY.*)* That's why you can't go look for him, Coney. If they've got him—well, go in there and they'll get you too. And us along with you.
CONEY: I should've stayed with him.
MAJOR: You had to get those maps back and you did. Now we've got to get off this island so we can bring those maps back. That comes first.
CONEY: So—to hell with Finch.
MINGO: Kid, the Major's right. We've got to take care of the job first.
MAJOR: Look, Coney—
CONEY: Yeah. I know. I know.
T.J.: I wish we were the hell out of here. . . . All of us. *(Slight pause.)* I don't suppose there's anything we can do.
MINGO: Sure. You know what we can do. We can wait.
T.J.: That's all you ever do in this man's army.
MINGO: *(Dryly.)* What man's army?

T.J.: You wait for chow, you wait for mail, you wait for pay. And when you're not waiting for that, you wait for something to wait for.

MINGO: Yeah. We wait. And back there, in those lovely forty-eight States—

(A scream from some distance off R.*)*

CONEY: What was that? *(Slight pause.)*

T.J.: Ah, a bird.

CONEY: That was no bird.

MINGO: Coney, you're just—

CONEY: That was no bird.

T.J.: A cigar to the boy with the ears.

CONEY: That was no bird! Listen! *(Slight pause. A bird.)* No. Listen!

MAJOR: Ease up, Coney. I know you—

(The scream again. And this time it is recognizable as)

CONEY: It's Finch! He's yelling for me! *(He picks up his gun and starts for bushes.* MAJOR *grabs him.)*

MAJOR: Coney—

CONEY: You heard him!

MAJOR: Yes, but—

CONEY: Please, sir. They're killing him. They're killing Finch!

MAJOR: They're not killing him and they won't kill him.

CONEY: Not them. Not much!

MAJOR: I tell you he won't be killed. It's just a trick. They're purposely making him yell.

CONEY: Please, Major, let me—

MAJOR: *(Holding tight.)* Coney, you can't go in there! They're sticking him just to make him yell like that. Just to make us come after him.

CONEY: All right!

MAJOR: But when we do—they'll get us. Don't you understand?

CONEY: I don't care!

MAJOR: Coney, listen to me. They're just trying to find out where we are. They're just trying to get us. It's a trick.

CONEY: I don't care, sir. Let me go, please!
MAJOR: Coney, will you listen to me?

(FINCH screams again.)

CONEY: You listen to him! *(With a savage jerk, he breaks away from* MAJOR *and starts into bushes.)*
MINGO: Coney! Stop trying to be a goddam hero! *(CONEY stops just as he is about to go into jungle. He doesn't turn around to face* MINGO, *who stands where he is and talks very fast.)* It's just a trick. A dirty, lousy trick. Sure, they're jabbing Finch and making him yell. But if you go after him—they'll kill him. And you too. *(CONEY turns around slowly.)* There isn't a lousy thing we can do, kid. *(Slight pause.* CONEY *walks toward* MINGO *very slowly, then suddenly hurls his rifle to the ground and sits by it.)*
CONEY: So—to hell with Finch.
MINGO: *(Going to him.)* No.
CONEY: Let them make hamburger out of him.
MINGO: Kid, there's nothing we can do.
CONEY: You can— *(FINCH screams again.)* O Christ!
MINGO: Don't listen. Try not to listen. You know—the way you do with guns. You don't hear them after a while.
CONEY: That isn't guns; it's Finch!
MINGO: Pretend it's just yelling. Hell, you ought to be used to yelling and noise. You're a city kid.
CONEY: What?
MINGO: You come from Pittsburgh, don't you? *(FINCH screams again.)* Don't you, Coney?
CONEY: Mingo, they're killing him.
MINGO: That bar you and he were going to have—was it going to be in Pittsburgh? *(FINCH screams.)* Was it going to be in Pittsburgh, Coney?
CONEY: Finch!
MINGO: Kid, it's not so bad if he's yelling. You got to be alive to yell.
CONEY: Major, please—
MINGO: Don't listen. Tell me about the bar.
CONEY: Major, let me—
MINGO: Talk.
CONEY: I can't.

MINGO: Remember that Jap knife I picked up? The one you wanted to—

CONEY: Mingo—let me—

MINGO: Say, whatever happened that night when you were on guard and—

CONEY: Mingo—

MINGO: You like poetry?

CONEY: Mingo, he's being—

(FINCH screams.)

MINGO: My wife writes poetry, Coney. Remember you always wanted to hear some?

CONEY: Please—

MINGO: Didn't you always want to hear some? Listen.

(FINCH screams again, weaker now.)

CONEY: Oh dear God!

MINGO: Listen. *(Quickly.)*

"We are only two and yet our howling
Can encircle the world's end.
Frightened,

(FINCH screams—weakly.)

you are my only friend.

(Slower now.)

And frightened, we are everyone.
Someone must take a stand.
Coward, take my coward's hand."

(Long pause. They sit waiting. Slowly, CONEY stretches out, buries his face in the ground and starts to cry. A bird screams. T.J. looks up.)

T.J.: *(Quietly.)* Lousy birds. *(T.J. begins to whistle "Shoo, Fly" very sweetly. Long pause. Then, MINGO gets up.)*

MAJOR: Helluva thing.

MINGO: Yeah. In the Marianas, I saw a fellow after the

Japs had gotten hold of him. They'd put pieces of steel through his cheeks—here—you know. Like a bit for a horse.

T.J.: You couldn't talk about something pleasant, could you?

MINGO: Sorry.

T.J.: We'll all have a chance to find out what the squints do if we keep sitting here.

MAJOR: Well, the plane won't come till after it gets dark and we can't dig up the canoes till sundown.

T.J.: There ought to be something we can do besides sit around here on our butts.

MAJOR: Suppose you go down the beach and see if the canoes are still where we buried them.

T.J.: Go out on the beach now? It's too light!

MAJOR: The canoes are right at the edge of the trees. You don't have to go out in the open.

T.J.: But even if they're not there, there's nothing I can do about it.

MAJOR: You can find out! Now you heard me. Get going, T.J.! *(*T.J. *hesitates, then picks up his rifle and starts upstage.)* If you run into trouble, fire four quick shots.

*(*T.J. *doesn't answer but storms off through path up* R. *During following, the lights begin to dim as the sun goes down.)*

MINGO: I think the big executive is a little afraid.

MAJOR: I guess he doesn't like to take orders from me.

MINGO: He doesn't like much of anything, Major.

MAJOR: Does he— *(Hesitates.)* Mingo, does he make cracks about the Jews?

MINGO: Yes, Major. He does. He does indeed.

MAJOR: To Coney?

MINGO: Coney's a Jew.

MAJOR: Funny. I never think of him as a Jew.

MINGO: Yeah, it is funny. I never think of you as a Gentile.

(Slight pause. Then MAJOR *speaks awkwardly—in a low voice.)*

MAJOR: Guess I said the wrong thing.
MINGO: I'm sorry, Major. I shouldn't've—
MAJOR: There are a lot of things you know, Mingo, that I guess I should but I—
MINGO: Look, sir, I didn't—
MAJOR: Wait. I'd like to get this off my chest. There are a lot of things I'd like to get off my chest. *(A pause.)* For one thing, I'd like to thank you, Mingo.
MINGO: For what?
MAJOR: For the rumpus just now with Coney . . . when you stopped him from running off half-cocked after Finch. . . .
MINGO: I just repeated what you'd said.
MAJOR: Yeah, but he— Well, you stopped him. Thanks.
MINGO: Nuts.
MAJOR: I shouldn't have needed you or anybody else to—
MINGO: It's no crime to get help, Major.
MAJOR: No. But it's lousy to think you need it. I know you fellows—well, take T.J. I know he thinks I'm too young to give him orders.
MINGO: He'd think God was too young.
MAJOR: I didn't know what T.J. was like before we started. I guess I should have.
MINGO: Yes. I think you should have.
MAJOR: I know what you think, too.
MINGO: What do you mean?
MAJOR: An officer's got to have the respect of his men. He's no good otherwise, Mingo.
MINGO: Depends what you think respect is.
MAJOR: You think I care about the job and not about Finch. I care about Finch! I do now! But the job comes first. And I know my job, Mingo. I know it darn well!
MINGO: Okay, sir.
MAJOR: This isn't what I started out to say at all. *(Pause.)* Look—I'm a Major . . . but I'm twenty-six. I don't know all the answers and I don't think I know 'em. Judas, I'm not even sure what this lousy war is all about. There are fifty million things I don't know that I wish I did. But I'm a Major. I've got to have the respect of my men. And there's only one way I can get it: by knowing my job and running it.
MINGO: Nobody wants to run the show, Major. Maybe

T.J.—but he's a first-class crud, anyway. We just want the same thing, too.

MAJOR: What?

MINGO: Respect. For us—as guys.

MAJOR: But an officer—

MINGO: An officer's a guy, isn't he, Major?

MAJOR: Yeah.

MINGO: Okay. All we want is for you—every once in a while to—talk to us—like this.

MAJOR: *(Smiling.)* Okay.

MINGO: *(Smiling.)* Okay.

*(*MAJOR *takes out a pack of cigarettes and holds one out for* MINGO. *Then he lights it for him, carefully shielding the flame.)*

MAJOR: How's the arm?

MINGO: Lousy.

MAJOR: Want me to change the bandage?

MINGO: No. I just want to get out of here. Thanks. *(For the cigarette.)*

MAJOR: Don't worry about it so. It'll be okay.

MINGO: I know, but I—well, I'd kinda hate to go back to the States anyway. And to go back with a—well, I guess I have too good an imagination.

MAJOR: I think you're just worried about going back to your wife with—well, a bum wing, say.

MINGO: *(Slightly bitter.)* Oh, my wife wouldn't care.

MAJOR: No. She sounds like a fine girl.

MINGO: How do you know?

MAJOR: From that poem. Wasn't that hers?

MINGO: What po— Oh. That. Yeah, that was hers.

MAJOR: Most people think it's sissy stuff but—I like poetry. I was trying to remember that last part. "Frightened, we are—"

MINGO: *(Reeling it off.)* "Everyone. Someone must make a stand. Coward, take my coward's hand."

MAJOR: I like that.

MINGO: Sure. It's great. My wife's a great little writer. Pretty, too. It's just a pity she doesn't read her own stuff once in a while.

MAJOR: What do you mean?

MINGO: She writes good letters, too. I remember the first one, the first one she wrote me in the Army. "My darling darling," it began. She likes repetition. "My darling darling, I will never again use the word love—except to say I love you."

MAJOR: That's nice.

MINGO: Oh, that's very nice. Almost as nice as her last letter. I can remember that one, too. I got that about a week ago. That began: "My darling, this is the hardest letter I've ever had to write. But it's only fair to be honest with you and tell you that—" *(He is too choked up to go on. Slight pause.)*

MAJOR: *(Embarrassed.)* Want another cigarette?

MINGO: No . . . thanks.

MAJOR: The sun's going down.

MINGO: They call that the G.I. letter, you know. Because there are so many of them.

MAJOR: I know.

MINGO: I can understand. Hell, I'm away and she meets another guy. But—Christ!

MAJOR: Well . . .

MINGO: It makes me want to hate all civilians. Then I remember I used to be one myself. A couple of million years ago. . . . Hell, they can't all be bad.

MAJOR: Of course not.

MINGO: Then I remember that we've got stinkers here too. Like T.J. And so I try to stay on the beam. It's kind of hard though, when I think of that bitch and what— *(He cuts off as there is a rustling noise from bushes* R. *They freeze. Rustling gets louder.* MAJOR *graps his rifle and, at same time,* CONEY *sits up with his rifle ready.)* T.J.

MAJOR: He wouldn't be coming from there.

(Rustling gets still louder. And then, in the fading light, T.J. *appears, scrambling through brush.)*

T.J.: The canoes are still there. I scratched holy hell out of myself though.

(Rifles are lowered.)

MAJOR: Why didn't you come back by the trail?
T.J.: I got lost. *(To* CONEY.*)* When did you wake up?
CONEY: Just now.
MAJOR: Are you hungry, Coney? Why don't you eat something?
CONEY: K ration isn't kosher.

(Slight pause. From now on, it begins to get dark rapidly.)

MINGO: The birds have shut up anyway.
MAJOR: *(Looking up.)* I think it's dark enough to dig up the canoes and get 'em ready.
MINGO: What about the gear?
MAJOR: There's no point in taking it until the canoes are ready . . . Only—we need someone to watch it. In case.
MINGO: I don't mind.
T.J.: How's your arm?
MINGO: My arm?
MAJOR: You couldn't use your rifle if—
CONEY: *(Getting up suddenly.)* I'll stay.
MAJOR: Oh, thanks, Coney, but you'd better—
CONEY: *(Harshly.)* What's wrong with me staying?
MAJOR: *(Quietly.)* Okay. Thanks.
MINGO: Maybe I'd better stay, too, Major. With this bum wing, I won't be able to—
CONEY: I'm not afraid to stay alone, Mingo!
MAJOR: You can help lift the canoes with your left arm anyway, Mingo.
MINGO: Sure.
MAJOR: Let's go. *(He starts for path up* L.*, followed by* T.J. *and* MINGO. *Just before he goes into trees, he turns and calls to* CONEY.*)* Four quick shots if anything happens, Coney.
CONEY: Yes, sir.
MINGO: Nothing will, kiddo. See you.

(He disappears after MAJOR *and* T.J. *into jungle. By now, the sun has gone down altogether. The jungle that rims the stage is pitch black, but there is pale light* C. *in clearing, dimming out to the edges.* CONEY *does not look after others when they go. He stands still for a moment, then takes out cigarette. He holds it, then suddenly shoves*

it in his mouth, holds rifle ready and whirls around. He listens sharply a moment, then slowly turns. His shoulders slump, rifle comes down, and he takes cigarette out of his mouth. He walks to pile of equipment, looks at it and is about to sit down when suddenly he freezes. Cigarette drops to ground, rifle comes up. Very slowly, he starts to turn and, when he is halfway around, leaps like a cat to dimly lighted edge of clearing, R. *He holds there for a moment, listening. Then leans forward a little.)*

CONEY: *(Softly.)* Finch? *(He moves closer to trees. Plaintively.)* Finch? *(He listens a moment, then suddenly whirls so that his gun is pointed up* R. *He whirls again so that it is pointed up* L. *He darts back across stage to pile of equipment and stands there breathing hard, moving rifle back and forth in a small arc. Then, suddenly, he hurls rifle down in front of him and sinks to his haunches.)* Your name is Coen and you're a— *(His voice cracks. He covers his face with his hands. He remains that way for a long moment, then sinks to ground, bracing himself with his* L. *hand and covering his face with his* R. *A second later, bushes down* R. *begin to rustle softly.* CONEY *doesn't hear this. Rustling gets louder; bushes move; then a body begins to crawl out very slowly; just the shape is discernible in the dim light by trees, but soon it is apparent that the body is not crawling, but dragging itself. It gets closer to lighted area and stops. A hand comes up and gestures—as though the man were trying to talk and couldn't. Finally, with a great effort, the body drags itself farther into the light. The clothes are slashed and splotched with blood and the face is battered—but it's* FINCH. *He sees* CONEY *and tries again to call to him. Again, his hand comes out in a pathetically futile gesture, he tries desperately hard to speak—but no sound comes. He tries to move farther but can't. Finally, in an outburst of impotent fury, he tries again to call, and now his voice shoots out in a shrill scream.)*

FINCH: Coney!

(Like a bullet, CONEY *drops his hands. His face is wide with terror, his body is rigid. He cannot believe he really heard anything. Then slowly, slowly, his head turns. He*

looks straight at FINCH*—but does not believe he sees him.)*

CONEY: *(Plaintively, with a suggestion of a tear.)* Finch? . . . Is that you, Finch?

FINCH: Coney!

CONEY: *(Frantically, he scrambles over and puts arm around* FINCH*, who groans in pain.)* Finch! Oh, Christ, Finch! Finch! *(He reaches for his canteen, quickly opens it and props* FINCH's *head in his lap. As he starts to give him water, he talks.)* Oh, I'm glad! I'm so glad, Finch! You all right? You're going to be all right now, Finch. You're going to be all right now— *(*FINCH *cannot hold the water and spews it up.)* Easy, fellow. Easy, Finch. *(*FINCH *begins to retch,* CONEY *holds his head.)* Oh, that's charming. That's really charming. You go right ahead. That's fine and charming, Finch. *(*FINCH *has stopped now and tries to talk.)*

FINCH: *(Just getting the word out.)* Delightful.

CONEY: Oh, you bastard! You damn son of a bitch bastard! I might've known they couldn't finish you off, you damn Arizona bastard. Let me see what they— *(He touches* FINCH, *trying to see his wounds.* FINCH *gasps in pain.)* I'm sorry. I'm sorry, kid, but I— What? What, Finch? I can't hear you. What? *(He bends down, his ear close to* FINCH's *mouth.)* Oh, for Chrissake, sure the lousy maps are all right. We've got to get you fixed up— *(Again he touches* FINCH *and* FINCH *groans.)* All right. Just lie still. The guys are getting the canoes now. The plane'll be here soon and you'll be back to the base in no time. You can goldbrick out the rest of the war in the hospital, you lucky bastard! You'll probably get a slew of medals, to say nothing of a big fat Purple Heart. And you'll go home and leave me stuck here. Hey, did I tell you I missed you, you jerk? O Jesus, I'm so glad, Finch. *(*FINCH's *head suddenly rolls over and flops to one side.)* I'm so glad, I'm so . . . *(He stops. He is absolutely quiet for a moment. Then, begging.)* Finch? Finch? Ah, Finch, please don't be dead! *(He turns* FINCH's *body slightly and ducks his head down so he can listen to* FINCH's *heart. A pause, then, with his head still on* FINCH's *chest, he says softly.)* O God. O God. O God. O God. O God. *(His voice cracks* *on the last and he begins to cry softly. Slowly, he straightens up. He is whimpering very quietly.* FINCH'S *body rolls back, stomach down.* CONEY *looks at it for a long moment and then, suddenly, stops crying and with a violent, decisive, brutal gesture, shoves body so it rolls over on its back. He stares at the horror he sees for a few seconds. Then, swiftly, he lifts the head into his lap with one hand and, with a long arclike sweep, cradles the torso with his other arm and bends across it. An anguished groan.)* Oh, no, Finch! *(He begins to rock the body as though it were a baby.)* Oh, no, Finch! Oh, no, no, no!

(Just at this moment, a voice cracks out from some distance off R. *It is a Jap voice.)*

1ST JAP: Hey, Yank! Come out and fight!

*(*CONEY *looks up sharply, cradling the head closer. From farther up* R. *comes another voice.)*

2ND JAP: Hey, Yank! Come out and fight!

*(*CONEY*'s head turns in direction of second voice.)*

CONEY: Finch, they're after you again! But I won't leave you this time. I promise I won't, Finch.

3RD JAP: Come and fight, yellow bastard.

CONEY: I won't leave you, Finch. I promise, I promise, I promise! *(He takes his bayonet out and starts to scoop up the ground furiously. At same time,* JAPS *continue yelling. Their shouts overlap with variations of the same cry. As he digs.)* Don't worry, Finch. I told you I wouldn't let them get you. I promised, didn't I? Didn't I? And I won't. Because I'm not a yellow bastard. I won't leave you, Finch. *(He is digging feverishly now, yelling is coming closer,* MAJOR *rushes on from path upstage, followed by* MINGO.*)*

MAJOR: Coney!

MINGO: He's got Finch!

MAJOR: *(To* MINGO.*)* Get the map case. *(*MINGO *quickly searches through pile of equipment for map case.* MA-

JOR *goes to* CONEY, *who is digging furiously.)* Coney, come on. We've got to—God, he's dead!

CONEY: They won't get him, though, Major. They want to but they won't. I'm going to bury him!

1ST JAP: Fight, you yellow bastard.

MAJOR: Bury— Listen, Coney, we— Coney, you can't bury him. We've got to get out of here.

3RD JAP: Heh! Yank, come out and fight.

MINGO: *(Coming over with map case.)* Got them, Major.
MAJOR: Coney—
MINGO: What's the matter with him?
MAJOR: Finch is dead and he's trying to bury him.

MINGO: O God! Coney, get up.

3RD JAP: Come out, you Yank bastard.

CONEY: I can't leave Finch.
MINGO: We'll take him. Come on. Get up.
CONEY: I can't leave Finch.
MINGO: Get up, Coney.
CONEY: Finch—
MINGO: Don't worry about him.
MAJOR: We'll take him.
MINGO: Come on, Coney.

(CONEY *tries to get up. He drags himself a few inches, but he cannot get up.)*

CONEY: I *can't.*
MAJOR: What do you mean you can't?

CONEY: I can't move, Major. I can't move!

3RD JAP: Yank, come out and fight.

MINGO: Holy God! Try.
CONEY: I am—but I can't.
MINGO: Now stop that. You've got to get out of here.

CONEY: I can't, Mingo. I can't walk. I can't move.
MINGO: Were you shot? Were you hit?
CONEY: No.

2ND JAP: Come out and fight.
1ST JAP: Yank, come out and fight.
2ND JAP: Fight, you yellow bastard.

MAJOR: Then why can't you walk?
CONEY: *(Building to hysteria now.)* I don't know!

MINGO: What's the matter with you?

3RD JAP: Yank, come out and fight.

CONEY: I don't know!
MINGO: Coney—
CONEY: I don't know! I don't know! I don't know!

(He is crying wildly now, MINGO *and* MAJOR *are trying to lift him, and the screaming of the* JAPS *is getting louder and louder. The* JAPS *continue through the blackness and gradually fade out.)*

Scene 3

SCENE: *Hospital Room. Pacific Base.*

Before lights come up, we hear CONEY *counting.*

CONEY: 85—84—83—82—81—80—79—
DOCTOR: 78.
CONEY: 78—77—76—75. *(Lights are up now.* CONEY *is on bed,* DOCTOR *sitting by him watching needle.)* 74—73—72—73—7— *(*DOCTOR *withdraws needle and gets up.)*
DOCTOR: Coney, do you remember how you got off that island?
CONEY: I think—Mingo. Something about Mingo.
DOCTOR: Yes. Mingo picked you up and carried you out.
CONEY: I—I remember water. Being in the canoe on water. There were bullets.
DOCTOR: Some of the Japs fired machine guns when they realized what was happening.
CONEY: I think maybe I passed out because—it's all kind of dark. Then I'm in the plane.
DOCTOR: T.J. lifted you in.
CONEY: T.J.?
DOCTOR: Yes.
CONEY: But Mingo . . .
DOCTOR: Mingo couldn't lift you in alone. His right arm was no good.
CONEY: Oh, yeah . . . yeah.
DOCTOR: That's all you remember, though?
CONEY: I remember being taken off the plane.
DOCTOR: I mean on the island. That's all you remember of what happened on the island?

CONEY: Yes.
DOCTOR: Then why can't you walk, Coney?
CONEY: What?
DOCTOR: You weren't shot, were you?
CONEY: No.
DOCTOR: You didn't break your legs, did you?
CONEY: No.
DOCTOR: Then why can't you walk, Coney?
CONEY: I don't know. I don't know.
DOCTOR: But you said you remember everything that happened.
CONEY: I—yes. Yes.
DOCTOR: Do you remember waking up in the hospital? Do you remember waking up with that bad feeling?
CONEY: Yes. *(Slight pause.* DOCTOR *walks next to bed.)*
DOCTOR: Coney, when did you first get that bad feeling?
CONEY: It was— I don't know.
DOCTOR: Coney— *(He sits down.)* Coney, did you first get it right after Finch was shot?
CONEY: No.
DOCTOR: What did you think of when Finch was shot?
CONEY: I don't know.
DOCTOR: You said you remember everything that happened. And you do. You remember that, too. You remember how you felt when Finch was shot, don't you, Coney? Don't you?
CONEY: *(Sitting bolt upright.)* Yes. *(Long pause. His hands twist his robe, then lie still. With dead, flat tones.)* When we were looking for the map case, he said—he started to say: You lousy yellow Jew bastard. He only said you lousy yellow jerk, but he started to say you lousy yellow Jew bastard. So I knew. I knew.
DOCTOR: You knew what?
CONEY: I knew he'd lied when—when he said he didn't care. When he said people were people to him. I knew he lied. I knew he hated me because I was a Jew so—I was glad when he was shot.

*(*DOCTOR *straightens up.)*

DOCTOR: Did you leave him there because you were glad?
CONEY: Oh, no!
DOCTOR: You got over it.

CONEY: I was—I was sorry I felt glad. I was ashamed.

DOCTOR: Did you leave him because you were ashamed?

CONEY: No.

DOCTOR: Because you were afraid?

CONEY: No.

DOCTOR: No. You left him because that was what you had to do. Because you were a good soldier. *(Pause.)* You left him and you ran through the jungle, didn't you?

CONEY: Yes.

DOCTOR: And you walked around in the clearing by the beach, didn't you?

CONEY: Yes.

DOCTOR: So your legs were all right.

CONEY: Yes.

DOCTOR: Then if anything did happen to your legs, it happened when Finch crawled back. And you say nothing happened to you then.

CONEY: I don't know.

DOCTOR: Did anything happen?

CONEY: I don't know. Maybe—maybe.

DOCTOR: But if anything did happen, you'd remember?

CONEY: I don't know.

DOCTOR: You *do* remember what happened when Finch crawled back, don't you? Don't you, Coney?

CONEY: *(Covers his face.)* Finch . . . Finch . . .

DOCTOR: Remember that. Think back to that, Coney. You were alone in the clearing and Finch crawled in.

CONEY: O God . . . O dear God . . .

DOCTOR: Remember. *(He gets up quickly, moves across room and in a cracked voice calls)* Coney!

CONEY: *(Plaintively—he turns sharply.)* Finch? . . . Finch?

DOCTOR: *(A cracked whisper.)* Coney . . .

CONEY: Oh, Finch, Finch! Is that you, Finch? *(He cradles an imaginary head in his lap and begins to rock back and forth.)* I'm so glad. I'm so glad, Finch! I'm so . . .

(He stops short, waits, then ducks his head down as though to listen to FINCH*'s heart. A moment, then he straightens up and then, with same decisive, brutal gesture as before, shoves imaginary body of* FINCH *so that it rolls over. He looks at it in horror, then* DOCTOR *calls out:)*

DOCTOR: Hey, Yank! Come out and fight!

CONEY: They won't get you, Finch. I won't leave you this time, I promise! *(He begins to pantomime digging feverishly.)*

DOCTOR: Come out and fight, Yank.

CONEY: I won't leave you this time! *(*DOCTOR *walks over deliberately and grabs* CONEY's *hand, stopping it in the middle of a digging motion.)*

DOCTOR: *(Curtly.)* What are you trying to bury him in, Coney? *(*CONEY *stops and stares up at him.)* This isn't earth, Coney. This is a bed. Feel it. It's a bed. Underneath is a floor, a wooden floor. Hear? *(He stamps.)* You can't bury Finch, Coney, because he isn't here. You're not on that island. You're in a hospital. You're in a hospital, Coney, and I'm your doctor. I'm your doctor!

(Pause.)

CONEY: Yes, sir.

DOCTOR: And you remember now, you remember that nothing happened to your legs at all, did it?

CONEY: No, sir.

DOCTOR: But you had to be carried here.

CONEY: Yes, sir.

DOCTOR: Why?

CONEY: Because I can't walk.

DOCTOR: Why can't you walk?

CONEY: I don't know.

DOCTOR: *I do.* It's because you didn't want to, isn't it, Coney? Because you knew if you couldn't walk, then you couldn't leave Finch. That's it, isn't it?

CONEY: I don't know.

DOCTOR: That must be it. Because there's nothing wrong with your legs. They're fine, healthy legs and you can walk. You can walk. You had a shock and you didn't want to walk. But you're over the shock and now you do want to walk, don't you? You do want to walk, don't you, Coney?

CONEY: Yes. Yes.

DOCTOR: Then get up and walk.

CONEY: I—can't.

DOCTOR: Yes, you can.

CONEY: No.
DOCTOR: Try.
CONEY: I can't.
DOCTOR: Try.
CONEY: I can't.
DOCTOR: Get up and walk! *(Pause.)* Coney, get up and walk! *(Pause.)* You lousy, yellow Jew bastard, get up and walk! *(At that,* CONEY *straightens up in rage. He is shaking, but he grips edge of bed and swings his feet over. He is in a white fury, and out of his anger comes this tremendous effort. Still shaking, he stands up, holds for a moment, glares at* DOCTOR. *Then, with his hands outstretched before him as though he is going to kill* DOCTOR, *he starts to walk. First one foot, then the other,* L., R., L.*—but he begins to cry violently and as he sinks to floor,* DOCTOR *moves forward swiftly and grabs him. Triumphantly.)* All right, son! All right!

CURTAIN

ACT III

Scene 1

SCENE: *Hospital Room. Two weeks later. There is a bright cheerful look about the room now. Window is open; sunlight streams in. Bed is pushed close against wall and has a neat, unused look. There is a typewriter on desk now.*

CONEY, *wearing a hospital "zoot suit," is seated at desk typing very laboriously. Door opens and* T.J. *comes in.* CONEY *stutters slightly in this scene when he is agitated.*

T.J.: Oh! Hi, Coney! *(A second's awkward pause.)*
MAJOR: *(Coming in.)* Coney! Gosh, it's good to see you, fellow!
CONEY: It's good to see you, Major.
T.J.: You're looking fine, just fine!
MAJOR: We've sure missed you. When are you coming back to us?
CONEY: I—don't know if I am, sir. I'm—working for the Doc now.
T.J.: Working?
CONEY: Yes. I type up his records and—sort of keep 'em straight for him.
MAJOR: Why, the dirty dog! Stealing my best man!
CONEY: *(With a smile.)* It's really not very much work, sir.
MAJOR: I didn't know you could type.
CONEY: Oh—hunt and peck.
T.J.: Well, it's great you're not a patient any more.
CONEY: I'm still a patient. In a way.
MAJOR: Do you—still get the—
CONEY: Shots? No. But the doc—well—he and I talk.

T.J.: Talk?

CONEY: Yes. Once a day.

T.J.: Why?

CONEY: Well, it's—part of the treatment.

T.J.: Brother, I'd like to be that kind of a patient.

CONEY: Maybe you should be.

MAJOR: *(Leaping in hastily.)* The doc's quite a guy, isn't he?

CONEY: Yes, sir. He— *(Slight note of appeal.)* he says I'm coming along fine.

MAJOR: Oh, anybody can see you are, can't they, T.J.?

T.J.: Sure.

MAJOR: We've got something to tell you that ought to put you right on top of the world. The island— *(He stops. Cautiously.)* You remember the island, Coney?

CONEY: *(Wry smile.)* Yes. I remember, Major.

MAJOR: It was invaded four days ago. And everything went off 100 percent perfect—thanks to our maps.

CONEY: Oh, that's swell.

MAJOR: We've gotten commendations a yard long.

T.J.: Wait till you get out of here! Your back's going to be sore from all the patting it's going to get!

MAJOR: The Doc wanted to tell you about it but . . . well . . .

T.J.: We felt since we were all in it together, Coney—

CONEY: Did you, T.J.?

T.J.: Sure. Weren't we?

CONEY: In a way, we were. And in a way, we weren't.

T.J.: Wait a minute, kid, don't forget how I . . .

CONEY: *(Getting a little unstable now.)* Don't you worry about my memory, T.J. The Doc fixed me up fine and it's all right.

T.J.: Sure, I know.

CONEY: Maybe it'd be better if I did forget a few things. If I forgot that— *(He breaks off as door opens and* DOCTOR *comes in.)*

DOCTOR: *(Kidding slightly.)* Well! Who said this was visiting hour?

MAJOR: We were looking for you, Doc. We wanted your permission to see Coney.

DOCTOR: *(Still the kidding tone.)* I'm afraid you can't have it.

MAJOR: *(Following suit.)* That's too bad. I guess we'd better run along, T.J.
DOCTOR: *(No smile now.)* Yes. I think you'd better.
MAJOR: Oh. I'm sorry, sir. I—
DOCTOR: That's okay. I'll tell you what. You're going to see Mingo this afternoon, aren't you?
MAJOR: Yes.
DOCTOR: Drop around after that.
MAJOR: Sure! Thanks, Doc. *(Turns to go.)* I'll see you later, Coney.
CONEY: Yes, sir.
T.J.: Take care, Coney.
CONEY: Yeah.
MAJOR: Thanks again, Doc.

(He and T.J. *go out.* CONEY *has edged toward desk when* DOCTOR *came in. Now, he goes behind it and sits down at typewriter.)*

DOCTOR: I'm sorry I had to run them out.
CONEY: *(Putting sheet of paper in typewriter.)* That's all right, sir. I didn't care.
DOCTOR: Nice boy, the Major.
CONEY: Yes, sir. *(He starts to type slowly.)*
DOCTOR: How'd you get on with T.J.?
CONEY: All right. *(A slight pause.)* No. Not really all right. He makes me think of things and I—want to jump at him.
DOCTOR: Why not? That's a good, healthy reaction.
CONEY: Honest, Doc?
DOCTOR: Of course. *(Indicating typing.)* Never mind that. This isn't your working period. It's mine.
CONEY: Now?
DOCTOR: Yes. Now.
CONEY: But we don't usually—
DOCTOR: *(Cutting him.)* I know. But we're going to work now. I'll tell you why later.
CONEY: Yes, sir. *(He gets up from behind desk and sits in chair* C.*)*
DOCTOR: How do you feel?
CONEY: All right.
DOCTOR: Did you dream last night?
CONEY: No.

DOCTOR: Good. The Major told you about the invasion?
CONEY: Yes.
DOCTOR: Well?
CONEY: I'm—afraid I didn't care very much, sir.
DOCTOR: You will. In time you'll feel that everything outside has some connection with you and everything in you has some connection with everything outside. . . . What bothers you now, Coney?
CONEY: That—feeling, sir.
DOCTOR: The bad feeling?
CONEY: Yes, sir.
DOCTOR: You still have it?
CONEY: *(Very low.)* Yes, sir.
DOCTOR: Yes, sir; yes, sir. Two weeks of psychotherapy and they expect—
CONEY: I'm sorry, sir. I try to get rid of it but—
DOCTOR: No, no, son. It's not your fault. I was just—come. We're going to talk about that bad feeling.
CONEY: Yes, sir.
DOCTOR: And we're going to get rid of it.
CONEY: Yes, sir.
DOCTOR: We are, Coney
CONEY: Yes, sir.
DOCTOR: *(Very gently.) We.* Not me. The two of us. I think we can do it, Coney.
CONEY: I wish we could, sir.
DOCTOR: I think we can. It's hard work. It's trying to cram the biggest thing in your life into a space this small. But I think we can do it. I want to try, Coney. I want to help you, Peter.

(Slight pause.)

CONEY: That's—the first time anybody's called me Peter since I've been in the Army. *(Pause.)* You're a right guy, Doc.
DOCTOR: I don't want you to think about anything except what I say now.
CONEY: Okay.
DOCTOR: Are you comfortable?
CONEY: Yes, sir.
DOCTOR: You still have that bad feeling?
CONEY: Yes, sir.

DOCTOR: It's sort of a guilty feeling.

CONEY: Yes, sir.

DOCTOR: When did you feel it first, Peter? Right after Finch was shot, wasn't it?

CONEY: Yes.

DOCTOR: And what did you think later?

CONEY: I thought I— Well, you know, Doc.

DOCTOR: Tell me.

CONEY: I thought I felt—like you said: guilty, because I left him. But then—then you told me what Mingo said—what they all said. That I did what I had to do. I had to leave Finch to get the maps back.

DOCTOR: And you know that's right now, don't you? You know that's what you have to do in a war.

CONEY: Yes, sir.

DOCTOR: But you still have that guilty feeling.

CONEY: Yeah.

DOCTOR: Then it can't come from what you thought at all. It can't come from leaving Finch, can it, Peter?

CONEY: No, but—what did it come from?

DOCTOR: Coney, the first time you were in this room, the first time you were under that drug, do you know what you said about Finch? You said: I hate him.

CONEY: But I don't, I don't!

DOCTOR: I know you don't. And later on, you said that when Finch was shot—maybe you can remember yourself now. How did you feel when Finch was shot, Peter? *(Pause.)*

CONEY: *(Low, very ashamed.)* I was glad.

DOCTOR: Why were you glad?

CONEY: I thought—

DOCTOR: Go on, son.

CONEY: I thought he was going to call me a lousy yellow Jew bastard. So—I was glad he got shot.

DOCTOR: Peter, I want you to listen hard to what I'm going to tell you. I want you to listen harder than you ever listened to anything in your whole life. Peter, *every soldier in this world* who sees a buddy get shot has that one moment when he feels glad. Yes, Peter, every single one. Because deep underneath he thinks: I'm glad it wasn't me. I'm glad *I'm* still alive.

CONEY: But—oh, no. Because what I thought was—

DOCTOR: I know. You thought you were glad because

Finch was going to make a crack about your being a Jew. Maybe later, you were glad because of that. But at that moment you were glad it wasn't *you* who was shot. You were glad *you* were still alive. A lot of fellows think a lot of things later. But every single soldier, every single one of them has that moment when he thinks: I'm glad it wasn't me! . . . And that's what you thought. . . . *(Gently.)* You see the whole point of this, Peter? You've been thinking you had some special kind of guilt. But you've got to realize something. You're the same as anybody else. You're no different, son, no different at all.

CONEY: I'm a Jew.

DOCTOR: This, Peter, this sensitivity has been like a disease in you. It was there before anything happened on that island. I only wish to God I had time to really dig and find out where and when and why. But it's been a disease. Oh, it's not your fault; the germ comes from the world we try to live in. And it's spread by T.J. By people at home in our own country. But if you can cure yourself, you can help cure them and you've got to, Pete, you've got to!

CONEY: Okay, if you say so.

DOCTOR: You can and you must, Pete. Believe me, you can.

CONEY: I believe you, Doc. *(He gets up and starts to desk.)*

DOCTOR: Peter . . .

CONEY: Are we through, Doc?

DOCTOR: Peter, don't you understand?

CONEY: Yes! Sure! I understand! I understand up here! But here— *(Indicates his heart.)* deep in here, I just can't. I just can't believe it's true. I wanta believe, Doc, don't you know that? I want to believe that every guy who sees his buddy get shot feels glad. I wanta believe I'm not different but I—I— *(The life goes out of him, and he goes behind desk to typewriter.)* It's hard, Doc. It's just damn hard. *(A slight pause.* CONEY *starts to type and then* DOCTOR *reaches across and tears paper out of machine.)*

DOCTOR: Coney, listen to me. I've had to try to tell you this fast, too fast. Because we haven't time, any more, Coney, we haven't time.

CONEY: What?

DOCTOR: It's like everything else in war, Coney. We live too fast, we die too fast, we have to work too fast. We've had two short weeks of this, thirty pitiful minutes a day. You've done wonderfully. Beautifully—but now—

CONEY: What are you getting at, Doc?

DOCTOR: I'm trying to tell you that we're almost through, son. You're leaving.

CONEY: What?

DOCTOR: You're being sent back to the States.

CONEY: *(Frightened.)* Doc!

DOCTOR: At the end of this week.

CONEY: Why? Why do I have to go, sir? Did I do something?

DOCTOR: You helped make some maps. Those maps helped make an invasion. And after every invasion, we need bed space, Coney. For cases very much like yours.

CONEY: But I—

DOCTOR: You see, you're not so different, son.

CONEY: But I can't go! I'm not better, Doc, I'm not all better!

DOCTOR: Son, sit down. Sit down. You'll get care in the States. Good care. Sure, you're leaving sooner than I'd prefer, but that's just part of war. That just means you've got to work now, every minute, every single minute you have left here, you've got to work, Pete, you've got to!

CONEY: I don't want to leave you, Doc!

DOCTOR: Peter—

CONEY: I'm scared, Doc!

DOCTOR: You won't be if you work. If you think every minute about what I told you.

CONEY: Doc, I'm scared.

DOCTOR: Every minute, Pete.

CONEY: Doc!

DOCTOR: Come on, Pete. Work!

CONEY: I—

DOCTOR: Come on!

CONEY: Every guy who sees his buddy get shot feels like I did. Feels glad it wasn't him. Feels glad he's still alive. . . . So what I felt when Finch got shot had nothing to do with being a Jew. Because I'm no different. I'm just— *(Breaks off in a sudden appeal.)* Oh, Doc, help me, will you? Get it through my dumb head? Get it through me— *(Indicates his heart.)* here? Can't you straighten me out before I go?

DOCTOR: I'll do my damnedest. But you've got to help me. Will you, Peter?

CONEY: I'll try. I'll try. *(In a burst.)* O God, I've got to try!

CURTAIN

Scene 2

SCENE: *The Office. Pacific Base.*

AT RISE: *The mid-morning sun fills room. A great air of bustle and activity. Odds and ends of equipment, records, papers are piled on desks, on chairs, on floor. Three or four packing crates are scattered about.* T.J. *is busy packing these crates and nailing them down. Right now, he is transferring records from cabinet upstage to one of the crates which is near desk, down* L. MINGO *is seated at this in dress uniform. He has his chair propped up against side wall and faces into room so that his* R. *arm cannot be seen. During following,* T.J. *bustles back and forth between crates and cabinet.*

T.J.: And if you think I'm going to shed any tears over leaving this hole, you're crazy.

MINGO: You and me both.

T.J.: Yeah, but we're moving on to another base. You're going home.

MINGO: Home is where you hang your hat and your wife.

T.J.: Ah, don't let that arm get you.

MINGO: Don't let it get you, bud. *(He gets up—showing an empty* R. *sleeve.)* These O.D.'s itch like a bitch. Poem.

T.J.: Whose idea were they?

MINGO: Some jerk who thought we'd catch cold when we hit the States.

T.J.: When do you leave?

MINGO: Pretty soon. If the Major doesn't get here pretty soon . . .

T.J.: *(Going into* MAJOR's *office.)* Oh, he'll be back in a minute. *(Brushing by* MINGO.*)* Excuse me.

MINGO: Well, I got a jeep coming by to take me to the airfield.

T.J.: *(Coming out with papers, which he puts in crate.)* Are you flying?

MINGO: On wings of steel.

T.J.: Say, that's a break!

MINGO: I'm the original rabbit's foot kid.

T.J.: I hear Coney's going back with you.

MINGO: Yeah.

T.J.: How is he?

MINGO: He's all right.

T.J.: They sending him back in your care?

MINGO: No! I said he's all right.

T.J.: Okay. I was just asking. You know as well as I do that cases like Coney get discharged from the hospital and then one little thing happens—and off they go again.

MINGO: Look—you leave that kid alone.

T.J.: Leave *him* alone! Why in hell don't you guys lay off me for a while?

MINGO: Huh?

T.J.: The whole damn bunch of you! Everything I do is wrong!

MINGO: Everybody picks on poor T.J.

T.J.: Not only on me! On anybody who made real money as a civilian.

MINGO: What? *(Phone starts to ring in* MAJOR's *office.)*

T.J.: Sure! That gripes the hell out of you, doesn't it? So it keeps us out of your little club. You and Coney and—

MINGO: The phone's ringing, T.J.

T.J.: *(Going inside.)* I hear it!

MINGO: If a man answers, don't hang up.

T.J.: *(Offstage.)* Corporal Everitt speaking— No, sir, he's not. *(Comes out.)* That Colonel's a constipated old maid.

MINGO: When are you pulling out?

T.J.: Oh—some time tonight or tomorrow morning; I'm not sure. *(Holding up two long pipelike metal map cases.)* Now what the hell am I going to do with these?

MINGO: *(Looks at* T.J., *then at cases, shakes his head.)* No. I guess not. Where's the outfit going?

T.J.: *(Stacking cases near crates.)* Damned if I know.

MINGO: Crap.

T.J.: I don't, Mingo.

MINGO: Crap.

T.J.: All right. It's a military secret then.

MINGO: Just because I'm leaving, T.J.— *(Phone rings again.)*

T.J.: *(Going inside.)* If that's the Colonel again, I'm going to tell him to screw off.

MINGO: Yep, yep. *(He gets up just as outer door opens and* CONEY *walks in. He, too, wears dress uniform and carries a barracks bag, which he sets down. He looks better now, but his stance, his walk, his voice, show that he is still a little unsure.)* Hi, kiddo!

CONEY: Hi.

MINGO: *(Kindly.)* It sure took you long enough to get here. *(Pulls chair over for* CONEY.*)*

CONEY: *(Sitting.)* I stopped to say good bye to the Doc.

MINGO: He's a nice gent. How do you feel, kid?

CONEY: Fine! How are you?

MINGO: Oh— *(Pokes his empty sleeve.)* a little underweight.

CONEY: Yeah.

MINGO: It feels kind of funny to be leaving, doesn't it?

CONEY: We used to talk so much about going home . . .

MINGO: Home? You mean back to the States.

CONEY: What do you mean?

MINGO: *(Snapping out of it.)* Oh! What the hell! We're going back to the land of mattresses and steaks medium rare! *(*T.J. *comes out of* MAJOR's *office.)*

T.J.: Well, Coney! How are you, fellow?

CONEY: Okay.

T.J.: *(Looking at him a little too curiously.)* You look fine, too, just fine. Feeling all right, eh?

MINGO: Want to see his chart, T.J.?

T.J.: All set to fly back to the States. Some guys get all the breaks.

MINGO: Yep. Some guys sure do.

T.J.: Well, what the hell! You fellows will be safe and sound in blue suits while we're still here winning the war for you.

MINGO: Thanks, bub.

T.J.: I don't know what you're beefing about.

CONEY: Nobody's beefing, T.J. Except maybe you.

T.J.: I got this whole mess to clean up single-handed.

MINGO: *(To* CONEY.*)* They're pulling out, too, but Montgomery Ward won't say where.

T.J.: You know we're not supposed to tell, Mingo.

MINGO: Yeah. Coney and I have a hot pipeline to Tojo.

T.J.: That's not the point. You're not in the outfit any more. You're—well, you guys are just out of it now.

MINGO: Don't break my Purple Heart, friend. *(Outer door opens and* MAJOR *comes in.)* Hi, Major.

CONEY: Hello, Major.

MAJOR: Gee, I was afraid I'd miss you fellows.

T.J.: The Colonel called twice, Major.

MAJOR: Oh, Judas.

T.J.: I told him you'd be right back.

MAJOR: Okay. *(To* MINGO *and* CONEY.*)* I'm glad you could come over and say good-bye. We've been together for so— *(Phone rings.)*

T.J.: Shall I get it?

MAJOR: No, it's probably the Colonel. I cornered that half-track. You can start loading these crates, T.J. *(To* MINGO *and* CONEY, *as he starts into office.)* This'll only take a minute, fellows.

MINGO: That's okay.

MAJOR: *(Inside—on phone.)* Major Robinson . . . Yes, Colonel. Yes, sir . . .

T.J.: *(Struggling to lift crate.)* Why the devil couldn't he get a detail to do this?

MINGO: T.S.

T.J.: Yuk, yuk. *(As he staggers toward door.)* Christ, this is heavy! *(*CONEY *walks swiftly to door and opens it for* T.J. *Slight pause.* T.J. *quietly.)* Thanks, Coney. *(He goes out.* CONEY *shuts door.)*

MINGO: Suddenly, it smells better in here.

CONEY: Yeah. *(*MAJOR *comes out of his office.)*

MAJOR: The Colonel's a wonderful man, but he worries more than my mother. . . . Well, Coney—

CONEY: Yes, sir.

MAJOR: Ah, forget that "sir."

MINGO: We're not civilians yet.

MAJOR: I didn't mean it that way and you know it, Mingo. I sure wish you were both going with us.

MINGO: So do we— *(Trying to find out where)* wherever it is.

MAJOR: That doesn't matter. I'm sure going to miss you, though.

MINGO: T.J.'s taken over pretty well.

MAJOR: The only reason he's taken over is that there isn't anyone else this minute. . . . Fellows, I— Oh, nuts!

MINGO: You don't have to say anything, Major.

MAJOR: I wish I knew how to say it. The three of us have been together for such a long time that it's—well, like saying good-bye to your family.

MINGO: Thanks.

CONEY: *(Simultaneously.)* Thank you, sir.

MAJOR: I ought to be thanking you, but I just can't. I—well, I wish both of you have all the— *(Outer door opens, and* T.J. *comes in.)*

T.J.: They want you over HQ, Major.

MAJOR: I was just there.

T.J.: Well, they sent Maroni for you.

MAJOR: O Lord! . . . *(To* CONEY *and* MINGO.*)* Look, will you two stick around for a little while?

MINGO: Well . . .

MAJOR: I'll be right back. *(To* T.J.*)* You can pack that stuff on my desk in there, T.J. *(He has started out and now trips against a barracks bag which was next to crate* T.J. *removed.)* What the devil is this doing here?

CONEY: I'm sorry, sir, that's mine.

MAJOR: *(Embarrassed.)* Oh . . . Okay.—I'll be right back. *(He goes out.)*

T.J.: I wish he'd make up his mind. Half an hour ago, he said not to pack the stuff on his desk. *(He starts for inner office.)*

MINGO: You really have it tough, don't you, T.J.?

T.J.: *(Going in.)* Oh, blow it, will you?

MINGO: *(Kicking his barracks bag out of the way—to* CONEY.*)* Well, G.I. Joe, I think we're just a little bit in the way around here.

CONEY: Yeah.

MINGO: I wish that jeep would come and get us the hell out.

CONEY: He'd like it, too.

MINGO: T.J.?
CONEY: Yeah.
MINGO: Oh, he's very happy playing King of the Hill.
CONEY: I get a kick out of the way he looks at me.
MINGO: *(Taking out cigarette.)* How?
CONEY: Like he's trying to see if I'm—still off my rocker.
MINGO: Oh! Forget it. *(He takes out a match and begins struggling to light cigarette.* T.J. *comes back into room and carries some papers over to crate.)*
T.J.: More crap in there.
MINGO: You're wasting your time. You can throw out half of it.

*(*CONEY *moves to give* MINGO *a light, then stops. He knows* MINGO *wants to do this alone.)*

CONEY: Mingo was going to throw it out but that mission came up.
T.J.: Look. You fellows are finished, so just let me do this my way, will you?
MINGO: Sure.
T.J.: *(Striking a match broadly.)* Here.
MINGO: It's more fun this way.
T.J.: Okay. *(Shrugs and starts to nail down crate.)* Does it bother you, the arm, I mean?
MINGO: No. It makes me light as a bird. *(Lights match finally.)*
T.J.: *(To* MINGO.*)* I didn't mean that. I meant does it hurt?
MINGO: Some.
T.J.: Well—
CONEY: *(Trying to change subject.)* What'd they put us in O.D.'s for?
T.J.: They'll give you a new arm back in the States, kid.
MINGO: I know.
T.J.: You ought to be able to work them for a good pension, too.
MINGO: Sure.
CONEY: *(Quietly.)* Shut up.
T.J.: What's eating you?
CONEY: Shut up.
T.J.: Why? Mingo's not kidding himself about—
CONEY: Shut up.
T.J.: Take it easy, Coney, or—

CONEY: Or what?

MINGO: Coney . . .

CONEY: No. *(To* T.J.*)* Or what?

T.J.: Are you trying to start something?

CONEY: I'm trying to tell you to use your head if you got one.

T.J.: If *I* got one? Look, friend, it takes more than a few days in the jungle to send me off my trolley. It's only your kind that's so goddam sensitive.

CONEY: What do you mean—my kind?

T.J.: What do you think I mean? *(A second's wait. Then* CONEY'S *fist lashes out and socks* T.J. *squarely on the jaw, sending him to the floor.* CONEY *stands there with fists clenched, trembling.* T.J., *getting up.)* It's a good thing you just got out of the booby hatch or I'd—

MINGO: You've got to get those crates out, don't you?

T.J.: Look, Mingo . . .

*(*T.J. *looks at him, then picks up a crate and carries it out. During this,* CONEY *has just been standing, staring straight ahead. His trembling gets worse. Suddenly, his head snaps up as though he hears* FINCH *again. His hands shoot up to cover his ears. At this point,* MINGO *shuts door after* T.J.*)*

MINGO: Nice going, kiddo. *(He turns, sees* CONEY, *and quickly crosses to him.)* Coney! Coney, what's the matter?

CONEY: *(Numbly. He is starting to lose control again.)* I'm just like anyone else.

MINGO: Take it easy, kid, sit down.

CONEY: I'm just like anyone else.

MINGO: Sure, sure. Sit down. *(He goes for a chair.)*

CONEY: *(Getting wilder.)* That's what the Doc said, Mingo.

MINGO: *(Bringing the chair over.)* And he's right. Ease up, Coney.

CONEY: That's what he said.

MINGO: Sure, sure. Take it easy.

CONEY: *(Sitting.)* I'm just like anyone else.

MINGO: That's right. You are.

CONEY: That's right.

MINGO: Yes.

CONEY: *(Jumping up in a wild outburst that knocks chair over.)* Yes! Who're you kidding? It's not right! I'm not the same!

MINGO: Kid, you gotta get hold of yourself.

CONEY: You know I'm not!

MINGO: Kid, stop it. Listen to me!

CONEY: No!

MINGO: Listen—

CONEY: I'm tired of listening! I'm sick of being kidded! I got eyes! I got ears! I know!

MINGO: Coney, you can't—

CONEY: You heard T.J.!

MINGO: And I saw you give him what he deserved!

CONEY: What's the use? He'll just say it again. You can't shut him up!

MINGO: What do you—

CONEY: You can't shut any of them up—ever!

MINGO: All right! So he makes cracks about you. Forget it!

CONEY: Let's see you forget it!

MINGO: What the hell do you think I'm trying to do? *(Slight pause. This has caught* CONEY.*)*

CONEY: What?

MINGO: He makes cracks about me, too. Don't you think I know it?

CONEY: But those cracks—it's not the same, Mingo.

MINGO: To him, it's the same. To that son of a bitch and all the son of a bitches like him, it's the same; we're easy targets for him to take pot shots at.

CONEY: But we're not—

MINGO: No, we're not the same! I really *am* something special. There's nothing in this sleeve but air, kiddo.

CONEY: But everybody around here knows you . . .

MINGO: Around here I'm in khaki, so they call me a hero. But back in the States, put me in a blue suit and I'm a stinking cripple!

CONEY: No. Not you, Mingo!

MINGO: Why not me?

CONEY: Because you're—you're . . .

MINGO: What? Too tough? That's what I keep trying to tell myself: Mingo, you're too tough to eat your lousy heart out about this. Okay you lost a wing, but you're not gonna let it go down the drain for nothing.

CONEY: You couldn't.

MINGO: No? You should've seen me in the hospital. When I woke up and found it was off. All I could think of was the close shaves I'd had; all the times I'd stood right next to guys, seen 'em get shot and felt glad I was still alive. But when I woke up—

CONEY: Wait a minute—

MINGO: *(Continuing.)* I wasn't so sure.

CONEY: *(Cutting again.)* Wait a minute! Mingo, wait! *(*MINGO *stops and looks at him.)* Say that again.

MINGO: Huh?

CONEY: Say it again.

MINGO: What?

CONEY: What you just said.

MINGO: About waking up in the hospital and . . .

CONEY: No, no. About standing next to guys when they were shot.

MINGO: Oh. Well, it was pretty rugged to see.

CONEY: But how you felt, Mingo, how you felt!

MINGO: Well, I—felt sorry for them, of course.

CONEY: No! No, that isn't it!

MINGO: I don't know what you mean, kiddo.

CONEY: When you saw them, Mingo, when you saw them get shot, you just said you felt—you felt—

MINGO: Oh. I felt glad I was still alive.

CONEY: Glad it wasn't you.

MINGO: Sure. Glad it wasn't me.

CONEY: Who told you to say that?

MINGO: Who *told* me?

CONEY: Yeah! Who told you?

MINGO: Nobody told me, kiddo. I saw it. I felt it. Hell, how did you feel when you saw Finch get it?

CONEY: *(Almost growing.)* Just like you, Mingo. Just like you! *Just like you!*

MINGO: Hey, what's got into you?

CONEY: I was crazy . . . yelling I was different. *(Now the realization comes.)* I *am* different. Hell, you're different! Everybody's different— But so what? It's okay because underneath, we're—hell, we're all guys! We're all— O Christ! I can't say it, but am I making any sense?

MINGO: Are you!

CONEY: And like what you said about your arm? Not letting it go down the drain for nothing. Well, I'll be damned if I'm gonna let me go for nothing!

MINGO: Now we're riding, kiddo!

CONEY: It won't be easy . . .

MINGO: What is?

CONEY: *(Grinning.)* Yeah. What is?

MINGO: Hey!

CONEY: What?

MINGO: Maybe this is cockeyed.

CONEY: What?

MINGO: That bar you were going to have.

CONEY: Bar?

MINGO: With Finch.

CONEY: Oh. Yeah. Sure.

MINGO: You want a partner?

CONEY: A—

MINGO: *(A shade timidly.)* A one-armed bartender would be kind of a novelty, Pete.

(A great smile breaks over CONEY*'s face. He tries to talk, to say what he feels. But all that can come out is:)*

CONEY: Ah Judas, Mingo!

(Offstage comes sound of a jeep horn.)

MINGO: Hey, that sounds like our chauffeur. Soldier, the carriage waits without!

CONEY: Yes, sir! *(He goes to his barracks bag.* MINGO *goes to his, but has to struggle to lift it with his* L. *hand.)*

MINGO: *(As he walks to bag.)* You'll have to keep an eye on me, you know. This arm's gonna— Dammit.

CONEY: Hey, coward.

MINGO: *(Turning.)* What?

CONEY: *(Coming to him.)* Take my coward's hand. *(He lifts bag up on* MINGO*'s back.)*

MINGO: Pete, my boy, you've got a charming memory. *(Slight pause.)*

CONEY: *(Softly.)* Delightful! *(He lifts up his own bag and the two start out proudly as—)*

CURTAIN FALLS

THE COLD WIND AND THE WARM

by

S. N. Behrman

Samuel Nathaniel Behrman, who would earn the reputation of "the Boswell of the overprivileged," was born into a lower middle class family in Worcester, Massachusetts, in 1893. Joseph Behrman, more devoted to studying Talmud than to running his grocery store, taught his son respect for acquiring book knowledge. As his early tastes—Shakespeare and Horatio Alger—indicate, Samuel grew up as a compulsive and comprehensive reader, the habit feeding his creative imagination until he went blind months before his death in 1973. His youth was also influenced by a friend, Willie Lavin, who would become the central figure in *The Cold Wind and the Warm.* Lavin guided Berhman's education and paid for his piano lessons.

Notwithstanding his interest in literature and the stage—by twenty, he had written and acted in a vaudeville sketch—Behrman entered Clark University in 1912 to study psychology. Three years earlier, Sigmund Freud had delivered a series of lectures in Worcester, energizing the psychology department at Clark. After two years, Behrman transferred to Harvard, where he studied playwriting in George Pierce Baker's famous 47 Workshop. Failing to find a job in journalism, Behrman enrolled at Columbia, where he worked with Brander Matthews, another renowned drama teacher. His graduate degree got him a position on the *New York Times Book Review*. However, when boredom with the obscure material he edited for a queries column prompted him to submit his own livelier questions, he was fired. He turned to book reviews, short fiction, essays—especially for *Smart Set*—and finally, plays.

The success of *The Second Man* in 1927 launched a theatrical career that spanned almost four decades. (Writing in 1965, theatre historian Allan Lewis saluted Behrman and Elmer Rice as "the elder statesmen of the Broadway stage.") In 1938, he joined Rice, Maxwell Anderson, Sidney Howard, and Robert E. Sherwood in founding the Playwrights Company, which produced many of his works. In addition to some two dozen plays, Behrman distinguished himself as the author of novels, biographies, memoirs, screenplays, a novel, and *New Yorker* essays.

S. N. Behrman is unique among American playwrights, particularly in the 1920s and 1930s. Instead of following the prevailing trend to realistic, generally proletarian drama, he made his métier high comedy. His plays are set in elegant drawing rooms, where the fashionable, cultivated elite exchange brilliant opinions and bons mots. These comedies of manners hardly seem native to the American stage; indeed, they are often likened to the glittering plays of British dramatist and actor Noel Coward, who, in fact, starred in the London production of *The Second Man.*

That comparison, however apt for the early Behrman plays, steadily loses applicability to those written in the years immediately preceding World War II. Behrman began to weight the subjects of his plays, though not their characteristic style. The polished carapace of the 1930s works does not conceal his opposition to all forms of inhumanity, his anger with the growing totalitarian crisis, and his anxiety about its threat to those whose activities or affiliations make them vulnerable. Behrman's deliberate infusion of urgent, ugly realities into the privileged world of high society prompted critic Joseph Wood Krutch to credit him with inventing "comedy of illumination." Though Behrman remained essentially loyal to his genre, the very title of his 1939 play *No Time For Comedy* reveals his awareness of the anomaly of high comedy in a world brutalized by fascism and darkened by war clouds.

Behrman first focused specifically on the fascist menace to Jews in *Rain From Heaven* (1934). In its cast is an exiled part-Jewish music critic who returns to his native Germany to fight with the underground. Inspired by an actual incident, the Jewish plot element manifests Behrman's outrage at Germany's turning against those who contributed so heavily to her civilization. Behrman's most extended dramatic treatment of anti-Semitism came in *Jacobowsky and the Colonel* (1944). Though this adaptation of Austrian Jewish dramatist Franz Werfel's play is hardly a comedy of manners, it is witty and insightful. The plot concerns a Jewish refugee and a Polish officer forced to become traveling companions by their mutual haste to escape the Nazis. Before their flight is over, the Colonel's hatred of Jews has melted as he benefits from Jacobowsky's resourcefulness and warmth.

In the 1950s and 1960s, Behrman turned increasingly to prose. Among the essays and memoirs he wrote for *The New Yorker* were a series of autobiographical reminiscences. Later collected and published as *The Worcester Account,* these pieces try, as critic Gerald Weales has noted, "to find the connection between the boy on Providence Street and the man on Broadway." *The Worcester Account* served as the basis for *The Cold Wind and the Warm.*

Wind opened on Broadway in 1958 and was selected by *The Best Plays* yearbook as one of the year's Ten Best. Strikingly, in adapting his memoirs for the stage, Behrman abandoned his signature theatrical style. The "Congreve of American letters" forsook geographically unidentifiable drawing rooms for parlors in modest western Massachusetts houses and New York City walk-ups. Roles written for sophisticated actors like Lynn Fontanne and Alfred Lunt were supplanted by widely assorted Jewish dramatis personae. The Behrman persona's deeply religious father was played by Morris Carnovsky; his unhappy mentor, Willie Lavin, by Eli Wallach. Their sobriety is offset by the braggadocio of the rich suitor, a role Sanford Meisner strutted through, and by the machinations of Aunt Ida, convincingly portrayed by Maureen Stapleton. Together with their neighbors, these characters won reviewers' hearts as "a closely knit Jewish community of warm and engaging people." Such praise must have represented a special triumph for Behrman, for *Wind* most resembles his other plays in its emphasis on characters rather than plot, and this time, he drew them from his own life.

There is satisfaction too in the evidence furnished by *The Cold Wind and the Warm* of continuity in the American Jewish theatre. Three members of the pioneering Group Theatre, which had closed shop in 1941, were prominently involved. Harold Clurman, a Group cofounder and its historian, directed *Wind*. Both Carnovksy and Meisner had been Group actors; Meisner, by then a renowned teacher of acting, had trained some of the cast with whom he appeared.

Wind was very much at home on the inwardly directed American stage of the 1950s, often fixated on the agony and ecstasy of youth. Decades later, this mid-century work can also be appreciated for its background, richly revelatory of changing patterns in American Jewish observance of traditional customs, especially those governing family life.

The Cold Wind and the Warm was first presented by The Producers Theatre and Robert Whitehead at the Morosco Theatre, New York City, on December 8, 1958, with the following cast:

TOBEY	*Timmy Everett*
WILLIE	*Eli Wallach*
JIM NIGHTINGALE	*Vincent Gardenia*
DAN	*Sidney Armus*
IDA	*Maureen Stapleton*
REN	*Jada Rowland*
MYRA	*Carol Grace*
AARON	*Peter Trytler*
RAPPAPORT	*Sig Arno*
MR. SACHER (FATHER)	*Morris Carnovsky*
LEAH	*Suzanne Pleshette*
NORBERT MANDEL	*Sanford Meisner*

Directed by HAROLD CLURMAN
Settings by BORIS ARONSON
Costumes by MOTLEY
Lighting by FEDER

SYNOPSIS OF SCENES

ACT I

Worcester, Massachusetts, summer 1908, early evening.

ACT II

SCENE 1. Sunday afternoon, two years later.
SCENE 2. Late afternoon the next day.
SCENE 3. A month later.
SCENE 4. Several days later.

Act III

New York City, five years later.

Scene 1. Tobey's and Willie's room. Ida's living room.
Scene 2. Next evening.
Scene 3. Immediately following.
Scene 4. Some time later—Worcester.

ACT I

As the curtain rises, the stage is dark. We hear Tobey's *voice. He is nearing sixty, and the voice comes from his meditation on a vanished past and particularly on the enigma of a lost but still-abiding friendship of his youth. Through the dissolving darkness we hear a lovely, plaintive melody: the oboe passage from the second movement of Handel's* Water Music.

Tobey's Voice: I find as I grow older that I keep going back to my friendship with Willie—when we were young and happy and living in Worcester, Massachusetts, in the early years of the century. Willie was always preoccupied with mystery—the mystery of life—the mystery of death. He used to illuminate all my childish problems for me. But he left me an inheritance of the greatest mystery of all: why he killed himself, why he felt he had to do it. What were the steep dark walls in Willie's mind that converged on him to destroy him? I don't know. What I do know, as I look back on my relationship with him—and on his relationships with others—was that he was the most life-giving person I have ever known. I remember still the first mysteries I brought him to solve: the mystery of infinity, the mystery of the True Name of the Lord. Did Willie, at the end, ponder these mysteries? Had he sought the True Name? Did he, I wonder, come too close? I don't know. I shall never know. I can only tell what I can remember.

(While Tobey's *meditation is going on, we gradually light up to the scene of the play: an early evening in the*

summer of 1908, in Worcester, Massachusetts. Then we see WILLIE LAVIN *and* TOBEY *standing at the foot of the hill.* WILLIE *is a young man of twenty,* TOBEY *is a boy of twelve, wearing glasses and carrying a strapped bag of school books. They are deep in talk. We can dimly see* DR. JIM NIGHTINGALE *in his office on the other side of the stage, engrossed in practicing his oboe. He continues playing the oboe passage from Handel.)*

TOBEY: Willie, my father is always telling me not to think about things.

WILLIE: What things?

TOBEY: All sorts of things.

WILLIE: For example? *(*TOBEY *stops, in the grip of the mystery.)*

TOBEY: Now, Willie . . . look . . .

WILLIE: *(Very sympathetic.)* Yes, Tobey?

TOBEY: We're standing here, aren't we—at the corner of Exchange and Green?

WILLIE: Precisely.

TOBEY: Above us is the sky. Right?

WILLIE: Right.

TOBEY: Now above that sky—let's say a million miles away—there's another sky.

WILLIE: I'll grant that.

TOBEY: Let's say there are a million skies beyond that sky. A trillion. All right?

WILLIE: I'm with you, Tobey—at the trillionth sky.

TOBEY: *(His voice rising in triumph.)* Well, what's beyond the *last* sky? There *must* be an end to it someplace. At night I build a big wall to end it. But what's beyond the wall?

WILLIE: Infinity.

TOBEY: *(Clinches it.)* That's what Father says I mustn't think about!

WILLIE: *(As they walk down the street.)* I disagree with your father. It's a problem—like other problems. It can be analyzed. Resolved into its component parts.

TOBEY: *(With sublime confidence in* WILLIE.*)* I *knew* you'd have some ideas about it, Willie! You're a scientist! You know everything.

(The sound of the oboe captures them.)

WILLIE: Dr. Jim Nightingale practicing his oboe. Let's look in on him. What else does your father tell you not to think about?

TOBEY: It seems that the Lord has many names but no one knows the *True* Name. He tells me not to try to find out the True Name.

WILLIE: Why not?

TOBEY: Because my father says that those who come close to it are destroyed. But infinity does bother me.

WILLIE: *(Musing aloud.)* Perhaps if you solved infinity you'd find out the True Name of the Lord also. Perhaps there's only one mystery—the key to everything—and you'd get it in one blinding flash—

TOBEY: Father says not to think of those things at all—

WILLIE: Your father and I are always arguing about that. I say there must be no limits to inquiry. *He* says—

(But by this time they are at DR. JIM NIGHTINGALE*'s door.* WILLIE *presses the bell and smiles at* TOBEY. *We see the outer room of* DR. JIM NIGHTINGALE*'s office. It is very shabby, with a dilapidated, sagging horsehair sofa.* DR. NIGHTINGALE, *a rusty dressed, stocky little man of about forty, with vivacious dark eyes and dark skin, cherry-cheeked, is standing before a music stand, tootling on his oboe with complete absorption. The doorbell rings. With tremendous annoyance the doctor puts down his oboe and opens the front door. When he sees* WILLIE *and* TOBEY, *his annoyance changes to pleasure.)*

JIM: Come in! *(Opens the door.)* Oh, you two! Delighted. I was scared to death it was a patient.

WILLIE: We heard the oboe. Knew you weren't busy.

JIM: *(With a gesture toward the sofa.)* Sit ye doon. I'd rather be interrupted when I *am* busy. Still, I'm always glad to see *you,* Willie.

*(*WILLIE *sits on a stool.* TOBEY *sits on the sofa.)*

TOBEY: *(Shyly.)* It's a sad sound, the oboe.

JIM: *(Points to music on stand.)* Handel's *Water Music*— Ought to hear my teacher play it. First oboeist of the Boston Symphony.

TOBEY: I'd like to be a pianist.

JIM: Why don't you?

TOBEY: No piano in the house.

JIM: *(Takes an obstetrical manual from a shelf.)* Here! Amuse yourself with this.

WILLIE: *(Curious.)* What's that?

JIM: *(Winks at* WILLIE.*)* Manual of obstetrics. The kids come in here and devour the illustrations.

TOBEY: *(Rises, moves back. Blushing furiously.)* No, thanks.

JIM: *(Urging it on him.)* Come on—nothing wrong with it. It's science. Maybe you'll be a gynecologist. Easier than being a pianist . . .

TOBEY: *(Hideously embarrassed.)* No, thanks.

WILLIE: Quit it, Jim. You're embarrassing him.

JIM: What's embarrassing about the facts of life? *(But he gives up as he sees* TOBEY*'s averted face, and throws the book on the sofa. He picks up a magazine instead and gives that to* TOBEY.*)* Well, here's *Puck.* You can look at the funny pictures . . . *(*TOBEY *grabs it, happy to absorb himself in* Puck. JIM *turns to* WILLIE.*)* Well, Willie, how're you getting on at W.P.I.? How's the chemistry? What are you on?

WILLIE: Knee-deep in colloids.

JIM: Who've you got?

WILLIE: Professor Jackson.

JIM: Oh, he's good, Professor Jackson. He comes in here. I have good talks with Jackson. Wish to hell I'd stuck to science.

WILLIE: *(Comforts him.)* Medicine's science.

JIM: Medicine may be science, but practicing medicine isn't. Good God—the women who come in here with their imaginary pains—they're bored with their husbands so they— By the way, Tobey?

TOBEY: *(Looks up from* Puck.*)* Yes, Dr. Nightingale?

JIM: How's your mother?

TOBEY: She's gone to New York to see Professor Jacobi.

JIM: I know that. When's she coming home?

TOBEY: I don't know.

JIM: All right, kid. *(*TOBEY *goes back to* Puck. JIM *turns to* WILLIE.*)* They haven't got the money to rent a piano for the kid, but to send his mother to New York . . .

WILLIE: Well, when it's a question of health . . .

JIM: She's got chronic asthma. I've done everything I can

for her. But they send her to New York to see Professor Jacobi! What a practice I have! *(Points to his oboe.)* Well, that little instrument . . . that little tube of wood and brass . . . saves my life. *(The telephone in his inside office rings.)* Damn that telephone! Well, let it ring!

TOBEY: *(Rises, shocked.)* But maybe somebody is dying!

JIM: *(Amused by* TOBEY*'s concern.)* All right, kid. *(*JIM *goes inside to take the call.)*

TOBEY: He must be the busiest doctor in Worcester and yet he finds the time for . . .

(He points to the music stand.)

WILLIE: Oh, Jim Nightingale's quite a character. With all his talk and cynicism he's very good-hearted.

TOBEY: *(Sits on sofa.)* No one ever pays him. I heard my father offer to pay him something. He always says no hurry. And he goes twice a week to Boston for music lessons. *(Dreaming for a moment.)* If there's one thing in the world I'd like to do . . .

WILLIE: What?

TOBEY: Play the piano.

WILLIE: Well—why not?

TOBEY: No piano. No teacher.

WILLIE: *(Musing.)* Pianos exist. Teachers exist. They are procurable.

TOBEY: I don't see how.

WILLIE: *(Cracks his knuckles.)* Let me consider this problem. Let me resolve it into its component parts.

TOBEY: Willie? What's a gynecologist?

*(*WILLIE *is stumped for a moment—he is saved the embarrassment of definition by* JIM*'s return.)*

JIM: *(Cheerfully.)* Well, the kid was right . . . somebody *is* dying! *(He picks up his oboe.)*

TOBEY: *(Aghast.)* Well—aren't you going to do something?

JIM: Oh, don't worry, it isn't going to happen tonight. *(To* WILLIE*, as he puts the oboe down.)* Diabetes.

WILLIE: *(Casually.)* Who?

JIM: *(Equally casually.)* Your friend Dan Eisner. There! I

violated a professional oath. Hippocrates will blackball me at his club.

WILLIE: *(Stunned.)* Dan Eisner!

JIM: Don't say anything. *(Wants to change the subject.)* Willie, speaking of colloids and Professor Jackson—

WILLIE: *(Rises.)* But Dan Eisner! It's not possible!

JIM: Why? Is he immortal?

WILLIE: *(Stupidly.)* But he's going to be married!

JIM: *(Flatly.)* Marriage is no cure for diabetes!

WILLIE: But, Jim—does Dan know it—have you told him?

JIM: I've told him what he's got. Let him draw his own conclusions. He's not an idiot.

WILLIE: Then how can he contemplate—how can he—

JIM: He doesn't trust me, I guess. Maybe he'll see Professor Jacobi.

WILLIE: But Myra—does she know?

JIM: If he's told her, she knows. If he hasn't, she doesn't. None of my business.

WILLIE: But if it's true—then Myra—

JIM: In three or four years she'll be a beautiful widow. That's a good kind of widow to be! *(He sees that* WILLIE *has been tremendously affected by the news about* DAN EISNER.*)* Oh, I forgot. You're in love with Myra yourself. Well, bide your time, Willie . . .

*(*TOBEY, *aware of* WILLIE*'s tension, looks up from his magazine.* WILLIE *is under a terrific strain and very much annoyed with* JIM *for dragging his emotional life into the open, especially in front of* TOBEY, *to whom he is a hero. He turns to go.)*

WILLIE: Well, Tobey, time to move on, I guess.

*(*TOBEY *gets up, at the ready.)*

JIM: *(Rises.)* What about dinner? I'll treat you both at Putnam and Thurston's.

WILLIE: No, thank you, Jim. We've eaten.

JIM: Sorry if what I told you . . .

WILLIE: *(Anything to get off that subject.)* That sofa is pretty dilapidated, Jim. Been here since I can remember. Can't you afford a new sofa?

JIM: Wouldn't give up that sofa for anything!

WILLIE: Certainly sags in the middle.

JIM: Symbol of conquest! I've been treating bored wives on that sofa for twenty years!

WILLIE: *(Shushes him, whispers.)* Please, not in front of the boy! *(To* TOBEY.*)* Come on, Tobey.

*(*TOBEY *is beside him;* JIM *walks them to the door.)*

JIM: *(To* TOBEY, *at the door.)* Come in any time—my medical library is at your disposal. *(He tousles* TOBEY*'s head. To* WILLIE.*)* You too, Willie—any time—we'll talk chemistry.

WILLIE: *(Can't wait to be off.)* Sure.

TOBEY: Good-bye, Dr. Nightingale. Thank you.

JIM: Good-bye, kid.

WILLIE: So long, Jim.

(The moment they go JIM *is back at the music stand and playing Handel's* Water Music. *This music carries us over to the first part of the next scene. Once they are outside,* WILLIE *and* TOBEY *start walking down the street.)*

TOBEY: You didn't answer my question—what's a gynecologist?

*(*DAN EISNER, *his manner defiantly athletic, walks by on his way to* JIM*'s office.)*

WILLIE: Hello, Dan—

*(*DAN *waves to them, goes on to ring the doctor's doorbell.)*

TOBEY: *(Full of wonder.)* But, Willie! How can Dan be dying? His tie, Willie—his collar and tie . . .

WILLIE: *(Very abstracted by* JIM*'s devastating revelation. To* TOBEY, *mechanically.)* What's his tie got to do with it?

TOBEY: *(Bubbles eagerly.)* Just like the posters of John Drew—you've seen them, Willie? A high stiff collar—with straight lines—and his tie, knotted so nice between them—

(His voice trails off in awe and wonder.)

WILLIE: I still don't see . . .

TOBEY: I mean—if he's dying—how can he take so much trouble with his tie?

WILLIE: Maybe he doesn't believe it. *(*WILLIE *and* TOBEY *walk on through the leafy summer evening—full of promise—of that evening, of the next day, of the veiled funnel of the future. The lights dim down and come up, revealing the façade of 31 Providence Street. The first and second floor piazzas are stage right. The porch and stoop are left of center.* WILLIE *and* TOBEY *enter stage right, walking up the hill.)* It could be done, you know.

TOBEY: What?

WILLIE: Piano lessons.

TOBEY: But who'd pay for it?

WILLIE: I would. I have great faith in your future.

TOBEY: All your friends wonder why you spend so much time with me.

WILLIE: Can't discuss abstract questions with my friends. Nice fellows, but they're a bit excessively down to earth.

TOBEY: I'm lucky to have a friend like you.

WILLIE: It's a natural affinity between sympathetic temperaments.

(He smiles at TOBEY. TOBEY *glows. By this time they have reached the stoop in front of the house. They sit down on it.)*

TOBEY: *(Suddenly.)* You know what I think Dan should do . . .

WILLIE: That's mental telepathy. I was thinking about Dan too . . .

TOBEY: I know just what he should do.

WILLIE: About Myra you mean?

TOBEY: No—about the angel. The Dark Angel. The Angel of Death. Dan should do what I do. He should hold on tight—to the bedposts. Like this. *(He illustrates, stretching his arms up and holding on to the railing of the steps on which they are sitting, in a kind of lopsided crucifixion.)*

WILLIE: *(Humors him.)* You don't think the Dark Angel might be stronger?

TOBEY: No. You can outfight him if you hold on fast enough. He comes at night. He's always at our house, you know, Willie—to take my mother. Every night Father says his night prayer, about those four good angels . . . and I have confidence in them, so I fall asleep. But then I wake up—and he's standing there, the Dark One, grabbing at me, to take me away . . .

WILLIE: *(Fascinated.)* What's he look like?

TOBEY: He hasn't got any face—yet he looks at you—with *something*. He's not angry or anything—he just wants to take you.

WILLIE: And you don't let him?

TOBEY: No. I hold on to the bedposts. The more he tugs, the more I hold on. That's what Mother should do and that's what Dan should do!

WILLIE: Have you told your mother?

TOBEY: When she has one of her attacks—I can't—her hands look so weak . . . her hands, Willie . . .

WILLIE: *(Quietly.)* Yes, Tobey?

TOBEY: Her hands look as if they already belonged to the Dark One.

WILLIE: *(After a moment.)* I think maybe, Tobey . . . I think maybe you read too much.

*(*IDA *comes out on piazza, anxiously looking up and down Providence Street. She is expecting someone.* IDA *is about forty, with large clear, candid blue eyes—she has the look of one of Holbein's matrons.)*

TOBEY: *(Calling up to her.)* Hello, Aunt Ida.

WILLIE: Good evening, Aunt Ida.

IDA: Tobey—Willie—what you two have to talk about all the time I don't know, but any minute I'm expecting Leah from Fitchburg.

WILLIE: Oh, I know. The entire hill is expecting Leah from Fitchburg.

IDA: She'll be on the Providence Street car. Wait till you see her, Willie, you'll right away melt.

WILLIE: Why do you dangle this paragon in front of me, Ida? You're marrying her off to somebody else, aren't you?

IDA: To a very rich millionaire from Atlanta.

WILLIE: Why should I melt in vain?

TOBEY: Why doesn't he go right to Fitchburg? Why does he have to come here?

IDA: Because he's very high-tone, the furrier from Atlanta, and Fitchburg is no place to meet a bride.

TOBEY: What's wrong with Fitchburg?

IDA: When your uncle—may he rest in peace—married me he took me for a honeymoon to Fitchburg on the streetcar. It spoiled the whole honeymoon. So be sure, Willie, and bring her up the moment she gets here. *(*IDA *goes inside. The lights come up, right, as part of the façade of the building is flown off, revealing* IDA*'s parlor.* REN, *her daughter, an attractive girl of fifteen, is lying on the sofa.* REN *is absorbed in* The Ancient Mariner. *A large framed photograph of* IDA*'s father, the Ramov, hangs on the wall: a venerable man with a full white beard, Moses with spectacles.* IDA *looks around her domain with satisfaction.)* It looks nice everything, you think so, Ren? She will like it, Leah from Fitchburg. Atlanta will like it? You like it, Ren?

REN: *(Without looking up from* The Ancient Mariner.*)* Fine.

IDA: *(Mild reproval.)* Why do you say fine when you don't even look? Maybe you will go up the hill to Lover's Lane and bring back some flowers?

REN: I'm trying to do my homework!

IDA: So you'll be a schoolteacher two weeks later!

REN: *(With scorn.)* I have a feeling that this furrier is nowhere near as high-tone as you think he is!

IDA: What are you talking, Ren? So rich is the furrier that his apartment is furnished by an interior man. I showed you his picture, Ren? *(She rummages in a drawer of a desk, takes out a photograph and shows it to the inattentive* REN.*)*

REN: *(Glances at the furrier's picture, disdainful.)* Looks more like a trapper than a furrier!

IDA: *(Studying the photograph with detachment.)* Handsome he is, but he has no neck.

REN: Why was Pa so anxious about Leah?

IDA: Before he went into the real estate your father used to peddle around Fitchburg. Leah's mother ran there a restaurant, and Poppa used to go there. Before she died she begged him, "Please, Harry, ask your wife she should find for Leah!"

REN: Well, that's your specialty. Finding! Why didn't you?

IDA: To find for Leah I didn't trust myself, so I went to a professional. I went to Rappaport, the matchmaker from Boston. So he found Atlanta. Leah's picture he sent to Atlanta. Atlanta's picture he sent to Leah.

REN: *(In a flare up of rebellion.)* Oh, Ma. It's so boring here. Why don't we go to New York to live?

IDA: Of this I am thinking. Already I wrote to my father, the Ramov.

REN: Well, what did he say?

IDA: He said wait till you get through high school. Then you can go to City College in New York!

REN: *(Dramatically.)* A whole year! It's ETERNITY!

IDA: A whole year goes by like five minutes!

REN: Maybe for you. Not for me. Besides, I don't think that's the real reason . . .

IDA: So what is?

REN: *(Accusingly.)* You're in love with Mr. Mandel, the landlord—that's why!

IDA: I am not in love till I find out if I am loved back!

REN: Well, I wish you'd hurry up and find out!

IDA: I have to go into the kitchen to make for Leah a snack.

*(*IDA *goes into kitchen.* REN *stretches out on the sofa again, props* The Ancient Mariner *in front of her and goes on reading. The lights dim down and come up on the stoop. We hear the sound of the passing streetcar.)*

TOBEY: I wonder if Leah is on this one?

WILLIE: The conductor didn't stop.

TOBEY: I love the sound of the streetcar. Especially at night. Don't you? I hear it go by when I'm in bed. I think of the people inside. I go along with them, inside the car, to the top of the hill. It stops at Lover's Lane. But I don't let it stop. I keep it going. Beyond Lover's Lane, down the other side, and on and on . . . all round the world—till it comes to Main and Pleasant again. When I hear it next time, it's been all around the world.

It must be wonderful to travel. Do you think I'll ever travel?

WILLIE: Why not?

(MYRA, *a lovely blond girl, and* AARON, *an intensely introspective young man, come down the hill.* MYRA *comes to* WILLIE, *bubbling and reproachful.* AARON *stands by, smoldering and sullen.)*

MYRA: Willie!

WILLIE: Good evening, Myra. Hello, Aaron.

AARON: Hello.

MYRA: I hate you, Willie! I just hate you. You never come to see me any more. Why, I haven't see you in ages!

WILLIE: Well, you are betrothed to another. You're practically a married woman.

MYRA: That's the awful thing about being engaged. Everybody drops you!

WILLIE: *(Virtuously.)* They should.

MYRA: *(With sudden apprehension of loneliness.)* Will it be like that *after* I'm married? Will no one come to see me? Oh gee, that would be awful.

WILLIE: You're supposed to "cleave unto" your husband. That's what the service says. You're gonna have to cleave—all the time—

MYRA: But I just love having boys around who adore me and I love to adore them back. That's all the fun—flirting— *(She giggles.)* With me flirting is almost everything. If I flirt with anybody that means I'm a little bit in love with them . . .

WILLIE: *(With some bitterness.)* Well, you've got Aaron, haven't you—while you're waiting to marry his older brother.

MYRA: But I love to flirt with *you,* Willie . . .

AARON: Please, Myra. I thought you wanted to read my poem.

MYRA: I'm just dying to read it. *(To* WILLIE.*)* Aaron's written a poem. It's dedicated to me. He dedicates all his poems to me!

WILLIE: When is the happy event to take place?

MYRA: *(Archly.)* That's for me to know and for you to find out!

WILLIE: Oh, come on! What's the big secret?
MYRA: *(Mysteriously.)* We may elope!
WILLIE: When?
MYRA: What's the point of eloping if I tell you when . . .
AARON: *(Miserable.)* Myra! Do you want to hear my poem or don't you?
MYRA: *(Takes his arm.)* I'm dying to read it, Aaron. *(She starts up stoop steps with* AARON. *To* WILLIE.*)* Don't forget me entirely, Willie—please . . .

*(*MYRA *and* AARON *disappear through the main doorway of the house.)*

TOBEY: Is Aaron in love with Myra too?
WILLIE: She drives him crazy. Cradle snatching. Dan's younger brother, too. She shouldn't have.
TOBEY: Is *everybody* in love with Myra? *(*WILLIE *doesn't answer.)* Are you really in love with her, Willie? *(*WILLIE *still doesn't speak.)* She's pretty. *(As* WILLIE *still says nothing.)* Aunt Ida's always arranging for people to get married. Is she arranging for Dan and Myra to get married?
WILLIE: No. Your Aunt Ida had nothing to do with that. That was spontaneous combustion.
TOBEY: What's that?
WILLIE: *(A moment.* WILLIE *is in a brown study, thinking about the news he has had from* JIM.*)* Tobey? I'm in something of a dilemma. *(Doesn't bother to explain.)* I think your father could help me. He's the only one I could think of. Is he home?
TOBEY: Well, he might be. But on Thursday nights he stays late at the grocery.
WILLIE: Let's go up and see.

(We see them go up the stoop steps, through the main doorway of house and into TOBEY*'s tenement, which is directly behind porch and continues left of it. Light comes up, revealing the parlor of* TOBEY*'s father's tenement. It is chiefly furnished with great Talmudic tomes.* TOBEY *and* WILLIE *sit down at a table.* WILLIE *sees two books, both open, which* TOBEY *has been reading. He picks one up, looking at it as* TOBEY *goes to the bedroom door, calling for his father. There is no answer. He comes back.)*

TOBEY: Father's not home yet.

WILLIE: There's a book I've been meaning to give you that I think you'll find very interesting. What are you reading now, Tobey?

TOBEY: *Hamlet* and Horatio Alger.

WILLIE: *Hamlet* is good. What a vocabulary that man had!

TOBEY: He certainly did!

WILLIE: *(Rises. Declaiming.)* "This majestical roof, look you, this brave o'erhanging firmament fretted with golden fire . . ." *(Pauses to give* TOBEY *a chance.)* How does it go from there?

TOBEY: "What a piece of work is man! How noble in reason! How infinite in faculty . . ."

WILLIE: *(Muses.)* "How infinite in faculty!" That's great. You won't find stuff like that in Alger.

TOBEY: What's the book you've got for me?

WILLIE: *Looking Backward,* by Edward Bellamy. Paradoxically enough, it's all about the future. Utopia.

TOBEY: *(Lit up with enthusiasm.)* Oh, I'd love to read it.

WILLIE: I'll run up the hill and get it for you now.

TOBEY: I'll come with you.

WILLIE: *(Pushes strapped school books toward* TOBEY.*)* No, you stay here and do your homework. I'll be right back.

*(*WILLIE *exits.* TOBEY *starts to unstrap his school books, but then the Alger catches his eye. He picks it up, reads aloud.)*

TOBEY: *From Canal Boy to President.*

(He puts the school books away and settles for the Alger. As he settles down absorbed, the lights dim. We see WILLIE *go down to the stoop. He bumps into* RAPPAPORT. RAPPAPORT *is a wispy little man dressed with seedy professional elegance. He carries a small nosegay.)*

RAPPAPORT: I beg your pardon, sir.

WILLIE: Well, I bumped into you.

RAPPAPORT: Oh, don't mention it! Do you happen to know where Mrs. Feinberg resides?

WILLIE: *(Points.)* In there on the left.

RAPPAPORT: I'm much obliged to you.

WILLIE: Are you the gentleman from Atlanta?
RAPPAPORT: No, Rappaport from Boston.

(He goes into the house and knocks on IDA*'s door.* WILLIE *goes on.* IDA*'s tenement lights up)*

REN: *(Jumps up. Calls to* IDA.*)* Ma, Leah from Fitchburg's here.

*(*IDA *runs in from kitchen, opens the door, aquiver with anticipation. But it is* RAPPAPORT *from Boston.)*

RAPPAPORT: *(With a gallant bow. Presenting his bouquet.)* Good evening, Mrs. Feinberg. I find you in good health, I hope.
IDA: *(All in one breath.)* You too. This is my daughter Ren. She studies. Mr. Rappaport, the matchmaker from Boston.

*(*REN *nods.)*

RAPPAPORT: *(Outdoes himself with* REN.*)* To meet the daughter of Mrs. Feinberg and the grand-daughter of the Ramov is a double pleasure, I assure you.
IDA: For her maybe when the time comes you'll find.
RAPPAPORT: *(Tartuffe.)* Where does there breathe anyone so worthy?
REN: *(To* RAPPAPORT.*)* Whoever he is, I hope he breathes in New York!
IDA: *(Dismisses her.)* Go, darling, study in the kitchen. *(*REN *picks up her homework and goes.* IDA *confronts* RAPPAPORT.*)* So, Rappaport, what is? Everything is settled, yes? Tomorrow you bring the furrier from Atlanta. So he'll see the furrier Leah has connections he shouldn't be ashamed. In the house of the daughter of the Ramov everybody *can't* come.
RAPPAPORT: *(Begins to sprinkle cold water.)* Your father is the most famous rabbi in the world. So famous is he that all over the world he is known by his initials . . . R-A-M-O-V. Ramov. So for me it is an honor. But for the furrier from Atlanta it is not such an honor.
IDA: *(Bridles.)* What is with the furrier that it isn't an honor?

RAPPAPORT: He is such a coarse fellow the furrier that, would you believe it Mrs. Feinberg, when I wrote him you are the daughter of the Ramov, he wrote me back: "And who is the Ramov?" Can you imagine such a coarse fellow?

IDA: A coarse fellow he is all of a sudden? Last time you told me he's the Prince from Wales. Stop beating, Rappaport. What time do you come tomorrow with the furrier? *(*RAPPAPORT *starts coughing to gain time.)* This coughing I don't like, Rappaport. *(*RAPPAPORT's *cough gets worse.)* This cough is not from a cold and it is not from a tickle. This cough is from not answering. With Leah from Fitchburg you wrote me it's fixed. *Is* it fixed or are you coughing yourself out of the fix?

RAPPAPORT: *(No way out, he masters his cough.)* With the furrier you should forgive me, Mrs. Feinberg, I have made a little mistake, though my fault it wasn't. An act of God took place.

IDA: *(Without emotion.)* He died the furrier?

RAPPAPORT: No, the furrier, thanks God, is alive.

IDA: Then what mistake?

RAPPAPORT: Mrs. Feinberg, I have to explain you. *(He starts coughing again)*

IDA: *(Very severe.)* Don't begin again with that coughing, Rappaport. Explain!

RAPPAPORT: With you, Mrs. Feinberg, matchmaking is a hobby. You don't make from it. But hobbies, *I* can't afford. From matchmaking I have to make a living, Mrs. Feinberg.

IDA: He won't pay you your commission, that stingy furrier?

RAPPAPORT: He pays.

IDA: So what are you grabbling me?

RAPPAPORT: *(In extremis.)* Pay he will, but not for Leah.

IDA: But with Leah—yourself you told me—when you sent the furrier Leah's picture—he right away melted.

RAPPAPORT: Of that, Mrs. Feinberg, there can be no doubt.

IDA: So give me direct!

RAPPAPORT: With Leah's picture—don't forget I have to make a living, Mrs. Feinberg—I sent along another picture to make smaller the risk.

IDA: *(Withering.)* Who did you send?

RAPPAPORT: Goldie from Revere Beach.

IDA: *(Full of scorn.)* Goldie from Revere Beach, then I'm not worried! To Goldie I brought myself three men. They all ran away. Goldie from Revere Beach speaks with a palate. With Goldie you can't tell whether she is saying yes or no.

RAPPAPORT: To the furrier she said yes.

IDA: *(Stunned.)* What are you telling, Rappaport?

RAPPAPORT: How should I know Goldie's mother will take it in her head to travel with Goldie to Atlanta? Moreandover, from the furrier Goldie's mother bought Goldie a fur coat—mink. Here mink, there mink, all mink.

IDA: *(With mounting fury.)* You wrote me it's fixed.

RAPPAPORT: *(With calculated sadness.)* It is. For Goldie.

(A silence. IDA*'s eyes flash.* RAPPAPORT *is quite nervous.)*

IDA: *(Murderously quiet, as she advances on him. He rises and slithers away from her.)* You know what I could do to you, Rappaport, and with pleasure—I could tear you from each limb!

RAPPAPORT: *(Pitiful.)* I beg you, Mrs. Feinberg, be a little bit reasonable. How could I tell that Goldie's mother . . . ?

IDA: *(Shouts.)* Why did you have to send that other picture?

RAPPAPORT: *(Pharisaical.)* That was my little mistake. Who isn't entitled to a little mistake?

IDA: *(Majestic, with great dignity, no anger.)* Rappaport! That you are a nudnick I always knew. Only now I find out that besides being a nudnick you are also—do you hear me Rappaport?—a no-good-Benedict-the-traitor!

RAPPAPORT: These are hard words, Mrs. Feinberg.

IDA: It is a strict report.

RAPPAPORT: Mrs. Feinberg, I promise you if you give me from Leah another photograph . . .

IDA: You will excuse me, Rappaport, but Leah's photograph is too private for a public matchmaker that deals with crooks. And as for this furrier—to him I do—*(She picks up Atlanta's photograph)* —what I'd like to do to you, Rappaport. A neck he hasn't got or I'd break it! *(She tears the Atlantan's photograph to pieces and hurls them into* RAPPAPORT'S *face)*

RAPPAPORT: *(Really desperate; he cannot afford to have* IDA *for an enemy.)* Mrs. Feinberg, I promise—on my late wife's memory, may she rest in peace—I promise you to make a match for Leah from Fitchburg. On my word of honor, Mrs. Feinberg, I swear you . . .

IDA: Don't swear, Rappaport, by what you haven't got.

RAPPAPORT: When you are more calm, Mrs. Feinberg, I am sure that . . .

IDA: *(Grandly.)* When I am more calm, Rappaport, I'll be sorry I didn't cripple you in the limbs. But it's good I didn't because a cripple can't walk out of the room. *(Dramatically she walks to the door and holds it open for him.)* So march, Rappaport, before I get calmer!

RAPPAPORT: *(Pleading.)* Mrs. Feinberg!

(His cough returns. Cowering, but with enough presence of mind to retrieve the nosegay, RAPPAPORT *makes an ignominious exit out the main doorway and up the hill.* REN *enters from kitchen. She looks at her mother with surprise; she has never seen her so angry.)*

REN: Why, Ma! What's wrong!

IDA: *(Sits at desk in despair.)* That dishonest crook from Atlanta, he isn't coming!

REN: *(Quite indifferent.)* Oh?

IDA: And any minute is coming Leah. What will I tell poor Leah?

REN: *(As she kisses* IDA.*)* Don't worry, Ma. You'll think of something. You always do.

*(*IDA *sits, dejected, pondering. The lights dim out on* IDA*'s parlor as* TOBEY*'s father comes to the stoop and goes up the steps, his eyes fixed on a newspaper. He is about sixty, still vigorous, with the look of a benevolent Saracen. As he walks into his parlor, the lights come up, revealing* TOBEY *still absorbed in Alger.)*

TOBEY: *(Without lifting his eyes from his book.)* Hello, Father.

FATHER: You're not reading in a good light, Tobey. You'll strain your eyes.

TOBEY: *(With excitement.)* Willie's coming to see you.
FATHER: Oh.
TOBEY: Yes. He's got a dilemma.
FATHER: *(Smiles faintly.)* I'm very tired. You should go to bed, too, Tobey. Go to bed, my boy.
TOBEY: When Willie comes, tell him I went to bed.
FATHER: I will.
TOBEY: Good night, Father.
FATHER: Sweet dreams.
TOBEY: You too. *(*TOBEY *starts toward the bedroom.)* Do you think Mother will be well when she comes back?
FATHER: I pray so.
TOBEY: The minute she comes back, I'll show her what I do against the Dark Angel—I'll show her just how to hold onto the bedposts. Good night, Father.

(He goes. FATHER *starts pacing the room, saying his night prayers.)*

FATHER: "And may the angel Michael be at my right hand, Gabriel at my left, before me Uriel, behind me Raphael, and over my head the divine presence of God." *(There is a knock on the door.)* Come in.

(It is WILLIE. *He has* TOBEY*'s book.)*

WILLIE: A book for Tobey.
FATHER: You're very good to him. I have a rather hard time with him you know. He's very . . .
WILLIE: Imaginative. At the moment he's got the Angel of Death on his mind. I'm going to make him cultivate a hobby.
FATHER: Anything to chase these morbid ideas out of his mind.
WILLIE: It's natural, you know. I read that children go through that stage . . . the fear of losing their parents—In Tobey's case, with his mother always.
FATHER: Yes. I know.
WILLIE: *(A moment.)* There's something I'd like to speak to you about.
FATHER: Yes?
WILLIE: A dilemma. An ethical dilemma.
FATHER: Yes.

WILLIE: *(Awkwardly.)* Just this afternoon—I found out something—by accident.

FATHER: What?

WILLIE: About Dan Eisner. He's very sick. He's got diabetes.

FATHER: I am very sorry to hear that. How do you know?

WILLIE: Jim Nightingale told me. It's only a question of time . . . And the thing is . . . *(He is flustered; he has difficulty getting it out.)* This is what I wanted to ask *you* . . .

FATHER: Yes?

WILLIE: Oughtn't I—tell Myra?

FATHER: *(Looks at him searchingly.)* With what motive, my son?

WILLIE: *(Embarrassed.* MR. SACHER *has touched a sensitive membrane.)* Why—to save Myra.

FATHER: Is this your motive? To save Myra?

WILLIE: *(Squirms.)* Whatever it is—don't you think she ought to be told?

FATHER: Is Jim Nightingale God?

WILLIE: *(With some heat.)* He's a damn good doctor!

FATHER: Can he read the future? How does he know that some cure will not be discovered? Or that Dan may not be the exception who recovers? My dear wife has been given up several times. Yet God has seen fit to spare her.

WILLIE: Jim says it's inevitable.

FATHER: Look into your soul, my boy. I know how you feel about Myra. If anyone tells Myra—it shouldn't be you.

WILLIE: *(Suddenly.)* Why don't *you* tell her?

FATHER: I'm a poor stumbling creature. I am not God. In any case, Willie—

WILLIE: Well?

FATHER: You know—according to the ancient law—if Dan should die . . .

WILLIE: *(Truculent.)* Well?

FATHER: Myra would be bound, unless released by Dan's family, to marry Dan's younger brother, Aaron, who professes to be in love with her too.

WILLIE: What is that law?

FATHER: It is called the levirate law. (FATHER *goes to bookshelves and hands him a book.)* There's been a great deal written about it. Here is something on it—in English.

*(*WILLIE *opens the book and starts to read it. The lights dim down and come up on the stoop.* MYRA, *leading* AARON *by the hand, walks out and sits on stoop.)*

MYRA: Isn't it much nicer here than in that hot parlor? This is better for reading your poem, isn't it? By moonlight! Like the *Moonlight Sonata*. Isn't it? You look so sad Aaron. Are you really so sad?

AARON: *(Staring at her in dumb adoration and misery.)* Yes. I look at you and I'm sad.

MYRA: Do my looks make you sad?

AARON: Yes. You're so beautiful, Myra. All the beauty of the world is in your face.

MYRA: No one says the things you do, Aaron. *(She gets up, stretches her arms in the moonlight in an ecstasy of narcissism.)* Shall I tell you something? I love to see in your eyes that I am beautiful. Oh, Aaron! You'll always love me, won't you? Even after I'm married to Dan? Won't you? When you become a famous poet you'll dedicate your poems to me and I'll tell you everything and you'll tell me everything. We'll have no secrets from each other—

AARON: *(Cuts in.)* My poems are no good! *(Shows manuscript.)* Look what the teacher wrote—in the margin.

MYRA: *(Peers at paper, reads.)* "Fine feeling. Expression . . ." *(Spells it out.)* "B-A-N-A-L." Is that good or bad?

AARON: It's bad. *(*AARON *stares hopelessly at his manuscript.)*

MYRA: What do you care what that old teacher says? The *feeling* is fine and that's the important thing. I go by *feeling*. With me everything is feeling. *(*AARON *is not comforted.* MYRA *rattles on.)* Aaron, do you know something? We're going to New York on our honeymoon! *(She giggles rapturously.)* Honeymoon! And guess where we're going to stay? Did Dan tell you? *(*AARON *shakes his head; with awe and delight* MYRA *tells him.)* THE HOTEL ASTOR! It's on Broadway and Forty-second Street—right in the middle of *everything*! I'll be Right There! Can you imagine? I've never been farther than Framingham. I'll miss *you,* darling; I wish you were coming. Do you think Dan would think it's funny if I asked him to bring you? *(In ecstasy at every prospect—stretching out her arms to the Universe.)* Oh, Aaron—Aaron!

AARON: *(In misery, mumbles her name.)* Oh, Myra—Myra . . .

MYRA: I love everything. All the world. I love myself—and everybody else. I love you, Aaron—in the most special way—I *love* you, Aaron!

AARON: If you loved me you wouldn't—

MYRA: *(Pedantically.)* Marriage is an experience every girl should have. You're too young to marry. Why, you're still in college.

(The lights dim down and come up in MR. SACHER*'s room. We go back to* WILLIE *and* FATHER. WILLIE *slams the book closed, throws it on the table.)*

WILLIE: Well, it's interesting as history. Fossilized social customs. No contemporary relevance whatever. Nonsense.

FATHER: *(Rather stern.)* If you analyze it, you'll find it is not nonsense.

WILLIE: We're living in Massachusetts in nineteen eight. We are not living in ancient times.

FATHER: This will only bring us back to our old argument . . . faith versus reason. You are a good boy, Willie . . . *(Smiles at him.)* though a scientist! You came to ask my advice. People who ask your advice usually want it to justify a course they have already decided on. You have probably decided, already, to tell Myra . . .

WILLIE: *(In self-defense.)* If I had, why wouldn't I just have gone and done it . . . why did I come to you?

FATHER: Then all I can say is . . . look into your heart—ask yourself why you're doing it. Is it to save Myra? Or to save her for yourself? *(Going to* WILLIE.*)* Go home, my son, and think.

(A silence. WILLIE *cracks his knuckles. He is in a turmoil of indecision; he knows that* MR. SACHER *has probed to the truth.)*

WILLIE: Well—thank you, Mr. Sacher.

FATHER: *(With tenderness for him.)* Good night, my boy. *(*WILLIE *goes out.* MR. SACHER, *deeply disturbed, begins again to repeat his prayer, pacing the floor. Intoning.)* "Before me Uriel, behind me Raphael, and over my head the divine presence of God."

(The lights dim out and come up on the stoop. WILLIE *comes down.)*

MYRA: Aaron's been reading me the most beautiful poem you ever heard! "In the wild garden of my heart a funeral urn is buried." *(Suddenly* AARON *tears up his manuscript and runs away.* MYRA *runs after him, calling.)* Aaron—what's the matter—Aaron! *(But he is gone, dashing down the hill.)*

WILLIE: Guess you're not satisfied with Dan. You want his brother, too.

*(*DAN *enters from the opposite side of stage. He greets* WILLIE *effusively but with condescension.)*

DAN: Ah, me bucko! *(He pounds* WILLIE *on the back.)* Up to your old tricks, eh? Trying to get Myra to change her mind . . .

WILLIE: On the contrary—I am trying to make her aware of her responsibility as a bride.

DAN: *(Masterfully.)* You don't have to worry about that. I'll take care of that. Got a little surprise for you, Myra. The ring. Want to see it?

MYRA: *(Overcome.)* Oh . . . Dan . . . *(*DAN *takes out jeweler's box and shows her the ring, flashing it in the moonlight. She coos with delight.)* Oh, Dan! It's beautiful.

DAN: *(With pride.)* Three carat! *(Waves it before her tantalizingly.)* Not yours yet, you know. *(He winks at* WILLIE. MYRA *giggles.)* Depends on your behavior. Want to try it on? *(He gives her the ring. She puts it on.)* Fits?

MYRA: Perfect. Just perfect. I love it. Oh, Dan!

(She stares at her ringed finger with delight.)

DAN: *(To* WILLIE, *as he takes the ring from* MYRA.*)* Went to the lake this afternoon. I swam from Jerry Daley's bath house to Parker's Point in an hour and twenty minutes!

WILLIE: *(Impressed.)* That's going some. Do you have a boat follow you?

DAN: No boat.

WILLIE: That's dangerous. You might get a cramp.

DAN: *(Omnipotent.)* I don't get cramps! *(He stretches himself, does a circular exercise with his arms.)* Never felt so well in my life. Tops! *(Postively crowing in triumph.)* Tell you, Willie, nothing like being engaged to put a fella in top physical condition. Recommend it. By the way, Myra—you haven't kissed me—as per usual . . .

MYRA: *(Disinclined.)* Not in front of Willie!

DAN: That don't make it worse—it makes it better!

(He kisses her. We see TOBEY *sneak out of his bedroom and come down steps to the stoop wearing a nightshirt.)*

WILLIE: *(Amazed.)* Tobey! I thought you'd gone up to bed.

TOBEY: I couldn't fall asleep. I heard you talking. I got up.

DAN: *(To* TOBEY.*)* Hello, kid.

TOBEY: *(Tense with his mission.)* I came down, Dan—to tell you what to do.

DAN: *(Smacks his lips.)* Just did it. Want to kiss Myra, Tobey? *(Pushes* TOBEY *toward* MYRA.*)* Willie's dying to. I won't let him but I'll let you . . .

TOBEY: I mean—about the Angel—

DAN: What angel?

TOBEY: The Angel of Death. I know he's after you.

WILLIE: *(Horrified, tries to shush* TOBEY.*)* Tobey—hush—

TOBEY: *(To* WILLIE.*)* I heard Father say—*you* mustn't do it—so *I* have to do it . . .

DAN: *(Has gone ashen in rage.)* What's the damn kid babbling about?

TOBEY: *(Not to be deterred.)* You must hold on tight to the bedposts . . . don't let him take your hand away . . . once you let him . . . you'll be . . . you'll be . . .

DAN: *(In a fury.)* Shut up, you little . . . *(He starts to strike* TOBEY. WILLIE *interposes, shielding* TOBEY. DAN *turns on* WILLIE.*)* You put him up to this, you bastard!

MYRA: *(Frightened.)* What does he mean? Dan . . . ?

WILLIE: *(Explains to both of them.)* You know with his mother sick all the time he has these fantasies at night . . . he's afraid he's going to lose his mother . . .

MYRA: But why to Dan?

DAN: *(To* WILLIE; *he is trembling with anger and with fear too.)* I won't forget this—I'll tell you that!

MYRA: Dan! Is there anything wrong with you?

DAN: *(Shouts.)* I'm in great shape I tell you! Never felt better in my life!

MYRA: Then why are you so . . . so . . . ?

DAN: *(In better control; with mechanical bravado, points to* WILLIE.*)* It's that jealous . . . He put the kid up to it. *(To* WILLIE.*)* Won't do you a bit of good, my friend. *(To* MYRA, *masterfully.)* You come upstairs with me. Away from these . . . How do you like the ring? Let me see it *on* you.

MYRA: *(Completely diverted, flashes the ring before her with a slow, undulating motion.)* It's just beautiful. I just love it! *(She takes it from him and slips it on her finger.)*

DAN: *(Jumps up the stairs.)* Come on, Myra.

MYRA: *(Hypnotized by the ring.)* They're bound to notice it, don't you think so, Willie, in the lobby of the Hotel Astor?

DAN: *(From the top of the stoop.)* I'm waiting for you, Myra!

MYRA: Coming, Dan . . .

(She follows him; they disappear up the steps into the house. A silence for a moment between WILLIE *and* TOBEY.*)*

TOBEY: Are you angry with me, Willie?

WILLIE: No, but your father will be if he finds out you're not in bed.

TOBEY: *(As he goes up on stoop and sits on the bench.)* How can Myra not love you, Willie?

WILLIE: *(Following him.)* She manages!

*(*WILLIE *has taken a little bottle out of his sweater pocket, uncorked it, and he now shakes some liquid onto his hands and rubs them dry.)*

TOBEY: What's that?

WILLIE: Alcohol. Air is full of germs. Protects the hands from germs. *(He replaces the bottle in his sweater pocket.)*

TOBEY: I'll be glad when Myra gets married.

WILLIE: *(Sits beside him.)* Why?

TOBEY: I don't know—I just feel—I don't know—I'll be glad.

WILLIE: I'm going to wait for her.

TOBEY: *(Shocked, scared.)* You mean you're going to wait—till the Dark One takes Dan away?

WILLIE: Yes.

TOBEY: Gee, that's scary.

WILLIE: *(Edgy.)* Why?

TOBEY: I don't know. It seems . . . something funny about it.

WILLIE: *(Gets up.)* I know what you feel. Tell you the truth, it kind of scares me too.

TOBEY: Then why do you do it?

WILLIE: Myra will need me. *(A moment.)* It's not for anything to happen to Dan I'm waiting. It's for Myra to be free I'll wait.

TOBEY: *(Quickly.)* But isn't it the same thing?

(This is unanswerable. WILLIE *is stumped.)*

WILLIE: *(Finally, with a sense of guilty evasion.)* You have a logical mind, Tobey!

TOBEY: Anyway, Father says if anything happens to Dan, Aaron will have the right—

WILLIE: I'd like to see them try it! I'm beginning to think you're much too preoccupied with angels. *(Sits beside him.)* Might be a good idea if you cultivated an outdoor hobby.

TOBEY: *(That would settle it.)* Have *you* got one?

WILLIE: I am beginning to think seriously about fishing.

TOBEY: Why don't you?

WILLIE: First I have to master the *theory* of fishing.

There's a considerable literature, you know, on fishing—different methods, different techniques.

TOBEY: Allie Seidenberg just fishes.

WILLIE: Well, he's just an empiricist.

TOBEY: What's an empiricist?

WILLIE: I'll explain that to you on one of our walks. *(Smiles at* TOBEY.*)* The peripatetic method.

TOBEY: *(Increasingly bewildered.)* What's that?

WILLIE: I'll explain that too.

TOBEY: All right. *(The sound of the streetcar has been heard, growing louder during the last few speeches. It comes to a halt in front of No. 31.)* Somebody's getting off. Could it be my mother? *(He jumps off the stoop and goes partway up the hill.)*

WILLIE: Oh, no. She's not expected yet.

TOBEY: *(Disappointed, peers through the gloom.)* It's only a girl! *(He comes back to the steps.)*

WILLIE: *(Peering also.)* Maybe it's Leah from Fitchburg. *(*LEAH*, carrying a cheap suitcase, walks into the shaft of light that comes from the tenement windows.* WILLIE *jumps to his feet.* LEAH *is an extremely attractive young girl. To* LEAH.*)* Can I help you, miss?

LEAH: I'm looking for a Mrs. Feinberg.

WILLIE: Are you, by any chance, from Fitchburg?

LEAH: *(Surprised.)* Yes. How did you know?

WILLIE: *(Jumps off stoop.)* I'm Sherlock Holmes! Mrs. Feinberg lives right there on the left. She's expecting you. *(Gallantly.)* You see! Your reputation has preceded you!

LEAH: *(Shyly.)* Thank you.

WILLIE: I'm Willie Lavin.

LEAH: I'm very glad to meet you.

WILLIE: This is Tobey.

LEAH: *(Smiles at him.)* Hello, Tobey.

WILLIE: Here, let me have your suitcase.

LEAH: Oh, thank you!

WILLIE: From what I hear—congratulations are in order.

LEAH: *(Intensely embarrassed.)* Really? Why?

WILLIE: *(Not noticing.)* May I say that the gentleman from Atlanta is a very lucky man?

(Her agitation is now so pronounced that WILLIE *does notice.)*

LEAH: Oh, Mr. Lavin—I—I—

WILLIE: *(Concerned.)* Do you feel faint, Miss—?

LEAH: —Long. I just felt a bit dizzy—I don't know why . . .

WILLIE: Here—sit down a minute . . .

LEAH: *(Accepts.)* Thank you. *(She sits on the stoop.)*

WILLIE: It's a long ride from Fitchburg. Were you, by any chance, carsick?

LEAH: Oh, no—it's just that—it's bewildering after Fitchburg to find myself in this big city all of a sudden—and—and—

WILLIE: As a bride? To a man you've never met. *(*LEAH *does not answer. She is miserable.* WILLIE *sees it.)* I'm sorry if I—

TOBEY: *(Cuts in.)* Worcester is built on seven hills, you know. Like Rome. Rome was built on seven hills.

LEAH: *(Smiles at him.)* Was it?

TOBEY: The highest is Mount Wachusett. You can see it from almost any place. I've been to the top twice. Willie can we take her to the top of Mount Wachusett?

WILLIE: Sure, why not?

LEAH: I'd love to go.

WILLIE: Fine. We'll go.

LEAH: You are the son of Lavin and Lupkin, aren't you?

WILLIE: *(With suave pomposity.)* That is an approximate statement. More accurately I am the son of Mr. Lavin, who is the senior partner of Lavin and Lupkin. Biologically speaking, I have no relationship whatever to Mr. Lupkin.

LEAH: *(She laughs.)* You are very funny.

WILLIE: *(After a moment.)* The gossip has it that the lucky gentleman is a very well-off citizen of Atlanta, Georgia.

LEAH: *(Acutely embarrassed.)* I see everybody knows it. That only makes it worse!

WILLIE: *(Comes right to the point.)* Have you got cold feet, Leah?

LEAH: Oh, Mr. Lavin . . .

WILLIE: Willie.

LEAH: Oh, Willie, I feel *so ungrateful*!

WILLIE: *(Cracks his knuckles.)* I can very well imagine a situation where at the very altar . . . *(Firmly.)* Where, at the very altar, the bride will relinquish the groom. I will go so far as to say . . . that unless the impulse toward this person is *overwhelming* it is your *duty* to break off this engagement.

LEAH: But Ida has been so kind and for a stranger, you might say. She hardly knows me. She's taken *so* much trouble.

WILLIE: Ida, out of the goodness of her heart, has found husbands for the halt, the lame and the blind—she will have no problem whatever with you, Leah.

TOBEY: *(Proudly.)* Ida's my aunt.

LEAH: Is she?

TOBEY: Oh, yes. Isn't she, Willie?

WILLIE: Beyond the shadow of a doubt.

LEAH: *(Gets up. Impulsively she kisses* TOBEY. *To* WILLIE.*)* I can't tell you how much better you've made me feel. You've taken such a load off my mind. I only hope I have the courage to—to . . .

WILLIE: *(Rises.)* Tell you what I'll do. In a few minutes I'll look in on you at Ida's. If you haven't summoned the courage to tell her by that time, I'll do it for you.

LEAH: I can't tell you how grateful I am!

WILLIE: It is the highest function of human beings to help each other—especially in moments of crisis. I venture to say that the opportunity may some day come for *you* to help *me*.

LEAH: Oh, I hope it does.

*(*NORBERT MANDEL *comes walking up the hill, swaggering and complacent. He carries a cane. He is around forty. He has a ginger-colored mustache—which he twirls elegantly, especially when he is meditating something—and ginger-colored, thinning hair.)*

WILLIE *and* TOBEY: Good evening, Mr. Mandel.

*(*MANDEL *nods condescendingly.)*

MANDEL: Good evening. Enjoying the moonlight? *(He notices* LEAH.*)*

WILLIE: This is Miss Long just arrived from Fitchburg.

MANDEL: Good evening, Miss Long.

LEAH: Good evening.

MANDEL: Are you the bride of the lucky gentleman from Atlanta?
LEAH: *(Greatly embarrassed.)* Well, I don't know . . .
MANDEL: I am Norbert Mandel. I am the proprietor of this property. My own residence is just on the top of the hill, very noticeable by its stained-glass window.
LEAH: How nice.
MANDEL: I am a close personal friend of Mrs. Feinberg and had I known she had so charming a client Norbert Mandel would have expressed a personal interest.
LEAH: *(In agony.)* Thank you.
MANDEL: I have just completed the purchase of a Winton Six. Consider it will be at your service any time should you care to see our fair countryside. Good night.

*(*MANDEL *continues his stately progress up the hill.)*

LEAH: Oh, dear. Everybody knows about it and now if it doesn't happen, what will Mrs. Feinberg say?
WILLIE: Don't worry about Ida. I will straighten it out with her.
LEAH: Well, I'd better be going up. Ida will be wondering. Which floor is it?
WILLIE: I'll show you.

*(*WILLIE *leads* LEAH *up the steps to the main door, carrying her suitcase.)*

LEAH: And you'll really come?
WILLIE: You may count on me.
LEAH: That's wonderful!
WILLIE: By that time you will have crossed the Rubicon. If not—I'll cross it for you.

*(*WILLIE *holds the front door open as he hands her her suitcase, and points the direction of* IDA*'s door.)*

WILLIE: *(Looking after* LEAH.*)* I venture the opinion that that is a very estimable young lady. Well, Tobey! Up with you. You've got to go to bed.
TOBEY: *(As they disappear into the hallway.)* Willie, what's the Rubicon?
WILLIE: Right through here—

(The lights dim down on stoop and come up in IDA*'s room.* LEAH *has knocked on* IDA*'s door.* IDA, *crossing her parlor, lets* LEAH *in. She greets her warmly.)*

IDA: Come! Leah darling! I was beginning to get worried there was an accident with the streetcar.

LEAH: Oh, no. Everything was fine. *(Looks around.)* What a beautiful tenement!

IDA: That's your room, and there's the piazza. *(Points.)* There from the piazza you can see the whole world.

LEAH: *(Goes out on the piazza and looks down the street. As she comes back into the room—)* I met your nephew.

IDA: Tobey?

LEAH: Yes.

IDA: So if you met Tobey you met Willie Lavin. If Tobey were Willie's own son he couldn't take more care. And how did you like Willie?

LEAH: He's a darling!

IDA: *(As a brilliant idea strikes her.)* He's very educated from the chemistry. To meet Willie Lavin that's a good start. I want you should have a good time in Worcester. You want perhaps to lie down for a nap after your trip?

LEAH: *(Has decided to take the plunge.)* Before I do anything—I want to talk to you about . . . about . . .

IDA: About the furrier from Atlanta.

LEAH: *(Faces her, prepared to speak the truth.)* Yes. I do. *(She sits on the sofa.)*

IDA: *(Sits beside her.)* So we'll talk. But first, Leah darling, I owe you an apology.

LEAH: Why?

IDA: Because about that furrier from Atlanta I found out such things that I apologize I ever got you mixed up with such a no-good.

LEAH: *(Feels greatly relieved.)* Really?

IDA: *(Squaring off.)* It's a miracle I found out in time. It's like a special delivery from God.

LEAH: What did you find out?

IDA: In the first place I met somebody who knows him close and his face is with pimples. In the photograph you can't see because the photographer took them all out with an eraser. This is right away dishonest. In his leg he has a vein. And, over and above, he's not even a furrier. What he sells is from cats. So now the mayor of Atlanta is after him with a subpoena.

LEAH: *(Happy to be absolved, playing along.)* Then how can I face him when he comes tomorrow?

IDA: *(By this time she firmly believes everything she is saying; her eyes flash with righteous indignation.)* You think I would let a no-good low-life that steals cats set foot in this house? Today I sent him a telegram he should save himself the trouble.

LEAH: *(Who could cry out for joy.)* To tell you the truth, I'm relieved.

IDA: Relieved is nothing. You are salvaged!

LEAH: I do want to get married. But somehow—I want . . .

IDA: You'll get!

LEAH: *(Smiles at her.)* Let's hope.

IDA: Take my word.

LEAH: Ida—it just occurred to me . . . now that the furrier is *not* coming, there's no reason really for me to stay here.

IDA: Stay you will for the company. Here are people coming and going. In the afternoon we go to Easton's Drug Store—five o'clock it's full of prospects with milk shakes. Already you met Willie Lavin. I bet he right away melted.

LEAH: *(Laughs, picks up suitcase.)* Well, all right, if you'll put up with me.

IDA: *(Opens bedroom door for* LEAH.*)* In here is your room.

LEAH: *(Surveying it from threshold.)* How pretty!

IDA: The flowers my daughter picked. Yellow I like in flowers, don't you? *(She closes the door after* LEAH, *and walks back into the parlor. She is full of thoughts, plans for* LEAH. WILLIE *comes in.)* Willie, for you I have the most wonderful news.

WILLIE: What about?

IDA: Leah from Fitchburg is free.

WILLIE: *(Teasing her.)* What about the furrier from Atlanta?

IDA: She don't like his picture. Already she sent a telegram to the furrier he should stay where he is!

WILLIE: Well, I'm glad that's disposed of. *(A moment; he doesn't have to help out* LEAH *now.)* I think I'll go home and do some work.

(He starts toward door. Ida, *in a panic that he will leave without seeing* Leah, *grabs him by the arm.)*

Ida: Leah darling. Willie Lavin is here!

*(*Leah *comes back.)*

Leah: Oh, Mr. Lavin, how nice of you to remember . . .
Ida: So why shouldn't he remember? A girl like you the problem is not to remember, the problem is to forget.

*(*Ida *goes out into the kitchen.* Leah *and* Willie *find themselves embarrassed at being left alone together.)*

Willie: *(Awkwardly.)* Well, Leah! Was the ordeal as formidable as you expected?
Leah: It wasn't an ordeal. Ida did it all. I can't tell you what a relief it is not to be a bride! *(An awkward pause, as she sits on the sofa.)* You know, I've never slept away from home before in my whole life.
Willie: *(Sitting beside her.)* Really?
Leah: It's a strange experience. I'm so excited I don't see how I ever will fall asleep tonight.
Willie: Under other circumstances I would take you to White City. That's what we call our Amusement Park on the Lake. There's dancing.
Leah: I'd love to go sometime.
Willie: I'll be happy to take you. It's just that tonight I—I have to get up early for a very important exam—I'm a senior, you know, at Worcester Polytechnic Institute.
Leah: *(Rises.* Willie *gets up.)* Of course. I understand perfectly. You've been more than kind to me already. I can't tell you how grateful I am.

(At this moment we see Myra *on her balcony and* Dan *on the stoop below. She calls down to him.)*

Myra: I hate your leaving so early, darling.
Dan: Got to be at the office early—got to be on my toes from now on—for my honey!

*(*DAN *waves to* MYRA *and disappears up the hill.* MYRA *leans over her balcony for a moment.)*

MYRA: Willie—Willie—

(On hearing MYRA*'s voice,* WILLIE *dashes across the room, out on the piazza, and looks up at* MYRA.*)*

WILLIE: Excuse me, Miss Long . . . Myra . . .
MYRA: Who're you with? Who're you talking to?
WILLIE: Ida's house guest. A Miss Long.
MYRA: Oh, Willie, I'm sad. I'm lonely.
WILLIE: Where's Dan?
MYRA: He got tired. He's gone home. Please come and talk to me.
WILLIE: Be right there! *(He has forgotten all about* LEAH*—remembers her only when he sees her as he runs back into the room from the piazza.)* Oh, excuse me, Miss Long! *(Lamely.)* It's an old friend of mine who lives upstairs . . .

(He runs out. LEAH *looks after him a moment, then she goes out to the piazza and leans over the rail to peer out into the darkness to catch a glimpse of the siren. When* LEAH *comes back into the room, her expression is wistful. She feels very lonely suddenly. She calls out.)*

LEAH: Ida! Ida!

*(*IDA *bustles in.)*

IDA: Where's Willie?
LEAH: A friend of his called him from upstairs. He went up to talk to her.
IDA: Myra?
LEAH: Yes. That's her name. Myra. I couldn't see in the dark. Is she attractive?
IDA: *(With contempt.)* She's thin and she giggles.
LEAH: Well, I guess she's attractive enough to make Willie forget his important examination tomorrow morning.

*(*Ida *comes to* Leah *full of sympathy and understanding, and comforts her.)*

Ida: Leah, darling, about that *hitzel-dritzel* you don't have to worry, Leah, because in two weeks she's getting married!

CURTAIN FALLS

ACT II

Scene 1

Two years later.

At rise, Tobey *and* Mr. Sacher *are in* Ida*'s parlor.*

Father: Well, Tobey, I have to be getting back to the grocery! *(Sighs.)* Though why I don't know.

Tobey: Is business bad?

Father: It's not flourishing! Well, there's one consolation, Tobey, in running an unsuccessful grocery. You can eat the inventory.

Tobey: Ida is very kind to us—having us to meals and everything—but I miss Mother. I dream at night that she is alive—then I wake up.

Father: I know, Tobey. So do I.

Tobey: *(Under great strain.)* Father!

Father: Yes, Tobey.

Tobey: There's something I've got to tell you!

Father: What is it, Tobey?

Tobey: I've done a terrible thing—a crime—

Father: Can it be so serious?

Tobey: I broke my glasses again last week.

Father: Did you? You didn't tell me.

Tobey: I was ashamed to tell you. I've broken them so often. I know things are not easy for you—and it's fifty cents a lens.

Father: How did you get the money to replace them?

Tobey: That's what's so terrible. I stole it.

Father: From the till?

Tobey: No. I wouldn't do that!

Father: How then?

Tobey: The Sweet Caporal packs from your shelves.

FATHER: Oh—you sold the cigarettes?

TOBEY: No, Father. The pictures. You know they have those pictures inside. Prize fighters like Bob Fitzsimmons and Jim Corbett. Allie Seidenberg is collecting the prize fighters. He needed Joe Choynski desperately. He offered me one dollar for Joe Choynski.

FATHER: A dollar for Joe Choynski?

TOBEY: So—I—

FATHER: Yes, Tobey?

TOBEY: I ripped open a dozen packs till I found Joe Choynski.

FATHER: Prize fighters? Why is trained violence so idealized? Why don't they put pictures in the cigarette packs of the philosophers: Spinoza, Descartes, Maimonides?

TOBEY: I guess they're not so well known, Father. I'm sorry, Father. I felt I had to tell you.

FATHER: *(Absently.)* Thou shalt not steal.

TOBEY: I'll never do it again, Father.

FATHER: It would have been better if you'd asked me for money, Tobey. Cheaper, too.

(He starts to go. WILLIE *comes in. He has just come from* MYRA*'s upstairs.)*

WILLIE: It's not to be believed what I hear.

FATHER: What do you hear?

WILLIE: The minute Dan died you all began to back Aaron's claim to marry Myra. And you justify it by invoking a dead law.

FATHER: Why do you accuse me?

WILLIE: I've just left Myra's mother. She says you approve of this monstrous engagement— *(*WILLIE *goes to* TOBEY, *and harangues* MR. SACHER *through* TOBEY.*)* Imagine, Tobey, you live in a community where they marry girls off by medieval rites. Now, in Worcester, Massachusetts in nineteen ten.

FATHER: Now, Willie—I hate to contradict a scientist because naturally scientists know everything, but you're wrong about this law. It's not medieval. It's Biblical.

WILLIE: Even remoter.

FATHER: You'll find it in the book of Ruth. I looked at it just this morning. *(He quotes.)* "Moreover Ruth the

Moabitess have I purchased to be my wife . . . that the name of the dead be not cut off from among his brethren, and from the gate of his place."

WILLIE: Exactly. Purchased. It was a real estate deal then. It's a real estate deal now.

FATHER: You simplify too much. There is a deeper reality behind it; a desire for immortality. Don't you see what threatens Mr. Eisner? That his name will be cut off from among his brethren and from the gate of his place.

WILLIE: It is brutal of Mr. Eisner to gratify his desire for immortality at Myra's expense. I'm studying law now and I've gone into this thing. Actually this law gives Myra the right to accept Aaron or refuse him. *She* has the right.

FATHER: That is so. But why are you so impassioned about this, Willie? Let Myra do what she wants.

WILLIE: Two years ago you stopped me from telling Myra the truth about Dan. With what results? Suffering and early widowhood for Myra.

FATHER: I ask you now what I asked you then—what is the motive behind your crusade?

WILLIE: All right. It's selfish. I love Myra. I intend to marry Myra. Had I behaved selfishly two years ago I'd have saved Myra from a horror that has left its mark. Good would have come from an impure motive. Your rigid code has resulted in disaster.

FATHER: *(With humor.)* Myra is adaptable. She'll get over it.

WILLIE: I'll see that she does!

FATHER: Willie—Willie—you've thrown over chemistry—now you're studying law—you change your profession overnight. But about Myra you're steadfast. I wish it were the other way round. *(A moment.)* Well, I've got to get back to the grocery. Tobey, I am disturbed by what you told me. I thought I was selling cigarettes. I didn't know I was selling prize fighters. *(He goes out.)*

TOBEY: *(To* WILLIE.*)* Father's so impractical. He doesn't know his own stock.

WILLIE: Tobey. I'm all worked up. Let's go for a walk.

TOBEY: Love to!

*(*IDA *comes in from the kitchen.)*

WILLIE: *(With affectionate reproach.)* You too, Ida. You too.

IDA: I too what?

WILLIE: Myra's mother tells me you're on her side. *(Goes to her, pinches her cheek.)* You too invoke the levirate law against me.

IDA: From laws I know nothing. I go by what is good for you, Willie, and to get Myra safely settled with Aaron would be a load off. Aaron I hope is healthy enough to stay for a while.

WILLIE: *(Laughs to* TOBEY.*)* No getting around Ida, Tobey. She pursues an objective with the tenacity of a—with the tenacity of a— *(Hung up.)* Of a what, Tobey?

TOBEY: With tenacity.

WILLIE: You see!

(They go out through the kitchen as MANDEL, *the landlord, knocks loudly and comes in. He is in smart riding costume: boots, whipcord breeches. He wears a carnation in the lapel of his tweed jacket, and carries a riding crop which he swishes occasionally, with nonchalance.* IDA *is in a fluster at seeing* MANDEL.*)*

IDA: Mandel! What a happy surprise!

MANDEL: Mrs. Feinberg.

*(*IDA *stares in admiration at* MANDEL, *taking in every detail of his bizarre costume.)*

IDA: Tell me, Mandel, in this suit are you coming or going?

MANDEL: Going.

IDA: It is a pleasure to look on you, Mandel. You smell from solid leather!

MANDEL: *(Formally.)* Thank you for the compliment, Mrs. Feinberg.

IDA: So tell me, with this suit where are you going?

MANDEL: Sundays is usual with me horseback. Sundays I canter. I am a habitue.

IDA: *(Stares at him, rapt.)* A peace on you, Mandel!

MANDEL: Thank you for the thought, but peace I don't want. Peace I'll have in my grave. Norbert Mandel wants action! *(He swishes his riding crop, by way of action.)*

IDA: *(Drinking him in with adoration.)* A long life to you, Mandel!

MANDEL: *(With restraint.)* Thank you, Mrs. Feinberg. Does Miss Long happen to be home?

IDA: No. Leah went out.

MANDEL: That's too bad because now I have an appointment with my groom.

IDA: Before the groom let me give you a piece of fish.

MANDEL: Thank you, Mrs. Feinberg, but before a canter I never eat.

IDA: But, Mandel! Why are you so formal? In the letter you wrote me from Revere Beach you call me Ida dear.

MANDEL: *(Swishing idly.)* In all the world—yes, I think I can say it Mrs. Feinberg—in all the world there is no woman I hold in the high regards I hold you.

IDA: So what interrupts?

MANDEL: *(Enjoys a Byronic melancholy—rotates his riding crop slowly.)* My experience of life has been so sad, dear friend. My wife—may-she-rest-in-peace—the good Lord took away. So I have decided from henceforth to concentrate on riding, hunting and real estate developments.

IDA: You are a young man yet—in the prime.

MANDEL: Norbert Mandel is old through suffering.

IDA: Mandel—listen to me—

MANDEL: *(Very cagey.)* Yes, dear one?

IDA: I have decided I would like, for a change, to be a private woman!

MANDEL: *(Affected incredulity.)* Give up matchmaking! You wouldn't. It's in your blood.

IDA: You should get married, Mandel—even if it's not me!

MANDEL: Is this your true opinion?

IDA: Whose true opinion isn't it?

MANDEL: Then I must tell you of a strange development that has developed lately in my psychology.

IDA: What development?

MANDEL: I am attracted, Mrs. Feinberg.

IDA: *(Dashed but game.)* By whom are you attracted?

MANDEL: *(Takes the plunge.)* Your lodger—Miss Long.

IDA: *(Flabbergasted.)* Leah!

MANDEL: Yes.

IDA: But Leah is a young girl—a child!

MANDEL: But didn't you just admit that I am in the prime?

IDA: *(With some heat.)* Even for the prime Leah is too young. Leah is in the beginning. Besides—for Leah I am already arranging.

MANDEL: *(Hard.)* The fact is, Mrs. Feinberg . . .

IDA: So what is the fact?

MANDEL: *(Tensely—Byron is cast away; Don Juan replaces him.)* The fact is that in Norbert Mandel your lodger arouses the flame.

IDA: At our age let me tell you from the shoulder, Mandel, marriage is no flame.

MANDEL: *(Swishes, flamelike.)* For less, Norbert Mandel will not settle!

IDA: *(Fighting a losing action.)* At our age a good marriage is to have steam heat in winter and an icebox in the summer.

*(*LEAH *comes in; she is surprised to see* MANDEL.*)*

LEAH: Oh, Mr. Mandel. How are you?

MANDEL: Happy to see you, Miss Long.

LEAH: *(To* IDA.*)* I just bumped into Willie Lavin and Tobey. Willie asked me to White City tonight.

IDA: *(Rises. Gives* MANDEL *a meaningful look.)* You see, Mandel! A fine canter to you, Mandel.

MANDEL: Thank you, Mrs. Feinberg. *(*IDA *goes out into the kitchen. For a few moments there is an awkward silence between* LEAH *and* MANDEL. *Finally—)* Do you ride horseback, Miss Long?

LEAH: *(Smiles.)* I'm afraid that's not for the likes of me, Mr. Mandel. I'm a working girl.

MANDEL: I have kept you under my eye for some time, Miss Long.

LEAH: *(Surprised.)* Have you?

MANDEL: You are a bright girl. Give you the opportunity you could shine in a bigger world than Providence Street.

LEAH: But I'm not ambitious to. I like Providence Street. Providence Street has been very good to me! *(A mo-*

ment.) And now—if you'll excuse me, I'm afraid I'll have to . . . *(She starts toward the door of her room.)*

MANDEL: *(Takes her arm as she starts to go.)* May I ask you something, Miss Long—something personal?

LEAH: Certainly.

MANDEL: May I ask how it happens—a lovely person like you—how it happens you are *not* married?

LEAH: *(Smiles at him.)* That is very simple to answer, Mr. Mandel. No one has ever asked me.

MANDEL: *(Ravished by her smile, touched by her candor.)* You are an honest soul, Miss Long—a very unusual soul.

LEAH: *(Embarrassed.)* Well—thank you. *(She starts to go again, but he holds her.)*

MANDEL: *(Very tense.)* No one, you say, has ever asked you?

LEAH: That's right.

MANDEL: I ASK YOU, MISS LONG!

LEAH: *(Startled.)* Surely, Mr. Mandel—you're not serious . . .

MANDEL: *(Still holding her arm.)* Norbert Mandel was never so serious in his life! I am in the prime of life, Miss Long . . .

LEAH: Congratulations!

MANDEL: I am able to satisfy your heart's desire—every which way. Give me yes and in a week you are living like a queen. You will find out that Norbert Mandel is a man of action. He don't let the grass grow.

LEAH: *(Rises.)* It is only fair to tell you—I am in love.

MANDEL: Willie Lavin? *(Cruel, inexorable, triumphant.)* Now that Myra is a widow you will get no place with Willie Lavin!

LEAH: *(Angry at him for saying this hard truth, and taking her own revenge.)* In any case, I could never marry you.

MANDEL: And why not? Do you intend, perhaps, to remain an old maid?

LEAH: Rather than marry you—yes!

(On the verge of tears she runs into her room. MR. MANDEL *is dumbfounded, furious. He swishes his riding crop savagely. With his free hand he twirls his mustache in anger.)*

MANDEL: *(Suddenly calling out in a voice of thunder.)* MRS. FEINBERG!

(IDA comes in.)

IDA: What's the matter? The house caught fire?
MANDEL: I AM ON FIRE, MRS. FEINBERG!
IDA: From the flame?
MANDEL: Yes, the FLAME. I am in the prime and in the prime the flame burns hotter than in the beginning!
IDA: So what do you want I should do?
MANDEL: Arrange for me with Leah Long, and Norbert Mandel will never forget you!
IDA: It's a funny way, Mandel, to preserve me in your mind!
MANDEL: For your benefit, Mrs. Feinberg, I can tell you in confidence—recently I took out a big policy with the Prudential Insurance Company.
IDA: You're sick, Mandel?
MANDEL: Norbert Mandel was never in better health in his life. But get me yes from Miss Long and overnight she becomes the beneficiary. On my policies with the Prudential Insurance Company is featured a big rock. Norbert Mandel is like that rock. Stable. Gilt-edged. Pass that to Miss Long; she should know on which side is the butter.
IDA: I'll pass.
MANDEL: Good day, Mrs. Feinberg! *(He goes.)*
LEAH: *(After he goes, from her room.)* Has he gone?
IDA: Gone he has. And, Leah, you should know if the worst, God forbid, comes to the worst, you have in reserve a BIG ROCK!

(The lights dim out and come up on the stoop. We see MYRA on the piazza, looking anxiously up and down the street. We see MANDEL's majestic exit. He encounters WILLIE and TOBEY on the stoop.)

WILLIE: Hello, Mr. Mandel.
MANDEL: Hello, hello. *(He goes quickly up the hill.)*
MYRA: Willie! I've been waiting for you!
WILLIE: I'll be right up.

MYRA: No. I'll come down. Mother's nagging the life out of me. I'll be there in a moment.

TOBEY: Willie?

WILLIE: Yes.

TOBEY: Before you go on this big fight, your object is to marry Myra. Right?

WILLIE: *(Humoring him.)* That is the dazzling objective—yes.

TOBEY: Don't you think then, that the *first* thing you should do is to find out how Myra feels? Oughtn't that to be the first step?

WILLIE: *(With the same tone of raillery.)* My impetuosity is so great that I'm taking the second step first.

TOBEY: *(Knows he is being chaffed.)* Seriously, Willie!

WILLIE: Seriously—Myra or no Myra—I've got to upset the CONCEPT—the concept of the dead hand. *(Thunder and lightning, the promise of a storm.)* Applause from Heaven! *(He sits on the bench.)*

TOBEY: *(Sitting beside him.)* I love before a storm. Willie, I want to tell you something: when I play the piano—Schubert and Chopin—

WILLIE: Well?

TOBEY: I think of Leah. The music's like Leah.

WILLIE: I see what you mean, Tobey. Leah's a wonderful girl. Loyal, self-reliant—

TOBEY: Isn't that a lot?

WILLIE: There's no mystery in Leah—in Myra there's mystery.

TOBEY: What's mysterious about Myra?

WILLIE: That's part of the chemistry of sex. Unexplainable.

TOBEY: Spontaneous combustion?

WILLIE: That's right.

TOBEY: *(Shyly.)* If I were older, Willie—

WILLIE: Yes, Tobey?

TOBEY: Well, I'd get more combustion out of Leah. I think about her at night.

WILLIE: Do you? It used to be the Dark Angel and holding on to the bedposts.

TOBEY: I've forgotten about them. It's Leah now.

WILLIE: That's progress.

TOBEY: It's troublesome too. *(A moment.)* I just don't understand, Willie, why you don't love Leah.

WILLIE: Neither do I, Tobey!

TOBEY: If things don't turn out—between you and Myra—will you turn to Leah?

WILLIE: Things *must* turn out for me and Myra.

TOBEY: One reason I love Leah is because she thinks you're wonderful. And when I talk to Myra about you—

WILLIE: Yes?

TOBEY: We always end up talking about Myra.

(MYRA appears on the stoop.)

MYRA: Hello, Tobey.

WILLIE: Well, go on up and practice your piece. *(TOBEY reluctantly goes.)* Where do you want to go?

MYRA: Anywhere . . . *(It begins to rain hard. Thunder and lightning. she shrinks against him for protection.)* Oh, Willie. I just can't stand the thunder. It frightens me so!

WILLIE: *(Holds her to him, adoring it.)* It isn't the thunder that's dangerous—it's the lightning that's dangerous. There—you see—it's over. It's just a summer shower . . .

(There is another great thunderclap. She buries her face against the lapel of his coat, stopping her ears with her hands.)

MYRA: Oh, Willie—I'm so scared!

WILLIE: *(Holding her.)* You were afraid of thunder. Since you were a little girl.

(A sudden lightning flash illuminates the stoop.)

MYRA: *(Removes her hands from her ears.)* Is it over?

WILLIE: Over. Now it's just the rain. Remember that awful thunderstorm—when we were out canoeing—a few years ago. Remember how scared you were! And you lived through it, didn't you?

MYRA: I remember *every* thunderstorm. Ever since I was a kid—they drove me crazy with fear.

WILLIE: I paddled to shore—we turned the canoe over—and lay under it—remember? Remember the noise the rain made on the canoe bottom—like bullets?

MYRA: I remember how wonderful it was when it went away.

WILLIE: I remember how wonderful it was—lying close to you.

MYRA: *(A little calmer now; there is the sound of steady rain.)* I know it's silly. Why is it? Why am I so scared?

WILLIE: *(Cracks his knuckles.)* I venture to say that if you analyzed it to its source you'd find some deep psychic . . .

MYRA: *(Interrupts him.)* Willie, why do you crack your knuckles like that? You're always doing it. Why?

WILLIE: *(Turning it off adroitly.)* Perhaps for the same reason you're afraid of thunder.

(They both laugh a little.)

MYRA: *(Sitting on the bench.)* Ever since Dan died—everything scares me even more. And now this with Aaron—and he's coming here any minute.

WILLIE: *(Sitting beside her.)* Why should you throw yourself away on somebody you don't love like Aaron?

MYRA: When it comes to that, I'd rather marry you than marry Aaron.

WILLIE: That's cold comfort!

MYRA: *(A moment.)* Sometimes I think of running away.

WILLIE: Where would you go?

MYRA: New York. I love New York. When I was there with Dan I met the manager of the Hotel Astor. Imagine—the manager!

WILLIE: Did he fall in love with you too?

MYRA: Oh, no. He's fat and old and has hundreds of children. But Dan fell ill—and this manager was so very kind. He said: if you want a job in New York, let me know.

(We hear TOBEY *playing Chopin.)*

WILLIE: But, Myra, I've waited for you.

MYRA: I know. I used to think—during that dreadful time—Willie loves me—Willie's waiting for me.

WILLIE: Did you, darling? Did you know?

MYRA: Of course I knew, and it consoled me. I thought—he's waiting—and I'm waiting.

WILLIE: For me? Were you waiting for me?

MYRA: I'm always waiting for a promise. That no one made me but which I've always felt. It's a kind of a feeling that there is—there must be—love—which will make life—which will somehow make life . . .

WILLIE: *(Suddenly miserable.)* I think I know what you mean.

MYRA: But *with* the promise I'm afraid of the future too—as if it were thunder.

WILLIE: I'll protect you from the thunder, Myra.

MYRA: Come closer to me. Talk to me, Willie. Tell me your innermost thoughts. *(He obeys her. He is tongue-tied, in an ecstasy of love.)* Say something to me—something soothing like the rain.

WILLIE: I love you. I've never loved anyone else. I never will love anyone else.

MYRA: How can you tell that?

WILLIE: I know it.

MYRA: What about Leah?

WILLIE: Leah's not you! No one in the whole world is you.

MYRA: Are you going to marry Leah?

WILLIE: How can I when it's you I love?

MYRA: Willie—Willie darling—

WILLIE: *(Downcast, knows what's coming.)* Yes, Myra?

MYRA: I love you. But shall I tell you something? Don't wait for me. Love me. Don't forget me ever. But don't wait for me.

WILLIE: No matter what you say, I'll wait for you. Always.

MYRA: I hate this mourning dress. Don't look at it. I feel that I'm pretending more than I feel when I wear mourning for Dan. I hate mourning like I hate the dark. I love light. I love bright colors. Oh, I'd love to be gay for you, Willie.

WILLIE: Be gay. Go up and change your dress.

MYRA: Oh, I'd be afraid to.

WILLIE: Don't be. Go up and change.

MYRA: I will. Why shouldn't I? I will.

(She goes in. AARON *enters from the right, holding an umbrella. He is sullen and attempts to brush by* WILLIE

without speaking to him. WILLIE *seizes his arm, holds him.)*

WILLIE: I want to talk to you, Aaron—seriously.
AARON: I don't want to talk to you. I dislike you.
WILLIE: I know that and I understand it. But I think for both our sakes we should declare an armistice and have a council of war.
AARON: What are you driving at?
WILLIE: Our tactics with Myra. I think they are wrong.
AARON: I have no tactics. My case is clear.
WILLIE: It may be clear but it has one defect. Myra doesn't consider you have a case at all. Don't you see, Aaron, we've both made a serious mistake. We have to change our whole plan of attack.
AARON: Why do you say we? I'm marrying Myra. You're not.
WILLIE: She'll marry neither of us if we don't change our tactics. You are basing your whole claim on this old law. I am basing mine on demolishing the law. We are both misguided, Aaron, and do you know why? Because Myra is lawless. She is ruled by instinct, not by laws. We have to drop our present campaign—regroup our forces—we—
AARON: Stop saying we! Stop saying our! This isn't a joint enterprise!
WILLIE: It is a joint enterprise until one of us eliminates the other.

(MYRA *comes back in a yellow dress.* AARON *is horrified.)*

MYRA: Oh, Aaron.
AARON: *(In a terrible voice.)* What are you doing in that dress?
MYRA: Why I just—Willie said I could stop mourning for an hour—
AARON: My brother is hardly in his grave and you—you put on this dress to tempt Willie. You're a harlot!
WILLIE: Tactics, Aaron—tactics!
AARON: You leave Myra alone.
WILLIE: I will when she asks me.

AARON: I'm Dan's younger brother. I have the right. She's mine by law. Get out!

MYRA: I never loved you, Aaron. And now I don't even like you any more. I don't care about the law.

AARON: Put on your mourning dress. *(To* WILLIE.*)* And you get out before I . . .

(There is a tremendous thunderclap. In terror, MYRA *clings to* WILLIE.*)*

MYRA: Willie—don't leave me—don't leave me with him—

WILLIE: Don't worry, darling. I won't leave you.

AARON: *(His voice drops, menacing and quiet.)* You'll pay for this—both of you. And I'm going up now to tell your mother! *(He goes into the house.)*

MYRA: *(Whispers to* WILLIE.*)* Willie—I'm scared—

WILLIE: *(Masterfully.)* Don't worry . . . He's like the thunder, darling—noisy but not dangerous.

MYRA: You are the only one who loves me— Don't leave me—please, darling, don't leave me.

WILLIE: *(Quietly, happy, holding her in his arms, kissing her hair.)* Never, Myra. Never, my love. I'll never leave you.

(As he caresses her hair, the sound of the rain fades and we hear the town clock strike six times.)

LIGHTS DIM OUT

Scene 2

MR. SACHER*'s room, late afternoon the next day. The parlor reveals a Rembrandtesque scene of* FATHER *and his fellow scholars at their annual session, celebrating the finishing of the reading of one of the books of the Talmud: the great, calf-bound volumes are propped up before each of the students, who are all men of* FATHER*'s age, or older: in their ordinary lives grocers, peddlers, petty artisans, tailors, but now, transmuted in their absorption, figures from a medieval print, with their skull caps, sober garments and absolute absorption, poring over the parchment-like pages. A cadenced warm hum comes from them: intermittent little flares of subdued argument in crises of interpretation; silence, then the hum again—it is a sound, not articulate speech. A Menorah, with lighted candles, furnishes the only—flickering—illumination.*

TOBEY *is sitting on the stoop, his head buried in a book.*

We hear WILLIE*'s whistle, his habitual signal to* TOBEY, *as he comes down the hill—the first notes of Beethoven's Fifth Symphony.*

WILLIE: Hello, Tobey. What are you up to?

TOBEY: Well, I thought of going to the lake with Allie and the boys as soon as my father gets through up there.

WILLIE: Oh, the annual session.

TOBEY: Does it take them a whole year to go through one of those Talmud books, Willie?

WILLIE: Well, they can only devote part time to it.

TOBEY: What's in them anyway?

WILLIE: *(Sitting beside him.)* The Talmud? A code of law and behavior—interpretation. Some of it's very funny.

TOBEY: Really? I never see my father or his friends laugh.

WILLIE: Well, it's a serious business for them. For instance, there is a speculation: Why did God make Eve out of Adam's rib? Well, the Talmud suggests if he'd made her out of his hand she'd be grasping; if he'd made her out of his tongue she'd be a gossip; if he used his eyes she'd be overcurious. In addition, God wanted Eve to be modest. So he used the rib because it was invisible. So, he stuck to this neutral material, the rib, with the result that she is now grasping, gossipy, incessantly curious and of disturbing visibility.

TOBEY: *(Laughing.)* I wish those books were in English. I'd love to read them.

WILLIE: You don't have time—not till you've finished that piece you're working on—*Opus One*.

TOBEY: *Opus One*. I'll never finish it. I knew I'd never be a great pianist, Willie. Now I guess I'll never be a composer either.

WILLIE: Stick to it. It'll come.

TOBEY: Are you free tonight?

WILLIE: No. I've got a date with Myra.

TOBEY: Everybody says Myra's given up Aaron for you.

WILLIE: So far, she's only given up Aaron.

TOBEY: Will she take you then?

WILLIE: That remains to be seen. You know Myra has an extraordinary faculty.

TOBEY: What's that?

WILLIE: She has the faculty of accepting you and rejecting you simultaneously.

(Meanwhile, in the parlor there is a small final crisis of interpretation; the hum stops suddenly. Everyone's attention focuses on FATHER; *obviously they look to him as the most learned, to bring them out of their dilemma. Complete silence.* FATHER *leans forward in concentration, his finger on the disputed passage. He repeats, reading the elusive sentence—first with one emphasis, then again with another, an entirely different emphasis. There is a sudden illumination among them; the difference in emphasis has dispelled the ambiguity, the meaning is now clear, irrefutable, to all of them. A great sigh of relief rises from the embattled table and then a kind of muted acclamation to* FATHER. *Laughter. Jubilation. They shut*

their books; they are like schoolboys released from an onerous task. Several of the men shake hands with FATHER, *congratulating him.* MR. SACHER *goes out to the stoop in the gloaming.)*

FATHER: Tobey—we're finished—come up—the tea and cakes—Tobey.

IDA: *(Comes out on the piazza. She sees* WILLIE *and* TOBEY *and* MR. SACHER.*)* You heard the news? Your *hitzel-dritzel,* Myra.

WILLIE: *(Apprehensive.)* What happened?

IDA: She flew away the coop!

WILLIE: What do you mean?

IDA: She ran away. A note she left that she'll write a note. So why didn't she write it now? For you too she left a note.

WILLIE: Where is it? *(*WILLIE *starts up toward her.)*

IDA: For the note you don't have to run because I read it!

WILLIE: You had no right to do that!

IDA: You, too, she tells when she gets settled she'll send you a note. What I have with Myra's mother I can't tell you. Dead Myra isn't I tell her. Better she should be dead she says.

WILLIE: I knew this would happen!

IDA: *(Matter-of-factly.)* So if you knew, why didn't you stop?

WILLIE: You've driven her out, all of you. The loveliest thing in this God-obsessed community—you've driven her out!

FATHER: No one forced Myra to go . . .

WILLIE: *(In despair—really to himself.)* All the bickering. All the wrangling. That fanatical father of Aaron's—Aaron himself.

FATHER: *(Gently.)* You are not fanatical, Willie. Could you keep her?

WILLIE: I'll go to New York. She asked me never to leave her.

FATHER: So then she promptly left you.

WILLIE: *(As he goes up the hill.)* I knew this would happen. I knew this would happen.

TOBEY: *(Starting after him, stops.)* Willie! Do you want me to come with you? Willie!

FATHER: He needs solitude, Tobey. It's no reflection on you. He's had a terrible blow.

IDA: No. It's a good blow. This blow will stop him from chasing that wild goose. Because don't you see, Tobey, for him Myra is no good. Now, I can arrange for him nice with Leah. *(She goes back into her house.)*

TOBEY: Father.

FATHER: Yes, Tobey.

TOBEY: Did you love Mother the way Willie loves Myra?

FATHER: You don't love like that when you're older.

TOBEY: But you did love Mother?

FATHER: Yes. I loved her very much.

TOBEY: Still you quarreled. I used to hear you quarreling. Mother never said anything. But your voice would go up—up—

FATHER: *(This makes him suffer.)* I am a sinful man, Tobey.

TOBEY: You pray all the time. You think about God all the time. That's why I could never understand about those quarrels.

FATHER: I suffer now over those quarrels. *(He stops, tries to explain.)* Look, Tobey, your mother lived in a silent world. She had been in this country as long as I, and yet she never learned the language. I was a student when I married her—had never left our village. And then I went away to study more—in France and Germany—and when I came back—

TOBEY: Yes?

FATHER: Your mother was still a village girl. And I was arrogant and impatient! I wish that I could have— But it's too late now.

TOBEY: Father, do you think Willie will get over this?

FATHER: That's a question I can't answer, Tobey. When I see the troubles of the young, it's a positive relief to be old.

TOBEY: Father—is it possible, Father, to be in love without being unhappy?

FATHER: It's possible, but highly unlikely.

(He motions to TOBEY *to come with him. They go into the house.)*

LIGHTS DIM OUT

Scene 3

At Ida*'s, a month later. There is a dress form with an attractive summer dress on it.* Ren, *discontented, full of Weltschmerz, is on the piazza, surveying the passing scene. From the Sachers' flat, we hear* Tobey *struggling with a composition of his own:* Opus One. *We hear* Allie Seidenberg *whistling for* Ren. Ren *turns her back on him disdainfully, and comes into the room.*

Ida: *(From the kitchen.)* Who is whistling?
Ren: *(With contempt)* Allie Seidenberg is whistling.
Ida: So why don't you ask him to come up?
Ren: Because he *disgusts* me, that's why!
Ida: Allie's father is a very fine man.
Ren: His son isn't. He has a dirty mind.

*(*Ida *enters from the kitchen, dressed to the nines in the style of Providence Street, 1910.)*

Ida: *(Shocked.)* Things like that you shouldn't say!
Ren: *(Very haughty.)* In school the other day he asked me what I was reading. I said, "The Lay of the Last Minstrel," and he made an offensive remark. I didn't even know what he meant!
Ida: *(Mildly.)* So how do you know it wasn't nice?
Ren: *(Very lofty, very elegant.)* By the tone!
Ida: *(Putting on a large hat, an odd confection which blooms with cherries and other fruit.)* You like my hat, Ren?
Ren: It's beautiful!

They listen for a moment to a crescendo in TOBEY'*s composition.)*

IDA: That's Tobey practicing. You hear, Ren?

REN: Oh, Ma, when are we moving to New York? I'm just stifled here.

IDA: When your grandfather's second wife dies—may she live to be a hundred and twenty—but she won't—she has a lung—then I'll . . . *(*WILLIE *comes in. He employes his usual tone of jocular levity with* IDA, *but he is under a cloud.)* Oh, Willie, life!

WILLIE: Why, Ida, you're dressed up like Queen Victoria. Where are you going?

IDA: Tonight I have with the Ladies Burial Improvement Society. It's too late I tell them to improve, but they like anyway to gossip. So where are you going?

WILLIE: I have a date with Leah. We're going to White City.

IDA: For a month already since Myra left you have dates with Leah, but where is the result? *(The sound of a shrill whistle from the street.* REN *runs out to piazza.* IDA *explains to* WILLIE.*)* Day and night they whistle for Ren.

WILLIE: Love call!

*(*REN *comes back and makes for the door.)*

IDA: Who is it?

REN: Allie!

*(*IDA *is a bit surprised at* REN*'s quick conversion.* WILLIE *listens to* TOBEY *playing upstairs.)*

WILLIE: *(Impressed.)* Say! Tobey's made progress.

IDA: *(Points to the dress form.)* Look at that dress Leah designed. Filene's in Boston want Leah should be a buyer.

WILLIE: *(Abstracted.)* I shouldn't wonder. Leah is clever.

IDA: Moreandover—from Field Marshall in Chicago you heard? A store he has in Chicago they say bigger than Filene's. To him Leah sent a design. Right away she got a letter for an interview. From a good family he is that Field Marshall—so latch on quick to Leah before he sees her.

WILLIE: *(Smiles at her.)* I adore Leah and it seems selfish somehow to interfere with such a brilliant match!

IDA: Yesterday Norbert Mandel came to see me.

WILLIE: Congratulations!

IDA: Don't scramble me up in my meaning. About Leah he came to see me. An expression from Florida he told me—Leah should fish or cut the bait. And to you too I tell the same thing, Willie—you shouldn't cut fish with Leah either.

WILLIE: Ida, darling, you're scrambling me up a bit—with your meaning.

IDA: What I mean you know.

WILLIE: I guess I do.

IDA: Did you hear, Willie—so crazy he is for Leah, Norbert Mandel, that last Sunday he fell off his horse!

WILLIE: I hope he recovered.

IDA: From the horse he recovered, but from Leah he didn't recover!

WILLIE: *(Enjoys teasing her.)* Oh, now, Ida, you know perfectly well that Leah is far too nice a girl to take the august Mr. Mandel away from you. It wouldn't be ethical.

IDA: In this department I have news. For Leah too. Something important: TO NORBERT MANDEL I HAVE GROWN COOL! So now for Leah with Norbert is ethical.

WILLIE: But Ida! You astonish me. How can you fall in and out of love like that? You're volatile. You're capricious.

IDA: Don't bamble me with those high-tone words. This I tell you, Willie. Educated you are. Bright you're not!

WILLIE: Never was truer word spoken.

IDA: From that Myra you're still looning? On me her mother cries all the time. In the hotel in New York where she spent her honeymoon half-undressed she's selling cigarettes. In the same hotel where she spent her honeymoon! Another hotel she couldn't find! About you, Willie, everybody on the hill is asking questions.

WILLIE: *(Smiles.)* So am I!

IDA: Everybody is asking: He's good with the chemistry.

Why does he all of a sudden switch to study for a lawyer?

WILLIE: Because I want to know for a lawyer.

IDA: Willie, I have loved you all your life—what is with you?

WILLIE: The surface is smooth. The interior's a bit untidy.

IDA: So everything tell to Leah. She'll fix.

WILLIE: I wonder.

IDA: If you won't tell Leah, at least tell me—in plain language.

WILLIE: The fact is, dear Ida, I am afflicted by a syndrome of perplexities. A syndrome, dear Ida—

IDA: Syndrome—pindrome, you've got to live!

WILLIE: That, darling, is the heart of my problem!

*(*LEAH *comes in from her room.* LEAH *and* WILLIE *greet each other warmly but with constraint.)*

LEAH: Oh, hello, Willie.

WILLIE: Hello, Leah.

IDA: *(Pointedly.)* Leah, Mandel was here. He plasters me where are you?

LEAH: *(Smiles at her.)* I'm right here.

WILLIE: Have you heard, Leah? Ida has grown cool to Norbert Mandel!

IDA: Me with Mandel is a romantic dream.

WILLIE: What's wrong with a romantic dream?

IDA: It's no good in the daytime! And I tell you this Willie . . . You should stop cutting fish. And I tell both of you, it's a sin to live alone.

(She goes out. LEAH *and* WILLIE *look at each other, smiling.)*

WILLIE: To be anchored to the bread and wine of life like Ida—to the near horizons—how enviable! Have you noticed? With Ida everything is factual—serious—a Heaven and Earth bounded by marriage.

LEAH: *(Lightly.)* Well, what *are* Heaven and Earth bounded by? *(She is conscious that this may sound like a lead, changes the subject quickly.)* Have you heard from Myra?

WILLIE: Once.

LEAH: In a whole month?

WILLIE: Well, she's very excited about being in New York. She's angling for a stage job. All the managers come to the Astor where she works.

LEAH: Myra is so—seductive. Something wonderful's bound to happen to Myra.

WILLIE: I hope so. *(Probing into his own mind, determined to be truthful.)* I hope so—and I don't hope so.

LEAH: What do you mean?

WILLIE: I love Myra. And yet, way down deep in my heart, I want her *not* to succeed—in whatever she's after—so that *I'll* have a chance. Egotism. Selfish egotism.

LEAH: *(After a moment.)* Willie?

WILLIE: Yes, Leah?

LEAH: I am going to ask you something dreadful.

WILLIE: You may ask me anything you like.

LEAH: Did you have an affair with Myra?

WILLIE: No. She wouldn't. She says if she'd sleep with me—she'd marry me. She's got something special about that. It was dreadful that way—I mean her experience with Dan—on their honeymoon . . . I gather it was something . . . she wants to forget about.

LEAH: Now I'll tell *you* something awful . . . I'm relieved to hear you didn't have an affair with Myra. I was sure you did. I was jealous over that, terribly jealous. How's that for selfish egotism?

WILLIE: You are a very fine person, Leah, I mean—to be so frank with me—to tell me about it . . .

LEAH: Well—so did you! So *you* are a very nice person also! *(*WILLIE *looks at her, troubled.* LEAH *has lost self-control, she pushes on, savage.)* That's what you are and that's what I am—what is Myra? *(She is obeying compulsively a masochistic impulse.)*

WILLIE: *(Disconcerted.)* What is Myra? Gosh, Leah, I don't know. It's like asking to describe a scent—an aroma. It's a kind of magic—a kind of . . .

LEAH: *(Inexorable.)* Well, what?

WILLIE: She will say to you—she's so eager—she's so eager for sympathy, for understanding—she says—she always says . . .

LEAH: Well?

WILLIE: She'll say, "Shall I tell you something, Willie?"

She's always saying that. It draws you into a kind of conspiracy with her, a cozy isolation, a secret shared only with her—from all the world . . .

LEAH: Don't you imagine she says it to everybody?

WILLIE: Of course. But that doesn't matter. But when she says it to you, then you're alone in the world with her. *(He is abashed at having said so much. Rises.)* I don't know what it is, Leah—but you make me talk a lot of nonsense! Let's drop all this. Let's go to White City!

LEAH: I don't think I feel like going any more.

WILLIE: Oh, come on now, Leah—you can't go back on me like that—we have a date.

(There is a moment of awkward silence between them. From upstairs we hear TOBEY *practicing* Opus One.*)*

LEAH: It was very sweet of you, Willie, to give Tobey that piano.

WILLIE: That's his own piece. I have an intuition about Tobey—that one day he'll do something. Tobey's creative. I'll study—he'll know. *(A pause.)* It's only fair to tell you, Leah, I'm going to New York, for good.

(The music fades out.)

LEAH: When?

WILLIE: Tomorrow. I have a feeling that Myra will one day come to a place where she'll need me—when that moment comes I must be there.

LEAH: There'll be other men in Myra's life. You know that. I know that. You'll wait—you'll wait—for the parade to pass.

WILLIE: Myra's vulnerable.

LEAH: She does what she likes. She takes what she likes. What's vulnerable about Myra? *(She gets up and faces him. Passionately—she is not in control of herself.)* Shall I tell you something, Willie? I'm glad you're going to New York. We've seen a lot of each other since Myra left. I look forward to the evenings when I have dates with you—but I dread them too. We talk. We make conversation. But with Myra at the back of your mind every second, it's an agony for me. I want no more of it. When Myra ran away I was happy, I thought—there, I'm rid of her. But I'm not. She's here. I'm not rid of her. I'll never be rid of her. If I felt there was any future in Myra for you I'd—I'd—

WILLIE: *(Comes close to her.)* Leah—dearest Leah—

LEAH: Don't come near me! I wish Myra were dead!

WILLIE: *(Whispers to her.)* Leah. Sweet Leah. I adore you. I love you. Darling Leah . . .

LEAH: She doesn't love you—but I do. That's why she won't sleep with you, because she doesn't love you—but I love you, Willie . . .

(He kisses her. The kiss becomes long and passionate.)

LIGHTS DIM OUT

Scene 4

Several days later.

The lights go up on MR. SACHER'*s room.* TOBEY *is curled up reading. From the next room we hear* MR. SACHER'*s nighttime prayer.*

MR. SACHER'S VOICE: ". . . May the angel Michael be at my right hand, Gabriel at my left . . ."
TOBEY: *(Looks up from his book, calls.)* Father! Father!
FATHER: *(Comes in.)* Yes, Tobey. What is it?
TOBEY: Those four angels you're always praying to—
FATHER: Well?
TOBEY: Why don't they *do* more?
FATHER: They do the best they can!
TOBEY: They couldn't save Mother. Is it because they're good that they can't do more?
FATHER: The good are not without power, Tobey. Their very existence is a power. *(We see* WILLIE *coming up the street with his suitcase.)* Otherwise the evil would have the field to themselves.
TOBEY: They certainly give those good angels a hard time!

*(*WILLIE *reaches the stoop and whistles his Beethoven signal.* TOBEY *jumps up and goes to the door.)*

FATHER: Here comes the oracle—turn over your questions to him.

*(*WILLIE *comes into the room.)*

TOBEY: Hello, Willie. You going someplace?
WILLIE: New York.

TOBEY: When?

WILLIE: *(Puts suitcase down.)* Tonight. I know it's late, Mr. Sacher. I just had to say good bye to Tobey.

FATHER: How long are you going for, Willie?

WILLIE: For good, I hope.

FATHER: What about your job here?

WILLIE: I'll get a better one in New York.

FATHER: Yes?

WILLIE: I've got plans for Tobey too. I know he wants to be a composer. When he gets through school I want him to join me in New York. That's where the opportunity is.

FATHER: Your plans are far-ranging, Willie. Now what made you reach this decision so suddenly?

WILLIE: It's not sudden. I've been planning this for some time.

FATHER: Myra?

WILLIE: I've had a telegram from her. She needs me.

FATHER: So this is your objective?

WILLIE: What's wrong with that?

FATHER: It isn't enough.

WILLIE: My other objectives are boundless.

FATHER: That's too much.

WILLIE: *(Teasing, with humor.)* Not for me. I'm insatiable. I'm going to cross all frontiers, master all the disciplines, then come back here and emancipate you.

FATHER: Oh, Willie, you won't be able to emancipate anybody until you've disciplined yourself.

WILLIE: *(In mock despair.)* I'm afraid my mission will fail. You live in a closed world.

FATHER: And you live in a limitless one.

WILLIE: It gives me more room.

FATHER: You joke, but that is your danger—too much room. Because there must be limits—that's what sanity is—a sense of limitation.

WILLIE: What are limits for you are chains for me.

FATHER: Words. Words. Admit it, Willie—you're chasing Myra. She doesn't love you. She'll never love you. Why don't you declare a loss and turn to someone else?

WILLIE: Because I'm afraid of bankruptcy. I can't expect you to understand what I feel for Myra. Myra's installed inside me, independent of me, feeding upon me, but it has nothing to do with Myra really.

FATHER: Evidently you prefer mystery to light—the riddle to the answer. And all your gifts will go for nothing. *(*WILLIE *turns away.)* I'm concerned about you, Willie. You run a grave risk.

WILLIE: *(Turns back.)* Life *is* a risk. Life *is* a danger. I'm not lucky the way you are—to be securely locked in a cell of faith. I wouldn't exchange my danger for all your security.

FATHER: You wave your danger like a banner. The facts of life may be pedestrian, but they are unalterable. You charge at them, but they will resist your charge, and you will come out the loser . . . Good-bye, Willie . . .

WILLIE: *(As he grabs his suitcase and runs out.)* I'll write you, Tobey!

(The lights dim down to come up on the stoop.)

TOBEY: *(Following* WILLIE *to the stoop.)* Willie! Willie! *(*WILLIE *stops.)* Willie, you're terribly angry with Father, aren't you?

WILLIE: Yes. I am.

TOBEY: Why?

WILLIE: Because he told the truth.

TOBEY: Then why are you going?

WILLIE: Because I must.

TOBEY: I see you must.

WILLIE: Whatever is ahead of me I've got to meet it—I've got to meet it head on.

TOBEY: Have you told Leah?

WILLIE: Yes. It's too late now, Tobey. *(A moment. He consciously lightens the mood.)* New York isn't Europe after all. You'll write. I'll write. We'll keep in touch. *(A pause. He reaches out his hand to* TOBEY. *They shake hands like two men.)* So long, Tobey.

TOBEY: *(Fighting tears.)* So long, Willie.

WILLIE: Work hard. Keep well.

TOBEY: You too, Willie.

WILLIE: *(Starts up the hill, stops.)* Finish *Opus One*.

TOBEY: I will. I'll finish it. *(*WILLIE *goes quickly.)* Don't go, Willie. Don't go.

CURTAIN FALLS

ACT III

Scene 1

New York City, five years later. The set consists of Ida*'s living room, stage right; and* Tobey*'s and* Willie*'s garret living room, stage left.*

Ida*'s flat is directly across the hall from her father's on West Eighty-sixth Street. A few pieces from Providence Street have been moved here. Prominently placed is the imposing, large photograph of her father, the Ramov.*

The lights come up on Tobey*'s and* Willie*'s flat, which is in Morningside Heights. On the easel of a cheap upright piano are* Tobey*'s music-manuscript papers. Nearby is a bridge table with a green-shaded light over it, over which* Tobey *is leaning, composing away. Every once in a while he experiments with a dissonant phrase on the piano, which he can do without moving from the table. He is in a profound concentration. The piece on which he is working is as far removed as possible in spirit from the melodious and pensive Chopin which we heard him play in Act II. His own composition is jagged, dissonant, very modern.*

When the telephone rings, Tobey *answers it. It is* Ida, *from the living room of her flat. As he reaches the phone and picks up the receiver, we light up on* Ida*'s flat.*

Tobey: Hello.
Ida: *(On the telephone.)* Hello, it's you, Tobey?
Tobey: Yes. How are you, Ida?
Ida: Fine. But this is not why I called you. Willie is there?
Tobey: Not just now. I know he has a date with Myra.

IDA: So why is he chasing with that Myra when she is crazy in love with another man?

TOBEY: That's a tough question to answer. I find it hard to pin Willie down these days—a bit like trying to put mist in a bottle.

IDA: But this is not why I called you. Why I called you is to tell you Leah is back from Chicago.

TOBEY: Oh, that's nice. How is she?

IDA: Wonderful. A wonderful job she has on Fourteenth Street. With me she is staying till she finds an apartment. The baby she adapted is here too. Wait till you see him, Tobey, you'll right away melt. What I want you should come to dinner and Willie he should come too.

TOBEY: *With* Myra?

IDA: Better without. But if I have to I have to. Leah is crazy to see you, Tobey, so come right away. Come quick.

TOBEY: Okay.

(She hangs up. We see TOBEY *hang up. He is smiling. He picks up his manuscript, looks at it, throws it down with a kind of disgust—then he picks up his coat and starts out for* IDA*'s. The light dims down on* TOBEY*'s apartment. Just as* IDA *leaves the telephone in her apartment it rings again.* IDA *turns to answer it.)*

IDA: *(On phone.)* So who are you? . . . Oh, Mrs. Grodberg from Fourteen F . . . Tell me, Mrs. Grodberg, do I know you? . . . At my stepmother's funeral was the whole city of New York so I'm sorry I don't remember you, Mrs. Grodberg . . . To my father you want an introduction? . . . Tell me, Mrs. Grodberg, are you healthy? . . . *(*REN *comes in, now an attractive young miss. She listens to her mother with some impatience.)* Are you pious? . . . I had in mind a Boston woman with whom my father could live out his life . . . well, promises I can't make, Mrs. Grodberg, but I will keep you in mind. . . . Yes, yes, I will mention to Poppa. . . . *(Kindly.)* On pins and needles you shouldn't be sitting because a long time you may be sitting. . . . So good bye, Mrs. Grodberg. *(*IDA *hangs up. She looks at* REN*, over-*

whelmed by her responsibilities.) Till I find for Poppa I won't have a moment's peace!

REN: Is Myra coming for dinner?

IDA: Maybe. That *hitzel-dritzel* is always with a maybe.

REN: *(Swooning over* MYRA.*)* She's so *glamorous*. Wasn't she beautiful in the show?

IDA: Beautiful she was, but so undressed I thought any minute they would turn the shower bath on her. What do you think, Ren? From Mandel I had a ring.

REN: Congratulations! Are you engaged?

IDA: On the telephone. He's coming.

REN: You're so busy marrying off other people you don't notice anything about *me*. I am going through a crisis. I'm crazy about this boy I met, a French major at Columbia.

IDA: So bring him.

REN: He keeps putting me off. He prefers *common* girls.

IDA: A Frenchman! What do you expect?

REN: Oh, Ma, you're hopeless.

IDA: Don't worry, darling, when the time comes for you I'll find.

REN: The time is *now,* Ma!

IDA: Now is the time I wish you would go in the kitchen and peel some onions.

REN: *(With disdain.)* Onions!

(The doorbell rings. IDA *gets up.)*

IDA: So here is Mandel.

(She goes out to the hallway. REN *looks at herself in the mirror, does something to her hair.)*

REN: *(Bitterly.)* Onions! *(But she yields to the exigencies of existence and goes into the kitchen.* IDA *comes in with* MANDEL. MANDEL *is tanned almost to blackness. He wears a sharkskin suit and twirls a cane.)*

IDA: *(Palpitating in spite of herself.)* A joy it is to see you, Mandel!

MANDEL: *(Very formal.)* Did you receive my communication from Florida?

IDA: I received but I did not answer because I was cool to you. Now I see you I tell you the truth my heart jumps. How can this be when I am cool? *(*MANDEL *twirls his ginger-colored mustache—does not deign to comment on this paradox.* IDA *stares at him with rapt admiration.)* Tell me, Mandel. This color you are all over?

MANDEL: *(With great delicacy.)* With certain considerations, Mrs. Feinberg. I understand Miss Long is now back from Chicago and residing on these premises.

IDA: She is.

MANDEL: I told you years ago Norbert Mandel has great willpower. He never gives up.

IDA: So what don't he give up?

MANDEL: Leah from Fitchburg. That's what he don't give up.

IDA: Leah put out of your mind.

MANDEL: Norbert Mandel is faithful! Norbert Mandel is steadfast! He don't switch!

IDA: With Leah you don't fit, Mandel.

(He walks away, swinging his cane debonairly. He abandons Romeo, becomes Machiavelli. IDA *watches him, fascinated.)*

MANDEL: *(Twirling his cane in large circles.)* While she was in Chicago, I understand Leah took it into her head to adapt a baby.

IDA: So what has that?

MANDEL: A very peculiar thing, you will admit, for a young girl to do.

*(*LEAH *comes in. She is older, but very handsome, assured and smart.)*

LEAH: *(Breathless.)* Oh, Ida, I'm so lucky. I've found a lovely apartment right— *(Sees* MANDEL.*)* Oh, Mr. Mandel.

MANDEL: *(All charm.)* Why so formal? After the length of our acquaintanceship you are surely justified in calling me Norbert.

IDA: *(Helping as far as she can.)* Yes, Leah. Call him Norbert. You'll feel closer.

LEAH: I've got quite a lot on my mind.

IDA: So how long does it take to call him Norbert?

MANDEL: *(To* LEAH.*)* You are starting in, I understand, as buyer in a dress shop on Fourteenth Street.

LEAH: Yes. I am.

MANDEL: Should be with luck.

LEAH: Thank you.

MANDEL: In Boston I have just acquired an important situation where I plan to put up a superior market.

LEAH: I'm glad. *(As she starts for the bedroom.)* I'm afraid you'll have to excuse me. I want to look in on my baby.

MANDEL: *(Flushes.)* Norbert Mandel is not used to being cut off in the middle. *(A moment. He glares.)* Norbert Mandel is a busy man! *(Looks at his watch.)* In a half-hour I have with a syndicate. *(He is simmering with fury. He moves to the door.)* Norbert Mandel knows when he is not welcome. *(A moment; revengeful.)* And how is your baby, Miss Long?

LEAH: Very well, thank you.

MANDEL: Norbert Mandel likes children, Miss Long. Maybe it is better for the baby you should the sooner the better be *Mrs.* Long.

(At this, IDA*'s eyes flash.)*

IDA: *(Rises.)* Mandel—what are you grabbling?

MANDEL: I think Miss Long knows.

IDA: Listen to me, Mandel! Cool I was to you already. Now I am frozen!

MANDEL: *(Drops* IDA, *addresses* LEAH.*)* At your feet, Miss Long, Norbert Mandel lays his heart—baby or no baby. Should you care to communicate with me I am in Rooms Two thirty-four, Two thirty-five in the Waldorf-Astoria Hotel on Thirty-fourth Street and Fifth Avenue.

IDA: *(In spite of herself, this tidbit fascinates her.)* Two rooms you have, Mandel!

MANDEL: Yes. Norbert Mandel always takes two rooms. One is for sitting.

IDA: Mandel, you should not come here again. Go to your rooms and sit in both of them.

MANDEL: *(Appeals to* IDA *with great sincerity.)* Mrs. Feinberg—tell her. What I feel for Miss Long is the kind of occurrence that occurs once in a lifetime. *(His voice rises.)* I am enamored. Deeply enamored.

IDA: You hear, Leah, what he is?

MANDEL: I want her to do me the honor to be my bride. *(He faces* LEAH. *He suddenly loses all his bravado. He has the courage, facing defeat, to reveal it as a façade.)* Miss Long, I am not a refined man. But my heart is in the right place. Miss Long, with you I could become refined. With you I could become educated. Please, Miss Long.

LEAH: *(Touched.)* I'm sorry, Norbert—I'm very sorry.

MANDEL: This is the last appeal of Norbert Mandel. What are you now? A buyer with an adapted baby that's not adapted.

(He goes out. IDA*'s eyes blaze. She turns to* LEAH.*)*

IDA: That he should let a thing like that drop from his mouth—never again will I arrange for Mandel!

LEAH: *(Quietly.)* It's true though, Ida.

IDA: To such slanders you shouldn't even listen!

LEAH: *(Very moved by* IDA*'s faith.)* But *I* am telling you, Ida.

IDA: *(Overcome with shock.)* Oh, I forgot. You I have to believe.

LEAH: I lied to you five years ago about my reason for going to Chicago. I was afraid it would be a shock to you.

IDA: So how could it be a shock if you did it?

LEAH: I went there—and got a job there—to have my baby.

IDA: *(Grasping at a straw.)* So it must be you're married?

LEAH: No, Ida, I'm not married.

IDA: *(Still struggling with the horrendous fact.)* But, Leah treasure! If you had a baby—even if all by yourself—he must have a father! *(Looks up at her.)* So who is the father?

LEAH: Willie Lavin.

IDA: *(Gets up indignantly.)* Willie Lavin! This from Willie Lavin I wouldn't believe.

LEAH: *(Smiles faintly.)* I had more to do with it than he did. Don't blame him! He was perfectly honest. He was always crazy about Myra. He never pretended.

IDA: But why didn't *he* tell me?

LEAH: Because he doesn't know. That's why I went to

Chicago in the first place. Because I didn't want him to know.

IDA: He must right away marry you!

LEAH: *(Very firm.)* He doesn't know and I don't want him to know and I trust you not to tell him.

IDA: But for the baby it's no good. Not to have even a father!

LEAH: I've been through all that. I had a terrible struggle about that. It's all I'll ever have of Willie's and I *wanted* it—because I wanted Willie.

IDA: *(Bewildered; it is too much for her.)* But, Leah angel, don't you *want* to get married?

LEAH: Not in the least.

IDA: *(Her universe overturned.)* A wonderful girl like you should be an old maid!

LEAH: *(Smiles.)* Well, not quite.

IDA: When you wrote me you adapted a baby, I said to myself, "How can you take in your house a perfect stranger?" Now I see he wasn't such a stranger!

LEAH: That's right—he's no stranger.

IDA: *(Moved.)* The poor little orphan.

LEAH: *(Laughs. Rises, starts toward bedroom.)* Not yet, Ida. I'm very much alive! *(Stops a moment at the door.)* I can trust you, can't I? Not to tell *anybody*—nobody in the whole world.

IDA: Who should I tell? *(Thinks a moment.)* I think I'll call up Mandel and invite him to dinner.

LEAH: What for?

IDA: Now that I know it's true what he said, I want to tell him he's a liar.

LEAH: *(Laughs.)* Oh, Ida!

(She blows IDA *a kiss and goes inside.* IDA *is in a daze. She sits, fans herself with the edge of her kitchen apron.* REN *comes in from the kitchen.)*

REN: I can't cope with any more onions, Ma. Let me arrange the flowers on the dining-room table.

IDA: *(Sits, overcome by her worry. To get rid of* REN*—)* Arrange! Arrange!

REN: What's the matter, Ma?

IDA: Everything! *(Catches herself.)* I mean nothing. *(The telephone rings.* IDA *rises, goes and picks up the re-*

ceiver.) Hello—the number you have right but the exchange is not right, so who are you?— It's too bad, Mr. Brown, you have a wrong number, but anyway call me later because now I'm busy. Glad to have met you, Mr. Brown. *(She hangs up and sits on the chair.)*

REN: Ma! It was a wrong number! Why did you ask him to call back?

IDA: A nice voice he had, very educated, and he sounded lonely.

REN: Oh, Ma! *(She goes out to the dining room as* TOBEY *comes in.)*

TOBEY: Hello, Ida.

IDA: *(Absently, without looking at him, her mind awhirl.)* Oh, come in Tobey life. *(She rises.)*

TOBEY: *(Kisses her on the cheek.)* How are you, Ida?

IDA: This don't ask me.

TOBEY: What's wrong?

IDA: *(Sitting on sofa.)* This don't ask me either.

TOBEY: Anything serious?

IDA: Tobey. To you I have to talk. To you I have to tell a secret. But first you must promise me—by your mother-may-she-rest-in-peace you must promise me—that what I'm telling you won't tell a living soul.

TOBEY: *(Sits beside her.)* I promise.

IDA: You heard that in Chicago Leah adapted a baby?

TOBEY: Yes. I did.

IDA: *She didn't adapt.* She *had.*

TOBEY: *(This* is *a surprise.)* Are you sure?

IDA: More sure I couldn't be! But I have your promise, Tobey—not to tell anybody in the whole world.

TOBEY: *(Sincerely.)* Of course you have!

IDA: *(Abruptly.)* Except Willie Lavin! Him you can tell!

(As he looks at her, he rises slowly, comprehension of the truth and of the meaning of her maneuver breaking in on him.)

LIGHTS DIM OUT

Scene 2

At TOBEY*'s. The next evening.*

WILLIE *is pacing in their room.* TOBEY *comes in, taut with determination to make* WILLIE *live up to his responsibilities.*

WILLIE: Hello, Tobey.

TOBEY: I'm glad I found you. I want to talk to you. I waited up for you last night.

WILLIE: I was with Myra. But I've been waiting for you too, Tobey. I have something I want to speak to you about.

TOBEY: Look, Willie, sit down.

WILLIE: *(Cuts in, doesn't sit, picks up* TOBEY*'s score.)* How's it going? *(*TOBEY *makes a gesture of disgust at his manuscript.)* Heard yet from that fellow you submitted your piece to?

TOBEY: George Slocum. I've been expecting a call all day but I haven't heard from him, probably never will. What the hell ever made me think I was a composer anyway? *(Sitting on piano stool.)* But that's not what I want to talk to you about.

WILLIE: *(Cutting in again.)* Congratulate me. I passed my bar exams.

TOBEY: Congratulations. But I'm not surprised. You can do anything when you set your mind to it.

WILLIE: But, Tobey, I want to ask you a favor.

TOBEY: What?

WILLIE: I want to go back to Worcester. I want you to come with me.

TOBEY: What for?

WILLIE: Impulse to revisit the scenes of our youth. Think things over. Get back to first principles. I've come to a kind of conclusion, Tobey—it'll probably seem strange to you. I passed the bar exam with flying colors, but the thought of practicing law revolts me. Now for the first time I feel I know what I want to do.

TOBEY: Now listen to me, Willie.

WILLIE: *(Sitting on the bed.)* Here's the thing. I'm sick of the endless revolutions of my thoughts. I'm sick of pondering the mysteries that are insoluble. Everything is a question, everything is a dilemma. I long, Tobey, for the simple, the finite, the concrete.

TOBEY: That's wonderful. I'm happy to hear you say that, Willie. That's exactly what I want to talk to you about.

WILLIE: *(Presses on. Passes his hand over his forehead.)* I don't sleep, you know, Tobey. I want to forget everything I've ever studied, ever thought. I want to go back to Worcester—get a job.

TOBEY: You better listen to me, Willie, before you fly off on another tangent.

WILLIE: No. But this is sound. No tangent. I want to go back and take a job in a factory. I want to do a job that requires no thought, tending a machine. I want to be tired at the end of the day, Tobey—spent—so tired that I'll fall into dreamless sleep. Will you know me in overalls, Tobey?

TOBEY: *(Deeply disturbed. A moment.)* Willie . . . I've got to have your attention about something vital.

WILLIE: Oh, by the way, Myra wants to have dinner with us.

TOBEY: Hasn't she gone to California yet?

WILLIE: That's all collapsed.

TOBEY: Really?

WILLIE: She doesn't project, it seems. That director she's in love with isn't taking her. All her hopes have vanished . . . to such a degree that she wants to marry me.

TOBEY: *(Thinks he sees it now.)* Will Myra consent to be the wife of a factory hand? I can't quite see her in that role.

WILLIE: If I married her now it would be out of pity and she deserves better than that. The truth is, I don't want to marry Myra.

TOBEY: I don't believe that.

WILLIE: Myra doesn't either. You know, Tobey, I've lived so long with this obsession for Myra that without it—I'd feel—unemployed.

TOBEY: Willie, now for God's sake listen to me. If you really want the finite, the concrete, you don't have to go to a factory in Worcester. Because they're all right here for you.

WILLIE: How?

TOBEY: You have a responsibility here—to Leah.

WILLIE: How can you trace responsibility to its ultimate source?

TOBEY: *(Rises.)* God damn it! Why do you talk about ultimate responsibility when you have an immediate one? Leah's adopted child is your child.

WILLIE: *(After a moment.)* That possibility has occurred to me, you know.

TOBEY: It has?

WILLIE: But I preferred to accept Leah's fiction.

TOBEY: Well, now you know it isn't fiction. It's a fact. A fact which you must face.

WILLIE: *(Suddenly docile, goes dead.)* Tobey—the True Name of the Lord your father used to forbid you to seek. Do you remember?

TOBEY: Yes. But what has that got to do with what we're talking about?

WILLIE: *(Sitting on bed.)* I used to think there was only one mystery, the key to everything, and you'd get it all in one blinding flash—

TOBEY: Willie—please—

WILLIE: *(In a spiral of amused speculation.)* No, Tobey, no, it's just an amusing idea I had—a vagrant idea— It just occurs to me—the heart of the mystery, the mystery that is the core of everything—supposing by some lucky chance I did hit on it—probed it—supposing it turned out, this terrible secret, to be quite simple really—even a bore? *(*TOBEY *is staring at him in desperation, in agony, in despair.)* I think that's funny. I thought it would amuse you. I see it doesn't.

TOBEY: *(Sitting on the stool.)* No, it doesn't amuse me.

WILLIE: What were you saying, Tobey, what were you telling me?

TOBEY: I was telling you about Leah.

WILLIE: I think about Leah—the suffering she must have gone through.

TOBEY: *(Jumps up, cutting him off.)* Listen, Willie. I owe you more than I can ever possibly repay: you made me see life as a wonder and as an adventure. I owe you everything—even the truth. And the truth is that you have wasted yourself—scattered your gifts, as my father warned you. I remember your arguments with my father. He was right—all the way. You feel this need for the concrete, so you turn to manual labor, which will probably bore you to death after one week. Another horizon, another mirage, another postponement. Chemistry. Law. What you know, what you have, you turn your back on. It is the unknowable that lures you. Even my talent is an unknown quantity and you made a concept out of that. Willie, the near things, the achievable things, the warm winds of affection, of friendship, of love, don't seem to touch you any more.

(A pause.)

WILLIE: You're right. I'm destructive to people—Leah—even Myra. I waited for Dan to die. He was my friend. When he died I couldn't repress a feeling of exaltation. Ethically speaking, I am a murderer.

TOBEY: Concepts again! That's distortion. *(Sitting beside him.)* Willie, for pity's sake, live your own life in *this* world. Attach yourself to something definite—with all the problems that go with it—Leah—your child—you could do for him what you've done for me.

WILLIE: You're right about everything. The pupil has outstripped the master. In the kid is wisdom. Tell me what to do, Tobey, and I'll do it.

TOBEY: I don't have to tell you. You know what to do.

WILLIE: I'll go to Leah and ask her to marry me. *(A pause.)* But what about Myra? She's coming here.

TOBEY: *(Rises.)* I'll take care of Myra. I'll take her to dinner.

WILLIE: Call me from the restaurant.

TOBEY: But you'll be proposing to Leah.

WILLIE: *(Rises.)* Then call me.

TOBEY: What for?

WILLIE: Just call me.

TOBEY: If you like.
WILLIE: I'll be waiting for your call.

*(*WILLIE *goes.* TOBEY *stares after him. He is deeply troubled, quite uncertain whether he has had a victory. He begins to pace the room, in unconscious imitation of his father—his hands behind his back. Out of a deep well of memory he begins to pray—as his father used to pray.)*

TOBEY: "At my right the angel Michael, at my left Gabriel, and over my head the Divine Presence of God . . ."

LIGHTS DIM OUT

Scene 3

At IDA*'s. The action follows the preceding scene at* WILLIE*'s. The doorbell rings.* LEAH *goes to open it, admitting* WILLIE.

LEAH: *(Very surprised, even a bit aghast. They stand face to face for a moment.)* Willie! Did you come to see me or Ida?
WILLIE: I came to see you.
LEAH: *(Doesn't believe it.)* Well, Ida's gone out.
WILLIE: *(After an awkward pause.)* Felt like seeing you.
LEAH: Well—thank you.

(Another awkward pause.)

WILLIE: *(Points to her dress.)* Pretty dress, Leah.
LEAH: Oh, it's just a little number I picked off my own racks on Fourteenth Street. *(A moment.)* Like a drink?
WILLIE: No, thanks.

(Another pause.)

LEAH: Well—sit down—relax. Working for the bar exams, I hear.
WILLIE: Just passed them. *(A moment. She looks at him; she is mystified by his visit. He starts walking around the room, suddenly wheels around, shoots the question at her.)* How would you like to be a lawyer's wife, Leah?
LEAH: *(A moment, lightly.)* Are you proposing to me?
WILLIE: *(Meets her look.)* Yes.

LEAH: *(It flashes through her mind that he has heard about the paternity of the baby.)* Why?
WILLIE: I've been thinking about you—and I want to.
LEAH: What about Myra?
WILLIE: Myra's out of my life.
LEAH: *(She smiles at him.)* Is *that* why you're proposing to me? Is Myra getting married?
WILLIE: Not as far as I know.
LEAH: Anyway—do have a drink.
WILLIE: Anything— *(*LEAH *moves at once to the little bar, fixes two drinks and hands one to him.* WILLIE *takes the drink and lifts the glass in a toast to her.)* Cheers!
LEAH: *(Touches her glass to his.)* Cheers!
WILLIE: To our future. *(She laughs.)* What's the joke?
LEAH: What a funny man you are!
WILLIE: *(Bleakly. Puts his glass down on bar.)* I can be funny on occasion.

(A moment. She keeps studying him.)

LEAH: You know, I suppose, that I've adopted a baby.
WILLIE: Yes. Ida told me.
LEAH: *(Points to bedroom.)* He's asleep. In there. Would you like a look at him?
WILLIE: No thanks.
LEAH: I know! Other people's babies are always a bore.
WILLIE: But you haven't answered my question.
LEAH: What?
WILLIE: How you would like to be a lawyer's wife?
LEAH: And you haven't answered mine.
WILLIE: What was that?
LEAH: About Myra. She's probably walking out on you again. So you come in here and ask me to marry you. *(Moves away from him.)* Well, I won't. I don't want to marry you. Nor anybody.
WILLIE: It seems unfair to yourself.
LEAH: You must understand my position.
WILLIE: I understand. You don't love me any more.
LEAH: *(In a low voice.)* I do though. I'll never love anybody else.
WILLIE: Then why? . . .
LEAH: I couldn't marry you because I don't think I could stand the perpetual threat of Myra.

WILLIE: *(With anger.)* It's all over—I've told you—between Myra and me. Over!

LEAH: I'd hate to put you to the test!

WILLIE: *(His voice rises.)* THEN STOP DOING IT! I've just been telling Tobey—Myra means nothing to me!

LEAH: I wonder.

WILLIE: *(Begins to lose control of himself.)* I BEG YOU, LEAH—DON'T CROSS-EXAMINE ME.

LEAH: *(Going to him. Relentless.)* Perhaps Ida told you something more. *(She waits. He says nothing. He sits on the hassock.)* I asked her not to. *(He is still silent.* LEAH *knows now.)* So that's why you're here! To make an honest woman out of me! Good, moral boy from Worcester!

WILLIE: *(In manic fury.)* You drive me crazy. Stop analyzing. I want you to marry me. I have the right to marry you. CAN'T YOU JUST ACCEPT THE FACT? I love you. I admire you. *(Rises.)* Isn't that enough for you? Have a heart, Leah! Give me a chance, can't you! *(Sitting on sofa.)* You don't risk anything.

LEAH: *(Turns to him. Her voice rises.)* I risk this hold Myra has over you!

WILLIE: Don't keep flinging Myra at me. It's broken, I tell you. How many times do I have to tell you? There's no hope in Myra—not only for me—for anybody. Nor for herself. Shall I tell you why? She's in pursuit of a romantic ideal. She'll pursue it endlessly. It will elude her endlessly.

LEAH: *(Beginning to be persuaded.)* It's taken you a long time to find this out about Myra.

WILLIE: No. I always knew it.

LEAH: *(Passionately.)* Then why, Willie . . . why have you let it drag on so long?

WILLIE: *(Quiets down, very clever, aware that he is pouring the word into an ear less subtle than his own.)* What I have felt for Myra was an obsession. Nothing more. What I feel for you—what I have always felt for you—is real. *(This does it. This persuades her. She goes to him, overcome with compassion and love for him.)*

LEAH: *(Kneeling beside him.)* Willie! Willie! *(She embraces him. A silence. Quietly—)* In my heart I have always been married to you. Don't you know that?

WILLIE: *(Numbly.)* It's all right, darling. *(With a little laugh.)* I accept you. I hadn't realized it was possible.

LEAH: What?

WILLIE: It's odd, with you I feel peace—security—a kind of peace.

(There is a long silence. She kneels beside him, holding his hand on the arm of the sofa.)

LEAH: *(Very moved.)* I can hardly believe it—I can hardly—oh, Willie, Willie, Willie—after all we've been through!

WILLIE: It's settled, isn't it, Leah, between us, the two of us—we're committed to each other, aren't we?

(The outside door is heard closing. IDA *comes in.)*

IDA: Did I stay away long enough?

LEAH: *(Gets up, smiles at her.)* Yes, you did, Ida. Just long enough.

WILLIE: There's no doubt about it, Ida—when you die, there will be joy in Heaven among all the unmarried angels.

IDA: *(Hugging* LEAH.*)* What I want there should be joy on *earth* among all the unmarried angels. *(Hugs* WILLIE.*)* With you, Willie, such a slow poke you are I began to give up hope.

WILLIE: *(Infuriated with his own bravura. Sits on sofa.)* Slow poke. Admitted. But you, Ida, you marry people off by instinct. You rush them to the altar. You seem unaware of the immense responsibility. For a girl like Leah the alternatives are endless. How can you settle on me? Think of it, Ida—consummation! *(He rises.)* "For as long as you both shall live." For eternity! That's a long time, darling. Who knows what lurks in the distance—for Leah? For me? What angers, what bitterness, accidents, disaster, deathknell sounding through the wedding bells!

IDA: Wedding bells you and Leah don't need. They'll wake up the baby! *(To* LEAH.*)* You told him yet that he's going to have a father?

LEAH: I'll wake him up now to break the news to him. *(*LEAH *starts out;* WILLIE *starts to follow. She stops at* *the door, kisses* WILLIE, *faces him toward* IDA.*)* I'll tell it to him gently. *(She goes.)*

IDA: Willie darling, so long I waited to see this day I thought it would never come.

WILLIE: *(After a pause.)* Perhaps it's come too late, darling.

IDA: What too late?

WILLIE: Too late for the near horizons—I abdicate!

IDA: What are you talking?

WILLIE: *(His exuberance gone—tender, and with abdication.)* Ida. Ida. Ida. *(He sinks into the sofa.)*

IDA: *(Rises, going to him.)* Willie! Willie!

(The telephone rings.)

WILLIE: That's Tobey.

IDA: *(Rises.)* So ask him to come over—so we can tell the good news—

(By this time WILLIE *is on the phone.)*

WILLIE: Tobey . . . where are you? At the restaurant? You got your call from Slocum—he's going to play it! Oh, Tobey, that's great! I'll meet you at the apartment . . . I'll tell you later, Tobey . . . Good-bye, Tobey. *(He hangs up. Goes to* IDA.*)* Tobey's having his first performance. Isn't that wonderful! I feel as happy about this as you do, Ida, when you pull off a match. It's a funny thing, Ida, that the only responsibility I have ever recognized is my responsibility to Tobey. He's grown-up—surpassed me, as I knew he would. But my faith in Tobey and what he might do . . . that was tangible—that was real—and not as Tobey thinks—a concept . . . Good-bye . . . I love you— *(He starts out.)*

IDA: What are you rushing?

WILLIE: *(Comes back.)* I want you to give Tobey a message for me.

IDA: But I just heard you—you're going to see Tobey.

WILLIE: In case I miss him, Ida—in case I miss him—

IDA: So what should I tell him? *(He stands silent, as if he hadn't heard her. To rouse him out of his trance, frightened—)* Willie life—look at me—what should I tell Tobey?

WILLIE: Tell him!

IDA: So?

WILLIE: Tell him he's right about the factory in Worcester—instead tell him I'm going to stop holding on to the bedposts. Can you remember that? Good-bye. I love you. *(He rushes out.)*

IDA: Willie! Willie! *(*IDA *starts for the bedroom, then runs to the telephone.)* Central, get me Schuyler nine-seven-four.

(The lights come up in TOBEY*'s apartment.* TOBEY *comes into his room as the telephone rings.)*

TOBEY: *(Sitting on bed, picks up the receiver.)* Hello.

IDA: Hello, Tobey.

TOBEY: Ida, where's Willie? I can't wait to talk to him about my concert!

IDA: Tobey, from Willie I'm worried—all settled he is with Leah and all of a sudden—

TOBEY: What?

IDA: You he runs to see.

TOBEY: That's all right. We arranged it that way—

IDA: All right it isn't.

TOBEY: Why?

IDA: He said good-bye to me as if he was saying good-bye . . . Go downstairs to the sidewalk—wait for him, Tobey—grab him, Tobey!

TOBEY: All right.

IDA: Something else he told me to tell you, Tobey. Crazy it sounded— He said I should tell you that no longer he's holding onto the bedposts. *(*TOBEY*'s hand holding the receiver goes limp. It falls to his lap.)* What does he mean? Tobey . . . *(As she gets no answer she jiggles the phone in terror.)* Tobey! Tobey! Tobey!

LIGHTS DIM OUT

Scene 4

Back in Worcester. The street leading to JIM*'s office. We hear the oboe:* JIM *is playing the melody from Handel's* Water Music, *as at the beginning of the play.*

Summer twilight. TOBEY *is walking to* JIM*'s office—as we saw him with* WILLIE *when he was a child.* TOBEY*'s walk is slow, dejected. He pushes the bell button.*

We light up on JIM*'s office, unchanged, and see* JIM *putting down his oboe, as we saw him do earlier when he admitted* TOBEY *and* WILLIE.

JIM: Well, Tobey! I've been expecting you! How are you?

(They shakes hands.)

TOBEY: Just about as low as you can get. Felt I had to come back here. I wanted to revisit the scenes where Willie and I were happy—when we didn't know what was ahead of us—doom for Willie—despair for me.

JIM: Now, Tobey! Tobey, pessimism is easy. Despair is a luxury you can't afford. Sit down. *(He points to the sofa.)*

TOBEY: Same old sofa.

JIM: Naturally.

TOBEY: Still a symbol of conquest?

JIM: Alas, only a symbol. The sofa is willing, but the flesh is weak.

TOBEY: Jim— *(He sits on the sofa.)*

JIM: *(Sitting beside him.)* Yes, Tobey.

TOBEY: Willie— *(But he can't. His head sinks in his hands and he shakes it in misery.)* No use, I can't.

JIM: Look, Tobey. You could have done nothing for Willie, I assure you.

TOBEY: He asked me to come here with him. Maybe if I had come—

JIM: It would have done no good. Willie was without an anchor—the anchor of reality. He couldn't face the everyday responsibilities of a permanent attachment—not only to a woman but to a job.

TOBEY: *(With bitter self-reproach.)* And yet—the last time I saw him—I pushed him into reality.

JIM: It had nothing to do with you. Suicide, you know, is self-criticism in its most acute form.

TOBEY: *(Gets up, starts to walk the room, flailing in self-abasement.)* The worst of it is—do you know why I didn't come with him when he asked me?

JIM: Why?

TOBEY: Because I was all excited over the performance of a piece I'd written.

JIM: How did it go, the concert?

TOBEY: Disaster.

JIM: Didn't anybody care for it?

TOBEY: A few fanatics for modern music like myself. One critic—

JIM: *(Rises.)* Wonderful! One whole critic!

TOBEY: You should have seen the others! I am a failure as an artist. A failure as a friend.

JIM: You can't be a failure at your age. It takes much longer to achieve solid failure. You're lucky to get your first failure over with so early. The sooner to get to your second!

TOBEY: But this is it, Jim—half the time it's not Willie I'm thinking of, it's that damned concert! *(Summing it up.)* Look, Jim—it is a world without Willie, and still the ego twitches.

JIM: Thank God. Once the ego stops twitching not even a great doctor like myself can do anything! What are you doing for dinner?

TOBEY: I'm free.

JIM: Come back at eight and I'll take you to Putnam and Thurston's.

TOBEY: *(Rises, starts out; stops.)* Jim, now that I'm back here, the whole past is like a heavy sack around me. All the dead—my father and mother—Dan and Willie—the anonymous dead. *(Sits on sofa.)* What does it all mean anyway?

JIM: Why does life have to have meaning? It's good in itself. That oboe is good. What Willie gave you was good. Dinner tonight will be good—I hope! *(Sitting beside him.)* You speak of the anonymous dead. They're not anonymous. They're figures in the tapestry in which we ourselves are figures. They've given us what we are. When you're young, you try to get away from them. But when you're mature, you return to them. You'll embrace them. And they'll support you, I promise you. Every breath you draw—every thought you have—every note you set down—you're living off them. *(Rises.)* Now, clear out!

TOBEY: *(Rises, goes to door.)* All right, Jim. I'll go. *(Stands at the door, looking out through the twilight.)* The seven hills of Worcester . . .

JIM: *(Brusquely.)* Lift your eyes to them! See you at eight!

*(*TOBEY *goes out.* JIM *starts playing his oboe. We see* TOBEY, *his stance more buoyant, his head up, walking down the street accompanied by the sound of Handel's melody.)*

CURTAIN FALLS

THE TENTH MAN

A COMEDY-DRAMA IN THREE ACTS

by

Paddy Chayefsky

He was Sidney Chayefsky at birth in New York in 1923 and as a student at City College and Fordham University. But on Sunday mornings in the Army, when he chose Mass over K.P., his buddies dubbed him Paddy. The nickname seems apt enough for a Jewish dramatist who set his early works in the Bronx and populated them with lower middle class ethnic characters. That focus contributed to Chayefsky's reputation as the Clifford Odets of the 1950s.

The comparison with Odets extends to a career that prominently included screenwriting. The film version of Chayefsky's *Marty* (1955), adapted from his TV play, won him the New York Film Critics Award, a Cannes Film Festival Golden Palm, and his first Academy Award. He collected two more Oscars for *The Hospital* (1971) and *Network* (1976). *Network*'s protagonist, a commentator frustrated by the illogic of a dehumanizing society who invited viewers to join him as he raged, "I'm mad as hell, and I'm not going to take it anymore," found a ready audience. The line echoed across the country, a national slogan for months. The satirical tone and the concentration on corporate bureaucracy in *Network* and *The Hospital* were new vehicles for themes Chayefsky had developed more simply and sentimentally in his early, explicitly Jewish works, like celebrating the power of love and the worth of people who only appear unremarkable in a society ruled by tinsel values.

Similarly, the later plays show that his vision had transcended the Bronx and its ordinary people. *The Passion of Joseph D.* (1964) is a "political burlesque" about Stalin's role in the Russian Revolution; *The Latent Het-*

erosexual (1968) portrays the bitter comedy of bureaucratic society. Chayefsky was reportedly writing a play about Alger Hiss when he died in 1981.

Universalism also characterized Chayefsky's activism in the 70s: he co-founded Writers and Artists for Peace in the Middle East and served as a delegate to the 1971 Conference on Soviet Jewry. His work, in and out of the arts, was shaped by regard for the individual and concern for a world outgrowing human scale and control. The seriousness of his convictions notwithstanding, he rarely failed to leaven them with the perspective and devices of Jewish humor.

Chayefsky first came to public attention during the golden age of TV drama in the 1950s. Typical of the acclaimed scripts he wrote for the Philco-Goodyear Playhouse is *Holiday Song* (1952). Here the piety of a disaffected cantor is restored when, on the eve of Rosh Hashanah, he is mysteriously led to reunite two Holocaust survivors. Several incidents in *Holiday Song* later found their way into *The Tenth Man* (1959): the rekindling of a disenchanted religious leader's faith, and the pilgrimage made by an elderly Jew through the New York City transit system to consult a chief rabbi. Chayefsky adapted his teleplay *Middle of the Night* to the Broadway stage in 1956 where it ran for 477 performances. Edward G. Robinson played the middle-aged Jewish widower who escapes loneliness and suffocating predictability when he marries a non-Jewish woman half his age, scandalizing his family and hers.

Chayefsky's most thoroughly Jewish plays are *The Tenth Man* and *Gideon* (1961), each cited among their season's Ten Best in the *Best Plays* series. Just as Odets had probed the contemporary relevance of an Old Testament story in *The Flowering Peach,* Chayefsky reworked the hero of the book of Judges as a man challenged both by divine favor and modern temptations. Like Odets's Judaized characters, Chayefsky's authentic Jew finds himself at odds with a God who demands unquestioning obedience of a man just learning to value and trust his own judgment. The God of *Gideon* also demands love, but the title character finds it easier to love man than God because, "To love you, God, one must be a god himself."

The source of *The Tenth Man* is the most famous of the

classic Yiddish plays, S. Anski's *The Dybbuk* (1914). Maurice Schwartz introduced the play to New York at his Yiddish Art Theater in 1922.[1] Three years later, the Vilna Troupe brought its legendary staging of *The Dybbule* to the United States, where various members of the company toured with it. Following its English language premier in 1925, the work has had countless productions and inspired several notable adaptations. While Chayefsky thus drew on material familiar to American Jewish audiences, he had much to do to fashion an American Jewish play of it.

The differences between the two works are as significant as the similarities. The very settings announce the divergences: Anski lays his play in the hermetic, cohesive world of the *shtetl,* where the generations interrelate within generally accepted values of Judaism. The source of dramatic conflict is, in fact, the unwonted challenge to those values. By contrast, *The Tenth Man* is set in a storefront synagogue whose hyphenated name proclaims a compromise, and whose affiliates, a cross section of American Jewry, represent the numerous implications of Jewishness, and even of Judaism, in mid-century America. A side-by-side examination of the two plays reveals the challenges Chayefsky met as he considered equivalences for the mysticism, the opposing forces, and the characters in the masterwork that inspired him. Such a comparison makes the alternate title of Anski's play, *Between Two Worlds,* apply to Chayefsky's with new layers of meaning.

Love plays a central role in both works. In *The Tenth Man,* it ranges from Hirschman's devotion to cabala to the more profane expressions of love that account for the presence of a dybbuk in the first place. Several of the congregants take responsibility for the Whore of Kiev who inhabits Evelyn Foreman. In doing so, they demonstrate a kind of love fundamental both to this play and to *The Dybbuk. The Tenth Man* celebrates the love of neighbor manifest in the individual's acceptance of responsibility to the community. Small wonder that when Arthur Brooks, paradigm of contemporary cynicism and anomie, finds himself in this rarefied atmosphere, he is totally disoriented. The miracle of Brooks's redemption and perhaps the only credible explanation for his swift confidence that he can cure Evelyn with his love stem from his reconnecting with the power of Jewish communal responsibility.

Although, as several reviewers noted, the redemption of a cynic through religion is a classic theme in Western literature, exorcisms are not routine events, not even in the Yiddish theatre. The enactment of this exotic Jewish ritual on the American stage warrants attention. So does the fact that the *entire* action of *The Tenth Man* is laid in a synagogue. One can question the playwright's substitution of "praying shawl" for *tallith,* or "quorum" for *minyan,* but it is impossible to ignore the fact that this Broadway play makes the morning service an integral part of its plot and the recitation of the confessional Al-Chait prayer a dramatic necessity. Chayefsky brought audiences into an orthodox synagogue as naturally as Odets and Regan had brought them into Jewish homes several decades earlier. *The Tenth Man* filled Broadway's Booth Theatre for 623 performances, an index of how far Jews had come in America as it entered the 1960s: Not only were the strangers welcome, they were no longer strangers.

The Tenth Man was presented by Saint Subber and Arthur Cantor at the Booth Theatre, New York City, November 5, 1959; directed by Tyrone Guthrie; setting and lighting by David Hays; costumes by Frank Thompson; with the following cast:

HIRSCHMAN	*Arnold Marle*
SEXTON	*David Vardi*
SCHLISSEL	*Lou Jacobi*
ZITORSKY	*Jack Guilford*
ALPER	*George Voscovec*
FOREMAN	*Jacob Ben-Ami*
EVELYN FOREMAN	*Risa Schwartz*
ARTHUR BROOKS	*Donald Harron*
HARRIS	*Martin Garner*
RABBI	*Gene Saks*
KESSLER BOYS	*Alan Manson and Paul Marin*
POLICEMAN	*Tim Callaghan*

SYNOPSIS OF SCENES

The action takes place in an Orthodox Synagogue in Mineola, Long Island.

ACT I

Before the Morning Prayers.

ACT II

SCENE 1. The Morning Prayers.
SCENE 2. Before the Afternoon Prayers.

ACT III

The Exorcism.

ACT I

SCENE: *Interior of the synagogue of the Congregation Ateret-Tifereth Yisroel. It is a poor congregation, and the synagogue is actually a converted shop. A raised platform surrounded by a railing contains the lectern and the Holy Ark. This altar is surrounded by rows of plain wooden folding chairs which constitute the seating accommodations for the congregation. On the far side of the altar is an old desk at which the rabbi presides when teaching Hebrew school. A partitioned area downstage right is the rabbi's study, a crowded little cubicle containing a battered mahogany desk and chair, an old leather armchair, a worn leather couch, and piles of black prayer books. On the walls are old framed pictures of bearded patriarchs in desolate obsession over their Talmuds and perhaps a few familiar scenes from the Old Testament. Downstage is a metal heating unit. There is a second heating unit upstage, and a door leading apparently to a bathroom. The front door is stage left.*

TIME: *It is 6:30 a.m. on a cold winter day.*

AT RISE: THE CABALIST *stands in the middle of the synagogue, entirely wrapped in a thick white linen praying shawl with broad black stripes, praying silently from a heavy prayer book that rests on the railing of the altar. Suddenly he pauses in his intense devotions, clutches at the railing as if to hold himself from falling. We have the impression that he is faint, near to swooning. He is a small, bearded man, in his seventies, his face lean and lined, his eyes sunken and hollow. He wears a small black skullcap from beneath which stick out gray forelocks and sidecurls—a testament to his orthodoxy. After a moment, he regains his strength and returns to his prayers. Three men hurry into the synagogue out of the oppressive cold of the street. They are* THE SEXTON, SCHLISSEL *and* ZITORSKY. *They all wear heavy overcoats and gray fedoras.* SCHLISSEL *and* ZITORSKY *are in their early seventies.* THE SEXTON *is a small, nervous, bespectacled man of 48. We know he is a sexton because he carries a huge ring of keys and is always doing something. They rub their hands for warmth and huff and puff and dart quick looks at* THE CABALIST, *who is oblivious to their entrance.*

SCHLISSEL: *(Muttering.)* Close the door. *(Light pours down on the synagogue as* THE SEXTON *raises the window curtains.* THE SEXTON *scurries upstage to fuss with the heater in the rear of the synagogue.* SCHLISSEL *and* ZITORSKY *shuffle downstage to a small naked radiator and stand silently—indeed a little wearily—for a moment;* SCHLISSEL *sighs.)* So how goes it with a Jew today?

ZITORSKY: How should it go?

SCHLISSEL: Have a pinch of snuff.

ZITORSKY: No, thank you.

SCHLISSEL: Davis won't be here this morning. I stopped by his house. He has a cold. His daughter-in-law told me he's still in bed.

ZITORSKY: My daughter-in-law, may she grow rich and buy a hotel with a thousand rooms and be found dead in every one of them.

SCHLISSEL: My daughter-in-law, may she invest heavily in General Motors, and the whole thing should go bankrupt.

ZITORSKY: Sure, go have children.

SCHLISSEL: The devil take them all.

THE SEXTON: *(Scurrying downstage; to* THE CABALIST *as he passes.)* Hirschman, are you all right? *(He flutters, a small round ball of a man, to the door of the rabbi's office, which he enters.)*

SCHLISSEL: Foreman won't be here today.

ZITORSKY: What's the matter with Foreman?

SCHLISSEL: His granddaughter today. This is the morning.

ZITORSKY: Oh, that's right. Today is the morning.

SCHLISSEL: Listen, it's better for everybody.

ZITORSKY: Sure.

SCHLISSEL: I told Foreman, I said: "Foreman, it's better for everybody." The girl is becoming violent. I spoke to her father. He said to me they live in terror what she'll do to the other children. They came home one night, they found her punching one of the little children.

ZITORSKY: Well, what can you do?

SCHLISSEL: What can you do? You do what they're doing. They're putting her back in the institution.

ZITORSKY: Of course. There she will have the benefit of trained psychiatric personnel.

SCHLISSEL: The girl is incurable. She's been in and out of mental institutions since she was eleven years old. I met the psychiatrist there, you know, when I was up there to visit Foreman last week. I discussed the whole business with him. A fine young fellow. The girl is a schizophrenic with violent tendencies.

ZITORSKY: *(Considers this diagnosis for a moment, then sighs.)* Ah, may my daughter-in-law eat acorns and may branches sprout from her ears.

SCHLISSEL: May my daughter-in-law live to be a hundred and twenty, and may she have to live all her years in *her* daughter-in-law's house.

(A fourth old Jew now enters from the street, a patrician little man with a Vandyke beard and a black homburg. His name is ALPER. *He bursts into shrill prayer as he enters.)*

ALPER: *(Chanting.)* As for me in the abundance of Thy loving kindness will I come into Thy house; I will worship toward Thy holy temple in the fear of Thee. How goodly are Thy tents, O Jacob . . . *(As precipitously as the prayer had begun, it now drops into nothing more than a rapid movement of lips.* THE SEXTON *acknowledges* ALPER*'s arrival from the rabbi's office, where he plunks himself behind the desk and begins hurriedly to dial the phone.* ALPER*'s voice zooms abruptly up into a shrill incantation again.)* . . . in the truth of Thy salvation. Amen!

SCHLISSEL: Amen.
ZITORSKY: Amen.

*(*ALPER *joins the other two* OLD MEN *and they stand in silent rueful speculation.)*

THE SEXTON: *(On phone.)* Hello, Harris? This is Bleyer the Sexton. Come on down today, we need you. Foreman won't be here. Davis is sick. We won't have ten men for the morning prayers if you don't come down— Services start in twenty minutes. Hurry up— Wear a sweater under your coat— All right— *(He hangs up, takes a large ledger from the desk and begins to nervously examine its pages.)*

SCHLISSEL: Hirschman slept over in the synagogue again last night. Have you ever seen such pietistic humbug?

ALPER: Well, he is a very devout man. A student of the Cabala. The Rabbi speaks of him with the greatest reverence.

SCHLISSEL: Devout indeed. I assure you this lavish display of orthodoxy is a very profitable business. I was told confidentially just yesterday that his board and food are paid for by two foolish old women who consider him a saint.

ALPER: It can't cost them very much. He's been fasting the last three days.

SCHLISSEL: And the reason he sleeps in the synagogue so frequently is because his landlady does not give him heat for his own room in the mornings.

ZITORSKY: Ah, go be an old man in the winter.

ALPER: I must say, I really don't know what to do with myself on these cold days.

SCHLISSEL: I'm an atheist. If I had something better to do, would I be here?

ZITORSKY: You know what would be a nice way to kill a day? I think it would be nice to take a trip up to Mount Hope Cemetery and have a look at my burial plot. A lovely cemetery. Like a golf course, actually. By the time one gets there and comes back, the whole day has been used up. Would you like to come? I'll pay both your fares.

ALPER: Why not? I have never been to Mount Hope. I have my burial plot on Mount Zion Cemetery.

ZITORSKY: Oh, that's a beautiful cemetery.

ALPER: Yes, it is. My wife wanted to buy plots in Cedar Lawn because her whole family is buried there, but I wouldn't hear of it.

ZITORSKY: Oh, Cedar Lawn. I wouldn't be buried in Cedar Lawn.

ALPER: It's in such a bad state. The headstones tumble one on top of the other, and everybody walks on the graves.

ZITORSKY: They don't take care in Cedar Lawn. My wife once said, she should rest in peace, that Cedar Lawn was the tenement of cemeteries.

ALPER: A well-turned phrase.

ZITORSKY: She had a way with words, God grant her eternal rest.

ALPER: I'd like you to come to Mount Zion sometimes, see my plot.

ZITORSKY: Maybe we could make the trip tomorrow.

SCHLISSEL: Listen to these two idiots, discussing their graves as if they were country estates.

ZITORSKY: Where are you buried, Schlissel?

SCHLISSEL: Cedar Lawn.

ALPER: Well, listen, there are many lovely areas in Cedar Lawn. All my wife's family are buried there.

ZITORSKY: Come with us, Schlissel, and have a look at my grave.

SCHLISSEL: Why not? What else have I got to do?

(ALPER *now slowly goes about the business of donning his praying shawl and phylacteries, which he takes out of a velvet praying bag. Among Jews, prayer is a highly individual matter, and peripatetic to the bargain. The actual ritual of laying on the phylacteries is a colorful one.* ALPER *extracts his left arm from his jacket and rebuttons his jacket so that his shirt sleeved left arm hangs loose. Then, the shirt sleeve is rolled up almost to the shoulders, and the arm phylactery, a long thin black leather thong, is put on by wrapping it around the arm seven times and around the middle finger of the left hand three times. All this is accompanied by rapidly recited prayers, as is the laying on of the head-phylactery. All the while* ALPER *walks bending and twisting at the knees, raising his voice occasionally in the truly lovely words of incantation. In a far upstage corner,* THE CABALIST *huddles under his enveloping white praying shawl, his back to everyone else, deeply involved in his personal meditations. The synagogue itself is a shabby little place, the walls yellowed and cracked, and illumined by a fitful overhead bulb. There is indeed at this moment, a sense of agelessness, even of primitive barbarism. During this* THE SEXTON *has dialed a second number.)*

THE SEXTON: Hello? Mr. Arnold Kessler, please— How do you do? This is Mr. Bleyer, the Sexton at the synagogue. Perhaps you recall me— Did I wake you up? I'm terribly sorry. As long as you're up, according to my books, your father died one year ago yesterday, on the eleventh day in the month of Schvat, may his soul fly straight to the Heavenly Gates, and how about coming down with your brother and saying a memorial prayer in your father's name?— Let me put it this way, Mr. Kessler. You know, we can't have morning prayers without a quorum of ten men. If you and your brother don't come down we won't have a quorum— As a favor to me— Kessler, may your children be such devoted sons, and bring your brother. You are doing a good deed. Peace be with you. Hurry up— *(He hangs up, sits frowning, totaling up on his fingers the number of men he has, scowls.)*

ALPER: *(His voice rises for a brief moment.)* and it shall be to Thee for a sign upon Thy hand, and for a memorial between Thy eyes . . .

THE SEXTON: *(Rises abruptly from his chair and bustles out of the office to the front door of the synagogue. To nobody in particular.)* Listen, I'm going to have to get a tenth Jew off the street somewheres. I'll be right back. Schlissel, will you please fix that bench already, you promised me.

(He exits. SCHLISSEL *nods and picks up a hammer. For a moment, only the sing-song murmur of the rapid prayers and the upstage tapping of* SCHLISSEL*'s hammer fill the stage. The front door to the synagogue now opens, and a fifth old Jew peers in. He is a frightened little wisp of a man named* FOREMAN. *He is obviously in a state. He darts terrified looks all about the synagogue, and then*

abruptly disappears back into the street leaving the synagogue door open. Nobody is yet aware of his brief appearance. A moment later he is back, this time leading a slim young Girl *of 18, wearing a topcoat, who is also distracted. The* Old Man *herds her quickly across the synagogue to the rabbi's office, pushes her in, and closes the door behind her. She sits in the rabbi's office, almost rigid with terror. Like his friends,* Foreman *wears a heavy winter coat and a warm fedora some sizes too small for him. He stands and watches the others apprehensively. At last* Alper *reaches the end of his laying on of the phylacteries, his voice climbing to a shrill incantation.)*

Alper: *(To* Foreman, *moving slowly as he prays.)* . . . and it shall be for a sign upon Thy hand, and for frontlets between Thy eyes; for by strength of hand the Lord brought us out from Egypt. Amen!

Foreman: *(Muttering, his head bobbing nervously.)* Amen!

Alper: I thought you weren't coming down today, Foreman.

Foreman: *(His mouth working without saying anything. Finally says:)* Alper—

Alper: You seem agitated. Is something wrong?

Foreman: *(Staring gauntly at his friend.)* Alper, I have her here.

Alper: You have who here?

Foreman: I have my granddaughter Evelyn here. I have her here in the rabbi's office.

Alper: What are you talking about?

Foreman: I took her out of the house while nobody was looking, and I brought her here. I am faint. Let me sit down. *(He sinks onto a chair.* Alper *regards him with concern.)*

Alper: Here, David, let me take your coat.

Foreman: Alper, I have seen such a thing and heard words as will place me in my grave before the singing of the evening service. Blessed art Thou, O Lord, King of the Universe, Who hath wrought the wonders of the world. *(Suddenly half-starting from his seat.)* I must speak to Hirschman! This is an affair for Hirschman who has delved into the Cabala and the forbidden mysteries of numbers.

ALPER: Sit down, Foreman and compose yourself. *(*FOREMAN *sinks slowly back onto his chair.)* Why did you bring her here? Foreman, you are my oldest friend from our days in the seminary together in Rumni in the Province of Poltava, and I speak to you harshly as only a friend may speak. You are making too much out of this whole matter of the girl. I know how dear she is to you, but the girl is insane, for heavens' sakes! What sort of foolishness is this then to smuggle her out of your son's home? To what purpose? Really, Foreman, a gentle and pious man like you! Your son must be running through the streets at this moment shouting his daughter's name. Call him on the phone and tell him you are bringing her back to him.

FOREMAN: *(Stares at* ALPER, *his pale eyes filled with tears.)* Alper—

ALPER: David, my dear friend, make peace with this situation.

FOREMAN: *(Whispering.)* She is possessed, Alper. She has a dybbuk in her. A demon! It spoke to me. *(He stares down at the floor at his feet, a numb terror settling over his face.)* It spoke to me. I went into my granddaughter this morning to comfort her, and I said: "How are you?" And she seemed quite normal. She has these moments of absolute lucidity. *(He looks gauntly at* ALPER *again.)* She seemed to know she was being taken to the institution again. Then suddenly she fell to the floor in a swoon. I said: "Evelyn, what's the matter?" And she looked up at me, and it was no longer her face, but a face so twisted with rage that my blood froze in my body. And a voice came out of her that was not her own. "Do you know my voice?" And I knew it. I knew the voice. God have mercy on my soul. I stood there like a statue, and my granddaughter lay on the floor with her eyes closed, and the voice came out of her, but her lips never moved. "David Foreman, son of Abram, this is the soul of Hannah Luchinsky, whom you dishonored and weakened in your youth, and the gates of Heaven are closed to me." And my granddaughter began to writhe on the floor as if in the most horrible agony, and she began to laugh so loudly that I was sure my son and daughter-in-law in the living room could hear. I flung the door open in panic, and my son and daughter-in-law were sitting there talking, and they heard nothing. And I tell you, shrieks of laughter were coming from this girl on the floor. And I closed the door, and besought God, and finally the dybbuk was silent. May God strike me down on this spot, Alper if every word I tell you is not true.

ALPER: *(Has slowly sat down on an adjacent chair, absolutely enthralled by the story. He stares at* FOREMAN.*)* A dybbuk?

FOREMAN: *(Nodding.)* A dybbuk. Could you believe such a thing?

ALPER: Who did the dybbuk say she was?

FOREMAN: You should remember her. Hannah Luchinsky.

ALPER: The name is vaguely familiar.

FOREMAN: You remember Luchinsky, the sexton of the Rumni seminary with his three daughters? Hannah was the handsome one, who became pregnant, and they threw stones at her, called her harlot, and drove her out of the city.

ALPER: *(Recognition slowly coming over him.)* Oohhh.

FOREMAN: I was the one who debased her.

ALPER: You? You were such a nose-in-the-books, a gentle and modest fellow. Dear me. A dybbuk. Really! What an extraordinary thing. Schlissel, you want to hear a story?

SCHLISSEL: *(Coming over.)* What?

ALPER: *(To* ZITORSKY, *who ambles over.)* Listen to this. Foreman is telling a story here that will turn your blood into water.

SCHLISSEL: What happened?

FOREMAN: What happened, Schlissel, was that I went in to see my granddaughter this morning and discovered that she was possessed by a dybbuk. Now, please, Schlissel, before you go into one of your interminable disputations on the role of superstition in the capitalist economy, let me remind you that I am a follower of Maimonides and—

SCHLISSEL: What are you talking about?

FOREMAN: A dybbuk! A dybbuk! I tell you my granddaughter is possessed by a dybbuk! Oh, my head is just pounding! I do not know which way to turn.

SCHLISSEL: What are you prattling about dybbuks?

ALPER: *(To* SCHLISSEL.*)* The voice of Hannah Luchinsky spoke to him through the lips of his granddaughter.

ZITORSKY: Oh, a dybbuk.

SCHLISSEL: What nonsense is this?

ALPER: *(To* FOREMAN.*)* Are you sure?

FOREMAN: *(Angrily.)* Am I sure? Am I a peasant who leaps at every black cat? Have I ever shown a susceptibility to mysticism? Have you not seen me engaging Hirschman over there in violent disputation over the fanatic numerology of the Cabala? Have I not mocked to his very face the murky phantasy of the Gilgul with its wispy souls floating in space? Really! Am I sure! Do you take me for a fool, a prattler of old wives' tales? Really! I tell you I heard that woman's voice as I hear the cold wind outside our doors now and saw my granddaughter writhing in the toils of possession as I see the phylactery on your brow this moment. I was a teacher of biology for thirty-nine years at the Yeshiva High School. A dedicated follower of the great Rambam who scoffed at augurs and sorcerers! For heaven's sakes! Really! I report to you only what I see! *(He strides angrily away, and then his brief flurry of temper flows away as abruptly as it flared.)* My dear Alper, please forgive this burst of temper. I am so distressed by this whole business that I cannot control my wits. I assure you that it is as hard for me to believe my own senses as it is for you.

ZITORSKY: When I was a boy in Lithuania, there was a young boy who worked for the butcher who was possessed by the dybbuk.

SCHLISSEL: *(Scornfully.)* A dybbuk. Sure. Sure. When I was a boy in Poland, I also heard stories about a man who lived in the next town who was possessed by a dybbuk. I was eight years old, and one day after school, my friends and I walked barefoot the six miles to the next town, and we asked everybody, "Where is the man with the dybbuk?" And nobody knew what we were talking about. So I came home and told my mother: "Mama, there is no man with a dybbuk in the next town." And she gave me such a slap across the face that I turned around three times. And she said to me: "Aha! Only eight years old and already an atheist."

Foreman, my friend, you talk like my mother who was an ignorant fishwife. I am shocked at you.

FOREMAN: Oh, leave me be, Schlissel. I have no patience with your pontificating this morning.

ALPER: Don't let him upset you, Foreman. The man is a Communist.

FOREMAN: He is not a Communist. He is just disagreeable.

SCHLISSEL: My dear fellow, I have never believed in God. Should I now believe in demons? A dybbuk. This I would like to see.

FOREMAN: *(Furiously.)* Then see! *(He strides to the door of the rabbi's office and wrenches the door open. The* OTHERS *gingerly follow him to the opened doorway and peer in. The girl,* EVELYN, *stares at them, terrified. In a thunderous voice,* FOREMAN *cries out:)* Dybbuk! I direct you to reveal yourself! *(*THE GIRL *stares at the four patently startled* OLD MEN, *and then suddenly bursts into a bloodcurdling shriek of laughter. The four* OLD MEN *involuntarily take one step back and regard this exhibition wide-eyed.)* What is your name?

THE GIRL: I am Hannah Luchinsky.

FOREMAN: Who are you?

THE GIRL: I am the Whore of Kiev, the companion of sailors.

FOREMAN: How came you to be in my granddaughter's body?

THE GIRL: I was on a yacht in the sea of Odessa, the pleasure of five wealthy merchants. And a storm arose, and all were lost. And my soul rose from the water and flew to the city of Belgorod where my soul appealed to the sages of that city. But since I was debauched they turned their backs on me.

FOREMAN: And then?

THE GIRL: Then my soul entered the body of a cow, who became insane and was brought to slaughter, and I flew into the body of this girl as if divinely directed.

FOREMAN: What do you want?

THE GIRL: I want the strength of a pure soul so that I may acquire that experience to ascend to heaven.

FOREMAN: I plead with you to leave the body of this girl.

THE GIRL: I have wandered in Gilgul many years, and I want peace. Why do you plague me? There are those among you who have done the same as I and will suffer a similar fate. There is one among you who has lain with whores many times, and his wife died of the knowledge.

ZITORSKY: *(Aghast.)* Oh, my God!

THE GIRL: *(Laughing.)* Am I to answer questions of old men who have nothing to do but visit each other's cemeteries?

ZITORSKY: *(Terrified.)* A dybbuk—a dybbuk—

FOREMAN: Evelyn—Evelyn— She is again in a catatonic state.

*(*THE GIRL *now sits in the rabbi's chair, sprawling wantonly, apparently finished with the interview. The four* OLD MEN *regard her a little numbly. They are all quite pale as a result of the experience. After a moment,* FOREMAN *closes the door of the rabbi's office, and the four* OLD MEN *shuffle in a silent group downstage where they stand each reviewing in his own mind the bizarre implications of what they have seen.* FOREMAN *sinks onto a chair and covers his face with his hands. After a long, long moment,* ZITORSKY *speaks.)*

ZITORSKY: Well, that's some dybbuk, all right.

SCHLISSEL: The girl is as mad as a hatter and fancies herself a Ukrainian trollop. This is a dybbuk?

ALPER: I found it quite an unnerving experience.

ZITORSKY: She caught me dead to rights. I'll tell you that. I was the one she was talking about there, who trumpeted around with women. Listen, when I was in the garment business, if you didn't have women for the out-of-town buyers, you couldn't sell a dozen dresses. Oh, I was quite a gamey fellow when I was in business, a madcap really. One day, my wife caught me in the shop with a model—who knew she would be downtown that day?—and from that moment on, my wife was a sick woman and died three years later, cursing my name with her last breath. That was some dybbuk, all right. How she picked me out! It gave me the shivers.

ALPER: Did you notice her use of archaic language and her Russian accent? The whole business had an authentic ring to me.

SCHLISSEL: What nonsense! The last time I was up to Foreman's the girl confided to me in a whisper that she was Susan Hayward. A dybbuk! Ever since she was a child, Foreman has been pumping her head full of the wretched superstitions of the Russian Pale, so she thinks she is a dybbuk. The girl is a lunatic and should be packed off to an asylum immediately.

ALPER: *(He regards* SCHLISSEL *with a disapproving eye; then takes* SCHLISSEL's *arm and leads him a few steps away for a private chat.)* Really, Schlissel, must you always be so argumentative? We are all here agreed that we have a dybbuk in our company, but you always seem intent on being at odds with everyone around you. Really, look at poor Foreman, how distraught he is. Out of simple courtesy, really, for an old friend, can you not affect at least a silence on the matter? And, after all, what else have you got to do today? Ride two and a half hours to look at Zitorsky's tombstone? When you stop and think of it, this dybbuk is quite an exciting affair. Really, nothing like this has happened since Kornblum and Milsky had that fistfight over who would have the seat by the East Wall during the High Holidays.

ZITORSKY: *(Ambling over.)* That's some dybbuk, all right.

SCHLISSEL: *(Frowning.)* All right, so what'll we do with this dybbuk now that we got it?

ALPER: It seems to me, there is some kind of ritual, an exorcism of sorts.

ZITORSKY: Maybe we should tell the rabbi.

SCHLISSEL: A young fellow like that. What does he know of dybbuks? A dybbuk must be exorcised from the body by a rabbi of some standing. You can't just call in some smooth-shaven young fellow fresh from the Seminary for such a formidable matter as a dybbuk. This rabbi has only been here two months. He hardly knows our names.

ALPER: He's right. You have to get a big rabbi for such a business.

SCHLISSEL: What has to be done is we must get in touch with the Korpotchniker rabbi of Williamsburg, who has inherited the mantle of the great Korpotchniker of Lwow, whose fame extends to all the corners of the world.

ZITORSKY: Oh, a sage among sages.

ALPER: I was about to suggest the Bobolovitcher rabbi of Crown Heights.

SCHLISSEL: Where do you come to compare the Bobolovitcher rabbi with the Korpotchniker?

ALPER: I once attended an afternoon service conducted by the Bobolovitcher, and it was an exalting experience. A man truly in the great tradition of Chassidic rabbis.

ZITORSKY: A sage among sages, may his name be blessed for ever and ever.

SCHLISSEL: It shows how much you know. The Bobolovitcher rabbi is a disciple of the Korpotchniker and sat at the Korpotchniker's feet until a matter of only a few years ago.

ALPER: Listen, I'm not going to argue with you. Either one is fine for me.

SCHLISSEL: The Korpotchniker is the number one Chassidic rabbi in the world. If you're going to involve yourself at all, why not go straight to the top?

ALPER: All right, so let it be the Korpotchniker.

ZITORSKY: For that matter, the Lubanower rabbi of Brownsville is a man of great repute.

SCHLISSEL: The Lubanower! Really! He's a young man, for heaven's sakes!

ALPER: Zitorsky, let it be decided then that it will be the Korpotchniker.

ZITORSKY: I only made a suggestion.

SCHLISSEL: The question is how does one get to the Korpotchniker? One does not drop into his home as if it were a public library. One has to solicit his secretary and petition for an audience. It may takes weeks.

ALPER: I do think, Schlissel, we shall have to get a more accessible rabbi than that. Ah, here is Hirschman, who I am sure can give us excellent counsel in this matter.

(THE CABALIST *has indeed finished his prayers, and is shuffling downstage, a small, frightened little man.* FOREMAN *leaps from his chair.)*

FOREMAN: Hirschman! *(Everyone crowds around* HIRSCHMAN.*)*

ZITORSKY: Oh, boy, Hirschman, have we got something to tell you!

ALPER: Zitorsky, please. Hirschman, you are a man versed in the Cabala, a man who prays with all the seventy-two names of the most Ancient of the Ancient Ones.

FOREMAN: *(Blurting out.)* Hirschman, my granddaughter is possessed by a dybbuk!

THE CABALIST: *(Starting back in terror.)* A dybbuk!

ALPER: Foreman, please, one does not announce such a thing as baldly as that.

THE CABALIST: Are you sure?

FOREMAN: Hirschman, as a rule, I am not given to whimsy.

THE CABALIST: Was it the soul of a woman wronged in her youth?

FOREMAN: Yes.

THE CABALIST: I heard her cry out last night. I awoke for my midnight devotions, and as I prayed I heard the whimpering of a woman's soul. *(A strange expression of bemused wonder settles over his face.)* I have fasted three days and three nights, and I dismissed the sound of this dybbuk as a phantasy of my weakened state. For only those to whom the Ancient One has raised his veil can hear the traffic of dybbuks. Is this a sign from God that my penitence is over? I have prayed for such a sign. I have felt strange things these past days. Sudden, bursting illuminations have bleached mine eyes, and I have heard the sounds of dead and supernatural things. *(He lifts his worn little face, his eyes wide with wonder. The others are put a little ill-at-ease by this effusive outburst.* FOREMAN, *indeed, is quite overwhelmed.)*

ALPER: Actually, Hirschman, all we want to know is if you knew the telephone number of the Korpotchniker rabbi.

THE CABALIST: *(With some effort, he brings himself back to the moment at hand.)* He is my cousin. I will call him for you. *(He moves slowly off, still obsessed with some private wonder of his own, to the wall phone, stage left.)*

ALPER: *(Quite awed.)* Your cousin? You are the Korpotchniker's cousin, Hirschman?

ZITORSKY: *(Hurrying after* THE CABALIST.*)* You'll need a dime, Hirschman. *(He gives* HIRSCHMAN *the ten cent piece.)*

ALPER: Schlissel, the Korpotchniker's cousin, did you hear? Apparently, he's not such a humbug.

SCHLISSEL: I tell you, he gives me the creeps, that Hirschman.

*(*HIRSCHMAN *has dialed a number on the wall phone.* FOREMAN *stands hunched with anxiety at his elbow.)*

THE CABALIST: *(To* FOREMAN, *gently.)* Where is she, the dybbuk?

FOREMAN: In the rabbi's office.

THE CABALIST: You are wise to go to the Korpotchniker. He is a Righteous One among the Righteous Ones. We were quite close as children until I abandoned the Rabbinate. *(On the phone, in soft gentle tones.)* Hello? Is this Chaim son of Yosif— This is Israel son of Isaac— And peace be unto you— There is a man here of my congregation who feels his granddaughter is possessed by a dybbuk and would seek counsel from my cousin— He will bless you for your courtesy. Peace be unto you, Chaim son of Yosif. *(He hangs the receiver back in its cradle, turns to* FOREMAN.*)* Give me a paper and pencil. *(The* OTHERS, *who have crowded around to hear the phone call, all seek in their pockets for a paper and pencil and manage to produce an old envelope and a stub of a pencil between them.)* That was the Korpotchniker's secretary, and you are to go to his home as quickly as you can. I will write the address down for you. It is in Williamsburg in Brooklyn. And you will be received directly after the morning services. *(He sweeps his praying shawl back over his head and retires upstage again for continued devotions.)*

FOREMAN: Thank you, Hirschman. The eye of the Lord will be open to you in the time of your need.

ZITORSKY: Oh, Williamsburg. That's quite a ride from here.

SCHLISSEL: What are you talking about? Foreman, you take the Long Island Railroad to Atlantic Avenue Station where you go downstairs, and you catch the Brooklyn subway.

ALPER: Maybe I should go along with you, David, because a simple fellow like you will certainly get lost in the Atlantic Avenue Station, which is an immense conflux of subways.

SCHLISSEL: What you do, Foreman, is you take the Long Island Railroad to the Atlantic Avenue Station where you take the Double G train on the lower level—

ALPER: Not the Double G train.

SCHLISSEL: What's wrong with the Double G?

ALPER: One takes the Brighton Train. The Double G Train will take him to Smith Street, which is a good eight blocks walk.

SCHLISSEL: The Brighton Train will take him to Coney Island.

ALPER: Foreman, listen to what I tell you. I will write down the instructions for you because an innocent fellow like you, if they didn't point you in the right direction, you couldn't even find the synagogue in the morning. Where's my pencil? *(He has taken the address paper and pencil from* FOREMAN*'s numb fingers and is writing the travelling instructions down.)*

FOREMAN: *(Staring off at the wall of the rabbi's office.)* What shall I do with the girl? I can't leave her here.

ALPER: Don't worry about the girl. She knows me. I'm like a second grandfather to her.

FOREMAN: I don't like to leave her. Did I do right, Alper? Did I do right, kidnapping her this morning and bringing her here? Because the psychiatrist said we must prepare ourselves that she would probably spend the rest of her life in mental institutions. The irrevocability of it! The rest of her life! I was in tears almost the whole night thinking about it. Perhaps, this produced a desperate susceptibility in me so that I clutch even at dybbuks rather than believe she is irretrievably insane. Now, in the sober chill of afterthought, it all seems so unreal and impetuous. And here I am bucketing off to some forbidding rabbi to listen to mystical incantations.

ALPER: The Korpotchniker is not a rogue, Foreman. He is not going to sell you patent medicine. He will advise you quite sensibly, I am sure.

FOREMAN: *(Buttoning his coat.)* Yes, yes, I shall go to see him. You shall have to hide her till I come back. My son has probably called the police by now, and sooner or later they will come here looking for her.

ALPER: Don't worry about it. I won't leave her side for a moment.

FOREMAN: I better tell her I'm going. She'll be frightened if she looks for me, and I'm not here. Ah, my coat— *(He hurries quickly to the rabbi's office, where he stands a moment, regarding* THE GIRL *with mingled fear and tenderness.* THE GIRL *has sunk into the blank detachment of schizophrenia and stares unseeingly at the floor at her feet.)*

SCHLISSEL: So the girl is a fugitive from the police. The situation is beginning to take on charm.

ALPER: Look at Schlissel. The retired revolutionary. As long as it's against the law, he believes in dybbuks.

SCHLISSEL: I believe in anything that involves a conspiracy.

(At this point, the front door bursts open, and THE SEXTON *returns with the announcement.)*

THE SEXTON: I've got a tenth Jew!

ZITORSKY: Sexton, have we got something to tell you!

SCHLISSEL: *(Shushing him abruptly.)* Sha! Idiot! Must you tell everyone?

THE SEXTON: *(He leans back through the open door to the street and says to someone out there.)* Come in, come in— *(A fine-looking, troubled young fellow in his middle thirties, dressed in expensive clothes, albeit a little shabby at the moment, as if he had been on a bender for the last couple of days, enters. His name is* ARTHUR BROOKS. *He stands ill-at-ease and scowling, disturbed in aspect. His Burberry topcoat hangs limply on him.* THE SEXTON *has scooted to the shelf stage right from which he takes a black skullcap, nervously talking as he does.)* Harris didn't come in yet?

SCHLISSEL: No.

THE SEXTON: The two Kessler boys, I called them on the phone, they didn't show up yet? *(Thrusts the skullcap on* ARTHUR*'s head.)* Here's a skullcap, put it on. *(*ARTHUR *takes the skullcap absently but makes no move to put it on. He is preoccupied with deep and dark thoughts.* THE SEXTON *heads for the front door.)* The rabbi's not here yet?

SCHLISSEL: He'll be here in a couple of minutes.

THE SEXTON: It's only seven minutes to the services. Listen, I'm going to the Kesslers'. I'll have to pull them out of their beds, I can see that. I'll be right back. *(To* ARTHUR.*)* You'll find some phylacteries in the carton there. Alper, give the man a prayer book. Sure, go find ten Jews on a winter morning. *(He exits, closing the front door after himself.)*

FOREMAN: *(As he comes out of the office, adjusting his coat about him.)* All right, I'm going. She didn't eat anything this morning, so see she gets some coffee at least. Let's see. I take the Long Island Railroad to Atlantic Avenue Station. Listen, it has been a number of years since I have been on the subways. Well, wish me luck. Have I got money for carfare? Yes, yes. Well—well—my dear dear friends, peace be with you.

ALPER: And with you, Foreman.

ZITORSKY: Amen.

FOREMAN: *(Opening the door.)* Oh, it's cold out there. *(He exits, closing the door.)*

ALPER: He'll get lost. I'm sure of it.

ZITORSKY: Oh, have you ever seen such excitement? My heart is fairly pounding.

ALPER: Oh, it's just starting. Now comes the exorcism. That should be something to see.

ZITORSKY: Oh, boy.

SCHLISSEL: Oh, I don't know. You've seen one exorcism, you've seen them all.

ZITORSKY: You saw one, Schlissel?

SCHLISSEL: Sure. When I was a boy in Poland, we had more dybbuks than we had pennies. We had a fellow there in my village, a mule driver, a burly chap who reeked from dung and was drunk from morning till night. One day, he lost his wits completely, and it was immediately attributed to a dybbuk. I was a boy of ten, perhaps eleven, and I watched the whole proceedings through a hole in the roof of the synagogue. A miracle-working rabbi who was passing through our district was invited to exorcise the dybbuk. He drew several circles on the ground and stood in the center surrounded by four elders of the community, all dressed in white linen and trembling with terror. The Miracle Worker bellowed out a series of incantations, and the poor mule driver, who was beside himself with fear, screamed and— Hello, Harris— *(This last is addressed to a very, very old man named* HARRIS, *who is making his halting way into the synagogue at this moment. He barely nods to the others, having all he can do to get into the synagogue and close the door.* SCHLISSEL *continues his blithe story.)* —and fell to the floor. It was a marvelous vaudeville, really. I was so petrified that I fell off the roof and almost broke a leg. The Miracle Worker wandered off to work other miracles and the mule driver sold his mule and went to America where I assume, because he was a habitual drunkard and an insensitive boor, he achieved considerable success. Our little village had a brief month of notoriety, and we were all quite proud of ourselves.

ALPER: Oh, it sounds like a marvelous ceremony.

SCHLISSEL: Of course, they don't exorcise dybbuks like they used to. Nowadays, the rabbi hangs a small amulet around your neck, intones "Blessed art Thou, O Lord," and that's an exorcism.

ALPER: Oh, I hope not.

SCHLISSEL: Really, religion has become so pallid recently, it is hardly worthwhile being an atheist.

ZITORSKY: I don't even know if I'll come to see this exorcism. I'm already shivering just hearing about it.

ALPER: Well, you know, we are dealing with the occult here, and it is quite frightening. Hello there, Harris, how are you? *(By now, the* OCTOGENARIAN *has removed his overcoat, under which he wears several layers of sweaters, one of which turns out to be one of his grandson's football jerseys, a striped red garment with the number 63 on it. For the rest of the act, he goes about the business of putting on his phylacteries.* ALPER *claps his hands.)* Well, let me find out if we can help this young Jew here. *(He moves towards* ARTHUR BROOKS, *smiling.)* Can I give you a set of phylacteries?

ARTHUR: *(Scowling, a man who has had a very bad night the night before.)* I'm afraid I wouldn't have the first idea what to do with them.

ALPER: You'll find a praying shawl in one of these velvet bags here.

ARTHUR: No, thank you.

ALPER: *(Offering a small black prayer book.)* Well, here's a prayer book anyway.

ARTHUR: Look, the only reason I'm here is a little man stopped me on the street, asked me if I was Jewish, and gave me the impression he would kill himself if I didn't come in and complete your quorum. I was told all I had to do was stand around for a few minutes wearing a hat. I can't read Hebrew and I have nothing I want to pray about, so there's no sense giving me that book. All I want to know is how long is this going to take because I don't feel very well, and I have a number of things to do.

ALPER: My dear young fellow, you'll be out of here in fifteen or twenty minutes.

ARTHUR: Thank you. *(He absently puts the black skullcap on his head and sits down, scowling, on one of the wooden chairs.* ALPER *regards him for a moment; then turns and goes back to his two colleagues.)*

ALPER: *(To* SCHLISSEL *and* ZITORSKY.*)* To such a state has modern Jewry fallen. He doesn't know what phylacteries are. He doesn't want a shawl. He can't read Hebrew.

ZITORSKY: I wonder if he's still circumcised.

ARTHUR: *(Abruptly stands.)* I'd like to make a telephone call. *(Nobody hears him. He repeats louder.)* I said, I'd like to make a telephone call.

ALPER: *(Indicating the wall phone.)* Right on the wall there.

ARTHUR: This is rather a personal call.

ALPER: There's a phone in the rabbi's office there. *(*ARTHUR *crosses to the rabbi's office.)*

SCHLISSEL: Well, look about you, really. Here you have the decline of orthodox Judaism graphically before your eyes. This is a synagogue? A converted grocery store, flanked on one side by a dry cleaner's and on the other by a shoemaker. Really, if it wasn't for the Holy Ark there, this place would look like the local headquarters of the American Labor Party. In Poland, where we were all one step from starvation, we had a synagogue whose shadow had more dignity than this place.

ALPER: It's a shame and a disgrace.

ZITORSKY: A shame and a disgrace.

(In the rabbi's office ARTHUR *is regarding the girl,* EVELYN, *with a sour eye.)*

ARTHUR: Excuse me. I'd like to make a rather personal call.

(THE GIRL stares down at the floor, unhearing, unmoving, off in a phantasmic world of her own distorted creation. ARTHUR sits down at the rabbi's desk, turns his shoulder to THE GIRL, and begins to dial a number.)

SCHLISSEL: Where are all the Orthodox Jews? They have apostated to the Reform Jewish temples, where they sit around like Episcopalians listening to organ music.

ALPER: Your use of the word "apostasy" in referring to Reform Jews interests me, Schlissel. Is it not written in Sifre on Deuteronomy, "Even if they are foolish, even if they transgress, even if they are full of blemishes, they are still called sons?" So, after all, is it so terrible to be a Reform Jew? Is this not an interesting issue for disputation? Oh, my God!

(He wheels and starts back for the rabbi's office. The same thought has been entering the other two old fellows' minds, as has been indicated by a growing frown of consternation on each of their faces. They follow ALPER to the rabbi's office, where he opens the door quickly and stares in at ARTHUR BROOKS. The latter is still seated at the rabbi's desk, waiting for an answer to his phone call, and THE GIRL is still in her immobilized state. ARTHUR bestows such a baleful eye upon this interruption that the three OLD MEN back out of the office and close the door. They remain nervously outside the door of the office. At last, someone answers the phone call.)

ARTHUR: *(On phone, shading his face, and keeping his voice down.)* Hello, Doctor, did I wake you up? This is Arthur Brooks— Yes, I know. Do you think you can find an hour for me this morning?— Oh, I could be in your office in about an hour or so. I'm out in Mineola. My ex-wife lives out here with her parents, you know. And I've been blind drunk for—I just figured it out—three days now. And I just found myself out here at two o'clock in the morning banging on their front door, screaming— *(THE GIRL's presence bothers him. He leans across the desk to her and says:)* Look, this is a very personal call, and I would really appreciate your letting me have the use of this office for just a few minutes.

EVELYN: *(She looks up at him blankly. Hollowly.)* I am the Whore of Kiev, the companion of sailors.

ARTHUR: *(This strikes him as a bizarre comment to make. He considers it for a moment, and then goes back to the phone.)* No, I'm still here. I'm all right. At least, I'm still alive. *(Hides his face in the palm of one hand and rubs his brow nervously.)* I've got to see you, Doc. Don't hang up on me, please. If my analyst hangs up on me, that'll be the end. Just let me talk a couple of minutes— I'm in some damned synagogue. I was on my way to the subway. Oh, my God, I've got to call my office. I was supposed to be in court twice yesterday. I hope somebody had the brains to apply for an adjournment. So it's funny, you know. I'm in this damned synagogue. I'll be down in about an hour, Doctor— Okay. Okay— I'm all right— No, I'm all right— I'll see you in about an hour. *(He hangs up, hides his face in the palms of both hands and slowly pulls himself together. After a moment, he looks up at* THE GIRL, *who is back to staring at the floor. He frowns, stands, goes to the door of the office, opens it, gives one last look at* THE GIRL, *and closes the door again. He finds himself staring at the inquiring faces of the three* OLD MEN.*)* Listen, I hope you know there's a pretty strange girl in there.

(The OLD MEN *bob their heads a little nervously.* ARTHUR *crosses the synagogue, his face dark with his emotions. The three* OLD MEN *regard him anxiously. After a moment,* SCHLISSEL *approaches* ARTHUR.*)*

SCHLISSEL: A strange girl, you say?

ARTHUR: Yes.

SCHLISSEL: Did she say anything?

ARTHUR: She said: "I am the Whore of Kiev, the companion of sailors."

SCHLISSEL: That was a very piquant statement, wouldn't you say?

ARTHUR: Yes, I think I would call it piquant.

SCHLISSEL: What do you make of it?

ARTHUR: *(Irritably.)* Look, I'm going. I have a hundred things to do. I—

SCHLISSEL: No, no, no, sit down. For heaven's sakes, sit down.

ALPER: *(Hurrying over.)* Don't go. Oh, my, don't go. We need you for a tenth man. We haven't had ten men in the morning in more than a week, I think.

ZITORSKY: *(On* ALPER*'s tail.)* Two weeks, at least.

(At this point, HARRIS, *who has finally divested himself of his overcoat, muffler, heavy-ribbed button-down sweaters which were over his jacket and is now enwrapt in a praying shawl, bursts into a high, quavering prayer.)*

HARRIS: Blessed art Thou, O Lord, our God, King of the Universe, Who hath sanctified us by his commandments and . . . *(The words dribble off into inaudibility.* ARTHUR BROOKS *darts a startled look at the* OLD MAN, *not being prepared for this method of prayer, and moves a few nervous steps away from the other* OLD MEN, *where he stands rubbing his brow, quite agitated.)*

ALPER: *(Whispering to* SCHLISSEL.*)* So what happened in there? Did she say anything?

SCHLISSEL: Yes, she said she was the Whore of Kiev, and the companion of sailors.

ALPER: Oh, dear me.

SCHLISSEL: I'm afraid we shall have to get her out of the rabbi's office, because if she keeps telling everybody who walks in there that she is the Whore of Kiev, they will pack us all off to the insane asylum. And let us be quite sensible about this situation. If Foreman has kidnapped the girl, he has kidnapped her, however kindly his motives—not that I expect the police to regard a dybbuk as any kind of sensible explanation. Whatever the case, it would be a good idea to keep the girl a little less accessible. *(The wall phone rings.)* Ah! I'll tell you who that is. That's Foreman's son calling to find out if Foreman and the girl are here. *(The phone rings again.)* Well, if you won't answer it, I'll answer it. *(He crosses to the wall phone.)*

ALPER: We could take her to my house. Everybody is still

sleeping. We'll put her in the cellar. *(The phone rings again.* SCHLISSEL *picks up the phone.)*

SCHLISSEL: *(On phone.)* Hello. *(He turns to the others, nods his head and makes an expressive face, indicating he was quite right in guessing the caller. The other two* OLD MEN *move closer to the phone.)* Mr. Foreman, your father isn't here— Listen, I tell you, he isn't here— I wouldn't have the slightest idea— I haven't seen her since I was up to your house last Tuesday. Isn't she home?— If he comes in, I'll tell him— Okay— *(Hangs up, turns to the other two.)* Well, we are in it up to our necks now.

ALPER: *(Stripping off his phylacteries.)* So shall we take her to my house?

SCHLISSEL: All right. Zitorsky, go in and tell her we are going to take her some place else.

ZITORSKY: *(Not exactly inspired by the idea.)* Yeah, sure.

SCHLISSEL: *(To* ZITORSKY.*)* For heaven's sake, Zitorsky, you don't really believe that's a dybbuk in there.

ZITORSKY: If that's no dybbuk, then you go in and take her.

SCHLISSEL: *(He shuffles slowly to the door of the rabbi's office. Pausing at the closed office door.)* It's getting kind of complicated. Maybe we ought to call Foreman's son and tell him she's here and not get involved.

ZITORSKY: Oh, no!

SCHLISSEL: Ah, well, come on. What can they do to us? They'll call us foolish old men, but then foolishness is the only privilege of old age. So, Alper, you'll deal with her. You know how to talk to her, and we'll hide her in your cellar. So we'll have a little excitement. Listen, Alper, let's get along, you know. Before the Sexton comes back and starts asking us where we're all going.

ALPER: *(He nods apprehensively and takes a few steps into the office. To* THE GIRL, *who doesn't actually hear him or know of his presence.)* How do you do, my dear Evelyn? This is Alper here. *(She makes no answer.* ALPER *turns to the other two.)* She's in one of her apathetic states.

ZITORSKY: *(Darting back into the synagogue proper.)* I'll get your coat, Alper.

SCHLISSEL: *(Looking around to see if* ARTHUR *is paying*

any attention to what's going on; he is not.) Well, take her by the arm.

ALPER: Evelyn, your grandfather suggested we take you to my house. You always liked to play with the children's toys in my cellar there, you remember? Come along, and we'll have a good time.

ZITORSKY: *(Giving* SCHLISSEL *an overcoat.)* Here. Give this to Alper. *(He hurries off to the front door of the synagogue.)*

HARRIS: *(In the process of laying on his phylacteries.)* And from my wisdom, Oh most High God, Thou shalt reserve for me— *(He dribbles off into inaudibility.)*

ALPER: *(Placing a tentative hand on* THE GIRL*'s shoulder.)* Evelyn, dear— *(She looks up, startled.)*

ZITORSKY: *(Leaning out the front door, searching up and down the street.)* Oh, it's cold out here.

ALPER: *(To* SCHLISSEL, *hurriedly, putting on his own overcoat.)* I have a feeling we're going to have trouble here.

SCHLISSEL: I've got your coat here.

ALPER: Evelyn— *(A strange animal-like grunt escapes* THE GIRL, *and she begins to moan softly.)* Evelyn, dear, please don't be alarmed. This is Mr. Alper here who has known you since you were born. *(He is getting a little panicky at the strange sounds coming out of* THE GIRL, *and he tries to grab her arm to help her to her feet. She bursts into a shrill scream, electrifying everybody in the synagogue with the exception of* THE CABALIST, *who is oblivious to everything.* ZITORSKY, *who has just closed the front door, stands frozen with horror.* ARTHUR, *sunk in despondency, looks up startled. The old man,* HARRIS, *pauses briefly as if the sound has been some distant buzzing, and then goes back to his mumbled prayers. Alarmed.)* Evelyn, my dear girl, for heaven's sakes . . .

THE GIRL: *(Screaming out.)* Leave me alone! Leave me alone!

ARTHUR: *(Coming quickly to* SCHLISSEL, *who has shut the office door quickly.)* What's going on in there?

SCHLISSEL: It's nothing, it's nothing.

THE GIRL: *(Screaming.)* They are my seven sons! My seven sons!

ALPER: *(Who is trying earnestly to get out of the office.)* Who closed this door?

ZITORSKY: *(Reaching for the front door.)* I'm getting out of here.

SCHLISSEL: *(To* ZITORSKY.*)* Where are you going? *(But* ZITORSKY *has already fled into the street.)*

ARTHUR: *(To* SCHLISSEL.*)* What's all this screaming?

ALPER: *(At last out of the office, he comes scurrying to* SCHLISSEL.*)* I put my hand on her arm to help her up, and she burst into this fit of screaming.

ARTHUR: *(He strides to the open doorway of the office.* THE GIRL *stares at him, hunched now in terror, frightened and at bay. To* SCHLISSEL.*)* What have you been doing to this girl?

SCHLISSEL: The girl is possessed by a dybbuk.

ARTHUR: What?

SCHLISSEL: *(To* ALPER.*)* Zitorsky ran out in the street like a kangaroo.

ALPER: Listen, maybe we should call somebody.

ARTHUR: Listen, what is this?

ALPER: My dear young man, there is no reason to alarm yourself. There is an insane girl in the rabbi's office, but she appears to have quieted down.

ARTHUR: What do you mean, there's an insane girl in the rabbi's office?

ALPER: Yes, she is a catatonic schizophrenic, occasionally violent, but really, go back to your seat. There is no cause for alarm.

ARTHUR: Am I to understand, sir, that it is a practice of yours to keep insane girls in your rabbi's office?

ALPER: No, no. Oh, dear, I suppose we shall have to tell him. But you must promise, my dear fellow, to keep this whole matter between us. *(To* SCHLISSEL.*)* Zitorsky, you say, took to his heels?

SCHLISSEL: Absolutely flew out of the door.

ALPER: Well, I really can't blame him. It was quite an apprehensive moment. I was a little shaken myself. *(Peeks into the office.)* Yes, she seems to be quite apathetic again. I think we just better leave her alone for the time being.

ARTHUR: Look, what is going on here?

ALPER: My dear fellow, you are, of course, understandably confused. The girl, you see, is possessed by a dybbuk.

ARTHUR: Yes, of course. Well that explains everything.

ALPER: Well, of course, how would he know what a dybbuk is? A dybbuk is a migratory soul that possesses the body of another human being in order to return to heaven. It is a Lurian doctrine, actually tracing back to the Essenes, I suppose, but popularized during the 13th century by the Spanish Cabalists. I wrote several articles on the matter for Yiddish periodicals. My name is Moyshe Alper, and at one time I was a journalist of some repute. *(*ZITORSKY *appears in the doorway again, peering nervously in.)* Come in, Zitorsky, come in. The girl is quiet again. *(*ZITORSKY *approaches them warily.)*

ARTHUR: Look, are you trying to tell me you have a girl in there you think is possessed by some demon? Where is her mother or father or somebody who should be responsible for her?

ALPER: If there were someone responsible for her, would she be insane in the first place?

ARTHUR: Of course, this is none of my business—

ALPER: You are a good fellow and let me put you at ease. The girl is in good hands. Nobody is going to hurt her. Her grandfather, who adores her more than his own life, has gone off for a short while.

ZITORSKY: To Williamsburg on the Brighton train.

SCHLISSEL: The Brighton train takes you to Coney Island.

ZITORSKY: You said the Double G.

ALPER: All right, all right.

ARTHUR: Of course, this is none of my business.

ALPER: *(To* ARTHUR.*)* I can understand your concern; it shows you are a good fellow, but really the matter is well in hand.

(The front door opens and there now enter THE SEXTON *and two young men in their thirties, apparently the* KESSLER BOYS, *who are none too happy about being roused on this cold winter morning. They stand disconsolately around in the back of the synagogue.)*

THE SEXTON: Here are two more, the Kessler boys.

ALPER: Now we'll have ten for a quorum.

ZITORSKY: Kessler? Kessler? Oh, yes, the stationery store. I knew your father.

(There is a general flurry of movement. THE SEXTON *hurries about the ritual of baring his left arm, donning the praying shawl and phylacteries, walking nervously about, mumbling his prayers rapidly.* ARTHUR, *quite disturbed again, looks into the rabbi's office at* THE GIRL *again, then moves slowly into the office.* THE GIRL *is again in a world of her own. He closes the door after himself and studies* THE GIRL. SCHLISSEL, ALPER *and* ZITORSKY *watch him warily, taking off their overcoats again and preparing to stay for the impending services.* HARRIS*'s shrill quavering voice suddenly leaps up into audibility again.)*

HARRIS: Thou shalt set apart all that openeth the womb of the Lord, and the firstling that cometh of a beast which Thou shalt have, it shall belong to the Lord—

SCHLISSEL: *(To* ALPER.*)* What are we going to do when the rabbi tries to get into his office? He'll see the girl, and that will be the end of our exorcism. What shall we tell the rabbi?

(The front door of the synagogue opens, and THE RABBI *comes striding efficiently in, right on cue. He is a young man in his early thirties, neatly dressed if a little threadbare, and carrying a briefcase.)*

ZITORSKY: Peace be with you, Rabbi.

THE RABBI: Peace be unto you.

ALPER: *(Intercepting* THE RABBI *as he heads for his office.)* How do you do, Rabbi? *(*THE RABBI *nods as he strides to the door of his office where* SCHLISSEL *blocks the way.)*

SCHLISSEL: We have ten men today, Rabbi.

THE RABBI: Good. *(Reaches for the door to his office.)* I'll just get my phylacteries.

ALPER: *(Seizing* ZITORSKY's *phylacteries from* ZITORSKY's *hand.)* Oh, here, use these. It's late, Rabbi.

THE RABBI: *(Taking the phylacteries.)* Fine. Well, let's start the services. *(He turns back to the synagogue proper.)*

(From all around, each man's voice rises into prayer, as the Curtain falls.)

ACT II

Scene 1

TIME: *Fifteen minutes later.*

AT RISE: ZITORSKY *is reading the prayers. He stands before the lectern on the raised platform singing the primitive chants:*

ZITORSKY: And we beseech Thee according to Thine abundant mercies, Oh, Lord—

THE SEXTON: Young Kessler, come here and open the Ark. *(The* YOUNGER KESSLER *ascends the platform and opens the Ark by drawing the curtains and sliding the doors apart.)*

ZITORSKY: And it came to pass, when the ark set forward, that Moses said, "Rise up, O Lord, and Thine enemies shall be scattered, and they that hate Thee shall flee before Thee. For out of Zion shall go forth the Law, and the word of the Lord from Jerusalem." *(Immediately, the rest of the* QUORUM *plunge into a mumbled response: "Blessed be Thy name, O Sovereign of the World! Blest by Thy crown, and Thy abiding place!" Jewish prayers are conducted in a reader and congregation pattern, although frequently the reader's vocalized statements and the congregation's mumbled responses merge and run along simultaneously. In this specific moment of prayer, where the Ark has been opened and the Torah is about to be taken out, the demarcation between reader and congregation is clearcut. The sliding brown wooden doors of the Ark are now open.* THE SEXTON *is reaching in to take out the exquisitely ornamented Torah, which, when its lovely velvet and brocaded cover is taken off, will show itself to be a large parchment scroll divided on two carved rollers. When* The Sexton *gets the Torah out, he hands it carefully to* Zitorsky, *who has been chosen this day for the honor of holding the Torah until it is to be read from.* Zitorsky, *who, as today's reader, has been reading along with the congregation although more audibly, now allows his voice to ring out clearly, marking the end of this paragraph of prayers.)* . . . May it be Thy gracious will to open my heart in Thy Law, and to grant my heart's desires, and those of all Thy people Israel, for our benefit, throughout a peaceful life. *(Pause.)* Magnify the Lord with me, and let us exalt His name together. *(Again, the* Congregation *leaps into mumbled response. "Thine, O Lord, is the greatness, and the power, and the glory, and the victory, and the majesty," etc.* Zitorsky *marches solemnly to the front of the lectern carrying the Torah before him. Each* Man *kisses the Torah as it passes him. There is now a ritual of removing the velvet cover, and the Torah is laid upon the lectern.* Zitorsky, Harris *and* The Sexton *make a hovering group of three old betallithed Jews over it.* The Rabbi *stands rocking slightly back and forth to the left of the lectern. Off the raised platform, but immediately by the railing stands* The Cabalist, *rocking back and forth and praying.* Alper *and* Schlissel *stand at various places, mumbling their responses. The two* Kessler Boys *have removed their coats and wear praying shawls but still stand as close to the front door as they can.* Arthur Brooks *stands, leaning against the wall of the rabbi's office, quite intrigued by the solemn prayers and rituals.* The Girl *is still in the rabbi's office, but she is standing now, listening as well as she can to the prayers. Her face is peaceful now and quite lovely. Again* Zitorsky*'s voice rises to indicate the end of a paragraph of prayer.)* Ascribe all of your greatness unto our God, and render honor to the Law.

(There is now a quick mumbled conference among the three Old Jews *at the lectern, and* The Sexton *suddenly leans out and calls to the two* Kessler Boys *in the rear.)*

THE SEXTON: Kessler, you want to read from the Torah?

ELDER KESSLER: No, no, no. Get somebody else.

THE SEXTON: Alper? *(*ALPER *nods and makes his way to the lectern.* THE SEXTON*'s voice, a high, whining incantation, rises piercingly into the air, announcing the fact that* MOYSHE, *son of Abram, will read from the Torah.)* Rise up, Reb Moses Hia Kohan, son of Abram, and speak the blessing on the Torah. Blessed be He, who in His Holiness gave the Law unto his people Israel, the Law of the Lord is perfect.

CONGREGATION: *(Scattered response.)* And ye that cleave unto the Lord your God are alive every one of you this day.

ALPER: *(Now at the lectern, raises his head and recites quickly.)* Blessed is the Lord who is to be blessed for ever and ever.

CONGREGATION: Blessed is the Lord who is to be blessed for ever and ever.

ALPER: Blessed art Thou, O Lord our God, King of the Universe, who hast chosen us from all peoples and hast given us Thy Law. Blessed art Thou, O Lord, who givest the Law.

CONGREGATION: Amen!

THE SEXTON: And Moses said . . .

(There are now four mumbling OLD JEWS *huddled over the lectern. It all becomes very indistinguishable, although* THE SEXTON*'s piercing tenor rises audibly now and then to indicate he is reading.* ALPER *moves into the reader's position and begins to read from the Torah, bending his knees and twisting his body and hunching over the Torah peering at the difficult little Hebrew lettering inscribed therein.* SCHLISSEL *and the* KESSLER BOYS *find seats where they were standing, as does* THE CABALIST. THE RABBI *and* HARRIS *are seated on the raised platform. In the rabbi's office,* THE GIRL *has decided to go out into the synagogue proper. She opens the door and moves a few steps out.* ARTHUR *hears her and turns to her warily.)*

THE GIRL: *(Quite lucidly and amiably.)* Excuse me, sir, are they reading from the Torah now? *(She peers over* ARTHUR's *shoulder to the* OLD MEN *at the lectern.)*

ARTHUR: Yes, I think so. *(He watches her carefully. She seems all right now. Still there is something excessively ingenuous about her, a tentative, wide-eyed, gently smiling innocence.)*

THE GIRL: Is my grandfather here? *(She peers nervously around the synagogue.)*

ARTHUR: Which one would be your grandfather?

THE GIRL: *(Growing panic.)* No, he's not here. I see Mr. Alper, but I don't see my grandfather.

ARTHUR: I'm sure he will be back soon. *(His calmness reassures her.)*

THE GIRL: *(She studies this strange young man warily.)* I think all synagogues should be shabby because I think of God as being very poor as a child. What do you think of God as?

ARTHUR: I'm afraid I think of God as the Director of Internal Revenue.

THE GIRL: *(She laughs brightly and then immediately smothers her laughter, aware she is in a solemn synagogue.)* You're irreverent. *(She goes frowning again into the rabbi's office and plops down on his swivel chair, and swivels back and forth, very much like a child.* ARTHUR *follows her tentatively, studying her warily yet taken by her ingenuousness. She darts a quick frightened look at him.)* Were you in here just before?

ARTHUR: Well, yes.

THE GIRL: Did I—did I say anything?

ARTHUR: *(Amiably.)* Well, yes.

THE GIRL: *(Sighing.)* I see. Well, I might as well tell you. I've been to several mental institutions. *(She looks quickly at him. He smiles at her.)* You don't seem very disconcerted by that.

ARTHUR: Oh, I expect it might be hard to find somebody who couldn't do with occasional confinement in a mental institution.

(In the synagogue, THE SEXTON *now calls* HARRIS *to read from the Torah.)*

THE GIRL: *(She frowns.)* Did my grandfather say when he would be back or where he was going? *(She starts from her seat, frightened again.)*

ARTHUR: I understand he'll be back soon.

THE GIRL: Are you the doctor?

ARTHUR: No. You don't have to be the least bit afraid of me.

THE GIRL: *(She brightens.)* My grandfather and I are very close. I'm much closer to him than I am to my own father. I'd rather not talk about my father, if you don't mind. It's a danger spot for me. You know, when I was nine years old, I shaved all the hair off my head because that is the practice of really orthodox Jewish women. I mean, if you want to be a rabbi's wife, you must shear your hair and wear a wig. That's one of my compulsive dreams. I keep dreaming of myself as the wife of a handsome young rabbi with a fine beard down to his waist and a very stern face and prematurely gray forelocks on his brow. I have discovered through many unsuccessful years of psychiatric treatment that religion has a profound sexual connotation for me. Oh, dear, I'm afraid I'm being tiresome again about my psychiatric history. Really, being insane is like being fat. You can talk about nothing else. Please forgive me. I am sure I am boring you to death.

ARTHUR: No, not at all. It's nice to hear somebody talk with passion about anything, even their insanity.

THE GIRL: *(Staring at him.)* The word doesn't bother you?

ARTHUR: What word?

THE GIRL: Insanity.

ARTHUR: Good heavens, no. I'm a lawyer. Insanity in one form or another is what fills my anteroom. Besides, I'm being psychoanalyzed myself and I'm something of a bore about that too. You are a bright young thing. How old are you?

THE GIRL: Eighteen.

ARTHUR: *(Staring at her.)* My God, you're a pretty kid! I can hardly believe you are psychopathic. Are you very advanced?

THE GIRL: Pretty bad. I'm being institutionalized again. Dr. Molineaux's Sanitarium in Long Island. I'm a little paranoid and hallucinate a great deal and have very little sense of reality, except for brief interludes like this, and I might slip off any minute in the middle of a sentence—into some incoherency. If that should happen, you must be very realistic with me. Harsh reality is the most efficacious way to deal with schizophrenics.

ARTHUR: You seem well-read on the matter.

THE GIRL: I'm a voracious reader. I have so little else to do with myself. Will you come and visit me at Dr. Molineaux's Hospital? I am awfully fond of you.

ARTHUR: Yes, of course, I will.

THE GIRL: It won't be as depressing an experience as you might think. If I am not in the violent ward, I will probably be allowed to go to the commissary and have an ice cream soda with you. The worst of an insane asylum is really how poorly dressed the inmates are. They all wear old cable-stitched sweaters. I do like to look pretty. *(A vacuous, atrophied look is beginning to come across her face.)* They ask me to be in a lot of movies, you know, when I have time. Did you see *David and Bathsheba* with Susan Hayward? That was really me. I don't tell anybody that. They don't want me to make movies. My mother, I mean. She doesn't even go to synagogue on Saturday. You're the new rabbi, you know. Sometimes, I'm the rabbi, but they're all afraid of me. The temple is sixty cubits long and made of cypress and overlaid with gold. The burnished Roman legions clank outside the gates, you know. Did you see *The Ten Commandments*? I saw that Tuesday, Wednesday. I was in that. I was the girl who danced. I was in that. Mr. Hirschman is here, too, you know, and my grandfather. Everybody's here. Do you see that boy over there? Go away. Leave us alone. He's insane. He's really Mr. Hirschman the Cabalist. He's making a golem. You ought to come here, Rabbi.

ARTHUR: *(Who has been listening, fascinated, now says firmly.)* I am not the rabbi, Evelyn.

THE GIRL: *(She regards him briefly.)* Well, we're making a golem and—

ARTHUR: You are not making a golem, Evelyn.

THE GIRL: *(She pauses, stares down at the floor at her feet. A grimace of pain winces quickly across her face and then leaves it. After a moment, she mumbles.)* Thank you. *(Suddenly she begins to cry and she throws herself upon* ARTHUR*'s breast, clinging to him, and he holds her gently, caressing her as he would a child.)* Oh, I can't bear being insane.

ARTHUR: *(Gently.)* I always thought that since the insane made their own world it was more pleasurable than this one that is made for us.

THE GIRL: *(Moving away.)* Oh, no, it is unbearably painful. It is the most indescribable desolation. You are all alone in deserted streets. You cannot possibly imagine it.

ARTHUR: I'm afraid I can. I have tried to commit suicide so many times now it has become something of a family joke. Once, before I was divorced, my wife stopped in to tell a neighbor before she went out to shop: "Oh, by the way, if you smell gas, don't worry about it. It's only Arthur killing himself again." Suicides, you know, kill themselves a thousand times, but one day I'll slash my wrists and I will forget to make a last minute telephone call and there will be no stomach-pumping samaritans to run up the stairs and smash my bedroom door down and rush me off to Bellevue. I'll make it some day—I assure you of that.

THE GIRL: *(Regarding him with sweet interest.)* You don't look as sad as all that.

ARTHUR: Oh, I have made a profession of ironic detachment. It depresses me to hear that insanity is as forlorn as anything else. I had always hoped to go crazy myself some day since I have apparently no talent for suicide.

THE GIRL: I always thought life would be wonderful if I were only sane.

ARTHUR: Life is merely dreary if you're sane, and unbearable if you are sensitive. I cannot think of a more meaningless sham than my own life. My parents were very poor so I spent the first twenty years of my life condemning the rich for my childhood nightmares. Oh, I was quite a Bernard Barricade when I was in college. I left the Communist Party when I discovered there were easier ways to seduce girls. I turned from reproaching society for my loneliness to reproaching my mother, and stormed out of her house to take a room for myself on the East Side. Then I fell in love—that is to say, I found living alone so unbearable I was willing to marry. She married me because all her friends were marrying somebody. Needless to say, we told each other how deeply in love we were. We wanted very much to be happy. Americans, you know, are frantic about being happy. The American nirvana is a man and his wife watching television amiably and then turning off the lights and effortlessly making the most ardent love to each other. Television unfortunately is a bore and ardent love is an immense drain on one's energy. I began to work day and night at my law office, and besides becoming very successful, I managed to avoid my wife entirely. For this deceit, I was called ambitious and was respected by everyone including my wife, who was quite as bored with me as I was with her. We decided to have children because we couldn't possibly believe we were that miserable together. All this while I drove myself mercilessly for fear that if I paused for just one moment, the whole slim, trembling sanity of my life would come crashing down about my feet without the slightest sound. I went to a psychoanalyst who wanted to know about my childhood when I could barely remember whether I took a taxi or a bus to his office that day. I began to drink myself into stupors, pursuing other men's wives, and generally behaving badly. One morning, I stared into the mirror and could barely make out my features. Life is utterly meaningless. I have had everything a man can get out of life—prestige, power, money, women, children, and a handsome home only three blocks from the Scarsdale Country Club, and all I can think of is I want to get out of this as fast as I can. *(He has become quite upset by now and has to avert his face to hide a sudden welling of tears. He takes a moment to get a good grip on himself, readopts his sardonic air and says.)* As you see, I have quite a theatrical way when I want to.

THE GIRL: *(Brightly.)* Oh, I think you are wonderfully wise.

ARTHUR: Oh, it was said best by your very own King Solomon, the wisest man who ever lived, when he wrote Ecclesiastes.

THE GIRL: Oh, King Solomon didn't write Ecclesiastes. That was written by an anonymous Jewish scholar in Alexandria. I wouldn't put too much stock in it. Weariness was all the rage among the Hellenized Jews.

ARTHUR: *(Staring at her.)* You are an amazing kid.

(She smiles back at him exuberantly, unabashedly showing her fondness for him. It embarrasses him, and he turns away. He opens the office door and looks out into the synagogue, where the reading of the Torah has come to an end.)

THE RABBI: *(Singing out.)* Blessed art Thou, O Lord Our God, King of the Universe, who has given us the Law of truth, and has planted everywhere life in our midst. Blessed art Thou O Lord, who givest the Law. *(There is a scattered mumbled response from the* OLD MEN *in the synagogue.)*

ZITORSKY: *(He now takes the Torah and holds it up above his head and chants.)* And this is the Law which Moses set before the children of Israel, according to the commandment of the Lord by the hand of Moses. *(The* FOUR MEN *on the platform form a small group as* ZITORSKY *marches slowly back to the Ark carrying the Torah. A mumble of prayer rustles through the synagogue.* ZITORSKY*'s voice rises out.)* Let them praise the name of the Lord; for His name alone is exalted. *(He carefully places the Torah back into the Ark. A rumble of prayer runs through the synagogue. All the* MEN *in the synagogue are standing now.)*

ARTHUR: *(Turning to* THE GIRL.*)* They're putting the Torah back. Is the service over?

THE GIRL: No. I have a wonderful book I want to give to you. Mr. Hirschman, our Community Cabalist, gave it to me. It is called *The Book of Splendor,* and it is a terribly mystical book. I never met anyone who wanted to know the meaning of life as desperately as you do.

ARTHUR: It sounds very interesting.

THE GIRL: Oh, I'm glad you think so. I have to get it for you.

*(*SCHLISSEL *pokes his head into the office and indicates to* ARTHUR *that he is needed outside.)*

ARTHUR: I think they need me outside. *(He moves to the door.)*

THE GIRL: Yes, we really shouldn't have been talking during the service.

ARTHUR: *(He goes out of the office, closing the door be-*

hind him. He joins SCHLISSEL, *who is a few steps away, muttering the prayers. Shaking his head.)* What a pity, really. A lovely girl. What a pity. Now, you look like a sensible sort of man. What is all this nonsense about demons? You really should call her father or mother or whoever it is who is responsible for her.

SCHLISSEL: Young man, if we called her father he would come down and take her away.

ARTHUR: Yes. That would be the point, wouldn't it?

SCHLISSEL: Then what happens to our exorcism?

ARTHUR: What exorcism?

SCHLISSEL: Listen, we've got to exorcise the dybbuk.

ARTHUR: *(Aghast.)* Exorcism!

THE SEXTON: *(He leans over the railing of the platform and admonishes them in a heavy whisper.)* Sssshhh!

*(*SCHLISSEL *promptly turns back to muttering his prayers.* ARTHUR *stares at him in a posture of vague belief.)*

ARTHUR: Are you serious?

ZITORSKY: *(His voice rises up loud and clear.)* . . . And it is said, and the Lord shall be king over all the earth; on that day shall the Lord be One, and His Name One.

(The CONGREGATION, *which had sat, now stands again.* THE SEXTON *leans over the railing and calls to the* KESSLER BOYS.*)*

THE SEXTON: Kessler, stand up. Now is the time for your memorial prayers.

(The two KESSLER BOYS *nod, stand, and look unhappily down at their prayer books.* THE SEXTON *pokes a palsied finger onto a page to show them where to read, and the two* YOUNG MEN *now begin to read painstakingly and with no idea of what they are reading.)*

KESSLER BOYS: Magnified and sanctified by His great Name in the world which He hath created according to His will. May He establish His kingdom in your lifetime and in your days, and in the lifetime of all the house of Israel, speedily and at a near time; and say ye, Amen.

CONGREGATION: Amen. Let His great Name be blessed for ever and ever.

KESSLER BOYS: Blessed, praised, and glorified, exalted, extolled and honored, adored, and lauded, be the Name of the Holy One, blessed be He, beyond, yea, beyond all blessings and hymns, praises and songs, which are uttered in the world, and say ye, Amen.

CONGREGATION: Amen.

(The front door to the synagogue bursts open and FOREMAN *thrusts himself in, obviously much distraught, not so distraught, however, that he doesn't automatically join in the "Amen.")*

KESSLER BOYS: May there be abundant peace from heaven, and life for us and for all Israel; and say ye, Amen.

CONGREGATION: Amen.

KESSLER BOYS: May he who maketh peace in his high places, make peace for us and for all Israel, and say ye, Amen.

CONGREGATION: Amen.

(The synagogue bursts into a quick mumble of prayers, except for SCHLISSEL, *who scurries over to* FOREMAN, *who stares back at him white with panic.)*

SCHLISSEL: What happened? You got lost? You took the Long Island Railroad to Atlantic Avenue Station, and you got lost in the Atlantic Avenue Station.

FOREMAN: What Atlantic Avenue Station? I couldn't even find the Long Island Railroad.

SCHLISSEL: Idiot! You are an innocent child! Really! Services are over in a minute, and I'll take you myself. *(*ALPER *is leaning over the railing of the platform making obvious gestures as if to ask what had happened. Even* ZITORSKY *looks up from his hunched position at the lectern.* SCHLISSEL *announces in a heavy whisper as he starts to put on his coat again.)* He couldn't even find the Long Island Railway Station. *(*ALPER *clasps his brow.* THE SEXTON *turns around to* SCHLISSEL *and* *admonishes him with a heavy "Ssshhh!!!"* FOREMAN *has begun walking about, mumbling the prayers by heart, automatically a part of the service again. As he passes* SCHLISSEL, *he indicates with a jerk of his head that he would like to know the well-being of his granddaughter.)* She's all right. Don't worry about her.

*(*FOREMAN *nods and continues mumbling his prayers. In the rabbi's office,* THE GIRL, *who has been sitting pensively, now stands, goes out of the office, calmly crosses to the rear of the synagogue, and exits out the front door. Absolutely no one is aware she has gone. The* CONGREGATION *now bursts into a loud prayer, obviously the last one of the service, since those* MEN *on the platform begin to meander off, and all those who are still wearing their phylacteries begin to strip them off, even as they say the words of the prayer.)*

CONGREGATION: He is the Lord of the Universe, who reigned ere any creature yet was formed. At the time when all things were made by His desire, then was His name proclaimed King. And after all things shall have had an end, He alone, the dreadest one shall reign; Who was, who is, and who will be in glory.

*(*SCHLISSEL, ALPER, ZITORSKY *and* FOREMAN *have all rattled quickly through this final paean, impatient to close off the service, while the others continue the slow, clear and ultimate recital. The four* OLD MEN *form a huddled group by the front door.)*

THE FOUR OF THEM: *(Rattling it off.)* And with my spirit, my body, also; the Lord is with me, and I will not fear. Amen.

ALPER: Amen, what happened?

SCHLISSEL: I'm taking him myself right away.

ZITORSKY: What happened, you got lost?

FOREMAN: I asked this fellow in the street, I said: "Could you—"

SCHLISSEL: *(To* ALPER.*)* Listen, keep an eye on that fellow there. He wants to tell the rabbi about the girl. All right, listen. I shall have to lead Foreman by the hand to the Korpotchniker. All right, listen, we're going. Good-bye. Peace be unto you.

ALPER: Take the Long Island Railroad to the Atlantic Avenue Station. Then take the Brighton train.

SCHLISSEL: Oh, for heaven's sakes. Are you presuming to tell me how to get to Williamsburg?

ALPER: All right, go already.

SCHLISSEL: *(Muttering as he leads* FOREMAN *out the door.)* The Brighton train. If we took the Brighten train, we would spend the day in Coney Island. *(He exits with* FOREMAN, *closing the door.)*

(The rest of the CONGREGATION *has finally come to the end of the service.)*

CONGREGATION: *(Their scattered voices rising to a coda.)* And with my spirit, my body also; the Lord is with me, and I will not fear. Amen!

SCHLISSEL *and* ALPER: Amen!

(There is a flurry of dispersion. The two KESSLER BOYS *mumble good-byes and disappear quickly out into the street, buttoning their coats against the cold.* HARRIS, *who is slowly and tremblingly removing his phylacteries, continues slowly to redress himself throughout the rest of the scene.* THE SEXTON *now scurries about gathering the various phylacteries and praying shawls and putting them back into the velvet prayer bags and then putting all the velvet bags and prayer books back into the cardboard carton they were all taken from, an activity he pursues with his usual frenetic desperation. Only* THE RABBI *and* THE CABALIST *continue to say a few prayers, "The Thirteen Principles of Faith," etc.* THE CABALIST *reads them sitting down, hunched over his prayer book.* ALPER *and* ZITORSKY *have genuine cause for alarm concerning* ARTHUR BROOKS, *for he has ambled down to the platform where he stands waiting for* THE RABBI *to finish his prayers. They watch* ARTHUR *warily.* HARRIS *suddenly decides to be communicative. He lifts his old face to* ALPER *and* ZITORSKY.*)*

HARRIS: Ah, am I thirsty!

ALPER: *(Watching* ARTHUR *carefully.)* Good.

*(*THE RABBI, *having finished his last prayer, now turns and starts down from the platform.* ARTHUR *steps forward to meet him.)*

ARTHUR: Rabbi—

THE RABBI: *(Walking by him.)* I'll be with you in just a moment. *(He strides directly to his office.* ALPER *leaps to intercept him.)*

ALPER: Rabbi—

THE RABBI: *(Continuing into his office.)* I'll be with you in a minute, Alper. *(He goes into his office and closes the door.* ALPER *clasps his brow and shrugs.* ZITORSKY *mutters an involuntary "Oy." They both nod their heads and wait with the sufferance that is the badge of all their tribe.* ARTHUR *moves a few steps to the rabbi's door and also waits. In the office,* THE RABBI *has sat down, all business, and has dialed a number. On phone.)* I'd like to make a person-to-person call to Rabbi Harry Gersh in Wilmington, Delaware. The number in Wilmington is Kingswood 3-1973— Thank you— *(He hums a snatch of the service.* ALPER *opens the door and comes into the office. He stares just a little open-mouthed at the absence of* THE GIRL. *He tugs at his Vandyke beard in contemplation.)* Yes, Alper?

ALPER: Well, I'll tell you, Rabbi— *(He scowls, a little flustered, then turns and goes out of the office.)* Excuse me.

THE RABBI: *(On phone.)* Locust 6-0932.

ALPER: *(To* ZITORSKY.*)* She's not there.

ZITORSKY: She's not there?

ALPER: I'll have to go out and look for her. *(Frowning, in contemplation,* ALPER *puts his coat on slowly and exits from the synagogue.)*

THE RABBI: *(His attention is abruptly brought back to the phone. His voice rises into that pitch usually used for long distance calls. On phone.)* Harry, how are you, this is Bernard here, I'm sorry I wasn't in last night, my wife Sylvia said it was wonderful to hear your voice after all these years, how are you, Shirley, and the kids? Oh, that's wonderful. I'm glad to hear it. Harry, my wife tells me you have just gotten your first congregation and you wanted some advice since I have already been fired several times— Good, how much are you getting?— Well, five thousand isn't bad for a first congregation although I always thought out-of-town paid better. And what is it, a one-year contract?— Well, what kind of advice can I give you? Especially you, Harry. You are a saintly, scholarly, and truly pious man, and you have no business being a rabbi. You've got to be a go-getter, Harry, unfortunately. The synagogue I am in now is in an unbelievable state of neglect and I expect to see us in prouder premises within a year. But I've got things moving now. I've started a Youth Group, a Young Married People's Club, a Theatre Club which is putting on its first production next month, *The Man Who Came to Dinner,* I'd like you to come, Harry, bring the wife, I'm sure you'll have an entertaining evening. And let me recommend that you organize a little league baseball team. It's a marvelous gimmick. I have sixteen boys in my Sunday School now— Harry, listen, what do I know about baseball?— Harry, let me interrupt you. How in heaven's name are you going to convey an awe of God to boys who will race out of your Hebrew classes to fly model rocket ships five hundred feet in the air exploding in three stages? To my boys, God is a retired mechanic— Well, I'm organizing a bazaar right now. When I hang up on you, I have to rush to the printers to get some raffles printed, and from there I go to the Town Hall for a permit to conduct Bingo games. In fact, I was so busy this morning, I almost forgot to come to the synagogue— *(He says gently.)* Harry, with my first congregation, I also thought I was bringing the word of God. I stood up in my pulpit every Sabbath and carped at them for violating the rituals of their own religion. My congregations dwindled, and one synagogue given to my charge disappeared into a morass of mortgages. Harry, I'm afraid there are times when I don't care if they believe in God as long as they come to Temple. Of course, it's sad— Harry, it's been my pleasure. Have I depressed you?— Come and see us, Harry— Good luck— Of course. Good-bye. *(He hangs up, stands, starts looking around for his briefcase, strides out into the synagogue still searching for it. He is interrupted by* ARTHUR.*)*

ARTHUR: Rabbi, I have to hurry off, but before I go I

would like to talk to you about that girl in your office. These old men tell me she is possessed by a demon and I think they are intending to perform some kind of an exorcism. I must caution you that that girl should be treated only by competent psychiatrists and the most frightful harm might come to her if she is subjected to anything like— Look, do you know about this exorcism, because I cannot believe you would tolerate any—

THE RABBI: *(Who has been trying very hard to follow all this.)* I'm afraid you have me at a disadvantage.

ARTHUR: I'm talking about the girl in your office.

THE RABBI: I'm somewhat new here and don't know everybody yet by name. Please be patient with me. Now I take it you want to get married.

ARTHUR: *(For a moment he briefly considers the possibility he is not really awake. Pensively.)* This whole morning is beginning to seem absolutely— Rabbi, there is a girl in your office, who is insane.

THE RABBI: In my office? *(*THE RABBI *is suddenly distracted by* ZITORSKY, *who has been wandering around the synagogue, looking up and down between the rows of chairs, and is now looking into the bathroom at the upstage end of the synagogue.)* Mr. Zitorsky, what are you doing?

ZITORSKY: *(To* ARTHUR, *who is moving quickly to the rabbi's office.)* Well, have you ever seen such a thing? The girl has vanished into thin air. *(He shuffles to* THE RABBI, *absolutely awestruck by it all.)*

ARTHUR: *(Now examining the interior of the rabbi's office.)* I suspect something more mundane, like simply walking out the door. *(He moves quickly to the front door, which now opens and* ALPER *returns, frowning with thought.)*

ALPER: *(To* ARTHUR.*)* Well, is that something or isn't it? I looked up and down, I couldn't see her.

*(*ARTHUR *scowls and goes out into the street, where he stands looking up and down.)*

THE RABBI: Mr. Zitorsky, if you will just tell me what this is all about.

ZITORSKY: *(His eyes wide with awe.)* Rabbi, Mr. Foreman

brought his granddaughter down this morning, and he said: "She is possessed by a dybbuk!" Well, what can you say when someone tells you something like that?

THE RABBI: Oh, Mr. Foreman's granddaughter. Yes, of course, I see.

ZITORSKY: So he took us into your office where she was standing, and it spoke to us! What an experience! You cannot imagine! The voice of the dybbuk spoke to us. It was like a hollow echo of eternity, and the girl's whole body was illuminated by a frame of light! Fire flashed from her mouth—all of us were there, ask Alper here, he'll tell you— I swear this on my soul!— The girl began to rise into the air!

ALPER: Actually, Zitorsky is coloring the story a little bit, but—

ZITORSKY: *(Riveted by the marvelousness of the fantasy.)* What are you talking about? You saw it with your own eyes!

ALPER: Well, it was an experience, I must say.

THE RABBI: And the girl has gone now?

ZITORSKY: Into the air about us.

THE RABBI: And where is Mr. Foreman?

ALPER: He went to Brooklyn.

THE RABBI: What in heaven's name for?

ALPER: To see the Korpotchniker Rabbi.

THE RABBI: *(Quite impressed.)* The Korpotchniker?

ZITORSKY: Certainly! Maybe you don't know this, but Hirschman is his cousin.

THE RABBI: Mr. Hirschman? I have to admit I didn't know that.

ZITORSKY: Oh, sure. Listen, Hirschman is the first-born son of the original Korpotchniker.

ALPER: I am afraid we are drifting from the point.

THE RABBI: *(Frowning.)* The girl probably went home. Why don't you call the girl's home, Mr. Alper, and find out if she's there? I think you are a very close friend of the family.

ARTHUR: *(Who has come back into the synagogue.)* Well, thank God, for the first rational voice I've heard today.

ALPER: *(Nodding his head sadly.)* Yes, I suppose I had better call her father.

ARTHUR: *(Buttoning his coat.)* Fine. *(Glancing at his watch.)* Gentlemen, if you don't need me for anything any more, I would like to get to my analyst. Good morning. *(He strides to the door.)*

THE RABBI: Peace be unto you.

ARTHUR: *(He pauses at the front door, a little amused at the archaic greeting.)* Peace be unto you, Rabbi. *(He opens the door and goes out.)*

THE RABBI: Who was that fellow?

ZITORSKY: Who knows? The Sexton found him on the street.

THE RABBI: *(Buttoning his own coat.)* Well, I have to be down at the printers. A dybbuk. Really. What an unusual thing. Is Mr. Foreman a mystical man? By the way, Mr. Alper—Mr. Zitorsky—you weren't at the meeting of the Brotherhood last night. I think you should take a more active interest in the synagogue. Did you receive an announcement of the meeting? Please come next time. *(Finds his briefcase.)* Ah, there it is, good. *(Heads for the door.)* I would like to know what the Korpotchniker said about this. Will you be here later today? I'll drop in. Let me know what happens. You better call the girl's family right away, Alper. Good morning. Peace be with you.

ALPER *and* ZITORSKY: Peace be with you, Rabbi.

*(*THE RABBI *exits. The two* OLD MEN *regard each other a little balefully, and then* ALPER *shuffles to the wall phone, where he puts his hand on the phone, resting it on the receiver, quite depressed by the turn of events. In the synagogue,* THE CABALIST *is huddled in prayer, and* THE SEXTON *is sleeping on bench up right. A long moment of hushed silence fills the stage.)*

ALPER: *(Hand still on the phone.)* Zitorsky, let us reason this out.

ZITORSKY: Absolutely.

ALPER: *(The Talmudic scholar.)* If I call the girl's home, there are two possibilities. Either she is home or she is not home. If she is home, why call? If she is not home, then there are two possibilities. Either her father has already called the police, or he has not called the police. If he has already called the police, then we are wasting a telephone call. If he has not called the police, he will call them. If he calls the police, then there are two possibilities. Either they will take the matter seriously or they will not. If they don't take the matter seriously, why bother calling them? If they take the matter seriously, they will rush down here to find out what we already know, so what gain will have been made? Nothing. Have I reasoned well, Zitorsky?

ZITORSKY: You have reasoned well.

ALPER: Between you and me, Zitorsky, how many people are there on the streets at this hour that we couldn't spot the girl in a minute? Why should we trouble the immense machinery of the law? We'll go out and find the girl ourselves. *(They are both up in a minute, buttoning their coats and hurrying to the front door, where they pause.)*

ZITORSKY: *(Regarding* ALPER *with awe.)* Alper, what a rogue you are! *(*ALPER *accepts the compliments graciously, and they both dart out into the street.)*

(Then, out of the hollow hush of the stage, THE CABALIST*'s voice rises into a lovely chant as he rocks back and forth, his eyes closed in religious ecstasy.)*

THE CABALIST: *(Singing slowly and with profound conviction.)* I believe with perfect faith in the coming of the Messiah, and though he tarry, I will wait daily for his coming. I believe with perfect faith that there will be a resurrection of the dead at the time when it shall please the Creator, blessed be His name, and exalted the remembrance of him for ever and ever.

(The front door opens, and THE GIRL *comes rushing in, holding a beautifully bound leather book. She looks quickly around the synagogue, now empty except for* THE SEXTON, *and then hurries to the rabbi's office, which is, of course, also empty. A kind of panic sweeps over her, and she rushes out into the synagogue again to* THE SEXTON.*)*

THE GIRL: Mr. Bleyer, the young man that was here, do you know— *(She whirls as the front door behind her again opens and* ARTHUR *comes back in. We have the feeling he also has been, if not running, at least walking very quickly. He and* THE GIRL *stare at each other for a moment. Then she says to him:)* I went home to get this book for you. I wanted you to have this book I told you about.

ARTHUR: *(Quietly.)* I just simply couldn't go till I knew you were all right. *(For a moment again, they stand poised, staring at each other. Then she sweeps across the stage and flings herself into his arms, crying.)*

THE GIRL: Oh, I love you. I love you. I love you—

(They stand, locked in embrace. THE CABALIST*'s voice rises again in a deeply primitive chant, exquisite in its atavistic ardor.)*

THE CABALIST: For Thy salvation I hope, O Lord! I hope, O Lord, for Thy salvation. O Lord, for Thy salvation I hope! For Thy salvation I hope, O Lord! I hope, O Lord, for Thy salvation! O Lord, for Thy salvation I hope!

(The Curtain quickly falls.)

Scene 2

TIME: *It is around noon, four hours later.*

AT RISE: *A silent, dozing quiet has settled over the synagogue. Indeed,* THE CABALIST *has dozed off over a thick tome at the upstage desk on the far side of the altar, his shawl-enshrouded head lying on his book.* THE GIRL, *too, is napping, curled up in the worn leather armchair in the rabbi's office.* THE SEXTON *is sitting like a cobbler on a chair at right.* ALPER *and* ZITORSKY *sit drowsily on two wooden chairs about center stage. Only* ARTHUR *moves restlessly around the synagogue. He looks into the rabbi's office, checking on* THE GIRL, *studies her sleeping sweetness, somehow deeply troubled. All is still, all is quiet. In the synagogue,* THE CABALIST *awakens suddenly and sits bolt upright as if he has just had the most bizarre dream. He stares wide-eyed at the wall ahead of him. He rises, and moves slowly downstage, his face a study in quiet awe. Apparently, he has had a profoundly moving dream, and he puts his hand to his brow as if to contain his thoughts from tumbling out. An expression of exaltation expands slowly on his wan, lined, bearded old face. His eyes are wide with terror.*

THE CABALIST: *(Whispering in awe.)* Blessed be the Lord. Blessed be the Lord. Blessed be the Lord. *(He stands staring out over the audience, his face illuminated with ecstasy. Then he cries out.)* Praise ye the Lord! Hallelujah! Praise ye the Lord! Hallelujah! It is good to sing praises unto our God; for it is pleasant and praise is seemly. Praise ye the Lord! Hallelujah! *(*ALPER *has been watching* THE CABALIST *with drowsy interest.* THE

CABALIST *turns and just stares at him.)* My dear friends, my dear, dear friends . . . *(Tears fill his old eyes, and his mouth works without saying anything for a moment.)*

ALPER: Are you all right, Hirschman?

THE CABALIST: *(Awed by an inner wonder.)* I was studying the codification of the Law, especially those paragraphs beginning with the letters of my father's name—because today is my father's day of memorial. I have brought some honey cake here, in my father's memory. I have it somewhere in a paper bag. Where did I put it? I brought it here last night. It is somewhere around—and as I studied, I dozed off and my head fell upon the Book of Mishna.— Oh, my dear friends, I have prayed to the Lord to send me a dream, and He has sent me a dream. I dreamt that I was bathing in a pool of the clearest mountain water. And a man of great posture appeared on the bank, and he said to me: "Rabbi, give me your blessing for I go to make a journey." And I looked closely on the man, and it was the face of my father. And I said unto him: "My father, why do you call me Rabbi? For did I not lustfully throw away the white fringed shawl of the Rabbinate and did I not mock the Lord to thy face? And have I not spent my life in prayer and penitence so that I might cleanse my soul?" And my father smiled upon me, and his bearded face glowed with gentleness, and he said unto me: "Rise from your bath, my son, and put upon you these robes of white linen which I have arrayed for you. For thy soul is cleansed and thou hast found a seat among the righteous. And the countenance of the Lord doth smile upon thee this day. So rise and rejoice and dance in the Holy Place. For thine is eternal peace and thou art among the righteous." Thus was the dream that I dreamt as my head lay on the Book of Mishna. *(He lifts his head and stares upward.)* The Lord shall reign for ever. Thy God, O Zion, unto all generations. Praise ye the Lord. Hallelujah! *(He stares distractedly around him.)* Where is the wine, Sexton? The wine! There was a fine new bottle on Friday! I have been given a seat among the righteous! For this day have I lived and fasted! I have been absolved! Hallelujah! Hallelujah!— Ah, the cakes! Here! Good!— *(He is beginning to laugh.)* I shall dance before the Holy Ark! Sexton! Sexton! Distribute the macaroons that all may share this exalted day! The Lord hath sent me a sign, and the face of my father smiled upon me! *(As abruptly as he had begun to laugh he begins to sob in the effusion of his joy. He sinks onto a chair and cries unashamedly.)*

ALPER: My dear Hirschman, how delighted we are for you.

THE SEXTON: *(Offering some honey cake to* ZITORSKY.*)* You want some cake there, Zitorsky?

ZITORSKY: I'll have a little wine too as long as we're having a party.

*(*THE SEXTON *scurries to offstage left to get wine.)*

ARTHUR: *(Who has been watching all this, rather taken by it.)* What happened?

ALPER: Mr. Hirschman has received a sign from God. His father has forgiven him, and his soul has been cleansed.

ARTHUR: That's wonderful.

ZITORSKY: *(To* THE SEXTON, *now pouring wine from a decanter.)* I'll tell you, Bleyer, if you have a little whiskey, I prefer that. Wine makes me dizzy.

THE SEXTON: Where would I get whiskey? This is a synagogue, not a saloon.

ZITORSKY: *(Taking his glass of wine.)* Happiness, Hirschman.

ALPER: Some wine for our young friend here. *(To* ARTHUR.*)* Will you join Mr. Hirschman in his moment of exaltation?

ARTHUR: *(Who is beginning to be quite taken with these old men.)* Yes, of course. *(*THE SEXTON, *who is pouring the wine and sipping a glass of his own as he pours, has begun to hum a gay Chassidic tune. He hands* ARTHUR *his glass.)*

ZITORSKY: *(Handing his glass back for a refill.)* Oh, will Schlissel eat his heart out when he finds out he is missing a party.

ALPER: *(Making a toast.)* Rabbi Israel, son of Isaac, I think it is fitting we use your rabbinical title—we bow in reverence to you.

THE CABALIST: *(Deeply touched.)* My dear, dear friends, I cannot describe to you my happiness.

ZITORSKY: There hasn't been a party here since that boy's confirmation last month. Wasn't that a skimpy feast for a confirmation— Another glass, please, Sexton. Oh, I'm beginning to sweat. Some confirmation party that was! The boy's father does a nice business in real estate and all he brings down is a few pieces of sponge cake and one bottle of whiskey. One bottle of whisky for fifty people! As much whisky as I had couldn't even cure a toothache. Oh boy, am I getting dizzy. When I was a boy, I could drink a whole jar of potato cider. You remember that potato cider we used to have in Europe? It could kill a horse. Oh, boy, what kind of wine is that? My legs are like rubber already. *(Suddenly stamps his foot and executes a few brief Chassidic dance steps.)*

ALPER: This is not bad wine, you know. A pleasant bouquet.

ZITORSKY: *(Wavering over to* ARTHUR.*)* Have a piece of cake, young man. What does it say in the Bible? "Go eat your food with gladness and drink your wine with a happy mind?" Give the boy another glass.

ARTHUR: *(Smiling.)* Thank you. I'm still working on this one.

THE CABALIST: *(He suddenly raises his head, bursts into a gay Chassidic chant.)*

Light is sown,
sown for the righteous,
and joy for the upright,
the upright in heart.
Oh,
light is sown,
sown for the righteous—

ZITORSKY: *(Gaily joining in.)*

and joy for the upright,
the upright in heart.
Oh!

*(*THE CABALIST *and* ZITORSKY *take each other's shoulders and begin to dance in the formless Chassidic pattern. They are in wonderful spirits.)*

and joy for the upright—

*(*THE SEXTON *and* ALPER *join in, clapping their hands and eventually joining the dance so that the four* OLD JEWS *form a small ring, their arms around each other's shoulders, their old feet kicking exuberantly as they stamp about in a sort of circular pattern.)*

ALL:

The upright in heart.
Oh!
Light is sown,
sown for the righteous,
and joy for the upright,
the upright in heart.
Oh!
Light is sown,
sown for the righteous,
and joy for the upright,
the upright in heart.

(Round and round they stomp and shuffle, singing out lustily, sweat forming in beads on their brows. The words are repeated over and over again until they degenerate from shortness of breath into a "Bi-bu-bu-bi-bi—bi-bi-bi-bi-bibibi." ARTHUR *watches, delighted. Finally,* ALPER, *gasping for breath, breaks out of the ring and staggers to a chair.)*

THE CABALIST: A good sixty years I haven't danced! Oh, enough! Enough! My heart feels as if it will explode! *(He staggers, laughing, from the small ring of dancers and sits down, gasping for air.)*
ALPER: Some more wine, Hirschman?
THE CABALIST: *(Gasping happily.)* Oh!

*(*ZITORSKY *looks up, noticing* THE GIRL, *who, awakened by the romping, has sidled out into the synagogue and*

has been watching the gaiety with delight. ZITORSKY *eyes her wickedly for a moment; then advances on her, his arm outstretched, quite the old cock-of-the walk.)*

ZITORSKY: Bi-bi-bi-bi-bi-bi-bi— *(He seizes her in his arms and begins to twirl around, much to her delight. She dances with him, her skirt whirling and her feet twinkling, laughing at the sheer physical excitement of it all.* ZITORSKY *supplies the music, a gay chant, the lyrics of which consist of)* Bi-bi-bi-bi-bi-bi-bi-bi— (etc.)—

THE CABALIST: The last time I danced was on the occasion of the last Day of the Holiday of Tabernacles in 1896. I was seventeen years old. *(A sudden frightened frown sweeps across his face. He mutters.)* Take heed for the girl, for the dybbuk will be upon her soon.

ALPER: *(Leaning to him.)* What did you say, Israel son of Isaac?

THE CABALIST: *(He turns to* THE GIRL, *dancing with* ZITORSKY, *and stares at her.)* Let the girl rest, Zitorsky, for she struggles with the dybbuk. Behold. *(*THE GIRL *has indeed broken away from* ZITORSKY *and has begun an improvised dance of her own. The gaiety is gone from her face and is replaced by a sullen lasciviousness. The dance she does is a patently provocative one, dancing slowly at first, and then with increasing abandon and wantonness.* ZITORSKY *recoils in horror.* THE GIRL *begins to stamp her feet and whirl more and more wildly. Her eyes grow bold and flashing and she begins to shout old gypsy words, a mongrel Russian, Oriental in intonation.* THE CABALIST *slowly moves to* THE GIRL *now, who, when she becomes aware of his coming close, abruptly stops her dance and stands stock still, her face now a mask of extravagant pain.* THE CABALIST *regards her gently and speaks softly to her.)* Lie down, my child, and rest.

THE GIRL: *(At this quiet suggestion, she begins to sway as if she were about to faint. Barely audible.)* I feel so faint, so faint. *(She sinks slowly to the floor, not quite in a swoon, but on the verge.* ARTHUR *races to her side.)*

ARTHUR: Do we have any water here?

ALPER: Wine would be better. Sexton, give her some

wine. (THE SEXTON *hurries to her with someone's glass.)*

ARTHUR: *(Holding* THE GIRL*'s head.)* Is she a sickly girl?

ALPER: *(Bending over them.)* She was never sick a day in her life.

THE SEXTON: Here's the wine.

ZITORSKY: *(To* THE SEXTON.*)* Did I tell you? Did I tell you?

THE GIRL: I feel so faint. I feel so faint.

ARTHUR: *(Bringing the glass of wine to her lips.)* Sip some of this.

THE GIRL: *(Murmuring.)* Save me—save me—

THE CABALIST: The dybbuk weakens her. I have seen this once before.

THE SEXTON: *(To* ZITORSKY.*)* When you told me about this dybbuk, I didn't believe you.

ZITORSKY: So did I tell you right?

THE SEXTON: Oh, boy.

ARTHUR: Help me get her onto the chair in there.

ALPER: Yes, of course.

THE SEXTON: Here, let me help a little.

(Between the three of them, they manage to get THE GIRL *up and walk her slowly to the rabbi's office, where they gently help her lie down on the leather chair.)*

THE CABALIST: *(To* ZITORSKY.*)* They haven't heard from Mr. Foreman yet?

ZITORSKY: No, we're waiting.

THE CABALIST: *(Frowning.)* It is not that far to Williamsburg. Well, the girl will sleep now.

(He walks slowly to the door of the rabbi's office, followed by a wary ZITORSKY. *In the rabbi's office* ARTHUR *is gently laying* THE GIRL*'s limp sleeping form down on the chair.)*

ARTHUR: *(To the others.)* I think she's fallen asleep.

ALPER: Thank heavens for that.

ARTHUR: *(Straightening.)* Look, I'm going to call her family. She may be quite ill. I think we'd all feel a lot better if she were in the hands of a doctor. If one of you will just give me her home telephone number—

(Just a little annoyed, for nobody answers him.) Please, gentlemen, I really don't think it's wise to pursue this nonsense any longer.

THE CABALIST: It is not nonsense. I do not speak of dybbuks casually. As a young man, I saw hundreds of people come to my father claiming to be possessed, but, of all these, only two were true dybbuks. Of these two, one was a girl very much like this poor girl, and, even before the black candles and the ram's horn could be brought for the exorcism, she sank down onto the earth and died. I tell you this girl is possessed, and she will die, clutching at her throat and screaming for redemption unless the dybbuk is exorcised. *(He stares at the others, nods his head.)* She will die. Wake the girl. I will take her to the Korpotchniker myself.

ALPER: Zitorsky, wake the girl. I will get her coat. Sexton, call a taxicab for Rabbi Israel. *(*ALPER, *who had been reaching for the girl's coat, is stayed by* ARTHUR. *He looks up at the young man.)* Young man, what are you doing?

ARTHUR: Mr. Alper, the girl is sick. There may be something seriously wrong with her.

ALPER: Young man, Rabbi Israel says she is dying.

ARTHUR: Well, in that case, certainly let me have her home telephone number.

ALPER: *(Striding into the rabbi's office.)* You are presuming in matters that are no concern of yours.

ARTHUR: *(Following.)* They are as much my concern as they are yours. I have grown quite fond of this girl. I want her returned to the proper authorities, right now. If necessary, I shall call a policeman. Now, let's have no more nonsense.

*(*ALPER *sinks down behind the desk glowering. A moment of silence fills the room.)*

THE CABALIST: The young man doesn't believe in dybbuks?

ARTHUR: I'm afraid not. I think you are all behaving like madmen.

THE CABALIST: *(He considers this answer for a moment.)* I will tell you an old Chassidic parable. A deaf man passed by a house in which a wedding party was going on. He looked in the window and saw all the people there dancing and cavorting, leaping about and laughing. However, since the man was deaf and could not hear the music of the fiddlers, he said to himself: "Ah, this must be a madhouse." Young man, because you are deaf, must it follow that we are lunatics?

ARTHUR: You are quite right. I did not mean to mock your beliefs, and I apologize for it. However, I am going to call the girl's father, and, if he wants to have the girl exorcised, that's his business. *(He has sat down behind the desk, put his hand on the receiver, and now looks up at* ALPER.*)* Well?

THE CABALIST: Give him the number, Mr. Alper. *(*ALPER *fishes an old address book out of his vest pocket, thumbs through the pages, and hands the book opened to* ARTHUR, *who begins to dial.)* There is no one home in the girl's house. Her father, who wishes only to forget about the girl, has gone to his shop in the city, and, at this moment, is overeating at his lunch in a diary restaurant. The step-mother has taken the younger children to her sister's. The girl's doctor has called the police and has gone about his rounds, and the police are diffidently riding up and down the streets of the community looking for an old Jew and his granddaughter. *(*ARTHUR *says nothing but simply waits for an answer to his ring.* THE CABALIST *sits down on the arm of the couch and contemplates mildly to himself. At last he says:)* I cannot understand why this young man does not believe in dybbuks.

ALPER: It is symptomatic of the current generation, Rabbi Israel, to be utterly disillusioned. Historically speaking, an era of prosperity following an era of hard times usually produces a number of despairing and quietistic philosophies, for the now prosperous people have found out they are just as unhappy as when they were poor. Thus when an intelligent man of such a generation discovers that two television sets have no more meaning than one or that he gets along no better with his wife in a suburban house than he did in their small city flat, he arrives at the natural assumption that life is utterly meaningless.

THE CABALIST: What an unhappy state of affairs.

ARTHUR: *(Returns the receiver to its cradle, muttering.)* Nobody home.

THE CABALIST: *(To* ARTHUR.*)* Is that true, young man, that you believe in absolutely nothing?

ARTHUR: Not a damn thing.

THE CABALIST: There is no truth, no beauty, no infinity, no known, no unknown?

ARTHUR: Precisely.

THE CABALIST: Young man, you are a fool.

ARTHUR: Really. I have been reading your book—the Book of Zohar. I am sure it has lost much in the translation, but, sir, any disciple of this abracadabra is presuming when he calls anyone else a fool. *(He produces the book the girl gave him.)*

THE CABALIST: You have been reading The Book of Zohar. Dear young man, one does not read The Book of Zohar, leaf through its pages, and make marginal notes. I have entombed myself in this slim volume for sixty years, raw with vulnerability to its hidden mysteries, and have sensed only a glimpse of its passion. Behind every letter of every word lies a locked image, and behind every image a sparkle of light of the ineffable brilliance of Infinity. But the concept of the Inexpressible Unknown is inconceivable to you. For you are a man possessed by the Tangible. If you cannot touch it with your fingers, it simply does not exist. Indeed, that will be the epithet of your generation—that you took everything for granted and believed in nothing. It is a very little piece of life that we know. How shall I say it? I suggest it is wiser to believe in dybbuks than in nothing at all.

ARTHUR: Mr. Hirschman, a good psychiatrist—even a poor one—could strip your beliefs in ten minutes. You may think of yourself as a man with a God, but I see you as a man obsessed with guilt who has invented a God so he can be forgiven. You have invented it all—the guilt, God, forgiveness, the whole world, dybbuks, love, passion, fulfillment—the whole fantastic mess of pottage—because it is unbearable for you to bear the pain of insignificance. None of these things exist. You've made them all up. The fact is, I have half a mind to let you go through with this exorcism, for, after all the trumpetings of rams' horns and the bellowing of incantations and after the girl falls in a swoon on the floor—I assure you, she will rise up again as demented as she ever was, and I wonder what bizarre rationale and mystique you will expound to explain all that. Now, if the disputation is at an end, I am going to call the police. *(He picks up the receiver again and dials the operator.)*

ALPER: Well, what can one say to such bitterness?

THE CABALIST: *(Shrugs.)* One can only say that the young man has very little regard for psychiatrists.

(The front door to the synagogue bursts open, and FOREMAN *and* SCHLISSEL *come hurtling in, breathing heavily and in a state of absolute confusion.* ALPER *darts out into the synagogue proper and stares at them.)*

SCHLISSEL: Oh, thank God, the synagogue is still here!

ALPER: Well?

SCHLISSEL: *(Can hardly talk he is so out of breath.)* Well, what?

ALPER: What did the Korpotchniker say?

SCHLISSEL: Who knows?! Who saw the Korpotchniker?! We've been riding in subways for four hours! Back and forth, in this train, in that train! I am convinced there is no such place as Williamsburg and there is no such person as the Korpotchniker Rabbi! I tell you, twice we got off at two different stations, just to see daylight, and, as God is my witness, both times we were in New Jersey!

FOREMAN: Oh, I tell you, I am sick from driving so much.

ALPER: Idiot! You didn't take the Brighton train!

SCHLISSEL: We took the Brighton train! *(He waves both arms in a gesture of final frustration.)* We took all the trains! I haven't had a bite to eat all morning. Don't tell me about Brighton trains! Don't tell me about anything! Leave me alone, and the devil take your whole capitalist economy! *(*ZITORSKY, THE SEXTON *and* THE CABALIST *have all come out to see what the noise is all about. Even* ARTHUR *is standing in the office doorway listening to all this.)* We asked this person, we asked that person. This person said that train. That person said this train. We went to a policeman. He puts us on a train. The conductor comes in, says: "Last stop." We get out. As God is my witness, New Jersey. We get back on that train. The conductor says: "Get off next station and take the other train." We get off the next station and take the other train. A man says: "Last stop." We get out. New Jersey!

(In the rabbi's office, THE GIRL *suddenly sits bolt upright, her eyes clenched tight in pain, screaming terribly out into the air about her, her voice shrill with anguish.)*

FOREMAN: *(Racing to her side.)* Oh, my God! Evelyn! Evelyn! What is it?!

THE GIRL: *(She clutches at her throat and screams.)* Save me! Save me! Save me!

*(*ZITORSKY *and* THE SEXTON *begin to mutter rapid prayers under their breath.)*

ALPER: *(Putting his arm around* FOREMAN.*)* David, she's very ill. We think she may be dying.

ARTHUR: *(He has raced to* THE GIRL, *sits on the couch beside her, takes her into his arms.)* Call a doctor.

FOREMAN: *(In panic to* ALPER, *who is standing stock still in the synagogue.)* He says I should call a doctor.

*(*ARTHUR *puts his hand to his brow and shakes his head as if to clear it of the shock and confusion within it.)*

ALPER: *(Crossing to* THE CABALIST.*)* Save her, Rabbi Israel. You have had your sign from God. You are among the righteous.

ARTHUR: *(He turns slowly and regards the silent betallithed form of the little* CABALIST. *To* THE CABALIST, *his voice cracking under emotions he was unaware he still had.)* For God's sake, perform your exorcism or whatever has to be done. I think she's dying.

THE CABALIST: *(He regards* ARTHUR *for a moment with the profoundest gentleness. Then he turns, and with an authoritative voice, instructs* THE SEXTON.*)* Sexton, we shall need black candles, the ram's horn, praying shawls of white wool, and there shall be ten Jews for a quorum to witness before God this awesome ceremony.

THE SEXTON: Just plain black candles?

THE CABALIST: Just plain black candles.

*(*ALPER *moves quietly up to* FOREMAN *standing in the office doorway and touches his old friend's shoulder in a gesture of awe and compassion.* FOREMAN, *at the touch, begins to cry and buries his shaking old head on his friend's shoulder.* ALPER *embraces him.)*

ZITORSKY: *(In the synagogue, to* SCHLISSEL.*)* I am absolutely shaking—shaking.

*(*ARTHUR, *having somewhat recovered his self-control, sinks down near pulpit, frowning, confused by all that is going on, and moved by a complex of feeling he cannot understand at all.)*

CURTAIN

ACT III

TIME: *Half an hour later.*

AT RISE: THE GIRL *is sitting in the rabbi's office, perched on the couch, nervous, frightened, staring down at her restlessly twisting fingers.* FOREMAN *sits behind the rabbi's desk, wrapped in his own troubled thoughts. He wears over his suit a long, white woolen praying shawl with thick, black stripes, like that worn by* THE CABALIST *from the beginning of the play. Indeed, all the* MEN *now wear these ankle-length white praying shawls, except* ARTHUR, *who at rise is also in the rabbi's office, deep in thought.* THE CABALIST *sits on pulpit, his praying shawl cowled over his head, leafing through a volume, preparing the prayers for the exorcism.* THE SEXTON *is standing by the wall phone, the receiver cradled to his ear, waiting for an answer to a call he has just put in. He is more or less surrounded by* ALPER, SCHLISSEL, *and* ZITORSKY.

ZITORSKY: How about Milsky the butcher?

ALPER: Milsky wouldn't come. Ever since they gave the seat by the East Wall to Kornblum, Milsky said he wouldn't set foot in this synagogue again. Every synagogue I have belonged to, there have always been two kosher butchers who get into a fight over who gets the favored seat by the East Wall during the High Holy Days, and the one who doesn't abandons the congregation in a fury, and the one who does always seems to die before the next High Holy Days.

SCHLISSEL: Kornblum the butcher died? I didn't know Kornblum died.

ALPER: Sure. Kornblum died four years ago.
SCHLISSEL: Well, he had lousy meat, believe me, may his soul rest in peace.

*(*THE SEXTON *has hung up, recouped his dime, reinserted it, and is dialing again.)*

ZITORSKY: *(To* THE SEXTON.*)* No answer?
THE SEXTON: *(Shakes his head.)* I'm calling Harris.
SCHLISSEL: Harris? You tell an eighty-two-year-old man to come down and make a tenth for an exorcism, and he'll have a heart attack talking on the phone with you.
THE SEXTON: *(Dialing.)* Well, what else am I to do? It is hard enough to assemble ten Jews under the best of circumstances, but in the middle of the afternoon on a Thursday it is an absolute nightmare. Aronowitz is in Miami. Klein the Furrier is at his job in Manhattan. It is a workday today. Who shall I call? *(Waiting for someone to answer.)* There are many things that I have to do. The tapestries on the Ark, as you see, are faded and need needlework, and the candelabras and silver goblet for the saying of the Sabbath benediction are tarnished and dull. But every second of my day seems to be taken up with an incessant search for ten Jews— *(On phone.)* Hello, Harris. Harris, this is Bleyer the Sexton. We need you badly down here in the synagogue for a quorum— If I told you why, you wouldn't come— All right, I'll tell you, but, in God's name, don't tell another soul, not even your daughter-in-law—
SCHLISSEL: My daughter-in-law, may she grow like an onion with her head in the ground.
THE SEXTON: *(On phone.)* Hirschman is going to exorcise a dybbuk from Foreman's granddaughter— I said, Hirschman is— A dybbuk. That's right, a dybbuk— Right here in Mineola— That's right. Why should Mineola be exempt from dybbuks?
ALPER: *(Thinking of names.)* There used to be a boy came down here every morning, about eight, nine years ago— a devout boy with forelocks and sidecurls—a pale boy, who was studying to be a Rabbi at the seminary.
THE SEXTON: *(On phone.)* Harris, this is not a joke.
SCHLISSEL: Chwatkin.

ALPER: That's right, Chwatkin. That was the boy's name. Chwatkin. Maybe we could call him. Does he still live in the community?

SCHLISSEL: He's a big television actor. He's on television all the time. Pinky Sims. He's an actor.

ZITORSKY: Pinky Sims? That's a name for a rabbinical student?

THE SEXTON: Put on your sweater and come down.

ALPER: *(To* THE SEXTON, *who has just hung up.)* So Harris is coming?

ZITORSKY: Yes, he's coming. So with Harris, that makes eight, and I am frankly at the end of my resources. I don't know who else to call.

ALPER: This is terrible. Really. God manifests Himself in our little synagogue, and we can't even find ten Jews to say hello.

THE SEXTON: I shall have to go out in the street and get two strangers. *(Putting on his coat.)* Well, I don't look forward to this at all. I will have to stop people on the street, ask them if they are Jewish—which is bad enough—and then explain to them I wish them to attend the exorcism of the dybbuk— I mean, surely you can see the futility of it.

ALPER: We can only get eight. A disgrace. Really. We shall not have the exorcism for lack of two Jews.

THE SEXTON: *(On his way out.)* All right, I'm going. *(He exits.)*

ZITORSKY: *(To* SCHLISSEL.*)* In those days when I was deceiving my wife, I used to tell her I was entertaining out-of-town buyers. I once told her I was entertaining out-of-town buyers every night for almost three weeks. It was a foolhardy thing to do because even my wife could tell business was not that good. So one night, she came down to my loft on Thirty-sixth Street and walked in and caught me with—well, I'm sure I've told you this story before.

SCHLISSEL: Many times.

*(*THE CABALIST *enters the office. Upon his entrance,* THE GIRL *stands abruptly, obviously deeply disturbed and barely in control of herself. She turns from* THE CABALIST *and shades her eyes with her hand to hide her terror.* FOREMAN *looks up briefly. He seems to be in a state of*

shock. THE CABALIST *sits down on the couch, lets the cowl of his prayer shawl fall back on his shoulders and contemplates his hands folded patiently between his knees. After a moment, he says:)*

THE CABALIST: *(Quietly.)* Dybbuk, I am Israel son of Isaac. My father was Isaac son of Asher, and I wear his fringed shawl on my shoulders as I talk to you. *(Upon these words,* THE GIRL *suddenly contorts her form as if seized by a violent cramp. She clutches her stomach and bends low and soft sobs begin to come out of her.)* Reveal yourself to me.

THE GIRL: *(In the voice of the dybbuk.)* I am Hannah Luchinsky.

(In the synagogue, ALPER, SCHLISSEL *and* ZITORSKY *begin to edge, quite frightened, to the opened office door.* ARTHUR *watches from his seat in the office.)*

THE CABALIST: Why do you possess this girl's body?

THE GIRL: *(Twisting and contorting; in the voice of the dybbuk.)* My soul was lost at sea, and there is no one to say the prayers for the dead over me.

THE CABALIST: I will strike a bargain with you. Leave this girl's body through her smallest finger, doing her no damage, not even a scratch, and I shall sit on wood for you for the First Seven Days of Mourning and shall plead for your soul for the First Thirty Days and shall say the prayers for the dead over you three times a day for the Eleven Months and light the Memorial Lamp each year upon the occasion of your death. I ask you to leave this girl's body.

THE GIRL: *(She laughs quietly. In the voice of the dybbuk.)* You give me short-weight, for you will yourself be dead before the prayers for the new moon.

(In the office doorway, the three OLD MEN *shudder.* FOREMAN *looks up slowly.* THE CABALIST *closes his eyes.)*

THE CABALIST: *(Quietly.)* How do you know this?

THE GIRL: *(In the voice of the dybbuk.)* Your soul will fly straight to the Heavenly Gates and you will be embraced by the Archangel Mihoel.

THE CABALIST: Then I enjoin the Angel of Death to speed his way. Dybbuk, I order you to leave the body of this girl.

THE GIRL: *(Her face suddenly flashes with malevolence. In the voice of the dybbuk, shouting.)* No! I seek vengeance for these forty years of limbo! I was betrayed in my youth and driven to the Evil Impulse against my will! I have suffered beyond belief, and my spirit has lived in dunghills and in piles of ashes, and I demand the soul of David son of Abram be cast into Gilgul for the space of forty years times ten to gasp for air in the sea in which I drowned—

FOREMAN: *(Standing in terror.)* No! No!

THE GIRL: *(In the voice of the dybbuk.)* —so that my soul may have peace! A soul for a soul! That is my bargain.

FOREMAN: *(Shouting.)* Let it be then! Leave my granddaughter in peace and I will give my soul in exchange.

THE CABALIST: *(With ringing authority.)* The disposition of David son of Abram's soul will not be decided here. Its fall and ascent has been ordained by the second universe of angels. The bargain cannot be struck! Dybbuk, hear me. I order you to leave the body of this girl through her smallest finger, causing her no pain nor damage, and I give you my word prayers will be said over you in full measure. But if you adjure these words, then I must proceed against you with malediction and anathema.

THE GIRL: *(Laughs.)* Raise not thy mighty arm against me, for it has no fear for me. A soul for a soul. That is my bargain. *(She suddenly begins to sob.)*

THE CABALIST: *(To* ALPER.*)* We shall have to prepare for the exorcism.

ALPER: I thought that would be the case.

THE GIRL: *(Sitting down on the couch, frightened, in her own voice.)* I am so afraid.

FOREMAN: There is nothing to fear. It will all be over in a minute, like having a tooth pulled, and you will walk out of here a cheerful child.

SCHLISSEL: *(Ambling back into the synagogue proper with* ZITORSKY *and* ALPER.*)* I tell you, I'd feel a lot better if the Korpotchniker was doing this. If you are going to have a tooth pulled, at least let it be by a qualified dentist.

ZITORSKY: I thought Hirschman handled himself very well with that dybbuk.

SCHLISSEL: *(To* ALPER *and* ZITORSKY.*)* If I tell you all something, promise you will never throw it back in my face.

ZITORSKY: What?

SCHLISSEL: I am beginning to believe she is really possessed by a dybbuk.

ZITORSKY: I'm beginning to get used to the whole thing.

*(*THE CABALIST *has stood and moved upstage to the rear wall of the synagogue, where he stands in meditation.* FOREMAN *is sitting again somewhat numbly beside his granddaughter.)*

THE GIRL: *(After a moment.)* I am very frightened, Arthur.

ARTHUR: *(Rises.)* Well, I spoke to my analyst, as you know, and he said he didn't think this exorcism was a bad idea at all. The point is, if you really do believe you are possessed by a dybbuk—

THE GIRL: Oh, I do.

ARTHUR: Well, then, he feels this exorcism might be a good form of shock treatment that will make you more responsive to psychiatric therapy and open the door to an eventual cure. Mr. Hirschman assures me it is a painless ceremony. So you really have nothing to be frightened of.

THE GIRL: Will you be here?

ARTHUR: Of course. Did you think I wouldn't?

*(*FOREMAN *moves slowly out into the synagogue as if to ask something of* HIRSCHMAN.*)*

THE GIRL: I always sense flight in you.

ARTHUR: Really.

THE GIRL: You are always taking to your heels, Arthur. Especially in moments like now when you want to be tender. I know that you love me or I couldn't be so happy with you, but the whole idea of love seems to terrify you, and you keep racing off to distant detachments. I feel that if I reached out for your cheek now, you would turn your head or, in some silent way, clang the iron gates shut on me. You have some strange dybbuk all of your own, some sad little turnkey, who drifts about inside of you, locking up all the little doors, and saying, "You are dead. You are dead." You do love me, Arthur. I know that.

ARTHUR: *(Gently.)* I wish you well, Evelyn. We can at least say that.

THE GIRL: I love you. I want so very much to be your wife. *(She stares at him, her face glowing with love. She says quietly.)* I will make you a good home, Arthur. You will be happy with me. *(He regards her for a moment, caught by her wonder. He reaches forward and lightly touches her cheek. She cannot take her eyes from him.)* I adore you, Arthur.

ARTHUR: *(With deep gentleness.)* You are quite mad. *(They regard each other,* ARTHUR *stands.)*

THE GIRL: You think our getting married is impractical?

ARTHUR: Yes, I would say it was at the least impractical.

THE GIRL: Because I am insane and you are suicidal.

ARTHUR: I do think those are two reasons to give one pause.

THE GIRL: Well, at least we begin with futility. Most marriages take years to arrive there.

ARTHUR: Don't be saucy, Evelyn.

THE GIRL: *(Earnestly.)* Oh, Arthur, I wouldn't suggest marriage if I thought it was utterly unfeasible. I think we can make a go of it. I really do. I know you have no faith in my exorcism—

ARTHUR: As I say, it may be an effective shock therapy.

THE GIRL: But we could get married this minute, and I still think we could make a go of it. I'm not a dangerous schizophrenic; I just hallucinate. I could keep your house for you. I did for my father very competently before he remarried. I'm a good cook, and you do find me attractive, don't you? I love you, Arthur. You are really very good for me. I retain reality remarkably well with you. I know I could be a good wife. Many schizophrenics function quite well if one has faith in them.

ARTHUR: *(Touched by her earnestness.)* My dear Evelyn—

THE GIRL: I don't ask you to have faith in dybbuks or gods or exorcisms—just in me.

ARTHUR: *(He gently touches her cheek.)* How in heaven's name did we reach this point of talking marriage?

THE GIRL: It is a common point of discussion between people in love.

ARTHUR: *(He kneels before her, takes her hand between his. He loves her.)* I do not love you. Nor do you love me. We met five hours ago and exchanged the elementary courtesy of conversation—the rest is your own ingenuousness.

THE GIRL: I do not remember ever being as happy as I am this moment. I feel enchanted. *(They are terribly close now. He leans to her, his arms moving to embrace her. And then he stops, and the moment is broken. He turns away, scowls, stands.)* You are in full flight again, aren't you?

ARTHUR: I reserve a certain low level of morality which includes not taking advantage of incompetent minors.

THE GIRL: Why can't you believe that I love you?

ARTHUR: *(Angrily.)* I simply do not believe anybody loves anyone. Let's have an end to this. *(He is abruptly aware that their entire love scene together has been observed by all of the* OLD MEN, *clustered together in the open doorway of the rabbi's office, beaming at them. With a furious sigh, he strides to the door and shuts it in the* OLD MEN's *faces. He turns back to* THE GIRL, *scowling.)* Really, this is all much too fanciful. Really, it is. In an hour, you will be back to your institution, where I may or may not visit you.

THE GIRL: *(She sits slowly down.)* If I were not already insane, the thought that I might not see you again would make me so.

ARTHUR: *(More disturbed than he himself knows.)* I don't know what you want of me.

THE GIRL: *(One step from tears.)* I want you to find the meaning of your life in me.

ARTHUR: But that's insane. How can you ask such an impossible thing?

THE GIRL: Because you love me.

ARTHUR: *(Cries out.)* I don't know what you mean by love! All it means to me is I shall buy you a dinner, take you to the theatre, and then straight to our tryst where I shall reach under your blouse for the sake of tradition while you breathe hotly in my ear in a pretense of passion. We will mutter automatic endearments, nibbling at the sweat on each other's earlobes, all the while gracelessly fumbling with buttons and zippers, cursing under our breath the knots in our shoelaces, and telling ourselves that this whole comical business of stripping off our trousers is an act of nature like the pollination of weeds. Even in that one brief moment when our senses finally obliterate our individual alonenesses, we will hear ringing in our ears the reluctant creaking of mattress springs.

THE GIRL: *(She stares at him, awed by this bitter expostulation.)* You are possessed.

ARTHUR: At your age, I suppose, one still finds theatrical charm in this ultimate of fantasies, but when you have been backstage as often as I have, you will discover love to be an altogether shabby business of cold creams and costumes.

THE GIRL: *(Staring at him.)* You are possessed by a dybbuk that does not allow you to love.

ARTHUR: *(Crying out again in sudden anguish.)* Oh, leave me alone! Let's get on with this wretched exorcism! *(He strides to the door, suddenly turns, confused, disturbed, would say something, but he doesn't know what. He opens the door to find the five* OLD MEN *patiently waiting for him with beaming smiles. This disconcerts him and he turns to* THE GIRL *again, and is again at a loss for words. She stares at the floor.)*

THE GIRL: We could be very happy if you would have faith in me.

ARTHUR: *(He turns and shuffles out of the office. To the* OLD MEN.*)* It was tasteless of you to gawk at us. *(He continues into the synagogue trailed by the* OLD MEN. *He sits and is immediately surrounded by the* OLD MEN.*)*

FOREMAN: Are you interested in this girl, young man, because my son is not a rich man, by any means, but he will give you a fine wedding, catered by good people, with a cantor—

ZITORSKY: And a choir.

FOREMAN: —Possibly, and a dowry perhaps in the amount of five hundred dollars—which, believe me, is more than he can afford. However, I am told you are a professional man, a lawyer, and the father of the bride must lay out good money for such a catch.

ALPER *and* ZITORSKY: Surely— Absolutely.

FOREMAN: Of course, the girl is an incompetent and you will have to apply to the courts to be appointed the committee of her person—

ALPER: —a formality, I assure you, once you have married her.

FOREMAN: As for the girl, I can tell you first hand, she is a fine Jewish girl—

ZITORSKY: Modest—

ALPER: Devout—

FOREMAN: —and she bakes first-rate pastries.

ARTHUR: *(Staring at the gay* OLD MEN *with disbelief.)* You are all mad, madder than the girl, and if I don't get out of here soon, I shall be as mad as the rest.

ZITORSKY: A beauty, young man. Listen, it is said—better a full-bosomed wife than to marry a Rothschild.

SCHLISSEL: Leave the man alone. We have all been miserably married for half a century ourselves. How can you in good faith recommend the institution?

ALPER: The girl is so obviously taken with him. It would be a good match.

FOREMAN: *(Anxiously.)* Perhaps he is married already.

ALPER: *(To* ARTHUR.*)* My dear fellow, how wonderful to be in love.

ARTHUR: I love nothing!

THE CABALIST: Yes. The girl is quite right. He is possessed. He loves nothing. Love is an act of faith, and yours is a faithless generation. That is your dybbuk.

(The front door of the synagogue opens, and THE SEXTON *slips quickly in, quietly closing the door after himself.)*

ARTHUR: *(To* THE CABALIST.*)* Don't you think it's time to get on with this exorcism?

THE CABALIST: Yes. *(He stands, moves to the pulpit, sits.)*

ALPER: *(To* THE SEXTON.*)* Did you get anybody?

THE SEXTON: *(He moves in his nervous way down into the synagogue. He has obviously been on the go since he left; sweat beads his brow, and he is breathing heavily. Unbuttoning his coat and wiping his brow.)* Gentlemen, we are in the soup.

SCHLISSEL: You couldn't find anybody?

THE SEXTON: Actually, we have nine now, but the issue of a quorum has become an academic one. Oh, let me catch my breath. The rabbi will be here in a few minutes.

ALPER: The rabbi?

THE SEXTON: I saw him on Woodhaven Boulevard, and he said he would join us. Harris is on his way already. I saw him coming down the hill from his house. But the whole matter is academic.

ALPER: You told the rabbi we need him to exorcise the girl's dybbuk?

THE SEXTON: Well, what else was I to say? He asked me what I needed a quorum for at one o'clock in the afternoon, and I told him, and he thought for a moment, and he said: "All right, I'll be there in a few minutes." He is quite a nice fellow, something of a press agent perhaps, but with good intentions. Oh, I am perspiring like an animal. I shall surely have the ague tomorrow. I have been running all over looking for Jews. I even went to Friedman the Tailor. He wasn't even in town. So let me tell you. I was running back here. I turned the corner on Thirty-third Road there, and I see parked right in front of the synagogue a police patrol car. *(The* OTHERS *start.)*

ALPER: *(Looking up.)* Oh?

THE SEXTON: That's what I mean when I say we are in the soup.

SCHLISSEL: Did they say something to you?

THE SEXTON: Sure they said something. I tell you, my heart gave such a turn when I saw that police car there. They were sitting there, those two policemen, big strapping cossacks with dark faces like avenging angels, smoking cigarettes, and with their revolvers bulging through their blue overcoats. As I walked across the street to the synagogue, my knees were knocking.

ALPER: When was this? It was just now?

THE SEXTON: Just this second. Just before I came in the door— Hello, Harris, how are you?

(This last to the octogenarian of the first act, HARRIS, *who, bundled in his heavy overcoat, muffler, and with his hat pulled down on his head, has just entered the synagogue.)*

ZITORSKY: *(To* THE SEXTON.*)* So what happened?

HARRIS: *(In his high shrill voice, as he unbuttons his overcoat.)* Gentlemen! Have you heard about this dybbuk?

SCHLISSEL: Harris, we were all here at the time he called you.

THE SEXTON: Harris, did you see the police car outside?

SCHLISSEL: So what did the policeman say?

THE SEXTON: *(Unbuttoning his collar and wiping his neck with a handkerchief.)* This big strapping fellow with his uniform full of buttons looks up, he says: "You know a man named David Foreman? We're looking for him and his granddaughter, a girl, eighteen years old." Well? Eh! Well, are we in the soup or not?

*(*SCHLISSEL *goes to the front door, opens it a conspiratorial crack, looks out.)*

ARTHUR: I don't think the police will bother you if you get your exorcism started right away. They won't interrupt a religious ceremony, especially if they don't know what it is.

THE CABALIST: *(Who has made his own mind up.)* Sexton, fetch the black candles, one for each man.

*(*THE SEXTON *scurries to the rabbi's office, where the black candles are lying on the desk, wrapped in brown grocery paper.)*

ARTHUR: *(Moving to the front door.)* I'll stand by the door and talk to the police if they come in.

SCHLISSEL: *(Closing the front door.)* They're out there, all right.

THE CABALIST: *(He looks about the little synagogue, immensely dignified now, almost beautiful in his authority. The* OTHERS *wait on his words.)* I shall want to perform the ablutions of the Cohanim. Is there a Levite among you?

SCHLISSEL: I am a Levite.
THE CABALIST: You shall pour the water on my hands.*

*(*THE SEXTON *scoots across the synagogue carrying black candles to everyone.)*

HARRIS: *(Looking distractedly about.)* What are we doing now? Where is the dybbuk?
ALPER: Harris, put on a praying shawl.
HARRIS: *(Moving nervously to the office door.)* Is this actually a serious business then? Where is the dybbuk? Tell me, because Bleyer the Sexton told me nothing—
THE CABALIST: There is nothing in the Book of Codes which gives the procedure for exorcism, so I have selected those passages to read that I thought most apt. For the purpose of cleansing our souls, we shall recite the Al-Chait, and we shall recite that prayer of atonement which begins: "Sons of man such as sit in darkness." As you pray these prayers, let the image of God in any of His seventy-two faces rise before you.
ALPER: *(Crossing into rabbi's office.)* I'll get the books.
THE SEXTON: *(Giving* SCHLISSEL *a metal bowl.)* Fill it with water.
SCHLISSEL: I'm an atheist. Why am I mixed up in all this?
ALPER: We do not have a quorum. Will this be valid?
THE CABALIST: We will let God decide.
THE SEXTON: When shall I blow the ram's horn?
THE CABALIST: I shall instruct you when.
HARRIS: *(Putting on his shawl.)* What shall I do? Where shall I stand?
ZITORSKY: *(To* HARRIS.*)* Stand here, and do not be afraid.
FOREMAN: *(He comes out of the rabbi's office carrying a long white woolen praying shawl which he gives to* ARTHUR.*)* I will show you how to put it on. *(He helps* ARTHUR *enshroud himself in the prayer shawl.)*

*(*SCHLISSEL *comes out of the washroom carefully carrying his brass bowl now filled with water. He goes to* THE CABALIST, *who holds his white hands over the basin.*

*Because Cohanim (Kohanim) and Levites are descendents of priests, they perform certain duties and are accorded first and second honors, respectively, in synagogue worship.

SCHLISSEL *carefully pours the water over them.* THE CABALIST *says with great distinctness:)*

THE CABALIST: Blessed are Thou, O Lord our God, King of the Universe, Who hath sanctified us by His commandments, and has commanded us to cleanse our hands.

ALL: Amen.

(The OTHERS *watch until the last of the water has been poured over his hands. A sudden silence settles over the synagogue. They are all standing about now,* SEVEN MEN, *cloaked in white, holding their prayer books.* THE CABALIST *dries his hands on a towel handed to him by* SCHLISSEL. *He puts the towel down, rolls his sleeves down, takes his long shawl and with a sweep of his arms cowls it over his head, lifts his face, and cries out.)*

THE CABALIST: Thou knowest the secrets of eternity and the most hidden mysteries of all living. Thou searchest the innermost recesses, and tryest the reins and the heart. Nought is concealed from Thee, or hidden from Thine eyes. May it then be Thy will, O Lord our God and God of our fathers, to forgive us for all our sins, to pardon us for all our iniquities, and to grant us remission for all our transgressions.

(As one, the other OLD MEN *sweep their shawls over their heads and begin the ancient, primitive recital of their sins. They* ALL *face towards the Ark, standing in their place, bending and twisting at the knees and beating upon their breasts with the clenched fist of their right hand. They each pray individually, lifting up their voices in a wailing of the spirit.)*

ALL OF THEM: For the sin which we have committed before Thee under compulsion, or of our own will; And for the sin which we have committed before Thee in hardening of the heart!

For the sin which we have committed before Thee unknowingly:

ZITORSKY: And for the sin which we have committed before Thee with utterance of the lips.

FOREMAN: For the sin which we have committed before Thee by unchastity.

SCHLISSEL: For the sin which we have committed before Thee by scoffing;

HARRIS: For the sin which we have committed before Thee by slander; And for the sin which we have committed before Thee by the stretched-forth neck of pride: *(It is a deadly serious business, this gaunt confessional. The spectacle of the* SEVEN MEN, *cloaked in white, crying out into the air the long series of their sins and their pleas for remission, has a suggestion of the fearsome barbarism of the early Hebrews. They stand, eyes closed, and in the fervor of communication with God, their faces pained with penitence. The last of the old men,* HARRIS, *finally cries out the last lines of supplication, his thin voice all alone in the hush of the synagogue.)* And also for the sins for which we are liable to any of the four death penalties inflicted by the Court—stoning, burning, beheading, and strangling; for Thou are the Forgiver of Israel and the Pardoner of the tribes of Jeshurun in every generation and besides Thee we have no King, who pardoneth and forgiveth.

(Again, the silence falls over the stage.)

THE CABALIST: Children of men, such as sit in darkness and in the shadow of death, being bound in affliction and iron, He brought them out of darkness, and the shadow of death.

THE OTHERS: Children of men, such as sit in darkness and in the shadow of death, being bound in affliction and iron, He brought them out of darkness, and the shadow of death.

(The repetition of these lines has its accumulative effect on ARTHUR. *His lips begin to move involuntarily, and soon he has joined the* OTHERS, *quietly muttering the words.)*

THE CABALIST: Fools because of their transgressions, and because of their iniquities are afflicted.

ARTHUR *and* THE OTHERS: Fools because of their transgressions and because of their iniquities are afflicted.

THE CABALIST: They cry unto The Lord in their trouble, and He saveth them out of their distress.

ARTHUR *and* THE OTHERS: They cry unto The Lord in their trouble, and He saveth them out of their distress.

THE CABALIST: Then He is gracious unto him and saith:

ARTHUR *and* THE OTHERS: Then He is gracious unto him and saith:

THE CABALIST: Deliver him from going down to the pit; I have found a ransom.

ARTHUR *and* THE OTHERS: Deliver him from going down to the pit; I have found a ransom.

THE CABALIST: Amen.

THE OTHERS: Amen.

THE CABALIST: Bring the girl in, Mr. Foreman. *(*FOREMAN *nods and goes into the rabbi's office.)*

ALPER: *(To* SCHLISSEL.*)* I don't like it. Even if the Rabbi comes, there will only be nine of us. I am a traditionalist. Without a quorum of ten, it won't work.

SCHLISSEL: *(Muttering.)* So what do you want me to do?

(In the rabbi's office, FOREMAN *touches* THE GIRL*'s shoulder, and she starts from the coma-like state she was in, and looks at him.)*

FOREMAN: Come. It is time.

THE GIRL: *(She nods nervously and sits up. There is a vacuous look about her, the vague distracted look of the insane. Quite numbly.)* Where are you taking me? My mother is in Rome. They put the torch to her seven sons, and they hold her hostage. *(She rises in obedience to her* GRANDFATHER*'s arm as he gently escorts her out of the office into the synagogue proper. All the while she maintains a steady drone of rattling gibberish.)* Where were you yesterday? I asked everybody about you. You should have been here. We had a lot of fun. We had a party, and there were thousands of people, Jerobites and Bedouins, dancing like gypsies. *(She suddenly lapses into a sullen silence, staring at the ground, her shoulders jerking involuntarily. The* OTHERS *regard her uneasily.)*

THE SEXTON: Shall I take the ram's horn out?

THE CABALIST: Yes.

*(*THE SEXTON *produces the horn-shaped trumpet from the base of the pulpit. The front door of the synagogue now opens, and a tall, strapping young* POLICEMAN, *heavy with the authority of his thick blue overcoat, steps one step into the synagogue. He stands in the opened doorway, one hand on the latch of the door, his attitude quite brusque as if he could not possibly get his work done if he had to be polite.)*

THE POLICEMAN: Is Rabbi Marks here?

*(*ALPER *throws up his arms in despair. The* OTHERS *alternately stare woodenly at the* POLICEMAN *or down at the floor.* ARTHUR, *still deeply disturbed, rubs his brow.* THE CABALIST *begins to pray silently, only his lips moving in rapid supplication.)*

THE SEXTON: No, he's not.

THE POLICEMAN: I'm looking for a girl named Evelyn Foreman. Is that the girl? *(He indicates* THE GIRL.*)*

ALPER: *(Moving away, muttering.)* Is there any need, officer, to be so brusque or to stand in an open doorway so that we all chill to our bones?

THE POLICEMAN: *(Closing the door behind him.)* Sorry.

SCHLISSEL: *(To* ZITORSKY.*)* A real cossack, eh? What a brute. He will take us all to the station house and beat us with nightsticks.

THE POLICEMAN: *(A little more courteously.)* A girl named Evelyn Foreman. Her father has put out a call for her. She's missing from her home. He said she might be here with her grandfather. Is there a Mr. David Foreman here? *(*NOBODY *says anything.)*

ALPER: You are interrupting a service, Officer.

THE POLICEMAN: I'm sorry. Just tell me, is that the girl? I'll call in and tell them we found her.

SCHLISSEL: *(He suddenly advances on* THE POLICEMAN.*)* First of all, where do you come to walk in here like you were raiding a poolroom? This is a synagogue, you animal. Have a little respect.

THE POLICEMAN: All right, all right, I'm sorry. I happen to be Jewish myself.

ALPER: *(He looks up quickly.)* You're Jewish? *(Turns slowly to* THE SEXTON.*)* Sexton, our tenth man.

THE SEXTON: Alper, are you crazy?

ALPER: A fine, strapping Jewish boy. *(To* THE POLICEMAN.*)* Listen, we need a tenth. You'll help us out, won't you?

SCHLISSEL: *(Strolling nervously past* ALPER.*)* Alper, what are you doing, for God's sakes?

ALPER: We have to have ten men.

SCHLISSEL: What kind of prank is this? You are an impossible rogue, do you know that?

ALPER: *(Taking* SCHLISSEL *aside.)* What are you getting so excited about? He doesn't have to know what it is. We'll tell him it's a wedding. I think it's funny.

SCHLISSEL: Well, we will see how funny it is when they take us to the basement of the police station and beat us with their nightsticks.

ALPER: Nightsticks. Really, Schlissel, you are a romantic. *(Advancing on* THE POLICEMAN.*)* I tell you, officer, it would really help us out if you would stay ten or fifteen minutes. This girl—if you really want to know—is about to be married, and what is going on here is the Ritual of Shriving.

ZITORSKY: Shriving?

ALPER: A sort of ceremony of purification. It is a ritual not too commonly practiced any more, and I suggest you will find it quite interesting.

HARRIS: *(To* SCHLISSEL.*)* What is he talking about?

SCHLISSEL: Who knows?

THE POLICEMAN: *(He opens the door* ZITORSKY *had shut and calls out to his colleague outside.)* I'll be out in about ten minutes, Tommy, all right? *(He opens the door further to allow the entrance of* THE RABBI, *who now comes hurrying into the synagogue, still carrying his briefcase.)* Hello, Rabbi, how are you?

THE RABBI: *(He frowns, a little confused at* THE POLICEMAN'S *presence.)* Hello, officer, what are you doing here? *(He moves quickly to his office, taking stock of everything as he goes, the* SEVEN OLD MEN *and* ARTHUR *in their white shawls—*THE GIRL *standing woodenly in the center of the synagogue.* ALPER *and* ZITORSKY *greet him with helloes, which he nods back.)*

THE POLICEMAN: They've asked me to make a tenth for the shriving.

THE RABBI: *(Frowning as he darts into his office.)* Shriving? *(He opens his desk to get out his own large white shawl, unbuttoning his coat as he does. He notes* ALPER *who has followed him to the doorway.)* What is the policeman doing here?

ALPER: We needed a tenth.

THE POLICEMAN: *(Amiably to* ZITORSKY.*)* This is the girl, isn't it? *(*ZITORSKY *nods his head a little bleakly.)* What's really going on here?

(In his office, THE RABBI *sweeps his large shawl over his shoulders.)*

ALPER: We have said Al-Chait and a prayer of atonement, and we are waiting now just for you.

*(*THE RABBI *frowns in troubled thought, slips his skullcap on as he clips his fedora off. In the synagogue,* ZITORSKY *shuffles to* SCHLISSEL.*)*

ZITORSKY: *(Indicating* THE POLICEMAN *with his head, he mutters.)* He knows, he knows.

SCHLISSEL: Of course. Did Alper expect to get away with such a collegiate prank?

THE RABBI: *(In his office, he has finished a rapid, silent prayer he has been saying, standing with his eyes closed. He looks up at* ALPER *now.)* I would rather not take any active role in this exorcism. I am not quite sure of my rabbinical position. But it would please me a great deal to believe once again in a God of dybbuks. *(He walks quickly past* ALPER *out into the synagogue.* ALPER *follows.)* Well, we are ten.

(A silence falls upon the gathered MEN.*)*

FOREMAN: May God look upon us with the eye of mercy and understanding and may He forgive us if we sin in our earnestness.

THE OTHERS: Amen.

THE CABALIST: Sexton, light the candles. *(*THE SEXTON *lights each man's candle.* THE CABALIST *advances slowly to* THE GIRL, *who stands slackly, her body making small occasional jerking movements, apparently in a schizophrenic state.* THE CABALIST *slowly draws a* *line before* THE GIRL *with the flat of his toe. Quietly.)* Dybbuk, I draw this line beyond which you may not come. You may not do harm to anyone in this room. *(The* OLD MEN *shift nervously in their various positions around the synagogue. To* THE SEXTON.*)* Open the Ark. *(*THE SEXTON *moves quickly up to the altar and opens the brown sliding doors of the Ark, exposing the several scrolls within, standing in their handsomely covered velvet coverings.* THE CABALIST *moves slowly back to his original position; he says quietly:)* Dybbuk, you are in the presence of God and His Holy Scrolls. *(*THE GIRL *gasps.)* I plead with you one last time to leave the body of this girl. *(There is no answer.)* Then I will invoke the curse of excommunication upon your pitiable soul. Sexton, blow Tekiah. *(*THE SEXTON *raises the ram's horn to his lips, and the eerie, frightening tones shrill out into the hushed air.)* Sexton, blow Shevurim. *(Again,* THE SEXTON *raises the ram's horn and blows a variation of the first hollow tones.)* Sexton, blow Teruah. *(A third time,* THE SEXTON *blows a variation of the original tones.)* Sexton, blow the Great Tekiah and, upon the sound of these tones, dybbuk, you will be wrenched from the girl's body and there will be cast upon you the final anathema of excommunication from all the world of the living and from all the world of the dead. Sexton, blow the great Tekiah.

(For the fourth time, THE SEXTON *raises the ram's horn to his lips and blows a quick succession of loud blasts. A silence falls heavily on the gathered* MEN, *the notes fading into the air. Nothing happens.* THE GIRL *remains as she was, standing slackly, her hands making involuntary little movements.* FOREMAN*'s head sinks slowly on his chest, and a deep expression of pain covers his face.* THE CABALIST *stares steadily at* THE GIRL. *Then, suddenly,* ARTHUR *begins to moan softly, and then with swift violence, a horrible atavistic scream tears out of his throat. He staggers one brief step forward. At the peak of his scream, he falls heavily down on the floor of the synagogue in a complete faint. The echoes of his scream tingle momentarily in the high corners of the air in the synagogue. The* OTHERS *stand petrified for a moment, staring at his slack body on the floor.)*

ALPER: My God. I think what has happened is that we have exorcised the wrong dybbuk.

THE POLICEMAN: *(He starts toward* ARTHUR*'s limp body.)* All right, don't crowd around. Let him breathe.

THE CABALIST: He will be all right in a moment.

ZITORSKY: If I didn't see this with my own eyes, I wouldn't believe it.

THE RABBI: Mr. Hirschman, will he be all right?

THE CABALIST: Yes.

SCHLISSEL: *(With simple devoutness.)* Praise be to the Lord, for His compassion is everywhere.

*(*THE RABBI *moves slowly down and stars at* ARTHUR *as* SCHLISSEL, ZITORSKY *and* ALPER *help him to a chair.)*

ALPER: How are you, my dear fellow?

ARTHUR: *(Still in a state of bemused shock.)* I don't know.

THE SEXTON: *(Coming forward with some wine.)* Would you like a sip of wine?

ARTHUR: *(Taking the goblet.)* Yes, thank you very much. *(Turning to look at* THE GIRL.*)* How is she? *(Her schizophrenic state is quite obvious.* ARTHUR *turns back, his face furrowed and his eyes closed now in a mask of pain.)*

SCHLISSEL: Was it a painful experience, my friend?

ARTHUR: I don't know. I feel beyond pain. *(Indeed, his hands are visibly trembling as if from cold, and the very rigidity of his masklike face is a frozen thing. Words become more difficult to say.)* I feel as if I have been reduced to the moment of birth, as if the universe has become one hunger. *(He seems to be almost on the verge of collapse.)*

ALPER: A hunger for what?

ARTHUR: *(Gauntly.)* I don't know.

THE CABALIST: For life.

ARTHUR: *(At these words he sinks back onto his chair exhausted.)* Yes, for life. I want to live. *(He opens his eyes and begins to pray quietly.)* God of my fathers, You have exorcised all truth as I knew it out of me. You have taken away my reason and definition. Give me then a desire to wake in the morning, a passion for the things of life, a pleasure in work, a purpose to sorrow— *(He slowly stands, for a reason unknown even to himself, and turns to regard the slouched figure of* THE GIRL.*)* Give me all these things in one—give me the ability to love. *(In a hush of the scene, he moves slowly to* THE GIRL *and stands before her crouched slack figure.)* Dybbuk, hear me. I will cherish this girl, and give her a home. I will tend to her needs and hold her in my arms when she screams out with your voice. Her soul is mine now—her soul, her charm, her beauty—even you, her insanity, are mine. If God will not exorcise you, dybbuk, I will. *(To* THE GIRL*)* Evelyn, I will get your coat. We have a lot of things to do this afternoon. *(He turns to the* OTHERS.*)* It is not a simple matter to get somebody released from an institution in New York. *(He starts briskly across to the rabbi's office, pauses at the door.)* Officer, why don't you just call in and say you have located the girl and she is being brought to her father? *(To* FOREMAN.*)* You'd better come along with us. Would somebody get my coat? We will need her father's approval. We shall have to stop off at my office and have my secretary draw some papers.

*(*MR. FOREMAN *has hurriedly gotten* THE GIRL*'s coat,* ARTHUR*'s coat, and his own. In this rather enchanted state, these* THREE *drift to the exit door.)*

THE POLICEMAN: Rabbi, is this all right?
THE RABBI: Yes, quite all right.
ARTHUR: *(Pausing at the door, bemused, enchanted.)* Oh—thank you all. Good-bye.
ALL: Good-bye.
ZITORSKY: Go in good health.
ALPER: Come back and make a tenth for us sometime.

*(*ARTHUR *smiles and herds* THE GIRL *and* FOREMAN *out of the synagogue. The door closes behind them.)*

SCHLISSEL: *(Sitting with a deep sigh.)* Well, what is one to say? An hour ago, he didn't believe in God; now he's exorcising dybbuks.
ALPER: *(Pulling up a chair.)* He still doesn't believe in God. He simply wants to love. *(*ZITORSKY *joins the other two.)* And when you stop and think about it, gen-

tlemen, is there any difference? Let us make a supposition . . .

(As the curtain falls, life as it was slowly returns to the synagogue. The three OLD MEN *engage in disputation,* THE CABALIST *returns to his isolated studies,* THE RABBI *moves off into his office,* THE SEXTON *finds a chore for himself, and* THE POLICEMAN *begins to button his coat.)*